HELEN FIELDING was born in Yorkshire. She worked for many years in London as a newspaper and TV journalist, travelling as wildly and as often as possibly to Africa, India and Central America. She has written three previous novels: *Cause Celeb* (1994), *Bridget Jones's Diary* (1996) and *Bridget Jones: The Edge of Reason* (2000) and co-wrote the screenplays for the movie of *Bridget Jones's Diary* and the forthcoming sequel based on *The Edge of Reason*. She now works full-time as a novelist and screenwriter and lives in London and Los Angeles.

Helen Fielding

OLIVIA JOULES

and the Overactive Imagination

PICADOR

First published 2003 by Picador

This edition published 2004 by Picador
an imprint of Pan Macmillan Ltd
Pan Macmillan, 20 New Wharf Road, London N1 9RR
Basingstoke and Oxford
Associated companies throughout the world
www.panmacmillan.com

ISBN 0 330 43408 X

9 8

A CIP catalogue record for this book is available from
the British Library.

Typeset by SetSystems Ltd, Saffron Walden, Essex
Printed and bound in Great Britain by
Mackays of Chatham plc, Chatham, Kent

To Kevin

Acknowledgements

With warm thanks to the following for their help with the writing of the book: for anecdotes, editing, expert knowledge, practical support and mysterious info re micro sub-aquatic GP locators: Gillon Aitken, Luis Anton, Craig Brown, Tim Burton, Andreas Carlton-Smith, Fiona Carpenter, Gil Cates, the CIA's Office of Public Affairs, Richard Coles, Marie Colvin, Nick Crean, Ursula Doyle, Harry Enfield, the Fielding family, Carrie Fisher, Piers Fletcher, Linda Gase, John Gerloff, Sarah Jones, Jules' Undersea Lodge, Key Largo, Andrew Kidd, Paula Levy, Hugh Miles, John Miller, Michael Monteroso, Detective Joe Pau of the LAPD bomb squad, Maria Rejt, Mia Richkind, Sausage, Lesley Shaw, the Sunset Marquis Hotel, Beth Swofford, Russ Warner and those who are too secret to be mentioned even with an x.

I'm particularly grateful to JC for his time, sharing of specialized knowledge and for showing me how to fire a gun using a biro.

And thanks above all to Kevin Curran for his enormous contribution in terms of plotting, characters, jokes, ideas, multiple reads and edits, spelling and punctuation, and most of all for advising me that the way to write a thriller was not to put the whole plot down in the first chapter as soon as you thought of it.

1

London

'The problem with you, Olivia, is that you have an overactive imagination.'

'I don't,' said Olivia Joules indignantly.

Barry Wilkinson, foreign editor of the *Sunday Times*, leaned back in his chair, trying to hold in his paunch, staring over his half-moon glasses at the disgruntled little figure before him, and thinking: *And you're too damned cute*.

'What about your story about the cloud of giant, fanged locusts pancaking down on Ethiopia, blotting out the sun?' he said.

'It was the Sudan.'

Barry sighed heavily. 'We sent you all the way out there and all you came up with was two grasshoppers in a polythene bag.'

'But there *was* a locust cloud. It was just that it had flown off to Chad. They were supposed to be roosting. Anyway, I got you the story about the animals starving in the zoo.'

'Olivia, it was one warthog – and he looked quite porky to me.'

'Well, I would have got you an interview with the

fundamentalist women and a cross amputee if you hadn't made me come back.'

'The birth of Posh and Becks's new baby you were sent to cover live for BSkyB?'

'That wasn't hard news.'

'Thank God.'

'I certainly didn't imagine anything there.'

'No. But nor did you say anything for the first ten seconds. You stared around like a simpleton, fiddling with your hair live on air, then suddenly yelled, "The baby hasn't been born yet, but it's all very exciting. Now back to the studio."'

'That wasn't my fault. The floor manager didn't cue me because there was a man trying to get into the shot with "I'm a Royal Love Child" written on his naked paunch.'

Wearily, Barry leafed through the pile of press releases on his desk. 'Listen, lovey . . .'

Olivia quivered. One of these days she would call him lovey and see how he liked it.

'. . . you're a good writer, you're very observant and intuitive and, as I say, extremely imaginative, and we feel on the *Sunday Times*, in a freelancer, those qualities are better suited to the Style section than the news pages.'

'You mean the shallow end rather than the deep end?'

'There's nothing shallow about style, baby.'

Olivia giggled. 'I can't believe you just said that.'

Barry started laughing as well.

'Look,' he said, fishing out a press release from a cosmetics company, 'if you really want to travel, there's a celebrity launch in Miami next week for some – perfume? – face cream.'

'A face-cream launch,' said Olivia dully.

'J-Lo or P. Binny or somebody . . . there we go . . . Devorée. Who the fuck is Devorée?'

'White rapper slash model slash actress.'

'Fine. If you can get a magazine to split the costs with us, you can go and cover her face cream for Style. How's that?'

'OK,' said Olivia doubtfully, 'but if I find a proper news story out there, can I cover that as well?'

'Of course you can, sweetheart,' smirked Barry.

2

South Beach, Miami

The lobby of the Delano Hotel was like a designer's hissy fit on the set of *Alice in Wonderland*. Everything was too big, too small, the wrong colour, or in the wrong place. A light in a ten-foot-high shade hung in front of the reception desk. Muslin curtains sixty feet long fluttered in the breeze beside a wall dotted with miniature wall-lamps and a snooker table with beige felt and ecru balls. A dark man was sitting on a white perspex chair that looked like a urinal, reading a newspaper. The man looked up as a slender girl with blunt-cut blonde hair stepped into the lobby. He lowered his newspaper to watch as she looked around, grinning, as if at some mischievous private thought, then headed for the reception desk. She was wearing jeans and a thin black top, carrying a soft tan-leather tote, and dragging a battered tan and olive carry-on behind her.

'Awesome name,' said the receptionist. 'Is that Jewels as in Tiffany?'

'No. J.O.U.L.E.S. As in the unit of kinetic energy,' the girl said proudly.

'No kidding? Ah yes, here we are,' said the receptionist.

'I'll have the bellboy bring in your luggage and send it to your room.'

'Oh, don't worry. This is all I've got.'

The dark man watched as the small, determined figure marched off towards the elevators.

Olivia stared in consternation at the elevator doors, which seemed to be made of quilted stainless steel. As they were closing, a beautiful bellboy in a white T-shirt and shorts forced his arm between them and leapt into the elevator beside her, insisting on helping her take her luggage – despite the lack of it – to her room.

The room was entirely white: white floor, white walls, white sheets, white desk, white armchair and footstool, white telescope pointing at a white venetian blind. The charmingly shaggable, white-clad whippersnapper pulled up the blind, and the startling aquamarines and petrol blues of Miami Beach burst into the room like a tiny bright-blue oil painting in the centre of a thick white frame.

'Yeees. It's like being in a hospital,' she murmured.

'Rather more comfortable, I hope, ma'am. What brings you to Miami?'

His skin was like an advert for youth, peach-like, glowing, as if it had been force-fed vitamins in a greenhouse.

'Oh, you know,' she said, moving closer to the window. She looked down at the lines of umbrellas and loungers against the white sand, the pastel lifeguards' huts, the surreally blue sea criss-crossed by yachts and wave runners, a line of big ships following each other along the horizon like ducks in a shooting gallery. 'My God, what's that?' One of the ships was three times as big as the others: oddly big, like a pelican in the middle of the ducks.

'That's the *OceansApart*,' said the bellboy with proprietary pride, as if he owned not only the ship, but Miami and the ocean too. 'It's like an apartment block – only floating? Are you here on business or pleasure?'

'They built it already?' she said, ignoring the nosy young whippersnapper's rudely interrogatory manner.

'They sure did.'

'I thought it was still just an artist's impression.'

'No, ma'am. This is the maiden voyage. It's going to be anchored in Miami for four days.'

'This is the one on a permanent cruise from Grand Prix to Australian Open to Masters kind of thing, and the people fly in by helicopter to find their Picassos and dental floss laid out waiting?'

'You got it.'

'Sounds like it might make a good story.'

'Are you a journalist?'

'Yes,' she said smugly, pride in her quasi foreign-correspondent status overcoming her discretion.

'Wow! Who for?'

'The *Sunday Times* and *Elan* magazine.' She beamed.

'Wow. I'm a writer too. What are you writing about here?'

'Oh, you know. This and that.'

'Well, if you need any help, just give me a call. My name's Kurt. Anything else I can do for you at all . . . ?'

Well, now you come to mention it . . . she felt like saying. Instead, she chastely tipped him five bucks and watched the delightful little white-clad bottom depart.

Olivia Joules liked hotels. She liked hotels because:

1. When you went into a new hotel room, there was no past. It was like drawing a line and starting again.
2. Hotel life was almost Zen-like in its simplicity: a capsule wardrobe, capsule living. No debris, no nasty

clothes you never wore but couldn't throw away, no
in-tray, no dishes full of leaky pens and Post-it notes
with chewing gum stuck to them.
3. Hotels were anonymous.
4. Hotels were beautiful, if you picked right, which, after
hours and sometimes days looking at hotel web sites on
the Internet, she inevitably did. They were temples of
luxury or rusticity, cosiness or design.
5. The mundanities of life were taken care of and you
were freed from domestic slavery hell.
6. No one could bother you: you simply put Do Not
Disturb on the door handle and the telephone and the
world had to bugger off.

Olivia had not always loved hotels. Most of her family
holidays had been taken in a tent. Until the age of twenty-two
her only hotel experience had been of dingy yet embarrass-
ingly formal Crowns and Majestics in northern British seaside
resorts – strange-smelling, with bizarrely patterned carpets
and wallpapers, where the guests spoke in intimidated whispers and forcedly posh accents, and her entire family would
freeze with shame if one of them dropped a fork or a sausage
on the floor.

The first time she was sent to a hotel on business, she didn't
know what to do or how to behave. But when she found
herself in an elegant, untouched room, with a mini-bar, crisp
white cotton sheets, room service, high-end soap, no one to
answer to and free slippers she felt like she'd come home.

Sometimes she felt bad about liking hotels so much, worried
that it made her a spoilt lucky bitch. But it wasn't just posh
hotels she liked. It wasn't really to do with poshness. Some
posh hotels were disgusting: snobbish; overly fancy; not
providing the things you needed at all, such as phones that
worked, food that arrived hot on the same date as the one on

which it was ordered; noisy air-conditioning units; views of car parks; and, worst of all, snooty, unfriendly staff. Some of her favourite hotels weren't expensive at all. The only real criterion of fineness she trusted was whether, on arrival, the toilet paper was folded into a neat point at the end. In the Delano, it was not only neatly pointed, it had a white sticker on saying THE DELANO in cool grey capitals. She wasn't sure about the sticker. She thought it might be taking things too far.

She put the case on the bed and started lovingly to unpack the contents that would make the room her home until she was forced back to London. Last thing out of the bag, as always, was her survival tin, which she tucked under the pillow. It wasn't clever to carry the survival tin through airports, but it had been with her for a long time. It looked like an old tobacco tin. She had bought it in an outdoor adventure shop on the forecourt of Euston station. The lid was mirrored underneath, for signalling. The tin had a handle to transform it into a miniature pan. Inside was an edible candle, a condom for water carrying, cotton wool, potassium permanganate for cleaning wounds and fire lighting, fish hooks, a rabbit snare, a wire saw, waterproof matches, a flint, fluorescent tape, razor blades, a button compass and a miniature flare. She hadn't used any of the items except the condom – which had been several times replaced – and the cotton wool in the occasional hotel that didn't offer cleansing pads. But she was certain that one day the tin would save her by helping her to collect water in the desert, strangle a hijacker, or signal from a palm-fringed atoll to a passing plane. Until then it was a talisman – like a teddy or a handbag. Olivia had never thought of the world as a particularly safe place.

*

She turned back to the window and the view of the beach. There was a laminated instruction card hanging from the telescope. She looked confusedly at it for a second, then gave up and peered into the eyepiece, seeing a green blur of magnified grass. She adjusted a dial to reveal the seafront upside down. She carried on, adjusting to the upside-down world moving down – or up? – to a jogger, ugh, without a shirt on (why boastfully revolt others?) and a yacht smacking awkwardly into each wave. She moved on upside-downedly sideways until she came to the *OceansApart*. It was like the white cliffs of Dover heading for Miami.

She dragged her laptop out of her bag and banged out an email to Barry.

Re: Fantastic new story
1. Miami Cool, going really well.
2. Great Style story: *OceansApart* – obscenely large new floating apartment block – docked in Miami on maiden voyage.
3. Can cover but would need one or ideally two more nights here? Over and out. Olivia.

She read it, nodding with satisfaction, pressed 'Send', then looked up at the mirror and started. Her hair was quite mad, and her face horrifying in its puffiness: the product of sixteen hours spent in planes and airports – five of them stuck in Heathrow because someone had left a laptop in the ladies' loo. The face-cream party was at six. She had twenty minutes to transform herself into a dazzling creature of the night.

3

Fifty-eight minutes later she emerged, breathless, from the elevator, scrubbed and polished. A line of white limos stretched from the front of the lobby all the way up the avenue, horns blaring. The hotel bouncers were in their bossiest of elements, throwing their weight around in little white shorts and talking into headsets with the gravitas of FBI agents. Two girls with huge breasts and no hips were posing with rather desperate grins on a red carpet. They looked like weird man–woman hybrids – the upper part buxom female, the lower adolescent boy. They were striking identical poses, standing side-on to the flashbulbs, one leg in front of the other, bodies forced into an S shape, as if they were trying to duplicate a diagram from *InStyle* magazine or were desperate to go to the loo.

The greeting table displayed a precarious pyramid of tubs of Devorée – Crème de Phylgie, very surgical-looking, plain white with plain green writing. Olivia gave her name, took one of the glossy press packs and headed, reading it, towards the throng, shuddering at the list of repulsive-sounding algae and sea-critter-based ingredients.

A woman in a black trouser suit powered over, arranging her face into the sort of frightening white-toothed smile that looks like that of an angry monkey. 'Hi! You're Olivia? Melissa from Century PR. Welcome. How was your trip over? How was the weather in London?' She marched Olivia towards the terrace, asking inane and ceaseless questions without pause for answer. 'How is your hotel room? How's Sally at *Elan*? Will you give her my regards?'

They stepped out on the deck. *Tout le* fashionista and muso Miami *monde* were artfully arranged around a selection of wrong-sized furniture and spilling down steps into the garden below, where white-covered comfy chairs, giant table lamps and cabañas surrounded the turquoise-lit pool.

'Have you tried the Devorée Martini? You got the press release about the chef who's prepared the special dishes we'll be sampling tonight?' Olivia let Melissa's auto-witter wash over her. Usually, she let annoying people do their thing and hoped they'd buzz off as soon as possible. Night had fallen with tropical suddenness. The landscaping was lit with flaming torches and beyond was the ocean, crashing in the darkness. Or maybe, she thought, it was an air-conditioning unit. There was something odd about this party. It felt controlling and tense, like Melissa. The wind was lifting press releases and napkins, ruffling dresses and hair. There were people around who didn't fit, moving and watching too anxiously for Party Funland. She focused on a group in the far corner, trying to figure them out. The women were actress slash model types: big hair, long legs, small dresses. The men were harder to place: dark-haired, swarthy, high moustache quota – they could have been Hispanic or Indian. They were making a show of being rich, but they weren't quite getting it right. They looked like an advert from Debenham's in-house magazine.

'If you'll excuse me, there's someone I need to bring over. Oh look, there's Jennifer . . .' Melissa powered off still talking, leaving Olivia standing on her own.

For a throwback second, she felt residual feelings of insecurity. She stamped on them hard, as if they were a beetle or

HELEN FIELDING

cockroach. Olivia really used to hate going to parties. She was too sensitive to the signals given off by other people to glide through any social gathering unscathed. She liked to have proper conversations, not mindless insincere moments, and she could never quite master the art of moving smoothly from group to group. As a result, she used to spend entire evenings feeling either hurt or rude. Dramatic events, however, made her decide she would no longer give a shit about anything. Over time, she had painstakingly erased all womanly urges to question her shape, looks, role in life, or effect upon other people. She would watch, analyse and conform to codes as she observed them, without allowing them to affect or compromise her own identity.

One of her favourites on her Rules for Living list was 'No one is thinking about you. They're thinking about themselves, just like you.' This was a particularly useful rule at parties. It meant, by implication, that no one was watching you either. Therefore, you could just stand on your own and observe, and no one would think you were a sad act. No one, for example, was thinking now that she was Olivia-no-mates-Joules just because she was on her own. Or worse, Rachel-no-mates-Pixley. No one would say, 'Rachel Pixley, you're a dropout from Worksop Comprehensive. Leave the Delano Hotel this instant and go to the Post House Hotel on the Nottingham bypass.'

When Rachel Pixley was a normal schoolgirl, living with two parents in Worksop, coming home to tea in a warm house, she used to think that an orphan was a glamorous thing to be, like Alona the Wild One in *Bunty* or *Mandy* – an orphan who was wild and free and galloped her horse bareback along the shoreline. For a long time after it all happened, she thought she had been punished for this fantasy.

When Rachel was fourteen, her mother, father and brother

were run over by a lorry on a zebra crossing. Rachel, having lagged behind buying sweets and a magazine, saw the whole thing. She was put in the care of her unmarried Auntie Monica, who had cats and read newspapers all day in her nightdress. Her flat smelt of something indefinable and bad, but despite the fag ash that festooned her like snow, and her eccentric and inaccurate application of lipstick, Auntie Monica was beautiful and had been brilliant. She had studied at Cambridge and still played the piano wonderfully – when she wasn't drunk. Playing the piano when drunk, as Rachel came to realize during the time she spent *chez* Auntie Monica, was like driving when drunk – inadvisable, if not criminal.

Rachel had had a boyfriend at school who was a couple of years above her but seemed much older than everyone else. His father was a nightwatchman and a maniac. Roxby was not exactly good-looking, but he was his own man. He used to work nights as a bouncer in Romeo and Juliet's. And when he came home – because by this time he and Rachel were living together in a room above the Hao Wah Chinese takeaway – he used to sit at the computer investing his bouncer earnings in stocks and shares.

Rachel, who had only ever understood money as something you earned in very small quantities by working, was initially resistant to the notion of making money out of money. 'Money doesn't buy happiness,' her hard-working father had told her. 'If you work hard and you're honest and kind, then nothing can harm you.' But it had. A lorry had run over him. So Rachel threw in her lot with Roxby and worked every weekend at Morrisons' supermarket, and did evening shifts after school in a corner shop run by a Pakistani family, and let him invest the money for her. When she turned sixteen, her father's life-insurance policy was turned over to her. She had twenty thousand pounds to invest. It was the beginning of the eighties. She was on the way to becoming, if not a rich woman, at least a woman of independent means.

When she was seventeen, Roxby announced that he was gay and moved to the canal district of Manchester. And Rachel, fed up with knock after knock, took a long hard look at life. She had seen her friends' older sisters, radiant and triumphant, flashing minuscule H. Samuel's solitaires on their engagement fingers, spending months obsessed with dresses, flowers and event-planning, only to be found a couple of years later in the shopping centre, fat, broke and hassled, pushing prams through the rain, moaning about being hit, or belittled, or left. And she thought: *Sod that*. She started with her name. 'Olivia' sounded glam. And the attractiveness of the word 'Joules' was the only thing she remembered from physics lessons. *I'm all I've got*, she thought. *I'm going to be complete in myself. I'm not going to give a shit about anything any more. I'm going to work out my own good and bad. I'm going to be a top journalist or an explorer and do something that matters. I'm going to search this shitty world for some beauty and excitement and I'm going to have a bloody good time.*

And this, Olivia Joules thought, leaning back against the Delano pillar, *is a lot more beautiful and exciting than Worksop. No one is watching you, just go with the flow and enjoy it.* Unfortunately for the Rule for Living, however, somebody *was* watching her. As she continued to scan the party, a pair of eyes met hers in a second of highly charged interest, then looked away. She also looked away, then glanced back. The man was standing alone. He was dark and rather aristocratic-looking. He was wearing a suit that was a bit too black and a shirt that was a bit too white – too flash for the Delano. And yet he didn't look like a flash person. There was a stillness about him. He turned, and suddenly his eyes met hers again with that thrilling unspoken message which sometimes transmits itself across a room and says, 'I want to fuck you too.' That was all that was needed: a look. No need to flirt, to manoeuvre, to chat. Just that moment of recognition. Then all you had to do was follow, like in a dance.

'Everything going OK?' It was the hyperactive PR woman. Olivia, realizing she was staring lustfully into space, remembered that she had a piece to file by tomorrow and had better get on with it. 'There's lots of people I want you to meet,' said Melissa, starting to bustle Olivia along. 'Have you had something to eat? Let me see if we've got some people for you to talk to. Have you met Devorée?'

Putting thoughts of shagging strangers firmly to one side, she turned her attention to the business of quote-gathering. Everyone wanted to be in British *Elan* and the launch was easy pickings for sound bites. After an hour or so she had vaguely face-cream-based quotes from Devorée, Chris Blackwell, the manager of the Delano, a couple of handsome men whom she suspected were for hire, the guy who did the list at Tantra, the PR for Michael Kors and P. Diddy. It was more than enough for the solitary paragraph which would inevitably prove the sum total of *Elan*'s coverage. Moving on to the *Sunday Times* 'Cool Miami' piece, she quickly filled her notebook with the grandmother of one of the models, who had lived on the South Shore Strip twenty years before it became fashionable again; a cop who claimed to have been on the scene after the Versace shooting and was plainly lying and – *la pièce de résistance* – Gianni Versace's former cleaning lady. Olivia even managed a moment with J-Lo, who gave her a few words. She was almost electrifying: radiant skin, great voice and attitude – *über*-cool. For a second Olivia started to want to *be* J-Lo, then caught herself and stopped.

'Olivia?' Damn, it was Melissa again. 'Can I introduce you to the creator of Devorée's Crème de Phylgie? Though,

HELEN FIELDING

of course, Devorée has selected the ingredients personally herself.'

Olivia let out an odd noise. It was the man who had been watching her. He was a compelling mixture of soulful and powerful: finely drawn features, a straight nose, fine, arched brows, hooded brown eyes.

'This is Pierre Ferramo.' She was disappointed. The name sounded like something you'd find in gilt-plastic faux hand-writing, pinned on an overpriced tie in a duty-free shop.

'Ms Joules.' He was wearing a ridiculously over-the-top gold watch, but his hand was rougher than she expected and the handshake strong.

'Pleased to meet you,' she said. 'Congratulations on Crème de Phylgie. Does it really contain sea slugs?'

He didn't laugh, he glinted. 'Not the sea slugs themselves, only an essence: an oil secreted by their skin.'

'It sounds like something you'd want to wipe off rather than put on.'

'Does it, indeed?' He raised his eyebrows.

'I hope you won't be writing that in your piece,' trilled Melissa with a brittle laugh.

'I'm sure Ms Joules will write with infinite subtlety and grace.'

'Infinite,' she said, putting her chin up cheekily.

There was an extremely charged pause. Melissa looked from one to the other then started twittering. 'Oh look, she's leaving. Will you excuse us? Pierre, I just want you to say hello to one of our very special guests before she leaves.'

'Very well,' he said wearily, murmuring to Olivia as he left, 'sea slugs indeed.'

Melissa introduced Olivia to more of her client base: two members of a boy band called Break whose gimmick was surfing and who had a 'Beach Boys meets Radiohead fusion vibe'. Olivia had never heard of the band, but the two boys were rather sweet. Beneath the surf-white hair, their complexions displayed a fascinating mixture of sunburnt crispiness and acne. She listened as they chattered on about their careers, Beavis and Butthead-type nervous sniggers punctuating a fragile veneer of bored arrogance. 'We're auditioning for parts in this, like, movie? With surfers?' Their strange interrogatory intonation seemed to suggest that someone as old as Olivia might not understand words like 'movie' or 'surfers'. 'It's going to launch the single off the album?'

Little sweetie ones, she thought. Two hits and they'd be off, but they didn't know it. She felt like giving them a motherly chat, but instead she just listened and nodded, watching Pierre Ferramo out of the corner of her eye.

'That's the guy who's, like, the producer? Of the movie?' whispered one of the boys.

'Really?'

They all watched as Ferramo made his stately way towards a mysterious-looking group of dark men and models. He moved gracefully, languid almost to the point of being fey, but exuding a sense of tremendous latent power. He reminded her of someone. The group parted like the Red Sea to receive him, as if he were a guru or god rather than a face-cream creator slash producer slash whatever. He settled himself down gracefully, crossing one leg over the other, revealing an expanse of bare leg, black shiny slip-ons and thin silky grey socks. A couple close to the group rose to leave their sofa.

'Shall we sit a bit nearer?' said Olivia, nodding towards the empty seats.

It was a silly, too-big sofa, so Olivia and the surf boys had almost to climb onto it, and then either virtually lie down or sit with their legs dangling like children. Ferramo looked up

17

as she sat and graciously inclined his head. She felt her senses quicken and looked away. She breathed slowly, remembering her scuba-diving training: just keep breathing, deep breaths, be cool at all times.

She turned back to the boys, crossing her legs and smoothing her hand across her thigh. She moistened her lips, laughed and played for a second with the delicate diamond and sapphire cross at her throat. She could feel his eyes on her. She raised her lashes, preparing to look straight into those penetrating dark eyes. *Oh.* Pierre Ferramo was staring down the cleavage of the tall, unbelievably beautiful Indian model on his other side. He said something to her and the two of them rose, his arm around her, his hand on her hip, guiding her away from the table. Olivia looked at one of the spotty boys and giggled foolishly. He leaned forward and whispered, 'It was doing it for me,' and traced a tiny circle with his finger on her thigh. She laughed her deep throaty laugh and closed her eyes. It had been a while.

Halfway across the terrace, Pierre Ferramo heard Olivia's laugh and raised his head, like an animal catching a scent. He turned to Melissa, who was hovering at his elbow and murmured a few words to her, then he continued his dignified progress towards the lobby, the tall, silken-haired Indian model at his side.

As she sipped her apple Martini, Olivia was struggling to think who it was that Ferramo reminded her of: the hooded eyes, the sense of intelligence and power, the languid movements.

She felt a hand on her arm and jumped.

'Olivia?' It was the wretched Melissa. 'Mr Ferramo would like you to join him for a small private party he is having in his apartment tomorrow night.'

Olivia could hardly breathe. The small hairs were rising

on the back of her neck and her forearms. She had suddenly realized exactly who Ferramo reminded her of. It was Osama Bin Laden.

'All right,' she said, brave and resolute, eyes darting this way and that in terror. 'I shall be there.'

Melissa looked at her oddly. 'It's only a party.'

4

Quivering with excitement, fear and lust, Olivia let herself into her room and flung herself on the bed. She kicked off her sandals and, rubbing a blister on her left foot with one hand, she dialled a number with the other. 'It's me,' she whispered urgently into the receiver.

'Olivia, it's the middle of the bloody night.'

'I know, I know. Sorry. But it's very important.'

'OK, what? Don't tell me. You've discovered Miami is a giant hologram designed by aliens? You're getting married to Elton John?'

'No,' said Olivia. She began to have second thoughts about asking Kate's advice if she was going to be like this.

'What? Come on.'

'I think I've found Osama Bin Laden.'

Kate started laughing. She laughed for quite a long time. Olivia's shoulders slumped and she blinked rapidly, hurt. Kate O'Neill was her friend but also a foreign correspondent on the *Sunday Times*. Olivia wanted her approval more than she could quite admit to herself.

'OK,' Kate said eventually. 'How drunk are you, exactly?'

'I am not,' Olivia said indignantly, 'drunk.'

'You're sure it's not a resurrected Abraham Lincoln?'

'Shut up,' said Olivia. 'But seriously. Just think about it.

Where better for Osama Bin Laden to hide than in plain sight where no one's expecting to see him?'

'I could think of, ooh, three, maybe four hundred places, just off the top of my head. Is he six foot four, late forties?'

'No, that's the whole point. He's had plastic surgery. He's completely altered his appearance. He could easily have had some length taken out of each leg and his face changed.'

'Right, right. So, if you look at it that way, Osama Bin Laden could be Oprah Winfrey, Britney Spears or Eminem. Why have you plumped for this guy?'

'It's something about him. He's sort of languid.'

'Oh, why didn't you say? *Languid?* Well that's definite then. I mean he is number one on the FBI's Most Languid List.'

'Shut up. He says he's called Pierre Ferramo. He's pretending to be French, but I don't think he is. He kind of rolls his *r*s, like an Arab. I mean, it's brilliant.'

'Right, right. Was Osama Bin Ferramo drinking alcohol?'

'Yes,' she said doubtfully.

'Did he flirt with you?'

'Yes.'

'Olivia. Osama Bin Laden is a Muslim. Do you know what a Muslim is?'

'Of course I know what a Muslim is,' Olivia hissed. 'What I'm saying is that it's a disguise. He's not in some cave in Afghanistan. He's moving around in fashionable circles pretending to be some international businessman slash playboy slash producer. I'm going to get to the bottom of it. I'm going to bring him to justice, save the world from terror and become a twenty-five-times millionaire.'

'Promise me something.'

'What?'

'Promise me you won't ring up Barry and tell him you've found Osama Bin Laden at a face-cream launch.'

Olivia said nothing. She was a believer in independent thought. She often wondered: when the Twin Towers were hit, when the authorities told everyone to stay where they were and not evacuate the building, would she have been one of the ones who did as they were told and stayed, or would she have thought for herself and got out?

'Olivia, are you listening to me? You remember the Sudan locust cloud? The Surbiton Moonies who turned out to be a Scout troop? The Gloucestershire ghoul which turned out to be steam from an air-conditioning vent? The *Sunday Times* has only just started to trust you again. So please: do your Miami story on time, to length, nicely, and don't bugger things up for yourself.'

'OK,' Olivia said sheepishly. 'Thanks and everything.'

But she couldn't sleep. She couldn't get over the brilliance of Osama Bin Ferramo's plan. Who would suspect? Everyone knew al-Qaeda operatives were geeky types: engineers in grungy clothes who lived in grim apartments in Hamburg, or faded thirties terraced houses in Cricklewood, eating Indian takeaways together, praying in makeshift mosques and faxing their instructions from post offices in Neasden. Al-Qaeda operatives didn't wander around being flash at parties in cool hotels and drinking apple Martinis. Al-Qaeda operatives didn't produce movies and have hyperactive PRs to up their profiles. It was the perfect cover. Perfect.

She jumped up and checked her email. No response from Barry. Then she Googled Pierre Ferramo.

There was nothing on him. Nothing at all. It was just *so* obvious why not.

She turned the lights off and tried to sleep again. Bloody jet-lag. She had to do something. Otherwise in forty-eight hours she'd be back in the London rain, writing articles about advances in knicker-line-hiding in the latest Marks & Spencer lingerie range. The computer glowed temptingly in the darkness. Where would be the harm in at least alerting Barry?

5

She sat outside a cafe on the South Shore Strip waiting for Barry's morning call and wishing it would stop being so windy. It was sunny and humid, but the wind was a roaring, flapping constant in the background. Breakfast was Olivia's favourite meal: coffee and something piggy like a muffin. Or a smoked-salmon and cream-cheese bagel. Or banana pancakes. And as many newspapers as possible spread before her. But this morning the *New York Times*, the *Miami Herald*, *USA Today* and two British tabloids had to be restrained under the salt and pepper. She had ordered cinnamon-apple French toast in order to eradicate the remnants of last night's apple Martinis. Treat apple with apple – like snake bite with snake venom.

Olivia believed that her first thought on waking was the one she should listen to. This morning, though, owing to an unfortunate bedtime struggle with the venetian blind, which had spoilt the designer perfection of the room by getting stuck with one end up and one end down, the slats splaying out in between, she had been woken at five thirty, after three hours' sleep, by the full force of the Miami sunrise, and thus did not have any thoughts as such. Technically, then, her first thought on waking would be her first thought after taking her first drink of coffee. That, she thought with relief, seeing the waiter appear with her order, would be now. She beamed her appreciation, poured herself a cup, took a delicious gulp and waited for the thought.

It's him, she thought. *It's Osama Bin Laden hiding in plain sight after extensive plastic surgery with six inches taken out of each leg.*

She poured maple syrup onto the cinnamon-apple French toast triangle, stuck her knife in and watched the puréed apple ooze out, imagining confronting Osama Bin Ferramo at his party that night: 'Killing is so very wrong. We, as nations, must learn to honour our differences and live in peace.' Osama Bin Ferramo, breaking down, would sobbingly agree that his Holy War must end and that he would work tirelessly in future for world peace alongside Paddy Ashdown, President Carter, Ginger Spice, et al. Olivia would be internationally fêted, elevated to foreign correspondent, awarded an honorary Pulitzer . . . her mobile rang.

'Hi,' she answered, in a tense, urgent voice, glancing behind her to check for al-Qaeda spies. It was Barry.

'OK, *numero uno*: this floating apartment-ship story . . .'

'Yes!' said Olivia, excitedly. 'It's a really good story. It's huge. And the people live on it all year round and just fly in by helicopter. I could do it in a couple of extra days.' Olivia had the phone wedged between her ear and shoulder while she tucked into the apple French toast.

'Oh, I agree it's a good story. So good, in fact, that, as you apparently failed to notice, we covered it in a full-page spread in the Style section last week.'

Olivia paused with her toast halfway to her mouth.

'That's a section of the *Sunday Times*, the newspaper you're supposed to be working for. Indeed, the very section of the *Sunday Times* you are supposed to be working for. You do, I assume, read the *Sunday Times* occasionally, you're familiar with it, at least?'

'Yes,' she said, brows lowered.

'And this other "fantastic news story" you've found. What might that be? Miami invaded by walking dolphins, perhaps? The Iraqi information minister spinning vinyl in the lobby?'

Thank God she hadn't emailed him after all.

'Well, actually it's something I've just started working on. I'll tell you more in a couple of—'

'Shut up. How are we getting along with the story we are supposed to be doing? The story we've been sent out to Miami, at considerable expense, to cover? Any chance of us turning our attention to that at some point? At all?'

'Oh yes, yes. I'm doing that. It's all fine. But I'm onto some really good leads for another story. I promise you, it's really good. If I could just stay one more night and go to this party, then . . .'

'No. En. Oh. No. You file "Cool Miami" by six o'clock your time tonight. Fifteen hundred words. Spelled correctly. With normal punctuation, not an assortment of strange markings put in randomly, to help. And then you do not go to parties, go shopping, or get waylaid by any other form of irrelevant entertainment. You go to the airport, get the night flight and come home. Got it?'

By a supreme effort of will, she refrained from telling him that:

1. He was missing the biggest story of the twenty-first century.
2. One day he would be sorry.
3. Re his punctuation slur: language was a beautiful free-flowing, evolving thing which should not be fettered by artificial rules, regulations and strange markings imposed from without rather than within.

'OK, Bazzer,' she said instead. 'I'll do it by six o'clock.'

*

Elan had not yet called to nix the *OceansApart* story, so she thought it wouldn't do any harm to nip quickly down to the harbour to take a look, just in *case*, so that if *Elan* did happen to call and say yes, then she would have some more material. Plus, she could be picking up more local colour for the *Sunday Times* piece while she was at it. It was nine already, but she figured that if she got back from the *OceansApart* by ten thirty, she'd still have seven and a half hours to write the article for Barry. And spell-check it. And email it. But it would definitely be fine. Definitely. That was only about two hundred words an hour. And she could run! It was, after all, vital to exercise.

Unfortunately, Olivia did not have a proper grasp of the passage of time. In fact, both Barry and Kate had noted on several occasions that Olivia thought time was personal, that it moved at the speed she wanted it to. Their view was that this was not a belief compatible with being a newspaper journalist with deadlines to meet and so on.

Jogging along the South Shore Strip, even at breakfast time, was like flipping through radio channels: a different beat blaring out from each cafe. Waiters were hosing down the pavements, gardeners blowing away leaves. The lines of hooting cars were gone, the party people only recently tucked into bed. Olivia passed a cafe playing salsa music; inside, everything – walls, tables, plates, menus – was covered in the same lurid jungle print; the waitress, even at that hour, was wearing a leopard-skin, halter-neck catsuit. She crossed the road to get a better view of the campy grandeur of the Versace mansion and the art deco hotels – whites, pinks, lilacs, oranges – the Pelican, the Avalon, the Casa Grande, curves and funnels suggesting trains and ocean liners. It was hot already, the shadows of the fluttering palm trees crisp against the white pavement. She started working out her piece as she ran.

27

'Think Miami is full of old people's condos, the hum of electric wheelchairs and people shooting each other? Think again!'

'Suddenly there are more revamped art deco hotels everywhere!'

'If Paris is the new elevator music, Miami is the new Eminem.'

'If Manchester is the new Soho, then Miami is the new Manhattan.'

'If Eastbourne had a makeover from Ian Schrager and Stella McCartney, then forced all its inhabitants into a giant tanning booth . . .'

Oh God. She couldn't do this stuff any more. It was nonsense. It didn't mean anything. She had to find a proper story.

At the south end of the strip were huge apartment blocks, and behind them, gliding smoothly, she could see a huge ocean liner. She must be close to the docks. She jogged along the street, the area becoming rougher and tattier, until she reached the water at South Pointe Park, where the deep shipping lane passed straight in front of the apartment blocks and marina. The liner was moving fast, its bulbous rear disappearing towards the docks: big, but not the *OceansApart*. She peered at the skyline beyond it: the tower blocks of downtown Miami, the arched bridges of the highways criss-crossing the big expanses of water, the cranes marking the docks. She started to run towards them, but they were further away than they seemed; she kept thinking she was so nearly there, it would be stupid to turn back.

She had stopped at the end of a traffic bridge, trying to get her breath and pushing a damp strand of hair from her forehead, when she suddenly realized that what she had thought was an office block beyond the liner was in fact the *OceansApart*. Here, in the harbour, it dwarfed all the other ships around it, making them look like toys or miniatures. It was monolithic. It looked too big to be safe, as though it might topple over.

Across the way, a small crowd of people was gathered on a patch of grass, a group of taxis parked alongside. Olivia made her way over. She counted the decks: there were fifteen of them, lines of portholes, then layer upon layer of balconies. There were people sitting out on white chairs at tables, eating breakfast. She glanced around at the crowd. Some of them were clearly passengers, taking photographs with the *OceansApart* in the background, dressed in the garish and bizarre outfits which seem to go with the cruising life. Olivia smiled at the sight of a lady with a bright orange face and red lipstick, which had missed her mouth, wearing a little white boxy jacket with epaulettes and a captain's hat, and an embarrassed husband in pastel, infantilized cruise gear beside her, posing while a taxi driver took their photos.

'Excuse me, love.' It was a northern English accent. Olivia turned to see an old couple, the auburn-haired lady in an elegant green dress with a cream handbag and matching cream shoes. The cream shoes made Olivia think of holidays in Bournemouth. The man, who was only slightly taller than the lady, and stockily built, was holding her jacket. It was sweet the way he was smoothing it proprietorially, as if he was proud to be holding it for her.

'Would you mind taking our photo in front of the ship?' The lady held out a disposable camera.

Olivia smiled. 'Where are you from?'

'Leeds, love. Just near Leeds.'

'I'm from Worksop,' said Olivia, taking the camera.

'Ee, 'ecky thump,' quipped the old man. 'You look out of

breath. Have you been running? Don't you want to get your breath back a minute?'

'No, I'm fine. Closer together,' said Olivia, peering through the viewfinder. 'Ooh, hang on. I'm going to have to move back a bit to get it all in.'

'Don't bother, love. Just get a bit in. We know what it is, don't we, Edward?' The lady was a charming mix of elegant looks and broad Yorkshire accent.

Olivia clicked the camera, looking at the beaming couple through the viewfinder. It suddenly felt as though all the scariness and bad things in life had receded, and she was in a lovely granny-and-grandpa world of biscuit tins and doilies. To her horror, she felt tears pricking her eyelids.

'There you go. Souvenir of Miami,' she said slightly too cheerily, handing back the camera.

The lady chuckled. 'Running. It makes me feel jiggered just looking at you. Do you want a cough sweet?' She began to rummage in her bag.

'So, love,' said the old man, 'what are you doing so far away from Worksop?'

'I'm a journalist,' said Olivia. 'I'm trying to get my magazine to let me write something about the *OceansApart*.'

'Eee, right fair. A journalist. That's grand, that is.'

'We can tell you all sorts about the ship, love.'

'Do you live on it?'

'Yes!' said the man proudly.

'Well, only part of the time,' said the lady.

'That's our cabin. Look, halfway up, in the middle, with the pink towel,' said the man, pointing.

'Oh yes, looks nice. Lovely balcony. I'm Olivia, by the way.'

'Elsie, and this is Edward. We're on our honeymoon.'

'Your honeymoon? Have you known each other a long time?'

'Fifty years,' said Edward, proudly. 'She wouldn't have me when she were eighteen.'

'Well, you started courting someone else. What did you expect?'

'Only because you wouldn't have me.'

Olivia loved people's stories. Scratch the surface of anyone and you'd find something strange and complicated going on.

'Do you want a lift anywhere?' said the man. 'We're taking a taxi to South Beach.'

'Ooh, yes please,' said Olivia. 'As a matter of fact, I've made myself a bit late.'

'So, carry on with the story,' Olivia said as the taxi pulled out onto the highway.

'Well,' said Elsie, 'anyway, he thought I weren't interested, and I thought he weren't interested, and we lived in the same town for fifty years and never said 'owt. Then my husband died, and Vera, that was Edward's wife as was, she died, and then . . .'

'Well, here we are. We was married two weeks ago and we've got a lot of missed time to make up for.'

'That's so sad,' said Olivia. 'All that time, wasted.'

'Aye,' said Edward.

'Nay, lass,' said Elsie. 'You can't go regretting stuff because there wasn't anything else that could have happened.'

'What do you mean?'

'Well, you know, it's cause and effect. Every time anything happens it's because of all the other things happening all over the world. Any time you make a decision, there wasn't 'owt else you could have done because it were who you were, like, and it was all the things that had happened up to then that made you decide that. So there's no point regretting 'owt.'

Olivia looked at her, nodding thoughtfully. 'I'm going to

add that to my Rules for Living,' she said. Her mobile rang, dammit.

'You can answer it, love, we're not bothered.'

It was a commissioning editor from *Elan*, barking at her that they wanted the *OceansApart* piece, and she could stay another two nights to do it. 'But we don't want any white shoes and blue rinses, right?' Olivia flinched, hoping her new friends couldn't hear. 'We want hip people, not hip replacements.'

Olivia said goodbye and clicked the phone off with a sigh. It rang again immediately.

'Where are you?' bellowed Barry. 'I've just rung the hotel and you're not there. What the fuck are you doing?'

'I. Am. Do. Ing. It,' she said. 'I'm just doing a bit of extra research.'

'Get the fuck on and write it,' he said. 'Six o'clock, finished, fifteen hundred words. Or that's the last time I'm sending you abroad.'

'He sounded a bit aereated,' said Edward.

'I don't like men what shout, do you?' said Elsie.

She arranged to come and talk to them the following morning at eleven. They said they'd introduce her to the residents' manager and show her round their apartment and 'all the amenities'. They dropped her off in front of the Delano. She looked at her watch and realized that, unfortunately, it was nearly quarter to twelve.

'If sex is the new elevator music, then Miami is the new Manhattan. If . . .'

It was quarter to four and she still hadn't got an opening paragraph. She sat back from the computer with her pen in her mouth. Then, glancing behind her guiltily, as if she was in the newsroom, she brought up AOL and hit Google, typing

in 'Pierre Ferramo'. Still nothing there. It was definitely weird.
If he was for real, there would be something at least. She
typed in 'Olivia Joules'. You see, even she had two hundred
and ninety-three entries. She started to read them: articles
from the years she'd been trying to make it as a journalist, the
first one about car alarms. Crufts Dog Show. She smiled
fondly at the memories. Then she thought she'd have a little
look through her clothes to think about what to wear for the
party. As she stood up, she caught sight of the clock.

OhmybloodyGodandfuck! It was four thirty-five, and she
hadn't written a word.

Olivia dived back to the desk and hit her sleek titanium iBook
with a sudden frenzy.

'In the capital of England the worlds of fashion, music, TV,
theatre, movies, literature, newspapers and politics combine in
one small city like a writhing knot of snakes. In America these
areas are separated out into capitals of their own. Traditionally, it was politics in Washington, literature, arts and fashion
in New York, entertainment in LA. But within the last few
years Miami – formerly the capital of guns, shady business
dealings, smugglers and sun-seeking geriatrics – has exploded
onto the capital-city scene in a burst of hot light, art deco and
leopard skin as the centre of extravagant cool, with the glitz
of music, fashion and entertainment increasingly drawn there
as if by the force of a giant pink and ice-blue magnet.'

There. Hahahaha. She would rephrase it and start with a bit
of colour. Easy-peasy. The phone rang. It was Melissa, the PR
girl, 'just asking' how she was getting on with the article and
checking that she was coming to Pierre Ferramo's 'little gathering'. Olivia tried to type with one hand, the phone tucked
under her chin, desperately waiting for a gap between sentences
which never came. No sooner had she got rid of Melissa than

the phone rang again. This time it was the commissioning editor from *Elan*, in a leisurely mood, wanting to talk more about the *OceansApart*: the angle, the length, the style, people who might be good for interviews. It was nearly five o'clock. It was hopeless, hopeless. Why the fuck had she got herself into this mess? She was doomed – doomed to write articles beginning: 'Suddenly there are more hats everywhere!' She would never be allowed out of the office again.

6

Back in London, in the *Sunday Times* office, Barry Wilkinson was pacing in front of the big old-fashioned clock, cursing Olivia.

He watched, furious, as the second hand clicked towards eleven o'clock, poised to pick up the phone.

'OK, the silly cow's flunked. We're going to have to run the standby.'

Barry's deputy burst into the room brandishing a printout. 'She's filed it!'

'And?' said Barry, witheringly.

'It's great,' said the deputy.

'Humph,' said Barry.

Meanwhile, Olivia too had been glancing furiously at the clock, but unlike Barry she had been doing so while trying on outfits. Why did people in America do everything so bloody early? Lunch at noon. Dinner at seven. It was like being back in 1960s Worksop. And now she was to face a scary party hosted by Osama Bin Laden. She giggled to herself, remembering an interview she had read with the wife of a British newspaper owner about how to deal with scary occasions. The woman had said, 'But surely one simply puts on one's Balenciaga and *goes*!'

It didn't take Olivia long. All she was doing was selecting a uniform. Eight years earlier, as part of the Rachel-to-Olivia metamorphosis, she had made one supreme effort to change herself from plump to thin, to arm herself with a great body as a useful tool in life. What had startled her was how differently the world had treated her old plump self and her new thin self. It was then that she realized she could manipulate reactions. If you wanted to create a stir and have everyone notice you, that wasn't so hard. You just wore something very small and attention-seeking, like a wannabe movie star does at a premiere. If you wanted no one even to realize you were there: ill-fitting jeans with hankies in the pockets, flat shoes and a baggy sweatshirt, no make-up, glasses, and hair all over the place. She became, in her instinctive way, a master of disguise. Dressing was all about uniforms and codes. People didn't look much beyond that outside Worksop, until you got to know them, if you ever got that far.

Tonight, she decided, she needed a look which was attractive, but not so tarty as to offend any possible Muslim sensibility (tricky), and shoes which enabled one to walk or at least stand still without getting blisters. She had packed her rich, attention-seeking uniform (designer slippy things, nice high shoes which you could walk in but not necessarily do stairs in, enough posh jewellery to carry off some flashier fakes) and also her usual equipment: pepper-spray pen, spyglass, hat pin (an old failsafe of her mother's to counter would-be assailants) and survival tin, of course.

After a very small number of attempts, she arrived at her joy-inducing Gucci borderline-bondage sandals, a simple pale slip dress and a Pucci wrap to cover her shoulders. She thought about covering her head as well, then realized she was getting carried away. She gave her reflection a rousing, almost cheerleader-like smile, and called downstairs for a cab. At the last moment, she stuffed the hat pin, pepper spray and survival tin into the Louis Vuitton clutch along with her miniature address book, just in case. She would show Barry.

She flicked on CNN just before she left to see if anything exciting had happened. They were doing a story about a time capsule from fifty years ago being discovered in a school.

'*A message from the past*' – dramatic pause – '*from those who lived in it*,' concluded the presenter sententiously. Olivia laughed. She loved the CNN riddle-me-ree phraseology: '*He's tall, he's got a moustache, and he wants to poison the world: Saddam Hussein!*' '*It's wet, it's see-through, but without it we'd die: waterrrrr!*' Then her eye was caught by the text strip running underneath the pictures: alongside '*Yankees 11: Redsox: 6*' it read: '*Osama Bin Laden sighted in southern Yemen. Sources call sighting "conclusive".*'

She stared at it, blinking, disbelieving. 'Oh,' she said eventually. 'Oh dear. Though, obviously, that's good.'

7

Olivia's feelings of sheepishness escalated as she arrived at Ferramo's apartment block and realized she had got a bit carried away. She had been expecting a cross between an overpriced Knightsbridge hotel and the interiors favoured by Saddam Hussein in his early promotional videos: fitted carpets, square beige sofas, stilted flower arrangements in front of long net curtains, curly gilt chairs and bulbous lamps. In her fevered mind, Ferramo had sprouted a beard, a turban, flowing robes and a Kalashnikov. She was expecting sweet Middle Eastern musks and perfumes, Turkish (for some reason) delight and Ferramo sitting cross-legged on a prayer mat next to one of the bulbous lamps.

But the block was an ultra-modern building, the public areas designed in a ruthlessly minimalist style with a nod in the direction of the nautical – everything was white or blue and dotted with porthole accents, i.e. round things. There were no bulbous lamps or curly chairs. Pierre Ferramo's penthouse occupied the entire nineteenth and twentieth floors. As she stepped out of the white metallic be-portholed elevator, she gazed awestruck at the spectacle in front of her.

The twentieth floor was one vast, glass-walled room, leading out onto a terrace which overlooked the sea. An illuminated lap pool – bright petrol blue – stretched the entire length of the terrace. At the back of the room, through one of the walls of glass, the sun was setting behind the Miami skyline in a flamboyant burst of oranges and salmon pinks.

Ferramo was seated at the head of a vast white table, where a card game was in play, an almost palpable air of gravitas and power emanating from his dark, elegant figure. Behind him, the tall Indian model was resting a hand, consort-like, on his shoulder. Her long black hair shone against a pure white evening dress, the whole effect set off by a dazzling array of diamonds.

Olivia looked away, ashamed, afraid that Ferramo somehow knew what lunacies had been running round in her brain. He looked like a clever, dignified businessman: a rich man, a powerful man certainly, but not a terrorist. Thank God she hadn't said anything to Barry.

'Your name?' said the boy at the entrance, holding out a list.

'Olivia Joules,' she said, fighting the urge to apologize, just in general.

'Ah yes, come this way.'

The young man led her to a waiter holding a tray. She carefully selected a glass of sparkling water – no drunken fuck-ups for her tonight – and looked round the room, reminding herself: *No one is thinking about you; they're thinking about themselves, just like you.*

Two young girls in T-shirts and tight jeans, the waistbands almost indecently low, were exchanging air kisses. She recognized them as the girls who'd been posing, S-shaped, on the red carpet the night before.

'Oh. My. God.' One girl's hand shot to her mouth. 'I have that T-shirt.'

'You're kidding me.'

'The exact same T-shirt.'

'Where did you get it?'

'The Gap.'

'So did I! I got it in the Gap.'

'Oh. My. God.'

The two girls stared at each other, overcome by this almost magical coincidence. Olivia felt she had to help them through this before one of them burst on the white carpet. She moved slowly towards them.

'Hi. How do you two know each other?' she ventured with a friendly smile, fighting down the sense of being the most unpopular girl in the playground. Would that she had the Gap T-shirt too.

'Oh, we both work at—'

'We're actresses,' snapped the other. They, like the T-shirts, were almost spookily identical: big breasts, tiny hips, long blonde hair, brown pencil outlining their glossed collagen pouts. The only difference was that one was much prettier than the other.

'Actresses! Wow,' said Olivia.

'I'm Demi,' said the less pretty one. 'This is Kimberley. Where are you from?'

'England.'

'England. Is that London?' said Kimberley. 'I want to go to London.'

'You're lucky, living here.'

'We don't live in Miami, we're just visiting. We're from LA. Well, not *from* LA.'

'My family's part Italian, part Romanian and part Cherokee,' explained Kimberley.

'Olivia,' she said, shaking hands and feeling awfully English. 'So you're just visiting? Are you working here?'

'No,' said Kimberley airily, pulling at her jeans. 'Pierre just flew us over for the launch.'

'That was nice of him. Gorgeous, isn't he?'

'Yes. Are you an actress?' said Kimberley suspiciously. 'Do you know him from Paris?'

'Can't act for toffee. I only met him last night. I'm a journalist.'

'Oh. My. God. Which magazine are you from?'

'*Elan*.'

'*Elan*? That's British *Elan*, right? You should come to LA. You should give us a call. You could maybe do a profile on us.'

'OK,' she said, taking her little book out of her bag, hiding the survival tin. 'What's the number?'

The two girls looked at each other.

'Actually we're between addresses at the moment,' said Demi.

'But you can reach us through Melissa. You know, who does Pierre's PR.'

'Or you can ring us at work, at the Hilton.'

Kimberley looked furiously at Demi. 'We're just working there temporarily,' she said sharply, 'to keep us busy between auditions and rehearsals.'

'Of course. Which Hilton?'

'The Beverly Hilton?' said Demi eagerly. 'On Santa Monica and Wilshire? Where they hold the Golden Globes? I usually get to host the ladies' powder room during the Globes. It's awesome: four make-up stations, every kind of perfume. All the big stars come in for touch-ups: Nicole Kidman, Courtney Cox, Jennifer Connelly, you get to meet them close up.'

Oh, for God's sake. Osama Bin Ferramo indeed. He was just a playboy . . .

'Wow. What's Nicole Kidman like?' said Olivia.

'Oh my God,' said Demi, hand to her heart.

'But actually,' Kimberley leaned forward conspiratorially,

41

'we're going to be starring in the movie Pierre's producing. You've heard about that . . .'

. . . a cynical playboy, playboying on the dreams of innocent little wannabes.

'May I interrupt you, ladies?'

Olivia turned. A short, swarthy man had joined them, dark chest hair protruding from a yellow polo shirt. The chest hair, like the hair on his head, was very tightly curled, like pubic hair. He smelt of nasty sweet perfume. He held out his hand, glancing at her breasts. 'Hi, baby. Alfonso Perez. And you are . . .'

'Hi, honeybunny. Olivia Joules,' she said, glancing at his crotch. 'I met Pierre last night at the Devorée launch.'

'Ah yes. And you are an actress too? Perhaps we can find a role for you?' He had a thickly accented voice with heavily rolled *r*s.

'No, thanks. I can't act my way out of a paper bag.'

'That's funny,' said Kimberley. Why did Americans say 'That's funny'? They said it instead of laughing, as if funniness were something you observed from afar rather than something you participated in.

'Really, Ms Joules? You do not wish to be an actress?' It was Ferramo, who had somehow joined them without anyone noticing.

There was a collective intake of breath from Demi and Kimberley. They gazed, lip-lined pouts momentarily ajar. Pierre Ferramo's legs were encased in neatly pressed blue jeans. His shoulders looked broad in a soft grey cashmere sweater. Olivia forced herself to breathe normally and looked into the dark, penetrating eyes. He raised his eyebrows quizzically.

'I tried acting once. I was given some roles in a comedy revue. One by one all my parts were taken away from me, apart from that of Miss Guided, the mute chambermaid.'

The wannabes and the little oily man looked at her, baffled.

Ferramo showed a glimmer of amusement. 'You will excuse us?' he said to the group, taking her arm and beginning to guide Olivia away.

As the wannabes glowered, Olivia had to fight down playground-level feelings of smugness and one-upmanship, feelings she deeply disapproved of in any circumstances. *Divide and rule*, she found herself thinking. Ferramo was dividing his roost of girlies in order to rule it.

A waiter hurried up with a tray of champagne.

'Oh, no thank you,' said Olivia quickly as Ferramo handed her a long-stemmed glass.

'But you must,' he murmured. 'It is French. It is the finest.'

Yes, but are you? His accent wasn't easy to place.

'*Non, merci,*' she said. '*Et vous? Vous êtes français?*'

'*Mais bien sûr,*' he said, with an approving glance. '*Et je crois que vous parlez bien le français. Vous êtes, ou – je peux? – tu es une femme bien educatée.*'

I wish. Worksop Comprehensive, she thought, but merely smiled mysteriously, asking herself if *educatée* was a proper French word and resolving to look it up later.

Olivia had an ear for languages, and had discovered that even when she couldn't speak a foreign tongue, she could often understand it. Even if the words were double Dutch, she could usually guess at what the person might be saying, or figure it out through her sensitivity to nuances of expression. There had been a time when her lack of university education had made her sad, so she had made up for it herself. With books and tapes and visits she had developed fluency in French and passable Spanish and German. A couple of visits to the Sudan and the Muslim islands of Zanzibar and Lamu had given her the rudiments of Arabic. Unfortunately, the world of style-and-beauty journalism was not giving her much chance to use all this.

Taking a large swig of champagne, Ferramo led her through the party, ignoring the bids for his attention. It was like being with the star at a film premiere. Eyes followed them, particularly those of the tall Indian beauty. 'But of course, Ms Joules, the French are not exactly *populaire* in your country,' he said, leading her onto the terrace.

'Less so in this.' She laughed. 'Cheese-eating surrender-monkeys, Homer Simpson called them.' She looked up at him, smiling flirtatiously while gauging his reaction. He leaned against the cruise-ship-type railing, and smiled back, gesturing for her to join him.

'Ah, Monsieur Simpson. The fount of all human wisdom. And you? You are at one with the French *sensibilité*?'

She leaned on the cool metal rail and looked out to sea. The wind was still raging. The moon appeared from time to time behind ragged, racing clouds.

'I was against the invasion, if that's what you mean.'

'Because?'

'It didn't make any sense. They were punishing someone for breaking international law by breaking international law themselves. I don't think Saddam had anything to do with the World Trade Center attack. He and al-Qaeda hated each other. There was no evidence that he still had chemical weapons. I kept wondering if there was something they weren't telling us, but there wasn't. It just made me think you shouldn't listen to anyone in charge.'

'You are right. You are not an actress.' Ferramo laughed. 'You speak from the heart.'

'That's a bit hard on the old actresses, isn't it?'

'Pah! Do you know that every day over five hundred young people arrive in Los Angeles expecting to be actresses, flocking after fame and wealth like so many locusts? There is nothing else of value in their lives.'

'You seem to have taken rather a lot of them under your wing.'

'I wish to help them.'

'Sure you do.'

He glanced at her sharply. 'It is a brutal profession.'

'Pierre?' The tall Indian beauty came out onto the balcony and touched him possessively on the arm. She was accompanied by a good-looking, well-toned man of maybe forty with a wide smile which turned up at the edges – a cross between that of Jack Nicholson and Felix the Cat. 'Can I introduce you to Michael Monteroso? You remember, the genius facial technician who's been helping us? He's the toast of Hollywood,' she added, wrinkling her nose at Olivia in an attempt to be girlishly conspiratorial. 'Backstage at everything.'

For a fleeting second a look of contempt crossed Ferramo's fine features, then he composed his face into a gracious smile.

'But of course, Michael. A pleasure. I am delighted to meet the maestro at last.' Monteroso and he shook hands.

'And may I introduce my friend from London, Olivia Joules,' said Ferramo. 'A writer of great distinction.' He pressed her arm as if to suggest a shared joke. 'And, Olivia, this is Suraya Steele.'

'Hi,' Suraya said coolly, running her hand through her hair at one temple and flicking back the long shiny curtain so that it cascaded over her shoulders. Olivia stiffened. She hated women who did hair-flicking. It seemed so sneakily vain: disguising hair-smugness and 'everybody look at me and my lovely hair' attention-seeking as hair-tidiness, as if they were flicking their hair back simply to keep it off their faces. In which case why not use a kirby grip or a sensible Alice band?

'Don't you write about beauty for *Elan*?' Suraya purred, slightly pitying.

'Really?' said Michael Monteroso. 'Let me give you my

card and my web site. What I do is a special microdermabrasic instant-lift technique. I gave it to Devorée three minutes before the MTV awards.'

'Didn't she look great?' said Suraya.

'Will you excuse me?' murmured Pierre. 'I must return to the game. There is nothing worse than a host who wins, apart from a host who wins and then runs off.'

'Yeah, we should definitely get back there.' Suraya's accent was odd. It was a fluid mixture of drawling West Coast American and bookish Bombay. 'Don't want rumblings of discontent.'

As Michael Monteroso watched Ferramo's retreating back with evident disappointment, there was no need for Olivia to remind herself that no one was thinking about her. Monteroso looked like a man who had clawed his way to success late in life and was hanging on to it for all he was worth. He nodded at her vaguely, turned to see if there was anyone more interesting to talk to and broke into a white-toothed smile.

'Hey, Travis! How you doing, man?'

'Good, good. Good to see you.'

The guy sharing a high five with Monteroso was one of the most overtly good-looking men Olivia had ever seen, with ice-blue, wolf-like eyes, but she sensed desperation.

'How's it going?' said Monteroso. 'How's the acting?'

'Good, good, you know. I'm doing like a little writing, and, you know, lifestyle management, and I'm making these kind of lifeline boxes, and, you know . . .'

So that would be bad, then, on the acting front, thought Olivia, trying not to smile.

'Olivia, I see you've met Travis Brancato! Do you know he's writing the script for Pierre's new movie?'

Heart sinking, Olivia listened politely to Melissa's schtick, then escaped to find the giggly Beavis and Butthead guys from Break, who told her excitedly that they were going to be extras playing surfers on Ferramo's movie and introduced her to Winston, a beautiful black diving instructor who worked for various hotels on the Keys and was in town to take out clients on the *OceansApart*. He offered to show her round the ship the following afternoon, maybe even take her out for a dive. 'I kinda get the feeling I won't be busy. I've only had one client so far, and I had to bring him back because he had a pacemaker.'

Unfortunately, she was interrupted yet again by Melissa bearing a press release and a barrage of autowitter about Ferramo's new movie, including the news that Winston was going to be underwater consultant. Eventually, Olivia was forced to conclude that the reason she was there was not that Pierre Ferramo had noticed her, but because she was supposed to write an article promoting his new movie.

She left the throng and stepped back out onto the terrace, struggling with feelings of disappointment and indignation at allowing herself to be manipulated like an idiot. Looking out to sea, there was nothing but blackness now. She couldn't make out where the dunes ended and the beach began, but she could hear the waves pounding the shore. She noticed a metal staircase winding up from the balcony to a higher level. A fire escape? She looked furtively around and headed up, finding herself on a small private deck, enclosed by a wooden screen. She sat down out of the wind, pulling her wrap around her. If Ferramo had been Bin Laden, that would have been one thing. If he'd been a clever, dignified businessman who'd taken a shine to her, that would have been another. But he was a playboy, surrounding himself with a harem of wannabes of both sexes and using some insane fabrication of a movie which would never come to anything to lure them in like innocent dupes.

For a second she felt lonely and sad. Then she reminded herself that she wasn't lonely and sad. She was Olivia Joules. She had rejected a life of frying eggs for some bossy man and pushing a pram through the Worksop shopping centre. She was a self-made woman, travelling the world in search of meaning and adventure. She needed to get out of this daft party and get on.

There was a sound on the metal staircase. Someone was coming up. She stayed where she was, heart pounding. She hadn't done anything wrong. Why shouldn't she come onto the roof?

'Why, Ms Joules. You are roosting up here like a little bird.'

Ferramo was carrying champagne and two glasses. 'Now you will join me, surely, in one glass of Cristal.'

She gave in. She took a sip of the exquisite, ice-cold champagne and thought: *Rules for Living number fourteen: sometimes you just have to go with the flow.*

'Now tell me,' he said, raising his glass to hers, 'can you relax? Is your work complete? Do you have your story?'

'Oh, yes,' she said, 'but I'm covering another one now. The *OceansApart*. You know? The giant apartment ship that's docked in the harbour.'

'Oh really? How interesting.' His face said the opposite.

'But I really want to cover proper news stories,' she said hurriedly, trying to correct the shallow impression. 'Real stories' – *oh, though* – 'not that the face cream isn't a . . .'

'I understand. It is hardly of global significance. And with the *OceansApart* you will do what? Interviews perhaps? A visit to the ship?'

'Yes. Actually, I met a really nice couple, from the north of

England like me. I'm going to go and see them tomorrow and—'

'At what time?'

'Um, in the morning at—'

'I really do not think that is a good idea,' he murmured, taking her glass away and drawing her closer.

'Why not?' He was so close she could feel his breath against her cheek.

'Because,' he said, 'I hope that tomorrow morning you will be having breakfast . . . with me.'

He reached out and touched her face, masterfully raising it to his, his eyes melting into hers. He kissed her, hesitantly at first, his lips dry against her mouth, then passionately, so that her body pulsed into life and she was kissing him passionately in return.

'No, no,' she said, suddenly pulling away. What was she *doing*? Snogging a playboy with a roomful of his other snoggees downstairs.

He looked down, composing himself, steadying his breathing. 'There is something wrong?' he murmured.

'I've only just met you. I don't know you.'

'I see,' he said, nodding, thoughtful. 'You are right. Then we will meet, tomorrow, at nine. I will come to the Delano. And we will begin to get to know each other. You will be there?'

She nodded.

'You are true to your word? You can delay your interview?'

'Yes.' She didn't need to. It wasn't until eleven.

'Then good.' He stood, held out his hand and helped her up, smiling with a flash of his perfect teeth. 'And now we must rejoin the party.'

*

49

As Olivia was leaving, she saw the guest list, abandoned under crumpled napkins and dirty glasses on a white table by the door. Just as she was reaching for it, a door opened behind the table and Demi emerged adjusting her top, followed by the dark youth who'd been in charge of arrivals.

'Hi!' giggled Demi sheepishly and headed back into the party.

'I think I gave you my jacket when I arrived?' Olivia said to the youth, giving him a conspiratorial grin. 'Pale blue? Suede?'

'Of course. I will look for it straight away. I like your accent.'

'Thank you.' She flashed him a dazzling smile. *I like your accent too*, she thought. *And it's no more French than your boss's.*

'Oh, gosh!' She hurried along the corridor after the youth. 'I'm really sorry. I didn't come in a jacket. I'm an idiot.'

'That's all right, ma'am.'

'Brain like a sieve. Sorry. Thank you,' she said, slipping him five dollars.

And she stepped into the elevator, the guest list folded safely inside her clutch.

8

'You *kissed* him?'

'I know, I know. Oh God.' Olivia was stretching the phone to the end of its cord, looking out of the window at the ships' lights on the ocean, wondering if Ferramo was looking out there too. The moonlight kiss had – to her embarrassment – been even more effective than the Yemeni Bin Laden sighting in making her suspicions seem ridiculous.

'I'm going to have to be quick. I'm in the newsroom,' said Kate on the other end of the phone. 'So, let's just get this straight. Last night you call me to say he's Osama Bin Laden. Not twenty-four hours later you call me to say you've been snogging him on a rooftop. You're the most ridiculous human being I've ever met.'

'Well, you were right,' said Olivia.

'You didn't tell Barry?'

'Nearly,' giggled Olivia. 'But no. I'm going to meet him tomorrow.'

'Who? Barry?'

'No, Pierre.'

'Pierre Bin Laden?'

She giggled again. 'Shut up. I know, I know. I'm an idiot. But listen. I'm not going to sleep with him. I'm just going to have breakfast with him.'

'Right, right, sure,' said Kate. 'Oh fuck, got to go. Call me after, OK?'

Olivia lay back happily and surveyed the room. It was so cleverly designed. *My flat could be like this!* she thought excitedly. I *could have a lampshade ten sizes too big. I could have a chain instead of a toilet-roll holder and a round stainless-steel bowl instead of a washbasin. I could have a chandelier and a giant chess set in the garden, when I get a garden. And I'm going to paint the whole flat white and get rid of anything that isn't white.*

Excited by her new design schemes, Olivia changed into her pyjamas, set the alarm for seven, closed the now-mended blind and logged on to her email. There was a message from Barry. 'Re: Miami Cool.'

Eagerly she clicked 'Read'.

'Good.'

That was all: 'Good.' She glowed with smugness and pride. Wildly encouraged, she clicked 'Reply' and typed:

Re: Good.
1. Thanks, Bazzer.
2. *Elan* keeping me on another day.
3. Do you want a story about wannabe actresses? 500 a day
arriving in Los Angeles hoping to make it?
Over and out. Olivia.

She knocked out seven hundred and fifty words on the face-cream launch for *Elan*, then impulsively sent them the idea for the Los Angeles wannabe article, as well as an article on making rash judgements when you first meet someone and how first impressions can be completely wrong.

*

The following morning Olivia was up and dressed freakishly early. By seven thirty, she was powering along the South Shore, determined to eradicate all foolish thoughts about Ferramo's terrorist alter ego from her brain while giving her cheeks a pleasing healthy glow. It was windier than ever; leaves and branches had fallen from the palms, shreds of them were littering the road. A waiter was running after a tablecloth as it flapped away from him.

She looked at the beach, where the hobos were starting to stir. One of them was staring in lewd delight at an oblivious beachside yoga class: seven girls on their backs, opening and closing their legs. She found herself following the same route as yesterday, telling herself she'd get a taxi back and have plenty of time to make herself pretty for breakfast.

She came to a stop when she reached the grassy island where she had met the old couple. She sat down on a concrete wall to look at the *OceansApart*, once more overwhelmed by its enormity. She heard the bing-bong of a tannoy on the boat followed by an announcement. A seagull dived into the water for a fish. There was the usual dockside smell, petrol mixed with fishy odours and seaweed. The warm wind was rustling the surface of the water, little frothy waves lapping against the man-made rocky shore. People were on the balconies. She raised her spyglass to her eye, looking for Elsie and Edward's cabin. There it was in the middle of the boat, third deck from the top. Elsie was sitting in a white wicker chair in a white bathrobe, her hair caught up loosely, robe fluttering in the wind. And there was Edward, also in his bathrobe, standing in the doorway. *Lovebirds*, she thought, *so sweet together*.

As she watched, a muffled boom came from deep under the water, making her jump. Suddenly the whole monstrous edifice gave a lurch like a drunken stagger, then righted itself, creating a huge wave which surged across the calm channel towards her, flinging itself against the rocky shore. She heard shouts and more figures appeared on the balconies, peering over the side.

Instinct told her to get away. There were some prefab shacks two hundred yards to her right, raised a couple of feet off the ground, and a steel storage container. She started to walk fast towards them. She was maybe twenty yards away from the steel container when there was a flash followed by a sound like a giant door slamming underground.

As she turned, a single large plume of water was rising beside the ship. She broke into a run, heading for the steel container, stumbling on the uneven ground. A siren started up, a blaring whoop like a nuclear alert from a fifties film. There were shouts, another siren, and then a blinding burst of blue light and a second boom, louder than anything she had ever heard. A great wall of hot air hit her, full of shards of metal and debris, flinging her forward onto the ground. Hearing herself gasping, her heartbeat banging in her ears, she dragged herself the final few feet towards the container. There was a gap underneath it, and she forced herself into it, wriggling to squeeze herself in as far as she could. She made a space around her mouth with her hands and breathed, trying to keep out the acrid smoke, trying to calm down, trying to shrink into herself to nothing, to hibernate like a tortoise in a cardboard box filled with straw.

NEVER PANIC. Rule number one, the chief survival rule, the major emergency rule for every place and for all time was Never Panic. Never let your mind be clouded by hysterics so you forget to look, forget to see what's really going on, or forget to do the simple, obvious thing.

As the sounds of destruction died down, leaving only screams and sirens, Olivia opened her eyes and peered out

A great wall of hot air hit her, full of shards of metal and debris, flinging her forward onto the ground.

from under the container. She was looking through bitter black smoke towards the dock, where a huge fire was raging. It was hard to see, but it looked as though the water itself was on fire. She could dimly make out the *OceansApart*, which seemed to have been blown in two. One side was still horizontal; the other had reared up until it was almost vertical, like the *Titanic* in the film. People were sliding down the deck and trying to cling to the railings while others were falling off into the flames. Elsie and Edward's balcony was right on the dividing line: where it had been was now a gash, showing the ship in cross-section like a diagram.

She decided to stay where she was. As she watched, the half of the ship which was still horizontal seemed to bend outwards. A wall of hot air hit her once more, as if she'd opened an oven, and there was another boom as the hull burst into a giant fireball. Olivia buried her chin in her chest, feeling the flesh on one hand burning. There was a deafening roar above her. She took a few seconds to make herself breathe properly, and then, saying, 'Calm, calm, never panic, calm,' wriggled out from her shelter, relieved to find her legs just about holding up beneath her. She ran for her bloody life, as behind her she heard the boom of the container exploding.

9

'You all right, ma'am?'

Olivia was crouched, her arms wrapped around her head, against a low building which was shielding her from the docks and the *OceansApart*. She looked up into the face of a youthful firefighter.

'Are you hurt?'

'I don't think so.'

'Can you stand up?'

She did and then vomited.

'Sorry about that,' she said, wiping her mouth. 'Not attractive.'

'I'm going to put this tag on you,' he said, hanging a yellow label round her neck. 'When the paramedics get to you, they'll sort you out.'

'I think they may have better things to do.'

The traffic had stopped on the highways and bridges. The city had come to a standstill. The air was filled with the sound of sirens. Helicopters were heading towards them from every direction.

He pulled out a water bottle. She took a small mouthful and handed it back.

'Keep it.'

'No, you keep it.' She nodded back towards the ship. 'You get out there. I'm fine.'

'Sure?'

'Sure.'

She leaned back against the wall and looked down at herself. She was black. The back of her left hand was burnt, although it didn't seem to hurt at all. She felt her hair gingerly. It was on the crispy side but still there – a miracle the peroxide hadn't combusted. Her eyes were smarting. There were hunks of torn metal and debris everywhere, and fires burning in dozens of places. *It's absolutely fine*, she thought. *It's perfectly simple. I'll just go into the water and find Edward and Elsie and bring them to shore*.

Olivia moved round the edge of the building, glancing for a moment out towards the open sea, the yachts in the marina, the blue sky. Then she looked back at the *OceansApart* and it was like switching from a TV holiday programme to a disaster movie. The vertical half of the ship was sinking fast, the water boiling around it. The other half had a vast blackened hole in the hull and was listing. Smoke and flames were still billowing from it. Between the fires that were burning all over the channel floated debris. In a surreal scene of carnage, human corpses were mixed up with those of sharks and barracuda. The firemen were starting to pour foam on the flames, and the bodies were floating in the middle of it all.

The paramedics had arrived and were setting up a help station. Olivia could see a man in the water close to the shore. Only his head was visible, his mouth wide open. As he looked in panic towards the shore, he went under. Olivia kicked off her trainers, took her sweatpants off and stepped into the water. Hot mud belched up between her toes. The water was hot too and dirty and thick. When she was close to where the man had disappeared, she took a big breath, steeled herself and plunged beneath the surface. She couldn't see a thing and she groped around in the foul murk for what seemed like an agonizingly long time until she finally felt him. He was barely conscious and he was a big man. She dived down again, put a hand on either side of his waist and pushed him upwards until he broke the surface. Then she let go for a second, burst into the open air beside him and took hold of his head. She held his nose and started rescue breathing, but it was too hard to keep them both buoyant. She turned to the shore and waved, then tried again. He took a huge, rasping breath and coughed up a spray of water, muck and vomit. She pushed it away in the water, put her arm around his neck as she'd been taught, and started to drag him towards the shore. The paramedics came out to meet her in the shallows and took him from her.

She looked back at the channel. It looked as though more people had been washed from the wreckage. A team of divers had arrived on the bank. She walked unsteadily over to where they were setting up. No one took any notice of her. She asked for a mask and some fins and a buoyancy-control jacket. The guy she spoke to looked at her for just a second.

'You OK?'

'Yes. Fine. I'm a diver.'

'You want tanks?'

She shook her head. 'No need to tank me. I'm doing it for the love of it.'

They looked at each other, both on the verge of an awful horror-induced hysteria.

'You certified?'

'Yes, but I think I'll be better working on the surface. Call me if you need another diver, though.'

'OK. Here,' he said, handing her the fins and the jacket, with its tubes and whistle attached. 'If you need help, just whistle.'

She walked back to the water's edge, putting on the jacket, blowing into the tube to inflate it until it felt tight against her ribcage, then letting the air out. For a moment Olivia felt nausea rising in her throat again. She thought she would find Elsie and Edward because they had been on their balcony on this side of the ship facing the shore. And although she had only just met them, they had brought with them all the comfort and familiarity of home. She realized dimly that trying to help them was some screwy attempt to heal the past: if she found them and saved them, then that would work a kind of alchemy on the trauma of her past and everything would be all right again.

Olivia brought back quite a few people, she didn't know how many. She felt as if she was on automatic pilot and none of it seemed quite real. She was too late with one woman; she saw her slip under the water, then come up, then go under again. By the time Olivia brought her to the surface, her face had a bluish tinge and there was foam around her mouth and nose. Olivia blew into the pipe to inflate her jacket, wiped the foam away from the woman's nose and blue-white lips and started the rescue breathing. The woman still had sunglasses round her neck on a gilt chain and was wearing a towelling top in red and white with a hood. After the third breath, the woman coughed and it seemed as if she would be all right, but as Olivia dragged her to shore she actually felt her dying. It wasn't much. It was like a shudder and then nothing. The paramedics took the woman away for CPR, but Olivia knew she was finished.

She sat down by a tree, suddenly exhausted. One of the paramedics came over with some water, got her to put her sweatpants back on, put a towel round her shoulders and rubbed her hands. He said she should go to the medical centre and helped her to her feet. The mobile phone in the pocket of her sweatpants rang as they walked along.

'Hey, Olivia. Listen, the *OceansApart* . . .'

'Hi, Barry,' she said wearily. 'The *OceansRippedApart*, you mean.'

'Listen, are you down there? What have you got for us?'

She gave Barry what he needed between his interruptions: what she had heard from the paramedics and divers and police, the fragments of recollections people had come out with as she brought them to the shore.

'Good. Any witnesses? Come on, where are you? Can you get me someone there? On the scene?'

She caught the eye of the paramedic who had brought her in. He took the phone, listened for a few seconds then said, 'You sure sound like one hell of an asshole, sir,' clicked off the phone and handed it back to her.

Olivia let the paramedics take her vital signs and cover the burns on her hand. She ate a piece of bread and took some rehydration salts. Then, with a blanket round her shoulders, she got up and walked around. In the makeshift centre were people who had been horribly burnt and people who had nearly drowned, or both. Then she saw a woman with auburn hair being brought in on a stretcher. Olivia stood there, bewildered, melting down, the pain from the last few hours reawakening the pain from the past – like hitting an old bruise. She found an empty corner, pulled the blanket over her, and curled into a ball. After a long time, she straightened up and wiped her fist across her face.

A voice said, 'Are you all right, love? Do you want a cup of tea?'

HELEN FIELDING

'Ooh, that looks too strong for her, love. Put a drop more milk in.'

She looked up and there, holding out a tray, were Edward and Elsie.

As darkness fell, Olivia staggered back into the foyer of the Delano, feeling like another unfathomable piece of furniture slash installation art herself, with mud, blood, debris, algae and God knows what else caked to her. She had a vision of herself crouched on all fours, with a chair or a lamp on her back. She made her way unsteadily, her vision blotchy, to the front desk.

'Can I have my key, please? Olivia Joules, Room 703,' she said thickly.

'OhmyGod. OhmyGOD,' said the receptionist. 'I'll call the hospital. I'll call the emergency services.'

'No, no. I'm fine, really. I just need . . . my key, and some . . . some . . . some . . .' She turned, clutching her key, looking for the elevator. She couldn't see where the elevator was. Then the beautiful bellboy was supporting her, then two bellboys, then total white-out.

For a second, when she woke, her mind was wiped clear, but then the memory of the disaster flooded her consciousness in a tangle of images: smoke, metal, heat, water, and the cold, dank feel of dead, drowned flesh against her own. She opened her eyes. She was in a hospital. Everything was white except for a red light flashing on and off beside her bed. She was Rachel Pixley aged fourteen, lying in a hospital bed, looking at a zebra crossing, running out of the newsagent's with a packet of Maltesers and a copy of *Cosmopolitan*. Running to catch up with her parents. There was a shout, a screech of tyres. She closed her eyes, thinking about a woman she had seen on television after the Twin Towers came down: a thickset woman from Brooklyn. She had lost a son and was talking tough. Then she said, 'I used to think I'd always want revenge: an eye for an eye, but now I just think, "How can the world be so ... cruel?"' And her voice broke on the 'cruel'.

The next time Olivia woke, she realized it was not a hospital but the Delano, and the red flashing light was not a heart monitor but the message light on the phone.

'Hi, Olivia! Hope I'm not calling too early. It's Imogen from Sally Hawkins's office at *Elan*. We got your email and we had a call from Melissa at Century PR about the wannabe story. Yes, Sally would like to go for it. We'll get onto the travel arrangements. Give us a call when you wake up. Oh, and good luck with the *OceansApart*.'

'Hi, Melissa here. I've spoken to your editor. We'll be holding auditions in the Standard Hotel in Hollywood over the next week or so, so I'm really hoping you'll be able to join us.'

'Olivia? It is Pierre Ferramo. I am in the lobby. Perhaps you are already on your way down for our rendezvous?'

'Olivia? It is Pierre at nine fifteen. I will be waiting for you on the terrace.'

'Olivia, it appears you have forgotten me. There has been the most terrible disaster, perhaps you have heard. I will telephone you a little later.'

'Olivia, oh God. It's Imogen from *Elan*. Oh God. Call us. Oh God.'

'Olivia, it's Kate. I'm just hoping you weren't anywhere near that ship. Call me.'

The hotel front desk, the doctor, Kate, nothing more from Pierre. Kate again. Then Barry.

'Where are you? Listen, can you get out there again? There's a press conference down at the dock at six fifteen your time. We've got a snapper there. I just need you to get a few quotes, then get off to the hospital for survivors and families. Call me.'

She fumbled for the remote, clicked on CNN, and lay back against the pillow.

'*More, now, on the* OceansApart *in Miami. As the death toll continues to rise, investigators on the scene say there are signs that the explosion may have been caused by a submarine, possibly of Japanese construction, packed with explosives. The submarine may have been manned by suicide bombers. Again, signs that the terrible explosion on the* OceansApart *may have been the work of terrorist suicide bombers.*'

The text strip underneath ran: 'OceansApart *explosion: 215 dead, 189 injured, 200 missing. Terror alert rises to red.*'

She swung herself awkwardly out of bed, moved stiffly to the laptop open on the desk and pressed a key. Nothing happened. She stared at it. It was plugged in, as she'd left it. But she hadn't shut it down. She'd left it on sleep, as she always did. It should have come on at the touch of a key.

Ignoring the pain in her hand and all her joints, she opened the curtains, flinching at the blast of white light, and looked round the room. She moved to the closet, rifled through the clothes, then opened the safe and checked the contents. She picked up the Louis Vuitton clutch. Her credit cards were there, the survival equipment, the business cards – she grabbed the side of a shelf to steady herself – the guest list was gone. The guest list she'd nicked from the party.

She staggered into the bathroom, picked up the phone by the loo and dialled the front desk.

'It's Olivia Joules.'

'Miss Joules, how are you? You have had a lot of telephone calls. The doctor asked us to contact him as soon as—. No, ma'am. We would not allow anyone to enter your room apart from the hotel staff. Housekeeping, of course, would have made up the room, but . . .'

She looked up at herself in the mirror. Her hair was standing up like a crest at one side. She reached for her hairbrush. From it was hanging a single, very long black hair.

'It's the housekeeper, you fool.'

Olivia sat on the floor of the bathroom, holding the phone to her ear, hanging on to the sound of Kate's voice.

'But why would she use my hairbrush?' Olivia's words came out in a whisper.

'You know, you look in the mirror, your hair's a bit off. Housekeepers have their pride too.'

'But shutting down the computer?'

'Maybe she unplugged it by mistake.'

'If it had shut down because someone pulled out the cord, it would have said, "Your computer did not shut down properly last time," when I started it up.'

'Olivia, you're exhausted and in shock. Go back to bed, get some sleep, and come home. You'll probably find the guest list in your pocket.'

'Kate,' she said haughtily, 'I didn't *have* a pocket.'

'No one's going to break into a room to steal a guest list from a party. Go back to sleep.'

Her eye fell on the slip dress she'd worn at the party, lying where she'd tossed it over the chair. A pocket indeed. But. Oh. Actually, she remembered sheepishly, there was a pocket in the clutch. Well, more of a pocket-type *feature*. She picked up the bag again. The guest list was there, tucked securely in the pocket-type feature.

She sat at the desk and rested her head on her arms. She felt deranged, exhausted, scared and lonely. She wanted comfort. She wanted someone to hold. She reached for a card on the desk and dialled a number.

'Hi.' It was a woman's voice, slight West Coast drawl.

'Could I speak to Pierre?'

'Pierre's not around. Who needs him?' It was the hair-flicking Suraya woman.

'It's Olivia Joules. I was supposed to meet him this morning but—'

'Sure. You want to leave a message?'

'Just, er, just say I was ringing to apologize about missing our meeting. I was down at the docks when the *OceansApart* blew up.'

'Yeah. God. That really sucked.'

Sucked?

'Will he be back later?'

'No, he had to leave town.' There was something odd about her tone.

'He left Miami? Today?'

'Yes. He had urgent business in Los Angeles. He's holding auditions for the movie. You want to leave him a message?'

'Just tell him I called, and, er, sorry about the meeting. Thank you.'

Olivia put down the phone and sat on the edge of the bed, the sheet screwed tightly in her fist, staring straight ahead, unseeing. She was thinking of the night before: Ferramo leaning close to her on the rooftop deck as she told him about the *OceansApart* story and her morning appointment with Edward and Elsie.

'I really do not think that is a good idea – ' his breath against her cheek – 'because I hope that tomorrow morning, you will be having breakfast . . . with me.'

She picked up the phone and dialled *Elan*.

'Imogen? Olivia. I'm fine. Listen, I'd like to go to LA and do the wannabe story. Straight away. As soon as you can. Get me on the first plane out.'

As Olivia looked down over Arizona, the sun was setting, turning the desert red. The great gash of the Grand Canyon was already in darkness. She thought of all the deserts she'd flown over before, in Africa, in Arabia, and all the things she'd seen. She thought about this asymmetric war that had suddenly touched her life and the way it was rooted in deserts and history and slights, real and imagined, which couldn't be eradicated by armies or bluster. And she wondered: *Did Pierre Ferramo know that the ship was going to blow when he kissed her that night?*

11

Los Angeles

So what was he doing in Hollywood? As the taxi rattled and bounced over the potholes towards the hills, Olivia wound down the window, enjoying the sense of freedom and vague lawlessness she always felt in Los Angeles. It was so deliciously shallow. She looked up at the giant billboards lining the road: 'Looking for a new career? Be a star! Contact the LA county sheriff's office.' 'We're back from Rehab and Ready to Party', said an advert for a TV guide. A bench at a bus stop featured a poster-sized shot of a grinning big-haired realtor: 'Valerie Babajian: your hostess for LA Real Estate'. Another billboard for a radio station said simply, 'Jennifer Lopez's brother, George', and another, which seemed not to be advertising anything at all, showed an artist's impression of a platinum blonde in a tight pink dress with a figure like Jessica Rabbit. 'Angelyne' was written underneath in giant letters.

'Is Angelyne an actress?' she asked the cab driver.

'Angelyne? No.' He laughed. 'She just pay for these posters of herself and then she do personal appearances, parties, things like that. She been doing that for years.'

Pierre must hate this place, she thought. As the grey-green hills grew closer, lights pinpricking through the dusk, they passed the Cedars-Sinai Medical Center with the Star of David raised on the side.

'I know what he's doing here,' she said to herself suddenly. 'The wannabe movie is bullshit. They're going to hit Los Angeles.'

Her mind began to whirr into a familiar overdrive: missiles launched from the top of the Runyon Canyon dog park, plummeting down into the executive offices at Fox Studios; suicide bombers at the *American Idol* final; manned torpedoes racing through the sewers. She felt like calling CNN and unilaterally announcing a red alert. '*He's handsome, he's sexy, but he's planning to blow us all sky high: Pierre Ferramo . . .*'

The sign for the Standard Hotel on Sunset, in a declaration of wacky subversiveness, was upside down. The hotel, once a geriatric home, had been recently converted to a temple of Hollywood retro chic. The contrast with its former clientele was dramatic. Seldom had Olivia seen so many beautiful young people gathered in one place talking on mobile phones. There were girls in camouflage trousers and bikini tops, girls in slippy dresses, girls in jeans so low their thongs were two inches above the waistbands, boys with shaved heads and goatee beards, boys in tight jeans which showed everything they had, boys in baggy jeans with the crotch at knee level. There were perspex pod-like chairs suspended from chains. Shag-pile carpet graced the floor, walls and ceiling. A DJ was spinning vinyl at the entrance to the pool deck. On the wall behind the reception desk a girl wearing only plain white underwear was reading a book in a glass box. It made Olivia feel like a seventy-year-old obese academic who would shortly be asked to move on down the road to the Sub-Standard.

The receptionist handed her a message from Melissa welcoming her to LA and saying that the auditions were starting in the morning, and the team would be easy to find around the bar and lobby. Once again, the bellboy insisted on accompanying her to the room, despite her lack of luggage. His head reminded her of a child's magnetic sketch pad, the sort where you add beards and moustaches to a face using metal filings. The boy, or rather man, had dyed black hair, a goatee beard, long sideburns and black-rimmed narrow glasses. It was a ridiculous look. His shirt was open almost to his waist, showing an Action-Man-like chest.

He opened the door to the room. There was a low bed, an orange-tiled bathroom, a bright blue floor and a silver beanbag. *Maybe I shouldn't paint the flat white*, Olivia thought. *Maybe I should do it more seventies with lots of colour and a perspex pod hanging from the—*

'How do you like the room?' asked the bellboy.

'It's like being on the set of *Barbarella*,' she murmured.

'I think that was before I was born,' he said.

Cheeky sod. He was definitely in his thirties. He had intelligent bright blue eyes, which didn't fit with his fashion-victim facial hair. He lifted her case onto the bed as if it was a paper bag. His body didn't fit with his facial hair either. But hey, this was LA: bellboy slash actor slash bodybuilder slash brainbox: whatever.

'So,' he said, pulling open the plate-glass window as if it was a net curtain. A blast of sound hit them. Below, the pool area was in full party mode, heat lamps were blazing, music pounding. Beyond was the LA skyline: a palm tree illuminated, a neon sign saying EL MIRADOR APARTMENTS, a jewel-box of lights.

'Looks like I'm going to get a lot of rest,' she said.

'Where did you just come in from?'

'Miami.'

He took hold of her hand, firmly, authoritatively, like a professional, looking at the burns.

'Been making fondue?'

'Yorkshire pudding.'

'What happened?'

'I burnt it.'

'What brings you to LA?'

'Do the words "air of mystery" mean nothing to you?'

He let out a short laugh. 'I like your accent.'

'They all talk like this where I come from.'

'You working here? You an actress?'

'No. What are you doing here?'

'Being a bellboy. Fancy a drink later?'

'No.'

'OK. Anything else I can do for you at all?'

Yes, rub sweet oils into my aching bones and change the dressings on my poor burnt hand, you wonderful, wildly strong, intellectual-looking beefcake.

'I'm fine.'

'OK now. Take it easy.'

She watched him go, then shut the door behind him, locked it and put the chain on. She was starting to feel like a family man on a foreign business trip: tempting young lovelies everywhere, luring her from the path of . . . well, what? A magazine piece about actresses? No. Not that. She was here on a mission. Maybe an investigative journalism mission – a mission of some kind, definitely.

She unpacked her things, colonizing the room. She stashed her valuables in the safe, thought for a moment, then took out her pot of Angel Dust illuminating face powder. It was very good stuff, affording a silken, light-reflecting sheen to the complexion. She dusted each number of the safe carefully with the powder, like James Bond. Well, James Bond probably wouldn't have actually given the numbers a silken, light-reflecting sheen. But still.

Then she turned on CNN.

'And the main headlines again. As the death toll continues to rise, it's believed that yesterday's explosion in Miami on the OceansApart, *which claimed the lives of over two hundred people, was in fact the work of al-Qaeda terrorists. The toll currently stands at 215 dead, 475 injured and over 250 missing. Do you suffer from reduced bladder control?'*

The shot had inexplicably changed to show a grey-haired woman giving a ballroom-dancing demonstration to a roomful of people. Olivia clicked off the TV in exasperation. Why couldn't they give you some clue as to where the news bulletin ended and the incontinence-remedy adverts began?

She called down and asked if the London *Sunday Times* was in yet: not until the following afternoon. She opened the laptop to look for it online.

There was a huge headline: OCEANS RIPPED APART. They had used her headline! She scanned the page excitedly for her byline. The byline at the top was Dave Rufford and Kate O'Neill. Kate! But what about *her* name? There were lots of her quotes in there and whole paragraphs of her description. Maybe her byline would be at the bottom. It said, 'Additional reporting by *Sunday Times* writers'. She ran a search for Olivia Joules. She wasn't credited anywhere at all.

'Oh, fuck it,' she said resolutely. 'At least I'm not dead. And neither are Elsie and Edward.' She opened the French doors, so that the sound of fun rose up from the pool deck, and sat down at the desk. It was the northern Protestant work ethic which had helped her escape from the land of the northern Protestant work ethic. Olivia clung to work to keep her safe, like her survival tin.

At midnight she leaned back, stretched and decided to call it a day. The desk was covered with the spoils from Miami: the party list, business cards, scribbled phone numbers on the backs of credit-card slips, a diagram trying to draw some meaning from connections which made no sense.

She clicked on Avizon.com in her favourites list. It was a low-rent actress slash model agency web site which she'd found amongst a horrifying 764,000 entries for 'Actresses Los Angeles'. There was Kimberley Alford, one in a whole page of startlingly similar Kirstens, Kelleys and Kims pouting provocatively at the camera for producers to mull over and the rest of the world to wank over. She clicked on Kimberley's nose and her pouting photo appeared full page, with her credentials:

Modelling level: professional
Acting level: professional
Ethnic look: Cherokee/Romanian

Then her bust size, waist size, shoe size, teeth quality ('excellent').

Professional skills: rollerblading, tap, speaks five languages. Has own cheerleader uniform.

Underneath was Kimberley's four-line personal message:

'*I am a true four-cornered all-rounder. I can sing, dance, act, model and play guitar! I'm on the right path, and waiting for the door to open that will lead to stardom. Acting is in my blood. My father has done the follow spot at the Academy Awards for twenty-five years. If you turn your spotlight on me, I will blow you away!*'

Olivia shook her head and turned to Travis Brancato, the wolf-eyed wannabe. His business card led her to a web site called Enclave, listing the hapless Travis as a 'lifestyle budget manager':

What is Enclave?

Enclave is a ground-breaking soft-science-based interface grounded in a qualitative value-increase-based proposition. Through this unique lifestyle enhancement program Enclave enables clients to increase qualitative lifestyle returns on investments to achieve maximum enjoyment.

Clients allow Enclave to manage a minimum annual lifestyle budget of $500,000, to advise and direct where the money is spent and to negotiate the purchase of qualitative-led concepts, experiences, goods and services.

From tickets to a major sporting event, premiere or award ceremony, a copy of a rarely heard early Floyd recording, to a table at the hottest new restaurant in Paris, many of LA's most senior CEOs, movie actors, producers and recording executives are already enjoying the science-based maximisation of pleasure interfaces which Enclave affords.

Olivia leaned back from the screen and grinned. The idea, it seemed, was that clients would 'give' Travis half a million dollars a year to spend, and in return occasionally receive a pair of tickets to a ball game or a free CD. She couldn't get anything but an answering machine on Enclave's twenty-four-hour hotline number. Presumably all the lifestyle managers were too busy managing hundreds of thousands of dollars into soft-science-based enjoyment maximization to pick up the phone.

She Googled Ferramo again. Nothing.

12

The indoor bar area of the Standard had a loosely desert theme: the walls were papered with a floor-to-ceiling frieze of Joshua trees, the floor was cork, the lamps like giant desert flowers. There were two – for some reason – fish suspended from the ceiling. Olivia sat enjoying her morning coffee and the sunlight blasting in from the pool area. Auditions were plainly about to start. A youth, sweating in the heat in thick camouflage trousers and a woolly hat, was wandering among the girls, sporting a clipboard and a rather confused expression.

Olivia saw Kimberley before Kimberley saw Olivia. Her unfeasibly large and perky breasts were bouncing in a thin white halter-neck above her non-existent hips, which were swathed in a miniature version of an ecru ra-ra skirt. Horribly aware of how attractive she looked, she was sliding her finger in and out of her mouth like a cross between a five-year-old and a porn queen. Suddenly she started talking to herself.

'I gotta get like, get something worked out. I don't want to wait tables any more ... Oh, yeah, she kept my reel and told me to call her and then she didn't take my call. She kept me on hold for ten minutes. I mean, I listened to three songs?'

Two men walked past, completely ignoring Kimberley's scantily clad perfection. Women who would turn heads in

London and New York scarcely seemed to warrant a second look in LA. It was as if they had a tattoo on their foreheads saying, 'Wannabe actress slash model. Will bore you with career aspirations: unstable.' The beautiful people in Miami were much more fun, Olivia thought. In LA, their beauty and semi-nakedness seemed to be saying, 'Look at this! Now make me a film star!' In Miami they just wanted to get laid.

'So,' Kimberley continued, 'when I finally got to meet with her she was so, like, not listening to me? She said the way I looked on the tape, I'm not, like – ' Kimberley's voice trailed off miserably – 'commercial enough.'

A wire was protruding from her ear. So at least she wasn't completely insane. But still, Olivia was starting to feel sorry for her.

'It's fine,' Kimberley said bravely. 'I'm thinking maybe I could do, like, body-part work? It's like body-double work, but they just use parts of you.'

But what about today? thought Olivia. *What about Pierre's auditions? I thought you were all lined up for a big part?*

She went over to Kimberley and said hi. Kimberley responded with the sort of defensive look which assumed that anyone who said hi was trying to hit on her.

'Olivia Joules. We met in Miami. I'm a journalist on *Elan*.'

Kimberley stared for a second, rasped, 'Gotta go,' into the hands-free, then turned on a dazzling smile and launched into an 'Oh. My. God.' routine.

'Where's Demi?' said Olivia, once the incredible nature of the coincidence had been dealt with. 'Isn't she auditioning for the film too?'

A strange froideur seemed to enter the proceedings.

'Has she been saying stuff about me? I mean, you know, I'm not going to say anything, like, bad about Demi. She has issues? You know? I mean, honestly? I think she's got a problem. But I'm not the kind of person who says anything bad about anyone.'

Olivia was confused, trying to work out how long it was since the party when they were the best of friends. Two days.

'I mean, she's still in Miami, right, with that Portuguese guy?'

'I've no idea.'

But Kimberley's attention had wandered. She had seen someone coming and started arranging her breasts in the halter top, like a bowl of fruit for a photo shoot. Olivia followed her gaze and found herself looking straight into the eyes of Pierre Ferramo.

He was dressed as an LA film producer in shades, jeans, navy jacket and whiter-than-white T-shirt. His manner, though, was as regal as ever. He was flanked by two dark-haired, flustered boys, who were trying to deal with a growing cluster of would-be auditionees. Ignoring the entourage, he made his way directly to Olivia.

'Ms Joules,' he said, slipping off his shades, 'you are two days late and in the wrong hotel in the wrong city, but as always it is a pleasure to see you.'

His liquid gaze burned into hers. For a second she was speechless, overwhelmed with lust.

'Pierre.' Kimberley teetered over and flung her arms round his neck. A fleeting glance of disgust crossed his features. 'Can we, like, go right away? I'm so, like, psyched?'

'The auditions will be starting shortly,' he said, disentangling himself. 'You may go upstairs and prepare if you wish.'

As Kimberley wiggled off, swinging her bag on her hip, Ferramo waved his aides away and spoke to Olivia in a low, urgent voice. 'You did not make our appointment.'

'I went for a jog first, down to the harbour . . .'

He sat down opposite her. 'You were there?'

78

'Directly across the water.'

'You are hurt?' He took her hand and examined the dressing. She liked the way he did it, like a doctor. 'You have had medical attention? Is there anything you need?'

'I'm fine. Thank you.'

'And how did you come to be in the vicinity of the explosion?'

'I was jogging. I often jog in the mornings. I was trying to get a good look at the ship. Did you know anyone aboard?'

She watched his face, like a detective watching a grieving husband make an appeal to his missing wife's abductor. Ferramo didn't miss a beat.

'No, thankfully I did not.'

What about Winston, your underwater consultant?

'I did.'

'You did?' He lowered his voice, leaning closer to her. 'I am so very sorry. They were people you knew well?'

'No. But they were people I very much liked. Do you know who did it?'

Was there a glimmer of a reaction to the oddness of her question?

'Some of the usual terrorist groups have claimed responsibility. It has the marks of al-Qaeda, of course, but we shall see.' He glanced around. 'This is not the time or place for this discussion. You are here for some days?'

One of the boys appeared behind him, hovering with papers. 'Mr Ferramo . . .'

'Yes, yes.' Different voice, harsh, authoritarian, dismissive. 'One moment. I am in conversation, as you can see.'

He turned back to Olivia. 'We can reschedule our meeting perhaps?' *a-rrreeeeshedull owah meeting.* He *so* did not sound French.

'I'm here for a few days.'

'You will join me for dinner? Tomorrow evening, perhaps?'

'Er, yes, I . . .'

'Good. You are staying here? I will call you and make the necessary arrangements. Until then. It is a pleasure to have you here. Yes . . . yes.' He turned to the boy, who was holding out a document apologetically.

Olivia watched as he looked at the document and rose to his feet, heading back to the wannabes. 'Actually, we should be through by four.' He handed back the paper. '*Shukran*. And then we can reconvene to discuss the call-backs.'

Shukran. Olivia looked down, steadying her hand, trying not to betray any reaction. *Shukran* was Arabic for thank you.

13

'Come home,' Kate said from London. 'Come home now. Call the FBI and get on the next plane.'

Olivia sat trembling on the silver beanbag, pushed up hard against the door to the room. 'But last time we spoke, you said I was jumping to conclusions.'

'The only evidence you offered was that he was "languid". You somehow overlooked the fact that he tried to persuade you not to go to the *OceansApart* the night before it blew up.'

'I didn't think about it before. I thought it was part of a crappy pick-up line about asking me to breakfast. You know: "Shall I phone you or nudge you?" kind of thing.'

'You are literally unbelievable. Listen. He lied. He told you he was French and then he starts talking Arabic.'

'He only said one word. Anyway, just because he's an Arab doesn't mean he's a terrorist. It might be just that sort of prejudice he was trying to avoid. I'm doing a story. *Elan* is paying my expenses.'

'They'll understand. You can always pay them back. Come home.'

'Al-Qaeda men don't drink champagne and surround themselves with beautiful half-clad women. They hang out in check shirts and grim flats in Hamburg.'

'Unbelievable. Look. Shut up. You're completely blinded by shag-lust. Get on the next plane. I'll call the FBI for you, and MI6.'

'Kate,' said Olivia quietly. 'This is my story. I found it.'

There was silence for a second. 'Oh God. It's that byline thing, isn't it? That was Barry. He said it would be a joint byline. I called him when I saw it and bawled him out.'

Then why didn't you call me too?

'He said they took your name out to save space. You're not on staff. I'm not trying to nick your story. Just come home and be safe.'

'I've got to go,' said Olivia. 'I'm supposed to be at the auditions.'

She pushed the Kate conversation to the back of her mind and started to work feverishly on a new list, which fell under two headings:

1. Reasons for thinking Pierre Ferramo is an al-Qaeda terrorist plotting to blow up LA.
2. Reasons why it is prejudiced, overimaginative or otherwise wrong to think Pierre Ferramo is an al-Qaeda terrorist plotting to blow up LA.

She paused, pen in mouth. Olivia thought of herself as a liberal-egalitarian humanitarian. And really, as she told Kate, he was hardly conducting himself like a true soldier of the jihad with his bottles of Cristal, beautiful women and expensive outfits.

She smiled grimly, remembering a friend of hers who had dated one of Bin Laden's sisters before the name Osama Bin Laden became inextricably associated with terrorist atrocities. The Bin Ladens were a huge, rich, cultured family with glamorous international connections and the sister was very posh. The friend had asked her about her brother's reputation as a black sheep.

'Oh, honestly,' the sister had replied. 'The worst one can say about Osama is that he's rather *socially difficult*.'

14

'You may be from the bright lights of LA, but here, in the desert, you will find out who you really are, what you mean . . . *mean.*'

'OK. Hold it there, hold it there.'

Olivia sympathized with directors. She wouldn't have the first idea what to say to an actress who was fucking up her lines except, 'Could you do it . . . better?' But this director didn't seem to have anything to say at all. He glanced feebly at Alfonso, who was there in some undetermined capacity, opened his mouth as if to speak, closed it again, then said, 'Um.'

Olivia looked at the director, bemused. His name was Nicholas Kronkheit. He didn't seem to have done anything at all except direct a couple of student music videos at Malibu University. Why pick him?

'OK,' Alfonso broke in bossily. 'Let's take it again, baby, from the top.'

The script, written by Travis Brancato, was, well, *worrying* to say the least. Entitled *Boundaries of Arizona*, it was the story of a Hollywood film star who realized Hollywood was meaningless and ran away to the desert, where he fell in love with a Navajo girl and discovered happiness and fulfilment through making ornamental lifeline boxes.

As Kimberley – dark, plaited wig doing its best to bring out the Cherokee in her – prepared to run through the lines yet again, Olivia slipped out of the room with a strange crab-like sideways gait which she'd never used before. It seemed to be a spontaneous and unconscious expression of guilt and apology for finding the whole thing so desperate.

She sat in the bar, sucking iced latte through a straw and pondering the various ways in which the production of *Boundaries of Arizona* made no sense. Was Ferramo going to finance the whole thing himself? In which case, why had he picked such an ill-qualified nitwit as a director? If he was looking for finance elsewhere, why would he have hired a director and started casting before he involved a studio? And how come he hadn't noticed that the script was total crap?

'Hi!'

Olivia started and choked on her latte at the sheer force of Melissa's arrival.

'How were the auditions? How did the interview with Nicholas go?'

Fortunately, there was no need to reply when Melissa was talking.

'Look, these are our surfers. Aren't they the cutest? They've been trying out at the beach all morning and now they're going to do lines. Are you going to come and watch? I'm sure you'll need a bit of that for the piece.'

A bunch of bleached-blond youths were ogling today's girl-in-her-underwear in the glass box behind reception.

'Oh, and this is our voice coach, Carol. Have you met her already?'

The woman looked interesting and rather nice. She actually had a wrinkled face, which looked completely out of place in

85

the Standard. It was like seeing someone in a rumpled old shirt in a room full of immaculately pressed outfits. Olivia started imagining the concierge rushing up, shrieking, 'Oh. My. Gaaaaaad. Give it to me! We'll have it pressed!'

'Pleased to meet you,' said the wrinkled one.

'You're English!' said Olivia.

'So are you. North-east? Nottingham? North of Nottingham?'

'Worksop. You're good.'

'So!' broke in Melissa. 'I've got you down for dinner with Pierre tomorrow night. This afternoon I want you to talk to the surfers, and then drinks early evening with some of the other boys.'

'Excuse me, Ms Joules.' It was the concierge. 'Just to say we have your appointment for a facial with Michael Monteroso at Alia Klum at three fifteen tomorrow. They do have a twenty-four-hour cancellation policy, so I need to give them a credit-card number. The cost is four hundred and fifteen dollars.'

'Four hundred and fifteen dollars?' said Olivia.

'Oh, I'm sure we can get Michael to give you a complimentary treatment,' said Melissa. 'And Kimberley and some of the other girls are going to meet you here at eight, take you out and show you some of the hangouts.'

'No, that's fine. I don't take freebies,' said Olivia. 'And I think I might have to skip the drink this evening. I've got some calls to make.'

Melissa pulled a nasty quizzical face, with her head on one side.

'Can't just write about this one production, you know!' said Olivia in a hearty voice. 'So many interesting things going on around here, don't you think?'

15

'Which city, please?' said the voice on the end of the phone.

'Los Angeles,' said Olivia, drumming her pencil on the desk.

'And the number you're searching for?'

'The FBI.'

'Pardon me?'

'The FBI.'

'I'm not seeing any listing for that. Is that a business or a private number?'

Olivia snapped the pencil in half. She had fifteen minutes before she was supposed to meet Kimberley for the night out and she hadn't done her make-up yet.

'No, the FBI. The Federal Bureau of Investigation. You know: cops, detectives, *X-Files*, hates the CIA?'

The other line started ringing. She ignored it.

'Oh, right.' A laugh. 'I got you. Here's the number now.'

'The number you require can be automatically dialled by pressing one now,' said a jerky, electronic voice. 'An additional charge will be made.'

'Hello, this is the Federal Bureau of Investigation,' said another recorded voice. Mercifully the other line stopped ringing.

'Please listen carefully to the following list of instructions.

If you are enquiring about employment possibilities, press one now; for existing cases, press two . . .'

Damn it. The other line started ringing again. She pressed hold and picked up line two.

'Olivia? It is Pierre Ferramo.'

'Oh, er, hi Pierre,' she trilled gaily. *I'm just calling the FBI on the other line to tell them you're an al-Qaeda terrorist.*

'Is everything all right?'

'Yes! Fine! Why?'

'You sound a little . . . tense, perhaps?'

'It's been quite a long day.'

'I won't keep you. I just wanted to make sure that we are still scheduled for our dinner tomorrow night? I would hate for us to miss each other again.'

'Absolutely. I'm looking forward to it.'

'Excellent. I will have someone pick you up at six thirty.'

Six thirty? That's a bit early for dinner, isn't it?

'That will be lovely.'

'And how were the auditions?'

By the time he'd gone, so had the FBI.

'Hi. Is that the FBI? I just wanted to report a suspicion I have in connection with the *OceansApart*.' Olivia was pacing the room, practising out loud. 'It's probably nothing, but you might just check out a man called Pierre Ferramo and . . .'

'Hi, Joules here. That the CIA? International terrorism, please. I've got a hot lead on the *OceansApart*. Ferramo, Pierre Ferramo. Arabic, certainly, possibly Sudanese . . .'

She couldn't do it. She felt as though she was about to go into an audition and had lost her motivation. She was Rachel Pixley from Worksop getting carried away and the operator would just laugh; at the same time, she was a treacherous Mata

Hari arranging dinner dates with her murderous lover then turning him over to her masters.

She decided to go out with Kimberley and pals and make the FBI call early tomorrow. She could order room service and make a morning of it.

16

Pierre Ferramo was wearing a green beret, speaking on al-Jazeera: 'She is a pigdog and an infidel. Her stomach is too fat to grill. It must be roasted.'

A phone was ringing in the background. Kimberley Alford produced an onion from her halter-neck and began to slice it, smiling to camera, blood oozing between her teeth. The phone was still ringing. Olivia fumbled for it in the darkness.

'Hi, Olivia? It's Imogen from *Elan*. I have the editor for you.'

She snapped the light on and sat up straight in bed, pulling her nightie over her boobs, running a hand through her hair and staring wildly round the room. Sally Hawkins. The editor of *Elan*. First thing in the morning. After a whole evening of, like, you know, like, Kimberley and her, like, friends. The horror, the horror.

'She'll be right with you.' Imogen's voice had that assistant's 'I-don't-need-to-be-nice-to-you-any-more-because-you've-fallen-from-grace' tone.

'Olivia?' Crisp, I'm-very-busy-and-important Sally Hawkins voice. 'I'm sorry to have to ring you so early. I'm afraid we've had a complaint.'

'A complaint?'

'Yes. I understand you called the FBI and suggested they should be checking out Pierre Ferramo.'

'What? Who told you that?'

'We don't know the source, but Century PR are absolutely furious and rightly so, if, indeed, you did call the FBI. I told Melissa I'm sure if you had some concern about one of her people, you would have called us first.'

Olivia panicked wildly. She hadn't called the FBI, had she? Or rather, she *had*, but she hadn't got through, or rather she *had* got through but she'd put them on hold and not said anything.

'Olivia?' Cold, nasty tone.

'I . . . I . . .'

'We work with Century very closely on a lot of celebrity interviews and shoots. We have the awards season coming up, for which we'll be relying on them very heavily and, and, really . . .'

'I didn't call the FBI.'

'You didn't?'

'Well, I *did*, but I never got through to a person. I can't understand why—'

'I'm sorry,' snapped Sally Hawkins. 'This really isn't making any sense. Did you call them, or didn't you?'

'Well, I started to call them, but . . .'

Olivia was staring at Century PR's press release for Ferramo's movie. Pierre Feramo, it said: Feramo with one *r*. No wonder she couldn't find him on Google. She had bloody well spelt his name wrong. Oh God. *Don't panic.*

'Olivia, are you feeling all right?'

'Yes, yes, it's just . . . I . . . I . . .'

Wedging the phone between her ear and her shoulder, she moved over to the desk and Googled Pierre Feramo. There were 1,567 entries. Oh dear.

'All right. I see.' The editor was now talking to her as if she was a retarded child. 'All right. Now you've had a very frightening experience in Miami. I understand that. I think the best thing is if you just take a good rest for a few hours and come home. You've done some of the research for the story?'

Olivia was scrolling down the first page of the 1,567 Google entries: producer credit on a French short which won the Palme d'Or; photographed with a model at 'the Oscars of the perfume industry'; quoted in the *Miami Herald* after the Crème de Phylgie launch.

'Yes. No, really I'm fine. I want to finish the story.'

'Well. *We* think it would be much better if you came home. Century PR are not happy about you continuing to work with their people. So perhaps you can write up your notes and email them to Imogen, and I'll have her arrange a flight for you this afternoon.'

'But, listen, I didn't say anything to the FBI . . .'

'I'm afraid I have to go, Olivia. I've got a conference call. I'll have Imogen call you with the flight details. Make sure you send the research over.'

Olivia stared around the room, disbelieving. She hadn't called the FBI, had she? She had only *practised* calling the FBI. Had they perfected reading people's thoughts over phone lines? No. The CIA possibly, but not the FBI. She sat down on the bed. Surely not. The only person who had known that she was going to call them was Kate.

Olivia was typing furiously, writing up as much of the wannabe story as she'd got together in the short time before she was so cruelly fired. Every few minutes she flicked to a document called *Kate: FURY: RE VENTING OF* and vented.

'I can't believe you fucking well did this to me. I thought our friendship was based on trust and loyalty and . . .'

Three more paragraphs of wannabe story. Back to *Kate: FURY: RE VENTING OF*: 'Kate, I hope I'm not jumping to conclusions unfairly, but I don't understand . . .'

Wannabe story again. *Kate: FURY: RE VENTING OF*, more considered this time: 'Listen, you fucking bitch-queen from hell, how the fuck dare you do me over by fucking telling them I called the fucking FBI when I fucking didn't, you fucking . . .'

Back to the article. She typed a final paragraph and read it over. She made a few changes, ran spell-check, pressed 'Send', then kicked the leg of the desk.

It wasn't fair. It wasn't *fair*. In a sudden moment of blind fury, she picked up the phone and dialled Kate's home number. It was on answerphone, but she decided to go for it anyway.

'Hi, it's me. Listen, *Elan* just called and fired me for calling the FBI about Feramo. I didn't call the FBI. The only person who knew I was even thinking of calling the FBI was you. I can't believe you just wanted to get me off the story so you could, you could . . .'

Olivia's voice cracked. She was really, really hurt. She put down the phone and sat on the beanbag, blinking and rubbing a tear away with her fist. She stared ahead for a long time, lower lip trembling, then marched over to the tan and olive carry-on case, took out a very old, tatty piece of paper, unfolded it carefully, and sat back on the beanbag with it.

Rules for Living by Olivia Joules

1) *Never panic. Stop, breathe, think.*
2) *No one is thinking about you. They're thinking about themselves, just like you.*
3) *Never change haircut or colour before an important event.*

4) *Nothing is either as bad or as good as it seems.*

5) *Do as you would be done by, e.g., thou shalt not kill.*

6) *It is better to buy one expensive thing that you really like than several cheap ones that you only quite like.*

7) *Hardly anything matters: if you get upset, ask yourself, 'Does it really matter?'*

8) *The key to success lies in how you pick yourself up from failure.*

9) *Be honest and kind.*

10) *Only buy clothes that make you feel like doing a small dance.*

11) *Trust your instincts, not your overactive imagination.*

12) *When overwhelmed by disaster, check if it's really a disaster by doing the following: a) think, 'Oh, fuck it,' b) look on the bright side and, if that doesn't work, look on the funny side.*

    If neither of the above works then maybe it is a disaster so turn to items 1 and 5.

13) *Don't expect the world to be safe or life to be fair.*

14) *Sometimes you just have to go with the flow.*

and then the new one from Elsie, added at the bottom:

15) *Don't regret anything. Remember there wasn't anything else that could have happened, given who you were and the state of the world at that moment. The only thing you can change is the present, so learn from the past.*

and then Olivia's own practical application of this:

16) *If you start regretting something and thinking, 'I should have done . . .' always add, 'but then I might have been run over by a lorry or blown up by a Japanese-manned torpedo.'*

Nothing is ever as bad or as good as it seems. There were always one or two of them which jumped out. *Trust your instincts, not your overactive imagination.* Did she really think, in her gut, that it was Kate?

No. She didn't. And the information hadn't come from the FBI because she never actually spoke to the FBI. The only place the information could have come from was right here, inside the room. She started systematically checking the lights, the phone, under the desk, in the drawers. What would a bug look like? She had no idea. Would it be like a microphone? Would it have batteries? She giggled. Or little legs?

She thought some more, then reached for the phone again and dialled information: 'The Spy Shop on Sunset Boulevard. Spy Shop. S.P.Y. You know, spies? James Bond? Kiefer Sutherland? English public-school nineteen-thirties homo-sexuals?'

Half an hour later, she was staring at a large bottom-cleavage, which was protruding from under the bed.

'Ohhh Kayyy. Here we go. This is basically your problem.'

Olivia took a few steps back as the bottom-cleavage started wriggling out towards her. Connor the counter-surveillance expert pulled himself awkwardly to his knees, joyfully holding out the square cover from the phone jack with the same smiley expression used by techies the world over – computer buffs, diving instructors, ski instructors, pilots – when they've found something only another techie would understand but which they have to explain to a lay person.

'It's a two-point-five MP with a pilger. Probably took him about ten seconds if he had a DSR.'

'That's great.' She tried valiantly to provide him with some sort of emotional reinforcement. 'Great. Er . . . so this was actually tapping the phone line?'

'Oh no. Oh no. No. This is just a microphone. Just a simple XTC four-by-two.'

'Right. So it would just pick up what I said? They wouldn't have any way of knowing whether I was actually on the phone or not?'

'You got it. They might pick up the dial tone but . . .' He sucked in air through his teeth and stared at the phone jack cover, then shook his head. 'No way. Not with a gimper. They would probably just pick up what you actually said. You want us to do anything else?'

'No, no. I'll pop in later and pick up the rest of the stuff.'

She had ordered a bug detector disguised as a calculator, an invisible-ink pen, a chemical-attack protection hood, an excitingly flat and tiny digital camera and, childishly, but most thrillingly, a spy ring with a mirror you could flick up to see behind you. It was an excellent stash of stuff to go with the survival tin.

After the counter-surveillance man had left, she immediately called Kate and left a message. 'It's me. I'm sorry. Really sorry. Brainstorm. Turns out the room was bugged. I owe you a big margarita when I get back. Call me.'

Then she started pacing the room, trying not to panic. It wasn't a game any more, and it wasn't her overactive imagination. Something really bad was going on and someone was after her. She glanced at the Rules for Living again, breathed in and out deeply, thought: *Oh, fuck it*, and tried to imagine the whole thing worked up into an amusing anecdote to tell Kate.

17

Thirty-eight minutes later, she was on Rodeo Drive, lying under a sheet in a white room with six separate jets of very hot steam hissing at her face.

'Er, are you sure these steam things are all right? They seem a bit . . .'

'They're perfect, trust me. We need to engineer a radiant temperature in order to micro-collapse the epidermal cella-feeds and stimulate—'

'Right. They're not going to leave big red blotches, are they?'

'Relax. You're going to be *sooo* adorable.'

She was feeling many tiny sucking movements all over her face, as if a set of toothless mini-piranhas had been let loose on it, along with the six Bunsen burners.

'Michael,' she said, determined to get at least something useful out of the hideous four-hundred-and-fifteen-dollar experience, 'how do you know Travis?'

'Travis? Who's Travis?'

'You know – Travis? The guy you introduced me to in Miami?'

'You've just flown in from Miami? Do you have jet-lag? I could ionize your face.'

'No, thank you. He's an actor slash writer, isn't he?'

97

'Oh, that guy. Right.'

'He's the guy who's written the screenplay for Feramo's movie.'

'You're kidding me. Feramo's movie is written by *Travis*? Would you like to take a jar of Crème de Phylgie? The larger one is excellent value; you get two hundred millilitres for only four hundred and fifty dollars.'

'No thank you. What's wrong with Travis writing the movie? Ow! What are you *doing*?'

'I'm lifting the initial resistance of your epidermis. You should try the ionizing. Even if you're not jet-lagged, it's an excellent rejuvenating exfoliant, hypoallergenic, totally free of free radicals . . .'

'No thanks.'

'. . . biocolic-balancing plant extracts,' he oozed on, ignoring her.

'How do you know Travis?'

'Travis?' Michael Monteroso laughed. 'Travis?'

'What's so funny?'

'Travis picks up the cash from the salon and takes it to the bank. He works for a security firm. Do you have a facial technician who works with you regularly?'

'No, I don't actually,' she said, momentarily thrown by the question.

'If you like, I'll give you my card when you go. I'm actually not supposed to work outside the salon, but for special clients I can come to your home.'

'You're very kind, but actually I don't live here.'

The Bunsen burners stopped, and she felt herself being lulled by the eucalyptus scents and the steady flow of gibberish into a half-asleep state. She tried to fight it and stay alert.

'I could come to your hotel?'

'No. So how do you all know each other – all the people at the party?'

'I don't really know them. I just help out with the facials for the events. I think some of them met at the dive lodge down in Honduras – you know, Feramo's place on the islands down there. Now this is eucalyptus and castor oil I'm putting on you here. I actually use a range of dermatologically tested organic products. This is totally organic, additive free. I'll make you up a pot to take with you.'

'How much is it?'

'Two hundred and seventy-five dollars.'

Olivia tried not to smile.

'Just the facial will be fine, thanks,' she said firmly.

When she got into the changing room, she looked in the mirror and let out a horrified sigh. Her face was covered in small red rings, as if she'd been attacked by a creature with tentacles or tiny parasites trying to suck greedily on her, tails wiggling. Which, in a way, she had.

It was quarter to six. She was to leave for dinner with Feramo in forty-five minutes. She was starting to feel very scared and she was still covered in red blotches. Thank God for concealer. By six fifteen, you could hardly see them at all. She was dressed, coiffed, made up and outwardly ready, but inside she wasn't ready at all. Her palms were sweating and her stomach kept being gripped by spasms of fear. She tried to stop, breathe, think, act calmly. She tried to think of positive scenarios: Feramo knew nothing about the phone call or the room-bugging. Maybe it was the nosy, overly chatty bellboy with the bulging muscles and strange facial hair. Maybe the bellboy was working for the tabloids and had thought a celebrity was going to be checking into Olivia's room, so had planted the bug and then grassed her up to Melissa. Maybe Feramo knew about the phone call and wanted to tell her he understood why she might be suspicious and would then explain everything and tell her that actually he was a half-Sudanese, half-French intellectual scientist slash doctor who just did film-making as a hobby and was sick of the whole nonsense and wanted to travel the Third World with Olivia and heal the sick and go diving.

By the time she was ready to go she had psyched herself up into thinking it was all completely OK. It was fine. She would just have this last fun dinner and then go back to London and start to rebuild the tattered remnants of her journalistic career.

Then she stepped out of her room and completely lost her cool again. What was she *doing*? Was she out of her *mind*? She was about to have dinner, alone, she didn't know where, with an al-Qaeda terrorist who knew she was on to him. There *was* no positive scenario. Feramo didn't want to have her to dinner, he wanted to have her *for* dinner. Still, at least the blotches on her face didn't show.

The elevator doors opened.

'Oh, my dear, what *has* happened to your face?'

It was the wrinkly voice-coach lady, Carol.

'Oh, nothing. I, er, had a facial,' said Olivia, stepping inside. 'Have you been working with the actors at the auditions?'

'Yes, well. Not just the audition people.'

Olivia looked at her quickly. She seemed to be troubled.

'Oh, really? So you're not just working with the actors then?' She decided to risk a bit of boldness. 'You work with the rest of the team as well?'

Carol looked her straight in the eye. She seemed to be thinking a lot of things that she couldn't say.

'I always thought it was only actors who needed voice coaches,' said Olivia lightly.

'People change their accents for all sorts of reasons, don't they?'

The elevator doors opened to the lobby. Suraya was crossing their line of vision, radiant against the white walls.

'What do you reckon?' said Olivia conspiratorially, nodding towards Suraya. 'Malibu with a touch of Bombay?'

'Hounslow,' Carol said. She wasn't laughing.

'And Pierre Feramo?' whispered Olivia, as they stepped out of the elevator. 'Cairo? Khartoum?'

'That's not for me to say, is it?' Carol said over brightly, never taking her eyes off Olivia's. 'Anyway. Have a lovely evening.' She gave a brittle smile and, pulling her cardigan around her, headed off towards the parking valet.

18

Olivia approached the reception desk and asked to have the charges since her arrival and all future charges taken off the *Elan* account and moved onto her credit card. It was turning into an expensive trip, but a girl has her pride. As she waited, the nosy bellboy with the goatee beard and muscles appeared.

'Leaving, Ms Joules?' he said. He *so* wasn't a bellboy. There was something far too clever and self-possessed about him. Maybe he was a brilliant young mathematician making money in his college holidays. No: too old.

'Not yet.'

'Enjoying your stay?'

'Yes, apart from the microphone in the room,' she said softly, watching his face.

'I'm sorry?'

'You heard.'

The receptionist returned just as a vaguely familiar, nastily sweet smell invaded her nostrils. Olivia turned. It was Alfonso, chest hair protruding from a polo shirt, which this time was pink.

'Olivia, I was beginning to think you would never appear. I was going to call up to your room.'

The accumulated stress erupted in a burst of irritation.

'Why? Are you coming to dinner as well?' she snapped.

For a second Alfonso looked hurt. He was a funny chap. All oiliness and bluster, but she had the feeling that underneath he was suffering from low self-esteem.

'Of course not. Mr Feramo simply wanted me to make sure you arrived safely. The car is waiting for you.'

'Oh. OK. Well, thanks,' she said, feeling a bit mean.

'My God, what happened to your face?'

It was going to be a long evening.

Alfonso led her out and proudly pointed to the 'car'. It was a white stretch limo, the sort that people from out of town ride up and down Sunset Boulevard in on bachelor nights, wearing brightly coloured wigs. As the driver held open the door, Olivia climbed in, or rather fell in, tripped over the bump in the middle, and found herself looking at a pair of Gucci stilettos. Her eyes moved upwards past delicate olive ankles and a dusty-pink silk dress to discover she was sharing the limo with Suraya. What was this?

'Hello again,' said Olivia, trying to crawl onto the seat while retaining some vestiges of dignity.

'Hi. My God! What happened to your face?'

'I had a facial,' she said, glancing round nervously as the limo purred off onto Sunset.

'Oh no.' Suraya started to laugh. 'You went to Michael, right? He's such a bullshitter. Come here.'

She clicked open her bag, leaned over and started dabbing at Olivia's face with concealer. It was an oddly intimate moment. Olivia was too startled to protest.

'So, you and Pierre, hey?' Suraya's voice didn't fit with the elegant beauty. She sounded stoned and oddly common. 'Are you guys an item?'

'Heavens no! Just a friendly dinner!' There was something about Suraya which was turning Olivia into a hearty Girl Guide.

'Oh, come on,' drawled Suraya, leaning forward. 'He thinks you're very intelligent.'

'That's nice!' she said brightly.

'Sure.' Suraya looked out of the window, smirking to herself. 'So you're a journalist, right? We should go shopping.'

'Right,' said Olivia, trying to work out the logic of this.

'We'll go to Melrose. Tomorrow?'

'I have to work,' she said, thinking how non-encouraging it would be trying on clothes with a six-foot, eight-stone model. 'What do you do?'

'I'm an actress,' Suraya said dismissively.

'Really? Are you going to be in Pierre's movie?'

'Sure. Movie, bullshit, whatever. Do you really think he's for real?' Suraya said conspiratorially. 'Feramo, I mean.' She opened her purse and checked her reflection, then leaned forward again. 'Well?' she asked, slipping her hand onto Olivia's knee and giving it a squeeze.

Olivia started to panic. Were they planning a hideous seventies-style sex romp as part of the smokescreen? They were passing the pink palace of the Beverly Hills Hotel now. She wanted to open the window and yell out, 'Help, help! I'm being kidnapped.'

'Pierre? I think he's very attractive. Are we going out to a restaurant?'

'I dunno. Restaurant, order in, whatever,' said Suraya. 'But do you think he's really a movie producer?'

'Of course,' said Olivia levelly. 'Why? Don't you?'

'I guess. How long are you going to be in LA? Do you like the Standard?'

If she was trying to get information, she wasn't very good at it.

'It's great, but not the sort of place you feel like putting on a bikini. It's like being on the set of *Baywatch*. Though that wouldn't be a problem for you.'

'Nor you,' said Suraya, pointedly eyeing her breasts. 'You've got a great little figure.'

Olivia adjusted her dress nervously. 'Where are we going?'

'Pierre's apartment?'

'Where's that?'

'On Wilshire? So why don't I call you on your cell tomorrow to fix up shopping?'

'Call me at the hotel,' said Olivia firmly. 'Like I said, I'll be working.'

Suraya looked nasty when she wasn't getting her own way. They lapsed into an uncomfortable silence as Olivia glumly imagined what was ahead: Olivia tied naked back to back with Suraya, while Alfonso strutted round them dressed as a baby in rubber pants and Pierre Feramo minced to and fro, cracking a whip. If only she'd stayed in the hotel and ordered room service.

Pierre's apartment in the Wilshire Regency Towers was the pinnacle of vertical luxury living. The elevator doors swung open on the nineteenth floor to reveal a gold and beige temple to understated bad taste. This was more like it – mirrors, gold tables, a black onyx statue of a jaguar. There was only one elevator. She slipped the hat pin out of her bag and hid it in her palm, looking round for another means of escape.

'You want a Martini?' said Suraya. She threw her bag casually onto the square beige-brocade sofa as if she lived there.

'Ooh, no. Just a diet Coke for me, thanks,' trilled Girl Guide Olivia.

Why am I being like this? she thought, walking over to the window. The sun was beginning to redden over the Santa Monica mountains and the ocean.

Suraya handed her the drink and stood ridiculously close. 'Beautiful, isn't it?' she purred romantically. 'Wouldn't you like to live somewhere like this?'

'Ooh! I think it might make me a bit dizzy,' joshed hearty Olivia, edging away. 'How do you find it?'

'You get used to it. I mean ... I don't actually live here, but ...' Hah! A flash of annoyance in the beautiful dark eyes. So Suraya *did* live here. She had given herself away.

'Where are you from?' said Olivia.

'Los Angeles. Why?' On the defensive now.

'I thought I heard an English accent in there.'

'I guess I'm mid-Atlantic.'

'How long have you known Pierre?'

'Long enough.' Suraya downed her drink in one, walked away and picked up her bag. 'Anyway, I gotta split.'

'Where are you going?'

'Out. Pierre will be here soon. Make yourself at home.'

'Right,' said Olivia. 'Well! Jolly good! Have a lovely evening.'

Olivia watched the elevator doors close on Suraya, listening for the groan and hiss as it moved downwards, until she was sure she was gone. It was silent now, apart from the hum of the air-conditioning. The apartment was either a high-end rental or it had been furnished by an insane designer. There was no personal stuff – no books, no dishes with pens in – just gilded mirrors, ornaments, miscellaneous onyx beasts of the jungle and strange paintings of women in peril from snakes and long, thin dragons. She listened, adjusting her hold on the hat pin, gripping the Louis Vuitton clutch tightly in the other fist. There was a corridor opposite the elevator. She padded silently across the plush carpet towards it, seeing a line of closed doors. Heart pounding and telling herself, if challenged, she could claim she was looking for the loo, she reached out for the first gilt handle and turned it.

She found herself in a large bedroom, one wall entirely window. The centrepiece was a four-poster bed, the pillars fashioned like thick ropes, bulbous lamps on either side. Again, there were no personal items. She pulled open a drawer, flinching when it creaked: nothing in there. She couldn't close it. It was stuck. Cursing herself silently, she left it open and continued her tiptoed search. The bathroom was huge, mirrored, ghastly, in pink marble. It led to a major closet lined with cedar shelves, a central island for laying out clothes. But no clothes. She leaned back against the wall and felt it move. A panel – two inches thick, steel – was sliding noiselessly to the left to reveal another room. A safe? A panic room? The lights came up. It was larger than the bedroom and painted white: windowless and empty apart from a line of small oriental mats lined up against the wall. The panel started to close and impulsively, just before it closed, she darted through.

She stood, heart beating, looking around. Was it really a panic room? Were they prayer mats? She turned to look at the wall behind her. There were three white posters with Arabic writing on them. She took out her camera, put the bag on the carpet, started to photograph them, then froze. There was a slight noise from the other side of the sliding wall: muffled footsteps! Someone was in the bedroom. The footsteps stopped. Then she heard the sound of someone struggling to close the drawer.

The footsteps started again, slow, still muffled, but moving closer. She felt as though she was trapped underwater, out of air. She forced herself to breathe, stay calm and think. Could there be a second exit? She tried to visualize the corridor outside: a long break, then a door. Another bedroom suite?

She heard the footsteps on the marble floor of the bathroom and looked back at the panel, noting the slight change in tone of the wall, then scanned the wall opposite. There! She tiptoed over and leaned her shoulder against it. It started to open. She slipped through the gap, willing the panel to move back, almost sobbing with relief as it did. She was in another closet, this time full of men's clothes. There was a faint smell of Feramo's cologne. They were his clothes: shiny, almost dainty shoes; dark suits; crisply ironed shirts in pastel shades; neatly folded jeans; polo shirts. Her thoughts came randomly and fast as she hurried through: *God, he had a lot of clothes for a guy. Very neat, almost anal. She could really mess up a closet like this. How was she going to explain her emergence into the corridor?* She stepped into the bathroom. *That was it: perfect. She could pretend she'd just come out to use the loo.* Her reflection looked back at her from every angle. She heard the slight, almost noiseless movement of the sliding panel. She tucked the miniature camera under her armpit and flushed the loo. Maybe good manners would keep whoever it was out of the bathroom.

'Olivia?' It was Feramo.

'Hang on a sec! Not decent!' she said brightly. 'OK.'

She smiled, trying to look as natural as one could, with one arm concealing a miniature camera under it. But Feramo's eyes were deadly cold.

'So, Olivia, I see that you have discovered my secret.'

19

Feramo moved past her, shut the bathroom door, locked it and turned to face her.

'Do you normally wander through your host's home without permission?'

Go with the fear, she told herself. *Don't fight it. Use the adrenalin. Go on the attack.*

'Why shouldn't I look around for a bathroom if you ask me for dinner and have me met by unexplained six-foot sex goddesses then leave me hanging around on my own?' she said accusingly.

He slipped his hand inside his jacket. 'I take it this belongs to you?' he said, holding out the Louis Vuitton clutch. Bugger. She had left it on the floor when she was taking photographs inside the secret room.

'You told me you were French,' she blurted. 'You made a great thing about speaking from the heart. And then you bloody well lied to me. You're not French at all, are you?'

He looked at her, impassive. His face, in neutral, had an almost aristocratic sneer.

'You are right,' he said eventually. 'I did not tell you the truth.'

He turned and unlocked the door. She thought she was going to faint with relief.

'But come. We will be late for our dinner,' he said, more pleasantly now. 'We will talk about these things then.'

He threw the door open, gesturing her out into his bedroom. It was a big bed. For a split second there was a blinding flash of desire between them. Olivia stepped determinedly into the room – there was his shirt on a chair, books by the bed – and out into the corridor. He closed the door and stood between her and the elevator, directing her the other way. She walked nervously ahead of him, trying to convey anger in her walk and wishing she'd had acting lessons. Diving lessons, self-defence lessons, language lessons, first-aid lessons: she'd spent her adult life pursuing her own university degree in life skills, but she'd never thought how useful acting might be.

At the end of the corridor was yet another closed door. He moved ahead of her to unlock it, and she grabbed the chance to slip the camera into her bag as he pushed the door open to reveal a stairwell.

'Up,' he said.

Was he planning to push her off the roof? She turned to look at him, trying to gauge if this was the moment to run. As her eyes met his, she saw that he was laughing at her.

'I'm not going to eat you. Up you go.'

It was very confusing. Reality kept shifting to and fro. Suddenly, now, with his laugh, it felt like a date again. At the top of the stairs he pushed opened a heavy fire door, and there was a rush of warm air. They stepped out into a strong wind and a tremendous roar. They were on the top of the building, the vast panorama of Los Angeles surrounding them. The noise was coming from a helicopter parked on the roof, rotor blades turning, the door open, ready.

'Your carriage awaits,' Feramo shouted above the noise. Olivia was torn between fear and wild excitement. Feramo's

*She scrambled into the helicopter, wishing she hadn't worn
a slip dress and the uncomfortable shoes.*

hair was streaming straight back from his face as though he was in front of a wind machine on a photo shoot.

Olivia ran across the concrete keeping low to dodge the rotor blades. She scrambled into the helicopter, wishing she hadn't worn a slip dress and the uncomfortable shoes. The pilot turned round and gestured towards the harnesses and ear protectors. Pierre was in the seat beside her, pulling the heavy door closed as the helicopter lifted into the air, the building shrinking away below them. They were heading towards the ocean.

It was impossible to speak against the din. Pierre didn't look at her. She tried to concentrate on the view. If this was going to be her last hour, at least she was going to spend it looking at something pretty. The sun was setting over the Santa Monica Bay, a heavy orange ball against a pale blue sky, red light reflecting back off the ocean's glassy surface. They followed the coast a little way, banking downwards against the dark line of the mountains towards Malibu. She could see the long line of the pier, the little half-built restaurant at the end, and beside it the surfers, black, seal-like figures, catching the last of the waves.

Feramo leaned forward, instructing the pilot, and the helicopter swung out towards the open sea. She thought of her mother, years ago when Olivia was only fourteen, chastising her for her sense of adventure, her interest in dangerous boys and life close to the edge: 'You'll get yourself into trouble; you don't understand the world, you only see the excitement. You won't see the danger until it's too late.' Unfortunately the advice was only given in the context of Catholic boys or boys with motorbikes.

The sun was slipping behind the horizon, separating in two, one orb on top of the other like a figure eight. Seconds after it

OLIVIA JOULES

disappeared the sky around exploded into reds and oranges,
the lines of aeroplane trails white against the blue high above.

Well, she wasn't having this. She wasn't just being whisked
out into the middle of the Pacific without so much as a by
your leave. She dug Feramo indignantly in the arm.

'Where are we going?'

'What?'

'Where are we going?'

'What?'

They were like a geriatric married couple already.

She wriggled further up in her seat and yelled in his ear.

'WHERE ARE WE GOING?'

He smirked. 'You'll see.'

'I WANT TO KNOW WHERE YOU'RE TAKING ME.'

He bent to say something in her ear.

'What?'

'CATALINA,' he bellowed.

Catalina Island – a day tripper's island twenty miles offshore. There was one little cheerful seaside town – Avalon; the
rest was wilderness.

Night fell quickly. Soon a dark shoulder of land was rearing
up out of the gloom. Far away to their left, she could see the
lights of Avalon – cosy and welcoming, cascading down to
the little curved bay. Ahead of them was only blackness.

20

Catalina Island, California

The chopper was descending into a deep, narrow bay on the ocean side of the island, well hidden from the Californian mainland and the lights of Avalon. She saw vegetation, palm trees flattening away from the chopper. As they landed, Feramo opened the door and jumped out, pulling her after him and gesturing at her to lower her head. The blades didn't stop. She heard the engine sound rise again and turned to see the chopper taking off.

He guided her along a path towards a jetty. There was no wind. The ocean was calm, the steep line of the hills on either side and the jetty black in silhouette against it. As the noise of the helicopter faded, there was silence except for tropical sounds: cicadas, frogs, the clink of metal against metal at the jetty. Her breath was coming short and fast. Were they alone here?

They reached the jetty. She noticed surfboards leaning against a wooden hut. What did he want with surfboards? Catalina was hardly fabled for its surf. As they drew closer, she realized that the hut was a dive shack, stocked with tanks and gear.

'Wait here. I need to get something.' As Feramo's footsteps died away, she gripped the railing weakly. Should she just grab a dive rig and make her escape? But then if this was, by any remaining chance, just an *über*-romantic date, it would seem like a pretty extreme piece of odd behaviour.

She tiptoed over to the dive shack. It was well ordered: a line of tanks, twenties, in brackets; BCDs and regulator rigs on hooks; masks and fins in neat piles. There was a knife lying on a rough wooden table. She picked it up and slipped it into her clutch, starting at the sound of Feramo's footsteps returning. She was in danger, she knew, of being overwhelmed by fear. She had to regain control.

The footsteps were getting closer. Terrified, she cried out, 'Pierre?' There was no answer, just the sound of the footsteps, heavy and uneven. Was it some thug or hired hit man? 'Pierre. Is that you?'

She drew the knife out of her bag and held it behind her back, tensed and ready.

'Yes,' came Pierre's liquid, accented tones. 'Of course it is me.'

She exhaled, her whole body relaxing. Feramo emerged from the gloom, carrying a clumsy bundle wrapped in black.

'What are we doing here?' she burst out. 'What are you *doing* bringing me to some isolated place and just dumping me and not answering when I ask if it's you when you're making weird footsteps? What *is* this place? What are you *doing*?'

'Weird footsteps?' Feramo looked at her, his eyes flashing, then suddenly whipped the black cover from the bundle. Olivia felt as though her legs were going to give way. It was an ice bucket containing a bottle of champagne and two flutes.

'Look,' she said, putting her hand to her forehead. 'This is very nice, but do you have to be so melodramatic?'

'You do not strike me as the kind of woman who seeks out the predictable.'

'No, but you don't have to scare me to death to keep me happy. What is this place?'

'It is a boat dock. Here,' he said, holding out the black cloth, 'in case you are cold. I should perhaps have warned you we would be putting out to sea.'

'To sea?' she said, trying simultaneously to take the wrap, which turned out to be very soft indeed as if made from the feathers of some rare bird, and hide the knife in it.

He nodded towards the bay, where the silhouette of a yacht could be seen gliding noiselessly round the headland.

She was relieved to find that there was a crew aboard. If Feramo was going to kill her, he would, one would have thought, have done it when they were alone. And the champagne would have been a very odd touch.

She was feeling slightly more relaxed, having managed to stash the dive knife in the Louis Vuitton clutch under cover of the black, ultra-fine pashmina. Feramo stood beside her at the stern, listening to the genteel phut-phut of the motor gliding them out into the blackness of the open sea.

'Olivia,' he said, handing her a glass, 'shall we drink a toast to our evening? To the beginning.' He clinked his glass against hers and looked at her intently.

'Of what?' she said.

'You do not remember our conversation in Miami? On the rooftop? The beginning of our getting to know each other.' He raised his glass, then drained it. 'So, tell me. You are a journalist. Why?'

She thought for a moment. 'I like to write. I like to travel. I like to find out what's going on.'

She wondered if this whole performance was designed to wrong-foot her, making her feel threatened and terrified one moment, and safe and pampered the next, like leg-waxing with a smooth-talking but incompetent beautician.

'And where have you visited on your travels?'

'Well, not as many places as I'd like: South America, India, Africa.'

'Where in Africa?'

'The Sudan and Kenya.'

'Really? You have been to the Sudan? And how did you find it?'

'It was brilliant. It was the most foreign place I've ever been. It was like *Lawrence of Arabia*.'

'And the people?'

'Nice.' The dance around danger in their dialogue was thrilling.

'And Los Angeles? How do you find it here?'

'Deliciously shallow.'

He laughed. 'That is all?'

'Unexpectedly rural. It's like the south of France only with shopping.'

'And this journalism you do, this froth for magazines, it is your speciality?'

'Froth? I've never been so insulted in my life!'

He laughed again. He had a nice laugh, rather shy, as if it was something he didn't quite feel allowed to do.

'I really want to be a proper foreign correspondent,' she said, suddenly serious. 'I want to do something that means something.'

'The *OceansApart*. Did you do a piece anyway?' There was a slight change of tenor in his voice.

'Humph,' she said. 'Yes, kind of. But they put it under someone else's byline.'

'Were you hurt?'

'Naah. Pretty trivial thing in that context. What about you? Do you like LA?'

'I am interested in what it produces.'

'What? Beautiful girls with giant fake breasts?'

He laughed. 'Why don't you come inside?'

'Are you trying to get fresh?'

'No, no. For dinner, I mean.'

A deckhand in a white uniform held out his hand to help her as she stepped down the stairs. The interior was breathtaking, if just a tiny bit naff. It was panelled in shiny wood with beige, deep-pile carpets and lots of brassware. It was like a proper room, not a cabin on a boat. The table was laid for two, with a white cloth, flowers and very shiny glassware and cutlery, which, disappointingly, was not gold-plated. The cabin was decorated with a Hollywood theme, and there were some interesting old photographs of stolen moments on set: Alfred Hitchcock playing chess with Grace Kelly, Ava Gardner soaking her feet in an ice bucket, Omar Sharif and Peter O'Toole playing cricket in the desert. There was a glass case with memorabilia inside: an Oscar statuette, an Egyptian headdress, a four-stranded pearl necklace with a picture of Audrey Hepburn in *Breakfast at Tiffany's* behind it.

'This is my passion,' he said. 'The movies. I watched so many with my mother, so many of the great old movies. Some day I will make a picture which will be remembered long after I am dead. If I can fight my way through the stupidity and prejudice of Hollywood.'

'But you've made movies already.'

'Small movies, in France. You would not know these films.'

'I might. Try me.'

Was that a fleeting look of panic?

'Look,' he said, 'this is a headdress worn by Elizabeth Taylor in *Cleopatra*.'

'Is that a real Oscar?'

'Yes, but I am afraid not the most distinguished one. My

dream is to obtain one of the statuettes awarded for *Lawrence of Arabia* in 1962. But for the moment I am having to make do with this, which is an award for best sound editing in the late sixties that I managed to find on eBay.'

Olivia laughed. 'Tell me more about your work. I might have seen something. I see quite a lot of French films in—'

'And look. These are the pearls that Audrey Hepburn wore in *Breakfast at Tiffany's*.'

'The real ones?'

'Of course. You would like to wear them for dinner?'

'No, no. I'd look ridiculous.'

He took them out of the case and placed them round her neck, fastening them with the dexterity of a surgeon, standing back to appraise the effect.

She caught herself feeling a stab of Cinderella syndrome and was furious. Dammit, she *was* impressed with the bloody yacht and the apartment and the pearls and the helicopter. She knew she was one in a long line of girls who had been wooed with this lot, and she didn't want to be. The ridiculous, delusional feelings which can afflict a girl in such situations were bubbling up. She was thinking: *I'm different; I don't like him for his money, I like him for himself. I can change him*, while simultaneously imagining herself installed on the yacht, an adored creature, slipping into the water for unlimited scuba diving with no additional charge for equipment rental, then emerging from the shower and fastening Audrey Hepburn's pearls around her neck.

Stop it, she told herself. *Stop it, you total sad act. Do what you're here to do*. 'Pierre Bin Feramo,' she felt like yelling, '*can we get this straight? Are you wooing me, or are you trying to bump me off? Are you a terrorist or a playboy? Do you think I tried to put the FBI onto you or not?*' Right, she was bloody well going to tackle him.

'Pierre,' she began, 'or perhaps I should I call you M- M-' she started to laugh, '. . . Moustafa.' The tension was making her hysterical. He looked at her angrily for a moment, which only made her want to laugh more. She felt like she was being childishly impudent to Osama Bin Laden.

'Olivia,' he said drily, 'if this continues, I shall have to have you stoned.'

'Buried up to my head in sand?'

'I suppose you think I am trying to recruit you as a suicide bomber.' He was leaning so close to her that she could almost taste his breath.

She stood looking at the Oscar and the Egyptian headdress in the case, trying to calm herself.

'Why did you lie to me?' she said without turning round.

He didn't reply. She turned to face him. 'Why did you tell me you were French? I *knew* you were an Arab.'

'You did?' He looked very cool about it all, even slightly amused. 'Might I enquire as to why?'

'Well, number one, your accent. Number two, I heard you say *shukran*.'

A second's pause. 'You speak Arabic?'

'Yes. Like I told you, I've been in the Sudan. I liked it there . . . but actually, mainly, it was your shoes and socks.'

'My shoes and socks?'

'Thin silk socks and shiny slip-ons – very Arab sheikh.'

'I must remember to change them.'

'Only if you're trying to hide your nationality. Was that a mosque in your apartment?'

The hooded eyes gave nothing away. 'It is actually a panic room. And it seemed an ideal place for privacy and contemplation. And as for the slight, shall we say, *inaccuracy* about my nationality, I was trying to do away with the encumbrance of racial stereotyping. Not everyone has your positive attitude towards our culture and religion.'

'Isn't that like politicians pretending not to be gay – the pretending in itself has the effect of suggesting there's something wrong with being gay?'

'You are suggesting I am ashamed of being an Arab?'

There was a hint of hysteria in his voice: a slight lack of control.

'I'm interested in why you lied about it.'

He fixed his dark, soulful eyes on hers. 'I am proud of being an Arab. Our culture is the oldest in the world and the wisest. Our laws are spiritual laws and our traditions rooted in the wisdom of our ancestors. When I am in Hollywood I am ashamed – not of my ancestry, but of the world I see around me: the arrogance, the ignorance, the vanity, the stupidity, the greed, the salivating worship of flesh and youth, the flaunting of sexuality for fame and financial gain, the lust for the new in the absence of respect for the old. This shallowness you joke of finding delicious is not sweetness but the very spores of rot within the ripe fruit.'

Olivia held herself motionless, gripping her clutch, thinking of the knife inside it. She sensed that the slightest misjudged word or move would trip the wire of his carefully controlled rage.

'Why are the richest nations on earth the unhappiest? Do you know?' he continued.

'That's a rather odd generalization,' she said lightly, trying to shift the mood. 'I mean some of the richest nations in the world are Arab nations. Saudi Arabia's rather well off, isn't it?'

'Saudi Arabia, pah!'

He seemed to be having some kind of private battle. He turned away, then looked back, composed now.

'I am sorry, Olivia,' he said in a gentler tone. 'But spending time in America, as I do, I am often ... hurt ... by the ignorance and prejudice with which we are pigeonholed and insulted. Come. Enough. This is not the evening for this discussion. It is a beautiful night, and it is time to eat.'

21

God, Pierre Feramo could drink. One Martini, a bottle of Cristal, an '82 Pomerol and the best part of a '96 Chassagne-Montrachet later, he was calling for a Reioto della Valpolicella to go with dessert. In most men, it would have seemed as though there was a problem. In a Muslim, it seemed down-right bizarre. But then, Olivia found herself thinking, just say for most of his life Feramo never drank a drop of alcohol. Just say he'd only started drinking recently, as a smokescreen. How would he know he had a problem? How would he know that everyone didn't drink like that?

'Aren't Muslims supposed not to drink alcohol?' she ventured. She was feeling rather full. The food was superb: scallops on puréed spring peas with white truffle oil, sea bass in a lightly curried sauce with pumpkin ravioli, peaches stewed in red wine with mascarpone ice cream flavoured with vanilla.

'Ah, that depends, that depends,' he said vaguely, filling up his glass. 'There are different interpretations.'

'Do you dive from this boat?' she asked.

'What, scuba dive? Yes. Well, actually, no, not from here, not personally. It is too cold. I like to dive in the Caribbean, on the reef off Belize and Honduras, and in the Red Sea. You dive yourself?' He moved to fill her glass, not noticing that it was already full.

'Yes, I love diving. Actually, I was thinking before I came of suggesting a diving story to *Elan*: diving off the beaten track. Belize, Honduras. I was thinking of the Red Sea coast of the Sudan as well.'

'But, Olivia,' he said, raising his hands expansively, 'you must come to my hotel in Honduras. I insist. The diving off the Bay Islands is unsurpassed. We have walls which fall for a thousand feet, intricate tunnels, the rarest of marine life. You must ask your magazine to let you cover it. And then go on to the Sudan. It is wonderful there, the visibility is the best in the world. It is totally untouched. You must do it. You must do it at once. I am leaving for Honduras tomorrow. You must telephone your magazine and join me there as my guest.'

'Well, there's a problem,' she said.

'A problem?'

'They've fired me.'

'They've *fired* you?'

She watched him carefully for signs of bluffing. 'Yes. Someone from your PR office called the editor and complained that I'd called the FBI to suggest they check you out.'

Just for a second he lost his composure, but quickly regained it.

'You? Call the FBI? How ridiculous.'

'Exactly. I didn't. But someone bugged my room and was listening to me talking to myself. Look,' she said, leaning forward, 'Pierre, I'll be honest. I did wonder about you after what happened in Miami. When we were together on your roof deck, you seemed so determined I shouldn't go down to the *OceansApart* the next morning. And after it was blown up you immediately left town. You told me you were French, and then I heard you speaking Arabic. I do get a bit carried away and talk to myself – imaginary conversations, I guess, because I spend so much time alone. But I can't understand who would have bugged my room.'

'You are certain the room was bugged?'

'I found a device in the phone jack.'

His nostrils flared.

'My dear Olivia,' he said eventually, 'I am so sorry that this has happened. I had no idea. I cannot imagine who would have done this, but as you know, we live in paranoid times.'

'Yes. And you can see how—'

'Oh yes, yes. Of course. You are a journalist and a linguist. You have an enquiring mind. I would probably have been suspicious myself. But then, I assume that had you retained these suspicions, you would not be here.'

'It would have been a bit daft to come,' said Olivia, carefully avoiding the lie.

'And now you have lost your job.'

'Well, it wasn't exactly a job. But apparently your PR people called them in a fury.'

'I will put this right immediately. You must write down the contact details of your editor and I will make a phone call in the morning. I am so sorry that this has happened.'

I think I'm falling in love with you, she thought. *Even if you are a terrorist. I'm like one of those female aid workers who falls for the leader of the rebel army or gets kidnapped and falls for her kidnapper. I've got Stockholm Syndrome. I'll end up being featured in a short report on* Woman's Hour.

He took her hand and looked into her eyes. He really was the most beautiful man: gentle, charming, gracious, kind. 'You will come? To Honduras?' he said. 'I shall organize a plane for you and you must be my guest.'

She steeled herself to resist. 'No, no. You're too kind, but I never accept hospitality when I'm writing a story. It interferes with the impartiality. I might find a cockroach in the soup and then where would we be?'

'Then this invitation to dinner must also interfere with your impartiality?'

'Only if I were writing a story about you.'

'And you are not? Ms Joules, you disappoint me. I thought you were about to make me into a star.'

'I'm sure you're the one person in LA who's not looking for stardom.' *Not in this life, anyway.*

'And you, I think, are the other one.'

He reached out and ran his hand delicately across her cheekbone. The melting brown eyes seemed to burn into her own. The touch of his lips on hers sent shock waves through her system.

'Ms Joules,' he murmured, 'you are so wonderfully, imperturbably . . . English.'

He stood up, took her hand, raised her to her feet and led her up to the deck.

'You will stay here with me tonight?' he said, looking down at her.

'It's too soon,' she murmured, giving in as he brought her head against his chest, putting his arms protectively around her, his hand moving to stroke her hair.

'I understand,' he said. The only sound was the soft lap of the waves against the side of the boat. 'But you will join me in Honduras?'

'I'll think about it,' she whispered weakly.

Los Angeles

'Weeesh tuminall?'

Olivia's cab was passing the oilfields on the way to the airport. Sand-coloured nodding donkeys bobbed up and down improbably, as if she was in southern Iraq, not on the outskirts of Los Angeles.

'Weesh tuminall?' yelled the cab driver again. 'Tuminall? Internassyunall? Or domestic fly? Weesh airline?'

'Oh, oh, er,' she stalled, having no idea where she was going. 'International.'

The sun was setting among the clouds with the detail and splendour of an oil painting, the tangle of telegraph wires silhouetted against it. She felt a stirring of premature nostalgia for Los Angeles and America: the America of deserts, gas stations, road trips and reinvention.

'Weesh airline?'

Oh, shut up, she felt like saying. *I haven't bloody well decided yet.*

She forced herself to think clearly and sensibly. It was a perfectly simple problem: she had fallen in love with a man. It was the sort of thing that could happen to anyone, apart from him being an international terrorist. The symptoms were familiar: only thirty per cent of her brain was operational. The rest was taken up with a combination of fantasy and flashback. Every time she tried calmly to evaluate her situation and make a plan, her mind was overwhelmed by images of an entire future with Feramo, beginning with scuba diving in crystalline Caribbean waters, followed by shagging in Bedouin tents in the Sudanese desert, concluding with Grace Kelly–Prince Rainer-style married life in yachts, palaces, etc., with a Feramo, who, in an astonishing feat of mental gymnastics, had been transformed from a terrorist into a major movie director slash philanthropist, and also possibly a doctor slash scientist slash other unspecified manly professional who could also fix cars. She should never have gone on the Catalina date. She tried desperately to pull herself together. *I am not*, she told herself, *going to follow a man anywhere. Women have evolved and learnt to do everything that used to be men's work, and they have responded by regressing. They cannot even mend things any more.* But by now Feramo, dressed in a rather fetching boiler suit, was tinkering with the engine of his helicopter, watched by an admiring crew. With a final twist of his spanner, the engine roared into life while the crew clapped and cheered. Feramo grabbed her by the waist, flung her head back and kissed her passionately, before sweeping her aboard his chopper.

Her mobile started ringing. The screen said OUT OF AREA. Feramo! Had to be.

'It's me,' said Kate. 'I was woken by transatlantic thought vibes. You're about to do something bad, aren't you?'

'No, no. Just, er, Pierre has a dive hotel down in Honduras and—'

'Don't you *dare* follow that man to Honduras. It's insane. What have you been working for all these years if you're just going to succumb to the charms of some ridiculous Dodi al-Fayed-style playboy? He's probably got a hairy back. Four years down the line he'll be forcing you to stay at home in a burka while he travels all over the world shagging wannabe actresses.'

'It's not like that. You don't know him.'

'Oh please. Neither do you. Just come home, Olivia. Mend your fences at the *Sunday Times*. Get on with building a career and a life that no one can take away from you.'

'But what if it's real? What if he is al-Qaeda?'

'Come home even quicker. You'll end up minus a head, let alone a career. And no, I'm not trying to nick your story.'

'Sorry about that,' said Olivia, sheepishly.

'It's all right.'

'I'm not planning to spend the rest of my life with him. I just thought I'd have a little . . .'

'You don't need to go to fucking Honduras to have "a little . . ." Get on a Heathrow flight tonight, and I'll see you tomorrow.'

The cab was rounding the concrete curve towards the departure bays.

'OK, we here. International tuminall,' the driver cut in. 'Weesh airline?'

'Just here.'

'You're too susceptible to men.'

'Well at least I haven't been married twice,' said Olivia, trying simultaneously to get out of the cab, tip the driver, get her carry-on and wedge the mobile under her ear.

'That's because you were startled into premature clarity by what happened to your family. Otherwise you'd have got married by the time you were twenty like everyone else in your school.'

Olivia had a sudden intuition. 'Have you had a row with

Dominic?' she said, trying to indicate to the taxi driver that she hadn't actually intended to give him a twenty-dollar tip on a thirty-dollar fare.

'I hate him.'

'Oh, you mean it's still on. Love and hate are the same thing. The opposite of love is indifference.'

'Shut up. I hate him. So you'll be landing about three tomorrow, right? Come straight round.'

'Yes, er, I'll call,' said Olivia doubtfully, heading into the terminal.

Olivia loved travelling alone: on the move, one small carry-on, responsible only for herself. She beamed as the automatic doors slid apart to receive her. How did they *know* to open? It made her feel so important.

She sat down on one of a row of plastic seats and watched the airport world go by: a worried family dressed in the comfy shoes, pastel jackets and bum-bag uniform of tourists, clutching their bags, looking around fearfully, huddled together against an alien world. A fat Mexican girl with a baby, following an angry-looking boy. She thought about what Kate had said. Would she have stayed Rachel Pixley and had an ordinary life if it hadn't been for the accident? *Naaah*, she thought. There *was* no ordinary life. Life was fragile and bizarre and turned on a sixpence. It was up to you to snuffle out the fun.

She pulled out a crumpled printout of an email and read it again.

Sender: editor@elan.co.uk
Subj: Pierre Feramo

My dear Olivia,
    We were contacted this morning personally by Pierre Feramo. M. Feramo explained that his people had made an unforgivable

mistake which was not in any sense your doing. He spoke of you in the highest terms and asked that we reinstate you on the story immediately.

I cannot apologize enough for misjudging you. We have received the copy you sent, which is excellent. There is enough there already, I think, to make the piece. Would you like to continue the piece yourself, or would you prefer to move on to the Honduras diving story M. Feramo mentioned? We could, if you wish, have the 'wannabe' copy cleaned up by the subs and you could retain your byline. Let us know.

Apologies again, and looking forward to many more superb pieces from you in the future.

Sally Hawkins
Editor, *Elan*

She put it back in her bag and pulled out the Expedia flight-detail printouts. There was a Virgin flight at 20.50 to London, and an AeroMexico flight to La Ceiba in Honduras at 20.40, connecting in Mexico City. All she had to do was decide.

23

Unfortunately, however, Olivia could not decide. She was plunged into the Land of Indecision, which she knew was a treacherous place where she could wander for days, increasingly lost in a maze of pros and cons and possibilities. The only way to escape was to make a decision – any decision – and then at least she could get out and see straight.

Brow furrowed with earnest resolve, she ran her eye down the departures board to check for the London flight: Acapulco, Belize, Bogotá, Cancún, Caracas, Guadalajara, Guatemala, La Paz. *What am I* doing? she thought. *If I go back to London, I'll be sitting in the pissing rain writing articles about dining rooms.*

She opened the guidebook to Honduras. 'A paradise of white-sanded beaches and rainforested peaks, surrounded by crystalline Caribbean waters. The Bay Islands offer the most spectacular diving in the Caribbean.'

Mmm, she thought, flicking through to find Popayan, the island which housed Feramo's eco-diving resort.

'The smallest island in the archipelago, Popayan offers a flashback to the Caribbean of the 1950s. Many of the population are a mixture of black, Carib, Hispanic and white settlers – the direct descendents of shipwrecked Irish pirates. The village's only bar, the Bucket of Blood, is the centre of all gossip and social life.'

Her eyes lit up. It sounded like major fun. Then, remembering her mother's remarks about excitement and danger, she took out another book, a book about al-Qaeda, and opened it at a turned-down page and a section headed 'Takfiri'.

> Intelligence officials warn that the Takfiri, an offshoot of al-Qaeda, belie their Islamic roots by drinking alcohol, smoking and even drug-taking, as well as womanizing and dressing in a sophisticated Western style. Their aim is to merge into what they see as corrupt societies with the goal of destroying them.
>
> Professor Absalom Widgett, a British scholar of Islam and author of *The Unlikelihood of the el-Obeid Plasma TV*, has described them as 'devastatingly ruthless: the hardcore of the hardcore of Islamic militants'.

Olivia had made her decision. She headed for the mailbox and dropped in an envelope addressed to her flat in London. It contained a CD copy of her hard drive, including the photos she had taken in Feramo's 'panic room'.

'One seat to La Ceiba, Honduras,' she said to the lady on the desk.

'Would that be single or return?'

'One way,' she said grimly.

24

Central America

The journey progressed from the anaesthetic cleanliness of
LAX to the craziness of Central America at a dizzying pace.
Olivia, excited, thought it was like a speeded-up version of
a Victorian exploration: Burton or Speke setting out from
London to Cairo in starched wing collars, then plunging
deeper and deeper into the African continent, losing their
sanity, possessions and teeth.

Mexico City's airport was wild: the seats were of worn
cowhide; men walked past in cowboy boots, sombreros and
big moustaches; women sashayed in tight jeans and stilettos,
bulging from sequinned tops like game-show hostesses; while
the game shows and music videos on the big screens teetered
on the wrong side of soft porn.

Olivia was busy. She called Sally Hawkins, said she'd like
to do the diving story, but stalled her for a few days. She
decided to snuffle round the Bay Islands incognito and find
out what she could before alerting anyone to her presence.
She bought cheap jeans and a sweatshirt, found a drugstore
and a shower and dyed her hair red and then switched to her
old passport (which she'd rather fraudulently claimed to have

lost when she changed her name) and became Rachel Pixley.
The thought of airline food usually repulsed her, but here she
was seduced by the smells and ate a giant plate of burritos
with refried beans, salsa, guacamole and chocolate sauce.

The ATAPA connection to La Ceiba in Honduras was five
hours late, the atmosphere at the gate increasingly festive. By
the time the motley bunch of passengers boarded the tatty
plane, the delay had turned into a full-scale party with styro-
foam sandwiches and tequila-laced lurid green drinks all
round. The man beside Olivia kept offering her swigs of
tequila from a bottle, but, as she explained, she was too full
of refried beans *au chocolat* to fit in anything else at all. Forty
minutes into the flight, the mindless movie, which had been
raucously ridiculed by the passengers, disappeared from the
screen and the captain's voice came over the address system –
first in Spanish, then in English.

'Ladies and gentlemen. Is your captain talking. I regret to
announce you that this plane is problem and no landing in La
Ceiba any more. We go another place. We let you know. Bye.'

Olivia immediately convinced herself that it was a hijacking.
Time seemed to slow down, like people said it did when you
were drowning. Her overwhelming feeling, she decided, was
sadness: sadness that she had never quite made it as a journalist
and never had her name on a story which counted. She tried
to remember the Rules for Living, then sulkily decided they
didn't count if you were dead. She brightened, briefly, thinking of a tearful reunion with her parents and brother, who
were dressed in angel outfits with wings. Then she thought:
*Oh, bloody hell, if I'd known this was going to happen, I'd
have had a last shag with Feramo on that yacht.*

25

Tegucigalpa, Honduras

Right, that's enough wallowing, she told herself briskly, reaching into her bag for her pepper-spray pen and looking towards the cockpit to work out a plan. The man next to her held out the tequila bottle. This time she gratefully took an enormous swig. She handed it back to him and was puzzled to see him grab it with a cheerful grin. Glancing around the plane, she realized that no one was behaving appropriately for those on the verge of death. The air hostess was making her way down the aisle with another tray of lurid drinks and a fresh bottle of tequila.

'Is OK,' said the man beside her. 'Is no worry. ATAPA Airlines is never know where they go. Is stand for Always Take a Parachute.' He roared with laughter.

The landing in Tegucigalpa was rather like a tractor hitting a corrugated-iron roof. But the assembled passengers clapped and cheered the pilot regardless. The first drops of rain were falling as they climbed onto a rickety bus, and soon, as they rattled through the scruffy streets of the town past crumbling colonial buildings and wooden shacks, a full tropical rainstorm was hammering on the roof. It was kind of cosy.

Olivia considered the El Parador hotel to be of the highest standard. The point on the toilet paper was faultless in terms of both sharpness and neatness. The only problem was that the bathroom floor was under two inches of water. The phone, when she tried to reach reception, gurgled in reply. She headed down herself, requested the speedy dispatch of a mop and bucket and returned to the room, where she sat cross-legged on the brightly coloured bedspread and started to organize her possessions.

She spread out her stuff in front of her and started two lists: *Essentials for Rest of Trip* and *Items Surplus to Requirements*. *Items Surplus to Requirements* now included the sweatshirt and ugly jeans (far too hot) and the beautiful this-year's Marc Jacobs tan-leather tote (too heavy, too identifiable and too posh).

There was a knock on the door.

'*Un momento, por favor,*' she said, concealing her research materials and spy equipment under the blanket.

'*Pase adelante.*'

The door opened, followed by a mop and a smiling Hispanic girl holding a bucket. Olivia made as if to take the mop, but the woman shook her head, and so the two of them did the floor together, Olivia emptying the bucket and the girl keeping up a steady stream of Spanish, mainly about what fun was to be had in the bar downstairs. When the floor was dry, the two of them stood back, beaming and admiring their handiwork. Olivia felt it was her honour – and hoped it wasn't neo-colonialist – to replace the tip for this happy spirit with the leather tote, as well as some clothes and other *Items Surplus to Requirements*. The woman was very pleased, though not quite pleased enough to suggest she realized it was actually this season's Marc Jacobs, or maybe she was just a spiritual person who eschewed labels. She embraced Olivia and nodded down at the bar.

'*Sí, sí, más tarde*,' said Olivia.

Better stay off the margaritas, Olivia told herself as she stashed her valuables in the safe and zipped her Essentials for Rest of Trip firmly in the tan and olive case. But hang it all, she thought when she reached the festive courtyard. Everyone else is as pissed as a fart. She took a sip of her first sensational margarita. *Salud*!

A handsome, white-haired man with a moustache, dazzlingly drunk, crooned along to his guitar as the shambolic crowd of hippy travellers, businessmen and locals joined in. When the inebriated *mariachi* started to lose the plot, he was abruptly replaced by blaring salsa. Within moments the dance floor was filled with locals dancing intricate, detailed steps exquisitely, and the indeterminate writhings of the tie-dye-clad gringos. Olivia, who had briefly gone out with a Venezuelan Reuters correspondent and developed a penchant for salsa, was mesmerized by the sight of dancers brought up on its rhythms doing the real thing. Through the mass of bodies, a guy with cropped, bleached-blond hair caught her attention. In the middle of all the festivity and mindless drinking, he sat at a table, leaning forward, chin on hands, watching the crowd intently. He was dressed in baggy hip-hop clothes, but he was too cool-looking and focused to be a backpacker. He reappeared a few minutes later, directly in front of her. He didn't smile; he just raised an eyebrow towards the dance floor and held out his hand. Sexy boy, cocky too; he reminded her of someone. He was a great dancer. He didn't move much, but he knew what he was doing, and all she had to do was follow. Neither of them spoke, they just danced, bodies close, his arm leading her where he wanted her to go. After a couple of numbers, an elderly local man cut in with immense courtesy. The blond guy ceded his position graciously. The next time she looked, he was gone. Eventually she took a break from the dancing; as she stood there, wiping her forehead, she felt a hand on her arm. It was the maid to whom she had given the tote bag.

'Go back to your room,' said the girl quietly in Spanish.

'Why?' said Olivia.

'Someone was in there.'

'What? Did you see someone?'

'No. I have to go,' she said nervously. 'You go and have a look. Go quickly.'

Sobering up fast, Olivia made her way to the room, taking the stairs, not the elevator. She slipped the key in the lock, paused and flung the door open. The room was a mass of strange shadows thrown by the street lights shining through the palm trees and the mosquito screens against her window. Still in the doorway, she reached for the light and clicked it on: nothing. She listened again, shut the door behind her and checked the bathroom: again, nothing. She went to the safe. It was untouched. Then her eye fell on her case. It was partly open; she knew she had left it zipped up. The clothes she had left folded inside were messed up. She slipped her hand underneath them and came across what felt like a polythene bag full of flour. She pulled it out, frantic, saw it was full of white powder and at the same moment heard footsteps in the corridor. She ripped open the bag, dipped in a finger and ran it along her gum, confirming her suspicion, with a not-unpleasant frisson, that it contained cocaine, and a sizeable stash of cocaine. Just then, the footsteps stopped outside her room, and there was loud shouting and banging on the door.

'*La policia! Abra la puerta!*'
'*Un momento, por favor.*'

It was a simple choice: open the door to the police with a large bag of cocaine in her hand, or take a jump straight down from the fifth floor.

26

Stop, breathe, think. She stepped into the bathroom and flushed the loo. With the flush masking the sound, she gently lifted the mosquito screen away from the window and stood back. Taking as long a run at it as possible, she hurled the plastic bag out of the window with all her might, thinking: *Someone over there is going to find their evening just looked up.* Then – hearing a distant splash – she replaced the screen and calmly opened the door.

Once she actually saw the police, they weren't scary at all. They were spotty teenagers and actually rather apologetic. She sat on an upright chair, watching them search the room, trying to work out if they knew what they were looking for and where it was. Were they real police? Military? Actors? Resting actors slash lifestyle coaches?

'*Todo está bien,*' said one of them finally. '*Gracias. Disculpenos.*'

'*No tiene importancia,*' she said, which wasn't strictly true, but then she was English and believed in the hot air of politeness, for, as the *Girl Guide Handbook* says, 'There's nothing but air in a tyre, but it certainly makes the wheels go round more smoothly!'

'*Un cigarillo?*' said the younger boy, holding out a packet.

'*Muchas gracias,*' she said, taking the cigarette and leaning

141

forward for a light. She hadn't had a cigarette in years. It hit her as though it was a joint. She wished she had some tequila to offer the policemen. They looked as though they'd be susceptible to getting drunk and telling her who sent them.

'*Por qué están aquí?*' she ventured anyway.

The two boys looked at each other and laughed. They had, they claimed, been tipped off. They all laughed some more and finished their cigarettes, and the two boys took their leave as if they were lifelong friends of hers who'd just been round for a party.

When she was sure they had gone, she sank down with her back against the door. Eventually, she pulled herself out of her funk of fear and confusion and asked herself, in accordance with Rules for Living number seven, *Does it really matter?* The answer, unfortunately, was yes. She decided to call the British Embassy in the morning. If there was a British Embassy.

Olivia had a terrible, hot, anxious, sleepless night. She was relieved when a rooster started crowing to signal that it was over. When the sun appeared through the glistening tops of the palm trees, it gave a disappointingly pale light, not full-on Caribbean morning sun. She opened the window, looking down on a tranquil harbour and corrugated-iron rooftops, smelling the heavy, spicy air. There was a group of local women talking and laughing in the street below. There was clumsy *mariachi* music coming from a radio. She realized there had been no word to the passengers as to how or when they might reach their intended destination. She wondered if they would all just stay there for ever, the party continuing day after day, until they did nothing but drink tequila and sleep under trees from dawn to dusk.

*

Down at reception, a scruffy piece of paper taped to the wall said:

Pasajeros de ATAPA para La Ceiba. El autobús saldrá del hotel al aeropuerto a las 9 de la mañana.

It was eight o'clock already. Olivia's mobile, it emerged, did not work in Honduras. She asked the receptionist if she could use the phone. He said the phones weren't working, but there was a call box outside. Down the road a dilapidated blue and yellow sign featuring what was either a telephone or a sheep's head was hanging at an angle off a wooden shed.

She started with Honduran directory enquiries, expecting a lengthy and frustrating round of engaged signals, non-answers and repeated yelling and spelling of words, culminating in a dial tone. Instead, the phone was immediately answered by a charming girl who spoke perfect English, gave her the number for the British Embassy and informed her that it opened at eight thirty.

It was eight fifteen. Should she wait? Or rush back and pack her bag so that she'd be in time for the bus? She decided to stay where she was. At eight twenty-five, a woman with two small children appeared, hovering insistently. Olivia briefly attempted to ignore her, but decency got the upper hand and she ceded her position. The woman began a lengthy emotional argument. By eight forty-five, she was yelling, and the smallest child was in tears. By eighty forty-eight, both the children were in tears, and the woman was banging the receiver against the wall of the shed.

She was going to miss the bloody bus and the plane and be marooned in Tegucigalpa. In the end, it was quite simple, really. She opened the door, said, 'You. Out,' and dialled the Embassy.

'Hello, British Embassy.'

'Hello, my name is' – dammit, what? – 'Rachel Pixley,' she

said quickly, remembering that was the name on the passport she had used when she booked the flight.

'Yes. What can we help you with?'

After briefly explaining her problem, she was put through to a man whose crisp English voice made her suddenly tearful. It was like bumping into a British daddy, or a policeman after being chased by brigands.

'Hmmm,' said the chap, when she had finished. 'I'll be honest with you, this is not uncommon with the flight from Mexico City. You're sure there isn't anyone who could have tampered with your bag there?'

'No. I had repacked it just before I left the room. The drugs weren't in there. Someone came to my room when I was down in the bar. I'm worried about some people I met in LA, a guy called Pierre Feramo and some rather odd things that happened . . .' There was a slight buzz on the line.

'Can you hold on a minute?' said the Embassy chap. 'Just got to take another call. Back in a mo.'

She glanced nervously at her watch. It was three minutes to nine. Her hope was that all the passengers would be so hung-over that everyone would be late.

'Sorry about that,' said the man, returning to the phone. 'Miss Pixie, isn't it?'

'Pixley.'

'Yes. Well, look. No need to worry about the drug business. We'll let the powers that be know. Any more problems, just give us a ring. Can you give us an idea of your itinerary?'

'Well, I was planning to get the plane today to Popayan, stay in the village for a few days, and then maybe move on to Feramo's hotel, the Isla Bonita.'

'Jolly good. Well, we'll let everyone know to watch out for you. Why don't you pop in on your way back and let us know how it all went?'

When she put down the phone, she stared straight ahead for a moment, biting her lip in concentration. Did the phone really buzz when she mentioned Feramo, or was it just her overactive imagination?

Back at the hotel the receptionist informed her that the bus had left ten minutes ago. Fortunately, she ran into the recipient of the Marc Jacobs tote, who said she'd get her husband to drive her to the airport in his van. He took a while to turn up. By the time they rattled up to the Departures area, it was ten twenty-two. The plane was due to leave at ten.

As Olivia careered across the tarmac, dragging the little case behind her and waving frantically, two men in overalls were starting to pull the stairs away from the plane. They laughed when they saw her and shoved them back again. One of them bounded up ahead of her and banged on the door until it opened. As she entered the crowded cabin, a ragged cheer went up. Her fellow passengers from the night before were pale and fragile, but still jolly. As she flopped gratefully into her seat, the pilot was making his way down the aisle greeting everyone individually. She felt quite reassured until she realized it was the drunken *mariachi* with the moustache from the salsa party the night before.

At La Ceiba airport she bought a ticket to Popayan and headed desperately for the news-stand, only to find no foreign newspapers except a three-week-old copy of *Time*. She picked up La Ceiba's *El Diario* and slumped into an orange plastic chair at the gate, waiting for the flight announcement, flicking through the paper and trying to find any update on the *OceansApart*. She was mildly cheered by the sight of her dancing partner from the previous night – the one with the serious expression and cropped peroxide hair. He reminded her of Eminem. He had the same combination of the grave and the subversive. He came over and sat beside her, holding out a bottle of mineral water.

'Thanks,' she said, enjoying the slight contact as he handed it over.

'*De nada.*' His face was almost expressionless, but he had compelling eyes, grey and intelligent. 'Try not to puke now,' he said, getting up again and heading for the news-stand.

Concentrate, Olivia, she said to herself. *Concentrate. We are not a skittish backpacker on our gap year. We are a top foreign journalist and possible international spy on a mission of global significance.*

27

Popayan, Bay Islands

The island of Popayan came into view, and soon they were descending over a crystalline turquoise sea towards white coral beaches and greenery. The little plane landed with a horrifying bounce, then veered off the unpaved airstrip and turned right over a rickety wooden bridge, quite as if it thought it was a bicycle, before coming to an abrupt halt next to a rusty red pick-up truck and a wooden sign which said WELCOME TO POPAYAN: DANIEL DEFOE'S ORIGINAL ROBINSON CRUSOE ISLAND.

There was a problem opening the door. The pilot was tugging at it from the outside, and inside a hippie backpacker was staring at the handle with unhurried fascination, poking at it from time to time as if it was a caterpillar. The blond guy got up, moved the hippie, gripped the handle, put his forearm against the door and opened it.

'Thanks, man,' muttered the backpacker sheepishly.

Someone had left a British newspaper on a seat. Olivia grabbed it eagerly. Outside, as they loaded themselves into the back of the pick-up, she sniffed the air happily and looked around.

It was fun sitting in the back of the truck with all the back-packers. They bounced along a sandy track, then hit the main street of West End. It was like a cross between a Western movie and the Deep South. The houses were clapboard, with porches. Some of them had swing seats, some of them had battered, comfy-looking sofas. An elderly lady with white permed hair and pale skin, wearing a yellow tea dress, was walking along with a parasol, a tall, extremely good-looking black guy a few paces behind.

Olivia turned back to the truck and found the blond man looking straight at her.

'Where are you staying?' he said.

'Miss Ruthie's Guest House.'

'You're here,' he said, leaning over and banging on the driver's door. She saw the muscles beneath his shirt. He jumped out to help her down, unloaded her bag and carried it up the steps to the green wooden porch. 'There you go,' he said and held out his hand. 'Morton C.'

'Thanks. Rachel.'

'You'll be all right here,' he said, shouting over his shoulder as he jumped into the back of the truck. 'See you at the Bucket of Blood.'

Spots of rain were starting to fall as Olivia knocked on the yellow door. A warm smell of baking wafted out. The door opened and a very tiny old lady stood before her. She had fair skin and red-gold hair in curls and was wearing an apron. Olivia suddenly felt as if she was in a fairy story and she would go inside to find a wolf in a red-hooded sweatshirt, several dwarfs and a beanstalk.

'What can I be doing for you then?' The old lady's accent had a strong Irish lilt. Maybe it was true about the Irish pirates.

'I was wondering if you had a room for a few nights.'

'To be sure,' said Miss Ruthie. 'Come in and sit yourself down. I'll get you some breakfast.'

Olivia half-expected a leprechaun to hop out and offer to help with her case.

The kitchen was constructed entirely of wood and painted in a fifties mixture of primrose yellow and pixie green. Olivia sat at the kitchen table as the rain hammered down on the roof and thought how making a home is nothing to do with a building and everything to do with how different people make it feel. She was sure Miss Ruthie could have moved into Feramo's minimalist Miami penthouse and still managed to turn it into Snow White's cottage or the Little House on the Prairie.

She ate a breakfast of refried beans and corn bread from a plate with two blue stripes, which reminded her of her childhood. Miss Ruthie said there were two rooms available, both looking out over the water. One was on the first floor and the other – which was a suite! – was on the top floor. The first room was the equivalent of five dollars a night, and the suite fifteen. She chose the suite. It had sloping ceilings, a covered deck and a view on three sides. It was like being in a little wooden house on the end of a pier. The walls were painted pink, green and blue. There was an iron bedstead and, in the bathroom, wallpaper which sported a repeat motif saying *I love you I love you I love you*. Most importantly, the toilet paper was folded to a faultless point.

Miss Ruthie brought her up a cup of instant coffee and a piece of ginger cake.

'You'll be diving later, will you?' said Miss Ruthie.

'I'm going straight away,' said Olivia. 'As soon as I've unpacked.'

'Get yourself down to Rik's shack. He'll take care of you.'

'Where is it?'

Miss Ruthie just looked at her as if she was mad.

Olivia took the coffee and cake on to the deck with the newspaper and lay down on a faded flowery daybed. There was a story headed AL-QAEDA LINK IN ALGECIRAS BLAST. She started to read, but fell asleep to the sound of the rain bouncing down on the calm waters of the bay.

28

Sixty feet below the surface, it was like being in a dream or on another planet. Olivia, dressed in a red swimsuit and diving gear, was on the edge of a precipice, a sheer cliff falling away a thousand feet into the abyss. You could simply throw yourself over and somersault and fall at your own pace. She was following an orange pufferfish. It was a lovable little thing, bright orange and shaped like a football, with huge round eyes and ginger eyelashes, like something out of a Disney cartoon. A shoal of extraordinary blue and green fish burst up around her like a design on a fifties bath towel. Dwayne, her diving buddy, a slight, twenty-two-year-old, long-haired hippy, banged his fists together for her to check her air. She held up the gauge. Fifty minutes had passed and it felt like five. She looked up to where the sunlight dappled the surface. It gave her a shock to realize that she was so far down; she felt utterly at home. All you had to do was remember not to panic and to breathe.

She made her way reluctantly upwards, following the wisp-like figure of Dwayne with his lankly flowing mane, keeping the pace slow, feeling the air expand in her BCD, letting it escape in short bursts. She broke the surface and stared, startled, at the other world: brilliant sunshine, blue sky, the cheerful line of clapboard houses on the shoreline deflatingly close. She had felt as though they were five fathoms deep, a million miles from civilization, and now the water was so shallow they could almost stand up.

She and Dwayne swam to Rik's Dive Shack jetty, where, holding onto the edge of the ladder, they took off their masks, euphoric from the dive. They swung their weight belts up onto the wooden platform, unfastened their tanks and waited for help to hand them up. A small group was huddled on the benches outside the shack, deep in conversation. No one had noticed them.

'Dudes! What's up?' Dwayne called over. He pulled himself onto the jetty, then helped Olivia up.

'Hey, Dwayne,' one of them replied. 'You see anything uncool down there?'

'No, man. It's beautiful. Blue water.'

Olivia's legs felt a little shaky as they walked along the warm wooden slats of the jetty. It had been a long dive. Dwayne was rinsing out the gear in a barrel of fresh water. He handed her a bottle of cold water. 'You've gone blonde,' he said.

She put her hand to her hair. It felt thick with the salt.

'Suits you better than red.'

'So much for six to eight washes,' she said, starting to dunk her gear in the barrel.

'Hey, Rik. What's up? Something happened?' said Dwayne, as he and Olivia moved over to the group.

Rik, a stocky Canadian with a moustache, was older than the rest. He had the air of a college lecturer about him.

'They've started on the marker buoys above Morgan's Cave,' said Rik, making a space for Olivia, then reaching into a cold box and handing her a soda. 'Frederic went down there with a bunch of clients and met a party of Arturo's from a Roatán boat in the tunnel coming the other way. Arturo said he'd left a marker buoy, but it wasn't there when Frederic went down. It has to be Feramo's lot.'

Olivia stiffened at the name but tried to act normally.

Another of the guys joined in. 'Saturday someone put a buoy there when no one was down. Arturo saw it and went down to check it out, and no one was in there. The only way to stop it is to sit on top of the dive sites all day with a boat.'

'Yeah, well, we might just have to do that and not just with a boat,' said Dwayne in a dark, threatening voice.

The party started to break up. Dwayne wanted to walk her back to Miss Ruthie's.

'Who were they talking about back there?' she asked innocently.

'Guys from the hotel over Pumpkin Hill. They've got this luxury eco-resort thing going. Some people say it's owned by an oil sheikh. They're trying to clear out all the other dive operations and take over the caves and tunnels for their own clients. It's a pile of shit.'

'Is it a dive hotel?'

'Well, yeah, but I think that's bullshit. He's got all these commercial divers and welders down there. He's got this fucking huge pier. I mean, what does he need a pier like that for on Popayan?'

Olivia's mind was racing.

'Welding? Can they do that underwater? What do they use for the blowtorches?'

'Acetylene.'

'Is it explosive?'

'It is if you mix it with oxygen.'

'Even underwater?'

'Oh sure. Anyway, here we are. You coming to the Bucket of Blood tonight?'

'Er, yes, OK,' she said vaguely. 'See you later.'

She hurried back to her room and leafed through the newspaper, looking for the Algeciras bomb story she had seen earlier. There had been a blast in a tourist complex, and it was being attributed to al-Qaeda.

'Preliminary investigations suggest that the device was acetylene-based. Acetylene is readily available and routinely used by divers in the field of commercial welding.'

The Bucket of Blood was quite a place. It was a wooden shack with a stone floor, a rough wooden bar and a barman with no teeth. There were three locals sitting at the bar. The tables and benches were filled with backpackers.

The sexual politics of the backpacker scene was something Olivia found relaxing. Obvious displays of sexuality or financial solvency were frowned upon. You would no more turn up to a backpacker party wearing a halter-neck top and a miniskirt than you would in a Marks & Spencer's business suit or fisherman's waders. The standard dress was faded, threadbare clothes which might have fitted when they left Stockholm or Helsinki but which, after six months of diving, rice and peas and dysentery, were now two sizes too big.

Dwayne gave her a wave as she walked in, beckoning her to sit beside him. A loud guffaw emanated from the three locals at the bar. She looked over and saw that one of them was telling an anecdote and was bent over with his arse in the air.

The gang from Rik's made room for her on the wooden bench. One of them was telling a jargon-filled dive story, which seemed to involve Feramo's people.

'So he catches one of them in Devil's Jaw without leaving a buoy, and the guy just turns off his air.'

Olivia lost her composure as Morton C walked into the bar.

'Jesus. What did he do?'

'He cut through the other guy's AS . . .'

She watched as he joined a group at the back of the bar, greeting the other guys in a manly fashion, like they were gang members from south LA.

'. . . and breathed from his BCD . . .'

Morton C caught her watching him and raised his beer bottle. There was a slight change in his expression which might or might not have been a smile.

'. . . then did an ESA until he managed to get his deck off and reopen the valve.'

A man approached their table; he had a seventies hippy look – a big handlebar moustache, long hair, bald on top. 'Hey, Rik. You wanna take a party out on the boat to Bell Key?'

'Any particular reason?'

The man gave a slow, delicious smile. 'We got the share.'

'Yay! Let's go. You coming, Rachel-from-England?'

It turned out that a large bag of cocaine had been washed up on the shores of Popayan the night before and was being shared democratically between the inhabitants of West End. Olivia wondered if it might be the bag that she had chucked out of the hotel window: highly unlikely, but there would be a pleasing circularity to that.

Most of the clientele of the Bucket of Blood headed out to the key in a small flotilla of dive boats, one of which conked out on the way. Olivia was aroused to observe that it was Morton C who came to the rescue. He pulled at the starter cord, messed around with the throttle, then hauled the outboard motor out of the water. After tinkering for a few minutes, he put it back, pulled at the starter cord a few times and the engine started perfectly.

There had been a whip-round for a plastic gallon-container of rum and a couple of gallons of orange juice. Once on the island, which was a hundred yards across and uninhabited, they lit a fire and mixed the drinks in coconut shells. Initially she was reminded of parties at school, everyone working out who they were going to snog later under a veneer of cool punctuated by bursts of nervous laughter. There was a bit of singing and guitar strumming while lines of coke were cut and joints passed around. People started to sit down around the fire and Olivia joined them.

She found herself acutely conscious of Morton C, watching him out of the corner of her eye and panicking slightly if she saw him talking to another girl. It was all deliciously teenage. He didn't acknowledge her at all, but their eyes met a couple of times, and she *knew*. He settled himself on the opposite side of the fire and she sipped her drink, declining the cocaine, but taking the occasional drag on a joint as it was passed round and watching his serious face in the firelight. Dwayne leaned over into her line of sight, his lank hair flopping over his face. 'Rachel,' he whispered solemnly, 'you see over there, those trees? There's a helicopter in there. You see it? They've covered it in cotton wool.' He glanced around furtively then loped off towards the trees in an ape-like manner.

It appeared that the cocaine was taking hold. An excited discussion started up to her right which consisted entirely of people agreeing with each other.

'That's it, that's it, man! That's it, that's it.'

'Yeah, I mean, like, that's, like, so, like . . .'

'That's what I'm saying! That's exactly what I'm saying! That is *exactly* what I'm saying!'

Someone started walking towards the fire, murmuring, '. . . the senses might give us an experience of reality that seems to be that reality and is actually related to that reality but is not literally that reality,' then stuck his toe in the fire, cursed and fell over.

Olivia lay back and closed her eyes. Someone had brought a boom box and put on French ambient music. The grass was great – very light, very giggly, very sexy.

'You changed your hair.'

She opened her eyes. Morton C was sitting beside her, staring into the fire.

'It was the sun.'

'Yeah, right.'

He slid back and leaned on one elbow, looking down at her, eyes moving over her face. He could have leaned forward just a couple of inches more and kissed her.

'You want to take a walk?' he whispered.

He helped her up and led her by the hand to the beach. She liked the feel of his hand: it was rough and capable. The path led round a rock, out of sight of the fire, and he stopped, brushing the hair away from her face, looking at her with those intense, grey eyes, the fine line of his cheekbone and jaw outlined in the moonlight. He looked adult and tough, as though he'd seen a lot. He took her face in his hand and kissed her, bold, insolent, leaning into her against the rock. He was a great kisser.

He moved his hands confidently down her body. She slipped her arms round his neck, drinking in the kiss, exploring the muscles of his back. There was a strap under his shirt. She followed it down towards his hip with her fingers and felt him push her hand away.

'Are you carrying a gun?'

'No, baby,' he whispered. 'Just pleased to see you.'

'It's in rather an odd place.'

'We aim to surprise,' he said, slipping his hand expertly into her jeans. God, it really was like being sixteen again.

There were shouts. Dwayne appeared round the side of the rock. He stared at them, chewing violently on a stick of gum. He looked really sad for a second then turned away. 'Hey, man, the boat's going back,' he said huffily.

They pulled themselves together, adjusting their clothing. Morton C put his arm round her and they walked back to join the others. He gave a short laugh. 'Jesus, how are we going to get this lot into the boats?'

Rik was halfway up a coconut palm, perhaps searching for a helicopter, cotton-wool bound or otherwise. Dwayne was darting skittishly along the beach, still chewing. A splinter group had taken to the lagoon, where they were dancing in the water, arms waving above their heads. By the dying embers of the fire, more people had joined in the excited agreement–discussion and were yelling over each other.

'That's *exactly* how I see it, that's *exactly* how I see it!'

'Exactly! That's it exactly!'

Morton C sighed and started to round everyone up.

The wind had dropped and the sea was inky black and calm. The talk turned to Feramo. Dwayne was agitated, staring off towards the lights at the end of the island, chewing frantically.

'You have to watch every fucking word you say on Popayan now because you never know who's working for them and who isn't. I'm going to go there tomorrow, man. I'm going to go down there and give them something to think about.'

'Hey,' said Morton C. 'You're loaded, man. Take it easy.'

'We should take them on,' said Dwayne. 'It's crazy, man. We know these caves better than they do. We should take them on.' He stared straight ahead, still chewing, one leg jiggling maniacally up and down.

Olivia shivered. Morton C pulled her close to him, wrapping his sweater round her shoulders. 'You OK?' he whispered. She nodded happily. 'You know anything about these people?'

She shook her head, not meeting his eyes. She was really embarrassed, suddenly, about the Feramo connection. 'Only what everyone says. Do you?'

Someone passed him a joint and, taking a heavy drag, he shook his head. Olivia noticed that he blew the smoke out straight away, without inhaling.

'Like to see the place, though. Would you?'

'I was going to go. I thought it would be good for my article. Sounds scary now, though.'

'You're a journalist?' Their fingers touched as he handed her the joint.

Dwayne was still going on about Feramo and Pumpkin Hill: 'We should set something up and really scare them. Like surprise them. Like do something really creepy in the caves so they won't go back.'

'Who do you work for?'

'Freelance. I'm doing a diving story for *Elan* magazine. What are *you* doing here . . .?'

Olivia caught her lower lip in her teeth as Morton slipped his hand onto her knee, pressing with his thumb as he slid his hand slowly up her thigh.

Outside Miss Ruthie's they made out in the shadows under a tree. For a second, looking over his shoulder, she thought she saw a curtain pulled aside inside the guest house, a head silhouetted against the glow of a lamp. She ducked back into the shadows.

'Can I come in?' he whispered into her neck.

With a tremendous effort of will she pulled away slightly and shook her head.

He looked down, composing himself, breathing unsteadily, then looked back at her.

'No overnight visitors, huh?'

'Not without a chaperone.'

'You diving tomorrow?'

She nodded.

'What time?'

'Around eleven.'

'I'll come and find you after.'

Back in the room she paced around, frantic. The nun-like self-denial was torture. She didn't know how much longer she would be able to keep it up.

29

As Olivia walked along the main street early the next morning, a rooster was crowing and the smell of breakfast cooking drifted out from the small wooden houses. Children were playing on the balconies, old people nodding on the porch swings. A lugubrious man with pale skin and an undertaker's suit raised his hat to her. At his side was a young, red-haired black girl and a fair-skinned child with a flat nose, broad lips and tightly curled hair. The blonde, pale lady she had seen when she arrived was walking elegantly along, still protected by her parasol and her handsome companion. Olivia started to imagine she was in a weird land of incest and interbreeding, where fathers would sleep with their nephews and great-aunts have secret affairs with donkeys.

She headed for a hardware shop and chandler's she had spotted the previous night, full of tin buckets, coils of rope and washing-up bowls. She loved the feeling that in hardware shops everything was useful and sensibly priced. Even if you spent really quite a large amount of money, it wouldn't be wasteful or extravagant. The sign above the window looked like something out of a funeral home in nineteenth-century Chicago: curly, intricate black writing which read *Henry Morgan & Sons* was peeling off now, showing the weathered wood beneath.

Inside, a tall man in a black suit was measuring rice out of a big wooden vat with a metal scoop – no Uncle Ben's boil-in-the-bag in Popayan. The man was muttering away to his customer in an Irish accent as thick as Miss Ruthie's. Olivia bent over the counter, fascinated by the array of things on sale: fish hooks, torches, string, small triangular flags, cleats, shoe polish. There was the jangling of a bell as the door opened; the conversation stopped abruptly and a heavily accented voice asked for cigarettes.

'We're all out of smokes. I'm sorry.'

'You do not have cigarettes?' It was a guttural, heavily accented voice, the *r* rolled, the *t* so emphasized it almost incorporated a spit.

Quick as a flash, Olivia flipped up the mirror on her spy ring, wild with excitement at a first chance to use it. The man, who had his back to her, was short and thick-waisted, clad in jeans and a polo shirt. She moved her hand slightly to get a better view and gasped as she saw the tightly curled black hair: it was Alfonso. She looked down quickly and peered into a cabinet, feigning an intent interest in a barometer. Alfonso was expressing some threatening-sounding scepticism about the alleged absence of cigarettes.

'Oh, but to be sure we'll have some Thursday when the boat comes in,' said the tall man. 'Try Paddy at the Bucket of Blood.'

Alfonso cursed then swung out of the shop, slamming the door behind him and making the bell jingle hysterically.

There was silence for a moment, then the storekeeper and customer started talking in lowered voices. At one point she picked out 'in the caves' and 'O'Reilly's goats are dead', but she thought that might be a line from an Irish ditty she had learnt at school and reminded herself sternly not to romanticize the situation.

Eventually she turned and asked for a ball of string, a map of the island, a bag of carrots and a large knife, adding casually, 'Oh, and a packet of cigarettes.'

'To be sure. What type will you be wanting?' said the shopkeeper.

'What have you got?'

'Marlboro, Marlboro Lights and Camels,' he said, casting a merry look out into the street.

Olivia followed his gaze. Alfonso was deep in a conversation, but Olivia couldn't see who he was talking to. He moved slightly to the left and she caught a glimpse of cropped peroxide hair and baggy hip-hop clothes. She gripped the edge of the counter, her cheeks reddening, feeling a lurch of pain. It was Morton C. Morton C was in cahoots with Alfonso. The sneaky bastard. How could she have been such an idiot? She couldn't visit Feramo now. Feramo wouldn't want a girl in his harem who had casually snogged one of his minions. She had managed to ruin the whole objective of her surveillance mission with one pathetic lapse of self-control.

The secret of success lies in how you emerge from failure, she told herself. She had two hours before her dive. That should be enough time to get to the top of Pumpkin Hill and see what was going on. She was determined to get *something* out of this.

Following the map, she headed out of the village along a path with numerous forks and turn-offs. At every point of potential confusion she left a carrot pointing the way back. Ahead of her, Pumpkin Hill rose up from the undergrowth like a grassy hillock on the South Downs, a sandy path zigzagging up it, exposed and unprotected. On the right, the undergrowth continued up a narrow valley on the side of the hill. As she grew closer, she crouched down and trained her spyglass on the summit. She caught movement behind a tree and peered through the glass, trying to focus. A figure stepped out in camouflage gear, carrying what looked like an automatic weapon, and surveyed the area. She whipped out her miniature camera and snapped. *This is outrageous!* she thought. *Pumpkin Hill is common land. People should have the right to roam and certainly should be able to do so without men pointing machine guns at them.* Olivia did not agree with weapons of destruction, mass, individual or otherwise.

Dropping a carrot to mark the spot, she left the main path and headed for the narrow wooded valley to the right of the hill. She marched along furiously, brushing branches aside, mind racing with notions as to what Feramo was cooking up in his fraudulent 'eco-lodge'. She was certain it was acetylene-based and headed for LA. Maybe he was training commercial diver–welders to take jobs in the cooling systems of power stations, where they would release gigantic acetylene and oxygen bubbles and put a waterproof match to them.

The trees and undergrowth reached almost to the summit. In places, the ground beneath was almost sheer. The climb left her covered in small cuts and scratches. As she neared the top, her spirits lifted, until she saw that her way was barred by a ten-foot fence with spikes on top. If she veered to the left, she would emerge onto the hill in plain view of the guard. She went to the right instead and came to a deep ravine. There was a ledge on the other side with a tree growing out of it, above which was a fairly easy climb. Olivia weighed things up. If it wasn't for the fifty-foot drop below, she told herself, she wouldn't think twice about jumping across. For God's sake, she had seen it done a thousand times by blonde-haired princes in tights in Disney cartoons.

Before she had really thought it through, she jumped and found herself on the other side, slithering on some incredibly slimy substance which smelt revolting. She only just stopped herself from falling into the ravine by grabbing the bottom of the tree, which was also covered in the disgusting slime. As she turned her head to look, she knew there was something bad about the slime. Her nostrils weren't having any of it. Calling on the training afforded by innumerable smelly Third World toilets during her hippy travelling years, she expelled her breath sharply and didn't take in any more air until she was out of stink range. Then, lungs bursting, she turned her head heavenwards, took a tentative sniff, then took a deep breath of delicious pure Popayan air and started peeling off her clothes.

She lay on her stomach in her bra and knickers, her slime-coated jeans, T-shirt and shoes hidden at a distance so she couldn't smell them. She was out of sight of the guards, round the side of the hill, and peering through her spyglass at Pierre Feramo's resort. A turquoise coral lagoon was ringed with a perfect white beach dotted with palms and wooden sun-loungers with cream linen cushions. In the centre, a square pool was set into a wooden deck. A large thatched structure behind was obviously the reception area and restaurant. A wooden jetty stretched over the lagoon, leading to a thatched bar. On either side two further walkways stretched over the water, three thatched huts leading off each. Each hut had a shaded wooden veranda with a wooden staircase leading directly into the sea. Six more guest huts were scattered among the palms on the edge of the beach. *Mmmm*, she thought. *Maybe I should visit, after all. I wonder if I could get one of the huts over the water. Or maybe it would be nicer to be back on the edge of the beach? But what about sandflies?*

The clientele dotted on the sun-loungers and bar stools looked like *Vogue* models. A couple paddled kayaks across the lagoon. A man was snorkelling. Two girls were wading to the edge of the reef in scuba gear, aided by an instructor. To the right of the resort was a parking area, where there were trucks and diggers, a compressor and tanks. A rough roadway snaked round a headland. Beyond, a substantial concrete pier led out past the coral to the point where the water turned from turquoise to darkest blue. She put the spy-glass down and took some more snaps. Then she put the spyglass back to her eye, but for some reason couldn't see anything.

'It's the wrong way round.'

She started to scream, but a hand was over her mouth, the other twisting her arm behind her back.

30

She wriggled round to find herself looking at her ex-favourite grey eyes. 'Oh God, it's you,' she grunted through his fingers.

'What are you doing?' Morton C sounded mildly amused, in sharp contrast to the hand over her mouth.

'Gerroff,' she demanded with as much dignity as she could muster under the circumstances.

Morton released his grip and rested one finger against her throat. 'Keep your voice down. What are you doing here?'

'Sightseeing.'

'In your underwear?'

'I am also sunbathing.'

'How did you get up here?'

'I jumped.'

'You *jumped*?'

'Yes, and I nearly fell in. The ledge is covered in slime and so are my clothes.'

'Where are they?'

She pointed. He scrambled down the slope. She could hear small sounds and rustling. She started to turn over.

'I said, don't move.' He reappeared over the edge of the hill. 'Is this yours?' he asked, holding up a carrot.

She glowered at him.

'Don't be sulky now. Come down here onto the ledge, slowly. Sit down on that rock.' As she did, she realized she was shaking. Morton C crossed his arms, pulled his shirt over his head and handed it to her.

'Put this on,' he said.

'Not with your stink on it.'

'Put it on.' He stood back, watching her put on the shirt. 'You're not a journalist at all, are you? What are you doing here?'

'I told you. I came for a walk up Pumpkin Hill. I wanted to see the lovely resort.'

'Are you out of your mind?'

'Why shouldn't I check out the lovely hotel? What if I want to stay there?'

'Well, you ask at the lovely tourist office in the lovely village, and if they have a lovely room, they'll take you round in a lovely boat.'

'Well, maybe I just will.'

'Well, get you.'

'Anyway, what are *you* doing here?'

'Are you always this difficult?'

'You're working for Feramo, aren't you?'

'What you need to do is get yourself back to the village without being spotted, and if you have any sense at all, you'll say nothing about coming up here.'

'What a shitty thing to do, hanging around all the divers, pretending to be one of the lads, then grassing on them to that horrible, sinister acolyte like a telltale tit.'

'I have no idea what you're talking about. Have you got any of that stuff on your skin?'

'My hands, but I wiped it off.'

He took hold of her hands, held them two feet from his

face and sniffed. 'OK,' he said. 'Off you go. I'll see you after the dive.'

No, you won't, you two-faced bastard, she thought furiously, sitting in the mangroves and watching through her spyglass as Morton casually smoked a cigarette with the guard at the top of the hill. *I'm going to have one last dive, then I'm going back to the British Embassy, tell them what I've found out and go home.*

When Olivia turned up for her eleven o'clock dive, a group was huddled around the crackly television in Rik's shack, watching the news.

'*They're small, they're green, they're widely available, but they're about to poison the world: castor beans!*

'*Experts believe these commonly grown beans may be the source of Tuesday's poison attack on the cruise ship* Coyoba, *an attack which has so far claimed the lives of two hundred and sixty-three passengers. The attack, believed to be the work of Osama Bin Laden's al-Qaeda network, has been traced to the poison ricin, placed in the salt pots in the ship's dining room.*'

Up popped a scientist in a white coat. '*Ricin, of course, was the substance used in the so-called "umbrella attack" on London's Waterloo Bridge in 1978. The Bulgarian dissident writer Georgi Markov was killed by a pellet filled with ricin and fired from an umbrella. The problem with ricin – which is highly toxic to humans – is that the source material, the castor bean, is widely grown in many regions of the world, and the poison can be produced in so many forms – powder, as in this latest attack, but also crystal, liquid and even gel.*'

'That's what O'Reilly says they're growing over the hill,' said Rik. 'He thinks that's what poisoned his goats.'

Fuuuuck, thought Olivia, sniffing her skin. 'Just going for a swim!' she said brightly. 'Very hot!'

She hurried to the edge of the jetty, stripped off her shorts and dived in. As she plunged deep into the lagoon, rubbing at her skin, her imagination was in overdrive: *Ricin, face cream, maybe Feramo was planning to poison Devorée's Crème de Phylgie with poison gel? Then Michael Monteroso would get it to catch on with his celebrity clients, and Feramo would slowly poison half of Hollywood before anyone suspected.*

As Olivia swam back, Rik was waiting at the end of the jetty with the gear. 'Fancy taking on a tunnel?' he asked, with a flash of his white teeth.

'Er . . .' Olivia was dead against diving tunnels and wrecks. As far as she could see, as long as you kept breathing and didn't panic underwater, you were fine. If you went where you could get stuck, it wasn't so simple.

'I'd rather do the wall again.'

'Well, I'm going to the tunnels. And Dwayne's not around. So if you want to dive today, you'll have to do tunnels.'

Olivia did *not* like being bossed around in this manner.

'Fine,' she said cheerily. 'I'll just go for another swim instead.'

'OK, OK. We won't go in any caves or tunnels. I might show you the odd crevice, though.'

Olivia tried to ignore the unattractive image this conjured up in her mind's eye.

31

Once underwater, Rik turned into a classic Smug Techie. He was the same breed as the man from the Spy Shop who had come to check out her room at the Standard, or the Smug Computer Expert who tinkers with your computer with a smirk and a vocabulary of unintelligible jargon, as if privy to a whole fabulous world which you cannot hope to understand, giving you a mere tasting menu of its delights suitable for a three-to-five-year-old, in order to bask in your childlike wonder and snigger about you with his techie friends later. Rik was somehow managing to convey a tech-esque smirk, in spite of the fact that he was eighty feet underwater and had a mask on his face and an oxygen pipe in his mouth.

Olivia followed him through a crevice and then, when she realized that the crevice was actually a tunnel and that it was getting too narrow to turn, panicked so much that she dropped the regulator out of her mouth. For a few seconds she broke the golden rule and started floundering. What if Rik was one of Feramo's men too and was going to kill her or lead her to Alfonso, who would perform female circumcision on her? What if she got trapped by an octopus? What if a giant squid wrapped its suckered tentacles around her and . . . *Calm, calm, breathe, breathe.* She collected herself, letting her air out slowly, and remembered what to do: lean to the right, run your hand down your thigh, and the regulator will be hanging just there – as indeed it was.

The tunnel was narrowing alarmingly. She started having fantasies about reporting Rik to the diving authorities and having him struck off. Could diving instructors be struck off? She wasn't breathing properly. A combination of fear and indignation was messing everything up. She had to force herself to do what she had been taught: breathe very very slowly and deeply, counter-intuitively, as if, instead of being almost trapped in an underwater tunnel, she was lying down at the end of a yoga class imagining a ball of orange light sliding down her body. Soon she was hearing her own heavy breathing, like a sound effect in a horror movie.

After what seemed an unconscionable amount of time, she emerged into blue water. They were in an enormous cavern. There must have been a pretty large hole somewhere above because the water was clear and illuminated by shafts of sunlight. She looked up, trying to see the surface, but all she could see was diffuse light. Shoals of brightly coloured fish darted this way and that. It was like being on some unbelievable acid trip. She swam to and fro, forgetting about time and reality, until she saw Rik in front of her tapping his hand on the air dial, communicating such patronizing sarcasm with each tap that she felt that the scuba world's gain had been the mime world's loss.

They had fifteen minutes left. She couldn't see the entrance back into the tunnel. Rik swam ahead of her, pointed to the gap and gestured to her to lead the way. It took longer than she remembered to get back. Something seemed wrong. She didn't recognize the route. The fear resurfaced: Rik was a terrorist, Rik had been talking to Morton, Rik was trying to get rid of her because she knew too much. As she turned a corner, she saw what was ahead and screamed into her regulator, screaming and screaming so that it fell from her mouth again.

32

Olivia was face to face with a diver whose entire head was covered in black rubber apart from holes for the eyes and an opening which flapped and sucked around his regulator like a fish's mouth. For a second, in the semi-darkness of the tunnel, they stared at each other, mesmerized, like a cat and a goldfish. Then the diver took his regulator from his mouth and held it to hers, blowing out bubbles, holding her gaze until her breathing steadied, then took it back and took a breath himself. He kept his eyes trained steadily on hers as she breathed out into the water, then put his regulator back in her mouth to let her take in more air.

The instinct to flail and gasp was overwhelming. They were eighty feet underwater, under rock. She could feel Rik behind her, clawing and shaking frantically at her leg, pushing her. Did he think she'd simply stopped to look at the view? She kicked her fins to signal him to stop as the diver gently lifted the regulator to her mouth again.

Diving is a constant fight against panic. The phrase repeated itself in her head. She had stabilized, she was breathing from the regulator, but another wave of terror was starting to overwhelm her. She was sandwiched between Rik and the hooded man in the narrowest part of the tunnel. Even if she and Rik pushed their way back to the cavern, they might not

*They stared at each other, mesmerized, like a cat and
a goldfish.*

make it in time. And if they did, they might not find air at the top; they might just die there.

The hooded man held up his finger for her attention. She kept her eyes on his, breathing his air, as he reached out along her body. Then he withdrew his hand and held up her regulator. Still holding her gaze like an instructor doing a demonstration, he breathed from it, then held it out to her. She thought there was something familiar about his eyes, but she couldn't make out the colour. Who was he? At least he wasn't trying to kill her, or if he was, he was prone to self-defeating behaviours. He reached forward again, found her gauge, looked at it, and showed it to her. At this depth she had seven minutes of air left. Rik was shaking her leg frantically. She tried to turn her head. When she turned forward again, the diver was moving away from her, backwards, at a steady speed, as if he was being pulled. She started to kick and moved ahead. She felt a massive stinging burn on her shoulder. Fire coral. She had an overwhelming urge to kick Rik in the face with her fin. If she had planned to go into a tunnel she'd have put on a wetsuit.

The tunnel widened. The light ahead had a different quality. She could no longer see the diver in front of her. She moved faster and faster, bursting out into the open sea, looking up to see the light and bubbles of the surface misleadingly close. Resisting the urge to race her way up there, she turned to check for Rik, who was emerging from the tunnel, making his thumb and index finger into a circle.

She wished there was a signal for, 'No fucking thanks to you, you irresponsible bastard.'

Rik raised a thumb signalling the ascent, then jerked his head in a sudden, panicky movement. She looked up to see the shadowy form of a shark.

The shark was maybe twenty feet above them. Olivia knew

that calm divers have nothing to fear from a shark. This one was moving fast and deliberately, as if towards prey. There was a flurry of movement and churning water, and then a red cloud started slowly to spread. She signalled to Rik to move away. His eyes were wide, terrified. She followed his gaze to see something falling down towards them, like a grotesque fish with a huge dark gaping mouth, trailing fronds which looked like seaweed. The object turned slowly to reveal a human face, the mouth open in a scream, bright red blood belching from the neck, long hair trailing behind. It was Dwayne's head.

33

Rik swam past her, thrashing dangerously, brandishing his knife and heading towards the shark. She reached out and grabbed his leg, pulling him back towards her. She held up the gauge, signalled with her fist across her throat to say out of air and pointed upwards. He looked down towards the head, still falling into the abyss, and then turned to follow her. She swam smoothly away from the scene, checking her compass for the direction of the shore, checking that Rik was still following, feeling the change in the regulator which told her that the air was almost gone, fighting the panic again. There were dark shadows above them. More predators were moving towards the bloodbath. She started a controlled, out-of-air ascent, blowing her air out very, very slowly, saying 'Ahhh' out loud. She felt the air in her buoyancy jacket expand and tighten against her chest and found the air-release hose, taking a lungful of air from it, discharging it slowly into the water, looking up, seeing the magical light and bubbles and blue of the surface beckoning, closer than it seemed, and forced herself to take her time: *Breathe, don't panic, slow your ascent to the speed of the slowest bubble.*

As they broke the surface, gasping for air and retching, they were still far from the shore – the dive shack was a good three hundred yards away.

'What did you do to him?' yelled Rik.

'What?' she said, pushing her mask up and dropping her weight belt. 'What are you talking about?'

She gave the signal for emergency towards the shore and blew her whistle. The usual bunch of guys were sitting around at the shack. 'Help!' she shouted. 'Sharks!'

'What did you do to him?' said Rik, through a sob. 'What did you do?'

'What are you talking about?' she said furiously. 'Are you mad? It wasn't Dwayne in that tunnel. It was someone in a rubber mask. He gave me his air and then just started zooming backwards.'

'For fuck's sake. That's impossible. Hey!' Rik started shouting and gesticulating towards the shack. 'Hey, get over here!'

She looked backwards and saw a fin.

'Rik, shut up and keep still.'

Keeping her eyes on the fin, she blew the whistle and raised her hand again. Mercifully, a sense of urgency had finally communicated itself to the dive-shack guys. Someone had started up the boat's engine, figures were jumping aboard and seconds later the boat was powering towards them. The fin disappeared under the water. She drew her legs up close, mushroom floating, thinking, *Hurry, please hurry*, waiting for a sudden muscular movement, the feel of her flesh being ripped apart. The boat seemed to take an interminable amount of time to reach them. *What were they doing? Fucking stone-heads.*

'Leave the tanks – get in,' yelled Rik, suddenly the capable dive instructor again, as the boat drew up. Olivia ditched her tank and her fins, reached out to the arms stretching over the side of the boat and, scrambling with her feet, got herself over and lay in the bottom, gasping for breath.

*

Back on the jetty, Olivia sat on the bench, a towel around her shoulders, her arms round her knees. The whole horrible ritual of death and its aftermath was unfolding around her. Out at sea, a shark cage containing Rik and a buddy was descending from a boat in a plainly hopeless quest to retrieve the remains of Dwayne. Popayan's only medical professional, an elderly Irish midwife, was standing helplessly on the jetty, holding her bag. At the sound of sirens, Olivia looked up to see a boat with flashing lights approaching: the medical boat from Roatán, the big island.

'You should be lying down, to be sure,' said the nurse, lighting a cigarette. 'We should be taking you off to Miss Ruthie's.'

'She must be interviewed first by the police,' said Popayan's one policeman grandly.

Olivia was dimly aware of the talk and theories gathering force around her: Dwayne had still been out of it on coke from the previous night; he'd gone down without a buddy; he'd been raving about teaching Feramo's lot a lesson. He could have made a mistake, cut himself and attracted the shark, or he could have taken on one of Feramo's people and got himself injured. Their voices lowered as they started talking about the figure in the tunnel. One of the boys touched her nervously on her shoulder, right on the fire-coral burn. She let out a slight moan.

'Rachel,' the boy whispered, 'sorry to ask, but are you sure it wasn't Dwayne in the tunnel? Maybe it was the shark pulling him back.'

She shook her head. 'I don't know. The guy was wearing a full body suit and head mask. I don't think it was Dwayne. I think if it had been, he would have let me know somehow. Sharks don't swim down tunnels, do they? And there was no hood on the h—' her voice broke, '. . . the head.'

*

Miss Ruthie was baking when she returned. Trays of buns and cakes were laid out on the stove and the yellow-painted dresser, and the smell was of cinnamon and spices. Tears started to prick Olivia's eyelids. Childhood images of comfort washed over her: Big-Ears's cottage, the Woodentops' house, her mother baking when she got back from school.

'Oh bejaysus, sit yourself down.'

Miss Ruthie hurried over to a drawer and fetched a neatly ironed handkerchief with a flower and the initial R embroidered in the corner.

'Holy Mary, Mother of God,' she said, taking a sticky-looking loaf out of a tin. 'There we go. Now let's make us both a nice cup of tea.' She cut Olivia a large slice of the loaf, as if the only response to a disembodied-head sighting was a sticky cake and a cup of tea. Which, Olivia thought, taking a bite of the most delicious, moist banana loaf, was quite possibly true.

'Is there a flight out today?' she said quietly to Miss Ruthie.

'To be sure. It goes in the afternoon most days.'

'How do I book it?'

'Just leave your bag out on the step, like, and Pedro will knock on the door when he passes with the red truck.'

'How will he know to stop? How will he know I want to get the plane? What if it's full?'

Once again, Miss Ruthie just looked at her as though she was stupid.

The knock came just after three. The red truck was empty. Olivia watched as her beloved tan and olive carry-on was loaded into the back, then climbed up in front, gripping her hat pin in the palm of her hand, running her thumb over the back of the spy ring, her pepper-spray pen tucked into the pocket of her shorts. The day was perfect: blue sky, butterflies and hummingbirds hovering above the wild flowers. The sweetness was unearthly, unsettling. She saw the Robinson Crusoe sign and the little bridge leading to the airstrip and started gathering her things together, but the truck turned off to the right.

'This isn't the airport,' she said nervously, staying firmly in her seat as they ground to a halt on a patch of scrub by the sea.

'*Que?*' he said, opening the door. '*No hablo inglés.*'

'*No es el aeropuerto. Quiero tomar el avión para La Ceiba.*'

'Yes, yes,' he said in Spanish, lifting the bags to the ground. 'The flight leaves from Roatán on Tuesdays. You have to wait for the boat.' He nodded towards the empty horizon. The engine was still running. He waited impatiently for her to step out.

'But there's no boat.'

'It will be here in five minutes.'

Olivia got out suspiciously. 'Wait just a few minutes,' he said and started to climb back into the cab.

'But where are you going?'

'To the village. It's OK. The boat will be here in a few minutes.'

He put the truck into gear. She watched forlornly as it rattled off, suddenly overcome with exhaustion, too weary to do anything. The sound of the engine gradually faded into silence. It was very hot. There was no sign of any boat. She dragged her case over to a casuarina and sat in the shade, swatting away flies. After twenty minutes she heard a faint whining sound. She jumped to her feet, joyfully scanning the horizon with the spyglass. It was a boat, heading towards her fast. She felt wild with relief, desperate to get away. As the boat drew closer, she saw that it was a flashy-looking white speedboat. She hadn't seen anything like it in Popayan, but then Roatán was much more of an international tourist hub. Maybe Roatán airport had its own private launch.

The boatman waved, cutting the engine and bringing the boat to the jetty in a perfect arc. It was beautiful, big, with white-leather seats and polished wooden doors leading to a cabin below deck. '*Para el aeropuerto Roatán?*' she said nervously.

'*Si, señorita, suba abordo,*' the boatman said, tying the boat up, swinging her bag aboard and holding out his hand to help her up. He pulled the rope loose, put the engine on full throttle and pulled out towards the open sea.

Olivia sat uneasily on the edge of a white-leather seat, glancing back as the coastline of Popayan faded into insignificance, then looking anxiously at the empty horizon ahead. The door to the cabin opened and she saw a dark head, slightly balding, covered in short, tightly curled black hair, emerging from the hold. He looked up and an oily, ingratiating smile spread across his features.

34

Olivia sat at the front of the boat in the white-leather passenger seat, fighting back surges of seasickness, her head bouncing up and down like a rag doll's as every few seconds she was slapped in the face by a wave. Meanwhile, Alfonso, also soaking wet, stood at the wheel, dressed in a ridiculous outfit of white shirt, white shorts, white three-quarter-length socks and a captain's hat. He was steering the boat inexpertly and much too fast into the prevailing wind so that it reared up and smacked into every wave head-on. He was gesticulating, oblivious, at the shoreline ahead and, completely inaudible above the roar of the engine, shouting things at her.

How, she thought grimly, *could I be such a bloody idiot? Miss Ruthie is working for Alfonso. Miss Ruthie probably poisoned the banana cake and cut Dwayne's head off. She's like the evil red-raincoated dwarf in* Don't Look Now. *She's going to reappear from the cabin in a Little Red Riding Hood outfit and cut my throat. What can I do?* The answer, she realized, was nothing. She still had the hat pin in her hand. The pepper-spray pen was in her pocket, but her chances of overpowering two burly men with a pen and a hat pin were, realistically, not very high.

'Where are we going?' she yelled. 'I want to go to the airport.'

'It is a surprise,' Alfonso said gaily. 'It is a surprise from Meester Feramo.'

'Stop, stop!' she said. 'Slow down!'

He ignored her, letting out a gurgling laugh and smacking the boat into another wave.

'I'm going to be sick!' she yelled, leaning towards the spotless white outfit and feigning a quasi-vomit. He jumped back in alarm and immediately cut the engine.

'Over the side,' he said, waving his hand at her. 'Over there. Pedro. *Agua.* Quick.'

She did a convincing dry heave over the side – not much acting required – and leaned back, hand to her head. 'Where are we going?' she said weakly.

'To Meester Feramo's hotel. It is a surprise.'

'Why didn't someone ask me? This is a kidnapping.'

Alfonso started the boat up again, looking at her with his oily smile. 'It is a beautiful surprise!'

She willed the vomit to rise again. *Next time I'll do it for real*, she said to herself. *Right onto his little shorts.*

As they rounded the headland, an idyllic holiday scene spread before them: white sand and turquoise sea, bathers frolicking and laughing in the shallows. Olivia wanted to rush ashore and slap everyone, yelling, 'It's evil, evil! This is all built on killing and death!'

The boatman approached the wheel, offering to take over, but Alfonso brushed him away impatiently, roaring towards the jetty as if in an advert for after-dinner mints, shower gel or tooth whitener. In the nick of time he realized he had misjudged it. He veered off to the left, scattering snorkellers and narrowly missing a jet ski, made a messy circle, churning up the sea, then cut the engine just a little bit too late so that he crashed into the jetty anyway, letting out a curse.

'Masterfully done,' said Olivia.

'Thank you.' He smirked, oblivious. 'Welcome to La Isla Bonita.'

Olivia sighed heavily.

Once she was on the stable surface of the jetty, feeling the sun drying her drenched clothes and the seasickness subsiding, things didn't seem quite so bad. A charming young man in white knee-length shorts took her bag and offered to show her to her room. Charming young bellboys seemed to be becoming a leitmotif of the trip. She thought back to the one at the Standard with the unnaturally bright blue eyes, large muscles, sideburns and goatee beard, whose face looked like one on a child's magnetic sketch pad, and made a mental note to check the room for bugs. And then suddenly it came to her: Morton with his bleached, cropped hair and grey, clever eyes; the hooded diver with the calm, steady eyes behind the mask; the Standard bellboy with the packed body, the bright blue eyes which didn't fit with his facial hair. There was such a thing as coloured contact lenses. They were the same person.

Trying to keep her composure whilst eyeing the current bellboy suspiciously, she followed him along a series of wooden walkways with ropes as handrails. The resort was fabulously eco, a barefoot paradise – pathways paved only with bark fragments, solar panels, signs carved in wood labelling the plants. She wondered whether there were neatly labelled castor-bean plants, and made a mental note to go for a nature walk in the morning and check for dead goats.

Her room – or, rather, ocean-view junior suite – was set back from the beach, standing on stilts on the edge of the jungle. She was disappointed not to be in one of the huts out over the sea, but even Olivia realized that in these circumstances it might not be appropriate to ask about a room change. The building was constructed entirely of wood and thatch, the linens and mosquito nets in soft whites and beiges. There were frangipani blossoms on her pillows. The walls were slatted to allow the sea breezes to join forces with the ceiling fan. The bathroom had modern chrome fittings, a deep porcelain bath with jacuzzi jets and a separate shower. It was all very stylish. The toilet paper, however, was not folded down to a neat little point. In fact, there was no fold in it whatsoever. It was simply left hanging against the roll.

'Mr Feramo has asked you to join him for dinner at seven,' said the boy with a sly smile.

He's going to poison me, she thought. *Feramo's going to poison me with ricin in the salt. Or he's going to serve me O'Reilly's poisoned goat. Or release an oxygen-acetylene bubble and set fire to me.*

'How lovely. Where?' she said smoothly.

'In his suite,' said the boy with a wink. She tried not to shudder. She hated people who winked.

'Thank you,' she said weakly. She wasn't sure if tipping was in order, but, deciding to err on the side of generosity, she handed him a five-dollar bill.

'Oh no, no,' he said with a smile. 'We don't believe in money here.'

Yeah, right.

It was excellent to have a proper shower: an up-to-the-minute rainwater-style power-shower with side jets and a chrome head the size of a dinner plate. She took her time, washing her hair in the high-end products, soaping herself, rinsing and moisturizing, then wrapped herself in the exquisite cream-coloured Frette robe and padded across the wooden floor to the balcony, where she sprayed mosquito repellent onto her wrists and ankles, hoping it would work for diver-murdering Islamic kidnappers as well.

It was dark now and the jungle was loud with the sounds of frogs and cicadas. Flaming torches lit the pathways down to the sea, the swimming pool glowed turquoise through the palms and the air was sweet with jasmine and frangipani. Enticing cooking smells drifted up from the restaurant area, along with the murmur of contented voices. It was the seductive face of evil, she told herself, marching determinedly back into the room to find the bug detector slash calculator she'd bought from the Spy Shop on Sunset Boulevard.

She took it out of her case with some excitement, then stared at it, frowning. She couldn't remember what you were supposed to do. She had decided to throw away the packaging of all her spy equipment in order to protect the various disguises, overlooking the obvious flaw in the plan, which was that she would no longer have the instructions. She vaguely remembered that you were supposed to press in a pre-agreed code. She always used 3637, which was the ages of her parents when they were killed. She punched it in: nothing. Maybe you were supposed to turn it on first? She tried pressing ON and then entered 3637, then waved it around the room: nothing. Either there was no bug, or the bloody thing was broken.

She snapped. One little thing too many had been added to the cumulative stresses of the day, and she found herself hurling the little calculator passionately across the room as if it was responsible for everything: Dwayne's head, Morton C, Miss Ruthie, the subaquatic hooded rapist, the strange slime on the hill, the kidnapping, everything. She shut herself in the wardrobe with her back to the door and curled up into a ball.

Suddenly, she heard a tiny beeping noise. Raising her head, she opened the closet door and crawled across towards the calculator. It was working. The little screen had lit up. She was overcome with a rush of affection for the tiny gadget. It wasn't the bug detector slash calculator's fault. It was doing its best. She dialled in the code again. It started to vibrate very slightly. Excited, she got to her feet and started to walk around the room, holding the calculator out as if it were a metal detector. She couldn't remember how you knew when it found the bug. It beeped again, as if it was trying to help. That was it! It would beep if it detected something and start to vibrate increasingly when it got closer to the bug. She tried waving it at the power outlets: nothing. There were no telephone jacks. She tried the lamps: nothing. Then she felt the vibration change. It led her to a wooden coffee table with a stone flower pot embedded in the centre, from which emerged a stubby cactus plant. The calculator started practically jumping out of her hand, completely overexcited with itself. She tried to look under the table, but it was a heavy, box-like thing. Should she disembowel the cactus with her knife? It would certainly be satisfying. She hated cacti. Spiky plants were bad feng shui. But then it was wrong to destroy life. What was it going to overhear anyway? Who was she going to talk to? She stared at the stubby little plant. Maybe it was a camera as well? She opened her case, took out a thin black sweater, pretended to put it on, then changed her mind and chucked it casually at the table, covering the cactus.

It was twenty minutes to seven. She decided she might as well try to look her best. A girl in a scrape had to use whatever resources were at her disposal. She dried her hair and then swung it around in the mirror in an imitation of the annoying Suraya, murmuring provocatively, 'Leaves my hair shinier and more manageable!' The combination of sea water, sun and the remains of the red dye had turned it a lovely streaky blonde. Her skin had caught some sun-glow too, in spite of the lashings of sunblock. She didn't need much make-up, just a bit of concealer to tone down the red nose. She put on a flimsy black dress, sandals and jewellery and surveyed herself in the mirror. The whole effect was quite good, she decided, at least for the end of a shit day like this one.

'OK, Olivia, you're on,' she said sternly, then shot her hand over her mouth, worrying that the cactus had picked it up. Tonight she had to put on a performance. She had to present Feramo with the woman he wanted her to be. She had to pretend to herself that she had kissed no blond, grey-eyed, double-crossing youths, seen no disembodied heads, understood nothing about the links between al-Qaeda bombs and acetylene, and had never heard the word 'ricin'. Could she pull it off? It was going to be like 'Don't mention the war' when dining with a German. 'Would you pass the ricin please?' 'It's very rice in the Bay Islands isn't it?'

She started giggling. Oh dear, was it possible she was hysterical? What was she *doing*? She was about to have dinner with a *poisoner*. Her mind raced wildly, trying to summon anti-poisoning strategies gleaned from movies: switching glasses, eating only from the same pot as the host. But what if the dishes arrived already on the plates? She stood still for a moment then lay down on the floor, repeating the mantra, 'My intuitions are my guide; I still my hysteria and overactive imagination.' She was just starting to calm down when there was a thunderous knock at the door. *Oh no, oh no. They're taking me away to be stoned*, she thought, scrambling to her feet, hopping into her strappy sandals and reaching the door just as the maniacal knock came again.

A small plump lady in a white apron was standing outside. 'You want turndown?' she said with a motherly smile.

As the lady bustled into the room, the bellboy appeared in the doorway behind her.

'Mr Feramo is ready to receive you,' he said.

35

Pierre Feramo was reclining on a low sofa, his hands resting on his lap with an air of controlled power. He was wearing loose clothes in navy linen. His beautiful, liquid eyes stared at her impassively beneath the finely arched brows.

'Thank you,' he said, dismissing the boy with a wave of his hand.

Olivia heard the door close, stiffening as the key turned in the lock.

Feramo's suite was sumptuous, exotic, lit entirely by candle-light. There were oriental rugs on the floors, ornate tapestries on the wall and a smell of burning incense which instantly took her back to her time in the Sudan. Feramo continued to stare at her scarily. Instinct told her to take control of the mood.

'Hello!' she said brightly. 'It's nice to see you again.'

In the flickering light, Feramo looked like Omar Sharif in *Lawrence of Arabia* when his blood was up.

'This is a beautiful suite,' she said, attempting to look around appreciatively, 'though in our country it is polite to get up when a guest enters, especially when you've had her kidnapped.'

She saw the slightest flicker of confusion pass over his features, quickly replaced by a stony glare. *Oh, sod him, sulky bastard*, she thought. On the table in front of him was a bottle of Cristal chilling in a silver ice bucket, together with two flutes and a tray of canapés. It was, she noted with interest, the same table as the one in her room, right down to the cactus embedded in the middle.

'This looks nice,' she said, sitting down and flashing him a smile as she glanced at the champagne glasses. 'Shall I be mother?' Feramo's face softened for a second. She was, she realized, behaving like a northern housewife at the vicar's tea party, but it seemed to be doing the trick. Then his expression changed and he fixed her with a fierce stare, like an annoyed bird of prey. *OK*, she thought, *two can play at that game*. She settled herself down and stared back. Unfortunately, however, something about the impromptu staring competition made her want to laugh. She could feel the giggles bubbling up from her stomach, and suddenly they burst out through her nose, so she had to put her hand over her mouth, shaking helplessly.

'Enough!' he roared, leaping to his feet, which just made her laugh even more. Oh God, she had really done it now. She had to stop. She breathed in deeply, looked up then collapsed in giggles again. Once something struck you as funny like that, when you really, really weren't supposed to laugh, you were doomed. It was like giggling in church or school assembly. Even the thought of him sweeping out a sword and lopping off her head struck her as hilarious as she pictured her head bouncing across the floor, still giggling, Feramo bellowing at it.

'Sorry, sorry,' she said, pulling herself together, both sets of fingers over her mouth and nose. 'OK, OK.'

'You appear to be enjoying life.'

'Well, so would you be if you'd narrowly escaped death three times in one day.'

'I apologize for Alfonso's behaviour with the boat.'

'He nearly killed a bunch of snorkellers and someone on a jet ski.'

Feramo's mouth twisted oddly. 'It was the fault of that accursed boat. Western technology, for all its promise, is designed to make a fool of the Arab.'

'Oh, don't be so paranoid, Pierre,' she said lightly. 'I really don't think that's the first priority in modern speedboat design. How are you, anyway? It's nice to see you.'

He looked at her uncertainly. 'Come, we must drink a toast!' he said, reaching to open the champagne. She watched him, fingering the hat pin hidden in the fabric of her dress, trying to assess what was going on. This was her big chance to get him drunk and find out what he was up to. She glanced around the room: there was a laptop closed on the desk.

Feramo seemed really quite desperate to get into the Cristal, but was having trouble with the cork. Clearly he hadn't had much practice either at opening champagne bottles or fucking things up. Olivia found herself frozen into an encouraging smile as if waiting for a man with a bad stammer to get the next word out. Suddenly the cork shot across the room and the Cristal spurted out, frothing all over his hand, the table, napkins, cactus and canapés. A strange curse burst from his lips as he started grabbing at things and knocking them over.

'Pierre, Pierre, Pierre,' she said, starting to dab at the puddle of Cristal with a napkin. 'Calm down. Everything's fine. I'll just take these . . .' she said, picking up the flutes and heading for the wet bar, 'and . . . rinse them, so that they're pristine. Ooh, what beautiful glasses. Are they from Prague?' She carried on babbling as she washed them in hot water, then gave them a good rinse and swilled out the bottoms.

'You are right,' he said. 'They are fine Bohemian crystal. Evidently, you are a connoisseur of beauty. As am I.' At this

Olivia almost started giggling again. Clearly the Arab mind could be as corny as the shopping channel.

She replaced the glasses on the coffee table, ensuring that what had been Feramo's glass was now hers. She watched him carefully for the gestures of a thwarted poisoner, but instead she saw only the eagerness of an alcoholic on the verge of his first drink of the evening.

'Let us drink a toast,' he said, handing her her glass. 'To our rendezvous.' He glanced at her seriously for a moment, then downed his champagne like a Cossack in a vodka-drinking competition.

Does he know you're not supposed to drink champagne like that? she wondered. It reminded her of Kate's mother, a lifelong teetotaller who, if she poured someone a G&T, would fill a tumbler almost to the top with neat gin with barely a nod in the direction of the tonic bottle.

'Come, let us eat. We have much to discuss.'

As he rose to lead the way out to the terrace, she emptied her glass into the cactus. Feramo pulled back her chair for her, like waiters do. She sat down, expecting him to push it forward, like waiters do, only somehow he got it wrong, and she sat down on nothing, plunging to the floor. She thought she was going to start laughing again until she looked up and saw the intensity of his humiliation and rage.

'It's all right, Pierre. It's all right.'

'But what do you mean?' As he towered over her, she imagined him commanding a mujahedin battalion in the Afghan mountains, pacing above prisoners, keeping his anger controlled, then suddenly blasting them with a machine gun.

'I mean it's funny,' she said firmly, starting to get to her feet, noting to her relief that he hurried to help her. 'The more a situation is geared up to be perfect, the funnier it is when something goes wrong. Things aren't *supposed* to be perfect.'

'So that is good?' he said, the trace of a small-boy smile appearing.

'Yes,' she said, 'it's good. Right, I shall sit down on the chair, not under it, and we'll start again.'

'I do apologize. I am mortified – first the champagne and then . . .'

'Shh,' she soothed. 'Sit down. You couldn't have found a better way to make me feel comfortable.'

'Really?'

'Really,' she said, thinking: *Now I don't have to worry about being poisoned every time I take a sip.* 'I was intimidated when I walked in. Now we know we're both just human beings and we don't have to pretend to be all fancy and perfect and we can just have a good time.'

He grasped her hand, kissing it passionately. It was as if something about her acted as a trigger for him. His mood swings made no sense. He was dangerous, clearly. But she didn't have a lot of options here. Maybe if she just brazened it out and followed her nose she could keep control of the situation. Especially if she was sober and Feramo was drunk.

'You are the most wonderful woman,' he said, looking at her almost wretchedly.

'Why?' she asked. 'Because I'm good at washing glasses?'

'Because you are kind.'

She felt terrible.

He downed another glass of champagne, leaned back and gave a vicious tug to a thick, dark-red bell-pull. Immediately, the key turned in the lock and three waiters appeared carrying steaming casseroles.

'Leave it, leave it,' Feramo barked as they twittered around, obviously terrified. 'I shall serve it myself.'

The waiters set down the dishes and hurried out, falling over each other in their haste.

'I hope,' said Feramo, unfolding his napkin, 'that you will enjoy our dinner. It is a great delicacy in our land.'

She gulped. 'What is it?' she said.

'It is curried goat.'

36

'You will take some more wine?' said Feramo. 'I have an 'eighty-two St-Estèphe which I think will go well with the goat.'

'Perfect.' There was a large potted fig tree conveniently placed beside her. As he turned to select a bottle, she quickly shoved a spoonful of goat from her plate back into the serving dish and emptied her glass into the plant pot.

'. . . and a 'ninety-five Puligny-Montrachet for dessert.'

'My favourite,' she murmured smoothly.

'As I was saying,' he said, pouring the wine before he had even sat down, 'it is the separation of the physical and the spiritual which is the source of the problem in the West.'

'Hmm,' said Olivia. 'But the thing is, if you have a religious government taking its cues from a deity rather than the democratic process, what's to stop any crackpot who takes power from saying it's the will of God that he spend the entire country's food money on eighteen palaces for himself?'

'Saddam Hussein's Ba'ath party was not an example of a religious government.'

'I wasn't saying it was. I was just plucking an example out of the air. I'm just saying who decides what the will of God is?'

'It is written in the Koran.'

'But the scriptures are open to interpretation. You know,

one man's "Thou shalt not kill" is another man's eye for an eye. You can't really think it's OK to kill in the name of religion.'

'You are pedantic. The truth does not require sophistry. It is as clear as the rising sun above the desert plain. The failure of Western culture is evident at every moment – in its cities, in its media, in its messages to the world: the arrogance, the stupidity, the violence, the fear, the mindless pursuit of empty materialism, the worship of celebrity. Take the people you and I have witnessed in Los Angeles – lascivious, empty, vain, swarming to feed off promises of wealth and fame like the locust on the sorghum plant.'

'You seem to be enjoying their company.'

'I despise them.'

'Then why do you employ them?'

'Why do I employ them? Ah, Olivia, you are not of their type and so you would not understand.'

'Try me. Why would you want to surround yourself with waitresses and security guards and divers and surfers who all want to be actors if you despise them?'

He leaned forward and ran a finger very slowly down one side of her neck. Her hand tightened on the hat pin.

'You are not of their type. You are not the locust, but the falcon.' He rose to his feet, moving to stand behind her. He started to stroke her hair, which made goose bumps rise on the back of her neck. 'You are not of their type, and therefore you must be captured and tamed until you will want only to return to one master. You are not of their type,' he whispered into her neck, 'and therefore you are not lascivious.'

Suddenly he wrapped her hair around his fist and jerked back her head. 'Are you? Are you open to the advances of another man, the kisses, hidden, in the darkness?'

'Ow, get off,' she said, pulling her head away from him.

'What is the matter with the men on this island? You're all as mad as buckets. We're in the middle of dinner. Will you please stop being so weird, sit down and tell me what you're talking about?'

He paused, his hand still on her hair.

'Oh come on, Pierre, we're not in a school playground. You don't need to pull my hair to ask me a question. Now come along, sit back on your chair and let's have our dessert.'

There was another moment's hesitation. He was prowling around the table like a panther.

'Why did you not come to me as you promised, my little falcon, my *saqr*?'

'Because I'm not a little falcon, I'm a professional journalist. I'm writing about diving off the beaten track. I can't cover the whole of the Bay Islands by heading straight for the most luxurious hotel.'

'Is it also necessary to check out the local dive instructors?'

'Of course.'

'Actually,' he said icily, 'I think you are perfectly aware of whom I speak, Olivia. I am speaking of Morton.'

'Pierre, you do realize that what Western boys do at parties, especially when they've had a lot of rum and free cocaine, is try to kiss girls. It isn't a stoning offence in our countries. And at least I fought him off,' she said, risking a white lie. 'How many girls have you tried to kiss since I last saw you?'

Suddenly he smiled, like a small boy who has got his toys back after a tantrum. 'You are right, Olivia. Of course. Other men will admire your beauty, but you will return to your master.'

God, he was nuts. 'Listen, Pierre. First, I'm a modern girl and I don't have masters.' She was thinking very fast, working out how to get the conversation back on track. 'Second, if two people are going to be together they have to have shared values, and I believe very firmly that killing is wrong. So, if you don't, we might as well sort it out now.'

'You disappoint me. Like all Westerners you are arrogant enough to entertain only your own naïve and blinkered view. Consider the needs of the Bedouin in the harsh and unforgiving desert lands. The survival of the tribe must take precedence over the life of an individual.'

'Would you support a terrorist attack? I need to know.'

He poured himself another glass of wine. 'Who in the world would prefer war to peace? But there are times when war becomes a necessity. And in the modern world the rules of engagement have changed.'

'Would you . . .' she began, but clearly he had had enough of this line of conversation.

'Olivia!' he said jovially. 'You have hardly eaten at all! You did not like it?'

'I still feel a little ill from the boat ride.'

'But you must eat. You must. It is a great offence.'

'Actually, I would love a little more wine. Shall we open the Puligny-Montrachet?'

That did the trick. Feramo continued to drink and Olivia continued to tip her wine into the potted fig. He remained lucid, his movements impressively co-ordinated, but his passion and eloquence grew. And always she felt as though he was teetering on the precipice of some violent mood swing. It was all so bafflingly different from his controlled, dignified, public persona. She wondered if she was witnessing the effects of some psychological bruise, some wounded underbelly like her own: an early trauma, the death of a parent, perhaps?

A patchy map of his history emerged. He had studied in France. He made references which suggested the Sorbonne, but he was not specific. He was more expansive about his studies at Grasse on the Côte d'Azur where he had trained as a 'nose' in the perfume industry. There had been a long period in Cairo. There was a father whom he seemed both to despise and fear. No further mention of a mother. She found it hard to draw him out on his work as a producer in French cinema. It was like trying to pin down one of the waiter slash producers in the Standard bar about his latest production. There was, clearly, a large amount of money sloshing around in his family and his life, and there had been major globetrotting: Paris, St-Tropez, Monte Carlo, Anguilla, Gstaad.

'Have you ever been to India?' she said. 'I'd love to go to the Himalayas, Tibet, Bhutan –' *don't hesitate* – 'Afghanistan. Those places seem so untouched and mysterious. Have you ever been up there?'

'Actually, Afghanistan, yes, of course. And it is wild and beautiful and raw and fierce. I should take you there, and we will ride, and you will see the life of a nomad, the life of my childhood and my ancestors.'

'What were you doing there?'

'As a young man I liked to travel, just as you did, Olivia.'

'I'm sure you weren't travelling just as I did.' She laughed, thinking: *Come on, come on: dish. Were you training in the camps? Were you training for the* OceansApart, *for something else? Now? Soon? Are you trying to make me a part of it?*

'Oh, but I was. We lived as poor men in tents. My homeland is the land of the nomad.'

'The Sudan?'

'Arabia. The land of the Bedouin: the gracious, the hospitable, the simple and the spiritual.' He took another large gulp of Montrachet. 'The Western man with his lust for progress sees nothing but the future, destroying the world in his blind pursuit of novelty and wealth. My people see that the truth lies in the wisdom of the past, and that wealth lies in the strength of the tribe.' He poured more wine, leaning forward and grasping her hand. 'And that is why I must take you there. And, of course, it will be perfect for your diving article.'

'Oh, I couldn't,' she said. 'No. I would have to get the magazine to send me.'

'But it is the finest diving in the world. There are cliffs and drop-offs plunging to seven hundred metres, coral pinnacle formations rising like ancient towers from the ocean floor, caves and tunnels. The visibility is unsurpassed. It is pristine! Pristine! You will not see another diver for the duration of your stay.'

Something in the latest bottle of wine appeared to have released the travel writer in Feramo.

'The pinnacle formations arise from great depths, attracting marine life in unbelievable numbers, including large pelagic species. It is an extraordinary technicolour experience: sharks, mantas, barracuda, dog-toothed tuna, dog-lips, jew fish.'

'So, lots of fish then!' she said brightly.

'And tomorrow we will dive à deux.'

Not with your hangover, we won't. 'And are there nice places to stay?'

'Actually, the majority of the divers stay on the live-aboards. I have several residential boats myself. But you, of course, shall have the full Bedouin experience.'

'That sounds wonderful. But I can only really write about what the readers can do themselves.'

'Let me tell you about Suakin,' he said. 'Suakin, the Venice of the Red Sea. A crumbling coral city, the greatest Red Sea port of the sixteenth century.'

After listening to a further twenty minutes of unbroken eulogy, she began to think Feramo's role in al-Qaeda might be boring his victims to death. She watched his drooping eyelids like a mother watches a child, trying to judge the moment when she could safely transport him to his cot.

'Let's go back inside,' she whispered, helping him to a low sofa, where he slumped with his chin on his chest. Holding her breath, wondering if she really dared do this, she kicked off her shoes and tiptoed over to the desk and the laptop. She opened it up and pressed a key to see if it was merely sleeping like its owner. Dammit. It was shut down. If she started it up, would it make a sound: a chord or, God forbid, a quack?

Olivia froze as Feramo gave a shuddering sigh and shifted position, rubbing the tip of his tongue against his lips like a lizard. She waited until his breathing steadied again then decided to go for it She pressed the start-up button and prepared to cough. There was a slight whirring, then, before she got the cough out, a female voice from the computer said, 'Uh-oh.'

Feramo opened his eyes and sat bolt upright. Olivia grabbed a bottle of water and hurried over. 'Uh-oh,' she said, 'uh-oh, you're going to have a terrible hangover if you don't drink some water.'

She held the bottle to his lips. He shook his head and pushed it away. 'Well, don't blame me if you have a horrible headache in the morning,' she said, making her way back to the computer. 'You should drink a whole litre of water at least and have an aspirin.' She kept up a steady stream of mumsy chatter as she sat down at the computer and checked out the desktop, trying to keep her cool. There was nothing there except icons and applications. She glanced over her shoulder. Feramo was sleeping soundly. She clicked on AOL, then went immediately to 'Favourites'.

She clocked the first two:

Hydroweld: for welding in the wet
Cut-price nose-hair and nail clippers

'Olivia!' She literally jumped an inch out of the seat. 'What are you doing?'

Calm, calm. Remember, he's had the best part of four bottles of wine.

'I'm trying to check my email,' she said without looking up, still clicking away at the computer. 'Is this on a wireless network, or are you meant to plug it into the phone socket?'

'Come away from there.'

'Well, not if you're just going to be asleep,' she said, trying her best to sound sulky.

'Olivia!' He sounded scary again.

'Oh, OK, hang on. I'll just shut it down,' she said hurriedly, quitting AOL as she heard him get to his feet. She put on an innocent expression and turned to face him, but he was heading for the bathroom. She darted across the room, opened a cabinet and saw a bunch of videotapes, some with handwritten labels: *Lawrence of Arabia, Academy Awards 2003, Miss Watson's Academy of Passion, Scenic Glories of the Bay Area.*

'What are you doing?'

'I'm looking for the mini-bar.'

'There is no mini-bar. This is not a hotel.'

'I thought it *was* a hotel.'

'I think it is time for you to return to your room.' He looked like a man who is just starting to realize how drunk he is. His clothes were crumpled, his eyes bloodshot.

'You're right. I'm very tired,' she said, smiling. 'Thank you for a lovely dinner.'

But he was crashing around the room, looking for something, and merely waved her goodnight.

He was a ruin of the dignified, mesmerizing man she had been so struck by at the hotel in Miami. *Drink is the urine of Satan*, she thought as she let herself back into her room. *I wonder how long before they start the al-Qaeda branch of AA?*

37

She had a hideous, sleepless night. She hadn't eaten anything since Miss Ruthie's slice of cake twelve hours before and, despite the luxury of the room, there was no mini-bar: no Toblerone, no jar of cashews, no giant pack of M&Ms. She turned her head this way and that against the pillowcase, which felt like it was finest Egyptian three-thousand thread count or something, but nothing helped.

At five a.m. she sat bolt upright and hit herself on the forehead. Caves! Al-Qaeda lived in caves in Tora Bora! Feramo was probably hiding Osama Bin Laden and Saddam Hussein in a cave under Suakin. There was probably a Donald Rumsfeld wet dream of weapons of mass destruction in a cave underneath her right now, all neatly marked PROPERTY OF S. HUSSEIN: WILL EXPLODE IN 45 MINUTES.

Eventually, as dawn was beginning to dilute the darkness over the sea, she drifted into confused dreams: headless bodies in wetsuits, Osama Bin Laden's head falling through the ocean in his turban while going on and on about fifteen-litre tanks, the virtues of neoprene drysuits, Danish BCDs and Australian drop-offs.

She woke to bright sunlight, the chirp of tropical birds and hunger pangs. There was the rich, humid smell that said 'holiday'. She pulled on the cotton bathrobe and slippers and padded onto her balcony. It was a perfect, almost cloudless Sunday morning. She could smell brunch.

The signs promising CLUBHOUSE led her to a tiki bar, where a bunch of young lovelies were laughing and joking together. She hesitated, feeling like the new girl at school, then recognized a familiar, like, Valley-girl voice?

'I mean, I, like, *get myself* so much more these days than I ever have?'

It was Kimberley with a huge stash of pancakes on her plate, playing idly with them with her fork and showing no interest in eating them at all. Olivia had to hold herself back from making a run at them.

'Kimberley!' she said brightly, barging into the group. 'Great to see you. How's the movie going? Where did you get those pancakes?'

It was one of the major pig-outs of her life. She consumed scrambled eggs and bacon, three banana pancakes with maple syrup, one blueberry muffin, three small slices of banana bread, two orange juices, three cappuccinos and a Bloody Mary. As she ate, trying to contain her excitement, she greeted more and more familiar faces from Miami and LA. As well as Kimberley, there was Winston, the beautiful black dive instructor – who, thankfully, had escaped the carnage of the *OceansApart* – Michael Monteroso, the facial technician, and Travis, the wolf-eyed actor slash writer slash lifestyle coach. All were displaying their fabulously oiled and worked-out bodies around the bar and pool. It was a recruiting camp, she was sure; it was the al-Qaeda version of Butlins. Winston was lying on a sun-lounger holding a loud conversation with Travis and Michael Monteroso, who were sitting at the bar.

'Was that the vintage Valentino year, with the white stripe?' said Winston.

'That was the Oscars,' said Michael bossily. 'The Globes she was in backless navy Armani. And she made that speech about honeys – "Everyone needs a honey to say 'How was your day, honey?' Benjamin Bratt does that for me."'

'And six weeks later they split up.'

'I was on security for the *Oceans Eleven* premiere and I'm thinking, I *so* can't ask Julia Roberts to open her purse, and she just goes right ahead and opens her purse for me.'

'You still doing that stuff?' said Travis the actor, Schadenfreude glinting in the ice-blue wolf eyes.

'Not any more,' snapped Winston. 'Are you still driving a van for that place in south LA?'

'No.'

'I thought you were,' said Michael.

'Well, only, like, part-time.'

'What place is that?' said Olivia.

'Oh it's, like, so not anything.' Travis sounded rather stoned. 'It sucks, man, but you can make good bread. If you do, like, Chicago or Michigan and sleep in the van, you can clock up, like *per diems* and overhours, but, like, the best stuff always goes to the old guys.'

'What's it called?' she said, then regretted it instantly. She sounded too much like a journalist or a policeman. Fortunately, Travis the actor seemed too out of it to notice anything.

'The security firm? Carrysure.' He yawned, got up from his perch and ambled over to a table by a palm tree, where several candles were burning in what appeared to be a giant sculpture made out of wax. He put a half-smoked joint into his mouth, lit it again and started to manipulate the wax, moulding it into strange, fanciful shapes.

'What's he doing?' said Olivia quietly.

Michael Monteroso rolled his eyes. 'It's his wax cake,' he said. 'It releases his creativity.'

Olivia glanced behind him and drew a sharp breath. Morton C was walking past the bar, wetsuit peeled down to the waist, muscles bulging. He was carrying a dive tank on each shoulder and was followed by two dark, Arabic-looking youths carrying jackets and regulators.

'I was at the Oscars that year,' said Kimberley. 'I was a seat-filler. I sat behind Jack Nicholson.'

Olivia saw Morton C spot her and looked away, furious. Two-faced git. He needn't think he was going to worm his way back into her affections now. She slipped the miniature camera from her wrap and surreptitiously snapped a few pictures.

'No kidding?' Winston was saying. 'Those guys who, like, sit in the seat when Halle Berry goes to the bathroom?'

Olivia nudged Michael, nodding at Morton's retreating back. 'Who's that?' she whispered.

'The blond guy? He's some kind of, like, diving instructor-type thing?'

'My dad gets me the gig because he does the follow spot,' Kimberley was saying proudly. 'The second time it was for Shakira Caine, but she only, like, went to the bathroom during one break. But last year I sat in the front row for the whole of the first half.'

'Anyone seen Pierre?'

'Alfonso said he was coming down for, like, for lunch, brunch, whatever. Hey! There's Alfonso. Hey, man. Come and have a drink.'

The troll-like figure of Alfonso, shirtless, was heading towards them. Olivia found herself unable to stomach the sight of his very hairy back.

'I think I'm going to have a swim,' she said, beginning to fear, as she slid off the stool, that she'd be drowned by the weight of the pancakes.

*

She plunged into the clear water, swimming strongly, holding her breath for as long as she could and surfacing a hundred yards further on. She had won a race at school for swimming underwater in Worksop Baths before it was banned because someone got dizzy. She surfaced, slicking back her hair so it didn't look mad, plunged down again and powered ahead for as long as she could, rounding the headland so that she could see the concrete pier. The sea was darker and choppier here; she was approaching the windward side of the island. She started to swim at a fast crawl until she was opposite the pier. It didn't seem to be in use. A tall fence with barbed wire along the top blocked entry from the hotel side. There were tanks and a storage shed close to the shore, and a surfboard which appeared to have been cut in half.

Beyond the pier was a long, windswept beach lashed by white-tipped waves. There was a small boat at anchor a couple of hundred yards out, tossing up and down. A diver stood up on the ledge at the back and stepped into the water, followed by three more. She dived down again and swam towards them. When she surfaced, the last of the four divers was beginning his descent. Thinking they'd be gone for a while, she started to swim towards the pier and was surprised, when she glanced back, to see all four of them had surfaced closer to the shore. Their pose was familiar as they waited in the water, like seals. Then one of them started paddling fast towards a wave and climbed onto a board. Surfers! She watched in fascination as they followed the wave in formation, zigzagging on the inner curve. They landed, laughing together, and set off towards the pier. Suddenly one of them shouted and pointed towards her.

Olivia plunged down about five feet and headed for the concrete pier. Her lungs were bursting, but she kept going until she rounded the pier and then surfaced, gasping for breath. The surfers were nowhere in sight. She plunged down again and swam back towards the resort until the water grew calmer, warm and blue, and she was above a sandy bottom back in the shelter of the bay.

She surfaced with relief, floating on her back, trying to get her breath back. There was a raft a little way ahead. She swam slowly towards it, pulled herself up and flopped down on the astroturf.

It was a cool raft. The astroturf was blue – the same type as they had around the Standard Hotel pool in LA. She stretched out, getting her breath back, looking up at the sky where the moon was already visible. She relaxed, feeling the sun on her skin, the raft rising and falling softly with the waves, the water slapping gently against the side.

She was woken abruptly from her daydream. A hand was clapped firmly over her mouth. Instinctively, she pulled the hat pin from her bikini and sank it deep into the arm, which jerked in shock and loosened just long enough for her to wriggle free.

'Don't move.' She recognized the voice.

'Morton, what is it with you? Have you been watching too many action movies?'

She turned and for the first time in her life found herself looking into the barrel of a gun. It was odd, really. She had wondered what it would be like, and, in the event, it was a strange, reverse-reality sensation. It made her think: *This is exactly like a film*, rather as when you see a beautiful view and you think it looks just like a postcard.

'What was on that needle?'

The grey eyes were icy, vicious. He was holding himself up on the raft with one elbow, still pointing the gun.

'That thing will never fire,' she said. 'It's been in the water.'

'Lie down on your stomach. That's right. Now – ' he leaned forward – 'what was in that fucking syringe?'

He was scared. She could see it in his eyes.

'Morton,' she said firmly, 'it is a hat pin. I'm travelling alone. You frightened me. You're frightening me even more now. Put the gun away.'

'Give me the pin.'

'No. Give me the gun.'

He shoved the barrel of the gun roughly into her neck and grabbed the pin with his other hand.

'This is very rude. I could easily just stand up and scream, you know.'

'You'd be too late and they'd never find you. What the fuck is this?' He was staring at the pin.

'It's a hat pin. It's an old trick of my mother's to ward off sexual assailants.'

He blinked at it, then let out his short laugh. 'A hat pin. Well, that's just great.'

'Bet you wish you hadn't pulled the gun, now, don't you?'

The grey eyes told her she was right. *Ha ha*, she thought.

'Shut up and talk,' he said. 'What are you doing here?'

'I wish I knew. I was kidnapped by Alfonso.'

'I know that. But what are you doing on Popayan? Who are you working for?'

'I told you. I'm just a freelance journalist.'

'Come on. A freelance fashion journalist who—'

'I am *not* a fashion journalist.'

'Perfume journalist, whatever. A perfume journalist who's a linguist?'

'In *our* country,' she said, drawing herself up indignantly, 'we realize the necessity of speaking other languages. We are aware of the existence of other nationalities. We like to be able to converse with them, not just to talk in a loud voice.'

'What are the languages? Gibberish? Bollocks? Gobble-degook? The language of love?'

HELEN FIELDING
She giggled in spite of herself. 'Come on, Morton, stop brandishing that gun. I don't think your boss is going to be very pleased if he finds out you've been shoving a gun down my throat.'

'That's the least of your worries.'

'I'm not talking about me. What were you doing in that tunnel?'

'What tunnel?'

'Oh, don't give me that. Why did you kill Dwayne? An innocent hippie like that – how could you?'

He looked at her dangerously. 'Why are you following Feramo?'

'Why are *you* following *me*? You're not very good at covering your tracks, are you? That fake beard and moustache you were sporting at the Standard were the worst I've ever seen in my life. And if you were going to stash a bag of coke in my hotel room in Tegucigalpa, it wasn't the brightest thing to sit making eyes at me five minutes before, then disappear and come back again.'

'Do you ever stop talking? I said, why are you following Feramo?'

'Are you jealous?'

He let out a short, incredulous laugh. 'Jealous? Over you?'

'Oh, I'm sorry. I was forgetting. I thought you might have kissed me because you fancied me. I'd forgotten you were a cynical, double-crossing, two-faced git.'

'You need to leave. I'm here to warn you. You're getting yourself into deep water.'

She looked down at him in the sea. 'If you don't mind me saying so, that's like the kettle calling the frying pan "dirty bottom".'

He shook his head. 'As I said, fluent in gibberish. Listen.

You're a nice English girl. Go home. Don't meddle in stuff you don't understand. Get your ass out of here.'

'How?'

'Oliviaaaaaaaaaa!'

She turned to look behind her. Feramo was calling from the shallows, wading towards her, the water waist high. 'Wait there,' he shouted. 'I will come.'

She turned back to Morton C, but all that was left of him was bubbles.

Feramo approached the raft with shark-like precision in a powerful freestyle and pulled himself onto it athletically. He was toned and perfectly triangular: clear olive skin and fine features devastating against the blue water. *It's raining men*, she thought. She wished Morton hadn't disappeared so she could have one on each side of the raft – one dark, one fair, both stunning against the blue water – and pick the prettier.

'Olivia, you look wonderful,' Feramo said earnestly. 'Wonderful.' The blue water was evidently doing it for her as well.

'Let me call for a boat and some towels,' he said, taking a waterproof bleeper from his pocket. Within minutes a speedboat drew up alongside them. A lithe Hispanic youth in swimming trunks cut the engine, handed them fluffy towels and helped Olivia aboard.

'That will be all, Jesus,' said Feramo, taking the wheel – at which Jesus walked to the back of the boat and simply stepped over the side, holding himself straight, as if he was going to walk back on the water.

Feramo turned to check that she was seated safely on the passenger seat and gently steered the boat in a wide curve through the millpond of the bay and off around the headland.

'I am so sorry I have left you alone all day,' he said.

'Oh, don't worry. I slept really late too. Did you have a hangover?'

As she spoke, she was trying to gauge his mood, looking for anything she could use to manipulate him and get away.

'No, it was not a hangover,' he snapped. 'I felt as if I had been poisoned. My stomach was churning like the innards of an ape, and I suffered a headache of such terrifying ferocity it was as if there was a metal brace grinding into my skull.'

'Er, Pierre. That's what we doctors call a hangover.'

'Do not be ridiculous. That cannot be.'

'Why not?'

'If that was a hangover,' he said imperiously, 'no one who has experienced it would ever drink alcohol again.'

She turned her face away to hide her grin. She felt like a wife whose husband insists he knows exactly where he's going, when he's going completely the wrong way. It made her feel stronger. He was just a man. She had two choices now. She could concentrate on getting more information, or she could concentrate on getting away. But simple psychology suggested that the more information she extracted, the less chance she had of getting away.

'I need to leave,' she blurted.

'That is not possible,' he said, without taking his eyes off the horizon.

'Stop, stop,' she said, allowing a note of hysteria to rise in her voice. 'I need to leave.'

Suddenly she knew exactly what she was going to do. She was going to cry. Under normal circumstances she would never dream of sinking so low, but a) this was a very unorthodox situation, b) she didn't want to die and c) she had a feeling that the one thing Feramo wouldn't be able to handle was a crying woman.

She thought back to her ill-fated locust story in the Sudan, when she had attempted to cover the starving animals instead. A minder from the Sudanese Ministry of Information had flatly refused to let her into the zoo until she accidentally started crying with frustration, at which point he caved in, flung open the gate and insisted on giving her a full tour, as if she were a three-year-old on a birthday treat. That had been an accident, however. She worked on the principle that she would never deliberately use tears to get her own way, and if they overwhelmed her by accident she would make sure she got to the loo before anyone saw. But at Khartoum Zoo there hadn't been a ladies'.

Now, though, she was planning to use tears in cold blood. It was a matter of life, death and global security. But then, did the end justify the means? Once you had violated a principle, where would it end? One minute you were crying in order to manipulate a man; the next you would be killing hippies.

Oh, fuck it, she thought and burst into tears.

Pierre Feramo stared at her in alarm. She sobbed and gurgled. He cut the engine. She cried more loudly. He recoiled, looking around for assistance as if under attack from laser-guided Scuds.

'Olivia, Olivia, stop, please. I beg of you, do not cry.'

'Then let me go home,' she said through paroxysms of tears. 'LET ME GO HOME.' She actually started keening, wondering if he would offer her a part in *Boundaries of Arizona* alongside Kimberley and Demi.

'Olivia . . .' he began and tailed off, staring at her helplessly. He didn't seem to have the capacity simply to comfort someone.

'I can't bear it. I can't bear to be trapped.' And then, in a burst of inspiration, she declared passionately, 'I need to be free, like the falcon.' She sneaked a look under her eyelashes to see what effect she was having. 'Please let me go, Pierre. Let me be free.'

He was agitated. His nostrils flared slightly, his mouth turned downwards at the edges. He reminded her more than ever of Bin Laden.

'Go where?' he said. 'You do not enjoy my hospitality? We have not made you comfortable here?' She sensed the danger in his voice – jangling raw nerves and imagined slights on every side.

'I need to come to you freely,' she said, softening, moving closer to him. 'I need to come by choice.'

She broke down again, this time for real. 'I don't feel safe here, Pierre. I'm tired, so many weird things have happened: the ship blowing up, Dwayne's head being bitten off – I just don't feel safe. I need to go home.'

'You cannot travel now. The world is not safe. You must stay here safe with me, *saqr*, until I have trained you always to return.'

'If you want me to return, then you must set me free. Free, to soar like the eagle,' she said, then wondered if she had overdone it.

He turned away, his mouth working.

'Very well, *saqr*, very well. I shall set you free and test you once again. But you must go quickly. You must leave today.'

Feramo took her to Roatán airport himself in the white speedboat. He cut the engine as they were still a way offshore to say goodbye.

'I have enjoyed having you as my guest, Olivia,' he said, touching her cheek tenderly. 'I myself will be leaving for the Sudan within a few days. I will telephone you in London and arrange for you to join me and I will show you the life of the Bedouin.'

Olivia nodded mutely. She had given him the wrong number.

'And then, *saqr*, you will begin to understand me better. And you will no longer want to leave.' He looked at her in a burning, insane manner. She thought he might try to kiss her, but instead he did the strangest thing. He took her index finger, thrust it into his mouth, and *sucked* on it, wildly, obsessively, as if it was a teat and he was a starving piglet.

38

As the Roatán–Miami flight became airborne, Olivia could not quite believe either what had happened, or that she had got away. She felt as if she had been under attack from a wild animal, burglar or violent storm, which suddenly, for no apparent reason, had gone away. It was not reassuring. She tried to tell herself that it was all her doing, that it was her brilliant psychological manipulation of Feramo which had won her her freedom. But she knew it wasn't. It was just luck, and luck could change.

There was one thing of which she was certain: she had been given a warning and a reprieve. She had moved too close to the flame and, fortunately, had escaped only slightly singed. Now it was time to go home and play safe.

Her confidence improved in direct proportion to her distance from Honduras. *Falcon, my arse*, she told herself as she boarded the Miami to London flight with thirty seconds to spare. *I've escaped the jaws of death through my brilliant psychological manipulation and now I'm free.* As the plane started its descent over Sussex, she was overcome with tearful relief. She looked down over rolling green hills, damp earth and chestnut trees, cows, lichen-covered churches, half-timbered houses, wiped a tear from her cheek and told herself she was safe.

But as she came through passport control and saw soldiers with guns, she remembered that you were never safe. People clustered around the television screens on the way through to the baggage hall. There had been another terror alert a few hours previously. The London Underground was closed. As she entered Customs, the doors to the Arrivals area opened and she saw the excited faces of waiting people and found herself irrationally hoping that someone would be waiting for her, someone's face breaking into a smile, hurrying up to get her case and take her home; or at the very least that there would be someone with a card saying OLIVIA JEWELS and the name of a minicab company. *Pull yourself together*, she said to herself. *You don't want to be taken home to cook supper in Worksop, do you?* But, actually, someone *was* waiting for her. She was pulled over at Customs, strip-searched, handcuffed and taken to the interrogation centre in Terminal Four.

Two hours later she was still there, her spy equipment spread out on the table before her: spyglass, spy ring, miniature camera, bug detector, pepper-spray pen. Her laptop had been taken away for examination. She felt as though she had gone over the story three hundred times. 'I'm a freelance journalist. I work for *Elan* magazine and the *Sunday Times*, sometimes. I went to Honduras to cover the cheap diving.'

Their questions about Feramo made her nervous. How did they know? Had the Embassy tipped them off? HM Customs were barking up completely the wrong tree anyway. They thought he was trafficking drugs and that she was his accomplice.

'Did he give you his number?'

'Yes.'

'Can we take it?'

'Won't that put me under threat?'

'We'll make sure it won't. Did you give him your number?'

'Nearly. I changed a couple of digits.'

'We'll need that number as well. The one you gave him. You're ex-directory, aren't you?'

'Yes.'

'Good. Why did you continue to follow him? Are you in love with him?'

She started to tell them about her terrorism theories, but she sensed she was dealing with the wrong people. They weren't taking her seriously. They were HM Customs and Excise. They were looking for drugs.

'I want to speak to someone from MI6,' she said. 'I need a terrorism person. I need a lawyer.'

Finally, the door opened and a tall figure swept in in a flurry of perfume, hair and covetable clothes. The woman sat at the desk, bent her head, took hold of her hair and threw it back so it cascaded over her shoulders in a glossy black curtain.

'So, Olivia, we meet again. Or should I call you Rachel?'

It took Olivia a second to realize that she recognized the woman and another second to realize where from.

'Hmm,' said Olivia. 'I wonder what *I* should call *you*?'

39

London

'I'm going to ask you again,' said Suraya in an annoying
primary-schoolteacher tone. 'And this time I want the right
answer.' She was as astonishingly beautiful as ever, but had
lost her West Coast drawl and replaced it with a posh girls'
boarding-school English.

Olivia's initial reaction to the revelation that Suraya was an
undercover spy was to think, *That woman could never be a
spy because no one would ever tell her anything because she's
also an Undercover Bitch.* But then she remembered how
stupid men could be when women were beautiful.

'I've told everyone about three hundred times. I'm freelance. I sometimes work for *Elan* magazine and the *Sunday
Times*, when they're not pissed off with me about something.'

'Born in Worksop.' Suraya started reading bossily from her
file. 'Witnessed parents and younger brother killed on a
pedestrian crossing aged fourteen.'

Olivia winced: horrible, cruel cowbag.

'Left school before A levels. Changed her name to Olivia
Joules. Started investing using parents' life insurance aged
eighteen. Extensive travel. Small apartment in Primrose Hill.

Freelance journalist, principally style and travel – ambitions to cover hard news. Plays piano, speaks fluent French, passable Spanish and German, some Arabic. Changes her appearance and hair colour with regularity. Frequent visits to the States and various European cities. Other visits to India, Morocco, Kenya, Tanzania, Mozambique and the Sudan.' She paused, then added, 'Currently unattached. So who are you working for?'

'Who are *you* working for?' snapped Olivia.

'MI6,' Suraya Exoceted back.

'Did you put the bug in my bedroom in the Standard?'

Suraya tossed her hair disparagingly and started reading from the file again. 'Rachel Pixley, writing under the name Olivia Joules, is considered by *Sunday Times* editorial staff to have an overactive imagination.' She closed the file and looked up with a nasty smile. 'So that explains the toys, yes?' she said, gesturing dismissively at the spy equipment. 'Jane Bond delusions.'

Olivia felt like hitting her on the head with a shoe. How dare she insult her spy gear?

Breathe, breathe, calm, Olivia told herself. *Do not stoop to the horrid witch's level.*

'So, tell me,' said Suraya. 'Did you enjoy sleeping with him?'

Olivia looked down for a moment, recovering her composure. It was fine, it was absolutely fine. Olivia's theory was that you could divide women into two types: those who were on the Girls' Team, and Undercover Bitches. If a woman was on the Girls' Team, she could be as beautiful, intelligent, rich, famous, sexy, successful and as popular as fuck, and you'd still like her. Women on the Girls' Team had solidarity. They were conspiratorial and brought all their fuck-ups to the table for everyone to enjoy. Undercover Bitches were competitive: they showed off, tried to put others down to make themselves look good, lacked humour and a sense of their own ridiculousness, said things which sounded OK on the surface but were actually designed to make you feel really bad, couldn't bear it when they weren't getting enough attention, and they flicked their hair. Men didn't get all this. They thought women took against each other because they were jealous. Quite tragic, really.

'Well?' said Suraya with a supercilious smile. 'Did you, or didn't you?'

Olivia felt like yelling, 'Oh, go fuck yourself, you ridiculous cowbag,' but managed to stop herself by digging her thumb into her palm.

'I'm afraid the closest I got was to see him in his swimming trunks,' said Olivia.

'Oh really? And?'

'They were quite baggy,' said Olivia sweetly. 'So sorry to disappoint, but I can't tell you much more. I'm sure you found all the information you needed from your own research. Why the interest, anyway?'

'That's for us to know and you to tell us more about,' she said, as if Olivia was a seven-year-old child. 'Now, I suggest you start by telling me why exactly you were following him.'

Calm, calm, breathe, don't go mental, Olivia told herself. *Look on the bright side. The fact that MI6 has arrived initially in the shape of this horrible public-school, hair-flicking, Undercover Bitch is neither here nor there. They are taking you seriously. Sooner or later, someone will lower his newspaper in a railway carriage, invite you for tea and biscuits in Pimlico, and pop the question.*

'I suppose you think staring into space like that is a clever technique,' said Suraya, stifling a yawn. 'Actually it's very childish.'

'Did you spend a *very* long time learning how to interrogate people?' asked Olivia. 'Did they tell you the best way to win people over was to really get on their nerves?'

Suraya froze for a moment, eyes closed, palms spread before her, breathing through her nose.

'OK, OK, freeze frame,' she said. 'Rewind, yah? Let's start again.' She held out her hand. 'Pax?'

'What?' said Olivia.

'You know: pax, yah? Latin for peace?'

'Oh! Yah, yah. I mean sometimes I, like, *dream* in Latin.'

'So look,' said Suraya, still keeping up the crisp English tone, 'let's come clean here. We've been looking at Feramo and his people for drugs. You know, Miami, Honduras, LA. It looked like a pretty obvious connection. As it turns out from our investigations, Feramo is as clean as a whistle – an international playboy with an eye for girls with not much between the ears.'

'You do yourself down.'

'What?' said Suraya. 'Anyway, you've mentioned a couple of times your suspicions about terrorism. We'd like you to tell us what that's based on.'

But Olivia wasn't going to tell her what that was based on, or not all of it, anyway. She would wait until she was interrogated by someone she could at least stand.

'Well, first of all, I didn't believe he was French,' she said. 'I thought he was an Arab.'

'Because?'

'His accent. And then, when the *OceansApart* blew up, I guess I, unfairly perhaps, put together some rather far-fetched clues to connect him to it. And then when I found out about the diving connection, I thought, ooh, maybe they'd used divers to blow up the ship. Silly, really, but there we are.'

Now, Olivia thought, if *she* had been doing the investigation, her next question would have been, 'And what do you think now?'

Instead, a tiny curl of satisfaction lifted the corner of Suraya's mouth. 'I see,' she said and got to her feet, picking up Olivia's file. She was wearing a very cool, short, seventies-style skirt with saddle stitching which looked like Prada, and a super-thin silk-knit sweater in an elegant shade of khaki.

'Excuse me one moment,' Suraya said with a smile and slipped out of the room, taking the file with her. Olivia could just make out the word Gucci woven into the knit at the back of the sweater. They must pay them a lot in MI6, she thought.

She sat looking round the room, imagining that Suraya had gone to talk to her superior. Any second now, she would return with an elderly M-like figure, who would lean forward and murmur, 'Welcome to MI6, Agent Joules. Now off you go to Gucci for the kit.'

The door opened, and Suraya reappeared. 'We're going to let you go,' she said with a brisk finality, sitting down.

Olivia sank down in her seat, crestfallen. 'I'll need these back, and my laptop,' she said, starting to gather her spy things together.

'We'll be retaining these for a few days,' said Suraya, putting out her hand to stop her.

'What about my laptop?'

'That too, I'm afraid. You'll have it back shortly.'

'But I need it to work on.'

'You can pick up a replacement and a copy of your hard drive on the way out. We'll contact you in a few days when we're ready to return the machine. In the meantime, Rachel' – Suraya had clearly picked up some pretty serious role-model stuff from the headmistress of her posh school – 'I'm sure you are aware of the importance of not mentioning this to anyone. No harm done, but in future remember it's an extremely silly idea to get involved with any sort of drugs issues. You got off lightly this time, but in future there might be more serious consequences.'

'What?' Olivia spluttered. 'It was the British Embassy people in La Ceiba who told me it was safe to go to Popayan. They said it would be all right to hang out at Feramo's hotel.'

'Well, how would they know?' said Suraya. 'Anyway, excuse me, I must be getting on. They'll give you another laptop on your way out.'

40

It was only back in the familiar surroundings of her flat – the plastic bottle of Fairy Liquid by the sink, the vacuum in the hall cupboard, the log McNuggets in the basket by the fireplace – that Olivia realized exactly how extraordinary the events of the last few days had been. Incredibly, it was less than two weeks since she had left London. The milk she had left in the fridge had gone off, but the butter was absolutely fine.

All the things that Olivia loved to escape to hotel rooms to avoid were here: an answering machine with thirty-one messages, the mail piling up in the hallway, the cupboard in the hall, which was full of things she hadn't got round to throwing away. It was freezing cold; the boiler had gone out, and she had to faff around pressing the ignition button over and over again, remembering as she did so how Morton C had pulled the starter cord on the boat on the way to Bell Key, until the thing suddenly ignited and made her jump. She stood in the kitchen with a can of Heinz baked beans in her hand: all the clues and theories, wild imaginings and suspicions of the last two weeks whirling round her head like clothes in a washing machine. *MI6 have made a mistake letting me go,* she thought. *They should be using me.*

She looked out of the small arched kitchen window onto

the familiar scene: the flat opposite with a piece of fabric instead of a curtain, and the floor beneath, where the man wandered around naked. In the street, she saw a man open the passenger door of a blue Ford Mondeo and get in beside the driver. The two of them looked up at her window, then, seeing her, looked quickly away. They didn't drive off. *Amateurs*, she thought, giving them a little wave, wondering who had made the bad employment decision: Feramo or MI6. She lit the fire, took a loaf of bread out of the freezer, made beans on toast and fell asleep in front of *EastEnders*.

Olivia didn't wake until noon the next day. The first thing she did was check the kitchen window. The men in the Ford Mondeo were still there. She was just wondering where they'd gone to pee in the night and hoping it wasn't on her doorstep when the phone rang.

'Olivia? It's Sally Hawkins. I'm so relieved that you're back safely.' This was odd. Sally, Olivia realized, had no way of knowing she was back unless either the security services or Feramo had tipped her off. 'How are you? How did the Honduras story go?'

'Well, er, I think maybe we need to talk about it,' said Olivia, frowning, trying to work out what was going on. 'I only got back last night.'

'Pierre Feramo telephoned me. I think he spoke to you. He's offered us a trip to the Red Sea to do another leg of the diving-off-the-beaten-track story. We're very keen to set it up. I just wanted to make sure that you'd be happy to make the trip, you know, so we can . . .'

This was too weird. Sally Hawkins sounded scared.

'Sure,' Olivia said casually. 'It sounds pretty exciting, and the diving's supposed to be great. I might need a couple of days to turn myself around, but I'm definitely up for it.'

'Good, good.' There was a pause. 'Er, just one more thing, Olivia.' She sounded strangely wooden, like a terrible actress reading lines. 'There's a chap I'd like you to meet, someone who's written for us a few times in the past. He's an expert on all things Arabian. Very interesting man. Must be in his eighties by now. He happens to be in London today. It might be a good idea if you could meet for tea and get a few, er, travel tips.'

'Sure,' said Olivia, pulling a 'she's mad!' face in the mirror.

'Excellent. Brooks on St James's. Do you know it? Just round the corner from the Ritz.'

'I'll find it.'

'Three thirty. Professor Widgett.'

'Oh yes. I've read his book on the Arab sensibility. Some of it, anyway.'

'Excellent, Olivia. Well, welcome back. And give me a ring tomorrow afternoon.'

Olivia put down the phone and reached for her bedside drawer. She was going to need another hat pin.

There were two different men watching her door now, from a brown Honda Civic parked across the road.

She raised a hand to them, turned on her new MI6-issue computer and Googled Professor Widgett: Arabist.

41

Widgett was a distinguished professor at All Souls and the author of forty books and more than eight hundred articles on various Middle Eastern topics including *The Sinister West: The Arab Mind and the Double-Edged Sword of Technology*, *Lawrence of Arabia and the Junior Suite: The Bedouin Ideal and Urban Hospitality* and *The Arabian Diaspora: Yesterday and Tomorrow*.

She spent a couple of hours online, reading what she could find of his work, then got dressed for a February day. It felt weird putting on tights, boots and a coat, but she kind of liked it. She glanced out of the window. The shadows were still there. She moved to the back of the flat, climbed out of the bedroom window and down the fire escape, scrambled over the wall of Dale's garden downstairs, went through the post office and came out on the busy main road of Primrose Hill. There was no sign of anyone following her. Whoever they were, they weren't very good.

Brooks was the sort of place which still didn't admit ladies, unless accompanied by a member, and offered three-course meals with savouries as dessert. It had a porter's lodge at the entrance, a black and white tiled floor and a real coal fire in an ornate Victorian fireplace. A doorman with a nicotine-lined face and a worn waistcoat and tails showed her up to the library.

'Professor Widgett is right over here, Miss,' he said. The room was silent apart from the ticking of a grandfather clock. Four or five old men sat on the worn leather armchairs behind copies of the *FT* or the *Telegraph*. There was another coal fire, an ancient globe, walls covered in books and a lot of dust. *Ooh, I'd like to take a cloth and a bottle of Pledge to this lot*, Olivia thought.

Professor Widgett got to his feet. He was immensely tall and old. He made her think of a poem she'd learned at school which began, 'Webster was much possessed by death / And saw the skull beneath the skin.' Widgett's skull was almost visible beneath his translucent, papery skin and the pattern of blue veins at his temples. His hair was all but gone.

The second he started to speak, though, Olivia was reminded of how ridiculous is the urge to patronize the old. Widgett was no kind, jolly old gentleman. As he spoke, she saw in his face the ruin of the beautiful roué he must once have been: the full, sensuous lips, the mesmerizing blue eyes – mocking, roguish, cool. She could see him galloping on a camel, scarf wrapped round his head, firing on some nineteenth-century desert fort. There was something theatrical about him: almost camp, but distinctly heterosexual.

'Tea?' he said, raising one eyebrow.

Professor Widgett's serving of the tea reminded her of someone doing a classroom chemistry experiment. It was such a performance: milk, tea strainer, hot water, butter, cream, jam. She suddenly realized why the English so loved their tea. It gave them things to fiddle with when they were bringing up other things which might stray into the difficult area of emotion and instinct. 'Ahm . . . that too strong for you? Drop more hot water?' Professor Widgett huffed and harrumphed between enquiries about her take on the Arab world, which seemed strangely irrelevant to a travel piece on diving off the beaten track. What had been her experience of the Arab world? What, in her view, was the motivating factor behind the jihad? Had she ever found it odd that there was no piece of technical equipment in general Western use – no TV, no computer, no car – which was manufactured by an Arab country? Little more milk? Let me top up the pot. Did she think it a result of an Arabic disdain for manual labour or a product of Western prejudice? Was it, did she feel, an ineradicable source of Arab resentment of the West, given the Arabs' insatiable urge to use and own the new technology? Drop more milk in that? Sugar lump? Ever had a love affair with an Arab? Oh my God, this stuff is like cat's piss. Let's get the waiter over for another pot.

'Professor Widgett,' she said, 'did Sally Hawkins contact you, or did you contact her and ask her to contact me?'

'Terrible actress, isn't she?' he said, taking a sip of tea. 'Absolutely appalling.'

'Are you from MI6?'

He took a bite of scone, scanning her with cool, insolent blue eyes.

'A bit clumsy, my dear,' he drawled in his slightly camp way. 'Traditionally, one waits for the spook to pop the question.'

He drank some more tea and ate some more scone, scrutinizing her. 'So,' he said. He leaned forward dramatically, putting his bony old hand on hers, and said in a stage whisper, 'Are you going to help us?'

'Yes,' she whispered back.

'You'll have to come now.'

'Where to?'

'Safe house.'

'How long for?'

'Don't know.'

'I thought those were your people watching outside my flat.'

'Yes. It's the others I'm worried about.'

'Oh I see,' she said, composing herself for a minute. 'What about my things?'

'Things, Olivia, things. One must never allow oneself to become attached to *things*.'

'I quite agree. But still, there are things I'll need if I'm going to come.'

'Make a list. I'll have someone –' he waved his hand vaguely – 'fetch the "things".'

'Why didn't you take me in at the airport and save all this trouble?'

'Operational blunder, darling,' he said, getting to his feet.

42

Widgett carried himself like a sultan. He strode through the gridlocked streets of St James's, elegant in a long cashmere overcoat, meeting anyone who crossed his path with a stare which was either hawk-like or fond, depending on the subject. Olivia thought how dazzling he must have been at forty. She could imagine rushing through the same streets with him in evening dress to dinner and dancing at the Café de Paris.

'Where are we going?' she asked, beginning to fear that Widgett was not MI6 at all, but just mad.

'The river, darling.' He led her on a complicated route through the back streets of Whitehall until they emerged onto the Embankment. A police launch was waiting. At the sight of Widgett, the officers, rather than loading him into an ambulance in a straitjacket, stood to attention. This was reassuring.

'Handsome fellows, aren't they?' he said, handing her into the launch.

'Where is the safe house?' she said.

'No need to know,' he said. 'Get some dinner and a good night's sleep. I'll be with you in the morning.' He gave them an elegant wave and disappeared into the crowd.

Immediately, the launch swung out from the bank and

into the central flow of the Thames, picking up speed and bouncing against the current. As they powered upstream, Big Ben and the Houses of Parliament were silhouetted against the moonlit sky. Olivia stood at the prow, heart leaping with excitement, the James Bond theme playing in her mind. She was a spy! She formed her fingers into a gun shape and whispered, 'Kpow! Kpow!' Then the boat banged down hard against a wave, and a spray of thick brown river water hit her in the face. She decided to spend the rest of the journey in the cabin.

There was a plain-clothes officer inside. 'Paul McKeown,' he said. 'I'm Scotland Yard's liaison with the security services. So, what do you make of Widgett?'

'I don't know,' she said. 'Who is he?'

'Come on. You know who he is.'

'I know he works for MI6 and that he's a well-known Arabist,' she said. 'That's all.'

'Absalom Widgett? He was a real old-school spy – the James Bond of his day. He seduced everybody's wives and daughters. He worked all over the Middle East and Arabia. He used to pretend to be a gay oriental-rug specialist. He had a store for years on the Portobello Road, and a Chair at Oxford. He was absolutely brilliant. A legend.'

'Is he the head of something?'

'He was. He was pretty high up. But he grew disenchanted in the seventies. It was never clear what happened in the end, whether it was someone's wife, or drink, or opium, or an ideological row. He was very much of the old school: chaps on the ground, native-lingo-speakers, trusting to instinct – that sort of thing. He thought all the new technology was the worst possible thing to happen to Intelligence. Anyway, whatever happened, it was a mistake on someone's part. The

She formed her fingers into a gun shape and whispered,
'Kpow! Kpow!'

Arabic section was never the same, and they pulled him out of retirement on the twelfth of September 2001.'

Olivia nodded thoughtfully. 'Would you tell me where I'm going?'

'Not allowed to say. Don't worry. I think you'll find it's pretty comfortable.'

At Hampton Court she was ushered from the boat to a helicopter and, after a short journey, into a car with darkened windows, which purred through the country lanes of Berkshire and the Chilterns. They crossed the M40 and she recognized the Oxford ring road, then they plunged deep into the Cotswold countryside, glimpsing flickering fires and cosy-looking scenes through the windows of pubs and cottages. Then they were following the high walls of a country estate, and Olivia heard the crunch of gravel beneath the wheels as wrought-iron gates swung slowly open, the headlights beaming up a long drive. It was the sort of journey which she imagined would end with a uniformed butler opening the door holding a silver tray of Bloody Marys, or a bald midget in a wheelchair, a cat on his knee being stroked with a metal claw.

She was, indeed, met by a butler, an excessively courteous man in uniform, who informed her that her bags had already arrived and ushered her up stone steps into a magnificent hallway. Oil paintings covered the panelled walls, and a wide staircase of dark wood led on to the upper floor.

He asked if she wanted dinner or a 'hot tray' in her room. She wasn't sure what a 'hot tray' was, but the image it conjured was so beguiling – potted shrimps, Welsh rarebit, Gentleman's Relish, sherry trifle – that she decided she *would* like one, thank you very much.

At the sight of the bed, she lost all interest in her surroundings and sank, exhausted, between the crisp white sheets, noticing to her intense joy that there was a hot-water bottle with a quilted cover in exactly the right position for her feet.

Olivia never discovered the constituents of the hot tray. The next thing she knew it was morning and she had the traveller's syndrome of not remembering where she was. She fumbled for the bedside lamp. The room was in darkness, but bright sunlight was flaring around the edges of the thick curtains. She was in a four-poster bed with heavy chintz drapes. She could hear sheep. It didn't seem to be Honduras.

She swung her legs around and sat on the edge of the bed. She ached all over. She felt dehydrated and vile. She padded over to the window, pulled the curtains aside and found herself looking at a splendid English country-house garden: lawns, manicured hedges in ordered lines, a honey-coloured stone terrace directly below her. Moss-covered steps, with a mock-Grecian urn on either side, led down to the lawn, on which there were croquet hoops. Beyond the lawn were chestnut trees, wintry and bare, and beyond that soft grey-green hills, dry-stone walls and smoke rising from the chimneys of grey rooftops clustered around a church spire.

She turned back to the room. Miraculously, her tan and olive case was there, containing the items from her flat she'd requested from Professor Widgett. There was an envelope under her door. It contained a map of the premises, a number to call when she was ready for breakfast and a note which said, *Report to Tech Op Room as soon as you have eaten.*

43

MI6 Safe House, the Cotswolds

Olivia blinked at the computer screen. She was sitting in a booth in a room full of computers and operators. A technician was going through the shots she had taken with her digital camera.

'What is this one of exactly?' he asked.

'Er . . .' she said. The picture was of a muscled black male torso and thighs emerging from an extremely well-packed pair of red swimming trunks.

'Shall we move on?' she said brightly.

'Lovely framing,' said a male voice. She turned. It was Professor Widgett, peering at the bulging red swimming trunks.

'I was shooting from the hip,' she said lamely.

'Obviously. Has he got a name, or just a bar code?' said Widgett.

'Winston.'

'Ah. Winston.'

'Shall we look at the next one now?'

'No. So these are all the wannabes around Feramo's pool? What were they doing there? Servicing him?'

239

'I don't know.'

'No.' He looked at the screen then sighed, as if bored, and looked at her with his head on one side. 'No, we rarely know. But what do you think? What do you scent?' He looked at her, opening his eyes wide and looking quite scary for a second. 'What does your gut tell you?'

'I think he was recruiting. I think he was using them for something.'

'Were they aware of that? Did they know what for?'

She thought for a moment. 'No.'

'Did you?'

'I think it's something to do with Hollywood.' She looked back at the bulging swimming trunks. 'Feramo hates Hollywood, and they all hang around there. Shall we move on to another shot?'

'Very well. If we must, we must. Next one, Dodd. Oh my word, what have we here?'

Olivia felt like crashing her head straight down onto the desk in front of her. What had she been thinking? The next shot was a close-up of a black rubber V with a zip at each edge. A bronzed, flat, rock-hard abdomen was emerging from the rubber.

'Oh dear. They're all a bit of a mess,' said Olivia, realizing she was looking at a close-up of the crotch of Morton C.

'Wouldn't say that, darling,' murmured Widgett.

'Try the next one. I'll be able to work out who it is.'

The technician sighed heavily and moved on. It was Morton C again, this time from the back, wetsuit peeled to the waist to show his impeccable torso. Morton C was glancing over his shoulder in a pose which was oddly reminiscent of a fifties pin-up.

'Very alluring,' said Widgett.

240

'He's not alluring,' she said, blinking angrily, humiliated. 'He's the guy I told you about who pulled a gun on me. He's a creep.'

Widgett's mouth twisted in amusement. 'Ooh! A creep? He's the one who works for Monsieur Feramo, we think? And in what capacity do we think? A pimp? A toyboy?'

'Well, it looked as though Feramo had taken him on fairly recently to do diving trips with the wannabes. To be honest, I think he was playing everybody off against everybody else. He was pretending to be one of the divers. He was schmoozing up to everyone in the bar and on the boat. He was just using everyone.'

Widgett leaned forward, raised his eyebrows wickedly, and whispered, 'Did you have him?'

'No, I did not,' hissed Olivia, staring furiously at the screen. The really annoying thing was that Morton C looked bloody attractive. He had that dangerous, focused expression on his face which had first caught her eye in Honduras.

'Pity. Interesting-looking fellow.'

'He's a shallow, double-crossing creep. He's little better than a common prostitute.'

There was a slight cough at the back of the room. Professor Widgett studiously inspected his fingernails as a figure rose up from one of the computer booths, a familiar figure in unfamiliar clothes: a hip-looking dark suit, tie and shirt loosened at the collar. The cropped hair was no longer peroxide. Widgett glanced around.

'"Little better than a common prostitute," she says.'

'Yes, sir,' said Morton C.

'What was it she stabbed you with again?' said Widgett.

'Hat pin, sir,' said Morton C drily, emerging from the booth.

Widget unravelled himself and rose to his feet. 'Ms Joules, may I present Scott Rich of the CIA, formerly of the Special Boat Service and one of the brightest stars of the Massachusetts Institute of Technology.' Widgett was overemphasizing his *ts* and *ss* as if he was Laurence Olivier on stage at the Old Vic. 'He's going to be at the helm of our current operation. Even though he was just *slightly* behind you in picking up on our target.'

'Welcome to the operation,' said Scott Rich, nodding slightly nervously at Olivia.

'Welcome to the operation?' she said. 'How dare you!'

'I'm sorry?'

'Don't look at me in that tone of voice. You heard.'

'Sorry about this,' said Widgett to the computer tech. 'Slightly wobbly moment approaching.'

'What were you *doing*?'

'Surveillance,' said Morton C slash Scott Rich of the CIA.

'I know that. I mean, what were you *doing*? If you were working for the CIA, why didn't you tell me?'

'Some might say you should have guessed.'

'I thought you were working for Feramo.'

'Likewise,' said Scott Rich.

'What do you . . . are you suggesting . . . ? How *dare* you?'

'Far be it from me . . .' Widgett murmured to the computer tech as if they were in a sewing circle. 'But didn't she just call him a common prostitute?'

'If I'd told you, you might have told him.'

'If you'd told me, we could have got to the bottom of what he was doing. I would have stayed.'

'I agree with her,' said Widgett, still in the gossipy voice to the computer tech. 'Can't imagine what he was doing pulling her out so quickly. Some misguided notion of chivalry.'

'Chivalry? Chivalry?' said Olivia. 'You used me from the moment you set eyes on me.'

'If I'd really wanted to use you, I'd have made sure you stayed.'

'You'd have used me before that if I'd let you, and you know perfectly well what I'm talking about.'

'All right, all right,' said Widgett, and Olivia heard the authority in his voice. The flash of cold detachment in his eyes told her he had given orders for harsh things in his time. 'Sort yourselves out, and I'll see the pair of you by the steps on the front lawn. You'll find wellingtons and Barbours in the boot room.'

'I have no idea what you're talking about,' said Scott Rich.

'Wet-weather gear, Rich. Can't have you tramping through the woods dressed like a waiter, can we?'

The housekeeper was waiting outside the operations room. Olivia and Scott Rich followed her down the dark, wood-panelled staircase and through to the kitchens, where there were scrubbed wooden tables, warm pipes and baking smells. The boot room was warm too and panelled in white-painted tongue and groove, with boots, scarves, socks and coats in neat lines on hooks and racks. It was soothing and comforting, but not enough.

'Why did you kill Dwayne?' hissed Olivia, putting on a pair of thick socks and green wellies.

'What are you talking about?' said Scott Rich, pulling a black sweater over his head. 'I didn't kill Dwayne. Jesus!'

'Don't pretend it was the shark,' she said, wriggling into a woolly jumper.

'If you really want the grisly details: Dwayne went after Feramo's divers on his own. He got into a fight underwater.

Someone pulled a knife. The sharks were coming in. Feramo's people pulled him up onto their boat. I was following at a distance. The next thing I knew, bits of Dwayne were dropping over the side and every predator this side of Tobago was heading for the scene. And, by the way, your sweater's inside out and back to front.'

She looked down uncertainly, then took it off and put it back on.

'It was you who put the cocaine in my bag in Tegucigalpa, wasn't it?' she said, as Scott Rich pushed open the door to let her go outside.

'No,' he said.

'Don't lie.'

He looked like a country squire. She realized she probably looked like a country squire's wife. The cold air hit her with a shock.

They rounded the corner and the full beauty of the house revealed itself: an Elizabethan manor with tall, square chimneys and mullioned windows, perfectly proportioned in honeyed Cotswold stone.

'I didn't put coke in your room.'

'Then who did?' she said. 'And what were you doing in that tunnel? You nearly killed me.'

'Killed you?' said Scott Rich. Widgett was standing waiting for them on the steps. He saw them and set off to meet them halfway across the lawn, coat and scarf flapping. 'I saved your life in that tunnel. I gave you my air. You guys were the idiots who went in without leaving a marker buoy.'

'Oh gawd. You two are not still arguing, are you?' said Widgett as he joined them. 'Come on, let's head for the woods. Olivia, when we get back to the house you'll be required to sign the Official Secrets Act. All right?'

'Yes, sir,' gabbled Olivia, thrilled. 'Absolutely, sir.'

'Yeees, I rather thought you'd like secrets,' said Widgett. 'Everything you hear here stays here, understood? Or you'll be taken to the Tower.'

It was a crisp winter day and the air was filled with English countryside smells, principally manure. Olivia followed the two spies along a path through the woodland, breathing in damp wood, rotting fungus, squelching through puddles in her wellingtons, remembering the joys of being wrapped up warm outside on a cold day. She noticed a camera fastened to a tree, and then another, and then, through the misty woodland, a high-security fence with four layers of barbed wire on top of it and a soldier in camouflage gear behind it. Scott Rich stopped and looked round at her.

'I'm sure neither of us wants to intrude on your private thoughts,' he said, 'but did you plan on adding anything to this conversation, or are you just going to play in the puddles?'

'I can't hear it, can I? You're just marching ahead and leaving me to catch up.'

'Oh God, I can't bear it,' said Widgett, turning round. 'It's like the opening scenes in a bad romantic comedy.'

In the cold, Widgett's face looked even odder. The red thread veins stood out through his skin, and there was a circle of blueish tinge, like a bruise, beneath each eye. He almost looked as if he was dead: a walking cadaver.

'There are two key questions,' said Scott Rich, ignoring him. 'One, what are they planning? We're picking up Intelligence chatter which points to—'

'Oh God, Intelligence chatter. I hate that term,' said Widgett. 'Intelligence chatter. Intelligence chatter. Retarded intelligence, more like. Men on the ground is what we need. Human beings with human reactions to other human beings.'

'We are picking up Intelligence chatter which strongly points to imminent attacks on London and Los Angeles.'

'As well as Sydney, New York, Barcelona, Singapore, San Francisco, Bilbao, Bogotá, Bolton, Bognor and anywhere else where people send emails,' muttered Widgett.

Scott Rich lowered his eyelids slightly. Olivia was starting to learn this would often be the only sign you got that he was rattled. 'All right. We've got a real human being here. She's all yours,' he said, leaning back against a tree.

Widgett appeared to be ruminating, chewing his lip or maybe his false teeth. He fixed her with his blue eyes. 'Two questions. One: what does Feramo have up his sleeve? Divers in sewers, reservoirs – nuclear cooling systems? Two: they're trafficking explosives from the hotel set-up in Honduras into southern California. How are they getting them in?'

'Is that what they were doing in Honduras?'

'Yes,' said Scott Rich, expressionless.

'How do you know?'

'Because I found C4 at the top of that cave you were on your way out of.'

Olivia looked down, frowning, thinking about herself swimming around in the cavern just looking at all the fish and thinking what bright colours they were.

'So . . . Agent Joules,' said Widgett. 'Any thoughts behind that stunning facade?'

She looked at him sharply. Her mind wasn't working properly. It had all got too important. She wanted to succeed as a spy too much.

'I need to think about it,' she said in a small voice. Widgett and Scott Rich looked at each other. She sensed disappointment from the one, and disdain from the other.

'Shall we walk on?' said Widgett.

The two mismatched figures walked ahead, talking seriously, the one precariously tall, trailing scarves, coat flapping, with theatrical gestures, the other powerful, contained, self-possessed. Olivia followed behind miserably. She felt like a fabled musical prodigy who had got onto the stage, made a few feeble squeaking noises on a violin and let everybody down. The stress of the whole bizarre experience started to crowd in on her. She felt exhausted and strung out, girly and useless. *Breathe, breathe, calm, calm, don't panic,* she told herself, trying to remember the Rules for Living.

Never panic. Stop, breathe, think.

Nothing is either as bad or as good as it seems.

When overwhelmed by disaster, think, 'Oh, fuck it.'

The key to success lies in how you pick yourself up from failure.

'Excuse me!' she said, hurrying to catch up. 'Excuse me! I know how they're getting the explosive in!'

'Oh goody,' said Widgett. 'Do tell.'

'They take it by road across Honduras, then up the Pacific coast by boat.'

'Yes, we had managed to get ourselves to that point,' said Scott. 'The question was how do they get the stuff into the States?'

'I think they transfer it to posh yachts and seal it inside surfboards, either on the yachts or at Feramo's place in Catalina.'

Scott Rich and Widgett stopped walking and looked at her.

'Then they take the surfboards close into the California coast on the yacht. They weight and dead-drop them under the ocean either on the bottom or on a line. Then their surfers go down in scuba gear, pick up the boards, dead-drop their

tanks, surf into shore at Malibu and drive off with the
surfboards full of explosives in their camper vans.'

There was total silence.

'Hmm, splendid piece of lateral thinking,' said Widgett.
'Based on . . .?'

'I saw them practising in Honduras. I swam round the
headland in Popayan and saw them dead-dropping the boards,
then surfing in.'

'Wasn't that what you were supposed to be looking for,
Rich?' said Widgett. 'Or were you too busy getting her
burgundy out of your electronic bug? Puligny-Montrachet,
wasn't it?'

'Shut up, please, sir.'

'So you put a bug in Feramo's potted fig tree?' said Olivia.

'And his cactus. And your cactus, come to mention it.'

'And you put a sweater over one, a glass of Cristal in the
other, and a white burgundy in the third. Louis Jadot 'ninety-
six, wasn't it?'

' 'Ninety-five,' said Olivia.

'Must have hurt, pouring it away,' said Widgett.

'It did,' said Olivia.

'Karl, hey.' Scott was talking into his phone. 'Get the H
section checking surfers on the SoCal coast, will you? Focus
on the Malibu Lagoon break. Check the boards for C4 inside.
And get some people onto Catalina – undercover – checking
out the boat docks. Where was this place, Olivia? Olivia?
Feramo's place on Catalina?'

'Oh, er. It was right of Avalon.'

'*Right?*'

'East. North, maybe; you know, right when you're facing
Catalina from LA. It's round the corner on the seaward side,
towards Hawaii.'

Scott Rich sighed. 'Just check all the landing stages,' he said into the phone.

'Jolly good. Well, that's all sorted then,' said Widgett. 'Now what about the target? Any thoughts?'

She told them about her theories, about the face cream with ricin in, the acetylene bubbles in the cooling pipes of the nuclear power stations, the attacks on the studios.

'But it's too broad,' she said. 'I need to spend more time with Feramo to narrow it down.'

'The perfect thing would be to take him up on this Sudan offer,' said Widgett. 'It would be fascinating under any circumstances.'

'He'd be crazy to bring you out there,' said Scott.

'He *is* crazy,' said Olivia.

'He's crazy to have let you go,' said Scott.

'Thank you,' said Olivia, thinking maybe Scott Rich wasn't so bad after all.

'I meant because it was obvious you'd turn him in. As you have.'

'He trusts me. He thinks I'm his falcon.'

Scott let out an odd noise.

'Is something the matter, Scott, Rich, Morton, or whatever your name is?'

'Yes, Rachel, or Olivia, or Pixie, or whatever the fuck yours is today . . .'

'Oh God in heaven,' drawled Widgett, taking out a hand-kerchief and wiping his forehead. 'It is rather the form for spooks to assume multiple identities. I mean some of us spent two full seasons as a drag queen at the Aswan Cataract Hotel.'

'*Spooks*, yes,' said Scott Rich.

'Which is what makes Ms Joules so interesting,' said Widgett. 'She's a natural spy. Now the question is, if *Pierre*

Feramo' – he said the name with an exaggerated French accent – 'telephones you as promised and beckons you to his Bedouin *lair* in the Red Sea hills, would you go?'

'Yup,' said Olivia solemnly.

'Would you?' said Scott Rich, fixing her with his intense grey eyes. 'Even if his only motive was to kill you?'

'If he wanted to kill me, he would have killed me in Honduras.'

'Oh, absolutely,' said Widgett. 'A fellow could have a lot of perfectly good reasons for wanting to whisk Agent Joules off to the desert. Surely you've read *The Arabian Nights*, Rich? Profoundly erotic book. A girl swept away by a Bedouin could look forward to some most imaginative nights in his tent, I would wager.'

'And then what?' said Scott Rich, striding angrily ahead.

44

It was five days since Olivia had left Feramo in the Bay Islands and he hadn't called. The team, which now, unfortunately, seemed to include Suraya the Undercover Bitch, had been holed up in a basement room since breakfast. Through some complex electronic manoeuvre, Scott Rich had routed the wrong number Olivia gave to Feramo through to the Tech Op Room so that, if Feramo rang, it would come to them direct.

The clock in the Operations Room was of the functional plastic type that Olivia remembered from school: a white face, black numbers and a red second hand. At school, she used to watch the clock, willing the hands towards four o'clock. The red second hand clicked into place. It was four p.m., nine a.m. in Honduras on the fifth morning since – with a badly sucked finger – she had taken her leave of Feramo.

Scott Rich, Professor Widgett, Olivia, Dodd the tech op and Suraya were all, with varying degrees of subtlety or ostentation, glancing at the clock in turn and – in Olivia's mind – all thinking the same thing: *She's made it up. He wasn't interested in her at all. He's not going to call.*

'Rich, my dear fellow. Are you absolutely sure you got that number wired up properly?' said Widgett, picking at a morsel of foie gras and toast he had had sent up. 'You seemed to be pressing an awful lot of buttons.'

'Yes,' said Scott Rich without looking up from the computer.

'He's not going to call, is he?' said Suraya.

'You should call him,' said Scott Rich.

'It will put him off,' Olivia insisted. 'He has to pursue.'

'I thought you were his falcon,' said Scott Rich. 'Or was it a budgie?'

He turned away and started talking to the technician, both of them focusing intently on the screen. One half showed Olivia's stolen shots of Feramo. The other was a slide show of known al-Qaeda terrorists. From time to time, they would stop and merge the shots to produce Feramo in a turban with a Kalashnikov, Feramo in a checked shirt in a bar in Hamburg, Feramo with a different nose, Feramo in a nightshirt with his hair standing on end.

'Actually, I agree with Scott,' said Suraya, putting her long jean-clad legs up on the desk.

'If he doesn't call, then there's no point in my calling him because it means he has lost interest.'

'Honestly,' laughed Suraya, 'this isn't *Blind Date*. You're just being insecure. He really likes you. Pierre prefers a strong woman. She should definitely call him.'

Scott Rich leaned forward, elbows on his knees, chin resting on his thumbs, and looked at Widgett with the same intense focus which had first startled Olivia in the bar in Honduras.

'So what do you think?' he said to Widgett.

Widgett scratched the back of his neck and sucked air through his teeth. 'There's an old Sudanese saying, "Wherever man and woman are present, the devil is the third." The Arab's stereotype image of a woman is almost as an animal: highly sexed and willing to have intercourse with any man, as if that is all they think about.'

'Really?' said Scott Rich, leaning back, smirking at Olivia.

'The feeling persists even today in some quarters that a man and woman alone together will inevitably engage in sexual intercourse.'

Olivia, infuriatingly, found herself flashing back to the night on Bell Key: Morton C kissing her, pressing against her, slipping his hand into her jeans. She caught his eye for a second and had the disconcerting impression that he was thinking about the same thing.

'There was a survey not long ago,' Widgett went on. 'A group of Sudanese Arabs were asked, "If you came home and found a strange man in your house, what would you do?" The answer came back almost unanimously: "Kill him."'

'Christ,' said Scott Rich. 'Remind me not to go out there as a plumber.'

'Thus the obsession, in some Arab cultures, with chastity – the veils, the burkas, the clitoridectomies. The woman is wholly eroticized: an object to be protected if she is one of your own, and pursued and conquered if she is not.'

'OK, so if in Feramo's eyes Olivia is an insatiable love beast anyway, why can't she just call?' said Scott Rich. 'But wait, how does sex outside marriage work with Islam?'

Olivia looked at him, thinking: *You really might have taken the trouble to find out some of this stuff.*

'Well, this is where it gets interesting,' said Widgett. 'Particularly with Feramo and all this Bedouin romanticism – wanting to sweep her onto a horse and gallop off into the desert sunset. The Bedouin ethos predates Islam. It's fundamental to the psyche. If you look at *The Arabian Nights*, you see that that way of thought, Bedouin desert-nomad mentality, overrides morality. When a hero's sexual conquests are the results of his courage, cunning or good luck, they are viewed not as immoral, but heroic.'

'Exactly. So he needs to break down my will and overwhelm me,' said Olivia. 'He's not exactly going to feel heroic if I phone and give him my flight number.'

Scott Rich handed her the phone. 'Call him.'

'Er, so the discussion we've just been having was meaningless?'

'Call him. Don't say anything about flying out there, or falcons. Just tell him you've got back safely and thank him for the fine wines and free hotel suite.'

'Hmm,' said Widgett, looking at Scott with cold blue eyes and chewing his toast.

'He's not going to call her,' said Scott Rich tersely. 'He's not going to ask her out to the Sudan, and we don't need her to go out to the Sudan. It's ridiculous. I just need to know where he is. Call him,' he said, holding out the phone.

'Of course,' said Olivia sweetly. 'Do I just dial?'

'No, I'll do it for you,' he said gruffly, turning back to the lines of screens and keyboards, giving a quick, disconcerted glance over his shoulder before going off with the tech op into some electronic zone-out, pressing and checking things and exchanging knowing looks. Scott Rich, for all his cool exterior, was a closet grungy techie. She tried to imagine him with a paunch and a big yellow T-shirt with something stupid written on it, drinking real ale with his mates.

He spun round on his chair. 'You ready?'

'Sure,' she said cheerily, putting the phone to her ear. 'Say when!'

Buttons were pressed. The phone started ringing. Olivia felt a rising flutter of panic.

'Hello?' she said, her voice quavering.

'Hi' – a woman's voice – 'my name is Berneen Neerkin. I'm calling from MCI Worldcom. We'd like the opportunity to introduce you to our new airtime package . . .'

Telemarketers! Olivia tried to compose her features. The infallible techno-god Scott Rich had got his wires crossed. She felt a giggle-bubble rising up as she caught a glimpse of his face. She tried to think of serious things, like death or getting a really bad haircut, but nothing worked. She started to shake and couldn't remember what position was normal for her own face.

Scott Rich got to his feet. He looked down at her very seriously, like a schoolmaster with a recalcitrant pupil. It just made her giggle more. He shook his head and turned back to the computer.

'I'll just get a glass of water,' choked Olivia, beetroot-red, and she staggered out into the corridor, where she leaned against the wall, shaking with laughter, wiping her eyes. As she made her way to the bathroom, the amusingness of the whole thing kept overcoming her. It wasn't until she'd splashed her face with water and stayed there a few minutes that she felt she had exorcized the last of the giggle-bubbles, and even then she didn't feel entirely safe.

As she made her way back along the corridor, she heard raised voices coming from the Tech Op Room.

'Look, we cannot shut down the whole of the state of California. We have C4, we have ricin, we have a possible commercial diving connection. Where does that take us? California is three times as big as your small, dark, benighted land.'

'Yes, all right, all right,' came Widgett's voice.

'Where do we start? In southern California alone we have major shipping ports in the Bay Area, Ventura, Los Angeles and San Diego. We have four nuclear-power sites and hundreds of miles of wide-bore tunnel water systems, sewage systems and drainage systems under every major city. We have aqueducts, bridges, reservoirs, dams and military bases. What do you propose we do? Evacuate the state? It's a needle in a haystack. Our only chance is to bust this Takfiri cell wide open and find out what they're up to. Now.'

'Listen, young man, if you bust the cell, the danger is that the plan or device, whatever and wherever it is, is already in place; they'll know they're rumbled and they'll detonate early. My hunch is that you won't get anything out of them anyway because none of them is party to the whole scheme of things. The only person who might know more is Feramo, and that's why the powers that be got him the hell out of Honduras at the first whiff of trouble. If I were you, I'd get your people on shutting down any non-essential underwater maintenance and repair projects right away, and get your chaps down there to check out employees, commercial diving schools, anything suspicious.'

'Have you any idea of the scale of that operation? All we need to do is find Feramo. If we find him, we can see into his freakin' laptop. We don't need Olivia.'

'Listen, Rich, if we can work out what the bastards are up to without spending thirty million dollars reducing the whole of eastern Sudan to a pile of smouldering rubble and at the cost of one girl, we should get on with it.'

No one heard Olivia slip back into the room

'Sir, she's a civilian.This is not an ethical path.'

'She's an agent and she's willing to go. Sharp as a tack, that one. Going to snap her up for the Service when this is over, if . . .'

'If she's still alive?'

Olivia gave a slight cough. Four pairs of eyes turned to stare at her. A split second later the phone rang.

'Jesus! Jesus!' Dodd the tech op started panicking, flapping around, trying to find buttons. 'It's him. It's Feramo.'

45

Scott crouched beside her, listening through his earphones. He held her gaze, steady, reassuring, just as he had in the underwater tunnel, then cued her to go.

'Hello?'

'Olivia?'

'Yes, it's me,' she said. There was frantic activity as Scott Rich and the technician attempted to trace the call. She closed her eyes and swung the chair so she had her back to them. She had to relate to Feramo as she had before, or it wouldn't work.

'Where are you?' she said, to save them the trouble. 'Are you still on the island?'

'No, no. I am en route for the Sudan.'

Olivia blinked, confused. Why was he telling her this on a mobile? Surely he couldn't be that much of an idiot? The old doubts returned. Maybe he wasn't a terrorist at all.

'Actually I cannot talk for long because my flight is departing soon.'

'To Khartoum?'

'No, to Cairo.'

'How fantastic. Are you going to look at the pyramids?'

'There will not be time. I will simply visit some business associates and then take a plane to Port Sudan. But, Olivia, you will visit me there, as we agreed?'

The quickening of attention behind her was almost tangible. 'Yessssss!' she felt like shouting, with her fist in the air. 'Yesssssssss!'

'Well, I don't know,' she said. 'I'd really like to come. I talked to Sally Hawkins, and she was keen, but I really need to get some more commissions to split the—'

'But that does not matter, Olivia. You will come as my guest. I will make the arrangements.'

'No, no. You can't do that, I told you. Oh, and thank you so much for your hospitality in Honduras.'

'Even though I had to kidnap you to force you to partake of it?'

'Well . . .'

'Olivia, my flight is about to depart. I must go, but I will call you from Cairo. You will be at this number tomorrow at around the same time?'

'Yes.'

'But wait. I will give you a number. These are the agents in Germany of my diving operation. They will organize your flights to Port Sudan and visas. You have a pen?'

Four separate writing devices shot out in front of her. She selected Professor Widgett's ancient gold Parker.

'I must go. Goodbye, *saqr*.'

Scott Rich was gesturing at her to keep him talking.

'Hang on. When are you actually arriving in Sudan? I don't want to arrive and find you not there.'

'I will be in Port Sudan the day after tomorrow. There is a flight from London on Tuesday via Cairo. You will take it?'

'I'll look into it.' Olivia laughed. 'You're so dramatic.'

'Goodbye, *saqr*.'

The phone clicked off.

*

She turned to the rest of the group, trying not to smirk.

Scott and the technician were still pressing things. Widgett gave her a fleeting, approving and vaguely lecherous smile.

'Rich?' he roared. 'Apologize.'

'Sorry,' said Scott Rich without looking up. Then he finished what he was doing, spun round on his chair and looked at her seriously.

'Sorry, Olivia.'

'Thank you,' she said. Then, feeling a rush of warmth and release from tension, she expanded. 'I like people who apologize straight like that, instead of that sort of double-talking, passive-aggressive "I'm sorry that you felt that . . ." fingers-crossed-behind-the-back non-apology which puts the blame on your own inaccurate understanding of the situation.'

'Good,' said Widgett. 'Now – and this is number one spook question at all times, Olivia – is he for real? Is *it* for real?'

'I know,' said Olivia. 'Why would he call from a mobile phone to say he's going to the Sudan if he's for real – I mean a real terrorist?'

'Well, I've always said he isn't,' said Suraya. 'He's a playboy who dabbles in smuggling, but he's not a terrorist.'

'Did you get any further with those photo-fits?' Widgett said to Scott.

'No. Nothing. No link to al-Qaeda.'

'There is one thing that I didn't say,' Olivia ventured hesitantly.

The cool grey eyes met hers. 'Yes?'

'Yes. It's just – you could check out his mother. I think he might have had a European mother, maybe someone vaguely connected with Hollywood. You know, a Sudanese or Egyptian father and a European mother, and I think she might have died when he was young.'

'Why do you say that, Olivia?'

'Well, he mentioned his mother, and it's just – he reacts in an odd way to me sometimes, as though I remind him of someone. And then, when he said goodbye at Roatán, he . . .' She screwed up her face. 'He shoved my finger in his mouth and sucked it, but manically, as if it was a teat and he was a piglet.'

'Oh Christ,' said Scott Rich.

'Anything else?' said Widgett.

'Well, yes. There is just one thing. He's an alcoholic.'

'What?'

Four pairs of eyes were staring at her again.

'He's an alcoholic. He doesn't know he is, but he is.'

'But he's a Muslim,' said Scott Rich.

'He's a Takfiri,' said Olivia.

They broke for dinner. As everyone was packing up and leaving, Olivia sat slumped at the table, thinking about the phone call. Widgett sat down opposite her, his mouth slightly twisted. He had an air of permanent disgust with the world which Olivia found refreshing.

'Your integrity – that's the fly in the ointment,' he rasped. The blue eyes were cold, like a fish. Suddenly they flashed into life. 'That's why you're a good spy,' he said, leaning across the table, wrinkling his nose. 'People trust you, which means you can betray them.'

'I don't feel good,' she said.

'Bloody good thing too,' he said. 'Never feel good. The corruption of the good by the belief in their own infallible goodness is the most bloody dangerous human pitfall. Once you have conquered all your sins, pride is the one which will conquer you. A man starts off deciding he is a good man because he makes good decisions. Next thing, he's convinced that whatever decision he makes must be good because he's a good man. So you've got Bin Laden hitting the Twin Towers and Tony Blair invading Baghdad. Most of the wars in the world are caused by people who think they have God on their side. Always stick with people who know they are flawed and ridiculous.'

46

The clock was ticking now. Suddenly there was high-level involvement on both sides of the Atlantic and a new air of gravity permeated the operation. Olivia had three days to prepare for her departure. She was being rushed through an intense programme of training in tradecraft, weaponry, desert survival and specialist equipment.

They were in what had been the servants' dining room, the full range of Olivia's equipment laid out on a long refectory table. She was inspecting a travel hairdryer, which had been doctored with ampoules containing a nerve agent attached to the front of the heating element.

'What about my real hairdryer?'

Professor Widgett sighed.

'I know you've gone to a lot of trouble, Professor,' she said, 'but the problem is, what am I going to actually dry my hair with?'

'Hmm. I see what you're saying. Is it conceivable that you might travel with two hairdryers?'

Olivia looked doubtful. 'Not really. Couldn't you make the nerve-gas thing be curling tongs? Or maybe a perfume spray?'

There was a snort. She looked up defensively. Scott Rich was leaning against the door frame, smirking.

'My dear Olivia,' said Widgett, ignoring Scott, 'we're trying to get the whole female thing right and so on, but this is a desert operation. Surely on such an expedition one would normally manage without a hairdryer?'

'Well, yes, but not if I'm supposed to be seducing the head of an al-Qaeda cell,' she explained patiently.

'You're crazy,' said Scott, straightening up from his leaning pose and joining the discussion.

'Well, it's all right for you two to say,' she said, looking at Widgett's bald pate and the cropped head of the smirking Scott Rich.

'Guys like women to look natural.'

'Wrong,' said Olivia. 'They want women to look how they do when they've finished doing their hair and make-up to *look* natural. I really think in this situation the hairdryer is a more important tool than the nerve-agent dispenser.'

'Take your point, Olivia. We'll look into some alternative,' said Widgett hurriedly. She had the feeling he was being soft with her because he felt guilty about sacrificing her, which was not an encouraging thought.

'Now,' said Widgett, 'I've got the list of your usual equipment, and we've tried to stick to it as closely as we can.' He cleared his throat. 'Cosmetics: lip gloss, lip pencil, lip balm, eyeshadow, eyeliner pencil, brushes, blusher, concealer, powder: matte, powder –' he paused slightly – '"illuminating shine", mascara: "radiant touch", eyelash curler.'

'Jesus Christ,' said Scott.

'It's all in very small containers,' said Olivia defensively.

'Yes, though actually that's rather a pity,' said Widgett. 'We're trying to keep your normal kit externally identical because his people undoubtedly checked it out in the Americas,

263

but we would actually do much better with normal sizes of all these things. Anyway: perfume, body lotion, mousse, shampoo, conditioner.'

'They'll have those in the hotel,' said Scott Rich.

'Hotel shampoos make your hair go funny. And anyway, I'm not going to a hotel. I'm going to a tent.'

'Then use asses' milk.'

'Mechanical items,' Widgett continued. 'Survival items, short-wave radio, digital micro-camera, spyglass and the usual clothing: footwear, swimwear and – Rich, no contribution required, thank you so much – underwear.'

'And jewellery and accessories,' added Olivia anxiously.

'Quite so, quite so. Now,' he said, striding to the other side of the room and clicking on a light. 'We have prepared a pretty extensive armoury based on these items. Actually quite interesting preparing a kit for a female.'

'You must have done that before.'

'Not in quite these circumstances.'

The total inventory was scary. She was really going to have to concentrate not to get things mixed up. Most of her existing stuff had been converted into weapons of – if not mass destruction, then short-range, specific destruction. Her ring had been fitted with an evil-looking curved blade which would flick out the second she pressed her thumbnail against one of the diamonds. Her Chloé shades had a spiral saw in one arm and a slimline dagger tipped with a nerve agent in the other. The buttons on her Dolce shirt had been replaced by minia-ture circular saws. She had a lipsalve which was actually a temporarily blinding flash, and a tiny blusher ball, which, when the fuse was lit, emitted gas which could knock a roomful of men out for five minutes.

'Good. Will I get my old things back afterwards?'

'If this goes as they hope it will,' said Scott, 'you'll get a supermarket sweep in Gucci, Tiffany and Dolce & Gabbana at the expense of Her Majesty's Government.'

She beamed.

One of her Tiffany starfish earrings now contained a tiny GPS locating beacon, which would track her movements throughout the expedition.

'Brand new, top of the range, this,' said Widgett. 'Smallest ever produced. Even works underwater to around ten or fifteen feet.'

'What about underground?'

'Unlikely,' said Widgett, not meeting her eye.

The other starfish earring contained a cyanide pill.

'And now the gun,' said Scott Rich. She stared at them aghast. They had gone over the daggers in the stilettos, the Dolce seventies retro belt made of real gold coins for buying her way out of a mess, the slim dagger and tranquillizer syringe made into bra underwirings. She'd rejected the brooch with the hand-ejected tranquillizer dart on the grounds that anyone under sixty wearing a brooch would immediately look suspicious.

'I'm not going to carry a gun.'

They stared at her blankly.

'It will get me into far more trouble than it will save me from. Why would I be carrying a gun if I'm a travel journalist? And, anyway, Feramo knows I don't believe in killing.'

Scott Rich and Widgett exchanged glances.

'Let me explain something,' said Scott. 'This isn't a romantic tryst. It's a highly dangerous, intentionally deadly and extremely expensive military operation.'

'No, let *me* explain something,' she said, quivering. 'I know how dangerous this is and I'm still doing it. If one of your specially trained expert operatives could do what you're sending me to do, you'd be sending them. You need me, like I am. That's how I've got this far with it, by being like I am. So either shut up and let me do it my way, or go and seduce Pierre Feramo yourself in the Sudanese desert.'

There was silence. Widgett began to hum a little song. 'Pom, pom, pom,' he went. 'Pom, pom, pom. Any more questions, Rich? Any more penetrating insights? Any more helpful comments? Or shall we get on? Good. Now let's look at how you fire a gun, Olivia, and we'll make a decision about whether to give you one later.'

47

Scott Rich stood behind Olivia, his hands over hers around the gun, easing her body into the right position.

'You're going to absorb the recoil through your arms without flinching. And then, *veery* smoothly' – he put her finger on the trigger – 'without jerking' – he placed his finger gently on top of hers – 'you're going to pull the trigger. Ready?'

The door burst open. It was Dodd.

'Sorry to interrupt, sir.'

Scott sighed heavily. 'What?'

'We've had a repeated caller on Ms Joules's mobile number, and Professor Widgett thinks she should call back straight away. He doesn't want her reported missing.'

Scott gestured at Olivia to take the phone.

'I'll play you the last message. Have to put it on speaker, I'm afraid, Ms Joules. That OK?'

Olivia nodded. Scott leaned back against the wall, arms folded.

'Olivia, it's Kate again. Where the *fuck* are you? If you've gone haring off to Honduras after your "little fling" with that ridiculous Dodi al-Fayed-style playboy, I'm going to have your guts for garters. I've called you four *hundred* times. If you don't ring me back by the end of today, I'm going to report you missing.'

'I'll call the number for you,' said the tech.

'Er . . . OK,' said Olivia. 'Could you not put it on speaker phone, please?'

'Sure.'

'Kate, hi,' she said sheepishly. 'It's Olivia.'

A barrage of indignation erupted from the earpiece.

'So anyway,' said Kate excitedly, when she'd finished venting, 'did you shag him?'

'No,' said Olivia, glancing at the two men.

'Did you snog?'

Olivia cast her mind back. Did she snog in Honduras? 'Yes!' she said. 'It was great, only it, er, wasn't him . . .' she tailed off, glancing embarrassedly at Scott.

'What? You followed him all the way to Honduras and then you snogged someone else? You are literally unbelievable.'

'Shhh,' hissed Olivia. 'Look, I really can't talk right now.'

'Where are you?'

'I can't . . .'

'Olivia, are you all right? If not, just say "no", and I'll contact the police.'

'No! I mean, yes, I'm fine.'

Scott leaned over and handed her a note.

'Hang on a minute.'

The note said:

Tell her you're having an erotic tryst – you're perfectly all right but you're in the middle of things and you'll call her tomorrow. We will pay her a visit to explain.

She looked up at Scott, who raised his eyebrows sexily and nodded encouragement.

'The thing is, I'm having an erotic tryst. I'm perfectly all right but I'm in the middle of things. I'll call you tomorrow and tell all.'

'You are the worst. What about Osama Bin Feramo?'

'I'll tell you tomorrow.'

'OK. Just as long as you're all right.' It seemed to have done the trick. 'Sure now?'

'Yes. Love you.' Olivia's voice wobbled slightly. At that moment she'd have given a lot to sit down with Kate over a couple of margaritas.

'Love you too, you incorrigible slapper.'

Olivia looked down at the note and laughed. Scott had signed it:

Uniquely yours – S.R.

48

Olivia sat by the fire in the snug, looking at a plate of plump truffles dusted with grated chocolate. She knew it was polite to wait, but the pressure was starting to get to her. She reached out and shoved two in her mouth. The daily recorded conversations with Feramo were making her feel like a creep. She had to concentrate on *OceansApart* flashbacks to keep her resolve. She had just stuffed another truffle into her mouth when the door opened and Widgett strode in, followed by Scott Rich.

'Something in your mouth, Agent Joules?' said Scott drily, sitting down on the sofa and spreading maps out by the tea tray.

'You'd better let me deal with this, or you'll put her off,' said Widgett, adding, in an aside to Olivia, 'He's got no affection for Africa and no understanding.'

'It'll take more than him to put me off,' said Olivia. 'I like it in the Sudan.'

'Good. So we're looking at the Red Sea hills here. Now the area is predominantly Arab, but with six per cent of the population Beja. Kipling's "Fuzzy-Wuzzies". Wily bunch of nomads, amazing vertical hair. Tremendously fierce and resilient. If you can get them on your side, you'll be all right in a crisis. The ones to watch out for are the Rashaida Bedouin nomads with satellite dishes on their tents and giant SUVs herding the camels. They're smugglers. No one can catch up with them. Hilarious bunch. I always had rather a soft spot for them.'

'This is where I think the caves might be,' said Olivia, nodding and pointing to the map.

'Ah, Suakin, the ruined coral port. Wonderful place.'

'Feramo told me all about it,' said Olivia. 'I think the al-Qaeda people are hiding there. I think they get into the caves underwater, like in Honduras.'

'We're looking into it,' said Scott Rich. 'Bin Laden was pretty cosy with the Sudanese regime in the mid-nineties.'

'I know,' said Olivia quietly.

'When the Sudanese finally kicked Bin Laden out in ninety-six, in theory the camps and cells were kicked out, but the more likely scenario is that they moved underground.'

'Or under water,' said Olivia.

'Exactly,' said Widgett excitedly. 'So your primary goal is to find out specifically what the threat is facing southern California. The secondary goal is to find who Feramo is hiding or visiting.'

'But it's still not too late to pull out,' said Scott Rich. 'It's important you know what you're getting into. We still don't know who Feramo is. But we know what sort of gracious hosts you'll be looking at in general. Port Sudan' – he pointed at the map – 'is directly opposite Mecca. Iran has leases on bases in Port Sudan and Suakin. So you've got thousands of Iranian soldiers in training, rebel NDA camps and a tinder-box of hydroelectrics to the north, a separate lot of interests coming in from Eritrea to the south, a bunch of crazy nomads in the mountains, and al-Qaeda, if you will, under the water. Still fancying a romantic mini-break?'

'Well, I thought it was very nice there last time!' said Olivia

271

brightly, to annoy him. 'I'm looking forward to it. Especially with all my new accessories.'

'Excellent. Have another chocolate,' said Widgett.

'Olivia, it's not safe out there,' said Scott Rich.

'Safe?' she said, eyes flashing. 'When is anything ever safe? Come on, you know how it is. It's like diving off that wall under the ocean.'

'Yeah,' he said softly. 'I know. Sometimes you just have to throw yourself over the edge, baby, and roll.'

49

As the plane approached Cairo, Olivia thought: *I wish I could freeze this moment in time and remember it for ever. I'm a spy. I'm Agent Joules. I'm on a mission for the British government. I'm in Club Class, drinking champagne with microwaved nuts.*

She had to stop herself grinning uncoolly as she strode through passport control. It was great to be on the road again. Away from the school-like atmosphere of the manor, she felt capable and as free as a bird of the non-falcon variety. The connecting flight to Port Sudan was delayed by six hours. *Ooh,* she thought. *I've never seen the pyramids.* The GPS wouldn't pick up her earring signal until she reached the Sudan. She cleared Customs and jumped in a cab.

Back at the safe house in the Cotswolds, Scott Rich was about to leave for RAF Brize Norton. He would be taking an RAF flight to the aircraft carrier USS *Condor* anchored in the Red Sea between Port Sudan and Mecca. He was packed and ready and he had an hour. He was alone in the Tech Op Room, working on the computer by a single light.

273

He leaned back from the search, screwing up his eyes and stretching, then leaned forward again, looked at the result and froze. As photographs and information began to appear on screen, he fumbled for the phone in his jacket and dialled Widgett.

'Yes, what is it, man? I'm in the middle of dinner.'

Scott Rich's voice was shaky. 'Widgett. Feramo is Zaccharias Attaf.'

There was a second's pause.

'Oh, God in heaven. Are you *sure*?'

'Yes. We need to get Olivia back from Africa. Now.'

'I'll be with you in forty seconds.'

Olivia's taxi was on a dual carriageway, weaving alarmingly between the lanes. There was a Christmas decoration hanging from the rear-view mirror and a pale blue nylon garland of some kind arranged across the dashboard. The driver turned to look at her, flashing a smile and one gold tooth.

'You hwan carrpeet?'

'I'm sorry?'

'Carrpeet. I geeve you verry good price. My brother have carrrpeet shop. Very close by. No go marrkeeet. In marrrkeet very bad man. My brother carrpeeet verry, verry beautifful.'

'No. No carpet. I want to go to the pyramids, like I said. Watch out!' she shouted, as cars started to swerve, horns blaring.

The driver turned back to the road with a curse, making a rude gesture out of the window.

'Pyramids. Giza,' said Olivia. 'We go to the pyramids then come back to the airport.'

'Pyramid verrry farr. Is no good. Is dark. No see. Better buy carpet.'

'What about the Sphinx?'

'Sphinx is OK.'

'So we'll go to the Sphinx, yes? And back to the airport?'

'Sphinx is OK. Very old.'

'Yes,' she said in Arabic. 'Old. Good.'

He roared off the dual carriageway at a crazy speed, plunging into a darkened residential area of dusty streets and mud houses. She wound down her windows, excitedly breathing in the smells of Africa: rotting rubbish, burnt meat, spices, dung. Eventually, the taxi ground to a halt beyond a labyrinth of unlit streets. The driver cut the engine.

'Where's the Sphinx?' said Olivia, feeling a twinge of alarm, flicking out her hook ring.

The driver grinned. 'No farrr,' he said, gassing her with his stinking breath. Suddenly, the total idiocy of her behaviour hit her. What was she *doing* deciding to sightsee on a mission like this? She took out her mobile phone. It said NO NETWORK.

'Sphinx very beautiful,' said the driver. 'You come with me. I show.'

She looked at him carefully, decided he was telling the truth and climbed out of the taxi. He took out a long object, which seemed to be a cosh. She followed him along the darkened road, feeling extremely dubious. There was sand underneath their feet. She loved the dry scent of the desert air. As they rounded a corner, the driver put a match to the cosh, turning it into a blazing torch. He held it aloft and pointed through the darkness.

Olivia gasped. She was looking at a pair of giant, dust-covered stone paws. It was the Sphinx – no barriers, no ticket counters, just *there*, in the middle of a dusty square, surrounded by low ruined buildings. As her eyes grew accustomed to the dark, the whole familiar shape began to reveal itself, smaller than she had imagined. The driver, raising the blazing torch, encouraged her to climb up onto the paws. She shook her head, thinking that if not actually illegal, it was certainly not right, and settled instead for following him around the perimeter, trying to get a sense of century upon century of oldness.

'OK,' she said, beaming. 'Thank you so much. Better get back to the airport now.'

It might not have been the most responsible decision, but she was awfully glad she'd come.

'You hwant carrpeet now?'

'No. No carpet. Airport.'

They turned the corner to head back to the car, and the driver cursed loudly. Another car was parked beside their taxi, headlights full on. Figures emerged from the darkness, coming towards them. Olivia shrank into the shadows, remembering her kidnapping training: the first moments of the kidnap attempt are key, on your territory, not theirs, when you have the last chance of escape. The men were focusing on the driver. There were raised voices. He appeared to be trying to placate them with an oily smile, talking very fast, heading towards his taxi. Olivia tried to melt away into the shadows. She was a hundred yards from the Sphinx, for God's sake. There had to be some other people somewhere. One of the shadowy figures saw her and grabbed her arm. At the same moment her driver got into his taxi and started the engine.

'Hey, wait!' yelled Olivia, starting to run towards him. *Now, make a noise, make a fuss, raise the alert while you're still in a public space.* 'Help,' she started to yell. 'Heeelp!'

'No, no,' said her driver. 'You go with him. Verry good man.'

'Nooooo!' she yelled, as he slammed the car in gear and moved off. A rough arm restrained her as she tried to run after the car, its tail lights disappearing into the labyrinth of streets.

Olivia looked round at her captors. There were three of them, young men in Western clothes. 'Please,' said one of them, opening the car door. 'Farouk must leave for other customer. You come with us. We take you to airport.'

As the man took hold of her, she jabbed him with the hook ring, breaking free as he yelled in pain, starting to run, yelling, as she'd been taught, in a way that left no doubt to anyone listening that she was under attack. 'Help me, oh God, please help me. Heeeeeeelp!'

It was a wet, windy night in the Cotswolds. On the tarmac at RAF Brize Norton, Scott Rich was yelling into the phone, trying to make himself heard above the roar of the jet engine. 'Where the hell is she? I said, where is she?'

'No bloody idea. Flight was delayed by six hours. Suraya's set up Fletcher in Cairo to watch for her: messages at the desk, et cetera, et cetera.'

'Suraya?'

'Yees. Anything wrong with that?'

Scott Rich hesitated. An aide approached, trying to rush him onto the plane. Scott waved him aside and headed into the shelter of the hangar. 'I want you to give me your word that you'll order Olivia back.'

Widgett gave a strange laugh. 'You're asking a spook to give you his word?'

'Zaccharias Attaf is a psychopath. He has killed eight women in exactly these circumstances. He becomes obsessed – as he is with Olivia – and when they fail to live up to whatever his insane fantasy happens to be, he kills them. You've seen the pictures.'

'Yes. He has a tendency to suck bits of them off, it would seem. Are you sure it's him? How did you get there?'

'It was what she said about Feramo's mother and the finger-sucking. There are no pictures of Attaf to go on, as you know, but everything else adds up. Pull her off the case. Bring her home. She's not a professional. Where is she now? Shopping? Getting her nails done? You can't knowingly send her out to meet a psychopath.'

'A psychopath who is also a senior al-Qaeda strategist.'

Scott Rich lowered his eyelids. 'You seem to view her as entirely expendable.'

'My dear fellow, Ms Joules is entirely capable of taking care of herself. We have all risked our necks in our time for the greater good. That,' said Widgett, 'is the business we are in.'

Calm, don't panic, breathe, calm don't panic breathe. Does it really matter? Yes. Oh fuck yes. Olivia tried to keep her head together and think as the kidnappers' car rattled through the blackness of the maze-like streets. They were Feramo's people, that much was clear. She'd failed on the first bit of kidnap training by allowing them to get her into the car. The next thing she'd been taught was to 'humanize the relationship with one's captors'. *Well, honestly*, she'd thought at the time, *how obvious could you get?* She fumbled in her bag for the pack of Marlboros she'd been given and held them out to the young man who had bundled her into the car. 'Cigarette?'

'No. No smoke. Very bad,' he said curtly.

'Quite right,' she said, nodding fervently. Idiotic. She was idiotic. They were probably devout Muslims. What next? 'Slug of whisky, Muhammad? Dirty video?'

There was a change in the streets outside: more light, figures, a donkey, a bicycle. Suddenly they burst out of the dark streets into a brightly lit souk. There were crowds of people, sheep, strings of fairy lights, music and cafes. The car ground to a halt at the entrance to a dark alleyway. The driver turned round. She clenched her fist, the hook ring outwards, clutching the hat pin in her other hand.

'Carpet,' said the new driver. 'You buy carpet? I give you good price, special for you.'

'Yes,' she whispered, slumping back against the seat, eyes closed, shaking with relief. 'Very good. I buy carpet.'

It was deemed necessary, unfortunately, to buy quite a large carpet. As they roared up the approach to the airport thirty-five minutes before take-off, the carpet protruded precariously from either side of the car boot. Olivia was so tense she was having to dig her fingernails into her palms in an attempt to stop herself yelling pointless things like, 'For God's sake, hurreeeeeeeeee.'

Then there were flashing lights, sirens, police cars and barricades and a line of red tail lights. It was a massive hold-up. Her mouth was dry. She had escaped death but, as is the way of things, her relief had immediately been replaced by another worry: missing the plane and therefore screwing up the mission. She felt herself trying to speed up the car by physically leaning forward as they slowed to a snail's pace. There'd been an accident, plainly. A man's body was lying on the tarmac, a pool of dark blood flowing from his mouth, a policeman chalking an outline around it. The driver leaned out of the window and asked what had happened. 'Shooting,' the driver yelled over his shoulder to Olivia. 'Englishman.'

She tried not to think about it. As the car pulled up at Departures, she almost threw the agreed fare of fifty dollars at the driver, grabbed her bag, leaped out and charged into the terminal, heading for the desk. Unfortunately, the two youths started to follow her, carrying the carpet.

'I don't want the carpet, thank you,' she called over her shoulder. 'Take it back with you. You can keep the money.' She reached the Sudan Airways desk and flung her passport and ticket down. 'My bag is already checked through. I just need a boarding pass.'

The youths triumphantly dropped the carpet onto the baggage scales.

'You want to check in this carpet?' said the Sudan Airways attendant. 'It is too late. You will have to take this carpet as hand luggage.'

'No, I don't want the carpet. Look,' said Olivia, turning to the youths, 'you can take the carpet. No room on plane. You can keep the money.'

'You no like carpet?' The boy looked devastated.

'I love the carpet, but . . . look. All right. Thank you, very nice. Please, just go away.'

They didn't go. She handed them each a five-dollar bill. They left.

The airline lady started typing into the computer in the way the ground staff do at airports when you're late for a flight – as if they're writing a contemplative poem, pausing to stare at the screen as if searching for exactly the right word or phrase.

'Er, excuse me,' said Olivia. 'It's very important that I don't miss the flight. I don't actually want the carpet. I don't need to check it in.'

'You wait here,' said the woman, who walked off and disappeared.

Olivia felt like swallowing her own fist. It was ten past nine. The departures screen for the delayed SA245 to Port Sudan said DEP 21:30. BOARDING GATE 4A. LAST CALL.

She was on the point of making a run for it and blagging her way through without a boarding pass when the woman returned wearing a sepulchral expression and accompanied by a man in a suit.

'All right, Ms Joules?' said the man in a slight east London twang. 'I'll see you through to the flight. Is this yours?' he asked, picking up the carpet.

Olivia started to protest, then gave up and just nodded her head wearily. The man rushed Olivia and the carpet past the queues and through security, taking her into an office a little way from the gate. He closed the door behind him.

'My name's Brown. I'm from the Embassy here. Professor Widgett wants to speak to you.'

Her heart sank. He had found out. She had fallen at the first hurdle. Brown dialled a number and handed her the phone.

'Where the hell have you been?' bellowed Widgett. 'Buying carpets?'

'I'm sorry, sir. It was a dreadful mistake.'

'Never mind now. Never mind. Forget it. A man who never makes a mistake never makes anything.'

'I promise it won't happen again.'

'All right. If it makes you feel better, a certain unpredictability of movement is no bad thing. The agent we had lined up to meet you just got himself shot.'

Oh my God. Oh my God. 'Was that his body I just saw on the way into the airport? Was it my fault? Were they trying to get me?'

A dispatcher in a luminous yellow jacket put his head round the door.

'No, no, nothing to do with you,' said Widgett.

'Better ring off,' mouthed Brown. 'They're about to shut the doors.'

'Professor Widgett, the plane's about to leave.'

'All right, jolly good. Off you go now,' said Widgett.

'Don't miss the flight after all this. Good luck and oh, er, with, er, Feramo ... Probably best to play along with this little fantasy he has about you as long as you can.'

'What do you mean?'

'Oh, you know ... these types that build a girl up, put her on a pedestal, are inclined to turn a bit nasty when the imaginary edifice crumbles. Just, er, keep him where you want him. Keep your wits about you. And remember, Rich is just a shout away in the Red Sea.'

Olivia rushed onto the plane, finding the carpet thrust into her arms as the doors closed. She tried vainly to shove it into the overhead locker under the baleful stare of the stewardess. It was only as the captain turned off the FASTEN SEATBELT signs and they were leaving the lights of Cairo behind, as she looked down at the vast, empty darkness of the Sahara, that she had time to digest what Widgett had said. She realized that the wiser course might have been not to get on board the plane at all.

50

Port Sudan, Red Sea Coast, Eastern Sudan

Scott Rich stood on the deck of the CIA dive ship USS *Ardeche* waiting for the lights of Olivia's approaching flight to appear in the night sky. The shoreline of the Sudan, dotted with the flickering red lights of fires in the desert, was a black shape against the darkness of the sky. The sea was utterly calm. There was no moon, but the sky was bursting with stars.

He heard the roar of the jet engine before the lights appeared, as the plane began its descent over Port Sudan. He slipped back below deck and flicked switches, the control deck before him humming into life. In a few minutes' time, the GPS would pick up the signal from Olivia's earring. Abdul Obeid, CIA agent, holding a Hilton sign, would pick her up in Arrivals and bring her to the harbour and a waiting launch. Before the first light of dawn, she would be aboard the USS *Ardeche* and out of reach of Feramo.

Scott Rich's face broke into a rare smile as a red light flashed up on the screen. He pressed a switch. 'We've got her,' he said. 'She's at the airport.'

*

As Olivia followed the line of somnambulant passengers into the scruffy Customs hall, she found herself drifting into her usual African-airport, hibernating-tortoise mode. She saw the passport control guys in their brown Formica booths, drowning in bits of paper. It always baffled her how they kept track of anything without computers, but somehow they did. The one time she'd tried to enter Khartoum without the correct visa she had found herself spending twelve hours in the airport. And the next time she had arrived, they somehow remembered and shoved her in the cage again. As she reached the front of the queue and handed over her papers, the man behind the desk stared at them, apparently blankly, and said, 'One moment please.'

Bugger, she thought, trying to maintain a pleasantly bland expression. There was no more stupid thing you could do than lose your temper with an official in Africa. A few minutes later the man reappeared, accompanied by a stout official in khaki military uniform, the belt squeezed far too tightly around his gut.

'Come with me please, Ms Joules,' said the stout man, flashing white teeth. 'Welcome to Sudan. Our honoured friends are expecting you.'

Good old MI6, she thought, as the portly officer ushered her into a private office.

A man dressed in a white djellaba and turban appeared at the door and introduced himself as Abdul Obeid. She gave him a quiet nod of complicity. It was all going to plan. This was the CIA local agent. He would take her to the Hilton, providing her on the way with a gun (which she had resolved to lose as soon as possible), and give her an up-to-date briefing incorporating any changes of plan. She would call Feramo, take a night to rest at the Hilton and prepare her kit and meet him in the morning. Abdul Obeid escorted her to a car park at the side of the office, where a smart four-wheel drive was waiting, a driver at the open door.

'You heard that Manchester won the Cup?' she said, settling into the back seat as the vehicle roared out of the car park. Abdul was supposed to reply, 'Do not speak to me of that because I am a supporter of Arsenal,' but he said nothing.

She felt a slight twinge of unease. 'Is it far to the hotel?' she said. It was still dark. They were passing corrugated-iron shanties. There were figures sleeping by the roadside, goats and stray dogs picking at garbage. The Hilton was close to the sea and the port, but they were heading towards the hills.

'Is this the best way to the Hilton?' she ventured.

'No,' said Abdul Obeid abruptly, turning to fix her with a terrifying stare. 'And now you must be silent.'

Eighty miles east, in the Red Sea midway between Port Sudan and Mecca, the full might of the American, British and French Intelligence services and special forces was gathered on the aircraft carrier USS *Condor*, focused on the whereabouts of Zaccharias Attaf and Agent Olivia Joules.

In the control room of the dive ship USS *Ardeche*, Scott Rich was staring, expressionless, at the small red light on his screen. He pressed a button and leaned forward to the microphone.

'*Ardeche* to *Condor*, we have a problem. Agent Obeid has failed to make contact at the airport. Agent Joules is travelling at eighty miles per hour in a south-westerly direction towards the Red Sea hills. We need ground forces to intercept. Repeat: ground forces to intercept.'

Olivia calculated that they were about forty miles south of Port Sudan and somewhat inland, following the line of the hills which ran parallel to the sea. They had long ago left the road behind, and she was conscious of rough terrain, land rising sharply to their left and desert scents. She had made several attempts to extract weaponry from her bag until Abdul Obeid had caught her at it and flung the bag into the back. She had weighed up the possible benefits of trying to kill or stun the driver and decided there was little to be gained. Better let them lead her to Feramo, if that was where they were going. Scott Rich would be on her trail.

The vehicle screeched to a halt. Abdul opened the door and pulled her out roughly. The driver took her bag out of the back and threw it to the ground, followed by the carpet, which seemed to have become even more unwieldy and landed with a heavy thud.

'Abdul, why are you doing this?' she said.

'I am not Abdul.'

'Then where is Abdul?'

'In the carpet,' he said, climbing back into the car with the driver and slamming the door. 'Mr Feramo will meet you here at his convenience.'

'Wait,' said Olivia, staring horrified at the carpet. 'Wait. You're not going to leave me here with a body?'

In response, the vehicle started to reverse, executed a dramatic handbrake turn and roared off back the way it had come. If she had had a gun, she could have shot out the tyres. As it was, she gave in, sank down on her bag and watched the tail lights of the four-wheel drive until they disappeared, and the roar of the engine faded into nothing. There was the cry of a hyena, then only the vast ringing silence of the desert. She glanced at her watch. The local time was three thirty a.m. Dawn would come within the hour, followed by twelve hours of unforgiving blistering African sun. She had better get busy.

*

As the first rays of the sun crept over the red rocks behind her, Olivia regarded her handiwork wearily. Abdul was buried under a thin covering of sand. Initially she had placed a cross of sticks at the head because that was what seemed normal on a grave; then she realized that this was a pretty major faux pas in these parts and changed it to a crescent made out of stones. She wasn't sure if that was right either, but at least it was something.

She had carried her belongings a good distance away, trying to escape from the smell and the aura of death. Her sarong was stretched between two boulders to make some shade. The plastic sheet was spread out on the rocky earth below, and on it was a chair made out of her bag and bundled sweatshirt. The embers of a small fire were burning beside it. Olivia was tending to her water-collection point: a plastic carrier bag stretched above a hole she'd dug in the sand, pebbles weighting it in the centre. She lifted it, carefully shaking down the last drops of water, and took out the survival tin from underneath. There was half an inch of cold water in the bottom. She drank it slowly, with pride. With the supplies she had in her bag she could survive here for days. Suddenly she heard hoofbeats in the distance. She scrambled to her feet and hurried to the shelter, rummaged in the bag and found her spyglass at the bottom. Looking through it, she saw two horsemen, maybe three, in coloured clothing. Rashaida, not Beja.

I hope it's Feramo, she thought to herself. *I hope he's coming to get me. I hope it's him.*

She ran a brush through her hair and checked her equipment. Fearing separation from her kit, she had stashed as much weaponry as possibly on her person – behind the booster pads in her bra, in the lining of her hat and the pockets in her shirt and chinos. The absolute essentials were in the bra – the dagger and tranquillizer syringe acting as underwiring. The flower in the centre hid another tiny circular saw and in the booster pad she had concealed the digital micro-camera, the blusher-ball gas diffuser, a waterproof lighter and the lipsalve, which was actually a flash.

She ate one muesli bar, slipped another two into her chinos and checked the contents of her bum bag: Maglite torch, Swiss army knife, compass. Hurriedly, she dismantled the water-collecting device, repacked her survival tin and shoved that in the bum bag too, with the carrier bag.

As the sound of hooves grew louder, she focused hard on her training – keep your spirits up by looking on the bright side; keep your mind alert and the adrenalin pumping by preparing for the worst – when she heard a single gunshot. She didn't have time to look, or think, as she flung herself flat on the ground.

51

At a little after nine a.m. the heat was still bearable. The Red Sea was glassily flat, the red rocks of the shore reflecting in the blue water. In the operations room of the USS *Ardeche*, the smell of frying bacon drifted over from the galley. Scott Rich sat slumped over the desk as the sibilant voice of Hackford Litvak, the head of the US military operation, oozed over the system.

'We have had no movement whatsoever within the last four hours. The possibility of finding her alive is rapidly decreasing. What is your view, Rich?'

'Affirmative. In all likelihood she is dead,' he said, without moving from his slump.

'Oh, don't be so bloody dramatic.' Widgett's camp bellow burst out from the desk. 'Dead? It's only nine o'clock in the morning. She's never been an early riser. Probably fast asleep with a Beja.'

Scott Rich straightened up, a flicker of life returning to his expression. 'This particular GPS is sensitive to an unprecedented degree. It picks up movements during sleep and at certain ranges can detect breathing.'

'Oh la-di-da-di-da. You sure the bloody thing isn't broken?'

'Professor Widgett,' purred Hackford Litvak creepily, 'in

November 2001, your British security services berated us for delay in reacting to intelligence that Bin Laden was hiding in the southern Afghan mountains.'

'Quite right too,' said Widgett. 'Bloody bunch of idiots. Our lot were ready to go in, but oh no, you had to do it. By the time you'd finished arguing about who was going to do the honours, Bin Laden had buggered off.'

'Which is why, this time, we want to move in immediately.'

'What's that English expression?' said Scott quietly on Widgett's private channel. 'Hoist with one's own petard?'

'Oh, do shut up,' said Widgett.

'Professor Widgett?' said Hackford Litvak.

'Yes, I heard. This is a completely different scenario. We have an operative on the ground, trusted by the target with whom she has a rendezvous. She is our best chance not only of finding him, but of finding out what he's up to. If you lot go barging in with all guns blazing, in this case I fear, quite literally, we'll get nothing. Hold back. Give her a chance.'

'You are suggesting we give a chance to a dead operative?'

'Jesus Christ, Litvak, you sound like a machine.'

'What is your view, Rich?' said Litvak.

Scott Rich blinked. It was a long time since he had found himself incapacitated by his emotions. He leaned forward, his hand on the microphone switch and paused for a second, collecting his thoughts. 'Sir, I think you should send the Navy Seals into the Suakin caves,' he said. 'And get undercover operatives into the hills immediately to retrieve the GPS and – ' a split-second pause – 'the body.'

'Oh dear,' said Olivia, 'I've lost my earring.'

Clutching her bare earlobe, she pulled hard on the reins to bring her stallion to a halt and looked down, appalled, at the sand.

The Rashaida behind her slowed his mount, shouting to his companion to stop. 'There is problem?' he said, bringing his horse alongside hers.

'I lost my earring,' she said, pointing first to one ear, then the other, in helpful illustration.

'Oh,' said the tribesman, looking genuinely concerned. 'You want I search?'

As the other Rashaida, who was riding ahead of them, pulled up his horse and started to trot back, Olivia and the first Rashaida looked back across the landscape of sand and scrub they had spent the last five hours traversing.

'I don't think we're going to find it,' she said.

'No,' he said. They continued to stare. 'Much money, he cost?'

'Yes.' She nodded very hard then frowned. Oh dear. This was very bad. The GPS cost very, very much money. They were not going to be pleased about this. Nor were they going to be able to find her.

She thought for a moment. There was a chance she could turn on the transmitter in the short-wave radio. Her orders were not to waste the battery and to use it only when she was transmitting an important message, but surely this qualified as an important message? Her bag was on the horse of the other Rashaida. The scarier of the two, he was dressed in a red robe and black turban. He was Bad Rashaida Cop. The Good Rashaida Cop, despite his fierce appearance, was turning out to be a sweetie.

'Muhammad!' she shouted. Both men looked up. Unfortunately they were both called Muhammad. 'Er, could I get into my bag?' she said, gesturing at the back of Bad Rashaida Cop's horse. 'I need to get something.'

He stared at her for a moment, flaring his nostrils. 'No!' he said, turning his horse back to the path ahead. 'We go.' He dug in his heels, cracked his whip and shot off, at which the other two horses whinnied excitably and shot off after him.

Olivia's exposure to higher levels of horsemanship had, hitherto, been limited to the occasional two-minute canter during a pony trek. The insides of her thighs were so agonizingly bruised that she didn't see how she could go on. She had tried every conceivable position: standing up, sitting down, sliding back and forth with the horse, sliding up and down with the horse, and had succeeded only in bruising herself from every possible angle so that there was no millimetre left of her legs which didn't hurt. The Muhammads, camel-like, seemed to require neither food nor drink. She had eaten three muesli bars since dawn. Nevertheless, the whole thing still struck her as something of an adventure. When else would she get to gallop through the Sahara alone with two Rashaida, unencumbered by tour guides, jeeps from Abercrombie & Kent, overweight Germans and people trying to sell you gourds and getting you to pay them to do dances?

But then, Bad Cop Rashaida ordered them to stop. He trotted a little distance ahead and vanished behind an outcrop of rocks. When he returned, he ordered Olivia to dismount and blindfolded her with a rough, evil-smelling black cloth.

Back on the USS *Ardeche*, Scott Rich was directing the onshore team towards the GPS. Three separate operatives, dressed as Beja, were approaching on horseback in a pincer movement. The line from Widgett in the UK crackled into life.

'Rich?'

'What?' said Scott Rich, eyelids lowering dangerously.

'Agent Steele, Suraya?'

'Yes?'

'She's working for Feramo.'

'The source?'

'A Deniable in Tegucigalpa. He was taken in on another count. The poor half-witted fellow tried to claim diplomatic immunity by saying he was working for us. He told them he'd planted a bag of the white stuff in Joules's room at our behest, then alerted the local police. The consular people got their local guys on the trail and it led straight to Suraya Steele.'

'Where is she now?'

'In custody. Debriefing. She spoke to Feramo late last night, it would seem. Maybe it was all for the best, eh?' said Widgett. 'They bumped Agent Joules off pretty quickly, it would seem. No time for Feramo to, you know, get—'

Scott brought his fist down on the switch, cutting Widgett off in mid-flow.

Olivia spent the last stretch of the journey clinging to Good Cop Muhammad on the back of his horse. Once they had left the flat sandy base of the desert floor and turned into the hills, the route had become steep and was pitted with rocks. Olivia, on her own horse but blindfolded, had become a danger to herself and everyone around her. Good Cop Muhammad was being very sweet and gentle, though, encouraging her, telling her that Meester Feramo was waiting to greet her, that all would be good and that there would be treats when she arrived.

Hours later, Olivia was to remember that even at this point, blindfolded and captive, she was idiotically oblivious to the gravity of her situation. Had she been less carried away by adventure, she might have tried to press her advantage with Good Muhammad, squeezing her arms a little more tightly around his waist, leaning in a little closer, playing on the Rashaida's gleeful lust for high-priced goodies by offering him the gold coins from her D&G belt. But she was light-headed from the heat and the jet-lag, excited and optimistic. Her imagination was full of the welcome ahead: Feramo with a bottle of chilled Cristal and a Bedouin treat prepared for the end of her journey – perhaps a torchlit feast with dancers, fragrant rice and three separate French vintages – in tented surroundings reminiscent of the trendier Marrakech holiday haunts featured in *Condé Nast Traveller*.

When she felt herself pass from sun to shadow, it was with relief. When Good Cop Muhammad dismounted and helped her down, even though her legs would barely straighten or bear her weight and her inner thighs were so bruised they were going to be black, she beamed with pleasure. She heard voices, both male and female. She smelt musk and felt a woman's hand slip into hers. The hand was guiding her forward. Olivia felt the brush of soft garments against her arm. The woman put her hand on the back of her neck, forcing her to bend it as Olivia caught her head against rock. There were hands behind her, pressing her forward. She was moving through a narrow, jagged entrance. She staggered unsteadily ahead, feeling the ground moving steeply down-wards and realizing, even through the blindfold, that she was in blackness. The air was cool and damp. It smelt stale and musty. The woman removed her hand from Olivia's neck. As Olivia stood to her full height, the woman's light tread retreated. It was only as Olivia heard the groan and crunch of a heavy object being moved behind her that she realized what was happening.

For once in her life, *stop, breathe, think* was of no use at all. Her bag was with the Muhammads. As she started to yell and grab at her blindfold, a hand caught her viciously across the face, flinging her against the rock. She was trapped under-ground without food or water, in the company of a madman.

52

Well, at least I'm not alone, she thought, forcing herself to look on the bright side as she lay in the dirt, struggling to get up, checking with her tongue to see if her teeth were still there. She fumbled at the blindfold.

'Leave it!'

Her heart started to beat frantically in her chest, her breath coming in short, ragged bursts. It was Feramo's voice, and yet it didn't sound like Feramo.

'Pierre?' she said, trying to sit up.

'*Putain!*' came the chilling voice again. '*Salope.*' He brought his hand down on her cheek again.

That did it. 'Ow!' she said, pulling off her blindfold and blinking furiously in the darkness. 'What on earth do you think you're doing? What's the matter with you? How dare you? How would you like it if I hit you?'

She pulled the hat pin out of her chinos and was almost on her feet when there was the crack of a whip and she felt the stinging blow of the leather across her arm.

'Stoppit!' she yelled and rushed at the dim figure in the darkness, sinking the hat pin into flesh, grabbing for the whip before retreating a few feet.

Her eyes were becoming accustomed to the dark now. Feramo was crouched before her, clad in the coloured robes of the Rashaida. His face was horrible, mouth working and twisted, eyes crazy.

'Are you all right?' Her words came out, quite unexpectedly, with tenderness. Olivia always had a problem, close up, with divorcing herself from the humanity of another person. 'What's wrong? You look terrible.' She reached out gently and touched his face. She felt him grow calmer as she stroked his cheek. He reached his hand up to hers, took hold of it, moved it towards his mouth and started to suck.

'Er, Pierre,' she said, after a few moments, 'I think that's enough now. Pierre? Pierre? What do you think you're doing?' She wrenched her finger out of his mouth and began nursing her hand.

His expression changed dangerously. He stood up, towering over her, ripped the tiny diamond and sapphire cross from her neck and threw it to the ground.

'Lie down, lie down flat, on your face. Your hands behind your back.'

He tied her hands with rope. There was a beeping sound. 'Sit up.'

He was sweeping her with a plastic detector stick. He took the hat pin, the belt and the bum bag containing the torch and the survival tin. He grabbed the remaining earring, the one containing the cyanide pill, from her ear, then twisted the hook ring from her hand and tossed it to the ground. He took hold of her blouse and ripped it, so that the circular-saw buttons fell to the ground, rolling in all directions.

'Where is the GPS?' he said.

'What?'

'The GPS. The tracking device. What are your people using to follow you? Do not feign innocence. You have betrayed me.'

She shrank back, cowering. How did he know?

'Your mistake, Olivia,' he said, 'was to believe that all beautiful women are as treacherous and disingenuous as you.'

Suraya. It had to be her. Undercover Bitch: undercover double agent.

'And now it is time for you to give us some information.'

Feramo dragged Olivia behind him for a long time through a low, narrow tunnel, shining his torch ahead. Whenever she stumbled, he jerked on the rope as if she was a donkey. She tried to detach herself from the situation and observe it. She tried to remember her training at the manor, but instead she saw Suraya instructing her sneeringly in tradecraft – the art of dead-drops, hiding film in lavatory cisterns, swapping briefcases with strangers, giving secret signals by leaving windows half open and displaying vases of flowers. She must have been really enjoying herself. Olivia turned her mind, instead, to the Rules for Living.

Nothing is ever as good or as bad as it seems. Look on the bright side and, if that doesn't work, look on the funny side. She thought back to telling Scott Rich she was Feramo's falcon and imagined his amused reaction if he could see her now – Feramo's mule or tethered goat. She still had a chance. She wasn't dead yet. Feramo was nuts and unstable and therefore things could change. If he wanted to kill her he would have killed her in the cave. Maybe she would kill him first, she thought, as he jerked on her rope again. She had plenty of weaponry in the Wonderbra.

The next moment she hit rock head on. Feramo cursed and jerked at the rope. The tunnel had turned a sharp corner. There was light and a change in the air and ... and ... she could smell the sea! As her eyes adjusted to the new light, she saw that the tunnel was widening into a cavern. There was scuba gear neatly stacked on racks and hooks: tanks, wet-suits, BCDs.

On the USS *Ardeche*, Scott Rich was watching the radar, monitoring the approach of a motor launch.

'Rich?' Litvak's puréed tones oozed over the speaker. 'I had a message. What's the problem?'

'They've found the GPS twenty miles west of Suakin. Plus a Rashaida acting friendly who says he'll take them to Olivia on horseback for fifty K.'

'Fifty K?'

'She's with Feramo. I've authorized it. I'm going in.'

'You need to stay on the *Ardeche*. You're commanding the intelligence operation.'

'Exactly. I'm commanding the intelligence operation. We need human beings on the ground. I'm going in.'

'Knew you'd come round to my point of view eventually,' came Widgett's voice.

'Shut up,' said Scott Rich. 'You're supposed to be asleep.'

Feramo had Olivia tethered to him twenty feet underwater with no air. She was reminded of a crocodile which weighs down its prey below the surface and comes back when it's ready to eat it. Feramo was making her breathe from his spare regulator – when he chose to let her. It was crazy, but good. It took all her mental energy to control her breath, to let it out slowly and not hold it. It slowed her into a rhythm and cleared her mind of panic. She allowed herself a moment to take in the extraordinary beauty surrounding her. Feramo was right. It was the best underwater landscape she had ever seen. The water was blue and crystalline, the visibility astonishing. Even this far down the rocks were red, and towards the open sea she saw coral pinnacles rising from the abyss. She caught

Feramo watching her and smiled, making her thumb and first
finger into an O to show her approval. There was a look of
warmth in his eyes. He held out the spare regulator and gave
her more air. He gestured to her to keep it, and they swam
forward together, sharing air, following the line of the cliffs,
for all the world like a couple in love. *Maybe it'll be all right*,
she told herself. *Maybe I can turn him round.*

A massive coral pedestal rock protruded from the shore
supported by a low, narrow stalk, eaten away by the current.
Feramo gestured to her to descend and swim underneath the
rock. It was unnerving: there were only three or four feet
between the rock and the seabed. Feramo swam ahead of her,
jerking the spare regulator from her grasp, and suddenly stood
up on the seabed, the top of his torso apparently melting into
the rock. Olivia looked up and gasped. Above her was a
square opening and a white room, lit by electric light.

Feramo was lifting himself up into the room. Olivia felt for
the bottom with her fins, straightened up and broke the surface,
pulling off her mask, shaking back her hair, gasping in the air.

There was an Arab boy dressed in swimming trunks whom
she recognized from the Isla Bonita. He took the diving
equipment from Feramo, and handed them towels.

'It's unbelievable,' she said. 'What is this place?'

Feramo flashed his white teeth proudly. 'The air pressure is
kept at exactly the same level as the water pressure, and
therefore the water will never rise above this point. It is
perfectly safe.'

And easy to escape, she thought, until he led her through a
solid-steel sliding door, opened by a punched-in code, and
then through another and into a shower room. He left her
alone to shower, telling her to change into the white djellaba
she would find inside.

*

He was waiting for her when she emerged. His face was angry again. 'And now, Olivia, it is time for me to leave you for a while. My people have some questions for you. I advise you to supply them with whatever information they need without resistance. And then you will be brought to me to say goodbye.'

'Goodbye?' she said. 'Where am I going?'

'You betrayed my trust, *saqr*,' he said, refusing to meet her eye. 'And therefore we must say goodbye.'

53

Olivia felt as though she'd been asleep for a long time. Initially, it was a woozy, not-unpleasant feeling, but as she regained consciousness sensation returned. The burnt spots on her hand were agonizing and there was new bruising on her back. She felt as though she had spent a night in a tumble-dryer. There was a sack over her head. It smelt of farmyards and barns, incongruously comforting. Her hands were tied, but hey – there was a mini circular saw behind the flower on her bra fastener

She made a few attempts to get at the bra with her teeth, realizing how ludicrous she must look, a white-robed creature with a bag on its head trying to eat its own bosom. She gave up and flopped back against the wall. There were voices not far off and the loud hum of the pressurized air supply. She strained to hear the voices. They were talking in Arabic.

I'm going to get out of this, she told herself. *I'm going to survive.* She sucked, pulling the sack-hood into her mouth, and started to bite. Before long, she had a small hole. Using her tongue and teeth and then her nose, she slowly made it wider, until she could almost see. There were footsteps. Quietly she flung herself down so she was lying on her face, hiding the hole. The footsteps came into the room, inches from her, and then retreated.

I've got to get into my bra, she thought. *I've got to get into the bra.* She carried on chewing at the sack, spitting out string and straw. She lowered her head and pushed the hole upwards until it was opposite her eyes. Bingo! She could see! She had to stop herself shouting, 'Yessss! Yessssss!'

She was in a passageway, hewn out of rock and lit by fluorescent strips. There were posters on the wall covered in Arabic writing and a Western calendar with, for some reason, a picture of a tractor on it. There was a date circled in red. She heard voices; they were coming from behind a curtain which hung over an archway to her left. Something was digging into her back. She twisted round. A valve protruded from a thin metal pipe running down the cave wall. She looked down inside the robe at her Wonderbra – it was a front fastener, which could be useful.

Very slowly, silently, she shifted herself round to face the valve and ripped at the sack, exposing more of her face. Then she shifted position, pushed the valve against the Wonderbra catch and pressed. Nothing. She tried again, and again, then tried to squeeze her shoulders and boobs together to loosen the pressure and leaned forward again. The Wonderbra sprang undone. It was such a relief not to have all the paraphernalia digging into her from the booster-pad pockets. She eased one cup against the valve to push it upwards and, after only three attempts, she caught the edge of the black lace in her teeth.

Olivia was unbelievably pleased with herself, so pleased she almost allowed herself to grin and drop the bra. She turned around too quickly so that her sandal scraped on the floor. The voices stopped in the next room. She was frozen with one half of a black Wonderbra in her mouth, like a dog holding a newspaper. Heavy footsteps started to move towards her. She shook the sack back over her face and lay down. The footsteps came very close. A foot poked her in the ribs. She shuddered and turned her head slightly, which she thought was a realistic touch. The footsteps retreated. She didn't move until the voices started again.

The Wonderbra cup was inside out, still held in her teeth. Slowly, she pulled it out from her djellaba and, still using her teeth, twisted round to hook it over the valve. It was awfully uncomfortable, but she managed to twist back and push the rope binding her hands against the saw. It was wretched, slow work. There was a horrible moment when the bra came away from the valve, and she had to go through the whole process of hooking it up there again. But, eventually, the little saw cut through enough fibres for her to break her hands free and untie her ankles.

Glancing anxiously towards the curtain, she opened the lipsalve she had stashed in her bra. She set the timer to three seconds, replaced the cap and, aiming carefully, rolled it under the gap between the curtain and the floor. Then she curled up, eyes tightly closed, squeezing her face between her knees and her arms. Even so, the flash was almost blinding. There were shouts, screams and crashing noises from behind the curtain.

She leapt to her feet, ran to the curtain and yanked it open. In that split second, she took in an astonishing scene. Twelve men were clutching their eyes, blinded, blundering in panic. There were photographs and diagrams on the walls. Bridges – the Sydney Harbour Bridge, the Golden Gate Bridge, Tower Bridge, another bridge spanning a wide harbour with sky-scrapers in the background. There were seven pictures in all. On a table in the centre of the room, there was what looked like the bottom of a round plinth facing towards her, and beside it a jagged piece of metal, gold on the outside, hollow inside, like a piece broken off a chocolate Santa. She thought about grabbing it to use as a weapon. Then, behind the table, sitting cross-legged on a carpet, she saw an unmistakable, tall, bearded figure. He was sitting perfectly still, eyes closed, blinded by the flash like everyone else, but totally calm and totally terrifying. It was Osama Bin Laden.

She had seconds. She photographed the bridges first – realizing halfway through that the flash wasn't working. Then she tried for a nice group shot. Then she tried Bin Laden. The camera was so tiny you couldn't see what you were doing – you had to guess. And it was hard to see anything after the flash. But she was sure it was him.

The man closest to her reacted to the sound of the shutter and turned towards her. She lit the fuse on the tiny gas ball and rolled it into the centre of the room, retreated through the curtain and ran. They would be able to see again in a couple of minutes, but the gas would knock them out for five.

Once she was out of the ante-room and round the corner, she stopped, leaned panting against the wall and listened. The corridor was white-painted rock, stretching as far as she could see in both directions. It was hard to hear above the air-pressure system, but the sound to her left seemed to have a different quality. Was that the sound of the sea or of machinery?

She decided to go for it. As she ran up the slight incline, it began to seem familiar and, yes, there was the shower room and, in the distance, the metal door. As she grew closer, she realized it was wedged open by a body, like a suitcase stuck between elevator doors. It was an injured, semi-conscious Feramo. He looked as though he had been trying to escape. She stepped over him, then hesitated. She put her face close to his. His eyes were slightly open. He was breathing with difficulty.

'Help me,' he whispered. '*Habitibi*, help.'

She pulled the dagger underwiring from her Wonderbra

and pointed it at his throat, as she had been taught, straight at the carotid artery.

'The code,' she hissed, jabbing him. 'Tell me the code for the door.'

'Will you take me with you?'

She blinked at him for a moment. 'If you're good.'

He could barely speak. She couldn't work out what they had done to him. What had he been thinking, bringing her here?

'The code,' she said. 'Come on, or you die.' It sounded silly when she said it.

'Two four six eight.' He could barely whisper.

'Two four six eight?' she said indignantly. 'Isn't that a bit obvious? Are both doors the same code?'

He shook his head and croaked, 'Zero nine eleven.'

She rolled her eyes: *Unbelievable.*

'Take me with you, *saqr*, please. Or kill me now. I cannot take the pain and indignity of what they will do.'

She thought for a second, reached into her bra and pulled out the tranquillizer syringe which formed the other cup's underwiring.

'It's all right, it's only temporary,' she said, seeing Feramo's frightened eyes. She whipped up the djellaba he was wearing and expelled the air from the syringe. 'There we go!' she said, matron-like, sinking the needle into his buttock.

Wow, it worked fast. She punched in 2468 and pulled him out from between the doors. Just before they closed, she had a brainwave, whipped off his sandals and shoved them between the doors, leaving a six-inch gap, too narrow to get through but wide enough to let water in. Dragging a prone Feramo behind her with her good arm, she tapped in 0911 at the next set of doors, feeling a great lightness of spirit as they opened to reveal the brightly lit entry room, the scuba gear and the square of sea water. This time she wedged a pair of fins between the doors.

She pulled off her djellaba and hovered for a second on the brink of the Land of Indecision. Should she just plunge into the water as she was, swim to the surface and wing it, or scuba? She reached for the BCD, weight belt and tanks, and put the whole kit together.

She was just stepping into the water when she glanced back at Feramo. He looked pitiful, crumpled and sleeping like a sad little child. She found herself imagining all the bossy men who try to organize the world – the Americans, the British, the Arabs – as fucked-up little kids: the Americans brassy and bullying, wanting to be stars of the baseball pitch; the British from their public schools priggishly determined to be righteous; and the Arabs, frustrated, repressed by their parents, blustering incoherently because there is nothing worse than losing face.

'He'll be more use alive than dead,' she told herself, banishing her feelings of tenderness. Listening out for the sound of anyone approaching, she ripped off his robe, pausing for an essential second to admire the sublime, olive-skinned body, checked him for shark-luring cuts and found him clear, weighted and buoyed him, shoved him in a full head mask and rolled him into the water, leaving him bobbing in the square of the entrance. There was a pressure gauge on the wall. She grabbed a tank and rammed it at the gauge, breaking the glass, then took a piece of glass to pierce the pipe. Immediately there was a change in the hum. She looked down at the square of water where Feramo was floating. It was starting unmistakably to rise. Yesss! Yesss! Eventually it would hit the lights and short the electrics, and with all that pressurized oxygen it might even blow the place to pieces. And if that didn't happen, the water would rush in and they would all drown. Hah!

She lowered herself into the water, letting air out of Feramo's BCD to make him sink, then, taking hold of the tranquillized floating terrorist, she started to swim, heading out from under the pedestal rock, dragging him behind her with her good hand in a gratifying reversal of roles.

I'm quite clever, really, she said to herself.

Unfortunately, it hadn't occurred to her that it would be dark. Diving at night, especially without a light and with a rather flimsy dagger instead of a harpoon, was not a great idea. She didn't want to break the surface too near the shore in case al-Qaeda had scouts. She didn't want to break the surface too far out because of sharks. She didn't want to use up her air in case she needed to go down again.

She swam directly away from the shore at a depth of ten feet for about thirty minutes, then surfaced and settled for letting air out Feramo's jacket so that he was neutrally buoyant two feet down. Then she pulled her legs in tight and sat on him. If the sharks came to feed, they could eat him first. All she could see was blackness: no lights, no boats. If the sharks stayed away, she could float here safely until dawn, but then what? She deliberated over whether to cut Feramo loose and swim back to shore, or further out to sea. She was so terribly tired. She felt herself beginning to drift off to sleep, when suddenly the force of a massive, living object burst to the surface from beneath her.

[illegible faded text from previous page]

54

'There's something down there.'

Scott Rich was in the navigator's seat of the Black Hawk watching the heat-seeking monitor. The electronic chatter filling the cockpit was crazy-making, but Rich was entirely composed, leaning forward, focused, intent, listening to simultaneous feeds from the ground forces, four separate air patrols and Hackford Litvak's Navy Seals.

'Sir, the ground patrol have found Agent Joules's clothing at the end of the tunnel. No sign of the agent herself.'

'Anything else?' said Scott. 'Signs of a struggle?'

'The clothing was torn and bloodstained, sir.'

Scott Rich flinched. 'And your position now?'

'At the coastline, sir, a ten-foot drop to the Red Sea.'

'Anything else you can see there?'

'No. Only scuba equipment, sir.'

'Did you say scuba equipment?'

'Yes, sir.'

'Then goddammit, get it on and get in the water.' He clicked off his microphone and turned to the pilot, pointing at the screen in front of them. 'There. You see it? Let's get down there. Now.'

*

Olivia screamed as Feramo burst up out of the water, forcing the dagger out of her grip with one hand, grabbing her round the throat with the other. She brought up her leg and kneed him hard in the balls, wriggling free the second he released her throat, swimming away and thinking fast. He had been under longer than her. He should be out of air – she had a good ten minutes' worth left. She could drop thirty feet and lose him.

She started to descend, pulling on the mask, clearing the regulator as she went down, but Feramo lashed out and caught hold of her wrist. She screamed in agony as he twisted the joint. She felt herself blacking out, drifting into welcome unconsciousness. The air was escaping from her buoyancy jacket, the weights were pulling her down, the regulator was yanked out of her mouth. Then, suddenly, there was an almighty clattering and roaring overhead, and bright lights shone into the water. A figure plunged towards her, silhouetted through the ghostly green water. It took hold of her, releasing the weight belt, and pulled her up towards the light.

'Falcon, indeed,' Scott Rich whispered in her ear as they broke the surface, strong hands around her waist. 'You look more like a baby frog.'

Then suddenly Feramo reared up again like a whale in a BBC special, lunging at them with the flimsy dagger.

'Float for a second, baby,' said Scott, as he grabbed Feramo's wrist and knocked him out with a single blow.

Olivia leaned nervously out of the Black Hawk. Scott Rich was still in the water, trying to tie up Feramo, who was slumped in the winch basket, but the rotor wash kept flinging him away.

'Leave him,' Olivia yelled over the radio. 'Come back up. He's unconscious.'

'That's what you thought last time,' came Scott's reply.

Feramo burst up out of the water.

Olivia gripped the edge of the open hatch, scanning the circle of light on the water for predators.

'Here, ma'am,' yelled Dan, the pilot, handing her a pistol. 'If you see a shark, shoot it, but try to avoid Special Officer Rich.'

'Thanks for the tip,' she muttered into the radio.

Suddenly, there was a dull boom back towards the shore and almost immediately a siren started blaring on the instrument panel.

'Jesus! Let's get him up, get him up, up!' yelled Dan as a missile lit up the sky around them.

'Scott!' Olivia yelled, as the sea ahead seemed to explode into a huge fireball, throwing out a blast of air which sent the chopper reeling.

Olivia could hardly breathe, but seconds later Scott's scowling face appeared over the edge of the hatch and the Black Hawk swung upwards, out of reach of the burning sea.

They were heading back to the aircraft carrier. It was steamily hot. Both Scott and Olivia were dripping wet. Neither of them looked at the other. Olivia was wearing only her underwear and a US Navy-issue T-shirt which the pilot had flung at her. She knew that if she leaned her cheek into the warm skin of Scott's neck, or felt his rough, capable hand brush the soft skin of her thigh, she wouldn't be able to control herself.

There was a burst of fire and a series of violent bangs against the airframe. 'Hold on, baby,' said Scott. 'We've taken a hit. Hold on tight.' The stricken helicopter shuddered and seemed to stop in its tracks. Then it lurched horrifyingly and plummeted straight down, throwing them onto the floor. There was a loud metallic bang and a jolt. Scott scrambled towards her, grabbing hold of her as the engine screamed and the pilot struggled to bring the aircraft under control. Ahead,

Olivia saw dark water rushing towards them, then the lighter colour of the sky, and then water again. The pilot was cursing and yelling, 'We gotta eject, we gotta eject!' Scott held her tight, pressing her head into his chest, trying to get them back towards a seat, yelling into his radio above the din, 'OK there Dan, hold steady. We're all right, bring her up, we're going to be fine.' Then, to Olivia, above the roaring and clattering, 'Hold onto me, baby. Whatever happens, just keep holding on as tight as you can.'

Yards from the water, suddenly, miraculously, Dan regained control. They hovered precariously for a few moments, stabilized, then swung upwards again.

'Phew, sorry about that, folks,' said Dan.

In the rush of adrenalin and relief, Olivia raised her head to see Scott Rich's grey eyes looking down at her with immense tenderness. For an astonishing second she thought she saw a tear, then he pulled her to him passionately, his mouth searching for hers, gentle hands sliding up beneath the US Navy T-shirt.

'USS *Condor* at five hundred metres ahead, sir,' said Dan. 'Shall we make the descent?'

'Give her another once around the block, will you?' murmured Scott into the radio.

As Olivia stood on the vast deck of the aircraft carrier, debriefed, showered and fed, taking a last look at the calm water and the star-filled night, Scott Rich appeared through the shadows.

'They found part of Feramo's leg,' he said. 'The sharks got him.'

Olivia said nothing, looking back towards the Suakin shore.

'I'm sorry, baby,' he said gruffly, allowing her the confusion of her feelings. After a few moments, he added, 'Not as sorry as the Administration are, though. And nowhere near as sorry as I am that I didn't get to do the job myself, with my bare hands, or perhaps my teeth, after I'd extracted every last morsel of information from that smooth bastard in the most painful manner possible.'

'Scott!' said Olivia. 'He was a human being too.'

'One day, I'll tell you exactly what sort of human being he was. And what he might have done to you if—'

'Done to me? What do you mean? I wouldn't have let him.'

Scott shook his head. 'They want you to go back to LA, you know that? They need you to help look into his entourage.'

She nodded.

'You going to go or have you had enough?'

'Of course I'm going to go,' she said, adding, as if it was an afterthought, 'Are you?'

55

CIA Safe House, Los Angeles

A solitary hawk gliding silently over Hollywood – above the Kodak Theater, ringed by cables and TV vans; the blaring horns of Sunset; the pre-Oscar parties thronging the turquoise-lit pools of the Standard, the Mondrian and the Château Marmont – towards the darkness and coyote cries of the hills, might have spotted a single lighted window high on a promontory. Behind the glass wall, a slight, fair-haired girl and a man with close-cropped hair were lying in each other's arms among rumpled sheets, lit by the flicker of firelight and CNN.

'Shhh,' said Scott Rich, putting his hand over Olivia's mouth and reaching for the remote, registering amusement at her muffled squeaks of protest as he turned up the volume.

'It was deadly, secret and would have brought the whole world to a standstill. Thwarted plans for a devastating al-Qaeda attack were revealed today by the White House,' said a newscaster, who looked like a swimsuit model. *'The planned operation, on an unprecedented scale, was uncovered and foiled by the CIA.'*

Olivia sat straight up in bed. 'It wasn't the CIA. It was me!' she said indignantly.

The shot cut to a White House spokesman pointing at a map with a little stick:

'Plans were well advanced for simultaneous attacks on key bridges in Manhattan, Washington DC, San Francisco, London, Sydney, Madrid and Barcelona. As bridges blew and panic spread throughout the major cities of the civilized world, a secondary operation to detonate explosives at key traffic intersections would have come into play.'

An excitable academic – captioned HEAD OF TERRORISM STUDIES, UNIVERSITY OF MARYLAND – replaced the man with the map.

'It had all the hallmarks of the al-Qaeda high command: simplicity of concept and audacious left-of-field thought. Within minutes of the news hitting the international media, panic would have spread, causing motorists in already traffic-choked cities to abandon their cars and flee the roadways, generating gridlock on an unprecedented global scale: a grid-lock made up of abandoned vehicles which would have proved a logistical near-impossibility to clear.'

Up popped the president.

'Hour by hour, minute by minute, the men and women of our Intelligence services, step by step, are winning the war on terror. Make no mistake . . .'

He paused with that odd look in his eye, which struck Olivia as that of a nervous stand-up pausing for a laugh.

'. . . the forces of evil who are conspiring in their holes against the mighty civilized world will not prevail.'

'Oh, shut *up*!' Olivia yelled at the screen.

'Hey, baby, relax,' said Scott. 'They all know it was you. But if they put your picture up on the news, there'd be an Olivia Joules jihad. And where would that leave us?'

315

'It's not that. It's that every time he says "civilized world", he converts another five thousand to the anti-arrogance jihad. It's just downright dangerous. If—'

'I know, baby, I *know*. If only they'd listen to you. If only there were more women in charge in the Western and Arab nations then none of this would have happened, and the world would live in peace, joy and freedom. You should have taken Bin Laden out in that cave. Then you could have launched your own presidential campaign with the twenty-five million.'

'I know you don't believe me,' said Olivia darkly, 'but Osama Bin Laden was in that cave. Once they get the water out of the camera, you'll see.'

'You will get something, you know, for Feramo and the other guys. You won't get the full whack because you were an agent. But I think you'll be able to buy as many insanely uncomfortable pairs of shoes as you like.'

She pulled the sheet around her and stared intently at the glittering lurex blanket of the city below. 'Scott?'

'What is it, my falcon, my desert frog?'

'Shut up. I still think they're going to do something else. I think they're going to do something in LA. Soon.'

'I know you do, but you're not going to figure it out by staring strangely into the abyss. You need to sleep. Why don't you rest your head right here and we'll get back on the case tomorrow?'

'But . . .' she began, as he pulled her into the strong, manly muscles of his chest. *I don't need men . . .* she told herself, feeling his strong arm drawing her closer, feeling warm and safe. *Oh fuck it*, she decided, as he rolled on top of her and started to kiss her again.

The safe-house Operations Room was a chaos of computers, wires, communications systems and men in shirtsleeves trying to look world-wearily cool. In the middle of it all Olivia Joules sat motionless, staring intently at her widescreen computer. Kimberley, Michael Monteroso, Melissa the PR, Carol the voice coach, Travis Brancato the out-of-work actor slash writer, Nicholas Kronkheit the unqualified director, Winston the divine black diving instructor, and as many of Feramo's wannabe entourage as could be located had been rounded up and taken to a local CIA interrogation centre, where they were all still in custody. Olivia had spent the last few hours going through the videotaped interrogations, cutting and pasting and scribbling notes. Sensing herself on the brink of a breakthrough, she paused, mind whirring.

'So I got the final take on Suraya.'

Dammit. She looked up with an irritation which was overtaken by lust. Scott Rich was leaning against the door frame, tie loosened, shirt collar undone. She felt like sliding up to him and removing the whole ensemble.

'What?' she said, catching his eye and looking away quickly. They were at that thrilling stage of early shagging when nobody else knows about it. Of course, it was hard to be sure in a CIA safe house, but then they *were* both established masters of subterfuge.

'Suraya Steele has been working for al-Qaeda for ten years.'

'No!' said Olivia. 'Ten *years*?'

'Al-Qaeda enlisted her when she was nineteen. She was hanging out in Paris trying to find modelling work and/or rich men. We don't know exactly who the contact was, but it was someone pretty high up. They gave her a lot of money, I mean a *lot* of money, up front.'

'That explains the Gucci and the Prada.'

'What? She was studying drama and media studies at Lampeter University. The deal was that she would switch her course to Arabic, then try to get into the Foreign Office with

317

a view to MI6. It sounds like naïve bullshit, but evidently it worked. It's sure put the wind up your security services, I can tell you. Every female operative under the age of seventy-five is going to be spending the next three months in intensive interrogation.'

'My God. Heads must be rolling. How could they not have spotted it?'

'Al-Qaeda are smart – no electronic communication, just whispers, winks, dead-drops, pen and paper – old-fashioned direct contact as advocated by Widgett.'

'How's he taking it?'

'He's fine. He was in retirement for most of her operational time. They rumbled her within months of him coming back on side.'

'So she was on a winner either way?'

'If she pulled off something big for al-Qaeda she'd get a new identity and a multi-million-dollar fortune. If she pulled one of them in for MI6, she'd be fêted and promoted. All the agencies were crying out for Arabic speakers. Once she was inside MI6 the cell kept feeding her enough to make her look like an ace spy. They set her up with enough inside info to swing her the Feramo case.'

'Did Feramo know she was working for al-Qaeda?'

'Sure. That's why he hated her.'

'He *did*?'

'They put her onto him because they were afraid he was a loose cannon. She was watching him for her superiors and watching him for his superiors.'

'So it was Suraya who bugged my room.'

'I told you it wasn't me.'

'No wonder she hated my guts.'

'Well, aside from the way you look.'

'That's not why girls hate each other.'

'And the fact that Feramo was hotter for you than her. If you had rumbled Feramo to MI6, it would have made her look incompetent. If you had got too close, Feramo might have rumbled her to you. Once you'd actually blown the whole thing for her by hooking up with Widgett, she couldn't wait to get you out to the Sudan, grass on you and have them bump you off.'

'What will happen to her now?' said Olivia, head on one side, feigning innocence. '*Please* don't tell me she'll be sentenced to fifty years in prison in a badly cut orange jumpsuit with all her hair cut off?'

'Probably a number of hundred-and-fifty-year sentences to run concurrently, if she's lucky and doesn't get shipped off to sample some Cuban cigars. Oh, and by the way, your friend Kate said hello.'

'Kate? Who's seen her?'

'Widgett did. He filled her in. She said to tell you she was very impressed and she wanted to know who the other one was.'

Olivia grinned. Kate meant the other snoggee.

'Excuse me, sir.' A slight, neatly dressed man was hovering in the doorway. Olivia found the reverence with which Scott Rich was treated in Intelligence circles a total turn-on.

'Mr Miller has requested that you see him in the lab immediately, sir, with Agent Joules.'

Olivia jumped to her feet. 'They must have got the photos out,' she said. 'Come on!'

She steamed along the corridor towards the lab, with Scott following, saying, 'OK, baby. You gotta calm down here. Must be cool at all times.'

Olivia burst into the lab, to find it filled with solemn faces. Every senior agency member in the area was gathered to see the proof that Bin Laden had been in the Suakin caves. The bodies of several senior al-Qaeda operatives had been recovered from the collapsed and waterlogged cave network. But not Bin Laden.

'Well done for getting them out of the wet camera,' said Olivia. 'Whoever did it.'

A small girl at the back with curly red hair broke into a grin. 'It was me,' she said.

'Thanks and everything,' said Olivia. 'Really clever.'

'OK, so shall we take a look?' said Scott Rich. 'May I?' He slid into the chair in front of the computer. The technician respectfully pointed out a couple of links, and Scott brought up the first photo.

'OK, what have we here?' It was entirely grey. 'Close-up of part of a whale?' murmured Scott.

'I hadn't got the flash working yet.'

He flicked to the next shot. Half of it was burnt-out white, but you could make out the photograph and diagram of Sydney Harbour Bridge. Olivia tried to remember the sequence of events in the cave. She'd phographed the pictures and then attempted a nice group shot. Then she'd gone for Bin Laden, then lit the fuse on the gas and bolted.

The CIA honchos crowded around the group shot. It was very hard to make anything out. All you could really see through the gloom were beards and turbans.

Scott glanced towards her. 'They'll be able to work on it,' he said encouragingly. 'They'll enhance it. Did you take a close-up of Bin Laden?'

'Yes,' she said. 'I'm pretty sure it's the next one.'

The chatter ceased. All eyes were on the screen. Olivia dug her fingernails into her palms. She had been sure, amidst the confusion and terror in the cave, that she was looking at Bin Laden. It was the demeanour: the sense of latent malevolent power, the intensity behind the languid calm. But then, as

Kate would no doubt remind her, at one point she had been equally sure that Bin Laden was Pierre Feramo.

Scott Rich leaned forward. She forced herself to breathe, watching Scott's weather-worn hand reach for the mouse and click. At first the image was hard to make out. Then it became clear. It was grubby white fabric, stretched across a pair of knees.

'Right,' said Scott Rich. 'It appears we have a shot of Bin Laden's crotch.'

56

Olivia was back on the computer within minutes, working off her fury and embarrassment, ploughing through the snatches of interviews she had bookmarked and the sections of transcript she had cut and pasted together. Then suddenly it was as if the sheer energy of her rage burst through the clouds of over-information and false leads like a shaft of light.

She leaned round the corner of the desk. 'Scott,' she hissed, 'come over here.'

'It's the Oscars,' she said, as he leaned on the desk beside her, so close that she almost put her hand on his thigh out of lust and newly acquired habit.

'I know it's the Oscars. Do you want to watch the show?'

'No, I mean they're going to *hit* the Oscars. That was what Feramo was planning; that's why he lured the wannabes. He hated Hollywood. It's the essence of everything his people despise about the West. The entertainment industry is predominantly Jewish-run. The Oscars is the—'

Scott rubbed his hand wearily across his forehead. 'I know, baby, but we've been through this,' he said softly. 'The Oscars would be the most incredible, obvious, fabulous symbolic target for al-Qaeda. Which means – with the possible exception of the White House or George W. Bush himself – the ceremony is also the best defended and most impossible to hit of all the potential targets in the Western world at this moment in time. The whole area from the sewers below to the airspace above is cleared and monitored. The full might of the FBI, the CIA, the LAPD and every high- and low-tech surveillance device on the planet and above is focused on the Kodak Theater. Any of those people will tell you: al-Qaeda are not going to hit the Academy Awards today.'

'Listen to this,' said Olivia, clicking on the screen. 'Michael Monteroso – you remember? The facial technician? He was backstage at the Oscars last year, performing his insane one-minute microdermabrasic non-surgical facial lifts to buff up the presenters before they went on. He would have been doing it again this year if he wasn't in custody. Melissa from Century PR worked on the PR team for the Academy Awards production office for three years before moving to Century. Nicholas Kronkheit, you remember? The director with no experience on *Boundaries of Arizona*?'

'Sure, but—'

'His father has been on the board of the Academy for twenty years.'

'These kids are trying to make it in Hollywood. Of course they're going to have – or try to have – some connection with the Academy.'

'Feramo had tapes of the Academy Awards at the lodge in Honduras.'

Scott Rich stopped talking. The sudden seriousness of his reaction made fear flutter up in her stomach.

'Can we warn them?' she said. 'Can we stop the show?'

'No. We don't get to stop the Academy Awards on a hunch from an operative. Go on. How do all these fit together?'

'They don't. That's the point. That's the mistake we've been making. I think Feramo was targeting the Oscars, but didn't have a plan. All these wannabes had a connection, and he was using them to find out how it works.'

He watched her with that familiar expression she loved, leaning forward, hands clasped against his mouth, focused, intent.

'Kimberley, you remember Kimberley?' she said.

'Oh. My. God. Oh *yeah*.'

'Shut up. Her father has done the follow spot at the Oscars for twenty-five years. If she wasn't in custody, this would have been her seventh year as a seat-filler.'

'Seat-fillers? Those are the guys who sit in when the stars go to the bathroom?'

She nodded. He looked at her carefully for a moment then picked up the phone. 'Scott Rich here, this is urgent. Get me a complete list of the seat-fillers at the Academy Awards this year ... I mean *urgent* urgent. Plus a list of all backstage passes issued this year.'

'Can we get in there?' she said, glancing at her watch and looking anxiously out of the big plate-glass window at the city below.

'Honey,' said Scott, 'the way the Chiefs of Staff feel about you at this moment, you could take the Best Supporting Actress award if you asked for it. What time does it start?'

'Half an hour ago.'

57

Los Angeles had been gearing up for the Academy Awards like London gears up for Christmas, although with rather less drunkenness. The windows of Neiman's, Saks and Barney's were dressed with evening gowns and Oscar statuettes. The front lawns of *le tout* Beverly Hills were covered with marquees. Publicists, agents, party planners, stylists, florists, caterers, facialists, trainers, hair and make-up artists, valet-parking organizers – all were in various stages of meltdown. Bitter phone calls had been exchanged over whether Gwyneth or Nicole had first call on the Valentino with the boxy pleats. In the Hermitage Hotel on Burton Way, the suites on two entire floors were converted into designer showrooms where any actress with the flimsiest claim to a red-carpet snap could wander in and help herself. The office in charge of the *Vanity Fair* post-Oscar party was in crisis, deluged by angry calls from agents and publicists. Charts on the walls showed a fluctuating schedule of what time each guest was allowed to arrive – the B-list arriving just before midnight, the C-list arriving before dawn next morning.

The Oscar race had been the traditional inter-studio contest of marketing budgets, newspaper ads, screenings, lunches and media bombardment. The lead contenders had emerged as follows:

1. *Insider Trade!*, a musical set on Wall Street during the boom of the 1980s, in which the heroine, a commodity trader who longs to be a dancer, spends most of the action asleep at her desk, dreaming about dancing with other commodity traders, the said dreams being shared on cue with the breathless movie-goers.
2. The story of Moses, starring Russell Crowe in a big white beard and a nightie.
3. A Tim Burton movie called *Jack Tar Bush Land* about mini-humans whose bodies are on top of their heads and who live underground in woodland areas.
4. *Existential Despair*, in which five different characters confront their own mortality during the period of one lunch hour in an upscale retailer.
5. *East Meets West*, a comedy-drama with a message, featuring Anthony Hopkins as Chairman Mao, who, through an ancient curse, switches bodies with a young Los Angeles student during the Cultural Revolution.

Some of the other notables contenders included:

- A film about the early Amish, which nobody had seen but was a cert for cinematography because the director of photography had just died.
- An adaptation of a book about Oscar Wilde, which was in the running for special effects for the scene in which Oscar Wilde bursts in his Paris hotel room, although that bit wasn't actually in the book, and the author was furious about it.
- Kevin Costner's comeback playing a man having a midlife crisis who, over a period of three and a half hours, lumbers towards the realization that he actually really loves his wife.

The atmosphere in the Kodak Theater moved from brittle nervousness at the start to restlessness as the minor awards went on and on, and too many wives, lawyers and agents were thanked. By the time Scott and Olivia arrived at the theatre, the show had been under way for nearly two hours. The stars were returning from the bar, the seat-fillers were being replaced by the real celebrities and tension was mounting for the big ones.

Scott and Olivia slipped quietly into the auditorium, standing in the shadows of a door stage-right, a few feet from the podium. Olivia tried to keep her composure in the face of such a spectacle. The whole of the entertainment industry's elite was before them: actors, directors, producers, writers, agents, executives were all gathered under one roof in a glittering display of self-congratulation. The front rows were filled with some of the most beautiful, recognizable faces on the planet.

As Olivia scanned the audience, Scott Rich watched her without seeming to watch, as only a secret agent can. Her face was silhouetted in the red light and had that familiar look of earnest determination. The long, shimmering dress that had been hurriedly provided clung to her form in a way which made him ache. She was wearing an insane auburn wig which made even Scott Rich want to smile. Her hands were clenched tighly around a smart leather clutch bag which, he happened to know, contained the following:

CIA ID
chloroform pad
syringe containing nerve relaxant
syringe containing instant sedative
stun gas pellet
mini-spyglass
tiny cellphone
and, of course, a hat pin

What Scott didn't know, because he was a man, and a man whose skills lay more in his powers of logical deduction and technical brilliance than in his intuition, was that Olivia was almost overwhelmed by fear. She was more scared than she had ever been in Honduras, Cairo or the Sudan. She had the awful feeling that there was about to be a catastrophe over which she had no control. She was here, at the epicentre of where it was going to happen, and she didn't know what it was, where it would come from or how to stop it.

She checked the faces in the auditorium, row by row. If she saw one face – one actress, one girlfriend, one security guard, one seat-filler, one usher – she recognized from Feramo's crew, she would know. She would have them arrested and interrogated while there was still time.

Helena Bonham Carter was taking the microphone. 'There are those who have argued that the nomination for Best Supporting Actor in *Moses* should have gone to the burning bush,' she began. There was a roar of laughter. The audience was excited, ready to laugh. Shots of the five supporting-actor nominees appeared onscreen in various poses of ferocious staring, weak smiles or studied nonchalance. The shot cut to one of them dangling from a helicopter above a choppy ocean, swinging to and fro, waving his legs wildly.

'If he carries on wriggling like that, the chopper'll be in the water,' muttered Scott. Olivia had a flashback to her rescue from the Red Sea: the noise of the Black Hawk above the surface, the lights turning the water green, Scott's silhouette plunging towards her, kicking Feramo away, grabbing her, hauling her up to the surface and the unexpected warmth of the tropical night, then him knocking Feramo out and winching her to safety.

As the tearful actor ran up the stairs, putting his hands to his heart then out to the audience, Olivia wanted to point at Scott Rich and shout, 'It should have been him, not you! He does it for real!' Then she imagined Scott attempting a sobbingly grateful 'without whom none of this would have been possible' speech, and Widgett arriving for his lifetime-achievement-in-heroic-deeds-of-espionage award, posing for the camera, arms and scarves flapping everywhere, and she wanted to burst out laughing.

The tearful actor held the Oscar above his head in a triumphant salute, and she saw the bottom of the plinth with the gold shape behind it, and suddenly nothing was funny about the situation any more because she knew exactly where she had seen the same image from the same angle before. It was in the al-Qaeda cave beneath Suakin: the plinth lying on its side, the jagged layers of gold-plated metal behind it, hollowed out like a chocolate Santa or Easter bunny.

'Scott,' she said, grabbing his arm. 'It's the Oscars.'

He patted her reassuringly. 'That's right, dear, yes, it's the Oscars.'

'No,' she hissed. 'The statuettes. They've doctored the Oscars. The Oscars are the bombs.'

58

Scott Rich neither changed his expression nor took his eyes off the audience. He simply drew Olivia into the shadows of the doorway and whispered, 'How do you know? Tell me quietly.'

'It was in the cave. They had an Oscar cut in half, hollow in the middle.'

'You're sure?'

'Well, it was kind of hard to see, but ... I'm pretty sure. And in Catalina he showed me an Oscar he'd bought off eBay.'

'Oh Jesus,' said Scott, scanning the audience, where the gold statuettes were scattered, cradled lovingly in the arms of the winners. 'How many are out there already? Fifteen? Twenty? Oh Jesus.'

He pushed Olivia through the door ahead of him and started walking fast along the corridor, taking his cellphone out, thinking aloud as Olivia tried to keep up.

'It has to be C4. It's the only explosive that's stable enough. A pound of C4 in each one and a timer sealed inside some sort of metal alloy. They must have switched the load at some point. They probably wouldn't even run the dogs over the statuettes. Even if they did, depending on when they put the stuff in there, they might not have picked it up.

Hello? Is that Central Control? Scott Rich, CIA. Give me the head of Law Enforcement. This is very urgent.'

With Olivia following, he headed out of the building, walking fast, the wrong way down the red carpet, flashing his ID. 'Hello?' he said. 'Tom. Scott Rich here. We have a tip-off. This is a secure line, right? OK, get this: the Oscars have been doctored. They're devices. IEDs. They're bombs.' There was a second's pause on the other end. Then Olivia heard the voice begin again. 'I know. We have the agent here,' Scott said. 'She remembers seeing a doctored statuette in the al-Qaeda hideout in Sudan. What? Yes, I know, I know. But what do we do?'

As they hurried along, Olivia's mind was working very fast. She suddenly interrupted him. 'Who're you talking to?' she whispered. 'Ask him the name of the company that transports the Oscars.'

A few seconds later the reply came back.

'Carrysure.'

'Carrysure! That was the company Travis Brancato worked for! You remember? The flaky actor slash writer slash lifestyle manager with the wolf eyes? The one who wrote the script? He was a driver for them when he wasn't writing.'

Scott blinked at her for a moment, holding the phone away from his ear. 'OK, Olivia, call the office,' he said. 'Tell them what you know and get them onto him in the interrogations unit.' Then back into the phone, 'Tom, OK, this lead is firming up. We need to move. Yeah, we're heading out towards you now. I can see the van, we'll be with you in two minutes.'

'Shouldn't they just stop the show and get everyone out?' Olivia said, glancing at her watch as she waited to be connected: twenty-eight minutes to go until the end of the scheduled broadcast.

Scott shook his head and scowled, still talking. Olivia's

connection came through, and she filled them in and told them to get onto the interrogation centre and grill Travis Brancato, adding a few helpful hints on how to get him to talk.

They were approaching the big white van of the Command Post. Scott clicked off his cell and looked at Olivia. 'OK, baby. This is not going to be pretty. You want to get out of here and go home?'

'No.'

'Good. So get back in there,' he said, nodding at the auditorium. 'If the statuettes are on timers, you can bet there'll be a very nervous al-Qaeda operative in the auditorium with a device which can override the timers and detonate the bombs. It's probably a cellphone or a very, very big watch. If he sees any attempt to stop the show, get the Oscars out or evacuate the theatre, his orders will probably be to blow the lot there and then, including himself. Just carry on looking for anyone you recognize from Feramo's entourage or anyone behaving suspiciously.They're going to be sweating, probably high on something, certainly very scared, like "Shit-I'm-about-to-die" very scared. Should stand out among a bunch of actors playing gracious in defeat.'

'Unless it *is* an actor.'

'Just get on with it,' he said, heading into the van. 'Oh, one more thing. When would you blow it, if you were them?'

'Best Picture?' she said. 'Just before the end.'

He looked at his watch. 'We have maybe twenty-five minutes.'

Inside the theatre, Olivia was silently repeating her mantra: *Don't panic, stop, breathe, think*; *don't panic, stop, breathe, think*, in a breathless, panicky fashion. She walked down the side of the auditorium, scanning the rows one by one, praying to whatever divine force was up there: *Please, please, whatever you are . . . just help me out one more time, then I won't ask you again, I promise.* She was conscious of a subtle increase in the security presence, people slipping through side doors, taking positions against the walls. Here and there among the audience, she could see the glint of the golden awards, each a ticking time bomb, cradled against a sequined bosom or passed admiringly from one celebrity to another.

Anthony Minghella was opening the envelope for Best Director.

'And the winner is, Tim Burton for *Jack Tar Bush Land*.'

Olivia spotted Burton as he rose to his feet, fringe flopping over his thick blue-tinted glasses as he made his way along the row. She headed swiftly down the aisle towards him, ignoring the odd glances, threw her arms round him as if she'd been his agent for fifteen years, flashed her ID and whispered: 'CIA. Major problem. Please keep talking as long as you can.'

He caught her eye, saw how scared she was and nodded. 'Thanks,' she whispered. 'Make it a long list.'

A shudder went through the crowds on Hollywood Boulevard as the white SUVs of the LAPD bomb squad raced the two blocks between the Command Post and the theatre. The Oscars still remaining backstage were being replaced. Guest lists, staff lists and plus-one lists were being scrutinized for clues. Officers were poised to remove the Oscars from the winners in the audience as discreetly as possible, as soon as the word came. But inside the Command Post there was silent pandemonium as the heads of the LAPD, the Fire Service, the FBI, the security firms and Scott Rich debated an impossible series of incalculable risks and decisions.

An attempt, however low-key, to extricate the Oscars from the clutches of their recipients, might trigger an operative to detonate them. Stopping the ceremony might do the same.

And in any case, evacuating an audience of three and a half thousand could take the best part of an hour. To send the full might of the emergency services hurtling to the scene would generate equal panic, a panic which would surely, inevitably, seep into the auditorium, into the consciousness of whoever it was who had his finger on that override button. Someone suggested gas.

'Yeah, that went great in Moscow,' murmured Scott.

'We'd have three dozen of the world's most famous celebrities choking on their tongues,' said the man from the FBI.

And so the ceremony was proceeding. With twenty minutes to go, there were eighteen metal bombs spread around the auditorium, which could blow the Academy Awards sky high with the whole world watching. But as far as anyone knew, it could all just be a figment of Olivia Joules's overactive imagination.

On stage, Tim Burton was giving the performance of a lifetime. 'What can you say about an assistant cinematographer who also makes a great pot of camomile tea, and I don't mean with tea bags . . .'

At the CIA special interrogations unit, Travis Brancato's formerly stunning ice-blue, wolf-like eyes were more like those of a drunk who has been on a four-day bender. His hair was wild, his chin against his chest. The interrogator's hand was poised to strike again, but he was getting nowhere. A woman appeared in the room and handed him a note – it was Olivia's suggestion for getting Travis to talk. The interrogator paused to read it, then leaned over to Brancato's ear.

'The head of every Hollywood studio is at that ceremony. You come up with the goods, you've saved the day. You don't, you'll never work in this town again.'

Brancato's head jerked up, alert. 'I didn't do anything,' he gabbled. 'All I did was leave the van unlocked for twenty minutes at a rest stop. That's all I did, man. I thought Feramo just wanted an Oscar for himself.'

Back on stage, an increasingly desperate-looking Burton was doing his best. 'Well, look at the time!' The audience was becoming restless, but he ploughed gamely on.

'But seriously,' he said, 'how many of us *do* stop to *really* look at the time? I hope my accountant Marty Reiss does, because I gather he works by the hour . . .'

As Scott Rich strode through the backstage area, a man hurtled past him with four Oscars in his arms. He was wearing a T-shirt which said IF YOU SEE ME RUNNING, TRY TO KEEP UP. Scott did as it said and was joined by a man carrying more Oscars, this one in full protection gear: a dark green, eighty-pound suit lined with bulky, ceramic, blast-proof plates and an air-cooled mask. They hurried out of the back of the building, where the area around the white bomb squad SUVs was cordoned off.

'Joe,' Scott shouted, seeing a seasoned, wise-looking man with greying hair and glasses. 'You run one through yet?' It was Joe Perros, a bomb-squad veteran of twenty-two years, now its head.

'Yup,' said Joe grimly. 'There's a pound of C4 in there with a Casio timer. We're just gearing up to open it by remote.'

'You going to take the rest away or blow 'em here?' said Scott. 'If they hear that lot go up inside the auditorium . . .'

'Yeah, that's the pucker factor,' said Joe. 'But as luck would have it, we brought a TCV.'

He pointed to a five-foot steel ball, which the techs were draping in bomb blankets in the back of one of the vans.

'We blow half a dozen in there, the audience won't know a thing.'

'You got a team inside to work on the overrider?' Scott said, nodding back towards the auditorium.

'What do you think?'

'Great. I'm going inside,' said Scott. 'Call me with the bad news when you get to the timer.'

Tim Burton had moved on to influences from his past. 'None of this would have been possible without my cousin Neil, who let me play with his painting-by-numbers in the school holidays. Thanks, Neil, this is for you. And finally, my first art teacher, a white-haired lady with the soul of Picasso. What the hell was her name? Mrs Something . . . Lankoda? Swaboda? Hang on, I'll get it in a minute . . .'

Olivia, lurking in the shadows of a doorway and sporting her newly borrowed seat-filler pass, was using the miniature spyglass to scan the upper levels of the balcony. There was no one she recognized. No one was behaving more oddly than was normal for an Oscar ceremony. The music started up. She saw the relief on Burton's face as he stumbled desperately towards the wings and, at his glance, flashed him a huge thumbs-up.

Stars were pouring back into their seats during the applause. Olivia watched the woman in charge of the seat-fillers shepherding her charges into the key gaps. They had less than fifteen minutes left now. As Bill Murray made his entrance to present the Best Actresss award, all eyes turned to the stage, and she saw a security guard bend towards an Oscar winner in the stage-left aisle. The order must have been given to get them out. Olivia did one last despairing sweep of the centre stalls – and there! There was a face she recognized, a blonde girl with big hair, heavy lip-liner and pneumatic breasts bursting out of a skimpy silver dress. It was Demi,

Kimberley's ex-best friend from the party in Miami. She was taking her seat in the middle of the stalls, a seat-filler's ID pass hanging round her neck, sitting down next to a dark-haired boy. Olivia recognized the boy – he had stumbled out of the cloakroom with Demi, all dishevelled, as she was leaving Feramo's penthouse in Miami. He was sweating. His eyes were darting wildly round the room. He had seen the security guard disappear with an Oscar, and his right hand was hovering nervously over his left wrist. Olivia dialled quickly and whispered into her cellphone, 'Scott, I think I've got him. Stage-right stalls, ten rows back, on the right of Raquel Welch.' She started moving up the aisle towards the boy and Demi, blood pounding in her ears.

Just then Brad Pitt appeared through the side door ahead and leaned against the wall, cool as fuck. Brad Pitt! Great. Olivia clocked his look of mild surprise as she approached. She flashed her new CIA ID and drew him back into the shadows of the doorway.

'We need you to do what I say,' she whispered. 'Just do whatever I say.'

He met her eye reassuringly. 'The girl in the silver dress,' she whispered, standing on tiptoes to reach his ear. 'Blonde hair in a bun thing, two to the right of Raquel Welch. You got her? Get her to leave her seat and go outside with you.'

'You got it.' He gave a delicious, sexy smirk and set off towards Demi. Olivia watched him play the moment like a pro. She watched Demi's head turn, as if drawn by Brad Pitt-vibes, saw him giving her a look and a nod. Demi's hand fluttered to her throat, disbelieving, then she got up, making her way along the row towards him. Olivia saw the dark-haired boy look round in a panic, and then back to the stage, where Bill Murray was giving the longest preamble to the Best Actress nominations in the history of the Academy Awards.

'Olivia?' Two men in dark uniforms appeared behind her. 'LAPD bomb squad. Where is he?'

She nodded towards the boy.

'OK. Separate him and the detonator before he knows about it. We're right behind you.'

There were murderous looks and shushes as Olivia pushed her way along the row, holding up her seat-filler pass, head down, making for the empty seat next to the boy, praying he wouldn't recognize her. She saw the bulge under his left sleeve, and the way his other hand kept moving towards it, covering it, as if protecting it. She had the chloroform pad concealed in her hand. She sat down, saw his face turn towards hers with a look of vague recognition, sweat dribbling down his temples. She gazed into his eyes and gave him her most dazzling smile, slipping her right hand onto his thigh as she did so. With one movement she covered his wrist and shoved the chloroform pad over his mouth, pulling the hand with the watch under her body, out of reach of his other arm, seeing his panicked eyes, hoping to God she was right. There was a commotion: heads turning, unbriefed security rushing towards them.

'Hold his other arm! Hold it! CIA,' she hissed to Raquel Welch as she held the pad closer over his nose and mouth, feeling the boy's struggles begin to subside.

Raquel Welch grabbed the boy's free arm, shoved it under her famous bottom and sat on it. It was so great working with an actress who could take direction.

'Hold this,' Olivia said, giving the arm with the watch on it to the startled man on her other side, whom, she later discovered, was a senior executive at DreamWorks. 'He's a terrorist. Don't let go.'

As the startled man gripped the boy's arm and up on stage the Best Actress finally got to find out who she was, Olivia pushed back his sleeve and wrested the watch off the now-limp wrist. A bomb-squad officer was halfway along the row, treading on people, pushing towards her. She reached out, handed him the watch, took her phone out and said, 'Scott. He's out cold. The watch is with the bomb squad. We can clear the auditorium.'

The danger of an override detonation was gone, but seventeen statuettes were still ticking away in the audience, primed to blow before the end of the show. They somehow had to get them out without starting a panic. Olivia saw officers appearing from the aisles and doorways and seats within the audience, attempting to collect the Oscars. Already it wasn't going well. The winner of the Best Foreign Language Film award, a lanky figure with a drooping moustache and striped bow tie, was refusing to hand his over, generating an unseemly tussle with a senior member of the Fire Department.

Out in the foyer, the area around the gentlemen's restrooms was cordoned off. Officers were ushering any remaining stray guests out into the street. An Englishman in a dinner jacket was arguing with a security guard who was refusing to let him back into the hall. 'But I'm nominated for Best Picture. My category's up next. I only came out to practise my speech in the bathroom.'

'Sir, if I told you what was happening in there, you'd be straight back into that bathroom.'

'I can't believe you're being so obtuse. What is your name and staff number?'

Two men in blast protection suits with BOMB SQUAD written on the back thudded at speed through the foyer, each clasping half a dozen Oscars in their arms. They dived into the men's restroom.

'You still wanna go back in there?' said the officer.

'Er, no, actually, no,' said the Englishman, 'no,' and he ran for his life out of the exit and down the red carpet. There were sounds of panic from the auditorium. Another bomb-squad tech appeared with two Oscars and ran for the restroom. 'Only one unaccounted for,' he yelled.

On stage, Meryl Streep was following orders, trying to surmount the rising pandemonium and keep the show running. 'And the winner of this year's Best Picture award is . . .' she said, drawing the card out of the envelope, '*Existential Despair*.'

Just then, a burly uniformed figure strode on stage and held up his hand for calm. 'Ladies and gentlemen,' he said, but no one could hear above the uproar. As Meryl Streep helpfully gestured the police chief closer to the microphone, an enormously wide man, the executive producer of both *Existential Despair* and the Wall Street musical, lumbered onto the podium, followed by the two men who had actually produced the movie. As he put himself between the police chief and Meryl Streep, lunging at the replacement statuette, Scott Rich appeared on stage scowling, marched up to the large producer and punched him full on the jaw. At which the other two men laughed. 'I've been wanting to do that for years,' one of them said rather loudly into the microphone.

'People,' Scott Rich said, taking the microphone. 'PEOPLE,' he bellowed. For a moment there was total silence.

'Scott Rich, CIA. We had a serious situation. It is under control. Whether it stays under control depends on you and whether you behave like adults. The world is watching. You need to leave the theatre by the front exits only: that's here, and the first balcony here, and the next two balconies here. You need to move calmly, you need to follow instructions and you need to move fast. OK, people. Over to you.'

*

As the audience filed out of the theatre, the combined security forces were frantically scouring the building. Seventeen Oscars were buried under blast plates and blankets in the gentlemen's restrooms, the surrounding area cleared. There were two minutes to go until the timers were set to blow, and one remaining Oscar was unaccounted for. The recipient, a thin, worried-looking girl who'd won the award for her role as Best Supporting Actress in the Chairman Mao film, was nowhere to be found. The crowds were still streaming out in a reasonably ordered fashion; only the security forces were aware of the bomb that might still be lurking in their midst.

Olivia stood flat against the wall, concentrating hard, then suddenly it came to her. She dialled her cellphone. 'Scott,' she said, 'I bet I know where she is. No one's seen her since she went backstage. I bet she's throwing up.'

'OK, I'm on it,' came Scott's voice. There was the sound of hurrying footsteps for a few moments. She glanced, terrified, at her watch again. 'OK. Now listen to me, Olivia. I'm right there. I see her; I'll get her out. I'll deal with it. There's nothing you can do. We have one minute left. Get out of the theatre. Now. I love you. Bye.'

'Scott!' she yelled. 'Scott!' But the line was dead.

She looked desperately around and started heading for the stage, trying to keep to the outside of the crowd as if it was a current – sticking to the edges where it was less strong, so she could move more easily. But as she moved forward, a huge rumbling roar began from the foyer, the ground beneath them shook, and the walls seemed to bend outwards. There were screams and panic and a smell of acrid smoke – like fireworks only more acidic – and then more explosions followed immediately by another blast ahead, from backstage.

Olivia jabbed frantically at her phone. 'Scott!' she yelled

desperately. 'Scott!' But it just rang and rang as the crowd started to scramble and surge in all directions. Olivia pressed herself against the wall and stood perfectly still in the middle of it, wide-eyed, watching. Slowly, she began to realize that it was all right. The bomb squad had done the job with the bombs in the restroom. The walls were still standing, the blast had not penetrated the auditorium, there was no shrapnel, no blood, no bodies. No one seemed to be hurt. Except for the one man she loved.

She dialled the number again. It rang and rang and rang. She sank down on the floor miserably, one big tear starting to roll down her cheek, then suddenly someone picked up.

'Scott?' she said, nearly swallowing the phone in her eagerness.

'No, ma'am, this ain't Scott, but he's right here.'

'He *is*? Is he all right?'

There was a silence. 'Yes, ma'am. I guess you could say he's looking a little dirty, but he seems to be all in one piece. He managed to get the Oscar right down into the lavatory bowl with a bunch of drapes on top, and he and the young lady almost got themselves under the bomb-squad van. Oh, ma'am, he wants to speak to you.' She waited, gulping, sniffing, rubbing her face.

'Is that you?' he said gruffly. 'I told you not to call me at work.'

'Can't trust you anywhere,' she said, smiling and wiping away tears at the same time. 'You just can't keep your hands off models and actresses, can you?'

59

Maui, Hawaiian Islands

As the air ambulance came in to land over the tropical waters of Maui, Olivia's mobile rang. She released her hand from Scott's for a second and pressed the button.

'Olivia?'

'Yes?'

'It's Barry Wilkinson here. Listen. Can you do us a piece? You were there, weren't you? The Oscars and the Sudan. We want a full I-was-there exclusive – front of the main section, whole of the News Review – and a piece for the daily, if you can run something off by eight o'clock. Just a few hundred words and some quotes. Olivia?'

'I don't know what you're talking about,' she said. Because if there was one thing she knew, it was that she didn't want her face on the front of any newspaper. She was probably going to have to live in disguise for the rest of her life as it was.

'Listen, lovey, I know. I know about MI6. I know you went to the Sudan, because *Elan* told me. I know you were at the Oscars because I saw you on camera in a red wig. And—'

She held the phone away from her ear, glanced out of the

window at where the plane was coming in to land over a curve of sparkling sea, palm trees and white sand, grinned gleefully at Scott Rich, put the phone squawking with Barry's irate voice back to her ear and said, 'Oh don't be silly, lovey. It's just a figment of your overactive imagination.'

MORE PHENOMENAL PRAISE FOR BILL SCHUTT AND J. R. FINCH'S R. J. MacCREADY NOVELS

The Himalayan Codex

"I reviewed [*Hell's Gate*] and compared it favorably to Michael Crichton's science-infused thrillers. This great sequel is more like Jules Verne's *Journey to the Center of the Earth* . . . There is a fantastic line in the book—'the strangest band of travelers since *The Wizard of Oz*.' Readers will find to their fascination that the description is completely accurate. Highly readable and great fun!"

—*The Historical Novels Review*

"While *Hell's Gate* was a brilliant start to this terrific new series, Schutt and Finch top themselves with this nerve-wracking, heart-thumping thriller that is perfect for fans of Michael Crichton and James Rollins."

—The Real Book Spy

"James Rollins and Steve Berry fans who relish a heaping dose of scientific and historical intrigue in their thrillers will find plenty of both here."

—*Library Journal*

Hell's Gate

"Scientifically accurate, and chillingly real; Schutt and Finch amplify the many perils that come with any expedition into the unknown. I dashed through this book—cover to cover—with white-knuckle fear of what might be lurking on the next page . . . Brace yourself, this is no ordinary thriller."

—Darrin Lunde, author of *The Naturalist*

"A World War II thriller with plenty of action and suspense in a most unusual setting. Just think Indiana Jones. For that matter, this yarn evokes more than a few reminders of Stephen King, Joseph Conrad, and Bram Stoker's *Dracula* . . . Fast-moving fun for thriller readers who enjoy a bit of horror and seeing bad guys get what's coming to them."

—*Kirkus Reviews* (starred review)

"The authors adeptly balance science and suspense, and a detailed afterword lays out how much of the story line is based in history. Michael Crichton fans will be pleased that the ending leaves room for a sequel."

—*Publishers Weekly* (starred review)

THE
HIMALAYAN
CODEX

Also by Bill Schutt and J. R. Finch

HELL'S GATE

By Bill Schutt

DARK BANQUET: BLOOD AND THE CURIOUS LIVES
OF BLOOD-FEEDING CREATURES
CANNIBALISM: A PERFECTLY NATURAL HISTORY

The
Himalayan
Codex

An R. J. MacCready Novel

BILL SCHUTT &
J. R. FINCH

wm

WILLIAM MORROW
An Imprint of HarperCollins*Publishers*

Excerpt from *The Darwin Strain* copyright © 2019 by Bakk Bone, LLC.

THE HIMALAYAN CODEX. Copyright © 2017 by Bakk Bone, LLC. All rights reserved. Printed in the United States of America. No part of this book may be used or reproduced in any manner whatsoever without written permission except in the case of brief quotations embodied in critical articles and reviews. For information, address HarperCollins Publishers, 195 Broadway, New York, NY 10007.

First William Morrow premium printing: February 2018
First William Morrow hardcover printing: June 2017

Print Edition ISBN: 978-0-06-241256-0
Digital Edition ISBN: 978-0-06-241257-7

Cover design by Richard L. Aquan
Cover artwork: © Shutterstock (mountains, DNA and background);
courtesy of Smithsonian Design Museum (engraving)
Photograph of Tibet by HelloRF Zcool/Shutterstock, Inc.
Chapter illustrations courtesy of Patricia J. Wynne

William Morrow and HarperCollins are registered trademarks of HarperCollins Publishers in the United States of America and other countries.

17 18 19 20 21 QGM 10 9 8 7 6 5 4 3 2 1

For our mentors.

To every man is given the key to heaven. The same key opens the gates to hell.

—A Buddhist proverb, approximately A.D. 700

In these matters the only certainty is that nothing is certain.

—Pliny the Elder

On the Shelf

1,500 feet above the East Himalayan Labyrinth
July 9, 1946

I hate fog," the helicopter pilot announced over his headset.

"I thought it was flies you hated?" answered a woman seated behind him.

"Yeah, I hate flies, too. But—"

The Sikorsky R-5 gave a sudden lurch in the wind and the pilot concentrated on steadying the cyclic stick in his right hand. He could feel the 450-horsepower Pratt & Whitney struggling to generate lift. "—but thin air is quickly movin' up my shit list. You see anything like flat ground?"

"No dice," said Yanni Thorne. "Still lookin'."

Behind a pair of polarized aviator glasses, the passenger on the woman's right side remained silent. He was also scanning the uncharted, mist-covered valley below.

"Jerry?"

"Bupkes, Mac."

"Swell," the pilot replied. "I *did* mention the potential for a high-pucker-factor landing, didn't I?"

The passengers quickly exchanged glances and head shakes.

"Not in the last two minutes there, Redunzle." Yanni continued to scan the mountainous terrain for a landing site free of fog or driving snow.

She was intense and insightful, two of Mac's favorite qualities. She was also an indigenous Brazilian with an incongruous Brooklyn accent that she'd picked up from her late husband, Bob. Much had happened to them in and around the plateau of Hell's Gate, most of which their passenger knew nothing about; yet the bottom line was that a lot of people died back in Brazil—including Bob.

But Mac and Yanni did not die, and after two years it was an outcome that still haunted them both.

The chopper's second passenger was Lieutenant Jerry Delarosa, a polymath, currently serving in the U.S. Army Special Forces. He and MacCready had last worked together three years earlier, during a South Pacific "suicide mission" to retrieve a kid with powerful East Coast connections whose torpedo boat was missing in action. The fearlessness and drive he had shown on that mission convinced Mac he would be a real asset to this team.

Presently, Yanni was pointing to something out the port-side window of the chopper's cramped cabin. "Mac, I think I see a place to land but it ain't on the valley floor. Three o'clock and down about five hundred feet." During the space of only a few seconds, sheets of wind-driven snow had begun dissipating in the direction Yanni was pointing.

Mac increased the pressure on the right tail-rotor pedal and a moment later the chopper responded by swinging its nose to that side. There *was* something—a shelf carved into a lower section of a cliff face twice the height of the Washington Monument. He feathered the cyclic control stick forward with his right hand, adjusting the pitch angle of the rotor blades. In response the R-5 struggled forward through the high-altitude air.

Mac swung into a satisfyingly incident-free flyby over the patch of flat, snow-covered ground. *So far, so good.*

The site they had chosen for landing was not quite three hundred feet long and extended into the mountain almost half as far.

"That's a pinnacle approach in a confined landing zone," Mac announced.

"English, please," Yanni said.

"A double bitch of a landing in these crosswinds."

Yanni nodded. "Check."

"Plus that shelf's not completely smooth," Mac continued, pointing to a pattern of elongated ridges where the snow seemed to be piled up higher. "Problem's going to be snow blowing up from the rotors and screwing up my visibility."

"What do you suggest?" Jerry asked.

"Switch seats with Yanni. You're gonna have to

put on a monkey belt and hang out that door a little bit."

"Hang out that what?" came the headset-distorted cry.

"Right before we land, I won't be able to see squat, so I'll need you to tell me when the wheels get close to the ground."

"You mean sit there with the door open?"

"Well, actually more like leaning. But—"

"I'm not switching seats with anybody," Yanni announced, cutting into the conversation. "Where's this so-called monkey belt?"

"Yanni—"

"Save it, Mac," she said.

MacCready knew that there was no time to argue, and that he'd never win this argument anyway. "It's tucked in behind your seat—pretty self-explanatory. The other end attaches to that hard point."

Yanni shot him a look. "*English*."

"To that metal *hook* to the left of your seat."

Less than two minutes later, Yanni was strapped into the canvas harness. From the moment she slid the side door open, the safety cable and clamp would become her only firm connection to the helicopter. Jerry double-checked the monkey belt and gave her a thumbs-up. Yanni nodded.

"It almost looks . . . man-made," Mac said as they flew in closer to the newly designated landing site. "Like it was carved right out of the mountainside."

"That's a lot of carvin'," Yanni added, adjusting her headset. "This could be quite the find."

"All right then," Mac called back, "Yanni, open that door slowly and *don't* let it go. It'll be a cold ride home if that slider comes off its track."

Yanni followed Mac's instructions and slid the lightweight door toward the rear of the fuselage, taking care to guide it into a fully open position before releasing it. The effect was instantaneous—it was as if someone had opened a car door at sixty miles per hour—in the Antarctic.

While Yanni maneuvered herself into position, MacCready slowly swung the R-5 around, bringing its nose just over the ledge at a height of only twenty feet. He nudged the craft forward and down, churning up swirls of rotor generated "whiteout."

Half-standing, half-crouching, Yanni braced herself on either side of the open door frame. "Fifteen feet, Mac," she called to the pilot, though the wind and increased engine noise made it even more difficult to hear. "Tail's nearly clear of the edge."

MacCready had decided to take the chopper in facing the mountain and hopefully into a headwind.

Unfortunately, the mountain had other ideas, summoning a massive gust that swept up the side of the ledge and slammed into the chopper's tail rotor. The force tipped the R-5's nose down and threw Yanni forward into the door frame. As she struggled to steady herself, vortices of snow buffeted the helicopter from below, sending a turbulence-driven blizzard into the cabin. With the rotors now spinning in their own downwash, the aircraft continued to jerk nose-downward and slip sideways.

Lift all but disappeared. Mac, desperate to abort the landing, pulled hard on the collective lever with his left hand while simultaneously fighting to move the wildly bucking cyclic stick to the right. It was clearly too little and too late.

"We're going in. Hold on!" Mac called over the headset.

Amid screaming engine parts, cracking rotors, and blasts of snow, and at the start of a violent clockwise roll, R. J. MacCready shot a glance back into the cabin.

He had but one thought. *Where's Yanni?*

After what seemed like five minutes, but was in actuality all of five seconds, the R-5 rolled to a sudden stop on its right side. Mac, uninjured, quickly undid his seat belt and scrambled aft into the cabin. Jerry seemed dazed but otherwise okay, and even now he was unbuckling himself from the overturned seat.

Turning to the open passenger door, which was now facing skyward, Mac could see the tether from the monkey belt extending out of the chopper. Giving it a tug, he felt a sickening lurch in the pit of his stomach as the safety line streamed through the door and into the cabin. There was no one attached to it.

"YANNI!"

MacCready quickly hoisted himself through the open passenger door frame, barely noticing that the craft had pitched up against a nub of rock only a few paces from the edge of a thousand-foot drop. He gave a quick glance over the precipice, then felt his guts tighten another notch.

"YANNI!" Mac called again. He clambered over the metal and Plexiglas framework of the cabin before staggering past the remnants of what had been a forty-eight-foot main rotor blade. He heard a grunt from behind, but it was only Jerry, who was making his own exit from the broken craft.

Mac frantically searched the snow- and debris-covered ground. Almost immediately, and to his great relief, he saw a figure lying prone in a snow-bank between the R-5 and the mountain. He struggled to run through the hip-deep drifts, pumping his arms as he went, then fell to his knees and began brushing the snow and long black hair away from Yanni's face.

"Yanni," he cried, his voice cracking. "Yanni?"

Amazingly, her violet-colored eyes popped open and blinked. "Nice landin' there, Ace," she said.

At this moment, Yanni mocking him again was the sweetest sound MacCready had ever heard.

S oon enough, Yanni Thorne was not only up and about, she was examining the perimeter of the oddly placed landing zone. It was, of course, surrounded by precipitous cliffs and bordered by what her late husband would have described as "a doozy of a first step."

Yanni, though, was far more concerned with the low line of rocks that had stopped the tumbling helicopter from rolling into the abyss. A similar bracework of block-shaped stones had shielded her body from flying debris after what they could now appreciate as an admittedly spectacular exit from the spinning chopper, this one involving a roll-generated whip snap that somehow flung her into a well-protected snowbank instead of against the rock wall that loomed just beyond it.

"It's a building foundation of some kind," Yanni told Mac, who was taking a break from helping Jerry recover supplies and the cold-weather gear they were now wearing. "And if you want my two cents, it ain't very recent and it could even be ancient."

Mac nodded toward the squat-looking wall adjacent to the former flying machine. "However old it is, I'd definitely call it fortuitously placed."

Yanni did not hear him. Instead she straightened her back as if just touched by a live wire.

Mac heard it, too, a strange whistling sound. "What the—"

"Shhhh," Yanni said, cocking her head to determine direction, but by then the haunting warble of notes had ceased abruptly. What they *could* hear was the crunch of snow underfoot, coming from behind them, and they both turned quickly, relieved to see that it was only Jerry.

"Hey, did you guys hear—"

Yanni held up a hand and the Special Forces officer quickly took the hint. After a half minute, and when the sound did not return, Jerry continued.

"Maybe it was just the wind, blowin' through the rocks or something."

Mac and Yanni did not respond, their eyes methodically scanning the rock wall.

As if on cue, the high-pitched whistling resumed again—alternating this time from several different points along the soaring cliff face.

"Call and response," Mac muttered.

"What?" Jerry asked.

"We ain't alone," Yanni said.

R. J. MacCready's eyes ticked back and forth, scrutinizing nooks and crannies in the cliffs of rock and ice. As Yanni confirmed what Mac already feared, the scientist part of his brain responded as it generally did in such situations—with a question of its own.

How in the hell did we get here?

CHAPTER 1

Mission Improbable

*Prepare for the unknown by studying
how others in the past have coped with the
unforeseeable and unpredictable.*
—GENERAL GEORGE S. PATTON

Metropolitan Museum of Natural History
New York City
June 18, 1946 (Three weeks earlier)

L ike most disasters, the chain
of cause and effect could be
traced backward through time
to an event that, to any outside observer, might
seem as dry and inconsequential as an old bone,
or as mundane as an elevator door sliding open.
As he stepped onto the museum's fifth floor, the
tall, red-haired man had no inkling that he'd just
initiated a wrong turn surpassing that of the Don-
ner Party some hundred years earlier. He carried
a four-foot-long, oilcloth-bound package in both

arms, bride-across-the-threshold style. A guard downstairs had offered him the use of a cart, but even though the package was awkwardly shaped and weighed upwards of thirty pounds, he had politely declined, uneasy about anyone getting too close to the objects he was hauling around.

Hurrying along a wide, cabinet-lined hallway, the man took a sharp right at a sign that read VERTEBRATE ZOOLOGY. He ignored a series of specimen-filled display cases, some housing mounted skeletons from animals he had no interest in identifying, and stopped finally outside a closed door. From inside he could hear a radio playing quietly—"The Gypsy," by the Ink Spots. He tapped out an arrival announcement with the side of his foot.

"Come in," called a familiar voice.

The red-haired man looked up and down the hall and, seeing no one, he gave the door a final hard rap with his shoe. "Open up, Mac," he called, impatiently.

From within, Captain R. J. MacCready followed the first of what would become an annoyingly lengthy list of orders issued by his longtime superior officer and friend, Major Patrick Hendry.

From a separate wing on the fifth floor, a second figure was also converging on MacCready's office. Charles Robert Knight was, without argument, the world's foremost natural history artist. Over a storied, five-decade career, the bespectacled seventy-one-year-old was renowned for the murals of prehistoric life he had created for museums across the country. Secretly, the Brooklynite was most proud of the fact that, while he had never been on the staff of any particular institution, his artwork had nearly single-handedly sparked a public fascination with long-extinct creatures— dinosaurs in particular. Just as fulfilling was the fact that the public's sense of wonder seemed to be growing stronger and more widespread with each passing year.

Knight had begun the day looking forward to wandering the halls of the great museum with his six-year-old granddaughter. But those plans were scuttled after an in-house phone call from one of the research fellows.

The old artist loved associating with the museum's array of taxidermists, exhibition builders, and curators, but R. J. MacCready was a different kettle of fish—a war hero, but one who never spoke a word about his military accomplishments. Mac was also a top-notch field zoologist, though Knight had admired the man's biting sense of humor most of all. He also appreciated, if only vicariously, Mac-Cready's refusal to suffer fools. Yet like so many young men these days, the friend who had come home from the war was not the same one who had gone off to fight nearly five years ago. Mac's unbridled enthusiasm had been tempered, and his wit—when he chose to display it—was darker now. Knight suspected that Mac had endured some unspeakable tragedy.

The goddamned war, Knight thought. *The goddamned war.*

The artist knocked and entered MacCready's small office without waiting. He always appreciated the unique view from just above the tree line and the cool breeze blowing in from Central Park. The office itself was nondescript, although a book lover might spend hours poring over the shelves here, which held everything from first editions of Darwin and Wallace to more recent works by "upstarts" like their museum colleague Ernst Mayr.

Today, Knight found that two others were already present. One was a military type he'd seen on several occasions previously. The artist remembered some recent museum scuttlebutt about a carrot-topped Army officer and so he needed no field guide to identify this particular specimen. The other was a strikingly beautiful young woman with dark, waist-length hair. Knight had seen her around as well, which he considered a far more pleasant experience.

"Afternoon, Charles," MacCready said, gesturing toward his visitors. "You've already met Yanni Thorne. And that's Major Pat Hendry, a friend."

Knight, an ever-present cigarette dangling from his mouth, acknowledged them with a nod, then noticed the room's other new addition: a tray holding an assortment of bones. The oilcloth and packing material, which had been carefully unfolded, told him that one of Mac's guests had likely brought the bones. Varying in size and shape, they were being illuminated by a pair of gooseneck desk lamps.

"Well hello," Knight said, stepping toward the

lab bench as both of Mac's visitors moved aside, providing him with some elbow room. Never one to make assumptions, Knight turned back to MacCready. "May I?"

"Go right ahead, Charles. Those are the specimens I called you about."

There was a partial skull, alongside approximately a dozen bones, the smallest of which spanned the length of Knight's pinky. Knight noticed that Mac had conveniently placed a magnifying glass beside the tray, a respectful nod to the fact that the artist possessed only one good eye—the other had been damaged at the age of six by a pebble-tossing playmate. These days an ongoing battle with cataracts raised fears that his bad eye might one day become his good eye, but he had vowed to do as much as he could, until he couldn't. With a degree of caution that he'd developed during decades of handing delicate (and indeed, priceless) fossils, Knight picked up the largest of the specimens—a nearly complete lower jaw that was a shade less than two feet in length.

"I must say, this is a wonderfully preserv—" Knight stopped suddenly, then, snatching up the hand lens, he began to examine the bone more closely. "This can't be," he said, shooting Mac-Cready an incredulous look.

Mac returned him a wry smile. "Yeah, that's what I thought, too."

"But Mac, this . . . this isn't a fossil."

"I figured you might find that an interesting feature."

Major Hendry cleared his throat, loudly. "How old *is* it, Mr. Knight?"

Knight responded by using the magnifying glass to carefully examine the complexly surfaced molars embedded in the thickened, rear portion of the jaw. "I can't be certain of course, but it's . . . it looks recent!" He turned to MacCready. "But this is impossible."

"Why's that?" Hendry asked. "It's an elephant, isn't it?"

"Well, no, not exactly," Knight replied, then paused for a moment. "It appears to be a type of mammoth."

Knight expected a chorus of skepticism, but instead, Mac's female friend stepped forward. "A baby mammoth?"

"What? Yes . . . I mean no," Knight replied, somewhat unnerved by their apparent acceptance of his outrageous pronouncement.

"Go on, Charles," Mac said, encouragingly. "Show us."

Knight held the upper portion of the jaw toward his small audience and pointed to the occlusal, or crushing, surface of a large flat molar. "Do you see this cusp pattern? It's quite different from that of a modern elephant. So yes, it's definitely a mammoth." Then he aimed the front end of the jaw at the trio. "But look at this mandibular symphysis."

"English, please," injected Major Hendry.

"The fusion of these dentary bones," Knight replied, turning toward the military man, who shook his head. "The right and left lower jawbones, for Christ's sake!"

Hendry nodded, flashing a smile that the artist found instantly irritating.

Knight continued, too excited to remain annoyed. "The way they're fused to each other at the . . . *chin* . . . tells me this specimen was an adult! Some unknown, dwarf species or a hell of a bizarre mutation."

"How bizarre?" the major asked, clearly trying to mask his concern.

Still holding the jawbones, the artist gestured to a pair of large openings in the front of the skull. "See those holes?"

His audience nodded.

"They're nasal cavities," Knight continued. "There's supposed to be one, with a septum running down the middle—like we have."

"And?"

"And this fella had *two*."

Hendry shrugged his shoulders. "A pair of nasal cavities. So?"

"So," Knight said, turning to the major, "I think this individual had *two* trunks. Is that bizarre enough for you?"

"But Charles—" MacCready began.

"Wait a minute, Mac," Knight interrupted. "It's my turn. Where on earth did you find this thing?"

MacCready nodded toward the redheaded officer, who was leaning against a rolltop desk. "Pat?"

The major crossed his arms. "That's classified information."

Knight, whose dislike for Hendry was growing by the second, began to throw his arms up, mock surrender-style, then, mindful of the specimen he was still holding, he gently returned the jawbone to the white-enameled tray.

"Classified, he says," Knight mumbled, using the Sherlock Holmes–style magnifier to scan across the spread of smaller bones. "Well, these *all* look recent," he said, mostly to himself but unable to hide the excitement in his voice. "Now how the hell can that—"

Knight held a long, narrow bone—approximately eighteen inches long and bent somewhat like an archery bow. "Remarkable," he said, examining one end of the object ever more closely. "*Unbelievable!*"

"What is, Charles?" Mac asked.

"This rib."

"What about it?"

"It's also from your mammoth. But you see these?" Knight asked, pointing to a section of the narrow shaft. "They're cut marks—made by tools."

"What kinds of tools?" Hendry asked, his interest ratcheting up a notch.

"Sharp ones," the older man answered, shooting the major a wry smile before shifting his gaze to MacCready. "We can examine these slashes for microscopic fragments and that'll tell us what made 'em. But at first glance I'd say this was a metal blade."

Deftly shifting the bone in his hand, Knight used a magnifier to examine one knobby end. "And there's something else going on. The epiphysis here's been gnawed on."

"Gnawed on—like, by a rat?" Major Hendry asked.

"No," Knight responded, squinting at a telltale

set of spatulate grooves that had been chiseled onto the bone. "More like a human—a big, hungry one."

Yanni stepped forward, watching as the artist ran an index finger along the tooth marks. "So, Mr. Knight, you're saying somebody butchered a miniature mammoth *recently* and then chewed on one of its bones?"

"As close as I can tell. But whoever did this is nobody you'd want to meet on the subway."

Yanni smiled. "Kinda like something out of your Neanderthal paintings?"

"Kind of, Yanni," Knight responded. "But different—much larger, with massive incisors and premolars. More humanoid than human." He turned to Mac. "Look, I've got some friends over in Paleontology who would literally trade five years of their lives to have a peek at these. Now if you'd just—"

Major Hendry shook his head. "I'm sorry but that won't be possible."

"What?" Knight said, exasperated. "For crying out loud!"

"Like I said, 'classified information.'"

Knight turned to Mac, who shrugged his shoulders, before turning his attention back to the officer. *This is definitely the same knucklehead the other curators had been jawing about*, Knight thought. "So classified that you let me handle them but I can't know where they came from?"

"For the time being, that's correct," the major answered, impassively. Then he prompted Mac-Cready with a nod.

"Um, Charles, we're asking you to please keep a lid on this—a tight lid."

"Tell no one," Hendry added.

"For the time being," Mac emphasized, trying to end things on a hopeful note.

Knight, who had a lifetime of experience dealing with decisions that made little or no sense, knew there was nothing to be gained from arguing—at least not now. Without acknowledging Mac-Cready or the major, he placed the rib back on the tray, bowed slightly to Yanni, and exited.

Yanni turned impatiently, aiming the stylus of a fountain pen at the officer. "So, Major, now that we've got that settled, where *did* these bones come from?"

"You mean, where are you going?" Hendry said. He stood beside a wall map, got his bearings, then moved a finger from left to right, crossing the Mediterranean and the Middle East. Slowing down as he reached India, he traced a path northeast but then stopped abruptly. "Those mammoth bones," he said, "came from here. A clan of Sherpas had them."

"Looks cold," Yanni said.

"Colder than the major's heart," Mac chimed in. He had abandoned his examination of the specimen and was looking over Yanni's shoulder. "Southern Tibet, huh?"

Hendry ignored Mac's dig. "It's a region the locals call the Labyrinth. Definitely on the chilly side climate-wise, Yanni."

"But quite the hotbed of political fuckery," Mac added, thoughtfully.

Yanni continued to examine the map. "So who's running the show in there?"

"If you ask the locals, *they* are," Hendry continued, "the Dalai Lama and his Buddhist pals. They're on number fourteen I think."

Yanni shot the major a puzzled look. "Fourteen what?"

"Dalai Lamas, spiritual leaders, head monks. Whatever you want to call them."

"Although this one's no more than a kid, right?" Mac asked.

"So I hear," Hendry said. "But whether he's eight or eighty, officially speaking, our government doesn't talk about Tibetan independence."

"And why's that?"

"Chiang Kai-shek wouldn't like it. He considers Tibet to be part of China."

Mac rolled his eyes. "I hear Chiang's got bigger problems brewing than Tibetan Buddhists."

"You got that right. Some of his Stalinist pals are chomping at the bit to take over, and pretty soon they might be chomping on Chiang's ass. It's the *real* reason we want you in there *yesterday*."

MacCready shook his head. "I was wondering why the Army had suddenly gotten all lathered up about miniature wooly mammoths."

Hendry let out a laugh, then gestured toward the tray holding the bones. "Just consider Dumbo there to be a perfect cover story. If anyone catches wind of this—then it's all just a museum-sponsored collecting trip. The famous zoologist and his Brazilian associate, well versed as she is in elephant talk—"

"—hot on the track of a living fossil," Mac added.

"Now you're talkin'," Hendry said, with a smile.

"But why send us now?" Yanni asked, ignoring his reference to her recent and highly publicized work on animal communication at the Central Park Menagerie.

"Like I said, we want you both in and out of there before the hammer falls on that whole region. Our intel is pointing towards a communist takeover—imminent, maybe."

"Nothing like cutting these things close, huh, Pat?" Mac said. "But you still haven't told us why we need to go in there in the first place."

Hendry held up his hand. "Before we get to that, I've got one question for you. This guy Knight, can we trust him?"

"A hundred percent," Mac replied, without hesitation. His impatience was now in full view. "Now are you gonna answer *our* question or what?"

"Yeah, spill it already," Yanni added, allowing her own annoyance to tick up a notch.

"I guess you'll want to take a gander at this," the major said, withdrawing a folded manila envelope from inside his jacket and spreading out several eight-by-ten photographs.

MacCready picked one up, Yanni took another, and they squinted at what appeared to be sections from an ancient text. Some of the writing was accompanied by carefully labeled drawings of plants and animals.

"Well, this is definitely Latin," Mac said,

squinting at the diminutive symbols. "What is this, Pat? It looks Roman."

Hendry smiled, clearly enjoying the proceedings. "It is. Somewhere between 70 and 80 A.D."

Mac thought for a moment, then used a hand lens to get a better look. "Well . . . the author's clearly a naturalist. Pliny the Elder?"

Hendry smiled. "Not bad, Mac."

"But where are these specimens supposed to be from?" MacCready continued leafing through the prints. "There's gotta be at *least* three different primate species here. And these plants? I'm no botanist but I sure as hell haven't seen any like the ones in these drawings."

"Me, either," Yanni emphasized. "Maybe this Pliny made 'em up."

"Or it could be a forgery," Mac said, picking up another of the photos. "I've read Pliny's *Naturalis Historia* but I'm not familiar with these writings."

"That's because we've only recently rediscovered them. The 'Omega Codex,' our boys are calling it."

"Codex?" Yanni asked, unfamiliar with the term.

"An ancient book," Hendry replied. "Usually made of papyrus."

"Or paper," Mac added. "The format allowed people to look stuff up randomly instead of having to unroll an entire scroll." Then he turned to the major. "Okay, so why's the Army all fired up about an ancient Roman text?"

"Well, for one, because Pliny evidently took a little side trip and then never talked about it."

Mac gestured to the map. "Lemme guess . . . Tibet?"

"You got it."

"And?" Mac and Yanni replied, simultaneously.

"*And* it's what he found there, and what the Chinese may have already found, that's got us worried."

"Which was what?"

"According to Pliny, the key to shaping life itself."

As the major expected, his audience of two paused to consider the statement before Mac slid into zoology mode. "Look, Pat, we've got departments full of researchers all over the country delving into the secrets of life: developmental biology, genetics, evolution. What could there be in a two-thousand-year-old codex that these folks don't already know about? And this 'shaping life' reference? I mean, ya gotta admit that's pretty damned vague."

The major waited until MacCready stopped for a breath. "Funny you should mention evolution, Mac. I've been reading up on your boy Darwin's theory about natural selection. What's your take? You buying it?"

"It's the engine that drives evolution," Mac recited, transitioning easily into science-speak. "Changing environmental conditions select the best-adapted individuals—the ones with fortuitous variations. They're faster or taller or better camouflaged than the norm."

Yanni chimed in. "Which also makes 'em less

likely to starve or get eaten and more likely to survive long enough to mate—"

"—and pass those adaptations on to the next generation," MacCready said, completing the thought.

"Hey, you two should work together one of these days," the major said, taking a moment to relish the twin frowns they flashed at him. "So this natural selection's a pretty perfect process, huh?"

MacCready shook his head. "It's far from perfect, Pat. Plenty of mistakes. Plenty of fits and starts along the way. Then there's the fact that most of the variations produced by mutations don't do shit. Others are harmful and some end up killing the individual. In fact it's so imperfect that a lot of species go extinct *before* they can adapt to an environmental change—a blight or a new predator or whatever."

"Well, thanks for the biology lesson, Mac. But what if there was a way to avoid the mistakes, a way to create a superior organism *quickly* and without all the trial and error?"

"You're talking about a perfectly adapted species?" MacCready shook his head. "They don't exist in nature."

"And how would you do that anyway?" Yanni asked. "Create this so-called perfectly adapted species?"

"There's selective breeding I suppose," Mac suggested. "Farmers and livestock breeders have been doing that sort of thing forever—bigger ears of corn, more breast meat on a chicken. But still—

it's never perfect, and more importantly, it takes generations. How would you deal with *that* little problem?"

"We don't know, exactly. But the brain trust down in D.C. suspect old Pliny may have stumbled onto something during his visit to Tibet—and it might be just the ticket."

"Something that speeds up the evolutionary process?"

"Speeds up. Smooths out. That's what I'm hearing. Unfortunately this codex of his is in shambles—sections missing, other parts completely confusing or impossible to translate."

Mac shuffled through the photos again. "But you *have* uncovered something that's important enough to send us into the middle of Frozen Nowhere?"

"Yeah, word coming out of China is that their scientists have started cranking up the bioweapons labs the Japs left behind. Now the Chinese army is swarming over the Tibetan plateau like ants—which has got the bigwigs in D.C. plenty scared."

Mac shot the major a hopeful look. "Did ya ever think that maybe this Omega Codex is just what Yanni suggested: a work of fiction—no more real than Plato's Atlantis?"

"In which case you and Yanni get to look for Dumbo's weird, pint-sized cousin, get him to pose for some pictures, then head home to shitloads of egghead acclaim."

"There *is* another possibility," Yanni added,

and the two men turned to her. "Since this codex is supposed to be two thousand years old, maybe what *was* there isn't anymore."

Hendry glanced at the photos, and then nodded. "Then I'd welcome that great news. But right now we just can't take any chances. I mean, how many soldiers they got in the Chinese army? A hundred million?"

"No . . . but far more than we've got," Mac replied, "or anyone else for that matter."

"Damn right. Now imagine jazzing up even a fraction of that army's next generation with something that makes 'em stronger or faster, or better adapted to operating at night."

"Didn't Hitler try that one already?" Mac shot back. "His super race?"

"Yeah, but the Paper Hanger and his psycho pals didn't have access to something that could speed up evolution, right?"

MacCready said nothing, knowing full well that this particular argument was over, and that the only things to be determined were the specifics of the mission.

"Mac, we can't take the chance that this shit *doesn't* exist. Like I said, the commies could overrun that entire region at any moment."

"And if it does exist?"

"If it *does* exist, then find it and bring it out of there."

"Bring it . . . out?"

"You heard me," Hendry said. "Shouldn't be too hard to put it on ice."

"And then what?"

"What you can't bring out—destroy."

"Destroy it?" Yanni asked.

"Right. We can't have it falling into the wrong hands—if it hasn't already."

"Whatever *it* is," Yanni said, quietly.

"Exactly," Hendry continued. "Whatever *it* is."

Mac held up a hand. "Look, Pat, I've only got a coupla thousand questions. But let me start with just one. Who did all the gnawing on that rib? From what I've seen so far, whatever it was isn't in Pliny's figures."

Hendry hesitated. "We don't know, Mac. Like I said, some of that codex is in shit shape or missing." Then he gestured toward the bone. "But from the look of those bite marks I'd say the current inhabitants of that region might be a lot more interesting than a herd of little elephants."

And a whole lot more dangerous, Mac thought.

Hendry turned to Yanni. He knew that her rather unique skills related to animal communication had landed her a job at the Central Park Menagerie, working with their elephants. He believed that those same skills might be perfectly matched to the mission he was planning. "And no offense about those pachyderms, Yanni."

The woman gave him the briefest of nods. "I've got a question for you, too, Major."

"Shoot," he replied.

Yanni pointed to the stack of photos. "What's Omega mean?"

The major flashed Yanni something Mac had been calling Hendry's "mortician smile" for years. "It's, um, one of the symbols they've been finding over and over again in this codex." Then the officer appeared to give the revelation a dismissive wave. "This Pliny guy seemed obsessed with it."

"It's the last letter in the Greek alphabet, Yanni," Mac said. "It often means, 'the End.'"

Yanni shot both men a quizzical look. "As in—?"

"As in the end of the world," Mac said.

He and Yanni turned toward the major.

"Yeah, that, too," Hendry replied, sheepishly.

CHAPTER 2

Cerae

Some mischievous people always there.
Last several thousand years, always there.
In future, also . . . always there.
—THE DALAI LAMA (#14)

*Terra incognita: three weeks sailing, and more
than 13,000 stadia* from Taprobane†*
April, A.D. 67

An early thaw.
Or so he believed.
That is how it began for Gaius Plinius Secundus. "A cataclysmic melting," he hypothesized, though it was strange to consider that without it, Pliny could not have hoped to complete his mission. During the past four weeks,

---

* According to the ancient Greek historian Herodotus, 1 stadium = 607 feet in length.
† Modern-day Sri Lanka.

he and his centuria of eighty soldiers had traveled uphill, using the channeled scablands as a well-placed trail, carved by nature. Nevertheless, it was a disquieting path, knowing as he did that the same water-blasted wounds over which they walked had been far from well placed for those living below.

The path of destruction descended from the mountains into what had previously been a fair-sized city, named after the family lineage of the late Prince Pandaya, the most recent and final governor. From what Pliny could determine, a new and terrible river, glutted with sediment and debris, had come roaring and frothing through the city, sparing none and leaving behind only traces of buildings torn from their foundations.

All of this, he concluded, had occurred within the past year.

But Pliny also knew that the surge of mud, trees, and other natural battering rams had been more effective than a thousand trailblazers and road builders. Had the doomed city not met its fate when it did, there would have been no way up through an obstacle course of local politics, forest, ice crevasses, and sheer cliffs—no matter how early in the season they tried, and no matter how many times Emperor Nero would have commanded them to *keep trying*.

For a time, Pliny was grateful. But now he realized just how easy it had been to mistake bad omens for good fortune.

Now listen, Proculus, because I record these words for your eyes, and for my conscience, and for the dust of the earth. So began Pliny the Elder's account of a lost expedition. *Remind me, old friend, that these strange and terrifying things really occurred. Remind me, Proculus, that you recall them as I do.*

Sailing forty days from Sinai past the horn of India we made landfall and trekked far inland. After a journey of great length but little intrigue or danger we arrived finally upon scenes of desolation and destruction. These evoked a new and immediate respect for a natural world that holds us so frighteningly at the mercy of its moods. Boulders, greater in size than Phidias' statue of Zeus at Olympia, were dislodged and carried downhill by the flood, with a single stone obliterating what had once been the royal palace. A city of frescoes and marble concourses, of sapphires and silk, built over generations, must have vanished in only a few heartbeats.

Climbing for twenty days along the path cleared for us by the catastrophe, we detected no blade of grass, no sign of life. I wonder if it will be possible for me, ever again, to be complacent about this world upon which we live. I cannot escape the feeling that Nature watches us all with the barely repressed fury of Poseidon and Talos, waiting to lash out.

Above an altitude of ten stadia and nearly reaching the snow line, the mudflow over which Pliny and his men walked had solidified into plains of semihardened earth. Already these had been cut through by new glacial streams and it was here, at last, that they began to encounter evidence of the local inhabitants—footprints and handprints along the water's edge. Most of the markings seemed to have been made by people of small stature, but even so, Pliny could see that they appeared so deformed in their extremities that they might only vaguely be called people. He shared an unspoken question with each of the men who saw the prints: *Are these the Cerae?*

Pliny's mind formulated another question, though this one he knew he could answer himself. During a decade in which he had survived African fevers, a shipwreck, pirates, and nearly every other disaster the gods could inflict upon him, the Roman asked himself:

How did I get here?

As a young man, Pliny had entered the army as a junior officer, demonstrating both heroism and keen intelligence in conflicts spanning all of Germania to the African provinces. Between a string of promotions, Pliny began to write extensively—of his travels, of military conquests, and natural history.

Beginning with Nero's paranoid stepfather, Claudius, Pliny's ability to write about anything more controversial than grammar and cooking had become a dangerous endeavor. Then, just when it seemed that life in Rome could not get any worse, the gods made certain that it did. With the death of Claudius (poisoned, it was rumored, by his own wife), the seventeen-year old Nero ascended to the throne. Standing before the Senate, he took the name Nero Claudius Caesar Augustus Germanicus—which became wildly popular with his sycophants and ghouls. Others, though, who spoke in hushed tones, came up with a more appropriate title—one that forced Pliny to realize that even writing a cookbook was now a risk. For neither Pliny nor any other reasonably sane person in all of Rome would knowingly attract special attention from the Cannibal Emperor. It was a name spoken only in whispers, and one Nero had earned from his penchant for dressing up in the skins and claws of a wild animal before attacking his terrified victims and consuming their genitalia.

Pliny was grateful, therefore, when Nero became obsessed with a mythical race of half-human grotesqueries said to inhabit an unknown land beyond the Emodian Mountains.* The obsession led the emperor to assign Pliny three ships, along with eighty battle-hardened soldiers and their officers. Nero's orders had been clear: "Find the Cerae, learn their many secrets, then return to Rome and teach them to me." As an afterthought, the emperor had added, "And bring me a Ceran head, pickled in spirits."

Pliny hoped that his immediate enthusiasm for what might seem to some a suicide mission hadn't betrayed a strong secondary motive—to embark on a trip of such duration that it might outlast Nero's rule.

But did the Cerae even exist? he wondered. *And if*

* Latin term for the Himalayan Mountains

so, were they people, minor gods, or perhaps even monsters? Pliny had tried to compare the strange markings in a patch of streamside mud with everything he knew about the Cerae. It wasn't much. They were said to have thrived in the time before the Ogygian flood described by Plato—a primeval deluge that brought with it calamity on a worldwide scale. Then, while the ice and water receded into the Emodian Mountains, so too did the Cerae recede from the rest of humanity. As legend told it, they lived at the gateway to Hades, a region home to all manner of fantastic animals, plants, and trees, some with fur or leaves of stark white—the color of death.

Beasts, they may be, Pliny wrote. *But beasts with skilled hands. What we discovered twenty days' march beyond the prints and scratches in the ground should have removed most every doubt of this. The scablands over which we had walked and the destruction of Pandaya were not created by a cataclysmic thaw of alpine ice and mud. Colossal and clearly hand-hewn blocks of stone had been formed into a dam, and then levered intentionally to either side.*

This alone should have been warning enough to turn back; but curiosity, and my own fatal pride, led us into thinning air and deepening snow, even as the mountain pass narrowed and the tall massifs on either side grew more imposing. Even after a level and easily traveled plain of ice collapsed beneath our feet, revealing itself to be a cleverly constructed trap bridging a bottom-

less ravine, I callously measured the lost (nearly half of our men) and the injured against those still able to continue the expedition. I sent the Medicus, *Chiron,* and nineteen deemed unfit to trek higher, back down to the ruins of Pandaya, and pushed the twenty who remained with me to higher ground.

One of our finest young engineers, the centurion from Libya known as Severus, held contrary views to everything I believed we had seen. To him, the ground that collapsed beneath our feet could have been a natural formation. In his mind's eye, the prints in the mud were made by ordinary animals—at least three different types. The great dam could have been built by the Pandayans themselves, to control the flow of water through their city—with the destruction that followed a result of flawed design rather than intent.

Then listen, Severus—for I can tell you now that conjuring what could have been, inevitably attracts its dark twin, what is.

CHAPTER 3

Morlocks

*I want to go ahead of Father Time with a
scythe of my own.*
—H. G. WELLS

*We are not retreating—we are advancing
in another direction.*
—GENERAL DOUGLAS MACARTHUR

On the Labyrinth's shelf, South Tibet
July 9, 1946

We ain't alone."
No sooner had Yanni
confirmed Mac's suspi-
cion than the strange whistling ceased as abruptly
as it had begun. He found this to be even more
unnerving than the sounds themselves.

Yanni's stare was fixed on one of the car-sized
boulders arrayed at the base of the nearest cliff face.

Mac nudged her with an elbow. "You see something?"

"I think so," she replied, quietly. "In the space between those two boulders."

Mac squinted. "I don't see anything. Just some—"

What he saw then was movement. A snow-packed section of the wall visible between the stones seemed to have shifted. Now, though, it was still.

"Some, *what*?" came a voice from behind, and Mac gave a start. It was Jerry.

"—rocks, ice, and snow," Mac said, completing the thought. "But they don't ripple in the breeze, do they?"

"Nope," Yanni responded. "But fur does."

Jerry sniffed at the air, which had picked up a thick, musky odor. "Jeez, you smell that?"

They did.

Yanni ignored the comment. "I'm gonna try something," she said, turning to Mac for approval.

He nodded without hesitation.

Yanni turned toward the space between the boulders again and began to whistle, pausing, to mimic as best she could the high-pitched sounds they had heard earlier.

There was no response, and the section of rock wall where they had seen movement was apparently unimpressed as well. Yanni resumed her whistling.

"I found the crate with the weapons, Mac," Jerry said, keeping his voice low. "And pretty much everything survived intact." By way of demonstration he opened his parka to reveal the Colt .45 he had holstered to his belt.

As he did this, an ear-piercing shriek rang out—then several more, coming from different directions. Mac caught a flash of movement from the rock wall and then another movement, farther away along the cliff face. Then another.

It appeared to R. J. MacCready as if eight-foot-tall, vaguely humanoid sections of snow and rock had stepped out of the very face of the mountain itself.

Metropolitan Museum of Natural History

FIFTH FLOOR

Charles Knight was clearly unimpressed with the typewritten communiqué Major Hendry had shown him several minutes earlier. In stodgy, official Army jargon, it gave the officer permission to appoint anyone he chose to an advisory role in "Project Kelvinator"—the mission title, a less-than-subtle nod to the ubiquitous household refrigerator company.

"So let me get this straight," Knight said, holding up a codex photograph. "You think these weird-looking simians Pliny drew might have been what chewed on that elephant rib?"

"With no other suspects, that's the current theory," Hendry replied.

"Well, it's not a theory. It's a hypothesis," Knight countered, sounding a bit too much like MacCready for Hendry's liking. "And it's wrong."

The major frowned.

"Anybody paying attention can see that the primates in your codex were man-sized or smaller. And whatever gnawed that bone was big—a lot bigger than a human."

Now the old guy was *really* beginning to remind him of MacCready. So instead of replying, Hendry eyed the sketches, paintings, and sculptures that seemed to cover every square inch of wall and every flat surface of the artist's office. "You did all these?"

Knight ignored the question. "And now you've lost contact with them as well."

"That's correct."

"But you're not too concerned about that?"

The officer answered with another question of his own. "You *do* know MacCready, right?"

Knight thought about it for a moment. "Okay, you've made your point. So what can I do for you, Major Discomfort?"

"I don't know, *Chuck*," Hendry said, pausing to relish the sour expression he'd hoped to generate. "But Mac seems to think you're a whiz and he trusts you. So . . . what *can* you do for me?"

"Let me think," Knight responded, still wearing an annoyed expression. "Well, for one, I can probably translate this goddamned codex faster than the clowns you've been working with."

"All right, you're in!" Hendry said, slamming his fist down on Knight's desk, the blow causing a sixteen-inch-high statue of *T. rex* to shift precariously. Then, just as suddenly, he turned to leave. "I'll have a photo set of all the originals here by tomorrow."

"Hold it," Knight said, adjusting the King of the Dinosaurs to its former position. "You'll have all the *originals* here by tomorrow," he responded calmly. "And I'll be working with an assistant."

The major hesitated. "An assistant? Wait a minute. Who?"

Knight waved the major away from the closed office door and the puzzled officer took a step to the side. "Patricia," he called.

Almost immediately, the door popped open and a bespectacled head appeared. "Well hello!" came a cheerful greeting.

Now it was Hendry who winced, before turning back toward the elderly artist. "You had this all planned out, didn't you? Right from the start!"

Knight flashed his best "who me?" look, then smiled. "Now if you'll excuse us Major, Miss Wynters and I have quite a bit of work to do."

Hendry dropped a handful of new photographs onto Knight's desk. "Here, start with these."

The artist picked up the first photo in the pile and used his hand lens to examine it. A passage by Pliny immediately drew him in and he roughed out the translation in his head.

"Unbelievable."

A moment later Knight's arm shot out and he passed half of the prints to his newly arrived colleague before returning to his examination of the photo.

"Well . . . I'll leave you to it then," Hendry said, but neither of the museum workers acknowledged him. The major considered emphasizing something about the top-secret nature of the project but instead he exited the office, making certain to close the door very quietly.

South Tibet
MAY, A.D. 67

During what Pliny eventually came to call his "last night of the old world," the notorious insomniac had joined Severus and the rest of the night guard, adding his watchful eyes to theirs. The hours passed slowly and in silence. On this night, the air was so thin that only by chewing a third of the way through his remaining ration of coffee beans was it possible for Pliny to maintain his breathing without growing faint. Observing the moon as it passed behind a fleet of rapidly advancing clouds told him that the uncanny stillness of the narrow mountain pass—through which not even breezes stirred—would not last much beyond dawn.

"A storm is coming," Severus said.

The commander nodded, weakly. Though they had reached a point at which the path could not possibly ascend more than a day's walk higher, to Pliny the absence of sounds was more oppressive than the thin air. He listened with increasing intensity, for noises that never came. As dawn approached, he discovered that, with the high-altitude absence of trees and life's usual background noise, the human brain created its own forests of the night. Something moaned threateningly among the nearer of the cliffs, and something howled back from the opposite cliff face. Pliny glanced at Severus with startled surprise, but he and the rest of the night guard had heard nothing.

"The sounds were born of my own imagination," Pliny explained.

"The mind is a skilled deceiver," Severus replied.

"Good line," said the historian.

"I'll be honored to have you steal it from me one day," the centurion joked, but Pliny did not respond. Instead of imaginary sounds, his oxygen-deprived mind had now begun generating imaginary figures—misty and white and vague, gliding within and between the rocky nooks and crannies overhead. The longer he peered into the distant shadows, the less distinct the shapes became, and thus he was able to cast them aside. *This is no different from reading animal shapes into cloud formations,* he convinced himself.

The ghosts on the massifs were gone and did not manifest again; after sunrise Pliny quickly forgot about them.

According to scraps of legend Pliny had been able to collect before their voyage, the Cerae, despite their secretive nature, had somehow arrived at an understanding with Prince Pandaya and his predecessors. Apparently this had come after his family's successful defense of the lowlands and their mountain passes from an attack by the Scythians—a tribe of horse-mounted nomads with an appetite for human flesh. But if the prince ever actually met with the Cerae, he had never recorded the encounter. Even the means of trade between the two groups was an enigma, since it did not appear to involve any actual exchange of goods. And while the white-leaved trees from the Ceran homeland yielded medicinal oils and something akin to silk, the Cerae apparently asked for nothing in return for their resources. Instead they deposited their treasures in secret, outside the city. Despite his centurion's belief that the Cerae might not even exist, Pliny suspected that what the prince had interpreted as a naïve generosity was really a message, a command: *Take these gifts but stay away*.

Far above the Pandayan ruins, during the last day in which Pliny's world still made sense, the storm Severus had predicted seemed determined to freeze them all to death. As their leather armor and shields became wet with snow, the remains of Pliny's regiment ascended to what he believed to be the uppermost reaches of the "trail" and it became possible to hope that soon they would be moving down into more breathable air. Presently, even without the burdens of deep snow and wet, ice-swollen gear, each step seemed to require three times as many breaths.

Though his men were far too exhausted to care about such things, Pliny wondered how high the tallest of the Emodian Mountains stood. At a guess, based upon what he had already seen, the mountain range rose so high that it rendered the earth an *imperfect* sphere. It was a scientific revelation he would have shared with like minds in Rome over wine and good food, but here and now, philosophy counted for nothing. Nature's flaws mattered only in the present reality of slippery rock walls and wind-driven snow.

Against his better judgment, Pliny unbuckled the scabbard holding his short sword, then passed both to his personal attendant. *Anything to lighten the load*, he thought. *Anything to help me draw another breath.*

"Remain at my side, Antoninus," he said, between gasps.

"Of course, sir," replied the dark-haired teen. A storyteller and poet who had been in his service for the past six years, Antoninus somehow managed a smile and a dutiful bow. Pliny, though, could read the plea written in the boy's eyes. *Can we turn around, sir? Can we go home now?*

But they did not turn back. Instead, Pliny led them to yet another rocky outcropping, from which sudden, snowy gusts threatened to launch them screaming into the underworld. Pliny decided that they should rest for an hour in the shelter of an icy overhang, consuming light rations of dried meat, taking turns warming their feet against a portable brazier, and melting snow into drinking water. After providing his own body with what he had calculated to be reasonable time to recover, Pliny began to scout the route ahead. Intermittent breaks in the obscuring veils of snow suggested that they had indeed passed the highest and most physically demanding point along the path. Pliny looked back at his men, their wind-chapped faces covered in turbans so that only their eyes were visible. Tugged and battered by the gusts, they had their backs pressed tightly against the cliff face that ran alongside the trail. Pliny shifted his grip on the rock wall as he descended, his own movements labored by exhaustion and the thick hides he wore. Through the worst of it, he allowed himself a moment of optimism. *By tonight, breathing will be easier,* he reasoned.

The moment passed, as he knew it would. Not very many paces from where he stood, a pair of opposing rock walls converged to form a narrow, V-shaped passage—as if a doorway had been thrown open.

"The lair of your Cerae, I suppose?" Severus grumbled, doing his best to restrain any actual expressions of anger or sarcasm.

"Perhaps," Pliny responded.

But with nowhere else to go, Pliny and the centurion led their party downhill and through the jagged entranceway.

Although they were still being buffeted by wind-blown snow, now and again the white veil parted for a moment, allowing tantalizing views of what lay ahead. Collectively, each glimpse built upon the previous one in Pliny's imagination, helping him to form a picture that could not be real. There appeared to be towers, sharp-edged and cleanly cut.

His men moved with an accelerated pace through the narrows, driven by a combination of foreboding and excitement. They could all see the structures now.

Descending into a mountain valley, Pliny watched

the entire curtain of snow draw back for several long seconds, granting them far more than a glimpse this time. His next thought was a revelation, for Pliny knew at once that even after coming to appreciate the strategic significance of the Pandaya-obliterating dam and the trap that had been sprung against his own group, he had vastly underestimated the Cerae. Sunlight striking the towers and domes was too bright and the wrong color to be illuminating mere works of stone. The turrets were composed of gleaming crystal or glass, or perhaps even ice—supported by foundations and ribs of granite.

Oddly, Pliny's next emotion was jealousy over an undeniable realization: *Rome's greatest architects could never have—*

A movement along the nearest rock wall drew his attention. Ghostlike, and so exquisitely camouflaged that the Ceran must surely have been standing only a few arm-lengths in front of his face all along, it—*they* moved as if they had been part of the snow and ice itself, summoned suddenly alive. Pliny instinctively reached for his sword then felt a flutter in the pit of his stomach as he realized he had given it to his young aide. He turned to Antoninus, who was still carrying the weapon, but in the next moment his view of the boy was obscured by a warm mist accompanied by the metallic scent of blood in the air.

In the space of five heartbeats, and in a silent whirlwind of arterial spray, the Cerae burst upon the Romans.

Metropolitan Museum of Natural History
FIFTH FLOOR

An hour after Major Hendry's departure, Knight looked up from his work, stretched, and yawned, realizing only now that the officer had gone. "Not the best writer, this Pliny guy," he said, removing his glasses to rub his eyes. "Not by a long shot," Knight emphasized. "Now his nephew, *he* could write."

There was no response from Patricia.

Squinting, Knight replaced his spectacles and turned around. He could see that Patricia had cleared a new space on a nearby lab bench and was using a desktop magnifier to examine the codex photos.

"He was confiding to Socrates in this section," she said, holding up a photo and without a hint of mockery. She wrote something down on a yellow legal pad.

"That's nice," Knight said. They both knew that by Pliny's time, the old Greek had himself been dead for nearly five centuries.

There was no further comment from the pair, and unaccustomed as the researchers were to small talk, they went silent and they went back to work.

I don't know what's more disturbing," Knight said at last, "this little dilly about what can happen to anyone bearing weapons, or this new stuff about worms?"

"I vote for the worms," Patricia replied, morosely.

"Well, either way, I'm starting to see why they sent Mac in there. I mean, if there's even the possibility that this world we're unraveling was real and that some of it could *still* exist—"

"Agreed," the black-clad woman replied, not bothering to look up from her own sample of codex photographs. "And Charles, about those worms—I think we need to bring in an expert on invertebrates."

Knight gave a mirthless laugh. "Yeah, that's gonna go over *real* well with Major Disaster. Let's just invite everyone we know."

"Speaking of invitations," Patricia said, "don't forget the concert Friday night and the tour afterwards with that movie guy."

Knight glanced over at the strange, cabinet-like instrument that had arrived two days before—a gift from its inventor. "Right, right," he said. "Remind me again. What's that movie guy's name?"

"Hitchcock," Patricia said.

Knight gave a brief nod. "That's it," he said. Then the pair returned their full attention to the codex.

I may truly say Socrates, that no one is meant to understand what I have seen. When you gaze upon the kingdom of which I speak, even wisps of snow gaze

back at you, and into you. My soul has
become a strange and dark companion.
In the course of our journey, I seem to
record my discourses more for the ancients
than in memory of those among whom
I travel. I suppose, in essence, I have my
dialogues with the dust. Then listen, dust.
Listen to a tale which, though difficult to
comprehend and more difficult to relate, is
a fact and not a fiction. And we know, we
who have seen. We know, we for whom the
tale began in a white blur, and gushes of
scarlet, and the whole of existence ceasing.

—PLINY THE ELDER (AS TRANSLATED BY
PATRICIA WYNTERS, MMNH)

South Tibet
MAY, A.D. 67

Pliny remembered struggling to regain consciousness in air that was too agonizingly
rarefied and cold. Until the awareness of pain set
in, he wondered if in fact he had perished during
the attack—wondered if he had become part of
the whirlwinds of red mist. The sudden confusing slaughter occupied the same instant of realization of *The Cerae have us*, and *This is the end of
me*. Then, stillness and nonexistence, without ice
or sky, darkness or light.

In the next moment, a breath was drawn in pain,

fear, and anguish—for he had caught a glimpse of the short but exceedingly muscular creature dragging him by one foot. Having nearly believed himself dead, Pliny had a new realization: *I have not been that lucky.*

Dropped at the base of a wind-sculpted snow dune, Pliny feigned death on ground that seemed unnaturally warm. A loud thud and a sickening crack forced him to give up the pretense. Opening one crusted eye, he found most of the view blocked by several pairs of legs, vaguely human yet covered with thick white fur. Here and there burlap-like strands of fabric had been braided into the fleece, camouflaging them against darker splotches of rock amid snow and ice. He also saw that Severus had been correct on one detail: there were at least three kinds of them among the dozen creatures present.

Grotesqueries. The Cerae are monsters.

With his senses beginning to clear, Pliny had a pair of simultaneous revelations: First, he had been discarded in a pool of coagulating blood— *the blood of my own men.* Second, the Cerae were building two orderly piles: the bodies of men whose heads appeared to be missing, and the weapons that had been taken from them.

A moan drew his attention elsewhere and Pliny realized that he was not the sole human survivor. A soldier whose name he could not presently recall was crawling toward a half-buried sword and, though already missing an arm, he was still determined to fight. In a flash of movement, one of the nearly man-sized monsters grabbed the

Roman by a foot and swung him headfirst into a pillar of ice, crushing the crown of his skull down to the level of his eyes.

"No!" Pliny cried out.

The murderous Ceran ignored him, focusing instead on the precise arrangement of the soldier's body on the pile of similarly "headless" men.

"Save your voice," came a weak call. It was Severus. "And your life."

South Tibet

JULY 9, 1946

S ensing that Jerry was about to withdraw his pistol, and in what seemed to Mac to be a single continuous move, Yanni blocked the man's right arm, grabbed the weapon, and flung it as far away as she could into the snow.

"What the *hell* are you doing?" Jerry cried, having acted just fast enough to stop a reflex to strike the person who had suddenly disarmed him. "Are you nuts?"

Yanni remained calm, exhibiting what Mac thought to be an equally extreme degree of self-control, considering there were four towering humanoids standing before them—their bodies covered from head to toe in long, translucent hair.

"Did you hear those shrieks when they saw that heater?" she replied quietly.

As MacCready watched the creatures closing in, he saw that any argument between Yanni and

Jerry had ended as quickly as it began. He could tell that Jerry's anger had already been circumvented by the fight-or-flight portion of his autonomic nervous system.

"What on earth are they?" Jerry muttered.

"Morlocks," Mac said, under his breath, reminded of H. G. Wells's fictional subterraneans.

"Pliny forgot to mention these big ones, huh?"

Mac did not respond. Instead he watched as the two figures to his far left and right shifted position—moving to encircle them. *Incredibly graceful*, he thought, noting that despite their size (which he estimated to be somewhere north of five hundred pounds), there was no wasted motion. They seemed to glide across the ground, and within seconds a pair of giants stood between the trio and their shattered helicopter—effectively cutting off any possibility of retreat. *Smart, too,* Mac thought. *Shit.*

R. J. MacCready slowly raised his hands, watching out of the corner of an eye as Yanni and Jerry followed suit. "*Bom dia!*" Mac said cheerfully in Portuguese, missing the brief incredulous look he'd gotten from his Brazilian friend.

The "Morlocks," whose faces and palms were apparently the only body parts *not* covered in thick, whitish fur, ignored him. Instead one of the creatures approached Jerry, who responded with a reflexive step backward.

"Do . . . *not* . . . move," Yanni said, through teeth clenched in what Mac thought was a rather scary-looking grin.

The man froze and closed his eyes. He never

saw the blur of movement as the giant brushed past him. Reaching into a snowdrift, it gingerly picked up the .45 and, without hesitation, flipped it off the side of the cliff. Then it gave a short whistle. Each of his hirsute colleagues responded by taking up positions behind one of the three humans. Then, simultaneously, the newly captive humans each felt what Bob Thorne would have considered a "somewhat less-than-gentle" poke in the back. All three obeyed the finger prods in exactly the same way.

They shuffled forward.

CHAPTER 4

First Impressions

*Somewhere, something incredible is
waiting to be known.*
—CARL SAGAN

*The greater our knowledge increases, the
greater our ignorance unfolds.*
—JOHN F. KENNEDY

Metropolitan Museum of Natural History
Fifth Floor
July 9, 1946

W ell this isn't very cheery," Patricia Wynters said, having just translated another section of the Pliny codex.

Charles Knight never looked away from the desktop magnifier. He was using a pair of rubber-tipped forceps to examine a tattered one-inch square of papyrus. "I never said we were going to be reading the funny papers."

"I'm terribly worried about Mac and Yanni," she said. "Aren't you?"

"Of course I'm worried," he replied. "I read about that attack on Pliny, too. But we've got a job to do here and the quicker we can—goddammit!" Knight's progress translating a fragment from a later section of the codex had been stymied by the fact that the second half of what looked like an important page was in tatters and mostly missing.

"For the first two paragraphs he goes on and on about worms again. Then there's a big hole in the next section. All that's left is something about 'molding life as if it were—' Then there's *another* hole."

"Oh, dear," Patricia said, quietly.

"I'm sure Hendry caused some of this damage himself," Knight muttered, before glancing over at his friend. "The codex spends two thousand years intact and in another week the Army would have turned it into powder."

Patricia kept quiet, knowing better than to interrupt Knight when he was on a roll. Not for the first time, though, she wondered if it would have been better for all of them if Pliny's work *had* been completely destroyed, long ago.

SOUTH TIBET

Y ou got a German cousin named Sergeant Schrödinger?" MacCready asked his towering Morlock shadow. There was no response (aside from another annoying finger prod) and no alternative, except to continue along the rocky trail that led them farther and farther away from the downed helicopter and—more disquietingly—farther away from their supplies.

Mac took the opportunity to retreat into zoology mode, mentally tweaking the standard mammalian field measurements for primates: They were all adult males ("Penis—pendulous; scrotum—primate-like," he would have written had he been filling out a field notebook). Arguably, their second most obvious trait was the long, dense hair that covered their bodies. This "pelage" ranged in color from pure white to a sort of cream, but remarkably, the creatures seemed to darken and lighten depending on their background. Mac noted that they looked almost slate gray when standing beside a rocky wall but within seconds of stepping onto the snow, the Morlocks blurred and changed before his eyes.

Textbook example of cryptic coloration, Mac thought, although he reasoned that the first trait he'd noticed might not make it into high school zoology texts.

As for *total* body size, in spite of the low oxygen levels, these guys had managed to pack on a great deal of high-metabolism beef. With muscular bodies of between seven and a half and eight feet in length, they made boxer Primo Carnera look like a toddler. Having had time to look them over, Mac *now* estimated that they'd weigh in at around six hundred pounds—or twice the weight of the six-foot-six-inch former heavyweight champion known to fans and foes alike as the Ambling Alp.

Of far more immediate concern were the creatures' oversize canine teeth, which reminded him more of a baboon's dentition than anything that might be considered human. MacCready also noticed that the tops of their heads came to a low front-to-back ridge. "Sagittal crest," he mumbled, knowing that the increase in bony surface area meant more room to attach a set of massive temporalis muscles—all of which translated into some *serious* jaw strength.

Although the mystery about what, exactly, had gnawed on the mammoth rib had been solved, Mac hoped to leave unresolved any questions about just how painful their bite could be.

After marching approximately three hours from the crash site, and to the point of exhaustion, MacCready realized that they were approaching what appeared to be a natural wall. It completely dead-ended what had, up till now, been a rugged path. Of course there were no handholds or, for that matter, anything that might give purchase to anyone insane enough to attempt climbing it. Mac guessed that any traveler taking this route would have determined the trail to have become impassable and, unless they possessed either a Buck Rogers rocket pack or sophisticated mountain climbing gear, been forced to turn back.

The Morlocks, though, continued herding the

humans forward, until they came within several arm lengths of the roughly ten-story-tall barrier of rock.

"Now where, pally?" Mac said under his breath. He looked over at Yanni, who shrugged her shoulders but remained silent.

"Looks like somebody forgot the map," Jerry said.

Mac suddenly felt himself being grabbed around the waist while almost simultaneously being swept off his feet. With an ease that circumvented all thoughts of escape, he found himself literally tucked under a hairy armpit, his body held roughly parallel to the ground. From this strange though not entirely uncomfortable vantage point, Mac glanced around as the giant effortlessly scaled the rock wall, paying no heed to the 180-pound load it was now carrying.

The creatures carrying Yanni and Jerry in an identical manner followed up the rock face in rapid order until they had deposited their cargo atop the wall, where the path resumed in a new direction. Glancing back over the edge, Mac could see the fourth climber literally running up the side of the sheer edifice.

"You see the dogs on these things?" Mac asked Yanni. He'd noted earlier that the Morlocks were equipped with huge, broad-soled feet and strange toes with rounded tips, the largest of which faced inward ("Great toe offset from digits II–V and directed medially!").

"Like a house gecko," Yanni said, sounding excited at the sight of the creature, though clearly struggling for air.

"You got it, Yanni," Mac added. "I wonder if they've got the same type of friction pads on their fingers and toes?"

"I'll bet," she countered. "More gecko mimicry."

"And can you imagine the lung capacity—"

Jerry cleared his throat. "Um, excuse me folks," he wheezed, pausing until they both turned to him. He caught his breath. "If you could possibly take a break from all this swell science talk, I've got about a million fucking questions—most of them dealing with us not getting killed."

Mac gave him the calm-down sign. "If they wanted us dead, Jerry, don't you think we'd *be* dead by now?"

Jerry thought about it for about a half second. "Yeah, and some cats will play with a mouse for hours before they finally decide to kill it."

"Well, they're definitely not feline, Jerry, but I do think they're as curious about us as we are about them."

Jerry frowned. "I suppose."

"Unless they plan on eating us," Yanni chimed in, a bit too cheerily.

Mac shot her a disapproving look. *Not quite the support I was looking for, kiddo.*

"Or . . . there's that," Mac offered, sheepishly.

"This is just great," Jerry responded, shaking his head and looking even more dejected—if that were possible.

Mac took the opportunity to shoot Yanni a quick

give the guy a break expression, and she returned it with a shrug of her shoulders. He knew she had initially voiced the opinion that Jerry was too young for this mission, but in that regard she wasn't alone. Back home, Mac had explained that although Jerry always looked a bit wet behind the ears, he had in fact mastered six languages by age twelve and graduated from Columbia at nineteen. But it wasn't all academics, and baby face or not, Jerry had saved Mac's life in the Pacific, and could therefore be counted on whenever the chips were down.

"Look," Mac said to his young friend, trying to sound confident, "we just play this by ear, right? There's no other option. I think *they* built this wall and now we're going to find out what's on this side of it." He looked Jerry in the eye. "You good?"

Jerry nodded.

"Well all right. Just don't look too threatening, huh?" Mac said, nudging his friend with a gentle elbow to the ribs.

Jerry managed to flash his trademark you-can-depend-on-me smile. "Got it."

"They eat the threatening ones," Yanni added, just before they each received another prod from behind.

South Tibet

MAY, A.D. 67

All told, Pliny counted just one other, besides himself and Severus, who had survived the massacre—*for only a liar would have described it as anything else.* The entire encounter could not have lasted more than the count of ten. Early in that count, a young Nubian cavalryman named Proculus had stumbled backward upon his own sword. In retrospect, the accident and an uncharacteristic fault in craftsmanship had saved his life—the sword tip breaking off as it struck his femur, and the blade itself cracking in two. The Cerae evidently considered the weapon to be useless, thus sparing Proculus a speedy trip to Hades.

"I'll be a Poseidon-cursed Cretan!" cried the wounded Roman. He was always one of the more profane members of the expedition but now he was lisping through a space where three front teeth were missing. Back home, before he became an adventure seeker, Proculus had been a much-sought-after architect, as stoic in striking deals with government officials as he was at hiding the pain of sucking in cold air over freshly broken teeth.

The three survivors and their captors were on the move now, setting out on a forced march toward whatever short and sorry future might await them. Trudging single file down a rocky path away from the carnage, each was shadowed by his own grotesque escort.

Pliny also noted that Proculus made a perfectly admirable display of hiding his limp, though muscle and even bone must have been pierced. The great blood vessels had remained unsevered, since the man had entirely stanched the blood flow by applying pressure to a well-placed rag.

"Why have they spared us, sir?" the wounded man asked.

"I think . . . because we lost our weapons," Pliny answered, between gasps of thin air.

"Perhaps," Severus said. "But I think you should *both* save your energy by not speaking."

A sharp prod to the centurion's back not only ended the conversation but reminded the Romans that there was no way to tell whether the vanquished were being marched toward their own executions.

Pliny concluded that any questions their captors might have about Roman fighting capabilities had already been settled. Now, it seemed, only pain thresholds were being explored with each successive prod—the latest, a thwack across his centurion's shoulder blades, had come from the flat side of a confiscated sword. Ahead, cradled in his well-muscled arms, a short-legged but disconcertingly stocky Ceran carried the remainder of the Roman weapons, and Pliny marveled that the creature exerted little if any extra effort.

"Who are these animals?" Pliny asked breathlessly. His companions, though, remained silent, as fresh waves of snow streamed in and broke upon them in stinging, blinding gusts.

After an especially strong blast of wind, Proculus began to stumble, teetering perilously close to the edge of a bone-shattering drop-off. A flash of movement followed but instead of falling, the soldier was dangling by an arm over the precipice, held aloft by his Ceran escort who, seemingly without effort, placed Proculus back on his feet and along the path.

During the episode, which had taken all of five seconds, the wounded Roman gasped but did not cry out, even though Pliny thought the "rescue" must have nearly disarticulated the man's arm at the shoulder. Instead Proculus brushed himself off in an exaggerated manner and threw the creature a nod. The only response from the Ceran was a gesture that could be interpreted as nothing other than *Keep moving*.

Proculus straightened his spine, obeyed the gesture, and gave an audacious nod that boasted, to his Roman onlookers, *Notice the restraint I have shown in not hurling this monkey over the edge.* "As you know," Proculus called back to his commanders, "for all warriors there are but two kinds of prisoners: assets and liabilities."

Severus shook his head. Despite the worsening conditions and their recent and unimaginable losses, he seemed truly amused by the man's audacity. "And which one are you?"

But the soldier's answer, if there was one, went unheard as the wind continued to roar and gale-animated blasts of snow whipped around them like maddened wasps.

JULY 9, 1946

The first thing R. J. MacCready noticed about the plants that ringed the walls and ceiling of the cave entrance was that they were stark white. The second was that they possessed teeth.

The Morlocks had deposited the trio of humans outside the fifteen-foot-wide opening and were currently huddled up nearby, deeply involved in what appeared to be a whistle-driven, hairy-arm-waving conversation.

"They almost look like snakes," Jerry said, pointing to the top of the opening.

"Yeah, but I think they're vines," Mac responded, squinting up at the impossibly weird life-forms.

"I don't know, Mac," the younger man went on, clearly unconvinced. "You ever been inside a bat cave?"

Mac and Yanni exchanged looks.

"I think I've got that one covered," the zoologist replied.

"Well, I was outside this cave in Puerto Rico once, and at dusk the boa constrictors would come out and hang down from the cave opening." He gestured upward. "Kinda like that—to snatch at the bats that flew out."

"Do they have bats in Tibet?" Yanni asked.

"Yeah, but nothing like the diversity you had in Brazil," Mac said.

"No vampire bats, though. Right?" Yanni asked.

"That we know of," Mac answered.

At that point the conversation died and the trio stood silently, peering into the cavern—which seemed to drop off a few feet just inside the entrance.

Moments later the finger prodders were back, and, having assumed their positions, they directed their captives in single file into the mountain itself.

Mac, who was the first one in line, paused for just a moment to get a closer look at the snake-headed vines—and as he did, something white and sparrow-sized streaked out of the cave, causing one of the plants hanging from the peak of the opening to snap closed.

"I think the breeze from that bird or whatever it was triggered those jaws," Mac commented.

Yanni squinted up at the vines as she passed beneath them. "Like the modified leaves of a Venus flytrap."

"Yeah, only this one seems to be lined with silica teeth."

"Interesting," Yanni responded. "Now, what was that you were telling Hendry about there being no perfectly adapted species in nature?"

Mac pondered the question silently as he entered the cave. "If it was a *perfect* adaptation, it would have caught that bird, right?"

"Well anyway," Yanni added, "do *not* buy one of those for my apartment."

Although a part of Mac's mind was still considering Yanni's comments about adaptation, another part concluded that the idea of having a few of these plants delivered to some of the bachelors living near her apartment made for some interesting visuals. Before his daydream could get *too* interesting, though, Mac received another finger poke in the back.

Had he and Yanni been allowed to stick around

for another thirty seconds, they would have been even more puzzled by some very un-flytrap-like behavior, as the snake vine's "mouth" snapped back open. Elsewhere in the world, the Venus fly-trap reset was a far more gradual process that could take up to two days.

Once inside the cave, the walls converged rather abruptly and the trio was soon being herded through a narrow passageway, roughly twenty feet high and less than half as wide. The straight sections led to a series of hairpin turns—and so the effect was one of continuous and gradual descent. *They really are subterraneans*, Mac told himself. Suddenly his funny nickname for them—Morlocks—seemed more apt than he had guessed, and his arms broke out in a chill of gooseflesh. Surprisingly, and to Mac's relief, instead of a nightmare march through a pitch-black maze, they soon discovered that there would be no need for torches or headlamps. The cave walls themselves were lit by what seemed to be a great multitude of bioluminescent microorganisms.

Bacteria and algae mostly, Mac guessed, *each giving off its own spectrum of light*. Remarkably, some of the colonies appeared to be blinking at different frequencies, while others were simply "on." He made a mental note that while blues and greens were predominant, there was definitely some red light as well. Mac knew that many nocturnal and cave species, including a certain population of vampire bats formerly thought to be extinct, had been blind to the red light emitted by specially designed lanterns. *But here at least some of the subterraneans seem to have evolved beyond that red insen-*

sitivity. Mac waited for Yanni's comment on the phenomenon but for now, at least, she was silent.

A stone arch under which they passed drove home the message that the world into which they were descending could be as strangely beautiful as it was dangerous. Along the arch's horizontal underside, hundreds of thumb-sized "glowworms" had draped an array of sticky silk feeding lines—each one baited with luminous beads that glistened like wet pearls on a string. The pearls were actually a gluey secretion and one of the lines was already being reeled in, having ensnared a chillingly vocal species of cave moth.

Another new species, Mac thought. Triphosa thorni—*Bob would appreciate that one.*

As if to emphasize the diversity of the cave environment, almost directly underfoot another previously unknown animal let out a squeak. MacCready, who reacted with a start, knew that this species was decidedly mammalian. About the size of a large white rat, it had nearly run across his boots before disappearing into the shadows. As their downward trek continued, Mac saw more vague shapes, scurrying in and out of the bioluminescence—but these, too, vanished into hiding places just before he could attempt to identify them.

I'd pay a million bucks to be able to stick around and study this ecology, Mac thought, before flashing back to his last caving experience—an outing that included voluntarily burying himself in a three-foot layer of living bat guano.

Well, maybe half a million.

But while R. J. MacCready focused on what was clearly a remarkable and unique troglodytic ecosystem, Yanni, as expected, was far more fascinated by the complex pattern of whistles and grunts that the Morlocks were exchanging with each other. More than once Mac looked back in response to a strange warble of notes only to find that it was Yanni who had made it.

None of the giants seemed to pay much attention to her linguistic exercises but at a brief rest stop beside a pool of what turned out to be deliciously cold water, one of the creatures did something remarkable.

After allowing the three captives to drink their fill, the alpha Morlock (a designation stemming from the fact that it did more whistling and no pulling of guard duty) ambled over and squatted down at the water's edge. Mac noted that its fur looked very different than when they were outside the cave—having darkened now to match the stony background. He currently suspected that, like polar bears, their hairs weren't really white. Instead they were likely pigment-free—transparent and probably hollow, thus providing them with the ability to scatter and reflect visible light. It would also explain, to one degree or another, how the Morlocks had taken camouflage to new levels of complexity and effectiveness.

This particular individual, who like the others gave off a strong musky body odor, was not looking for a drink. Instead it dipped its hand into the shallow water and appeared to fish around for a few seconds, as if gathering something. Once the lead Morlock withdrew his arm, Mac could see that its forefinger was now covered in a dense mat of cottony material.

Was it algae? MacCready wondered. *Probably, but it certainly isn't getting its energy from sunlight.*

Unconcerned about such questions, "Alpha" glanced over at Yanni before slurping the mess off its finger. Then it directed a short series of whistled notes at her.

Yanni hesitated for a moment, apparently not wanting to interrupt the big guy's meal. Then she shook her head and emitted a single, whistled note of her own. The creature responded with something that was *clearly* an expression of exasperation—which Mac thought was actually a distinct improvement over the aggressive, bared-canines look they'd generally been sporting up till now. The giant followed up by thrusting its hand back into the water and withdrawing a baseball-sized handful of the white glop. This time, though, instead of eating it, the big guy flipped the material through the air, the flight path ending with a splatter against Jerry's chest. The man's fear of the creatures had abated not at all since their initial encounter, but now he forced a phony-looking smile. The others, Morlock and non-Morlock, watched as the sticky mass plopped down onto his lap.

The algae flipper's three colleagues responded with what sounded very much like a hissing laugh, and though their expressions were anything but comforting (a return of the flashing fangs made that a certainty), the absurdity of what had just taken place caused Yanni and Mac to laugh as well.

Jerry responded by popping a chunk of the strange slime into his mouth. "Thi tuff ess great," he managed.

Less than a minute later, they were all eating the white stuff and all agreeing that despite its mucus-like consistency, it was indeed quite palatable.

Another new species, Mac noted, though he knew he'd never be mistaken for an algae expert.

After quickly eating his fill, Mac stood up, eyeing a semicircular alcove just up ahead.

"Gotta see a man about a horse," he said.

Jerry nodded, knowingly, while Yanni threw him a puzzled look.

Alerted by the movement, Mac's personal bodyguard broke away from his own group and followed, uttering an angry grunt as he did. Mac-Cready turned and held up his hands, in what he hoped was *still* the universal sign for peaceful guy. Then, making sure that Yanni wasn't looking, he used a somewhat ruder gesture to explain why he had wandered off. The creature made no response except to move into its familiar position behind him.

"Hey, spread out, huh? Ya know how hard it is to pee when someone's st—"

MacCready's wisecrack was halted by the sight of a neat pile of unfamiliar bones in the alcove, sitting beside a small circular pool. As he moved in closer, the water was clear enough for him to see that a similar geometrically arranged mound sat submerged about two feet below the surface.

Mac wondered why anyone would create such an arrangement, but before he could get a better look, his hirsute shadow was back and a less-than-gentle shove (instead of a prod) followed. Adding to Mac's annoyance was the fact that he had been forced to leave the alcove without carrying out his original mission.

Yanni was studying the cluster of Morlocks rather intently, so Mac took a seat next to Jerry. "There's something over there on the ground that I really want you to see."

Jerry responded by scrunching up his face in an odd way. "I'll pass," he said.

Mac threw him a puzzled look that ended with a head shake. *What the hell's wrong with him?* he thought, before turning to see what had drawn Yanni's attention.

Off to one side, the now-reunited Morlock quartet continued to converse in their vaguely birdlike language, and Mac noticed yet again that the giant who'd dodged guard duty was doing most of the whistling.

He's definitely *the* jefé, Mac thought, wondering if his personal bodyguard was now taking flack from the boss for allowing one of the humans to poke his nose where it probably didn't belong.

Yanni acknowledged MacCready's return and gestured toward the Morlocks. "If you think about it, Mac, whistling's the perfect means of communication over long distances and mountainous terrain. I wouldn't be surprised if they were using low frequency as well."

"Like your elephants?" Mac said.

"And those musky secretions are probably some kind of scent marker," she added.

"Sounds about right," Mac replied with a nod. "Hey, I saw an interesting arrangement of animal bones in that alcove."

"An arrangement?"

"Yeah, one stack on the ground, another one submerged in a smaller pool."

Yanni paused for a moment. "*In* the water?"

"Sittin' there in a neat little pile."

"Maybe they're feedin' their algae friends."

Now it was Mac who hesitated. "Calcium, phosphorus, and protein. Could be," he said. Then he gestured toward the lead Morlock, who seemed to be in monologue mode. "Can you make out what he's saying?"

"Not yet," Yanni replied, "but I'm workin' on it."

CHAPTER 5

The Shape of Things to Come

To be a naturalist is better than to be a king.
—WILLIAM BEEBE

The happier the moment, the shorter.
—PLINY THE ELDER

Metropolitan Museum of Natural History
Fifth Floor
July 10, 1946

Major Patrick Hendry was peering over Charles Knight's shoulder—which provided no little annoyance to one half of the Army's new Codex Translation Team.

"Can you make out what he's saying?" Hendry asked.

Knight turned and shooed the officer back a

few steps, having just worked on a particularly ratty-looking section of ancient papyrus. "Well, it's not just strange primates they'll need to be concerned with. As you've suspected, the bad news comes in a smaller package."

"And that is?"

"It's in the valley Pliny keeps talking about. That seems to be where the real trouble is."

"Was," Patricia chimed in. "Two thousand years is a long time. Who knows what's going on there now?"

"Okay, 'was,'" Knight said, relenting.

Patricia cleared her throat and, after a pause that went on a beat too long, Knight got the message. "So, Major," he continued, "what about sending some additional men in there? In case half the stuff Pliny described turns out to be true."

Patricia nodded in agreement, though it was obvious whose idea it had been.

Hendry simply folded his arms, assuming what had quickly become Knight's least favorite example of body language. "This mission doesn't exist, folks."

"Yes, I know," the artist said, struggling not to lose his temper. "But how do you expect our people to handle something that can reshape flora and fauna the way we shape modeling clay?"

"Especially when they have no road map to the source of that kind of power—no clue what they're searching for?"

"I understand, Miss Wynters," Hendry replied. "Even looking at the sketches of these weird apes, I can see as well as you, that . . . that . . ." The major did not know what to say next. The words did not exist yet, to articulate how, nearly two thousand years ago, someone had discovered and used an advanced genetic engineering system.

Hendry continued—slowly this time, as if measuring each word. "From what I can gather," he said, "some as-of-yet-unknown people in ancient Tibet learned how to fiddle around with their plants and animals—like those monkeys and apes that Pliny drew. And they used this . . . whatever it is . . . to make 'em smarter and nastier."

Now Knight stood, turning to face the much larger man. "First of all, Major, you *don't* understand—any better than any of us can really understand, yet. But more importantly, those are our friends and colleagues you sent in there."

"Mac's my friend, too, Knight," Hendry shot back. "And he knew *exactly* what he was getting into. So did his two pals."

"Did you not just hear me?" The artist held up a yellow legal pad filled with their recent translations. "They *knew*, you say? Well, according to this, they didn't."

Knight handed the note pad to the major, who began reading immediately.

"I hate worms," the officer muttered. "Shit."

"Yeah, shit," the Codex Translation Team replied in unison. It was the first time that Charles Knight had ever heard his old friend utter a curse.

In the Valley of the Cerae

MAY, A.D. 67

When Pliny turned his open mouth into the gale, the just-past-his-prime and slightly asthmatic Roman discovered that the wind brought a certain amount of relief, for it squeezed higher-pressure air into his lungs. But he also felt the cold air biting deep within and knew that if the Cerae did not allow him shelter by nightfall, he would be a frozen corpse—with Proculus to follow, despite his outward defiance.

Too many deaths, Pliny thought. *Forty in the Ceran trap. Almost twenty more today. I'm the leader of a ghost expedition.*

Gasping and now mute, Pliny tried to peer over the heads of his shadowy captors and through the whiteout conditions. There was little to see. His other senses told him only that their trek had veered gradually and more sharply to one side of the mountain pass before turning downhill. Trying to drive thoughts of a death march out of his head, Pliny stiffened his spine, coughed, and, with renewed determination, picked up his pace. *I've visited dangerous new lands all my life and I've always survived. And somehow I always will.*

Pliny tried to search through the storm—hoping to see some additional hint of Ceran architecture, and the possibility of shelter. But though the wind stalled from time to time, the light remained dull and gray, the air itself still angry and driving a billion tiny needles of ice.

"*Maggot!*" Proculus cried out against another prod. Though his call was muffled and distant, it served to bring Pliny back to a new concern: even in the soldier's wounded condition, he and his escort were now a full hundred strides or more ahead of his own slog.

Pliny exerted all his strength to keep moving forward, quickening his pace trying to catch up. His short and lanky guard kept up as well. A sharpened spear point, formerly one of their own, remained within jabbing distance of Pliny's spine, following his motions with remarkable precision.

"What in Hades?" It was Proculus, again—nearer, this time, though his shout conveyed surprise, not anger. "Stop, you mother of whores!"

Now *he is angry*, Pliny thought, wondering what the man had seen.

"Poseidon's teeth!" Severus called, also from somewhere ahead.

Though his lungs ached and he felt his own heartbeat throbbing against his temples, Pliny threw each leg more quickly before the other until he was closing the distance at a trot. The gale, as he advanced through it, shuddered, stalled, rose strong again. His vision reeled, coming and going with the on-again, off-again blasts of blinding snow, until finally he stumbled and rolled forward into clear air, as if tumbled out through a ghostly white lens.

Immediately, Pliny glanced backward. The wind and snow were abandoning him, racing back up the hills and along the mountain pass through which the three survivors had marched.

Pliny's Ceran captor allowed him to approach his men, who were on their knees in the snowfield, both of them staring in the same direction. Pliny put a hand upon Severus's shoulder and gripped. The centurion's breathing was hard and fast, not so much from exertion as from astonishment.

"Do my eyes deceive me?" Severus asked.

Pliny ignored the question, for the sight that lay before them had replaced all other words and all other thoughts.

Spanning the entirety of a wide valley floor, what appeared to be a frozen lake was in fact a form of frozen mist. Though the mist lake was strange and beautiful to the point of being spellbinding, it was the enormous spire extending upward through its center that had stolen Pliny's voice. Seemingly constructed out of crystal and stone, the glittering tower stood far higher than anything he had expected to see in this part of the world—a cyclopean spire assembled from stacked terraces, narrowing at each successive tier. Adding another facet to the power of this landscape came the revelation that the crystalline tower was clearly inhabited, for Pliny could detect movement—figures within the structure itself as well as on the outside of it, the latter clambering acrobatically between the terraces on a meshwork of branchlike supports.

Although the tower alone could easily have

held Pliny rooted to the spot, his attention was drawn back across the mist to a wider view of the valley, where scores of less lofty though no less impressive structures were clustered—elongated domes, each taller than the Imperial Palace in Rome.

There was plant life as well. Most of it was ghostly white, but the pattern was occasionally broken by more familiar-appearing cables of thick greenish vine, climbing into the hills surrounding the valley. Pliny noted that the latter very much resembled the outer architectural elements of the tower, which the Cerans used to move with ease from level to level.

"What is this place and who are these . . . people?" It was Proculus, and once again, Pliny could not and did not respond.

Despite the difficulty of breathing the thin air, Pliny was able to concentrate on the details of the level overlook onto which they had been led. He began to suspect that the Cerae had reshaped the entire valley. Out there, in the center of the fog lake, the tower's lower terraces were awash in gently rising and falling swells of white. He wondered how much deeper below the mist the actual foundation must stand. The portion that stood above the strange vapor was taller than the lighthouse at Alexandria, and yet the abrupt cessation of the blizzard revealed even nearer wonders.

Here, along the "shore" of what he would come to call "the Opal Sea," one of the domes appeared to be undergoing the final phase of construction. Once their captors decided that their rest period was over and marched them forward toward shelter, the astonishments continued to add up. Overhead, dozens of Cerae were moving busily to and fro along handholds and footholds set into branches and ribs that served as buttresses. Pliny noted that these were members of a leaner and more graceful race than their captors.

They seem as different from those brutes as we are different from the people of Asia or Nubia. Perhaps even more *different.*

Within the mountains of southern Tibet

JULY 10, 1946

I think I see daylight," Mac said, noting that several hundred feet ahead the passageway became suddenly brighter. This seemed impossible. By everything he knew, nightfall had certainly overtaken the world above. So he was surprised but not completely shocked to discover that the impression of daylight was illusory—nothing more (*or less*) than an intensely bioluminescent, cathedral-like chamber. All around, crystalline arches and carefully hewn rock walls bore the marks of being shaped in the recent geologic past. Whoever the Morlocks were, they had obviously chosen to hide at least a portion of their civilization deep beneath snow and rock.

As they moved toward the center of the immense space, they passed below rows of thick glassy pillars that were strangely organic. Each of them soared a hundred feet upward before splitting into branches that reinforced an arched ceiling, which was itself shaped from sections that resembled leaves.

"Feel familiar?" Mac said to Yanni.

"I feel like I'm in a forest," she replied.

"No forests up here though, right?" Jerry asked.

Yanni continued to stare upward. "Not anymore."

Jerry rapped gently on a column base. The Morlocks did not stop him.

"It's mostly ice," he said, "mixed in with some sort of plant matter. Cute trick. I've heard of experiments with this sort of stuff in the Aleutians, during the war."

Yanni gave him a quizzical look. "Where?"

"Off the coast of Alaska," Jerry replied, and she shot him a nod. "So anyway, you mix ice with the right material—even cotton balls or sawdust— and you can make it as flexible as steel beams and strong enough to take a direct hit from a cannon."

"Or from an earthquake," Yanni suggested.

"Definitely a high likelihood of quakes round here," Jerry said, without looking away from the architecture.

"Well, whoever built this was thinking long-term," Mac said. "Perfectly functional yet—"

"—constructed with an eye for beauty, too," Yanni finished for him.

Jerry nodded toward their escorts. "Do you think *they* built these?"

Mac shrugged. "I don't know. But I'm bettin' their origin story turns out to be a real doozie."

"Mac, your breath," Yanni said.

"What?"

"Your *breath*," she repeated, more forcefully this time, before turning to Jerry. "Yours, too."

"Jeez, I'm sorry," Jerry snapped back, clearly annoyed now. "This has all been a bit too stressful for me to worry about brushing my—"

"No, you ninnies," Yanni said, shaking her head. "Your breath—you've gotten it back."

Jerry stopped in mid-rant. "Hey, she's right," he said. "No more wheezing."

"Now that *is* odd," Mac followed. "Especially since we haven't been up here long enough to crank out the extra red blood cells that mountain types have in their bloodstreams."

"You mean Sherpas and the like," Jerry chimed in.

"You got it. More erythrocytes equals more hemoglobin."

"Then what coulda—"

"Wait a minute!" Mac interrupted. "When Pliny mentioned the reshaping of life itself, we were all thinking about speeding up evolution by skipping over a few steps. Maybe cutting down on the number of generations required to develop new adaptations."

"So?"

"What if this works a lot faster than generations?"

"You mean evolutionary change within an individual?" Yanni asked.

"Hold on," Jerry interjected. "Didn't a guy named Lamarck get hung out to dry for that one?"

"You lost me," Yanni said, with a shrug. "La-who?"

"Early-nineteenth-century Frenchie," Mac said, picking up the story. "Lamarck believed in evolution but thought it worked when individuals needed or desired specific adaptations. He even incorporated environmental change."

Jerry jumped in. "When the ground foliage died, short-necked giraffes stretched their necks to feed from higher branches. Then they passed those longer necks on to their progeny."

"Exactly," Mac followed. "Only evolution doesn't work like that."

"So then why would it work in this case?" Yanni asked.

"Okay, I'm only hypothesizing here," Mac said, "but what if there's something in the water or in that glop they fed us—a bacterium—something that initiates a positive feedback system? In other words, once inside our bodies, it somehow calculates what needs fixing, then fixes it, maybe even improves it."

"That would be a *new* one," Jerry said.

"Yeah," Mac went on, "but our own immune system adapts to fight thousands of foreign invaders every day—some of them brand-new. This could be a take on that mechanism."

Yanni shot Mac a skeptical look. "Okay, assumin' this is an organism we're talking about here—what does *it* get out of the deal?"

"Especially," Jerry added, "when you consider the seriously hazardous digestive system this 'what-zit' runs into after being ingested."

Mac considered the imagery for a moment. "Well, maybe some of it *doesn't* get digested.

Maybe it can withstand the acid wash and enzyme rinse, pass through the walls of the digestive tract, and find a nice safe place to live and reproduce."

"And the more it reproduces, the more positive effect it has on the individual?"

"Could be."

Yanni shook her head. "Yikes."

Mac let out a loud whistle, and failed to notice the stares of the Morlocks as he continued his thoughts aloud. "Hendry was right. Back when Hitler dreamed of a master race, they would have needed generations. But with this kind of biological tool kit—damn!"

"That's assuming your hypothesis holds water," Jerry added. "I'm wondering how these individual changes get passed on to the next generation?"

Before they could bring their debate to the origin of Morlocks, the Morlocks themselves were pushing and poking again. As they moved forward, Mac began to suspect that their captors understood the rapidity with which the organism (if indeed it was an organism) produced its effect. It seemed to him that they realized their captives could be prodded along more quickly now. This added to a growing list of evidence indicating that the Morlocks were far from a pack of dull brutes who had stumbled into the ruins of someone else's lost civilization.

More archways loomed ahead, and beyond them still more galleries—forest cathedrals with walls supported by a dense meshwork of Jerry's "ice composite." In the distance a whole arboretum of columns and branching arches marched away into lurid shadows and phosphorescence.

They followed a long, narrow incline, which led, finally, down into the strangest space of all. Just how strange, Mac could not have guessed, at least initially.

"This thing is huge!" Jerry exclaimed. A fog appeared to have rolled in, completely obscuring the roof of the cavern. "Like something out of *Journey to the Center of the Earth*. The biggest cavern behind us could easily be lost in a small corner here."

"No more arches," Mac observed.

"So no more ceiling," Yanni said.

"Then we're outside," Jerry said, finishing the thought.

"I think you're right," Mac added.

"Could be the valley we were supposed to land in," Yanni suggested.

Mac managed a smile. "Now I think you're *both* right."

As they stepped out of the stony passageway, their feet crunched on a carpet of ground frost covering a surprisingly rich-looking layer of soil. Dusk and a thickening fog seemed to be closing in, limiting visibility to perhaps forty feet in any direction. Upon closer inspection, the incoming fog appeared to be a misty suspension of snow. Mac held out a hand and indeed some of the tiny crystals clung to it. Others, though, took the opportunity to demonstrate some very unsnowflake-like behavior by swerving away just before contact. As he watched spellbound, the pseudo-flakes, which MacCready now believed to be insects, resumed their mimicry, blending seamlessly into the frozen fog.

There were other amazements, and these were terrestrial in nature—loud, trumpetlike sounds coming from something unseen within the mist.

"Don't tell me, Yanni," Mac said. "Mini-mammoths with two trunks."

"Could be," Yanni replied. "But those calls are very different from anything you'd hear from an Indian or African elephant."

Much nearer than the unseen trumpeters, colorless plants were peeking up through the soil in clusters. The predominant flora reminded Mac of a drooping rosebud grafted on to the end of an asparagus stalk. Waxy and pallid, the plants stood just a little higher than Mac's knees. *No chlorophyll here, either*, Mac thought, as yet another set of bitonal calls, haunting and even mournful, emanated from somewhere behind the veils of fog.

"I think it's a type of corpse plant," Yanni said, having seen Mac's interest in the white clusters.

"That's pleasant."

"They're also called Indian pipes," she continued, in the lull between the presumed woolly mammoth calls. "They steal the energy they need from ground fungi."

"Parasites, huh?"

"Yeah, but compared to anything I've seen or read about, these specimens are on the extra-large side."

The botany lesson ended rather abruptly when the quartet of Morlocks pushed the trio of humans into a tight cluster, which they then immediately surrounded.

Even Alpha's getting into the act, Mac thought as

the presumptive Morlock leader took up a position at the head of the formation and they set off along a trail that ran uphill.

At first the march reminded MacCready of three people simultaneously entering a revolving door, but the giants backed off a bit once their intentions became clear: the single-file line they had assumed in the mountains and through the subterranean cathedrals of ice had been replaced by a more compact grouping that would circumvent any thoughts the captives might entertain about suddenly breaking rank and tearing off into the frozen mist.

In reality, thoughts of running had not occurred to either Mac or Jerry, although Mac wasn't anywhere near as sure about Yanni, who seemed entirely enthused at the prospect of meeting up with some new pachyderm pals. Soon enough, however, the point became moot.

Approaching a field of ghostly white grass, the Morlock leader began shuffling his feet, kicking up clumps of frost and earth. In response, the carpet of ground cover before him began to part. Some of the blades scuttled off in high-speed inchworm style, exposing a narrow trail of bare soil bordered by frantic movement.

"Swell way to cut the lawn," Mac said, nodding to the Morlock leader. But the look on the creature's face revealed that he considered the proceeding to be anything but humorous. Instead, it was clear that Alpha was uneasy about the strange new path, and his enormous associates appeared even more wary.

A second revelation was olfactory in nature: the unpleasant, musky odor the Morlocks gave off had been ramped up to borderline nauseating. Further intensifying the stench, all four of the creatures began moving their arms up and down, as if performing jumping jacks.

"That's a nice touch," Jerry said, joining Mac and Yanni in what had turned into a group wince.

"I think that skunk scent they're giving off repels these grass mimics," Mac said, watching as the blades nearest the Morlocks beat an even hastier retreat.

The lead giant then turned to his captives, wordlessly calling for their attention, before withdrawing something live and squealing from a fur pouch it had evidently been carrying. Mac recognized one of the rodentlike creatures he had seen earlier. It resembled an eyeless albino squirrel but before he could get a better look, the Morlock casually flipped the animal into the field of white blades. The "squirrel" let out a series of yelps, cut off by a flurry of motion as the tiny troglodyte was stripped to the bone. Seconds later there came a new sound, a disquieting crunching communicating that the bones, too, were being consumed.

The message was simple: *This can happen to you.*

"So noted," Mac acknowledged.

The group moved slowly along the trail, whose boundaries seethed backward, then ever so threateningly forward—giving every indication of being held barely in check—before closing in behind the last (and indeed the most nervous looking) of the Morlocks, only seconds after it had passed by.

MacCready was drawn back to the Old Testament and what he'd always considered to be the most cinematic of biblical tales. The imagery was unavoidable once he saw the "grass" creeping in hungrily behind them. Now the trio of humans drew deliberately closer to their captors for the very first time—despite the inherent threat they posed and despite their god-awful smell. Glancing back, R. J. MacCready watched the turbulent swarm flowing around the Morlock footprints and closing off the path they'd traveled. He recalled an ancient description of the Red Sea rushing in to wash away the footprints left by Pharaoh's troops and carrying off the terrified men who had made them.

"They'll need to do that one in Technicolor someday," Mac muttered to himself.

In the Valley of the Cerae

MAY, A.D. 67

Gaius Plinius Secundus came to the realization that any concerns about the Cerae looking upon him as a potential meal might have been unfounded—at least for the moment. The curiously lithe race he called "architects" seemed so focused on their work that if they glanced in Pliny's direction at all, they regarded the odd-looking strangers with contemptuous indifference.

"Who *are* these people?" Proculus asked, yet again. "And what will they want with us?"

"I don't know," Pliny said. "At this point, the only certainty is uncertainty."

A strangely high-pitched growl in three syllables and a sharp thump from behind communicated that there was to be no further talking. It did not matter. In this strangest of strange lands, Pliny found that there was little left to say. What he could not shake, however, was the guilt that his mind should choose to be more dominated by a sense of wonder than by the all-too-recent loss of more than sixty men.

The structure toward which they were being ushered was a dome, built on a scale Pliny had never seen—even in the most imaginative architectural designs. At the base of the dome's nearest arched buttress, a wall was being constructed. Blocks of ice were being broken out of molds and set into an interlocking arrangement.

Those Cerae doing the building were strikingly different from any of Pliny's brutish captors. The "architects" had longer, more spidery arms and legs than the others, larger eyes, and higher foreheads. Now that the Romans were being led directly beneath them, one of the workers finally seemed to take notice. Without thinking, Pliny raised a hand, as if greeting an acquaintance. Standing amid a pile of recently poured and frozen blocks, the creature seemed to disappear before his eyes. Pliny squinted into the shadows.

Can it move that quickly? he wondered.

The answer came to him as the architect reappeared just as suddenly in the exact position and pose it had occupied a moment before, staring back at him again in open daylight.

It's playing some sort of game with me—trying to frighten with a demonstration of muscles and reflexes so powerful that it can indeed move in a blur.

Pliny reminded himself that he had, at almost every step, continued to underestimate the Cerae and that every one of his assumptions about them was probably wrong.

Failing to ask the right questions.

He supposed there were enough new questions to be discovered just outside the threshold of the great dome to keep him busy through the next two or three imperial reigns. But there was no time even to begin working on the first few questions before he and the other two captives were shepherded inside.

But inside of what? Pliny asked himself.

Under the dome, tiers of arched supports had been grown, rather than built. A colossal and unfamiliar form of vegetation, looking like a cross between a paper birch and a mushroom stem, was being carefully directed in its growth by the Cerae. They had managed to guide these buttress trees with far greater knowledge of nature than any *vinetarius* ever applied to guiding grape vines along trellises.

The interior was illuminated by millions of ice-refracted glimmers from the setting sun. Pliny's mind, too, was illuminated—asking the right questions now: *Are these Cerae animals that think like men, or men who look like animals?*

Proculus paid less attention to the Cerae, but their architecture seemed to hold him completely in its spell. He was a cavalryman, and under Roman law, every equestrian or equestrian candidate was required to achieve an expert rank in at least one trade. Before Pliny had begun his mentorship of Proculus, he had already watched him advance at a very young age from gifted artist to designer, specializing in the rapid construction and dismantling of boats and bridges. Pliny knew this was the reason for their shared appreciation of the skill necessary to raise structures such as these. He had noticed a similar genius and hunger for adventure in Severus, and had carefully mentored him as well.

"I suppose you both think this is a good place to die?" Severus asked.

"Better than most," Pliny responded.

"Then find me a sword," the centurion said. "So that I can die like a soldier."

"Go easy, my friend," Pliny said. "Were you to reach for anything remotely resembling a weapon, you would die here and now—but with no purpose."

Pliny thought that Proculus was about to say something but instead he lost his footing and stumbled against him. Blood continued to seep from his leg wound, pooling beneath his left foot.

Alarmed, they eased him down into a sitting position.

"I'm fine," Proculus said, attempting unsuccessfully to regain his feet.

"Remain seated," Pliny commanded, observing

how difficult it had suddenly become for Proculus to fill his lungs.

As if in response, a score of hirsute brutes appeared, quickly surrounding the Romans with their bodies. As the Cerae encircled them in a living fence of flesh and fur, Pliny felt as if he were being enclosed in a corral.

"What now?" Severus asked.

Three of the newly arrived Cerae stepped into the circle with such suddenness that Pliny scarcely had time to follow their movements before Proculus was lifted to shoulder height. Just as swiftly, two more creatures, white-furred and noticeably lankier than the rest of their kind, sprang like acrobatic children onto the backs of the individuals securing the wounded man. Advancing with quick precision, they began probing and examining their prisoner. All the while, three pairs of hands clamped Proculus's arms and legs, rotating his body beneath the inquisitive new arrivals as Pliny and Severus watched in confusion and amazement.

The two examiners—Pliny immediately identified them as female—ran their fingers over Proculus's chest, back, and legs as he was rotated for their inspection. Thoughts of being consumed crept into Pliny's mind because he found it impossible not to think of a pig being slowly turned on a spit over a cook fire. Thankfully, the thought was fleeting, as it suddenly occurred to him that the more thickly muscled Cerae (*a warrior caste?*) were acting in tandem as a form of living medical instrument, allowing the two physicians to clamber around and examine their patient in the most efficient means possible.

Proculus's two examiners had more elongated faces than the other Cerae, a characteristic that gave the impression of being less brutish and more civilized. Pliny classified them as "a physician race." He noted that their more enlightened countenance was counterbalanced by short white fur covering the entire face (while the facial skin of the other Cerae he'd encountered was bare and leathery). Oddly, even the lids of the "physician" eyes were furred, and Pliny hypothesized that, out in the snow, the covering might be needed to protect and camouflage the eyes themselves, which were disquietingly large and intense. Similarly striking were the great manes of hair that framed their faces—combed and, curiously, either dyed or dusted in unnaturally dark hues.

Initially, Pliny wondered how these particular markings tied into their penchant for camouflage, until he realized that the dark streaks would resemble natural features of the landscape had they been set against snow and rock.

Despite the distinctive and terrible odor their bodies gave off, along with the inescapable sense that from certain angles they looked more animal than human, there was something dreadfully beautiful about the big-eyed physicians, who were currently smearing a yellowish waxy substance into Proculus's leg wound. Pliny observed that it seemed almost immediately to halt the seepage of blood and he wondered if it had squelched the man's pain just as instantly. One of them, keeping a hand planted firmly upon the cavalryman's chest, produced a small leathery pouch with a nozzle, through which she squirted a black, molasses-like substance into his mouth. That quickly, the refreshment the patient received from each intake of air was improved enormously.

"What form of magic is that?" Severus exclaimed.

"Real phenomena, poorly interpreted," Pliny said, quietly. "It's not magic. It's medicine."

For a while longer, the two physicians commenced to run their hands over every part of Proculus's body, monitoring his responses to their salves and elixirs. One of them flashed her patient an expression that in Pliny's view was a disquieting smile. *As if she enjoys the feel of his smooth bare skin.*

Proculus, for his part, reacted with disgust, deciding to focus his attention elsewhere by looking away from his caregivers. As his breathing became progressively easier, he was lowered to the ground. He stood, shakily at first, then seemingly recovered to a degree that Pliny would have found difficult to comprehend, even if his thoughts had not been interrupted by attention from the physicians. Thankfully he received a quicker examination than Proculus—which concluded with one of them squirting the same black elixir into his mouth. It was horribly bitter but almost immediately he could feel his breathing improving.

Finally, Severus was snatched up and raised high for inspection. As the centurion was being rotated and examined for wounds, Pliny noticed that the physician who had earlier taken an inordinate interest in Proculus's almost completely hairless skin was now demonstrating an even more unsettling interest in the Roman officer's well-muscled arms and legs.

Pliny observed that Severus did not seem at all unsettled by the prolonged physical inspection. In fact his attitude was undergoing a puzzling reversal.

Proculus, his color having returned to normal, sidled up to Pliny and together they watched as the Ceran physician brought her face close to the centurion's, brushing one side of her mane across a cheek. She stared directly into his eyes and he returned the stare.

Pliny nodded toward Severus and spoke under his breath. "He seems to have snuck in a weapon after all."

Proculus managed a smile. "His short sword, apparently."

In the Valley of the Morlocks

JULY 10, 1946

I s it me or do you feel like we've just landed on another world?"

MacCready nodded absently at Jerry's comment, having been thinking something along those very lines.

Major Patrick Hendry had once brought up the topic of what might happen if the aliens from an Asimov or Heinlein science fiction story ever landed on earth for real.

"Maybe they'd be friendly," Mac had suggested.

Hendry shooed away the comment as if it were a fly. "It wouldn't matter how friendly they were."

"But—"

"Just look in the mirror, Mac. That'll tell you all you need to know about what our reaction would be. People are people."

"So what do *you* think would happen?"

"Look, if Orson Wells's Martians landed in New Jersey and tried to cross the Hudson, they'd be on the daily 'Specials Board' at the Fulton Fish Market by noon. And if by some luck they happened to taste like crap, they'd be peering out from behind bars at the Bronx Zoo."

Mac forgot the rest of the conversation (*something about hating calamari*) but the bottom line was that he himself had some serious reservations about how humanity would react to an alien encounter. And now that they'd met the Morlocks, the closest thing to an alien civilization anyone had ever seen, he was even more skeptical.

But who must be more alien to whom? he wondered. It was a trio of humans, after all, who, much like Wells's Martians, had fallen into *their* world aboard a flying machine. And just as the fictional Martians coveted the earth, Hendry's "bigwigs in D.C." coveted the organism Morlocks (or their ancestors) presumably used to shape life. MacCready supposed it spoke volumes about Morlock temperament that upon capture, he and his friends were not treated immediately to Major

Hendry's fish market solution. Instead, they were escorted through a sea of carnivorous grass to an igloo-like structure that apparently served as the local version of a county jail.

Their "cell" was undergoing some final assembly by a pair of Morlocks. The last of the freshly cut blocks were being set into place atop the nine-foot-high dome—which glistened through the mist and the shifting tide of snowflakes like an improbably large gemstone.

Mac looked around thoughtfully as they reached the arched entrance. The inchworm grass seemed to be keeping its distance, which he counted on the plus side. Yanni was listening intently to something out there in the mist, and though Mac and Jerry tried to listen in with her, neither of them was able to detect anything more than a barely perceptible, low-frequency murmur. They both shot Yanni a quizzical expression. "Whatcha got?" Mac asked.

"Those ain't Morlocks," she whispered.

R. J. MacCready managed a smile, having flashed once more, in his imagination, to the skull they'd shown Charles Knight back at the museum—the midget mammoth with its strange mutation hinting at two elephantine trunks. More interesting by far, he thought, was that the "mutation" suggested the possibility of *two* manipulative limbs, serving perhaps the same function as human arms and hands.

Yanni made a low-frequency sound that caught the sudden attention of all four of their captors.

What could be more fantastic? Mac wondered,

watching Yanni as she called to the unseen mammoths. But before he could say a word, he had become airborne.

Flung through the igloo entrance, Mac thrust out his hands to avoid plowing face-first into the floor.

What the hell?

Jerry and Yanni were similarly tossed into the structure, landing beside and on top of him. Within that same second, one of the Morlocks pushed a slab along a groove at the threshold of the arch, sealing the prison door.

Rising to his feet, Mac observed that the portal was crystal clear, and so precisely cut that it fit perfectly into the curve of the dome.

"That doesn't look very secure," Yanni said, gesturing toward the now closed doorway. "Can't weigh more than a coupla hundred pounds."

"I'm thinking they put it there to keep the grass off the people—if you know what I mean," Mac said.

"You're right," Jerry added. "These monsters probably couldn't care less if we did decide to stage a jailbreak."

As indeed they could not.

This became as crystal clear as the ice door itself. Seconds after sliding it into place, the Morlocks simply walked away, leaving no guards behind.

Dusk descended quickly, and in response the local "streetlights" came on. Fungi glowed in the loamy soil, and bioluminescent plants and animals were active as well. But beyond a range of forty or fifty feet, every detail was hidden by the fog—which absorbed and scattered the phospho-rescence.

Where dusk ended and where nightfall began had been difficult to define. Through the ice and not more than two yards away, they watched the lawn trying to close in—repelled by the scent, spread by the jail's architects over their prison's ice blocks. As the carnivorous blades continued testing the chemical boundaries of the igloo, a fist-sized, crablike creature burrowed up out of the ground. After flicking off a few shreds of shimmering plant matter, it began emitting a blue phosphorescence, then skittered toward the ig-loo's outer wall. A breakaway swarm of grass fol-lowed it, closing in quickly.

"This is gonna be ugly," Mac muttered, but he squatted down anyway to get a closer look. *Watch out, little guy.*

The crab scurried to within a foot of the struc-ture, the blades continuing their hot pursuit of the pulsating blue light. *If anything,* Mac thought, *it's attracting even more of them.* Suddenly the crus-tacean flashed a stunning strobe of white.

"What the—" MacCready cried, snapping his eyes shut—too late.

"You all right?" Yanni said, moving in beside him.

"Just swell," he replied, shaking his head. A circular green afterimage burned brightly in his right eye. "Did you catch that?"

"I think so," Yanni said, watching as the for-mer predators inchwormed their way backward in double-time fashion. Apparently, though, not all of them were successful, since the crab was now casually munching on one of the creatures, spaghetti-style, while brandishing several more, clamped tightly in a second claw. As the vanquished lawn mimics made an uncomfortable transition from hunter to main course, the crab continued to glow—blue to deep violet to blue again.

"Gotta admit, this prison has a coupla interesting features," Yanni said.

"*And* practical," Jerry added. "Who needs guards when the local grass can cut *us* down?"

"Unless, of course, you happen to be a light-emitting crustacean," Mac countered.

"I'm tellin' ya, this place is amazing. Beautiful, too," Yanni gushed. "So why the hell would we want to run?"

Jerry started to answer but Yanni turned to Mac. "Would *you* run? If we could get out of here?"

Mac shrugged his shoulders. He knew exactly how his friend would respond and she did not disappoint.

"Look, maybe you two are scheming to take a powder, but I plan on leavin' with a whole lot more knowledge and with my—you know—" She got stuck on a word.

"Dignity," Mac finished for her.

"Right," she said. "We're explorers, aren't we? And there's so much to learn here. So much to *do*."

Jerry gestured toward the walls of their prison. "If we weren't locked in an icebox."

Yanni turned toward the color-shifting crab outside—which seemed to have finished its meal. Jerry and Mac followed her gaze, watching as the creature sank back into the frost and earth, its light diminishing to a dull blue glow before blinking out.

"No argument there, Yanni," Mac said. "That was certainly an interesting little floor show. I'm guessing the blue color serves as an attractant while that flash functions as an offensive weapon."

"How do you figure?" Yanni asked.

"You ever heard of William Beebe?"

"Sounds familiar," she replied.

"He used to be a curator at the Bronx Zoo. Birds."

"Neighbor of yours, too," Jerry added, and Yanni shot him a quizzical look. "Brooklyn boy."

MacCready continued. "'Bout twelve years ago, Beebe and another guy took a diving bell down to three thousand feet. One of the things he described was a fish that used a phosphorescent lure to attract its prey."

"Which is certainly the *obvious* explanation for what we just saw," said Jerry.

Mac raised an eyebrow. "But?"

"But I'm starting to think that calling anything around here *obvious* is the first reason we should doubt it."

"Speaking of which, I don't know if you've noticed," Yanni announced, "but the lights are shuttin' down."

She's right, Mac realized. *It is getting darker.*

"Well, there ya go, Mac," Jerry said. "So much for any similarity to William Beebe's strange fish. When it's darkest, bioluminescent life should be at its brightest."

Mac peered into the mist and knew that his

friends were right. At first, shortly after the last cloud-penetrating rays of sunset had retreated behind mountains and heralded dusk, the mist shimmered brightly from every direction—more brightly than the twilight itself. Now some lurid and heatless fire still burned out there, providing scarcely more illumination than a clear, starry night far from the city.

Outside, shadows held sway over the world, and these alone—whether imagined or not—became the real inhabitants of the Morlock's lair. Mac believed he observed a large figure moving in the distance, against the barely perceptible light, but he became reasonably certain that it had been something no larger than a cat, prowling only fifteen or twenty paces away. Surely it must have walked among the grass mimics, and he wondered what defense *it* might have evolved to avoid being eaten by the lawn.

"You know, if you think about it, it kinda makes sense for the local biolumes to feed at dusk, then shut it down in the evening."

Jerry thought about it for a moment. "Biolumes, huh?" Then he gave the name an approving nod. "So how do you figure, Mac?"

"Well, it's no stretch that there are probably aerial predators out there, doing their night-owl act over this valley. And if so, then anything illuminating up through these clouds at night could go from being hunter to hunted before you can say, 'Talon time.'"

"And so . . . they dim their lights," Yanni said.

Jerry stared out through the panoramic "window," lost in thought for several seconds. "All right," he said at last. "I'll give you that. So the little bit of shadow glow that remains must be completely invisible from above the fog."

Mac nodded. "Ding. No more calls."

Jerry, though, hadn't quite finished with their exercise in hypothesis building. "Also seems to me that shutting off the lights when it gets *really* dark preadapts the local wildlife to avoiding nighttime eyes of another sort."

"You mean, human eyes?"

"Yeah, nighttime recon from the air."

Mac found himself agreeing with his friend once again. Unlike the far more luminous world they had seen in the underground cathedrals, the denizens of the valley had no light-blocking layers of rock overhead. And neither was the snowy fog dense enough to completely block out bioluminescence. Without a carefully timed cycle, the lake of mist would glow as brightly as the twilight sky itself—easily seen from the cliffs above, *and nowadays by passing aircraft.*

"It's either a preadaptation or one hell of a coincidence," Jerry said. "I suppose—"

Yanni jabbed him in the side with an elbow. "Did you see that?"

"I saw it. But what's with the elbow?"

"Keep looking," she replied.

Mac stifled a laugh, knowing that part of the reason she'd thrown the jab was to prevent another round of *Who knew more shit*. Staring through the broad lens of ice, he saw nothing. "I missed it. Whatcha see?"

"A shadow about the size of a horse," said Jerry. "But it was gone in only a second or two."

"Out there with our chompy-grassy pals? You sure?"

"That's what I saw, too, Mac," Yanni affirmed.

If the prison's internal temperature being down near freezing was not enough to make them step away from the ice window, phantasms on the other side decided the issue.

They retreated to the center of their cell and sat back-to-back on the floor, each facing outward to cover one-third of their 360-degree view through the ice. The darkness, and fleeting glimpses of the mysteries it concealed, should have made sleep impossible, but their minds had been in a state of information overload all day, and now, even as their breathing had become easier with each passing hour, they were exhausted. And so one by one they began to slump and doze off.

MAY, A.D. 67

After the acrobatic doctors were finished examining the three Romans, after sunlight had ceased filtering down through the dome's crystalline panes, the living corral of Ceran guards opened up on one side and the trio of humans were shepherded uphill. They were moved toward a central, spiral horn of strong, fiber-infused ice. It was crystalline art, a tower in which perhaps hundreds of Cerae dwelled. Pliny and Proculus were led across a broad balcony to an open-air room, with bowls of warm food laid out beside comfortable-appearing animal pelts. One of the little doctors separated Severus from his friends and two of the race Pliny had begun to call the "warrior caste" ushered Severus along behind her. Without any chittering, any words, or any fuss at all, she disappeared with him into an adjoining chamber.

Pliny puzzled over this for a moment, then looked around.

Where are we?

On the landscape below, only three or four small fires had been lit after sunset, yet Pliny could see clearly. A heatless, opalescent light gradually brightened the interior, highlighting the artistry of the grown arches, and the world over which those arches towered. Aside from a handful of multistoried structures (*indecipherable as to their purpose*, Pliny decided), most of the dome's interior space appeared to be devoted to a concentric arrangement of presumably agricultural gardens. Their captors farmed ghostly white plants varying greatly in height, all of them unfamiliar to the naturalist. A thin, waist-high mist hung over the gardens of the Cerae, filling the air with an underscent like rotten eggs.

The light grew almost bright enough to read by, then brightened further.

"Where are we?" Pliny asked again—this time aloud.

Proculus did not answer him. He had just discovered that some of his flesh was falling away.

For as far back as anyone could remember, the

young man's face was marred by warts—most of them blacker than his Nubian skin, others alarmingly shifting toward an ugly, reddish purple. During the past year, Proculus had come to peace with the dawning reality that some of the growths had been worsening into a condition commonly called "the rocks." To a few, though, the mysterious affliction was known by another name. Pliny knew that, centuries earlier, when Hippocrates had examined victims, the pattern of veins on the solid, malignant tumors reminded him of the legs and claws of a crab. Accordingly, the physician named the condition after the Greek word for the creatures—*carcinos*. Recently, Pliny heard the condition called by the Latin word for crab—cancer.

Proculus scratched at a growth near his lip that had lately begun bleeding. But now, like the large warts that had simply fallen from his cheek, the mass of hardened flesh also came away, leaving behind only the faintest patch of scar tissue.

Surprise and disgust creased the cavalryman's face, and Pliny returned it with his own look of astonishment. "Amazing. And how are you recovering from those smashed-out teeth of yours?" he asked.

He ran the tip of his tongue over the gap in his smile, pressing hard. "Painless," Proculus replied. "Completely painless."

"I would not be surprised to see those teeth trying to grow back," Pliny said, failing to notice that two physicians had mounted the balcony ledge, far more stealthily than any leopard.

"If we can learn *how* they do this, and bring it back to—" Proculus began to say, but cut his words short.

Both men had heard the sound—if only barely—*like parchment shifting in a breeze*. They turned toward the ledge and were startled by the presence of the statue-like visitors.

Pliny wondered if the Cerae had captured additional Westerners over the years. *And if so, might these creatures understand some measure of Latin?*

"It's nice to see you healing so well, Proculus," he said. "Now rest your mouth and speak no more."

The cavalryman looked puzzled for a moment but then nodded.

Yes, Proculus, Pliny told himself. *There is a power here. And a wealth any emperor would envy.*

His new hope was that the Cerae could not read his mind.

PREDAWN, JULY 11, 1946

Not even a shove from the alpha Morlock could have been more startling than the sound that awoke Yanni. It seemed that the very sky had called out to her, first as a low-frequency drone, followed quickly by trumpeting and moaning and clicking.

Jerry, looking alarmed, was on his feet in seconds, staring up at the manhole-size vent in the ceiling.

"What's happening, Yanni?"

"Elephants," she said, noting that while they sounded similar to the unseen animals they had heard upon first entering the valley, these calls were louder and more beautiful. Yet it was also a mournful beauty.

Jerry shook his head. "Elephants can make a sound like that?"

"These can," she said, before gesturing toward the hole at the top of the dome. "Give me a boost, huh?"

The men responded instantly and the lithe Brazilian was soon standing on their shoulders, an ear tilted toward the circular opening.

"Whatcha hear, Yanni?" Mac asked.

"Shhhhh!" she replied, then said quietly, "The calls are bitonal. Each individual can sing the melody and harmonize at the same time."

"Guess it pays to have two trunks," Mac said.

Jerry shook his head. "And these are the same little guys Hendry showed you two at the museum?"

"Yep, miniature mammoths," Yanni replied, impatiently. "Now will you pipe down already?"

The calls were certainly very different from anything Yanni or any other human being had heard, yet at the same time they would have been eerily recognizable to anyone familiar with elephant vocalizations. She was still trying hard to decipher the chorus when the calls changed suddenly before fading away, leaving behind only silence.

Yanni, who had been craning to hear the

sounds through the partially open ceiling of the igloo, slowly sank down into a sitting position—the reason readily apparent to her friends.

Even Jerry, who knew little more about elephants than the typical New York City denizen, seemed to recognize the final notes of this opera. Like a dirge, they communicated the low, painful lamentations of slaves.

R. J. MacCready was about to move in to comfort his friend when, simultaneously, the lights began to come on again outside their prison. Yanni, ever the fascinated visitor to an increasingly strange world, put aside her sadness, if only for a moment, and watched.

Bioluminescent life was preparing to greet the morning twilight.

S oon it was nearly as bright as a full moon outside, bright enough to give depth and shape to shadows moving to and fro in the night. The Morlocks were awake now—if in fact they ever slept at all. One or two of them occasionally came into view, seeming to leer at the prisoners. The combination of their utter alienness and the unusual optics of the ice blocks made it impossible to really know whether their expressions conveyed anger or curiosity—or possibly both. They simply tended to show up on the other side—silently, without any warning or fuss. After a second or two, they vanished like creatures in a dream.

Eventually one of them showed up and did *not* go away. Mac believed it to be the same individual he had come to call Alpha. It slid the door seal effortlessly to one side and entered carrying something.

A few moments later their jailer laid down crudely hewn bowls full of cold soup with generous helpings of the same stringy white fungus that they had been served the day before. In addition, there was a single slab of tough-looking red meat, served on a thin stone platter.

"What, no steak knife?" Jerry asked the giant, who was standing beside the door, arms at his sides. "Jeez."

Mac managed a laugh. "Yeah, why don't you ask him to leave us a pistol, too?"

Jerry shrugged his shoulders before taking a sip of the fungus soup. Moments later he was gulping it. "This is even better than yesterday's," he announced.

Mac's attention, though, was on Yanni, who was clearly gearing up for another of her patented attempts at interspecies communication. As usual, she did not disappoint.

"Rrrr-rhea," Yanni half-said, half-trilled—the same whistling note with which she had exasperated Alpha in the caves.

The Morlock turned its full attention on Yanni. "Rrrr-ah-rhea," it replied.

Yanni nodded, and after only two more attempts she echoed it perfectly.

"That's amazing," Mac said, quietly.

"Yeah, thanks," Yanni replied proudly.

"What's it mean?"

She shrugged her shoulders, all the while keeping a smile directed at her hirsute instructor. "I have no idea."

What Mac *did* understand was that the level of tension in their igloo prison had dropped several notches.

Yanni, eager to continue the lesson, pointed to herself and pronounced her name.

Alpha repeated it.

Not bad, Mac thought. Then, as he watched, the creature pointed at its own chest and sang out something that seemed far too long and cumbersome to be a name. *Perhaps*, he guessed, *it's a recitation of ancestry?*

Yanni stifled a laugh at the unpronounceable string of warbles and quickly decided to steer the linguistic exchange in a different direction. She passed her hands over the bowls and the meat, all the while smiling and keeping her movements slow—avoiding anything that might suggest dominance or aggression.

"Food," Yanni said, the giant still watching her intently. Then she bowed her head slightly for a moment. "Thank you."

Once again, Alpha appeared to consider her combination of gesture and sound before pointing toward the soup. He chirped a few syllables and Yanni began to repeat. Then, without pausing, Alpha gestured toward the meat and pronounced a word, distorted by high pitches that barely passed for syllables. Still, Mac noticed something surprisingly familiar despite the language barrier.

"Alapas?" Yanni repeated, wrinkling her nose questioningly.

"Alafas. *Alafas*," the Morlock said, then turned and departed.

Yanni looked to Mac, noticing that he was suddenly less enthusiastic about the prospect of a linguistic breakthrough than he'd been only moments earlier. "Why the puss, Mac?"

The expression MacCready returned told Yanni that something was definitely wrong. "I think that last bit was Latin."

"Latin?"

"Yeah, a sort of big, hairy, bastardized Latin."

"Alafas," Yanni repeated, slowly, but this time the excitement drained from her voice.

"Well, whatever it is," Jerry announced from behind them, "*this* stuff tastes better than beef."

"I think he was trying to say *Elephas*," Mac said, quietly.

Jerry had a flash of recognition and dropped the meat as if it had stung him.

"It's the little elephants," Yanni whispered.

MacCready suspected that something in the late afternoon soup the Morlocks had brought slowly converted tension and exhaustion into an overpowering sense of relaxation, making it impossible for him to remain alert. The rest of their second day in the igloo prison passed without their captors showing themselves at all. Mac was not quite finished digging a latrine when sleep overtook him. Hours after midnight, with a faint glow from the setting moon filtering down, he and Jerry awoke to find Yanni staring out into the ever-present mist.

"I'll tell you one thing," Jerry said, with as much nonchalance as he could muster, "I'd give just about anything for a smoke and a cuppa joe."

Yanni said nothing. Both she and Mac were members of a minority who did not smoke cigarettes, although neither of them would have turned down a steaming mug of coffee.

Outside, the strange air-suspended snow had thickened, and though there was no wind, some of the flakes moved with a life of their own, swirling like plankton.

"Snowflake mimics," Mac said, to no one in particular. He rose and took up a position several feet from Yanni, close but not crowding her. "Ya gotta wonder what percentage of this snow is actually alive?"

Mac had thrown out what he hoped would be a distraction, however brief, from the recent revelation about their breakfast, the remains of which he had hidden out of sight.

They stood together for a long time, even after the moon had gone down and there was nothing left to see. Like clockwork, as dawn approached the sea of fog, the world gradually filled with phosphorescence, then dimmed its lights with daybreak. Soon there would be only the dull, silvery glow of fog-obscured sunlight.

The sounds of the mammoths were back as well. Coming from somewhere beyond the carnivorous grass, they rose to a slow and steady murmur.

Like a communal moan, Mac thought, but did not say.

Yanni had a similar thought, and occasionally she was able to snatch glimmers of meaning from an individual call. "It sounds to me like most of them are being put to labor," Yanni announced. "Others sound like they're grieving."

"Grieving?" Jerry asked. "How can you tell?"

"Jewell."

"That's the old elephant in Central Park—the one you worked with, right?"

"She died recently," Yanni said, in a disturbingly uncharacteristic monotone. Then, after a pause, "These calls are like the ones Jewell made when she was reminded of her sister."

Jerry looked puzzled, but said nothing.

"Jewell's sister was put down right in front of her," Mac explained quietly.

"And these mammoths are using the same language?" Jerry asked. "Fascinating, given their geographic distribution."

"Well, sort of," she responded, seeming to recover a bit from her gloom. "These calls are more complicated and more—*subtle*—like songs of mourning."

The two men remained silent, allowing Yanni to finish her thoughts.

"And the Morlocks breed them like cattle," Yanni continued, her anger now rising to the surface. "How very *human* of them."

Mac tried to think of something to say that

might soothe his friend, but he found it impossible to get the words out. Yanni wasn't someone who cried easily, but she was on the verge of tears when Alpha returned.

The Morlock was looking none too happy himself, upper lip drawn back to expose a pair of no-nonsense canines, body hair erect and bristling.

This form of communication required no words. It was a language as ancient as the meeting of predator and prey. *Hair-lifting arector pili muscles in full contraction. Fangs bared in a message straight from the sympathetic nervous system.*

Mac did not have to look at Yanni to know that she was experiencing a similar array of involuntary responses—now, thankfully, held in check.

As apparently unconcerned as he was unaware of Yanni's current mental state, Alpha tossed a piece of multigeared machinery at their feet. The metal parts showed no signs of wear and still bore portions of paper tags affixed with a bit of wire.

"Let me guess," Jerry said. "He wants to know who left a mess at the crash site."

"Not quite," Mac added, "although that *is* a spare helicopter part."

"What? They scavenging our bird now?"

Mac shook his head, then moved in and prodded the device with his foot. "That ain't from ours."

"Well whose is it, then?"

CHAPTER 6

Yeren

Whatever we believe about how we got to be the extraordinary creatures we are today is far less important than bringing our intellect to bear on how we get together now around the world and get out of this mess we've made. That's the key thing now. Nevermind how we got to be who we are.
— JANE GOODALL

We become what we do.
— CHIANG KAI-SHEK

Shennongjia Forest, Northwest Hubei Province, China
June 16, 1946 (Four weeks earlier)

A gust of warm, humid air rushed up from the valley floor—from five thousand feet below the overlook on which Wang Tse-lin had set up his tent. It was well past midnight, and once again the biologist was having a difficult time falling asleep. On most nights he could blame his insomnia on the forest sounds—the breeze rustling through stalks of dead bamboo, the high-pitched chatter of bats, or the incessant call of insects he could not identify. But tonight a new sound came to him—and so he sat up in his low cot, cocked an ear, and waited.

With his eyes acclimated to the dark, Wang realized that the canvas flap at the foot of his pup tent was closed, although he distinctly remembered tying it open before he lay down.

Beyond the confines of the tent, from the direction of the small pit of embers where he'd earlier roasted a hare, came a faintly whispered "eh" sound. It was followed by something he made a mental note to record as "a short guttural growl." A response came from a different direction, high-pitched and composed of but a single brief note.

Wang had been in the forest for nearly five weeks now, relocating his campsite every three or four days and only occasionally crossing paths with another soul—usually a villager or a hunter, eager to take him up on his offer to buy the skins and skulls of the strange and unique creatures that inhabited the pristine Shennongjia wilderness. One of the endemic mammals was the *takin*—a large goat antelope whose thick blond coat was said to have inspired the legend of Jason and the Golden Fleece.

The *real* prize, if it existed, was the white bear. Some of Wang's colleagues believed that it existed in legend only, while others suggested that it was an albinic form of brown bear, pointing to the fact that there seemed to be an inordinate number of albino species in this particular forest. Wang, however, hypothesized that the bear was neither legend nor mutant but rather a separate species of *Ursus*. This, of course, would be a major coup for anyone who could provide physical evidence—*especially* if that someone was a young university faculty member like himself.

Now, however, his night visitors seemed a real and present obstacle. Though Wang's bounty for the skin and skull of a white bear was the highest he had offered for any specimen, experienced hunters would not likely have entered his camp at night. And in these parts, few (even if well armed) would have dared move too deeply into the forest after sundown.

Locals, he thought, *desperate to steal my supplies.*

Wang swung his feet toward the tent opening and, having slept in his boots, he reached for the bayonet he'd recovered from a Japanese soldier, dead now for just over three years. The sounds outside his tent had stopped but somehow he could still feel the presence of someone creeping about the campsite.

Who else could it be? Can't be my coworkers, he told himself. None of his three colleagues in the Yellow River Irrigation Committee would have ventured this far into the mountains. Immediately realizing his mistake he shook his head. *Make that two colleagues.*

"The River of Sorrow Flood Committee," is how one of his coworkers had jokingly referred to it on the day the team of four was to depart by boat from the city of Yi Chang. On that same day, the unfortunate jest rendered his colleague a "former associate," reducing the survey team to a trio. Wang knew that there was no way to make even an educated guess at how many friends back home might now be under arrest or had simply disappeared for committing lesser infractions.

The great moment of freedom from the yoke of Japanese occupation lasted precisely that long—a mere moment, so quickly did liberators become oppressors. Men known to Buddhist and Christian survivors as "sainted ones" were vilified each day. Fearless acts that saved lives during the war could be transformed, without warning, into examples of "social incorrectness" or even criminality. The fact was that whoever or whatever happened to be prowling his campsite could induce no more terror in Wang than he himself had already seen in postwar Peking and Shanghai. As civil war raged across China, men and women of every age were rounded up in the night, for any reason at all, or for no reason at all.

The Second Sino-Japanese War had left Wang Tse-lin's country clinically insane. As a scientist, he had concluded: *A human creature driven crazy is a most frightening sight in itself. But when we go crazy together, we are the most terrifying power in all of creation.*

Military and paramilitary mobs now roamed well-paved, big city streets and muddy backwater villages, given free range by whatever gifted abomination of an orator happened to be in command at any given moment. There were intimidating, openly circulated stories about whole families executed, with the parents granted the mercy of death only after watching their children precede them.

Which should I fear more, the rabid mobs or what might lurk right outside, among the rattling bamboo?

For Wang (himself a Ph.D. recipient at Northwestern University in Chicago), a months-long assignment in a primeval deciduous forest was a blessing, specifically because it took him far away from the madness that had so tightly gripped much of his country.

Could my visitors be soldiers sent to arrest me? he wondered, his body reacting to the question with an involuntary shudder. Pulling aside the tent flap, he stepped outside and stood, holding the bayonet.

The River of Sorrow—not a misnomer, Wang Tse-lin had thought upon hearing his coworker's joke, though his own response was stony indifference. He knew that the accumulated sorrows of more than two millennia occurred at the whim of the Tibetan Plateau's glaciers and vast underground springs. Although these were hundreds of miles to the west, without warning they frequently changed the Yellow River from a muddy stream into a flood-blasted channel.

Currently Wang's two remaining colleagues were stumbling around in the humidity and heat of the river valley below.

"What a waste of time," he told himself. *Drafting details of riverbank profiles that might disappear even before those maps can be sent home—only to be ignored by bureaucrats more concerned with not joining "the disappeared" than with the lives of those living along the river.*

Nonetheless, Wang knew that it was important for him to keep the charade going, for to place scientific reality or good sense above political reality could be just as fatal as a coworker's casually tossed joke.

Wang Tse-lin looked in every direction around the campsite, noticing at once that it was completely fogged in. The full moon, which would have been only intermittently visible through the canopy, was covered in thick gray gauze. Even the night sounds seemed to have been swallowed by the heavy wet mist.

No one here, Wang thought. *Maybe it was my—*

The sound of a misplaced footfall on a dead bamboo stalk stopped the thought and he spun in the direction of the disturbance. Flicking on a battery-powered lamp, he aimed the beam into the forest. The fog consumed most of the light before it could reach the source of the sound; it threw the rest of the rays back at him, producing a shapeless white glare.

Villagers, Wang told himself again, though he was inwardly certain that this was not the case. As if to confirm his suspicion, he noticed something else—a musky smell that had not been there earlier. And though he would never come to understand how, it was a scent that chemically circumvented any inclination he might have had to head off into the forest in search of his visitors.

Ten minutes later the biologist was back in his tent, and despite the musky night visitor, and the discomfort that a sheathed bayonet made for a bedmate, physical and emotional exhaustion had done their work. He was soon fast asleep, and at peace.

It did not last—could not last, in a time and place such as this.

Before the moon had moved halfway across the sky, he was awakened by a single gunshot. The blast echoed up the canyon like a reverse thunderclap. It was followed several seconds later by the distant baying of dogs—incessant and aggressive. *They smell blood*, Wang thought, a moment before another sound pierced the night. It was an almost human cry—high-pitched and conveying fear. Simultaneously muffled and echoed, magnified and distorted by the combination of fog and valley walls, the shriek passed through his campsite like a ghost. The reaction from below to this sound was completely different from the response to gunfire. It was as if someone had flicked a switch— the forest and indeed what seemed to be the entire canyon went completely silent: no dogs, no bats, and no insects. Even the windblown clacking of the dead bamboo seemed to have stopped.

At dawn, Wang quickly broke down his campsite and began a descent toward the nearest village, in the direction of the previous night's gunshot. As usual, the hike was treacherous. The Silurian karstic limestone that made up the Daba Mountains was riddled with cavities ranging from finger length to cavernous—nearly all of them hidden by dense scrub and a thick layer of humus. One false step could easily lead to a broken leg—which in these regions was often indistinguishable from a sentence of slow death. An even faster route to the afterlife might be found in a crash through the thin ceiling of an uncharted cavern system—a spectacular but final discovery for an unlucky explorer.

Even before he reached the village, Wang Tse-lin could see the smoke from its morning cook fires. Though the settlement, a half-dozen bamboo huts with thatched roofs, defined remote, there was no fear of being treated as an intruder. Having visited before, he entered the clearing and found slightly more than a dozen people standing together.

Nearly the whole village.

They were gathered around something on the ground. The men crowded in close—the women and children on the periphery. As Wang approached, heads turned in his direction. Recognizing their strangely dressed visitor, the tight cluster of men parted, allowing him a first look at what appeared to be a body lying prone and wearing an elaborate ceremonial costume. Raising a hand in greeting, Wang nodded and advanced.

His first revelation was that the figure lying before him wasn't wearing a costume at all. It was in fact covered from head to foot in dense, grayish-red hair. And, although the body was clearly bipedal, it was definitely *not* human.

"Yeren!" the leader of the village cried. He was a wiry-looking man, with a bowl haircut. Immediately the others followed with their consensus opinion: "Yeren! Yeren!"

Wang dropped his backpack and knelt to examine the creature, lying facedown on a patch of wet earth. A fist-size hole in the lower back showed how it had died—its spine severed by a single gunshot and most of the abdominal organs blown through.

He estimated it to have stood around six feet tall, perhaps a shade taller. Extending a hand, he touched one of the elongated arms—which had been thrown forward, completely obscuring the face.

The body is still supple, Wang realized, before being startled by what he thought was the heavily muscled limb beginning to move. His momentary alarm gave the assembled crowd a good laugh, and he quickly realized that two of the men were turning the corpse over to get a better look.

Later, Wang Tse-lin wrote in his field notebook:

The creature turned out to be a mother with a large pair of breasts, the nipples being very red as if it had recently given birth. The hair on the face was shorter and the face itself was narrow with deep-set eyes, while the cheekbones and lips jutted out. The scalp hair was roughly one foot long and untidy. The appearance was very similar to the plaster model of a female Peking Man.

After examining the body, Wang questioned the villagers, who told him that the Yeren had *always* lived in the forest and that two of them, a male and a female, had been in the area for over a month. The creatures were reported to have great strength and "were very brisk in walking," with the ability to move as rapidly uphill as on a plain.

"This," the chief explained, "makes it difficult for normal people to catch up with them."

The biologist nodded and forced a smile. *Unless those normal people have rifles*, he thought, but left unsaid.

"They do not have a language," the head local assured the biologist, with his "expertise" regarding the Yeren beginning to wear a bit thin. "They can only howl."

Wang requested and was granted a meeting with all three of the village leaders. He presented his university ID card again, reminding the men that he was on a government-sponsored mission and that his superiors would certainly express their gratitude for the sale of the Yeren's body, though the payment could be no more than he had previously offered for a specimen of white bear.

"These are hard times," Wang added in a grave tone. "And there is little funding for this sort of

work, especially since we have several similar specimens donated by villages in the western portion
of the district." This last part was, of course, not
true but it quickly produced the desired effect.

"Of course you may have the wild woman,"
the chief said, with the wave of a hand and a gap-
toothed grin. "The forest has plenty of game and
there are plenty of Yeren."

Though Wang was puzzled at the mention of
game, the thought was soon forgotten in the excitement of having so easily procured a specimen
of such monumental scientific importance. The
chief even volunteered to provide him with the
salt necessary to dry the "Yeren's" pelt and the services of a pair of stout villagers who were said to
be "the finest skinners in the region." Wang expressed his gratitude, then insisted on paying extra for an oversize clay jar half-full of the potent
local home brew, into which he intended to preserve as many samples of the organs and other soft
tissue as he could.

The day proved to be very long and very bloody
and by the end of it Wang was not only exhausted
but also covered in gore. The amiable chief, noting the weight of the now specimen-filled jar,
assigned two porters to transport it—first to the
river, then by canoe to the town of Yi Chang.

"When you arrive, you can tell your bosses
about us!" the chief suggested enthusiastically.
"How generous we were."

"Your people are indeed generous," Wang
said, "but telling my supervisors might send the
wrong message." He paused, thinking about the

coworker who disappeared after having uttered a single, harmless joke. Wang could see that the chief was confused, so he continued. "What if . . . more and more *guests* arrived . . . trapping your forest animals, killing the Yeren?"

The local nodded, solemnly. "That would be bad."

By nightfall, the specimen had been completely packed, as had an array of sharp, newly washed instruments used to skin and prepare the creature. Wang bowed deeply, thanking the chief for his generosity before presenting him with a brass pocket compass that he'd owned since childhood.

Shortly before dawn, the biologist and his two porters began their descent out of the Shennong-jia Forest. Although there would be no specimens of white bear to study and describe, Wang Tse-lin knew he would be returning to civilization with something of *far* greater value—the salt-packed skin, alcohol-preserved entrails, and partially disarticulated skeleton of an unknown primate—a creature that by all appearances had evolved along a branch somewhere between humans and apes. In all likelihood it would become one of the greatest scientific discoveries of the twentieth century. But while this was certainly a cause for celebration, another emotion was creeping into his consciousness. These days, even in the presence of a discovery that put his greatest childhood dreams to shame, darkness lurked beneath the excitement—a sense of fear and dread that would not go away.

The inland port city of Yi Chang
Western Hubei Province, China

JUNE 20, 1946

A trip from the Shennongjia Forest to Yi Chang required four full days. During the second day, Wang and his escorts arrived at a larger village where he was able to hire a motor launch. He also contacted his supervisor at the Irrigation Committee as well as his university department chairman. The former instructed him to check into a hotel in Yi Chang and wait for further word. The latter, after determining that Wang had not lost his mind, urged him to "safeguard the specimen at all costs."

"Someone will meet you," he was assured, "when you disembark at the Yi Chang's central harbor."

Two days later, as his boat approached the crowded dock, he saw a line of ten or twelve soldiers, standing at attention behind an impatient-looking army officer.

"Are you Dr. Wang Tse-lin?" the man called.

"I am," the biologist replied.

The officer gestured to one of his men and immediately the soldier stepped forward to receive the bowline from the frightened-looking boat pilot, who immediately retreated and checked the fuel level of a gas tank he had planned to refill after getting paid.

"You and your specimen must come with me," the officer snapped at Wang.

"Yes, but—"

The military man held up a hand. "Enough talk!" With that, he signaled for his men to remove the scientist, his bags, and the containers containing the Yeren from the vessel. "Take them to the trucks."

Within minutes, Wang was sitting in the back of a seven-passenger, armored scout car. He knew that the Americans had been supplying Chiang Kai-shek's National Revolutionary Army with outdated and sometimes barely functional vehicles and equipment since 1942. The scientist noted that the interior of this particular model was so poorly ventilated that the engine fumes became almost immediately nauseating. Of more concern to Wang was his precious Yeren specimen—which had been loaded into a second vehicle. Now, as both truck drivers gunned their engines, Wang glanced back to see the motor launch pilot doing exactly the same thing—rapid departure. Their vehicles were now speeding in opposite directions, throttles open. What disturbed him most was that the boatman had never even bothered to collect his fee.

Less than a half hour later, the two trucks slowed down at a checkpoint outside the Yi Chang airport. The guards there quickly ushered them through and the vehicles made their way toward the runway. Wang could see that the few planes present had been shifted to one side, and the reason for this was immediately and perplexingly apparent. Three of the strangest-looking helicopters he had ever seen—or imagined he would ever see—were arrayed along the blacktopped runway.

They look like enormous bananas, Wang thought.

CHAPTER 7

A Hitch in the Plan

*Civilization is like a thin layer of ice
upon a deep ocean of chaos and darkness.*
—WERNER HERZOG

I see technology as a Trojan Horse.
—DANIEL GREENBERG

*Trojan is a horrible name for a
brand of condoms. Why name it after
something that, after penetrating the
wall, broke open to let [an army] of
little guys pour out and [mess] things
up for everyone?*
—ANON.

Metropolitan Museum of Natural History
Theodore Roosevelt Auditorium
July 12, 1946

Did you know that Selznick
cut ten minutes out of that
Dalí dream sequence?" The

film director had used a slight pause in the musical program to inform Charles Knight of this seemingly important fact about his most recent motion picture.

"Really," Knight whispered back, hoping his guest would keep his lugubrious, and soon-to-be-world-famous, voice down.

Onstage, composer Bernard Herrmann had just finished conducting a full symphony orchestra in the *Prologo* to what would become his only solo opera, *Wuthering Heights*.

"Now this is what I've *really* come to hear," said Alfred Hitchcock.

With the aid of an assistant, a young musician carried something that more resembled an odd piece of cabinetry than a musical instrument, to a spot adjacent to where the conductor stood.

Herrmann, already famous for scoring *Citizen Kane*, and *Jane Eyre*, basked in the applause of a sold-out audience before introducing the newly arrived musician with a wave of his hand.

"It's a theremin, my dear man." Hitchcock continued his monologue, every syllable given its own moment, even as the rest of the auditorium went silent.

Knight flashed a tight smile, then turned quickly toward the stage.

"Miklós Róza used one in *Spellbound*."

Someone in the row behind them shushed the director, who immediately pivoted in his seat. Appraising the considerable size of the "shusher," whose biceps seemed a serious threat to burst his tuxedo jacket, Hitchcock chose survival, turning back again toward the stage himself. "Riffraff," he mumbled.

From her seat on the other side of Charles Knight, Patricia Wynters quietly let out a breath she felt like she'd been holding for several minutes. As she breathed in again, sounds that might have come from a ghost orchestra filled the auditorium, although oddly, the musician producing the notes was not even touching the instrument—instead passing his hands in the proximity of a pair of metal antennae.

How chillingly wonderful, she thought, watching as the "thereminist" (as he would later be introduced to her) seemed to wring eerie swoops and flutters from the very air.

H is majesty awaits," Knight warned Patricia, in a whisper.

Patricia had grown accustomed to giving tours of the museum's Vertebrate Zoology Department. What she found most amusing was the fact that dignitaries of every ilk, in addition to all manner of the rich and famous, reacted in precisely the same way—leaving their titles and self-importance in the elevators as they stepped onto the museum's legendary fifth floor. Once there, each of them was a child again—from kings to stuffy British directors—and each was thrilled by the opportunity to visit a part of the museum they knew few people would ever see.

And tonight is no different, Patricia thought, unable to suppress a smile. For while Alfred Hitchcock was being given a personal tour of the paintings and dinosaur statuary in Charles Knight's office (by the artist himself), "Call Me Benny" Herrmann was demonstrating a theremin (which had recently been gifted to Knight) for an uncharacteristically bemused Major Patrick Hendry. Choosing to avoid the aural torture that soon followed—as the major initiated a series of rude-looking contortions in a vain attempt to play theremin "Chopsticks"— Wynters and the composer wandered over to where Hitchcock was admiring Knight's *Tyrannosaurus rex* model.

"There's something terribly familiar about this creature," the director said, stretching the sentence out so that it seemed like a paragraph.

Knight laughed. "I agree. My colleague Edwin Colbert thinks they're birds, or rather that birds are dinosaurs. A fascinating concept, no?"

Bernard Herrmann nudged his corpulent new acquaintance. "Alfred, can you imagine these horrors running wild across the earth today?"

The director said nothing, apparently lost in thought, so Knight responded, "I guess we should be thankful the modern versions have lost both their size and their teeth."

"I'm not sure that would matter, my dear Charles," Hitchcock replied. "They do have numbers on their side."

Patricia was just about to chime in when the sound of a crash from across the room caused them all to jump.

Four pairs of eyes turned toward the commotion, which found the redheaded Army officer holding his hands up as if in surrender. The theremin lay tipped over and splintered on the floor, emitting a thin trail of smoke and a brief sizzle before it died.

"I barely touched it," the major exclaimed, defensively.

At that very moment, in a small dark room less than a block away on Central Park West, a man screamed and fell backward off his chair, tearing at the headphones he had been wearing and kicking over a monitoring device—which flew in the opposite direction.

"Are you out of your mind, Julius?" came the loud whisper of a second man, spoken in Russian.

The man on the floor moaned and rubbed his ears.

"I assume you've lost contact," the other man said.

"*What?*" the man on the floor said, in a voice that was far too loud considering where they were and what they were doing.

Suddenly, a bang on the wall, followed by an only slightly muffled voice, "Hey! How 'bout shuttin' up in there?"

"Yes . . . sorry," the man who was standing called back in unaccented English.

"My kids are tryin' ta listen to Fibber *fucking* McGee and Molly!" the plasterboard explained.

"Okay then. We are just fine in here," the man reassured the wall. "Thank you." Then, when there was no further response, he turned to the man on the floor. "You see what you have done?" he hissed in Russian. "Wait until Comrade Theremin hears how you've destroyed his prized bug."

The man on the floor nodded but then quickly shook his head. "*What?*"

CHAPTER 8

Foreign Parts

*Time destroys the speculation of men, but
it confirms nature.*
—MARCUS TULLIUS CICERO

In waking a tiger, use a long stick.
—MAO ZEDONG

South Tibet
July 12, 1946

R. J. MacCready held up his
hands "peaceful-guy" style,
waited a beat to gauge Alpha's response, then knelt beside the machinery
that the Morlock had dumped on the ground.

"This looks like part of a helicopter transmission," he said, shifting the object onto its side.
"Definitely American made."

Yanni moved in beside him. "How can you tell?"

"Serial numbers are in Arabic numerals. But take a gander," he said, pointing to a flat section of metal with a set of characters stamped in red.

"Well, that's definitely *not* American," she replied.

"Chinese, from what I can tell."

"It *is* Chinese," Jerry confirmed.

Yanni shot them a confused look. "But how did the Chinese get their mitts—"

"Lend-Lease," Mac said. "Back in '41, we started sendin' shitloads of supplies to the Brits, French, and Soviets—trucks, railroad equipment, helicopters, and the like. Some of it went to China."

The Morlock, who had been standing by silently, now took the opportunity to emit an impatient-sounding growl.

"I guess somebody needs to explain that to Alpha here," Jerry suggested, doing his best imitation of "the least threatening human in Tibet."

Mac pointed to the machinery, shot the creature a quizzical look, and then shrugged his shoulders. "No clue, big guy," he said.

The Morlock emphasized his next growl with a facial display that caused Mac to momentarily imagine being driven into the ground like a screaming, six-foot-long tent peg.

Sensing calamity, Yanni stepped between her friend and the giant. "I've got this one," she said to Mac and Jerry. Rather than speaking to the creature, or even looking it directly in the eye, she knelt down and smoothed a section of the dark loamy soil into a sort of canvas. Then, using only her index finger, she began to draw.

The figure was clearly meant to depict the face of a Morlock. Mac noted that Yanni correctly portrayed the long hair but had decided to leave out the snarl and the canines.

"Nice touch with the smiley kisser," Mac said quietly, and by way of support.

Yanni did not bother to respond. Instead she pointed to the portrait and then to Alpha. She repeated the move, checking to make sure that the Morlock had made the connection. Apparently he did.

Next, she drew a rather decent facsimile of MacCready's face and reenacted the pointing-from-picture-to-object pantomime, while Mac tried as hard as possible to resemble the caricature. Finally, she drew a third figure, this one with what appeared to be exaggerated Asian features. Completing it, she pointed at helicopter parts and then to the last section of her artwork.

The response by the Morlock, whose initial transition from jailer to art critic seemed to have diminished his anger, took an unexpected turn. With canines in full threat display again, the giant moved forward and used its foot to stamp out the last figure.

"Serr-rah!" Alpha growled.

"I'm guessing he's not a big fan of Impressionism," Jerry muttered. Mac and Yanni followed up by flashing him a matching pair of *shut the hell up* looks.

"SERR-RAH!" Alpha emphasized, in a tone that was simultaneously a roar, yet part of a curiously birdlike language.

"Sarah?" Mac wondered out loud. "Sure doesn't sound Chinese."

"Jesus," Jerry said. "I don't think he's saying Sarah."

"SERR-RAH!"

"Lemme guess," Yanni said. "More bastardized Latin."

"You got it. *Sere* is the Roman word for Chinese."

"But how the hell do the Morlocks know Latin?"

The trio exchanged glances, each of them sharing the same thought: *Pliny.*

MAY, A.D. 67

For a creature of such short stature, the little doctor was astonishingly strong.

Moments after the female Ceran physician separated Severus from his two friends and led him indoors, she pushed him to the ground. Then she brought her face close to his—holding him spellbound, as if by the stare of a cobra. Severus found it impossible to determine, from the Ceran's expression, what to expect. All he knew for certain was that, at any chosen instant, she could strike him dead.

Pliny, what did you get me into this time?

"The only certainty is uncertainty," Pliny had said. Severus, however, was not so sure. One certainty *did* gnaw at him: that he was losing, forever, everything that his family had built for him back home. It occurred to the young Roman that Pliny had planned to seduce him away from art and engineering, into doomed expeditions such as this. By the time the voyage was planned, his family owned the Bay of Naples's most educated and artistic slaves. They counted themselves among the city's wealthiest architects and engineers.

All those carefully planned connections and all that hard work—wasted.

Looking back, he could see that once Pliny caught sight of an explorer's uneasiness in him, he had begun stoking the fires of confusion. The older man had recognized in Severus a student torn between wanderlust and the desire to design great machines. Eventually Pliny convinced him that there was no need to choose one love over the other. Like a half-dozen others in the handpicked expedition team, Pliny had deceived him into believing that he could live out all of his dreams.

And how have those dreams rewarded me? Severus asked himself, and tried to avert his eyes from the beastly physician. But she would not let him turn his head away. *I'm dead*, the centurion thought. And for a single, nightmarish moment, true fear welled up like a punch against his heart. By the time the Roman shook aside that emotion, two other physicians had descended into the dwelling. They flitted in with such fluid and silent motion that he failed to notice their presence, or their exit. He simply realized, with a start, that someone else had draped a warm robe over his shoulders—incomparably soft to the touch and woven from a delicate fiber that was neither wool nor cotton.

Perhaps I will not be joining our honored dead quite yet, he thought.

He had no sooner realized how hungry he was when the physician who had apparently chosen him as her own personal captive produced a bowl of hot broth. Surprisingly tasty, it contained generous helpings of a strange grain that defied identification.

"*Gratiam*," Severus said, thanking her in Latin. The Ceran locked her large, almond-shaped eyes with his again, trying unsuccessfully to imitate the sound he had just made. She studied his expression, then raised a hand and shoved him hard on one shoulder.

Message received, Severus told himself. *Repeat.*

"*Gratiam*," he said.

"*Graaa-tee-yum*," she shot back at him, though far more accurately this time—even down to the parroting of his accent and the slight speech impediment that served to further bastardize his Latin. Again the physician struck his shoulder with the "repeat" signal.

He said the word again, slowly raising the bowl and sipping from it. This time she pronounced it even more precisely, though Severus wondered if the physician believed herself to have learned his word for the bowl of soup, or the thanks he had expressed for receiving it.

She motioned toward her eye and uttered a long, trilling whistle. After his third try at parroting it back to her, he began to realize that the word—if it was a word—contained multiple whistled inflections in *more* than six syllables. He tried . . . and failed. Then failed again. He hoped their words for a simple "yes" or "no" would prove easy enough to at least start something like a conversation. They were—just barely.

After mastering a handful of Latin words in only a few tries, it became clear that whatever passed for Roman language was far simpler (and perhaps more primitive) than the Ceran tongue.

The lessons continued until dawn. By then, only occasionally did she attempt to teach him her own words, and each time, he failed. At one point Severus became vaguely aware that the stench from the one he would henceforth refer to as "Teacher" had become a nearly tolerable background odor. As daylight began flooding in, Teacher's cobra stare was still horribly apparent, yet not quite so threatening as it had seemed to him at sunset. Now he noticed that when the pupils of her eyes narrowed, they revealed irises like those of an alpine wolf, flecked with speckles of blue-green. Those eyes, and the dyed stripes of the creature's mane, were the only signs of pigment on her entire body.

Belonging to a people who could deliver death with both speed and cunning, Severus knew that this rendered Teacher was as fascinating as she was dangerous. He saw in her a being who was at once amazing and obscene, terrifying and wonderfully mysterious.

CHAPTER 9

The Missing

*What seest thou else, in the dark
backward and abysm of time?*
　—WILLIAM SHAKESPEARE, *THE TEMPEST*
　(ACT 1, SCENE 2)

*South Tibet
July 12, 1946*

This is some seriously perplexing shit," Jerry said, after Morlock "Alpha" singled out and obliterated the last of the three caricatures Yanni had drawn in the soil, then left with the Chinese helicopter parts.

"What's up?" Mac said, though clearly preoccupied with his own thoughts.

"I'm still wondering what they've got against the Chinese."

Mac shrugged, and looked through the curved wall of ice at the swarming field of inchworm grass just beyond. Distracted by it, he thought aloud, "Some sort of hive organism—like wasps."

"Huh?" Jerry said, puzzled. Then he turned his gaze to the seething, carnivorous lawn. "Oh, them. Gotcha."

Together the two men watched silently, lost in thought, until Jerry spoke. "So here I am, Mac, thinking you've already been through enough strange shit to last a lifetime. Like that little adventure you had in Brazil."

"And?"

"So do you ever get the feeling that we're being dragged down Alice's rabbit hole?"

MacCready paused for a moment. "I suppose it feels like that sometimes, although that 'adventure' in Brazil was certainly no fantasy." Then he gestured to the activity taking place just outside. "And neither is this one."

"I guess what I mean is . . . do you ever get *used* to it?"

MacCready thought about it for a moment, and then for another. "I don't know if 'get used to it' is the right phrase," he said at last. "You travel to incredible places—dangerous places—and too often you don't come back with as many people as you went in with. But somehow you feel honored to be there."

"Even though the story can end badly," Yanni added, before falling into stony silence.

Mac knew that her thoughts were drifting back to another time and another place.

Ashamed that he'd done something to upset the

only person in the world he *never* wanted to upset, Mac backpedaled. "Jerry, have I told you about Bob Thorne's diaper invention?"

Jerry, who also noticed what had just occurred, shook his head.

"Sparties!" Yanni blurted out, with a laugh.

Now Mac's face broke into a wide grin. He supposed that this might have been the first time since Bob's death that Yanni could recall something about him more with laughter rather than pain.

"Sparties?"

"Yeah, Jerry—a diaper you only have to change every month!" Mac announced proudly.

"The Spartan thirty-day diaper," said Yanni, picking up the story. "The baby fits inside—"

"—except for their head," Mac added, with a laugh.

"Right," Yanni continued, "and you kind of secure it around the kid's neck." She made a string-tying motion around her own neck. "Done!"

Jerry threw his friends a skeptical look. "Then what?"

Mac continued the pitch. "Then thirty days later, you take Junior out of his diaper, hose him down, and leave 'em out in the sun to dry."

Yanni finished up, "Then ya stick 'em into a new Spartie and he's good to go."

Jerry laughed before shaking his head at the imagery. "Sparties, huh? Sounds like your Bob was a real hoot."

Yanni nodded, and gave Jerry a rare compliment, a showing of respect that would have gone over the heads of most outside observers. "I'm sure you two woulda become great friends," she said. "I'm startin' to think you're our kind of stupid."

The trio lapsed into silence as the here-again, gone-again white shapes they had been watching converged menacingly outside the igloo.

The ice-sculpted door slid open. This time Alpha and two other giants entered without uttering any sounds. Each took a prisoner under an arm, exited, then started off at a fast jog—the sea of grass mimics parting before the three Morlocks. Mac glanced around in every direction, trying to get his bearings. His best guess was that they were headed back toward the cave system they had passed through earlier. He tried to take in more details but "the armpit express" was moving with such haste that there was time enough only to *think* he had seen something large and white foraging in the mist—but the moment passed so quickly that now he could not be sure.

Soon they were once again in among the tunnels and cathedral-like caverns, the supporting ribs and buttresses lit brightly by heatless fire. After passing through a chamber system so large that St. Patrick's Cathedral could easily have been contained in one of its side branches, the prisoners were taken into an alcove and unceremoniously dropped to the floor.

What Mac saw confirmed beyond all doubt that the Morlocks had been the architects of this undiscovered realm. But of morality and wisdom, no matter how intelligent these beings might be, they could easily match humanity's own savage impulses, black for black. The stalagmites told it so—row upon row of polished ice columns.

No, Mac reminded himself. *Not merely polished— planned and constructed.*

From the floor up, it was an atrocity of rare design. In this most brilliantly illuminated of subterranean chambers, the pinnacles spoke, in crystal clarity, of the savage brain. There were hundreds of the artificial stalagmites, each cut into a perfect cylinder, each enclosing and preserving one or more "specimens." Some were zoological, some were botanical, while others were clearly man-made. But by far most of the shapes entombed in ice were human—sometimes dozens of people in a single enormous column.

"Like—"

"—flies trapped in amber." Yanni completed Mac's thought.

The Morlocks prodded their three human captives, as if to say, *Go and see.*

And so they did.

"Holy shit!" Jerry blurted out. "Their equipment is here, too!"

"Who?" Mac asked, trying to keep up with Jerry as he ran from one pillar to the next, barely pausing at each for more than a glance. To Mac it seemed as if his friend was trying to fill his mind with everything he could glimpse before the Morlocks stopped him—and he looked that way because, in fact, he was. Jerry finally came to a momentary halt at one of the tallest cylinders. Inside, no fewer than twenty soldiers were arranged in a semicircle amid broken pieces of military equipment—artillery, firearms, and swords.

Mac could see, in at least a dozen of the pillars standing nearby, that all the bodies encased within were wearing the same uniforms.

Jerry, who had resumed his flitting back and forth between columns, followed silently by the trio of Morlocks, finally came to a stop.

"Chinese," he said, pointing to one of the icy displays, then turning to his captors. Their expressions seemed to be wavering somewhere between mild amusement and annoyance, but Jerry appeared unconcerned. He repeated the word, then shrugged, clearly hoping that the gesture conveyed three truths to the Morlocks: confusion, surprise, and finally, a message: *We are not Chinese and we are not your enemies* (the latter Jerry emphasized with some hand-waving that reminded Mac of an interpretive dance).

Jerry turned to his friends. "Ever heard of the Yangtze disappearance?"

Mac and Yanni both shook their heads.

"You mean the Nanking disappearance?" Mac asked.

"No," Jerry said, quite unable to hide his excitement. "Although it did happen around the time Nanking fell to Japan back in '37."

"And?"

"And there's even less known about this one. Nothing but rumors, really. What we *do* know is that the Chinese sent a large force up into the mountains, beyond the source of the Yangtze. Tremendous undertaking—with all sorts of equipment. Huge generators. Cannons. They hauled it all up there."

"The proverbial 'force to be reckoned with,'" Mac said.

"Exactly. Something like three thousand men. Anyway—"

Mac held up his hand. "Jerry."

"Yeah, Mac?"

"Take a breath."

"Oh, right," Jerry said, looking slightly embarrassed. "At any rate, from the way Alpha responded to Yanni's drawing, I'm guessing these Yangtze guys must have killed more than a few Morlocks before they fell."

Yanni looked around. "And there were three thousand of 'em, huh?"

"I know what you're thinking," Jerry responded quickly, and, as Mac and Yanni exchanged glances, he made a quick recount of the Chinese-laden columns. "There's not nearly enough bodies here, right?"

"War trophies?" Yanni suggested.

"Or maybe museum pieces?" Mac said with a shrug. "Who can tell what's really going on here?"

"*They* can," Yanni said, gesturing toward the Morlocks. "If we can learn to speak their language."

She paused at a particularly gruesome pillar that seemed to tell the fate of a similarly armed group, though these were wearing different uniforms. Young men had been tied in a circle with their feet at the axis—and above them, another layer had been tied likewise, with their heads facing outward. There were twenty such layers, encased one upon another within the column of ice. Yanni could see that those on the lower layers had the life crushed out of them by the layers above. A Japanese war flag left no mystery as to their origin.

Yanni pointed to the banner. "Maybe these guys tracked the Chinese up into the mountains?"

"And ran into quite a surprise." Mac finished the thought.

Jerry continued moving forward into the forest of crystalline display cases. Yanni followed, then Mac, without any discouragement from the Morlocks.

He halted at a display of what was apparently a lost German expedition, pre–World War II. "I'd say your Morlocks have been playing this gig for a long time."

Mac found himself overwhelmed by the sheer variety of organisms, tools, and people on display. The chamber really did remind him of a museum—full of historical clues, and with nothing random about it. In fact, the deeper they walked from the alcove entrance, the deeper they traveled backward in time.

"Holy mackerel. Will you look at that," Jerry exclaimed. "I mean, who knew that Templars made it this far?"

R. J. MacCready nodded, his puzzlement giving way to something else. He had sometimes felt inadequate against the broad canvas of Jerry's knowledge—which seemed to span every arcane subject and, by comparison, often left the zoologist feeling a little too specialized in his own field. This was hardly a cause for despair. Mac hoped, as any true teacher or explorer hoped, that Jerry and others who followed would surpass him.

Only a few short paces from the Templar knight, Jerry paused at a display of men and their horses. They seemed to have died together, in twisted agony, within the ice itself.

"Khan's men," Jerry announced.

Mac peered through the ice. "So Genghis lost an army, too, huh?"

"His grandson Kublai did. Or so say the legends," Jerry replied.

"Well, they might be from the right time, in this sequence, but they certainly took a wrong turn somewhere."

Jerry led Mac and Yanni farther down through the centuries until a carved golden eagle, encased in ice, brought him to a stop. Behind the winged symbol of Rome, the rest of the column contained a tangle of bodies.

"Those Pliny's men?" Yanni asked.

"I don't think so," Jerry said as he moved in for a closer look at the eagle. Turning to Mac, he said, "You've been boning up on your Roman history. Who do you think they are?"

There had been damage to the inscription beneath the talons of the sacred icon, but even through the distorting lens of ice, Mac was able to read enough. "Not Pliny's Romans, that's for sure."

"You give up?"

"I think it's the Ninth Legion."

"Excellent!" Jerry said. "The *Legio nona Hispana*."

"Show-off," Mac said, under his breath. "Jeez, that would be about what—forty years *after* Pliny?"

Jerry replied, with a smile. "Yeah, something like that—forty, fifty." He was about to place a hand on the ice containing the Romans but a glance at the Morlocks made him stop. "This one's a real head-scratcher though."

"How so?"

"I sure as hell wouldn't have expected to find the Ninth Legion anywhere near Tibet."

"So how'd they get here?" Mac wondered.

"Dunno," Jerry said. "According to historians, the Ninth was either annihilated in northern Britain by Celtic tribes or they were transferred."

Yanni moved in for a closer look. "I'd vote for number two. But transferred where?"

"Possibly to the Jordan Valley," Jerry said, continuing the tale. "One rumor has them moving east from there into India."

"And what were they doing in India?" Yanni asked.

Mac shrugged and turned to Jerry, who shook his head. "Who knows? Like I said, it was pretty much just a rumor, sung by ancient poets. What is clear is that there's no trace of the Ninth after A.D. 120. After which they *did* pick up a new moniker."

Jerry waited, but the pair remained silent.

"Go on," Mac said at last.

"Rome's Ghost Legion."

"So they just up and disappeared?" Yanni asked.

"All five thousand of them, poof—gone."

Yanni gestured toward the columns. "Until now."

She knelt down near the base of the pillar, where a Roman leg had been thrust close to the surface of the ice—thrust at an angle so awkward that she supposed it would have been extremely painful were he alive in that final moment. Dozens of yellowish strands seemed to have sprouted out of the leg, tearing at the flesh before he died.

"Talk about your shitty transfers," Mac chimed in.

Yanni squinted at the bizarre wounds. "What are those things?"

A shove at Jerry's left shoulder blade communicated that Alpha was finally becoming impatient with the conversation. Obediently, the trio moved in the direction indicated by the shove, down through the second century B.C. into Hannibal's time. Far ahead, Mac could see bodies whose faces were pressed near the outer surface of an ice pillar. They displayed distinctly Asian features but their hair was bright red.

Mac was certain that the Morlocks' collection went back at least through the Bronze Age—past the incongruous-looking redheads and beyond the first dynasties of emperors and pharaohs alike. "Jerry," he asked, "you've heard of Howard Carter, right?"

"Sure, Mac. Why? He sure as hell didn't get this far."

"No, but I was just thinking that discovering Tutankhamun's tomb completely intact might take a backseat to a thirty-foot walk in any direction down here."

Jerry was about to respond when his attention was suddenly diverted by something near the very center of the chamber. The Morlocks allowed him to sidetrack past a display of Jin Dynasty infantrymen and their rockets, toward the tallest and widest of the pillars they had encountered thus far.

It stretched high above the backs of the elephants entombed within—and in fact four of the neighboring pillars also contained elephants, along with their drivers. The frozen pachyderms were outfitted in protective plating and the warriors astride them also wore battle armor and thick furs. Mac was just telling himself that the soldier nearest to him looked either Chinese or Cambodian—and possibly female—when Yanni distracted him. She had knelt down beside one of the entombed elephants. Clearly, she was deeply immersed in her own thoughts.

Despite the distinct possibility that the remainder of their lives would henceforth unfold under the whim of the Morlocks, and despite certain grim details of their immediate surroundings, Mac had at least some small measure of success in convincing himself that being here was an astonishing turn of good luck. For now, even Jules Verne's fictional Captain Nemo and his discovery of the ruins of lost Atlantis could not compare to this.

"Hannibal's army?" Mac spoke, not quite believing his own question.

"I don't think so," Jerry replied, when Alpha's call startled them both.

The Morlock had been watching intently as Yanni sketched yet another figure into the earth—

this time it was an elephant's head. And after emitting a rather loud call, the giant was kneeling down beside her, using an index finger to draw his own version of the figure.

He looks almost enthusiastic, Mac thought.

"*Alafas*," Yanni said, then quickly sketched one of the two-trunked mammoths Knight had described back in New York.

But the Morlock did not respond to Yanni. Instead, Mac saw that Alpha's attention was drawn to the pair of Morlocks who had been standing by silently. One of them displayed what had been a seriously deep and recent wound, running from above his left temple down to the jawline. Now almost completely healed, the wound was discernible mostly as a line of slightly mismatched fur. Alpha and "Scarface" had both begun uttering low-frequency growls.

The pair exchanged a series of whistles and canine-flashing grunts that concluded with Alpha looking frustrated and even angry. Turning back to Yanni, the creature erased the drawing of the bi-trunked *Elephas* before lifting her up gently. Then, as swiftly as she had been carried into the chamber of ice and lost souls, Yanni was whisked away from its center, and up again through time.

The two men exchanged frantic looks before MacCready turned and caught a last glimpse of Alpha retreating out of the chamber. Their own escorts approached quickly, each of them hefting their human cargo before setting off at a trot. To Mac, however, it seemed as if they were being handled more roughly this time.

"Where do you think he's taking her?" Mac asked, straining in vain to see around the Morlock's bulk.

"Search me," Jerry responded, "but she'll be okay, buddy."

Something's up, Mac thought. And now he realized that it had been Alpha's reaction to his own brethren that he'd found most disturbing.

Near the chamber threshold, among what they had determined to be the youngest pillars, Mac saw that a new pedestal of ice, wood, and rock was being constructed adjacent to a column containing what appeared to be a British explorer and his Sherpa guides. A pair of Morlocks looked up from their work.

Jesus Christ, Mac thought, but kept to himself.

"Hey," came a concerned voice, "I don't like the way that one guy is—"

There was a crack—loud and unmistakable, and Mac reflexively turned toward the sound. The Morlock who was carrying Jerry had dropped him to the ground. His friend's eyes were open—wide open—and Mac immediately felt a sickening feeling in his guts.

R. J. MacCready had just begun to scream when a hand clamped over his mouth and nose.

His world went black.

CHAPTER 10

The Gathering

With man, most of his misfortunes are occasioned by man.
—PLINY THE ELDER

Only two things are infinite: The universe and human stupidity. I'm not sure about the former.
—ALBERT EINSTEIN

Yi Chang Airport
Western Hubei Province, China
June 20, 1946, 11:40 A.M. (22 days earlier)

W here are you taking me?" Wang asked the army officer. The man, who appeared to be about forty years of age, had a long scar that ran from just below his right eye to the point of his chin. He said nothing but responded by gesturing to the first of three strange-looking helicopters tethered to the tarmac.

Climbing down from the armored scout car, Wang noticed that their arrival had set off a flurry of activity at the airport. Members of the ground crew were sprinting from a rust-stained hangar toward each of the aircraft. They were followed by three pairs of serious-looking men in flight suits—*pilots*, Wang assumed—who began double-checking the outsides of their respective machines. Each of the helicopters had a pair of rotors—one centered on the roughly fifty-foot-long fuselage, the other mounted at the rear, atop a section of the body that curved upward to an angle of approximately 40 degrees. The front of the craft was roughly triangular in shape, with large windows. Approaching the open aft cargo door, Wang noticed with a sense of alarm that the ship's outer shell appeared to be made of nothing more substantial than fabric that had been stretched over a thin tubular frame.

After a prod from behind, the zoologist entered the craft, the officer and his men following through the same cargo door.

Wang shuffled forward, carrying his backpack, and took a window seat near the cockpit. Behind him, the earthen jar containing the Yeren specimen was loaded into the cargo hold, along with the small wooden crate containing the creature's skin. The skull sat at the bottom of Wang's backpack, cushioned by clothes.

As the pilots strapped themselves into their seats, and just before the noise from the dual engines rendered any conversation impossible, Wang turned to the army officer, who was seated across from him. "Is this trip related to the specimen I found?" he said, pitching his voice above the increasing whine. "The Yeren?"

At the mention of the creature, the officer's eyes widened in a momentary flash of anger, but just as quickly his face returned to its previously passive state. Then, in a gesture that only served to increase the unease Wang had felt since his arrival in Yi Chang Harbor, the military man turned silently and faced forward in his seat. Glancing aft, Wang began to see that every step he had taken was degenerating into a string of poorly chosen actions. All conversation between the soldiers had stopped, but it was clearly more than the rise of engine noise that silenced them. Each of the men was glaring at him. Like the officer, Wang turned and stared straight ahead, letting out a deep breath.

Underfoot, river and forest gave way to more rugged terrain. After several hours, the helicopter began a descent and Wang could see that they were approaching a field of well-irrigated farmland, located on the outskirts of a small village. The great peaks had been looming ever larger as the trio of aircraft flew steadily southwest but now, descending into a landscape lit by the last rays of the setting sun, the vast mountain range dominated the entire western horizon. Directly below, Wang watched three torch-waving figures arraying themselves across a field of ripening crops. As the helicopters made their final approach, each of the torchbearers scrambled out of the way, just before the downwash from the six enormous blades destroyed a month's supply of the village's squash crop.

Wang was escorted hastily to a small yurt and he was thankful to see that it was equipped with a chair and a little table, upon which sat a lantern. There was also a straw-filled mattress, and after setting his pack beside it, he lay down. Exhaustion had come upon him like a wave.

Only for a moment, he thought, closing his eyes. *Only for a—*

He awoke to the sounds of men singing—a drunken chorus, as near as he could tell. Crossing to the open doorway, Wang saw soldiers gathered around a sizable campfire. Some of them were dancing and all of them seemed to be making quite a great time of it. He caught the glint of bottles being passed around and the smell of meat cooking. The villagers were watching the festivities as well, but they stood grim-faced and silent. *This is not their party.*

Afraid that someone would see him, he withdrew quickly, closing off the doorway, then lighting his lamp. Retrieving the Yeren skull and his notebook from the backpack, he sat down. Examining the anterior aspect of the skull, he began to sketch. His descriptions of the incredible find filled ten pages by the time a knock on the door frame interrupted him and an officer entered, carrying something.

Captain Mung Chen placed a plateful of food beside the notebook. He waited for a lull in the alcohol-fueled din taking place just outside. "You should eat something."

"Captain, why am I being held prisoner?" Wang asked.

"You are *not* a prisoner here," the officer responded, his voice calm and measured.

Wang then managed a smile, before gesturing toward the plate, which contained rice and vegetables. "If that is as you say, then why am I not being fed the meat I've been smelling—fed like the other men?"

Captain Mung had already turned to leave but now he stopped to address the scientist again. "Because, Wang Tse-lin, I did not think you would enjoy eating your specimen. My men, on the other hand, *are* enjoying it. They'll be stronger now. And where we are going, they will need strength."

Wang stood. "But—"

The captain held up a hand. "Of course they had no idea that we were carrying the flesh of the mountain ogres with us—until you told them. So before you say another word, know that *you* did this."

Wang's mind flashed back to the helicopter and the careless words he had spoken just before takeoff. Then he slowly lowered his head into his hands.

"*You did this.*"

Wang Tse-lin had been sitting in stunned silence for many long and uncomfortable minutes when the officer reappeared and took a seat at the bamboo-framed table. He gestured toward the skull. "Tell me more about how you tracked the Yeren."

The scientist's worried expression shifted to puzzlement. "Tracked? I don't understand."

Captain Mung crossed his arms. "It's no secret. Your university colleagues couldn't stop talking about you—how you had tracked the Yeren across the mountains. How you followed it into the Shennongjia wilderness."

Wang sat silently for a moment, then shook his head. "Who was it? Dr. Yi?"

Mung said nothing but reacted as if the chair had suddenly become uncomfortable.

The scientist managed a wry smile. "It *was* Dr. Yi."

"Explain yourself," Mung commanded.

"My work was to survey the valley. I used the opportunity to collect zoological specimens. I was hoping for a white bear but instead—"

"But instead you killed a Yeren?"

"The villagers killed the creature. I tried, as I said, to . . . purchase it."

"You *bought* it?"

"They gave it to me."

Captain Mung sank back into the chair, closed his eyes, and let out a deep sigh. A minute passed, but to each of the men it seemed far longer, until a burst of drunken laughter outside brought them back to present reality: a damp hut in a nameless village.

Finally, the officer spoke. "My family came from

a settlement not much bigger than this one," Mung said. "Outside Harbin."

Wang winced involuntarily at the name.

"You've heard of it, I see," the captain said, briefly wearing a humorless smile.

"To my sadness, I have."

"My wife was killed there, as was my youngest child."

Wang bowed his head.

The officer continued. "My two remaining children are sick—poisoned with candy. Can you believe that? Candy."

"I am sorry," Wang said, quietly. Like many people, he was familiar with the rumors about what took place at Harbin during the war— rumors whose details became far too specific to have been made up. The Japanese invaders had constructed a vast complex of buildings—"a lumber mill," inquiring local leaders were told. Then the walls went up—razor wire and guard towers— the perimeter patrolled by soldiers and vicious guard dogs. Stranger still were reports of a ceaseless rumble of trucks moving into and out of the facility in the dead of night and long after construction was completed.

Through it all, and in what would become the most disturbing development, was the oddly charitable nature of the Japanese occupiers—who provided regular deliveries of food to the perplexed and war-starved locals: fresh vegetables, meat, even cookies and candy. Soon after, many of the villagers became horribly sickened and most of them died. The few who survived were taken in the night by teams of men who arrived and departed like phantoms, men clad from head to toe in strange suits.

The officer had gone silent, his attention seemingly focused on a cockroach that was making its way down one of the hut's wooden support beams.

"But why are you here, Captain? What do you and your men want with me?"

Mung stared at him, severely. "It seems we were sold a rather inaccurate bill of goods."

"How so?"

"Your colleagues exaggerated your role in the discovery of the Yeren."

"Out of fear, I am certain," Wang said, trying not to appear too defensive.

Mung paused for a moment, then gave a slight nod. "A logical suggestion."

"And so what will become of me now?"

"Now, Wang Tse-lin, to survive you must play the game. And no matter how little you *do* know about the biology and habits of the Yeren, you must quickly become an invaluable expert on the topic."

"But, Captain, why are you so concerned with these creatures? Why all the soldiers? Why the helicopters?"

"It seems physicians in Peking have concluded that the stories passed down through the centuries about the Yeren are true."

"Which is why your men ate my specimen?" Wang responded, his anger surfacing for only a moment.

"Precisely," the officer said. "In this case, to increase their strength."

The scientist looked perplexed. "But why 'in this case'?"

"Because the flesh of the Yeren is also said to have unsurpassed curative powers."

"Surely you don't—"

Mung held up his hand. "I *do* believe it. I believe that the flesh of the Yeren can cure the sick. That it can cure my children and others like them."

"But if this is true, then why aren't you combing the Shennongjia valley for more Yeren?"

"The reason, Wang Tse-lin, is that the forest ogres—like the one I mistakenly presumed you had tracked and killed—are far too rare. The Shennongjia population is small and scattered, and soon it may be extinguished."

"Then with all respect, Captain, I'm confused as to why you allowed your men to consume such a rare find."

The officer rose and moved slowly toward the door, unable to hide his fatigue. "Because you have changed everything," he said. "None of us ever believed in legends told by the khans about the Yeren—or that any Yeren could actually exist—until you made belief possible. I allowed my men to eat your specimen because, where we are going, there should be many more of them—each one composed of life-giving flesh, and in possession of secrets that can cure every affliction."

CHAPTER 11

Things We Lock Away

*When we think we have been hurt by
someone in the past, we build up defenses
to protect ourselves from being hurt in the
future. So the fearful past causes a fearful
future and past and future become one.*
—ALFRED HITCHCOCK

South Tibet
July 12, 1946

After leaving the cavern and
its strange museum of the
dead, Alpha carried Yanni
down a snowy incline. She craned her neck, hoping to see Mac and Jerry, tucked under the hairy
arms of their own escorts. But there was no one
following them and soon the cave opening was
obscured by mist.

Yanni's sense of unease increased further when,

instead of being returned to the igloo with her friends, Alpha had set off in a wholly new direction. Stopping several minutes later at the edge of a corral-like structure, they were met by two female Morlocks.

Even as Alpha gently set her down outside the "fence," she could hear the mammoths, somewhere beyond the veil of perpetually suspended snowflakes. The enclosure (as much as she could see of it through the mist) was a series of chest-high, semi-rectangular granite columns, connected by thick cords of something resembling woven silk. The material was drawn piano-wire tight, and the carved granite had become weatherworn long ago. The calls of the creatures within the enclosure grew louder with their approach—clearly elephantine, but unique and more complex. Though still wondering about Mac and Jerry—back in the "Trophy Room from Hell"—Yanni prepared her mind for the approach of yet another first-contact situation.

Her initial view of them was shadowy—the shifting of ghosts in the mist. But as the phantoms stepped forward and out of the snowy cloud, they resolved themselves into a dozen white-furred mammoths. None of them stood higher at the shoulder than a Shetland pony, but one, slightly taller than the rest, lumbered cautiously toward the edge of the corral.

Yanni's initial impression was confusion. *This can't be them*, she thought, as the largest animal approached. *They've only got one—*

As if to allay her concern, the creature slowly extended its trunk toward her, and, as it did so, the appendage began to split from tip to base.

—*trunk*.

Then, as the appendage's right-hand section gripped a horizontally arranged cord with its digitlike tip, the left-hand section reached out and came to a pause inches above Yanni's shoulder. The entire movement was as graceful as any dance move Yanni had ever seen.

Her second impression, during the first moments of the encounter, was that their limbs were clearly built for agile locomotion. *You'd never know it, though,* Yanni observed, from what appeared to be an almost deliberately lumbering gait. *The Morlocks may have superior numbers on their side, but the mammoths are clearly hiding something.*

"Yasss, tang-gerr," one of the female Morlocks said, in its bastardized version of Latin. The words were accompanied by a hand signal, and Yanni was immediately reminded of the trainers at the Central Park Menagerie.

The mammoth, a male with beautiful brown eyes, reacted to the command by resting the tip of one trunk gently on Yanni's shoulder. Its tusks were noticeably stubbier than those of the other individuals, and one eyelid appeared to be healing, from some sort of tussle.

"You don't look like a bruiser," she said, her voice calm as she stroked one of the muscular and lightly furred trunks.

"Conversssa-can-tah-bo," the Morlock commanded, using yet another hand signal. Yanni was able, just barely, to decipher something specific from the directive.

Was she trying to say, Conversa? Yanni wondered. If so, a word that meant "conversation" among the miners of Brazil and *cantar* in the Brazilian dialect of Portuguese was the Latin-derived word for "sing."

The mammoth's response left no room for doubt as it began to vocalize in a strange bitonal language. Four others of his kind followed his lead.

Presently Yanni realized she might have an easier time understanding Morlock-Latin than the language of the mammoths. Still, the miniature pachyderms were effortlessly conveying emotions in their tones, in much the same manner that a talented violinist conveyed moods without words. And likewise, they were doing it to equal or greater effect.

No one who hears this will ever forget the sound, Yanni thought.

The low notes and the high notes swooped down and spiraled up in a lament that vibrated through her ribs as if they were tuning forks. Yanni did not fully comprehend that the heritage of more than two thousand years was being recalled and sung out to the mists, much of it, she suspected, below the range of her own hearing. She felt the emotions within the tones but could not quite decipher the cries of loves lost, of freedoms lost, and all the loneliness of slavery.

Yanni could not know that the composer, who paused to rest a pair of trunks gently on her shoulders, was reaching across broken foundation stones from the great tower Pliny had seen protruding above the sea of mist. The tower was now a roughly circular ruin, converted into a corral. Its actual dimensions were difficult to determine, the far reaches of the enclosure remaining obscured by the ever-present flakes and the fog.

She tried to communicate back to the mammoths, in tones of her own, but she felt wholly inadequate. As the twelve slaves stared back at her, there was no escaping a clear sense that minds the equal at least of men and Morlocks lived behind those gentle eyes. The mammoths responded encouragingly to her effort, and the Morlocks seemed as curious as she was about the encounter.

The song continued, a dirge that belonged to the white mammoths, and to the white mammoths alone—the incomprehensible song-story of generations long ago lost yet preserved in memory. Yanni was beginning—and only just beginning—to perceive the depth of detail, but the mammoths looked up suddenly and the lamentation died in the mist.

She started to raise a hand toward an outstretched trunk and was about to say something when a growl from the other "elephant keeper" sent the creature back several steps. The mammoth let out a low-frequency hiss as it withdrew.

"No need to translate, kiddo," Yanni spoke quietly to the retreating mammoth. Its companions spread their ears wider and looked past her, with a new and sudden concern.

The Morlocks heard it, too, then Yanni.

A helicopter was approaching.

"Mac," Yanni said to herself. "Where the hell are you?"

IN THE IGLOO

S he'll be okay, buddy."

"Yeah, whatever you say, Jerry," Mac replied, squeezing the head of an inchworm blade up through the skin of his leg like a pimple. He watched his friend pulling evenly and gently along the remaining two-inch length of the creature's body.

Despite the reassurance, and through the pain, Mac's thoughts were with Yanni and her sudden departure from the cave with Alpha. Meanwhile, Mac's own escort had apparently all but killed him during a particularly rough ride back to the igloo and through the field of bitey grass mimics. One of the creatures had latched on and was stubbornly resisting eviction from its new home—Mac's leg.

"Are you making a career out of this, or what?" Mac asked his friend, impatiently.

"Mostly *or what*—especially if I break this critter off inside of you."

Once again, Mac's mind wandered, and for at least the third time Jerry seemed to read his thoughts. "She'll be okay, buddy."

Mac nodded, less than entirely convinced.

"You *know* Yanni," Jerry continued, "and the effect she has on animals."

"Yeah, that'd be fine," Mac said, squeezing

harder against the creature under his skin, "if the Morlocks were animals."

"Nah, come on. She's probably got Mr. Alpha wrapped around her little finger by now."

"Do ya . . . *ow!* . . . think?" Mac said, as the creature in his leg came out another fraction of an inch, bit at him, was drawn out a little farther, bit again. "Shit!"

"Sorry!" Jerry said. "And just in case you haven't noticed, Yanni is already working on them. I mean, compared to the way they treat us, they're treating her like royalty."

Mac gritted his teeth. "I suppose . . . they have been giving her the kid-glove treatment. Not like that hammering you took back there in 'Lost and Found.'"

"What are you talking about?" Jerry replied, calmly. "You're the one they smothered half to death—and that was *before* you picked up your little passenger on the return trip."

Mac vaguely remembered being hauled back to their igloo jail like a sack of potatoes, and he remembered pain. Evidently, the Morlock had also been somewhat less than efficient in clearing a path through the inchworm grass and one of the miniature predators had managed to gain purchase. Its mouthparts, having pierced skin and muscle, felt like a thorn dipped in electric fire.

Somehow this all made sense, except for Jerry's comment about being suffocated—Mac had no recollection of that at all.

"I think Alpha's taken a real shine to her," said Jerry, *still* trying to sound cheery—a tone that was definitely starting to piss Mac off.

"Yeah, well, just keep that shit to yourself, okay. Now about that smothering they laid on me, I'm wondering why— *Ouch!*"

The head of the little monster, which had dug deep into the muscle of his thigh, was now almost out through the skin surface, and with its battle nearly lost, it felt like the thing was spitting more venom. Mac already had an advanced education in pain, but this creature was helping him to write a whole new thesis.

"So, why *wouldn't* Alpha be smitten?" Jerry said, in a further attempt to distract his stricken friend. "He sorta reminds me of those Brooklyn musicians you're always complaining about—only with more hair and no guitars."

"Stop trying to make me laugh!" Mac replied. Jerry was one of the only people he knew who could pry something funny out of even the gravest situation, who could laugh and be afraid at the same time.

"And stop trying to change the subject!" Mac added. "Tell me what happened—back there."

Jerry feigned an offended look. "Okay, Mr. Sensitive. Now just hold on. This bugger's almost out."

Mac felt another surge of venom and his subconscious seemed suddenly more in control than his conscious mind, seeking out a lighter place—a place he hadn't thought about in—

"Well, it's about time, Yanni," Mac said, absently. He had been pressing a handkerchief to his wounded leg but started dabbing clumsily at the air several inches above his knee. "Whoops," he said, flashing a lopsided grin. "Missed."

"Say, you're looking a little pale there, Mac." Jerry's voice seemed to be coming from far away.

Mac felt as if he were being lowered into a prone position, strangely relieved to be drifting off, as a heretofore-unknown chemical compound did its work. Semiconsciousness allowed worry to slip away and into the distractions of random and sometimes absurd details, bubbling up from the subconscious—*Long Island . . . Fresh bagels! . . . the smell of Mom's perfume . . . Tamara . . .*

Mom's grave.

"Stop."

He drove his thoughts away from his mother and from loss—wondering for a moment what force of natural selection had led to the evolution of grief and regret.

"Stop!"

Instead, Mac latched on to the now barely felt but nonetheless paralyzing sting. He wondered why an animal that could so quickly swarm over and strip its prey down to the bone, before consuming those very bones, needed a toxic bite as well. Thus far he had only seen the inchworm grass consuming small game—the "squirrel" Alpha had used for demonstration purposes.

Perhaps something special for larger prey, he guessed, *like us.*

The blade pulled out another fraction of an inch and Mac struggled to focus his thoughts on helping Jerry to remove the grass mimic.

"Jeez, this sucks!" Mac called out, against a sharp, acidic sting, followed by relief at the final withdrawal of his tormentor.

"She'll be okay, buddy," Jerry said, holding the creature as it snapped and contorted into fantastic S-shapes—trying unsuccessfully to latch on to a new prey item.

"Huh?" Mac asked. "What'd you say?"

"She'll be okay, buddy."

"Pally, you are startin' to sound like a broken record," Mac said, feeling the venom-induced fog beginning to lift rapidly.

Jerry put an end to the creature's relocation attempt by crushing its head between his thumb and forefinger. Then, as Mac watched, his friend took a sniff of the dead animal.

"Smells like antifreeze," Mac told Jerry, while another part of his brain recognized, *Something's wrong.*

MacCready realized that what he had just experienced was like watching his friend down a tumbler of Jack Daniel's, but with *Mac* being the one who tasted and felt the effects of the whiskey.

She'll be okay, came a voice in his head, startling him.

Mac stared down at his own thumb and index finger. *They* were covered with the blood of the grass mimic.

Fully conscious now, he glanced frantically in

every direction. The igloo had gone completely silent and he was alone.

"Jerry? *Jerry!*"

Mac lurched up and tottered over to the ice wall. Recollection and realization were slow to emerge. When they did, he knelt down hard— mentally groping for retreat into a private world of denial.

He failed.

Instead, Mac relived over and over again the awful crack of Jerry's neck breaking.

He's still in the trophy room.

Outside the ice prison, a great shadow passed overhead, making a mechanical commotion.

R. J. MacCready did not perceive it, over the sound of his own weeping.

CHAPTER 12

Dracunculus Rising

One death is a tragedy; one million is a statistic.
—JOSEPH STALIN

Extinction is the rule. Survival is the exception.
—CARL SAGAN

Somewhere above the south Tibetan Labyrinth
July 12, 1946

S hould we be doing this, sir?" the Chinese helicopter pilot called back to the officer standing behind him in the cockpit.

The pilot, whose name was Po Han, was gradually easing the "Dogship" toward a sea of mist that seemed to rise threateningly, filling more and more of his visual field.

"You have your orders," snapped the officer, a lieutenant named Lee Song.

"But, Captain Mung told us—"

"These orders did not come from Captain Mung."

"Of course, sir," Po Han said, wondering only briefly *who* was giving the orders now. What he did know was that he had already developed a strong dislike for this particular helicopter. And then, as if those in charge had not already pressed far enough into the limits of crazy, he was being asked to push the craft—an American prototype known as a Harp—beyond what any sane person would consider to be safe limits.

Safety, though, appeared to be the last thing on the lieutenant's mind. The original orders had been simple: drop off additional equipment and fuel at a previously established supply site near the labyrinth's edge. The plan fell apart, however, once they discovered that someone had ransacked the initial cache of fuel and spare helicopter parts. But instead of returning to the village where they'd established their primary base camp, the officer on board had taken a sudden interest in tracking down the perpetrators—especially after their guides insisted that the thefts were the work of the Yeren.

"I see where they've gone," the lieutenant had said, pointing to what he believed was a trail through the mountainous terrain. Po Han and his copilot had serious doubts but the officer left no room for discussion. The new supplies were dumped hastily into the already compromised site ("to lighten the ship and extend our range for the hunt").

This makes no sense, Po Han thought. *Heading deeper into the mountains is madness.* For a while he was certain they were following imaginary trails—*shadows in the stone*—and then the helicopter crested a ridge and the earth fell away into a wide valley, the bottom of which was completely obscured by dense mist. The officer ordered them to fly toward the center of the valley and so, reluctantly, they did.

Within minutes, the mist was rising all around them, and as the rotors pulled down dual columns of clear air from above, the pilot was expecting to see solid ground, but there was none. "It looks bottomless," he said, grimly.

"Keep going," commanded a voice behind him.

"Sir, we need to put a man in the doorway right now. And tell him to start shouting the moment he sees the valley floor."

The officer shouted an order back to one of his soldiers and moments later two others wrestled open the aft cargo door.

Po Han took the helicopter down, skillfully, a foot at a time. The rotors were no longer bringing down clear air. The world was a white blur, with nothing ahead and below except fog. "See anything?" he shouted back into the cabin.

A moment later the officer scrambled forward. "There's grass!" he cried excitedly. "You've got a spot for your landing, now take us down!"

Po Han nudged the helicopter lower, and for a change, he thought, the craft handled smoothly. *No wind at all down here.*

With the lower portion of the cockpit now hovering a mere six feet above the ground, Po Han could see that the officer had been right about the landing zone. It was a flat field, covered in frost-laden grass but otherwise unimpressive. He eased the helicopter even lower, relieved as the tricycle landing gear contacted the ground and at the near certainty that whoever the officer might have been chasing would have been long gone by now. These thoughts had barely registered when, remarkably, he saw three tall figures standing at the extreme edge of visibility. At first the pilot thought they were wearing strange costumes.

"Do you see what I'm seeing?" he asked his copilot, even as the shadowy figures seemed to disappear before his eyes.

There was a pause, followed by a stunned, one-word reply. "Yeren."

Though the word brought a deep churning in his bowels, it was a shriek from behind, louder even than the considerable engine noise, that shifted Po Han's fight-or-flight response into overdrive. The lieutenant's voice rose above the commotion—strangely high-pitched and frantic: "Take us up!"

Glancing back over a shoulder, Po Han glimpsed the officer and the other five soldiers writhing in a tangled mass on the cabin floor—tearing at their own uniforms and at their own bodies.

Forward and below, through the Plexiglas, the pilot imagined he saw (and his mind told him that he *had* to be imagining) frost-covered grass moving toward him in a wave. *Like a school of ravenous fish*.

Reflexively, he throttled the engines up, desperate to get away from a landing spot that had become more like a descent into a hive of angry bees. But as the screams of the men in the cabin actually grew to rival any he had heard during the war, Po Han began to believe that landing in a field of hornet's nests would have been preferable.

The sudden throttle-up, and the rebound effect of the rotors' downwash against the ground during an abrupt change of both thrust and direction, suddenly revealed a design flaw that had rendered the "Dogship" undesirable to Americans and Russians alike—the hull was nothing more than canvas, stiffened with dried glue. The entire starboard side tore open and as Po Han instantly corrected the tilt to his right, the port side too was suddenly all open air. The ship's aft end bounced down hard but during the next instant, another throttle-up seemed to have them safely airborne again.

The pilot allowed himself to believe that they might still complete this cursed excursion and escape with their lives, but this belief was shattered the moment he heard (and felt, through his controls) the shreds of his ship's membrane being tornadoed into the rotors.

"We're going in!" Po Han called out, breaking radio silence. As the aft section pounded down again and the rotors began to die, and as he tried to describe his location to anyone listening at base camp, it became all too horribly clear that more and more debris from the ground was being whirled into the cabin.

The screams behind Po Han continued to rise above the grind and whine of failing engine parts and as he glanced again over his shoulder he recoiled at what he saw. The men—all of them were covered in white grass turning red.

But it's not grass, he realized at last. *They're worms! And they're everywhere!*

The pilot kept his microphone open and broadcasting till the very end, even after he looked down and realized that the monsters had begun drilling into his own arms and legs and were swarming toward his face.

During the seconds in which Po Han broke radio silence, the helicopter windmilled out of control and slid in Yanni's direction. It was still a vague shape in the mist when it bounced to a stop, its rotors whipping her with a fierce gust laden with soil and something else—something alive.

It took only another moment for Yanni to fully realize what was happening.

Grass mimics!

Throwing both hands up to protect her face, Yanni fell backward against the corral's fence. Alpha, seeing immediately that something had gone terribly wrong, stepped in front of her, forming an effective but incomplete wall against the flying debris and hungry predators. Yanni could smell the musk he was releasing but the inchworms were already crawling along the shoulders of her parka and becoming tangled in her hair.

At the moment in which she was about to scream, a familiar sound came from behind and she turned toward it. Yanni's cupped hands obscured her view but she knew there was nothing else keeping the ravenous biters away from her eyes.

Suddenly, twin blasts of liquid struck her shoulders from separate directions, then her head and hands were similarly sprayed. When Yanni realized that she could no longer feel the grass wiggling toward her scalp and her face, she spread her fingers slightly, peeking out between them. Two of the little mammoths had come up behind her. She felt a series of tugs as some of the grass mimics were blown out of her hair while others were flicked off by the fingerlike projections that tipped the muscular bifurcated trunks.

Get them all. Every single—

The thought was interrupted by two more blasts in the face with the foul-smelling liquid. Yanni became aware that the last of the white blades were springboarding off her neck and fleeing. She exhaled, unaware of the breath she'd been holding.

Saved by the mammoths, she was dismayed that two of their Morlock keepers were already herding them away, tugging on leashes attached to what appeared to be woven choke collars.

"Thanks, guys," she said quietly, as they disappeared back into the mist that hid the rest of the corral.

Turning again toward the downed helicopter, Yanni was prodded forward, now surrounded closely by Alpha and two female Morlocks. Their musk was stronger than she thought possible and the inchworm grass reacted predictably, moving apart and forming a barren trail in the debris-strewn soil.

Once the helicopter rotors stopped spinning and breaking, the machine had apparently keeled gently over to one side, its membranous outer covering in tatters. A figure tumbled out, screaming weakly and wrapped in what appeared to be a cape of inchworm grass. The man's cries did not last much beyond the moment one of his arms broke off near the shoulder joint. The horde of now red-tinted blades seemed to vie for possession of the limb, its previous owner even making a desperate grab for it before falling face-first into the welcoming carpet.

An eerie quiet began to settle over the valley.

Lifting Yanni and carrying her with them, the Morlocks approached the dead machine and its dying crew, but they clearly refrained from moving near enough for their scent—which shepherded the inchworm grass before them—to repel the predators from their prey. With nothing to interrupt their feast, Yanni heard new sounds—faint and horrible—like corn being milled with a grinding stone. And now, as a distinctly queasy feeling crept into her, the grass mimics penetrated humerus, femur, and brow and continued to gorge themselves.

Alpha broke the spell, giving Yanni an un-characteristically rough shaking and uttering a familiar, mispronounced exclamation in Latin, "*Serr-rah.*"

"Serrah," Yanni repeated, under her breath. "Chinese," she whispered.

Alpha followed with a more primal form of body language that left no room for misinterpretation. He snarled at the disintegrating men.

Though it ranked with some of the most horrible things she had ever seen (and perhaps because of this), Yanni was unable to turn away.

As a chill ran up her back, Yanni swept her gaze around as far as the fog allowed, searching for warning signs of a second, shadowy wave of carnivorous grass—but none appeared. The combination of Morlock and mammoth stench was evidently maintaining its repellent effect.

But for how long? she wondered.

Nearby, the skeletons of the Chinese intruders caved in like children's sand castles and were swept swiftly away by the hungry blades.

Metropolitan Museum of Natural History

FIFTH FLOOR

A nd how old is this Lost Codex supposed to be?" said Dr. Nora Nesbitt. She was the invertebrate zoologist Wynters and Knight had requested, now officially and freshly approved by Major Hendry. She was also one of the Metropolitan Museum's rising stars.

"It dates back to not very long before Vesuvius buried Pompeii," replied Patricia Wynters. "Now is that a humdinger, or what?"

Nesbitt, who had been examining a grainy photograph of the ancient text, peered over the top of her stylish horn-rimmed specs. "*Definitely.* Too bad these photos are for shit."

Wynters glanced at the closed office door, then flashed a wry smile. Today Charles Knight was off exploring the museum with his granddaughter, which meant that in all likelihood he would not be back until after lunch. "Want me to show you the original?" she said, with conspiratorial glee.

Nesbitt, an attractive thirty-something brunette, returned a wide smile of her own. "Sure thing."

Wynters led her thoroughly amused guest to a map table. Opening the top drawer, she carefully sorted through a saga of yellowed and browned pages that had been skillfully mounted between acetate sheets. "Here we go," she said, selecting one, then handing it to the biologist. "This work a little better for you?"

Nesbitt studied an ancient illustration—which showed a human figure pulling what appeared to be a strand of spaghetti out of another man's foot and winding it onto a spool. The second man seemed to be in great pain. "Is that supposed to be a nematode?" she said, at last.

"That's above my pay grade," Patricia replied. "You tell me. Charles thought that maybe these guys were doing some strange knitting."

Nesbitt flashed a *you've got to be kidding me* expression, then saw that indeed Wynters *had* been. She squinted at the codex. "It looks a lot like *Dracunculus*."

"Lovely!" Patricia replied. "That's a worm, right?"

"Yes, a guinea worm."

"Well, Pliny *does* mention worms quite a bit."

Nesbitt nodded toward the ancient text. "Which is, I suppose, the reason you called me in."

Patricia responded with a wry smile.

Nesbitt continued. "Europeans named these critters for the Guinea coast, where they first encountered them in the seventeenth century. You gotta like the Latin, though—'little dragons.'"

"That *does* sound pleasant. And what's their deal?"

"It's more of a horror story, really. *Dracunculus* is a parasite. You pick it up by drinking water containing copepods—tiny crustaceans."

"You mean those little one-eyed critters they call Cyclops?"

"Exactly."

"Yum," Wynters said, scrunching up her face. "Let me guess, the copepods carry the *Dracunculus* larvae?"

"You got it," Nesbitt replied. "And by the way, Egyptian physicians described dracunculiasis in medical papyri dated to thirty-five hundred years ago."

Patricia repeated the disease name to herself. "Interesting. What are the symptoms?"

Nesbitt grimaced. "Well, here's where things get a little grim. The larvae are released when the ingested copepod dies. Then they penetrate your stomach and intestinal wall, and mate in your abdominal cavity."

"And how do I feel about all this?"

"Not so good—fever, nausea, vomiting, diarrhea."

"Oh my."

"But after the nematodes have their little honeymoon—that's when the real party begins."

"Do tell," Patricia said, clearly enjoying the narrative.

"The females start to migrate, burning a path through your soft tissue, and following the long bones out to the extremities. Eventually they make their way to your feet, then up through the skin, where they form a blister—which happens to burn like hell."

"Ah," Patricia exclaimed. "Hence the term 'little dragons.'"

"Exactly. And of course you are now looking for any relief possible, so—"

"—so I dip my dragon-scorched piggies in a cool stream."

"Now you're cookin'!" Nesbitt exclaimed. "Eggs get laid, little swimming Cyclops gulps them down—"

"Water gets drawn by some unsuspecting human, and the whole shebang starts up again."

"Bingo."

"But what does this have to do with what a Roman expedition found two thousand years ago?" Patricia wondered aloud. She returned her attention again to the codex, sorting carefully through several mounted leaves, until she came to and withdrew a page she had been seeking. "Okay, what do you make of this one?" she said, and handed it to Nesbitt.

The zoologist examined the figure for half a minute but remained silent. The badly damaged papyrus depicted what looked like a hair-covered and vaguely human arm using a stick to hold a coiled mass of spaghetti above a shallow pool of water.

"Beats me," Nesbitt said at last.

"It looks like whatever this creature is, it's harvesting guinea worms, no?"

Nesbitt looked more closely at the codex, then shook her head. "If that tangle at the end of the stick is supposed to be *Dracunculus*, then what we're seeing here is the adult stage—which can get up to forty inches long."

"So . . . you're saying these things wouldn't be coming *out* of the water?"

"Right," Nesbitt agreed.

They exchanged puzzled looks, then turned back to the ancient, humanoid figure. It was Nesbitt who spoke first. "Then why's Mr. Fuzzy here placing parasites *into* a pool of water?"

Patricia thought about the question, then shrugged her shoulders. "Maybe he's breeding them."

"Breeding them? Jeez, for what?"

Wynters shrugged. "I have no idea. But Pliny does go on about shaping the substance of life. Now what if these Cerae were shaping the guinea worms?"

"Why on earth would they do that?"

"What if they were designing a weapon?"

Both women gave a start at the creak of the office door opening. It was Charles Knight, with his little blond granddaughter in tow.

"Patricia, I thought you might want to accompany us—" He stopped, realizing that she had a guest. "Ah, Nora," he said, but with a glance at the codex she was holding, the cheer drained from his face. The pair had obviously been doing quite a bit of work without him.

"Charles, we'd *love* to go to lunch with you," Patricia chirped. Then she bent over and gave the child a welcoming smile. "Well, hello. This is Dr. Nesbitt. She studies animals with no backbones."

"You mean invertebrates—like insects and worms," the girl replied, with an assurance that belied her age.

"Absolutely," Nora responded, cheerfully. "Now, who's ready for lunch?"

"*I am!*" the girl cried happily. "I'm starving!"

"Me, too," Nora said. "Thank you for the invitation, Charles."

Knight turned to the trio, his demeanor apparently restored. "So, ladies, what would you like to eat?"

"Anything but spaghetti," Patricia replied.

An unnamed village on the Tibetan Plateau

JULY 12, 1946

As Captain Mung left the hut that held their shortwave equipment, Wang thought he resembled someone who had just suffered a swift kick to the solar plexus. Since their arrival at the Tibetan village six days earlier, the officer had opened up to him even more, about the mission and even about his family. Aside from the haunting memories of diseased children, the unusually large and complicated expedition had been progressing quite smoothly. The relay of supplies to and from this westernmost outpost was not even an hour behind schedule. But now Mung stormed past the scientist, jaw set and silent. After clapping his hands twice, his path was quickly intercepted by two of the three junior officers who had accompanied him from Yi Chang. As Wang watched, the captain spoke quietly to the men—who, moments later, ran off in opposite directions.

Mung stood perfectly still, arms at his sides, then turned and motioned for Wang to approach.

Something has happened to the other helicopter, Wang thought.

"Captain Mung, what is it? How can I help?"

"They were ordered to drop off supplies," the officer said quietly. "That's all. Drop off supplies and fuel, then return."

"But—"

"But this time they went off course—far off course, according to the distress call."

"And why would your men do that?" Wang asked.

"Apparently, they received orders that superseded my own."

"But who would have—"

"That's not important now. What is important is that they discovered a valley—fogbound. For some reason they either decided to land the helicopter—or it crashed. Then they were . . . attacked."

"By the Yeren?"

"No," the captain said, then hesitated. "By the earth, or the ground—or something *on* the ground."

"By the earth?" Wang repeated, to himself.

"Only parts of their message came through," Captain Mung said. "It's difficult to know what really happened."

"But maybe they—"

"They could not have survived what I heard."

Wang bowed his head but said nothing.

"We will be leaving this place," Mung said. His voice belonged to a commander who had just lost seven of his men, including a pair of pilots. "And we will find out who or what attacked them."

CHAPTER 13

The Taken

> *You need the ability to fail. . . . You cannot*
> *innovate unless you are willing to accept*
> *some mistakes.*
> —CHARLES R. KNIGHT

In the igloo
July 12, 1946

R. J. MacCready never heard
the tandem-rotored helicopter until it crashed some-
where in the distance. Even muffled by snow and
fog, the smashing of steel framing against rock
and earth was unmistakable. It also provided the
minor favor of allowing him to concentrate on
something else—anything else.

Mac flashed back to their own crash only days
earlier. Given everything that had transpired
since then, the event felt oddly distant—as if it
had happened to someone else.

But it didn't, he thought. *I'm the one who got us stuck here. And now Jerry's—*

"All right, cut!" Mac said, shaking his head as if to clear it of the very thought. The cold, hard fact was that Jerry was gone—having done nothing at all that might have provoked his captor.

The Morlocks are completely unpredictable, he thought, realizing that now there could be only *one* concern—*finding Yanni and getting her the fuck out of here.*

But is she even alive? Mac wondered. *Or are they both gone?*

"She's alive," he told himself.

Mac moved across the silent interior of the igloo and pressed his hands against the freezing walls, trying in vain to see beyond the mist.

"So whose chopper was that?" he asked himself, before mentally reconstructing what he'd just heard. *Six sequential blows—six blades, two rotors.* Mac knew the sound of a double-rotor set was consistent with the spare chopper part Alpha had thrown down at their feet. *Probably Chinese,* he thought, remembering the stamped metal and Hendry's warning that those guys were swarming over the region like hornets.

What *wasn't* swarming, he noticed, were the grass mimics. In fact the entire white horde that seemed to be permanently camped outside the igloo was gone.

Mac approached the slab that served as a door, squinting through the thick, polished ice as he went, but he could detect no movement at all. He put his shoulder to the portal and immediately felt it begin to move. *I can do this*, he thought, now giving serious consideration to pushing it open and taking his chances outside. The more rational part of his brain decided to wait *a few minutes more*.

"But where the hell is—" Mac said, his question interrupted by sudden movement. It came from deep within the mist, which swirled upward, displaced by a new wave of grass mimics. *There's something different about them*, Mac thought, straining to determine exactly what that could be.

It's their color, he realized, aware now that many of the blades rushing toward him had a distinctive crimson tint. Mac felt his insides beginning to twist in an all-too-familiar manner. *Is that Yanni's blood?*

The answer arrived barely more than thirty seconds later, but for R. J. MacCready those seconds were longer than any hour.

Out of the snowy mist strode one of the Morlocks. It was the same individual, the one they'd been calling Alpha, who'd prevented Yanni from seeing what had taken place in the cavern. Now the grim-faced creature was carrying her on his shoulder.

"You are shittin' me," Mac muttered, to himself.

Predictably, the sea of white and red pseudo-grass parted before the Morlock as he advanced toward the igloo entrance, simultaneously closing behind once the giant had passed.

Stopping just shy of twenty feet from the ice prison, Alpha set Yanni down gently and gave her a slight nudge forward. Yanni glanced back for a moment, as if to confirm what she was being asked to do. Then, seemingly without giving it another thought, she began walking toward the igloo.

Mac pounded against the ice—screaming out against the realization that she was being forced to walk into her own execution.

"No!"

Looking quite calm, Yanni responded with a wry smile and a wave of her hand. Then she stepped away from the Morlock and into the seething carpet of grass mimics.

Mac cursed, throwing his weight against the door and pushing for all he was worth. The slab fell forward. By then Yanni was so close that she had to jump back a step to avoid getting her feet crushed by the ice.

Mac threw his arms around Yanni and spun her toward the opening. She responded with a look of surprise at what turned out to be his unnecessary attempt to use his body as a shield. The zoologist had failed to notice that the grass had parted before Yanni, fleeing in such haste that not a single mimic stood within ten feet of them.

"Mac, what on earth are you doin' out here?"

Before he could reply, a shove from behind sent them both tumbling into the igloo and immediately the Morlock reset the door and slammed it back into place.

"I . . . I thought he was trying to kill you, *too.*"

"What? I was perfectly safe," she said. "Take a whiff. I call it *Eau de Elephas.*"

Mac responded to her joke with unexpected silence.

"Mac, what did you mean 'kill me too'?" Yanni said, amid a very sudden realization that they were no longer a trio.

Mac turned away from her.

Normally, the friends would have talked for hours about Yanni's twenty minutes at the corral. Instead, in utter silence, they thought only about Jerry.

1,500 feet above the south Tibetan Labyrinth
JULY 13, 1946

D o you see that ledge ahead of us?" the Chinese helicopter pilot asked. He was pointing to the exact spot that Yanni had indicated to Mac, on the day their trek began.

Captain Mung Chen took off his aviator glasses and squinted through the cockpit window. "Yes, take us down lower."

As the shelf came nearer, the copilot contacted the crew of the second chopper, who put their ship into a slow holding pattern circuit as Mung's craft went in for a closer look.

The resulting flyby revealed the same low wall of stones that had prevented Mac and his friends from tumbling off the ledge. This time, however, the rocks and snow gave silent testimony to more than the work of a past civilization.

"There's another helicopter down there," the pilot said. "Or at least part of one."

Once again, Captain Mung strained to see, but this time he shook his head. "Where? I can see nothing but those low ridges."

"Lying at the base of that rock wall flanking the terrace," said the pilot.

"Nature hates straight lines, sir," the copilot added. "Those two long shadows in the snow appear to be rotors—and over there, maybe a wheel assembly."

Now Mung saw them as well. "Ours?"

"Impossible to say from here," the pilot responded.

"Can you put us down, *safely*?"

The pilot flashed a brief but confident smile. "I think there is just enough room for both ships, sir."

"Good. Inform our sister ship, then take us in."

Only after Mung had returned to his seat in the cabin did the two flyers exchange looks. "*Both* ships?" the copilot repeated, somewhat incredulously.

"He was just about to ask us anyway," the pilot responded. "And you . . . 'Nature hates straight lines'? Who said that? Certainly not you!"

The copilot shrugged. He knew it was either Buddha or some long-dead English landscape architect. Though he could never quite remember which.

JULY 14, 1946

The pair of prisoners from New York never heard the new arrivals. The Chinese were a long way off, miles beyond the maze of underground passages and high above a sound-muffling sea of snowy fog.

What they *did* notice, just before nightfall on the second day after Jerry's death, was an increase in the activity outside their prison.

"What do you think they're up to?" Yanni asked.

Mac shrugged his shoulders but remained silent. She had yet to draw anything like a normal response from him.

"Mac?"

Silence.

"You really should eat something," she followed, although even she had left her food mostly untouched and neither of them had slept.

"Please leave me alone," Mac said at last. Then he curled up on the ground with his back turned.

Previously, the three prisoners had reluctantly begun sleeping in what Mac referred to as "a thermodynamically efficient position." Yanni had actually preferred Jerry's term, *spooning*, although they were careful not to use that description around Mac.

Yanni approached her friend and lay down behind him. She could sense his shoulders tensing up and he inched himself away from her.

"Good night, Mac," she said gently. Then, moving to fill the space between them, she placed a hand on his shoulder. Mac allowed it.

"He's gone, Yanni," he whispered.

"Shhhh," she whispered back. "Good night, Mac."

Mac supposed he should have dropped off into sleep from sheer exhaustion, but it seemed unimaginable to him that his thoughts could stop racing for even a few seconds. He had become so accustomed to stepping into and out of improbable shit storms with Jerry that it had become possible for both of them to let down their guard—even here, among creatures no more predictable than tigers.

Yanni had only recently accepted Jerry as "our kind of stupid," but she did not know the half of it. Their first mission together had begun in the Pacific, after Jerry received word that "Captain America"—actually a lieutenant jg—and his crew *might* have survived the total destruction of their torpedo boat. No one at the time seemed willing to believe it. The "proof of life" was a message found by a local fisherman, carved into a coconut. Against a "no-go" decision from their superiors, Mac and Jerry went into freelance mode, eventually stealing a canoe from under the noses of ten thousand Japanese soldiers stationed on the nearby island of Kolombangara. Following a set of cryptic directions and a familiar surname carved onto the shell, they found the grateful lieutenant and most of his crew on a tiny island that Jerry had aptly described as "a pile of sand with visions of grandeur." Ultimately, Mac took a spearhead in the leg for his troubles—from a friendly native.

"You definitely can't make this shit up," Mac later told a less-than-pleased senior officer. Eventually it took a personal call from Captain America's father to get him and Jerry off the hook for disobeying an order.

Jerry was also present when, during an interlude between missions and while the spear-pierced muscles of his leg healed, Mac met a youthful genius named Tamara, who saw in ants and bees the intelligence of "superorganisms," and who would certainly have been helpful in figuring out inch-worm grass and Morlocks. Mac had noticed only during their first two minutes together that Tamara bore the childhood scars of smallpox. From the instant they began speaking, he could remember only her unforgettable grace, her kindness, her brilliance.

And Jerry was there with him, in that place of tropical beaches and grief, wonder and loss, beauty and regret. He was at Mac's side when he no longer needed a crutch to walk, was healed to the point of "mission ready" and sailed away, vowing that he would return to the island.

Only three weeks later, the beaches and the forests belonged to carrion-feeders, the island having been overrun by the enemy. Tamara, her family, and more than two thousand civilians disappeared, with less mystery but even more all-embracing thoroughness than Rome's Ninth Legion.

Jerry had been there to console him.

"Tamara—"

Mac's arm thrashed involuntarily, just as he began to doze off. "Shhhh," Yanni whispered again. "It's all right."

He'd never spoken to Yanni about Tamara. Back then, he scarcely had time to grasp the fact she was gone when he received word that another of the war's evils had claimed his mother and sister. Jerry had been there for that, too.

In one way or another, bit by bit, the world had taken everyone Mac loved. There seemed little left to do about it, except to keep everyone else at arm's length and attend to the job: *Save lives, where you can. Keep exploring and writing, exploring and writing.*

"Some men *can* be, and maybe *should* be, islands," Mac had recently told Jerry.

Slow to trust and emotionally emaciated, Mac came to regard himself as the human equivalent of a remote island—a place where nature itself veered off into different and unexpected directions. His way of thinking had likewise evolved along its own directions, and perhaps even flourished. It was, he suspected, what had turned him into a think-outside-the-box type of explorer, and so useful to the military.

"*Jerry*—" Mac's arm lashed out, awakening Yanni again. She was still there, trying to console him.

"It's okay, Mac. Try to rest."

I can't, he thought, and wondered if it would be possible ever to rest again. He let out a deep breath and felt Yanni's hand on his shoulder. Somehow Mac knew that she would not remove it. And she did not, even after sleep eventually reached out and took him into its house.

L ong past midnight, yet before the phosphorescent world outside came alive, Mac and Yanni were awakened by the loud arrival of several Morlocks outside the igloo.

The pair sat up as the ice door was pulled aside.

They saw a blur of movement in the dark and something large was flung onto the ground. Landing with an audible grunt, it became immediately apparent that this late-night delivery was another person, and as the ice door slid closed, the fur-clad figure sat up and shook his head—as if trying to convince himself that what he had just experienced was simply a bad dream.

The man turned to the two silent figures sitting on the floor. He spoke a few words in Chinese, seeming to ask a question.

MacCready, who had only a rudimentary knowledge of the language, tugged at an earlobe as he tried to work out the dialect and the translation. He replied at last, with a short phrase of his own.

Yanni nudged Mac with an elbow. "What'd he say?"

"I think he wants to know where he is."

"And what'd ya tell him?"

"I *think* I told him 'Up Shit Creek.'"

"That's helpful, Mac," Yanni said, with a head shake, although she did consider the first sign of a "Mac-like" response to be a welcome improvement.

Their guest needed a few seconds to rough out the meaning of Mac's slang. Then he sighed and lowered his head into his hands.

Only a day before, the helicopter pilot (whose name was Li Ming) believed that he was prepared for anything. He knew that strange encounters had been part of the region's mythology for centuries, and after the carved-up remains of a Yeren were actually loaded aboard his craft he began to accept that the old stories about monsters in the hills were not merely warnings, contrived to keep people away. Yet when one of the mythical giants finally stood before him, Li Ming was taken completely by surprise.

In the end, they *had* been able to land both of the remaining helicopters on the challengingly small table of flat ground. After Captain Mung's initial plans unraveled with the disappearance of their third aircraft, Li Ming's commanding officer had decided to consolidate his remaining force of thirty men. They would explore the mountain pass, leading away from the landing zone—the very spot where an American helicopter had recently crashed, and where someone or something had attempted to hide the wreckage.

Captain Mung's men set up camp on the improbably located terrace, their tents hidden among the rocks and as far away as possible from the vertigo-inducing cliff. The pilot and four other men were selected to remain behind. They would safeguard the helicopters from intruders and from the engine-degrading effects of the harsh winds and temperature changes.

Li Ming's first sunrise at the base camp broke clear and relatively warm. Within an hour, Captain Mung, accompanied by twenty-three heavily armed soldiers, marched away from the landing site. Wang Tse-lin, the scientist Mung had evidently coerced into joining the expedition, went along as well.

The two flyers who had safely landed Captain Mung's "Dogship" watched as the last members of the expedition disappeared around a bend.

"Well, this is going to be fun," Li Ming mumbled after briefly touring the perimeter of their new home base.

"Would you rather be going with them?" his copilot countered.

The pilot shrugged. "At least we'd be doing something exciting, instead of babysitting a pair of Russian bananas."

The copilot was just about to express his preference for bananas when Li Ming gestured toward the helicopters. "Which reminds me," he said, "you should check those safety tethers. I'm sure Captain Mung wouldn't be pleased to find that a sudden gust caught us unprepared, and that his ride had left without us."

The copilot nodded and trudged off toward the nearer of the two aircraft, then stopped and shot Li Ming a quizzical look. "*Me* check the safety tethers? And what are you going to do, stand around here and brood?"

"No," Li Ming said, pointing to a rock near the base of the sheer wall. "I'm going to stand over *there* and piss."

During the next three minutes, and with disorienting rapidity, the air shifted from dead calm to snow-driving gusts. The copilot, meanwhile, had double-checked the straps that secured the two helicopters' landing gear to a set of thick pegs, driven into solid bedrock. He was annoyed to find that he actually had to tighten one of them.

"Nice job those two did on this thing!" he called out to his friend.

There was no response, so he called again, walking through knee-deep snow to the beginning of the footprint trail left by his partner. The trail ended at a puzzling pattern of markings and fresh-frozen urine, *as if he had started pissing against the base of a boulder that was no longer there.*

Perplexed, he glanced to a spot just beyond Li Ming's trail before letting out a frighteningly childish cry that echoed along the full length of the rock wall.

It took a fellow copilot and two other men a good five minutes to calm him down. By then they had all seen the footprints in the snow—far larger than those of any human and with an oddly placed big toe.

Approximately three hours into their trek down the mountain pass, Captain Mung and his group came to a dead end. An enormous wall of stone and ice stood blocking their path.

Wang stared up at the imposing formation, then took a peek over the edge of the "trail"—which fell off into clouds and vast open space. "Do we go back?"

"No," the officer replied, "we go up."

"But—"

"Get those climbers up here," Mung called out. "Everyone else form a defensive perimeter. Be ready for an attack at any moment."

Instinctively, a part of him already knew that

the enemy would choose its own ground, its own striking distance, in its own good time. He also believed that a difficult cliff ascent, led by climbers burdened with coils of rope, harnesses, and an array of strange-looking gear, might bring the Yeren out. But after four hours, the twenty-five men and their supplies had made it uneventfully up the sheer wall and onto flat ground.

Mung was able to plot another trail almost immediately, and there was even a broad "tabletop" formation along the wall, where they could pitch their tents and spend the night.

As Wang began to unpack his one-man pup tent, the officer approached, shaking his head.

"I want you to set yours up there," he said, pointing to a patch of ground away from the cluster of soldiers' tents, and slightly up a "trail" that was now mostly obscured by lengthening shadows.

"But why?" Wang asked, clearly unnerved.

"Some of the men think your presence here is bad luck," he responded, though far from convincingly. "Just do as I say."

The scientist glanced over at the others. None of them appeared to be paying the slightest attention to him. Knowing that it would be senseless to argue, he picked up his pack and trudged away.

"And stay in your tent, once it gets dark," the captain called after him. "Until I tell you to come out."

By way of affirmation, Wang gave the officer a wave without turning around. *Wonderful*, he thought. *And here I was planning on a midnight tour of the place.*

About twenty before midnight, and as a nearly full moon was setting, Wang Tse-lin dreamed he went again to the Shennongjia Forest.

His dream of Shennongjia night began with the metallic clamor of insects that he could not identify, and the barely audible high-frequency calls of the bats hunting them. Then the night sounds died—as if someone had turned off a switch. For a while all that could be heard was his own breathing, until something began rustling through the brush, just outside his tent—something strangely familiar. This time, when Wang tried to sit up, he discovered that he was trapped inside a canvas-covered cage. Straining to hear what might be happening beyond the tent, he suddenly wished that he could not hear at all.

Outside his cramped prison, the gentle rustle of stealthy movement had been transformed into the slurping and crunching of a bestial meal. Growing louder and more disturbing with each passing second, the merriment of a ghoulish feast quickly became terrible beyond words. Wang started tearing at the canvas and screaming. The sounds did pause, as if in response, but for some reason Wang found this even more disturbing than the dark banquet. Slowly, someone dragged the tarp away from his cage. The scientist could see figures huddled around a campfire now, their bodies naked, slick with grease and blood. One of them was holding a severed arm, and as the reveler stood and shambled toward the cage, his face broke into a hideous grin. The other monsters began to rise and—

An explosion jolted Wang into semi-wakefulness and he struggled to free himself from the hungry embrace of the revelers. By the time the second blast came, the captive knew that he had been wrestling with his own sleeping bag. Freeing himself, he threw back the tent flap and stumbled outside. Beams of light alternated between his tent and the trail, one of them sweeping upward and hitting him square in the eyes.

"I ordered you to stay in your tent until I called you out!" said Captain Mung. Then, in what had quickly become the conscious extension of his still-vivid nightmare, the voice and the light were gone, leaving Wang momentarily blind.

Another man rushed past him without stopping.

"But I—" Wang called after the officer. As his eyes adapted to the haphazard sweep of flashlight beams, he could see Mung and two of his men, each holding rifles and staring down at a large figure on the ground. Eventually, three separate beams converged on the kill—which glistened wetly under the flashlights. Wang squinted and stepped closer. His first impression was that someone had just shot the largest bear that he had ever seen. But he already knew that this was no bear.

"These are not your grandmother's Yeren," Mung told the crowd of soldiers, as they gathered three deep around the body.

The officer went down on one knee and used both hands to lift the creature's head out of the spreading puddle of blood. Mung turned the fur-covered face toward his men. For a few seconds more, it continued to pulse blood through a gap-

212 Bill Schutt & J. R. Finch

ing hole where the right eye had been. The left eye seemed to have been following the movements of Mung's electric lantern.

A trick of the light, perhaps? the scientist thought.

But now Wang was able to see clearly (too clearly) the moment the life went out of that eye.

"*This* is what we are up against!" the captain said.

As Wang Tse-lin watched, and as the officer continued to address his men, several facts were becoming apparent. First, Mung had not hesitated to use him for bait. But, as unnerving as this was, it also made perfect sense. *He needs warriors to carry out his mission. My presence here is an afterthought.* Second, the officer had been *expecting* a visit from the Yeren. The two marksmen Mung had assigned to lie in wait were all the proof he needed of this. Despite his being set out as bait, Wang's respect for Captain Mung's tactical and logistical skills had actually gone up a notch. The third realization concerned the Yeren themselves, for Wang could see that while there were certainly characteristics shared by this creature and the Shennongjia specimen, it was like comparing a howler monkey to a gorilla.

By the time the captain had finished his examination, Wang Tse-lin knew that these beasts were *not* the mischief makers of deep-forest lore. This species was the supremely adapted denizen of a dangerous and unfamiliar world. It was also a world in which the scenario for any meaningful contact was now completely redefined. In the eyes of the Yeren, he, Captain Mung, and all of the others had been transformed from intruders into murderers.

In the Valley of the Morlocks

4:00 A.M., JULY 15, 1946

H e says he's a helicopter pilot," Mac told Yanni, as they sat across from a disheveled-looking Asian man dressed in an insulated flight suit.

"Can you ask him what he's doing here?"

Mac resumed his duties as a reluctant translator, first trying to work out the question, then listening to the rapid-fire response.

"No dice," Mac said with a shrug, before deciding to take another tack. "Yanni, could he have gotten out of the chopper that came down in the valley?"

"No way, Mac," Yanni said. "I told you what happened to those guys. *All* of them."

"Then our friend here got snatched from a separate group—Chinese army, from the looks of it."

Yanni gestured to the new arrival, who looked not quite thirty years old. "How 'bout we lay off him for a while? Ya gotta figure this guy's just gone through some serious shit."

"Serious shit," the man repeated.

Two sets of eyes turned toward the pilot.

"You understand us?" Mac asked.

The man nodded. "I go to flight school in Hawaii," he said, in heavily accented but perfectly understandable English. "Before war."

"What's your name?" Yanni asked.

"Li Ming," the man replied, and gestured toward a gourd sitting on the floor. "Water, please."

Mac passed him the container, then watched as the man gulped down the contents. When he finished drinking, Mac held out a wad of foil, filled with the crushed remains of a chocolate bar he had been saving for a "special occasion."

"And how did you wind up here, Li Ming?" he asked, nonchalantly.

Instinctively, the man reached for the candy bar, but he then hesitated and pulled back his hand. "Would you disclose your mission . . . if *you* are sitting here instead of me?"

Mac smiled. "No, I wouldn't." Then he gestured for the man to take the chocolate anyway— which he did, unfolding the wrapper.

"How did *you* . . . wind up here?" the pilot asked, between bites.

"You're kiddin', right?" Yanni said, stepping forward.

"Helicopter," Mac responded, surprising her.

"Not so much a good hiding job," the Chinese pilot responded quickly—*too quickly*.

"So your men landed up there as well," Mac said, though it was clearly not a question.

Li Ming immediately realized what had happened. Turning away, he directed his stare to a point beyond the igloo's wall of ice.

Mac flashed Yanni a short, knowing nod.

She returned it with a nod of her own, then moved in to stand beside the downcast newcomer.

"Don't be so hard on yourself, Li Ming," she said. "Mac's a professional ball-breaker."

Li Ming did not respond. His only concern appeared to be the three white-furred giants that had suddenly appeared out of the snowy mist, and who were now striding toward the igloo door with what seemed to Yanni to be a lot like grim determination.

CHAPTER 14

Strange Days

> *I learned from my dog long before I went
> to Gombe that we weren't the only beings
> with personalities.*
> —JANE GOODALL

> *We misuse language and talk about the
> "ascent" of man. We understand the
> scientific basis for the inter-relatedness of
> life, but our ego hasn't caught up yet.*
> —JILL TARTER

*Pliny's chamber
June, A.D. 67*

L ong before the first rays of
dawn began slanting across
the floor of the Ceran dome,
Severus's language-teaching physician entered the
living quarters and roused the groggy historian.

As Proculus stood by, trying to assess what was happening, she forced Pliny's mouth open and squirted the contents of a small, wine-bag-like pouch into his throat. Another Ceran entered carrying a bowl of thick, stringy soup and the physician gave Pliny a wordless prompt to consume it. Proculus noted that this time there would be no force-feeding, though the Cerae stood by anyway, as if to ensure that Pliny would finish every drop.

Within an hour, Pliny came to realize that whatever Ceran medicines had healed Proculus's wounds and caused the tumors to fall from his face were vastly improving his own breathing. The sinus pain and asthma that had begun troubling him before the voyage and worsened with increasing altitude were now gone seemingly beyond recall. He longed to record these amazements in ink and papyrus, but even the absence of such materials seemed no cause for despair, since his normally sharp memory had suddenly become noticeably sharper.

After sunset, when he stepped out onto the balcony with Proculus, Pliny discovered that even his vision had improved enormously. He was now able to discern new details in the luminous vegetation—as diverse in its abundance as it was in variety.

At dawn, on the third day of their imprisonment, three attendants brought bowls with combs and washcloths soaked in warm water. One of them began tugging at the back of Pliny's head, and it occurred to him that she not only wanted to comb his hair but to braid patterned fur into it. She had long, agile arms and a far more slender body shape than the brutish warriors. Yet somehow he knew that she did not belong to the physician caste.

"*No!*" he heard Proculus shout, and as Pliny gently pushed away the hand that held a comb near his head, the attendants apparently got the message that neither man wanted his hair pulled or braided with camouflage. The three Cerae backed off, made something vaguely like a polite bowing motion, then sat on their haunches and stared at the two Romans.

After Pliny was handed a fresh serving of the soup and began to eat, a moan reached him from the adjoining cell.

It sounded as if the language lessons next door had continued throughout the night again—that, and apparently much more.

The attendants heard it too, and, aroused momentarily from their sphinxlike silence, they chittered back and forth in what could easily be interpreted as knowing, mischievous laughter.

Pliny could not shake the imagery from his mind, so he attempted to steer his thoughts elsewhere, wondering about the fate of his *medicus* and the other survivors they had left along the trail. *They must be in a safer place than up here*, he assured himself. Another grunt sounded from the other side of the black ice wall and Pliny tried to imagine what his *medicus* would make of Severus's current "entanglement."

"He'd think you're possessed, Severus," Pliny muttered to himself.

A high-pitched scream gave the historian an involuntary start, and glancing over at a thoroughly unnerved Proculus, Pliny knew that he too was uncertain if the scream had been human or not, pleasure or pain.

Pliny's *medicus*, Chiron, was not a betting man, but if anyone had told him at the time of Pliny's departure into the highest reaches of the snow line that his commander could still be alive, he would certainly have wagered against it.

Chiron and nineteen of his men had settled in and waited beside the ruins of a fortified wall overlooking the city of Pandaya—what was left of it. The fragment of wall, which survived above the surge of water and boulders, was equipped on one side with a stone tower. Atop its observation platform, the *medicus* shared guard duty with the other survivors. The task had become an exercise in boredom, primarily because, with the exception of weeds and cottonwoods taking over the ruins, none of those on watch noticed any signs of life—human or otherwise.

And for a short while, it remained that way.

On the third day of Pliny's captivity, Chiron struggled back to consciousness in the aftermath of an attack that began with silent foot soldiers and ended with a dozen elephants striding forward, two by two. Adorned in elaborate body armor, their tusks had been outfitted with swordlike blades. But even beyond this menacing sight, it was the appearance of their fearsome riders that stunned the battle-tested *medicus* and his men.

These warriors were the last thing he saw before a blow to the back of the head flashed his world to black, and they were the first thing he saw when someone pulled him brutally to his feet. With long ebony hair streaming backward, the wild-eyed elephant riders had removed most of their body armor to display an array of tattoos and self-inflicted scars. Their forearms and hands bore grotesque wounds as well—*oddly similar*, he thought—until a sudden realization solved the riddle. The brutish cavalrymen were wearing gauntlets fashioned from human flesh.

Ten of the *medicus*'s men had survived, and stood bound with him.

He could see that the foot soldiers were creating a bed of coals that now glowed bright enough to drown out the starlight. The entire area around the fire pit was crowded with the strangely garbed invaders. They reminded Chiron more of hyperkinetic insects than soldiers—some gyrating wildly against the shadows of dead Pandaya, others simply bashing into their brethren. All appeared to be intoxicated but nothing about their actions resembled conventional drunkenness. There were guttural chants and the sounds of a strange language coming from all around. Though it hurt to look up, Chiron could see that there were figures all along the top of the wall. Several fell and smashed to the ground amid wild laughter, only to be replaced by a constant stream of revelers pouring out of the former observation platform.

Then, in what Chiron could have sworn was a simultaneous action, the entire crowd went si-

lent, the wild gyrations transforming into fright-
ful whole-body vibrations that ran back and forth
through the sea of human figures like a wave. The
wave parted and six of the elephant riders, all of
them women, advanced upon the Romans. Chiron
squinted, not quite believing his own eyes. Each
of the women had but a single breast. Where the
one on the right side had been there was instead
a hypertrophied pectoral muscle bearing the unmistakable scar of an old cautery wound.

"They burn away their breast to make themselves
better archers," said the man next to Chiron.

"How do you know this?" the *medicus* asked, under his breath.

"They're Scythians," he said, and then, noticing
that many of them had Far Eastern features, added,
"or some strange offshoot."

"Scythians? I thought they were as extinct as
the Babylonians."

The cavalryman nodded toward three of the
approaching female warriors. "Maybe you can ask
them about that."

CHAPTER 15

Fear of Pheromones

Each piece, or part of the whole of Nature
is always an approximation of the complete
truth, or the complete truth so far as we
know it. In fact, everything we know is only
some kind of approximation because we
know that we do not know all the laws yet.
—RICHARD P. FEYNMAN

Evolution is opportunistic, hence
unpredictable.
—ERNST MAYR

Metropolitan Museum of Natural History
New York City
July 15, 1946

D r. Nora Nesbitt believed
no astronomer discovering
a new planet beyond Pluto

could have been filled more with a sense of wonder than she was every time she translated a newly puzzled-together page from Pliny's Omega Codex and made a connection no one had made before.

"This is pretty strange," she said, pushing her chair back from the lab bench where she had been working with Patricia Wynters. "*Too* strange."

"Compared to what?" asked Patricia.

"So, you know this apish doctor Pliny mentions?"

"You mean, Severus's favorite member of the Physician race?"

"That's the one. What if she infected our centurion with a mind-controlling parasite?"

"Severus?"

Nesbitt nodded, then they both stared in silence at a particularly well-preserved Pliny sketch depicting the Ceran version of a *medicus*. Although nearly half of the papyrus sheet had been lost to ancient disintegration and modern mishandling, the pair could make out enough to sum the portrait up in a few words: *bestial* was one they both agreed upon, and yet they also perceived a strange beauty in those barbaric eyes.

According to Pliny, even he eventually had to resist an inexplicable attraction to the little doctors. In one part of the codex, the famed historian/naturalist had dedicated nearly a half page of his near-microscopic penmanship to descriptions of their uniquely disgusting odor—"difficult to relate, how strongly it emanated from sweat-slicked fur." In a later entry, Pliny recalled that the cavalryman Proculus had developed a tolerance to it, while he himself had first become accustomed to the stench, before claiming to have actually come to like it. To Nesbitt, though, poor Severus seemed hopelessly bound to the musk of a very specific physician, and perhaps even addicted to it.

"Have you ever heard of the cat-rat paradox?" Nesbitt asked at last.

"No, but do tell."

"Well, you know how much I love protozoa?"

"Don't we all?" Patricia answered, without a hint of sarcasm.

"So, one of my recent favorites—*Toxoplasma gondii*—seems to have evolved a particular talent for toying around with the wiring of rat's brains. Normally, it's no stretch to infer that rodents must be born with an instinctive fear of cats, and all the smells associated with them."

"Okay."

"But in rodents infected with *Toxoplasma*—"

"Let me guess," Patricia interjected. "The rats end up being attracted to them."

Nesbitt smiled. "Yes, though it's more than just an attraction. Once infected with the parasite, male lab rats respond to cat hair, dander, skin oils, and even urine in the same way they respond to the pheromones female rats release to attract mates."

"That's interesting. Go on."

"And in my lab we've even seen the *Toxoplasma* parasite make the rat run *toward* the cat."

Patricia looked at the Pliny drawing with increasing amazement. "So . . . you're saying Pliny's man Severus became the lab rat in this equation."

"Could be," Nesbitt replied.

Patricia, who was clearly excited, continued the mental exercise. "Then the lab rat gets eaten, right?"

"Yes, and—?"

"And the parasite reproduces in the cat."

Nesbitt nodded. "It certainly appears so."

"Incredible."

The invertebrate biologist continued: "I'm beginning to think Pliny's Cerae were doing something similar, but of course operating on an even more complex level than a microbe infecting lab animals."

"You mean, the Cerans were consciously altering the responses normal humans *would* have had to being in close contact with them?"

"Right," Nesbitt said. "Maybe this Ceran version of a similar parasite started switching circuits in regions of the human brain that control emotions like fear or anxiety—or even sexual attraction?"

Both of the researchers took another look at Pliny's figure of the physician, and winced simultaneously.

"Do you realize how nutty this is beginning to sound?"

Nesbitt nodded. "I know, but just because this little hypothesis *sounds* crazy doesn't mean it's not crazy enough to be correct."

"Scary to imagine, really," Patricia replied. "A tiny invertebrate puppeteer, pulling Severus's and Pliny's strings—yuck."

"Yuck is right. Like I said, though, for now it's hypothetical. But the closer you look at our world, the more apparent it becomes that we live in a dancing matrix of hosts, parasites, and symbionts. And if Pliny wasn't just penning a fantasy, if this codex is more than some ancient myth—"

"You mean the part about a race that could 'mold life the way we mold clay'?"

Nesbitt took a moment to consider Pliny's quote again—important enough for him to have repeated at least a half-dozen times up to this point in the manuscript. She nodded her head slowly. "That does seem to be the line that got us into this mess."

Patricia stood silently for a moment before responding. "Pliny's physicians could have designed that response themselves—based on something learned from prior encounters with people or animals outside the valley."

Dr. Nora Nesbitt, who now wore a wry smile, gestured back to the rest of the codex. "So, what does Pliny say finally happened to the centurion?"

"Hard to tell," Patricia said, and shook her head. "That's the frustrating thing. The codex breaks away into five or six missing pages, just when that part of Pliny's story gets most interesting."

AUGUST, A.D. 67

During the weeks since the capture, Pliny noticed that Severus and "Teacher" had become more inseparable than he ever imagined possible—or healthy.

In any case, no matter how far Severus might

have pushed long-held taboos, Pliny believed he owed a depth of gratitude to that very same relationship. He had no doubt that Severus and the Ceran physician were the reason he and Proculus were still taking in air through heads that had not been smashed flat against a pillar of ice.

Language-wise, for all of their efforts, the Romans had learned no more than a score of Ceran words. *It was*, Pliny thought, *a maddeningly difficult exercise*. Inexplicably, teaching the Cerae Latin was only marginally easier—even basic things like colors. *Did they even interpret them in the same way?* Pliny wondered.

On some levels, it seemed easy to understand the Cerae—as in their mastery of architecture. On other levels, though, Pliny believed he might have had greater success trying to understand the thoughts of a housefly.

For a time, the Romans were allowed to walk freely through the garden plots, tasting all of their fruits, grains, and meaty gourds at will—and there Pliny learned that the word for each plant seemed to have its own unique series of Ceran whistles and inflections. *Each individual plant has its own name?*

Pliny guessed that more than two or three weeks must have passed before he began to acclimate, emotionally, to the utter alien nature of this hidden world. The rough treatment—pokes and prods mostly—from their chaperones continued even after they were reunited with Severus. It served to remind him that this was not the tour of wonders he had once hoped for. There were, of course, wondrous sights to behold—the wall of mountains surrounding the valley, the tower of stone and ice rising with intimidating majesty from the center of the fog lake. Despite the often-boorish treatment by their captors, Pliny might have even found some serenity in the view—if not for a few contrary facts.

The Cerae were clearly disturbed about something. Scores upon scores of them were hurrying up and down through the mist layer. And, fewer than forty paces from Pliny's overlook, two men staked out for Ceran target practice had been reduced to little more than smears on the ground, their distinctive garb revealing them to be Scythians.

"Though horrible, it brought great relief, to see immediately that they were not my men," Pliny would write later.

There was little time, however, for relief or reflection. Teacher, two other physicians, and seven members of the race Pliny had come to call "the warrior caste" ushered them along a path that descended below the lake of snow fog. The historian noted that though they usually displayed little emotion, the Cerae now exhibited undeniable signs that indeed something new had intruded upon their well-ordered and strangely lit world—something next of kin to chaos. Briefly, they approached and then passed the base of the central tower.

"There's something wrong with it," Pliny thought aloud.

Proculus replied, "It looks like no one is home."

Pliny shook his head, trying to peer through the floating snow—listening for sounds of a population that was no longer present.

"Severus, ask your friend where everyone went."

The centurion hesitated.

"Go on," Proculus urged, employing a tone that Pliny found as surprising as it was lacking in respect.

Severus waved his hands and flicked his fingers in what appeared to be developing into his private language with Teacher, reinforcing hand signals with a series of high-pitched syllables that barely passed for Latin.

The Ceran made a sound that only Severus could begin to understand, accompanied by a sharp hand motion. Once again the officer hesitated.

"Well?" Proculus said, now openly displaying impatience toward his superior.

Severus returned a stern expression that had nothing to do with Proculus's insubordination. "We would heed well, all of us, not to speak unless spoken to."

This time both Pliny and Proculus obeyed the order. Neither man had any way of knowing what was really happening. There was too little information available, no basis on which to conclude that the great building's inhabitants were fanning out into the wilderness—that they were preparing for war.

Ten or twelve stadia beyond the tower, the group came to the edge of an unusually quiet river, from which warm mists were rising and crystallizing in midair. Pliny hypothesized that this process, here and at similar bodies of water, functioned to regenerate the snow fog.

Teacher raised a hand, signaling, *Halt.*

Two more of the physician caste arrived, along with one of the more spidery-limbed Cerae that Pliny had identified as architects. At Teacher's urging, Severus unraveled a maplike sheet of unusually flexible paper and spread it out on the ground. It bore a set of immediately recognizable designs, illustrated from multiple angles, and rendered in Severus's precise hand.

"*What?*" Proculus asked. "You're showing them how to build catapults?"

"*No,*" said Pliny. "This cannot be true!"

A glare from a Ceran physician put an end to the comments while the "architect" unfurled a second sheet on the ground. The Romans could see that this too had been drawn in Severus's hand. The creature ran her fingers back and forth over both sets, clearly making careful comparisons between the two drawings.

He's not only showing them how we build our weapons, Pliny realized, *he's improving the designs.*

"You treasonous dog!" Proculus cried, and lunged toward his commanding officer and former brother-in-arms.

Teacher appeared between them in a white blur and before Pliny could even begin to track her motion, Proculus was airborne—with his face bleeding and two more teeth flying out of his mouth.

NIGHTFALL, JULY 15, 1946

Although Mac was still asleep—albeit fitfully—Yanni Thorne found herself in a state of hyperalertness. Something more than the loss of their friend Jerry kept her from eating or sleeping, but she struggled to determine exactly what her instincts were trying to tell her. Certainly, there were the many possibilities. High on the list were the three angry Morlocks who had removed the Chinese helicopter pilot. Complicating *this* particular issue was Mac's insistence that one of the giants, a beast he began referring to as "Scarface," was the same individual who had killed Jerry.

On the other side of their icy window, the Morlock world was an unending parade of strange inhabitants. Even now she was watching a flower-mimicking animal that appeared near the outer edge of the igloo wall. The newly arrived "whatzit" attacked one of the grass-eating crabs they had seen previously, trapping it in a net of glowing red petals. Only a few days earlier she would have looked upon the flower mimic with a sense of wonder. Now, though, her thoughts were dark.

Yanni looked away to where Mac was sleeping, and was reminded of the fact that just a single grass mimic possessed enough toxin in its bite to nearly kill him. *There's widespread lethality here*, she concluded, and wondered how many deadly organisms they'd walked by already without any concern at all—the stand of Indian pipes, the strange little creature that darted across their path in the cave.

Yanni understood now that she had been looking at the world of the Morlocks through innocent eyes, but the reality was, *There is no innocence here.*

Outside, as if to support her newly acquired view, the "flower" was suddenly writhing on the ground like a viper bitten by something even *more* poisonous. The little crab scuttled away, carrying with it one of the petals.

Yanni reasoned in passing that if evolution *were* being sped up here, then the arms race between predator and prey had also been sped up. *But were the Morlocks controlling any of this? Or had they somehow dropped the reins?* From their unease with the grass mimics to their relationship with the little elephants, Yanni believed that any control the locals might have once wielded was now tenuous at best.

In the center of the igloo, R. J. MacCready was finally awake—staring up at the circular opening in the ceiling.

"Did something just scream?" he wondered.

"Yeah, a flower," she replied.

"Oh, okay."

"How's that leg of yours?"

"Feels a lot better, actually," he reassured her.

Yanni did not continue the conversation. A sudden movement had drawn her attention outside, again.

The world tonight was so black that it was impossible to see beyond the limited range of bioluminescent speckles on the ground. No moonlight filtered down through the fog. Yanni could just barely recognize the shape of a Morlock walking out of the mist, eclipsing the little ground "stars" as it approached. It was Alpha and he was not alone. Trotting beside him were three of the bi-trunked mammoths, still wearing their choke collars but now without leashes.

Very quickly, and with deliberate stealth, Alpha slid the cell door aside and motioned for Yanni to come out. Mac hesitated, then followed her, expecting at any moment to be pushed forcefully back through the opening, but Alpha did not seem to care. The ground around the igloo was strangely free of grass mimics, though the harsh scent of the elephant-generated repellent Yanni had described previously provided an explanation for their absence.

There was no rumbling or snorting from the mini-mammoths, and no loud, whistling Morlock-speak, making it even more apparent that whatever the reason might be for this middle of the night visit, it was happening in secret. Alpha and the mammoths stood in utter silence and Yanni took the hint, signaling Mac to do likewise. Then the Morlock led her and the three little elephants to a spot some thirty feet away, for what R. J. Mac-Cready supposed must be the strangest conference of all time.

Mac checked their surroundings—on the lookout for less friendly visitors. *One hairy son of a bitch in particular.*

On previous nights, at about this time, phantom shapes, wider than the stretch of his arms, had fluttered overhead. Tonight, he noticed, there were no flyers. In fact the only trace of nightlife, besides their mammalian visitors, was the "poisoned flower" Yanni had been watching earlier. Mac felt a sudden unease that its phosphorescent blush was returning and as the minutes passed, the creature had rekindled brightly enough to illuminate a broadening swath of the mist. The meeting participants seemed too busy to notice.

Not so fast there, son, Mac thought, before moving quickly toward the steadily strengthening glow and stamping the bogus flower flat, as a smoker might stamp out a cigarette on a sidewalk. Then he kicked some dirt on top of the glowing red bits.

"Evolve your way out of that one," he muttered to himself.

Mac's mind-set was "all mission" now and his only mission was to get Yanni out of this valley alive. He was also starting to hope against hope (something Mac did very rarely) *that Yanni's pals might have the very same thing in mind.*

Soon after Mac finished his novel impersonation of "lights out," the meeting ended. Yanni took a moment to give an approving nod to his handiwork before Alpha motioned them back into the igloo.

"What's going on?" Mac asked.

"Shhhh," Yanni whispered. "You're not gonna believe this."

They scrambled inside. The seal was closed silently behind them, and the four night visitors disappeared, in perfect silence.

"Okay, spill it," Mac said.

"Seems that Alpha wants to learn more about the mammoths—and he wants my help."

"Oh?" Mac replied, unable to hide either his skepticism or his concern.

"Yeah, well, apparently at least one Morlock has discovered that these little elephants are a lot smarter than they've been letting on."

"How smart?"

"*Very*. Maybe smarter than us."

Mac shook his head, amazed and incredulous at the same time. "And remind me again how you figured this all out, in what—five minutes?"

"I don't know how to explain it," Yanni said. "Trying to understand both of these species is kinda like pounding at a cement wall. At first you don't get anywhere. Then this little crack appears—and maybe there's a hint of feelings or a specific emotion. You keep hammerin' away and suddenly there's light shining through it. Now when you move closer to that tiny crack of light, you can start to see a whole lot, even stuff on the other side."

Mac remained silent.

"Like I said, it's tough to describe. But toss in the bit of Latin that Alpha and I share, and I just *know* what's going on now."

"But, Yanni," Mac said, then hesitated, "the Morlocks *eat* these elephants. And they—"

"And your point is what?"

"My point is, why all this sudden interest in co-operating with a menu item?"

"I think things are different with these individuals," said Yanni, firmly. "I get the sense from Alpha, *and* from those three mammoths, that they've been treating each other as equals."

"What about Alpha's brethren?" Mac added. "What about the asshole who—"

"I think Alpha's in this by himself," Yanni replied, cutting off Mac's thought before it went any further. "I really believe he sees the outside world closing in. First us, now the Chinese are back again, this time in flying machines. I get the feeling he's looking at cooperation as a necessity—for both species."

Mac nodded. "Well," he said, grudgingly, "I suppose if anyone can help get you out alive, it'd be the Morlock *jefé* and his mammoth posse."

Yanni managed a quiet snort of a laugh. "Now *there's* a sentence I'll bet you never thought you'd be uttering."

With the stakes as high as they had become, Mac pushed the irony of their situation aside and decided to play the skeptic. "Look," he began, "what do we know for sure? These Morlocks are sentient creatures. Right?"

"Right," Yanni replied, quickly recognizing where Mac was taking the conversation.

"Well, then they can lie and deceive just like everybody else."

"Sure," Yanni said, "but if I missed the boat on this one, then Alpha's got the elephants fooled, too. And why bother doing that? They've already got 'em completely enslaved."

"All right, good point," Mac acknowledged, "even if their way of thinking should turn out to be completely alien to us . . ." He trailed off into thought for a while, adding up the facts. "Two wildly intelligent species," he said at last.

"Existing side by side as master and slave for who knows how long? Can it even *be* changed?"

Yanni stared into the night. "Of Morlocks and mammoths," she said to no one in particular.

"It'll be tough," Mac added. "And even more dangerous with the third species elbowing its way in."

Yanni shook her head. "Yeah, the ones with rockets and atomic bombs."

Mac shuddered inwardly. "In a few years, the question won't be about masters and slaves. It'll be about whether this world of theirs exists at all."

"Or ours for that matter," Yanni added.

"Or ours," Mac conceded.

On the floor of Pliny's Mist Lake
AUGUST, A.D. 67

The catapults were still under construction when Pliny and Proculus, now separated from Severus by members of the soldier caste, were led to what Pliny would later christen, for his codex, "The Pink and White Terraces."

He had never imagined, much less seen, the like. For many centuries, perhaps for many thousands of centuries, steaming hot water must have been rising from somewhere deep beneath the valley walls, trickling downhill and depositing pink and white minerals in tier upon tier of gently overflowing pools. It was, to Pliny, a stairway to the gods. He could not see the top of it.

But all thoughts of beauty were soon squashed

as their own survival again became a matter of grave doubt. The abrupt transition occurred once Pliny saw what the Cerae had been cultivating in the pools, and once he realized what was being dragged out from beneath mounds of crushed ice. He closed his eyes, trying to calm his mind against the atrocity and taking several deep breaths before opening them again. When he did, the view became even more overwhelming.

Severus, what have you brought us into?

Against the haunting beauty of terraced pools, against strata of fog that obscured everything above and beyond the nearer pools and subdued a valley's usual level of noise, the area around the catapults was a scene drawn from the deepest and busiest level of Hades.

Pliny felt sick with anger, watching as pieces of naked Roman bodies were hauled from beneath mounds of crushed ice by Ceran physicians and elephants—each of which, though small, possessed a powerful trunk, more muscular than a physician's arm. The body parts were from his own soldiers, the ones who died all around him during that first afternoon at the valley entrance. Five of the so-called physicians were separating muscles from bones—peeling them into long strips, which were immediately scrutinized, as if the examiners were searching for gold.

One of them pulled something yellowish and stringy from a ribbon of curled flesh. The "string" was about the length of a man's forearm, and though still ice-chilled, the physician pinched it just hard enough to provoke a wormlike wiggle, verifying that the parasite was indeed very much alive.

Pliny looked away; but it seemed there was no direction in which he could turn his head and avoid a new vision of hell. The explorer knew very little about the pain-dealing guinea worms, little beyond a warning from his *medicus* that some of the men had apparently contracted them while on leave in Alexandria.

At the edge of a pink and white terrace, three more physicians had been spooling worms out of the water and onto the ends of long sticks. Although closely resembling the parasites Pliny had seen pulled from Roman flesh, these creatures were different—each equipped with a short, needle-like probe at one end. Judging from the caution exhibited by those doing the spooling, these worms were a far more aggressive and dangerous lot.

Pliny attempted to reason out what he was seeing, struggling to accept what he feared was the only logical conclusion. *Weeks ago, the Cerae must have begun extracting parasites from Roman bodies. Now they have succeeded in breeding them.*

Nearby, a familiar voice cried out, but Pliny never heard it. As the reality of what he was seeing invaded his brain, Pliny failed to notice that Proculus was no longer at his side.

"They're not just breeding these worms," Pliny said to no one in particular. "They've processed them into something new."

"May the sands lie softly on your grave, Severus!" came the familiar voice, and Pliny gave a start as if snapping awake from a nightmare. "So the dogs may dig you up!"

The historian turned away from the worm spoolers to face yet another vision from the depths of hell. Proculus, now bound hand and foot, was being dragged by two Ceran warriors toward a series of circular pits in the ground. Less wide than the span of a man's arm, each of the excavations was deep enough to hold a Roman soldier, up to the level of his chest.

"Spawn of Cretan whores!" cried Proculus, who, despite the dire circumstances, continued to roll out an impressive litany of curses.

At first the Cerans simply stood the cavalryman before a row of the holes. Then, in a move that surprised Pliny (at a time when he feared nothing could any longer come as a surprise), a particularly large member of the warrior caste rubbed Proculus's face in a fur-tangled armpit. It followed up this rude exercise by chest-butting the centurion back and forth between itself and another Ceran. Having anointed the Roman with a stench that could be smelled even at Pliny's distance, they lowered Proculus into one of the pits.

On either side of Proculus were similar holes containing bodies, though they did not appear to be Romans. Any further identification was impossible, because their heads, shoulders, and armor breastplates were cloaked in seething masses of what Pliny believed to be white ants.

"Remain *calm*," Pliny told his friend. "We've survived worse situations than this" (*even if I cannot think of one right now*, he left unsaid).

Then, naturally, the situation became worse. Three new prisoners were herded out of the snowy fog and dropped into pits. Spewing what were curses in their own tongue, Pliny was able to identify their tribal origins: *Scythians*. He observed that the pit-bound corpses flanking Proculus were also Scythians, a point made clear as the living veils of white fell away—revealing similar tunics and armor, draped upon bloodless husks. One of the dead's armor plates had been scavenged from a slaughter. It bore the crest of a Roman *medicus*.

Chiron . . . Pliny did not have time to utter the word. Proculus's movements suddenly became frantic and it was all so clearly too easy to know why. In that moment, a small part of him would have traded for a quick death at the mountain pass, if in the bargain he would never have lived to see this. Having fallen from their wraithlike former hosts, the veils of white ants now reappeared from below, streaming over the ground and toward Proculus. Pliny prepared himself to turn away at the last instant—but to his utter surprise, instead of pouring down around the centurion, the miniature horde hesitated, then began to retreat.

Any solace Pliny received from the realization that Proculus might live did not outlast the revelation that the miniature army was now advancing on his own position—with the only buffer being the freshly trenched Scythians. Pliny squashed growing panic beneath his ever-present urgency to observe and record. His latest revelation was that the "ants" had never been ants. They were in fact some form of tick, each no larger than his pinky nail.

This time, the same veil of parasites that had spared Proculus spilled like milk down the three Scythian pits. The Easterners strained erratically against their bonds. Their struggle was not an escape attempt. It was a combination of anger and what the historian regarded as an honorable defiance. Within only forty beats of Pliny's racing heart, the ghostly white swarm began rising from beneath the prisoners' armor—streaming out in waves and then coalescing into tentacle-like branches across shoulders, necks, and finally heads. As the seconds passed, the branches began to change color—from pallid white to pinkish white, then finally, red.

They have refused to let out a single cry of pain, Pliny dictated to his mind's expedition log.

A new commotion at the stalactite-lipped terraces—concentrated at a pool filled with dark water and white worms—drew his attention away from the pits. Three large sticks, their ends coiled round and round with glistening trapped worms, were withdrawn from yet another black pool by physicians, who brandished the worm sticks like spears and moved toward the already parasite-covered prisoners.

The addition of transformed guinea worms to the already incomprehensible hellscape removed all doubt: *The Cerae have forged weapons from life itself.*

By the time worms were introduced to the carnivorous mix, the three Scythians in the pits were not nearly so drained of blood as to be spared by merciful unconsciousness. The ticks seemed to invade only the skin; now with the worms added, their bodies were being invaded from within and without. The end did not come quickly. For too many minutes, the Easterners continued to burble and quiver.

Pliny knew what he was watching, but true understanding was difficult. The term *biological weapon* did not yet exist. But there was a term for the engineering prowess that had produced ball bearings, and the movable pattern printing press that was the pride of Neapolis (Naples), and which Pliny had known until now as "superior technology." *That* term, for the moment, served him.

At last, Pliny turned his gaze back toward the catapults, where shoulder-width casks were being carefully stacked and arrayed nearby—empty and awaiting the addition of their deadly cargo. But while the engineer in him admired the subtle design modifications to the machines, a far greater part of him was sickened by Severus's actions, clearly directed at enhancing range and accuracy to serve an enemy of Rome. More sickening yet were the raw materials—the worms—contributed by the flesh of his own men.

"Severus, what have you done?"

Severus did not answer. Despite his work on the catapults, he was seized by the Cerae, covered in their stink, and thrown into a pit just like Proculus.

The bastard deserves it, Pliny told himself. The worms and ticks, he was certain, would soon spill in upon Severus—weapons of biological alchemy, made possible by an elixir hidden in those hellish pools of black water. Pliny remembered Proculus's initial suggestion that medicines used by the Cerae to repair his body were a form of magic. Pliny was the first naturalist to observe how easily an advanced technology could present the stubborn illusion of witchcraft. In much the same way his fellow Romans had learned to control steam, forge iron, and make concrete, the Cerae had plucked something out of nature, studied it, and built a thing the world had never seen before.

At the moment Pliny believed he could understand what was happening, two physicians lowered him into his own pit. They spared him the humiliating smearing with their stink, to which Proculus and Severus had been subjected.

In another moment, he saw two more Easterners shepherded out of the fog and lowered into pits. They too were spared the greasy-fur-smearing. This time the weapons burrowed into the newcomers' bodies with such astonishing rapidity that Pliny supposed, if these Scythians worshipped gods, they did not survive long enough to pray.

Pliny became transfixed by the small line of ticks that climbed out of the killing pits and began moving steadily, and apparently still hungrily, in his direction. Another trail fell in behind it. Then another. And yet another.

Pliny's world was reduced again to tunnel vision. So completely was he focused on the approaching blood-feeders that if not for the grunt she emitted, he would have failed to notice Teacher's immediate presence.

He looked up at her, his eyes trying to convey defiance.

She responded to him with an incomprehensible trill. Then, hefting a jug filled seemingly to the brim with weaponized life, she strode off directly toward Severus—the man Pliny vowed would, in a just universe, be written down into history as the modern-day Brutus.

Now the puzzle pieces were lining up, but analysis of their meaning remained elusive. Four things, he noticed. First: The ticks were avoiding the Cerae and even the tracks made in the ground by their feet. Second: They were avoiding Severus (who was covered in the stink of the Cerae). Third: They seemed to be consistently avoiding Proculus (also covered). Fourth: They swarmed straight to the Scythians (not covered). This led Pliny to know a fifth thing he had not quite pieced together before: He was not covered; he was, like the Scythian enemies, unprotected by the stench of the Cerae.

More trilling drew him away from these thoughts. He saw Severus bowing his head and even managing a submissive smile as Teacher laid a hand gently on his shoulder. Then, suddenly and without any warning or expression of emotion, she emptied the contents of her jug over his head.

Finally, more thorough analysis became possible. *Even unprotected, I might live through this after all*, Pliny realized. There was actually a bizarre logic behind what he was witnessing. *They have a plan*, he told himself. And the implications for the future of man were terrifying.

CHAPTER 16

Adam Raised Cain

Things fall apart. The center cannot hold.
—WILLIAM BUTLER YEATS

Things do not happen. Things are made to happen.
—JOHN F. KENNEDY

Show me the man and I'll find you the crime.
—LAVRENTIY BERIA

In the Valley of the Morlocks
July 17, 1946

W here's Alpha?" Yanni asked. Her words were uttered in surprise, underscored by alarm. She and Mac had been shepherded by three Morlocks to a hill, along a path clear of grass mimics. As deeply as either of them could peer through the fog-suspended snow, they saw no sign of the giant.

This was the third time in two days that they had been taken out of their icehouse jail for what, at least on its surface, appeared to be the start of another leg-stretching exercise routine. During each outing, they were encouraged and even prodded to run through knee-deep dunes of snow. And each time, Alpha had led the way—until now.

Today they were led by a Morlock Yanni had never seen before, and accompanied by another Mac instantly recognized by a distinctive irregularity in the hair along one side of his face.

"What's wrong?" Yanni asked.

"Scarface here," Mac said, "is the asshole who—" He stopped short, having just taken a hard jab to the kidney. *Do these things murder each other, too?* he asked himself. *Is Alpha even alive?*

Though this new dilemma was bad enough, Mac realized that something more subtle had been troubling him. While Yanni still reeked of Alpha musk, even from two arm lengths away, he'd noticed that neither of them stank quite so much as the day before, or the day before that. He glanced around, looking for grass mimics— thankful that the repellent was still working— *for now.*

Without any threatening sounds, without any warning at all, Mac was grabbed from behind and forced face-first down into the snow.

Within that same moment, Yanni was lifted off the ground and, turning toward Mac, watched as dozens of snowflake mimics swarmed away from his face, separating themselves from the real snow that only partially obscured his features. The Morlock who held Yanni let out a series of whistles that sounded to her like approval—as if some sort of test were taking place, the nature of which was utterly inexplicable. What had become clear was a feeling that their chances of ever leaving this valley alive had just descended deeper into what her late husband would have designated as "the shitter."

"Mac?" she called out, recognizing that his abuser was the one he had come to call "Scarface."

"Listen, Yanni, just roll with it," he managed, as the beast hoisted him up under one arm and set off at a jog.

The last thing Yanni wondered, before Mac and Scarface disappeared into the mist, was whether those would be the last words she ever heard from him.

R. J. MacCready knew exactly where Scarface was carrying him, long before the entrance to the subterranean world came into view. He saw few other Morlocks during the trek, but those that they did pass appeared to turn away.

Within the earth, and even before they approached the newest of the "trophy room's" ice columns, Mac felt an all-too-familiar churning in his guts. He caught a glimpse of Jerry's parka and closed his eyes tightly, forcing himself to think about something else—anything else. *A way out of here or at least a way to put a dent in this guy's day.*

MacCready's ride ended with a fling along the ground and he skidded into a violent shoulder slam against an object he already understood too well.

Refusing to look at the freshly constructed stalagmite, Mac sensed the approach of his tormentor. Defiant, he stared up at the beast, right in the eye. Although Mac always detested the habit many people had of anthropomorphizing, at that moment he would have sworn on a first edition of Darwin's *Origin* that Scarface was gloating.

"Yeah, fuck you, too!" Mac snarled, calculating that this would probably be his very last second of conscious existence.

The creature reacted with something approximating a laugh, removing from Mac's mind any doubt that his sentence in Scarface's court was about to be carried out. During another of his rare hopes against hope, he wished that Jerry and everyone else he had lost would somehow be there to embrace him, even if only during a near-death hallucination.

Yanked off the ground by one foot, Mac drew a bead on the creature's genitals and lashed out with his free leg. Scarface sidestepped the attempt and slammed Mac's body into the pillar of ice—just hard enough to hurt, but not with enough force to break bones or to kill. *Not this time*, Mac told himself, before he was flung again along the ground.

Shaking his head, the zoologist struggled to

his knees, using the nearest column for support. He was unable to avoid the sight of a modern Chinese soldier in an ice pillar—recognizable only by his uniform. *One of Li Ming's buddies*, he thought.

There was also no doubt in his mind that Scarface was drawing a malicious joy from this new exercise.

With a speed that, despite everything he had already witnessed, caught Mac by surprise, his tormentor rushed forward and hoisted him into the air, this time by both arms. Again he kicked at the giant, who spun him around and brought his face within mere inches of a gaping mouth. The close-up threat display of Morlock teeth was enhanced by a skull-vibrating roar, accompanied by the hot stench of decayed meat.

"Jesus Christ," Mac roared back, fighting off dizziness. "A little Listerine wouldn't kill you!"

The creature ignored him, flipping his body around again like a rag doll before forcing his head finally to face, at close range, the ice column containing his friend. Mac looked past the familiar figure, doing everything he could to *not* see what they'd done to Jerry.

It did not help.

Beyond the ice-suspended body, his eyes focused on an open space in the cylinder—clearly meant for him. What took Mac to the very precipice of madness was not his own soon-to-be permanent niche, but what lay just behind it. The beast lifted him higher, to see it more clearly—a second unfilled cavity, meant for Yanni.

Author - Thou shalt not take the name of the Lord thy God in vain. (2nd Commandment)

Now, held immobile and with a Morlock hand tightening around his neck, R. J. MacCready began to give in, for the first time ever, to a sense of utter hopelessness. Emphasizing the point, he heard the arrival of a second Morlock, accompanied by an even more skull-vibrating roar. Scarface reacted by dropping Mac to the ground and kicking him backward with a leg sweep.

As he came to rest beside the Chinese soldier's column, Mac looked up and beheld a suddenly tamed killer. He was reminded of a guilty teen kicking a risqué magazine under his bed. But instead of a shocked parent, the surprise visitor was Alpha, who rushed forward to confront Scarface.

Making certain that the Big Guy knew exactly what had been happening in the Trophy Room, Mac pointed at the space prepared for Yanni, struggled to sit upright, then gave up.

Even from his prone position, the zoologist could see that the changes in Scarface's stance and demeanor were as immediate as they were dramatic. Head bowed, the Morlock took a step backward, letting his arms drop to his sides.

"Subservient, my ass," Mac muttered, sensing even without Yanni's abilities that Alpha could not trust this particular beast. "Watch out for that one," he called to Alpha, saddened that he might just as well be warning him in Yiddish. Then he collapsed in exhaustion.

Alpha snatched up the human rag doll, tucked him under an arm, and carried Mac out of the subterranean maze.

Yanni had been nervously pacing the interior of the igloo when, at last, Alpha approached through the fog. She let out a small cry as she saw that he was carrying Mac—bloodied and seemingly in shock but very much alive.

Pushing aside the ice door, Alpha, with Yanni's assistance, eased Mac down onto the floor. The giant communicated something that approximated a sigh, then exited without any further attempts at communication. She watched him through the ice wall until he disappeared into the mist.

Yanni brought Mac some water and squatted down to help him drink.

"I'm all right," he said, noting the look of concern she wore.

"Oh, yeah," Yanni replied gently. "You look great."

"Really," he said, stopping when she put a finger to his lips.

Mac looked past her.

What did you see out there? Yanni thought, but could not bring herself to ask. MacCready's entire body seemed to shudder for a moment, then he closed his eyes, very tightly.

Whatever it was, she told herself, *it sure as hell wasn't in Pliny's codex.*

METROPOLITAN MUSEUM OF NATURAL HISTORY

The weak never become top dogs. This is an unbreakable rule. Be they Roman, or

*Ceran, or Easterner, any people capable
of building a civilization will be highly
intelligent, vigilant, and (when necessary,
from their point of view) thoroughly
ruthless. Thus, their survival will always
be more important than our survival.
And in the end, we must remember
above all else, that when we encounter
any foreign civilization for the first
time, their people will know that these
same unbreakable laws define our way of
thinking about them.*

—PLINY THE ELDER (AS TRANSLATED BY
PATRICIA WYNTERS, MMNH)

So began a concluding chapter of Pliny's hidden codex. Patricia Wynters knew that the collision of three civilizations had led the historian to believe that whenever Rome or one of its descendant cultures met another so alien as the Cerae, "the very few things that can be predicted for certain, render the outcome certainly unpredictable."

"Sheesh, this guy rambles on like nobody's business," Patricia told Charles R. Knight. "It's all pretty obvious nowadays but I guess two thousand years ago, this might have been an example of hitting the nail square on the head."

"A few things never change, I guess," Knight replied.

"But most things do," she added, her friend sensing more than a hint of sadness in her voice.

The Kremlin

JULY 17, 1946

I have called this meeting," Joseph Stalin began, "because the young man in charge of decoding transmissions from our people in New York has something important to tell us."

A young electronics prodigy named Anatoly handed out transcripts to the other two men who had been called into the office.

"Our problem is named MacCready," Anatoly said. "The same MacCready sent to the wilds of Brazil in '44 by this Major Hendry. The theremin device transmitted at least two references confirming this fact. There was no mention of what he did there, but we feel he was somehow involved in the destruction of a missile base—but not before a high-altitude rocket launched from there dropped bacteria bombs on our troops in the Ukraine."

"And what is his job now—this MacCready?" Stalin asked.

"Officially, he is a zoologist," Anatoly continued.

"And *is* he—a zoologist?"

Anatoly's boss, a bespectacled man, stepped forward and cleared his throat. Although he would have looked at home stacking canned goods in a market, Lavrentiy Beria was more feared in his country than Stalin himself. Only three years earlier, he had been introduced to President Roosevelt by the Soviet leader as "our Himmler." It was a designation that had much to do with the fact that Beria not only oversaw Stalin's dreaded secret police, but was also in charge of the gulag labor camps.

"Recently, this American was planning a return to Brazil—to look for prehistoric horses. At first, I believed it to be just a stupid cover story—but there is a solid paper trail."

"Go on," Stalin said, gesturing to the transcript.

Beria continued. "The man—MacCready—wherever he goes, is a human lightning rod for trouble."

Anatoly nodded in agreement. "The incident two years ago killed thousands in the Ukraine—and, in the end, the Nazis trapped there were able to break out of the encirclement our brave comrades had fought to create."

"I know all about this disgraceful incident," Stalin bellowed. "One in which our 'brave comrades' *failed to carry out their orders*!"

"Of course you're right, sir," Anatoly said, with a submissive bow.

Stalin continued, his voice noticeably slurred by alcohol: "And did anyone take the time to examine these dead *heroes*? To determine just what killed them?"

There was an uncomfortable silence until Lavrentiy Beria cleared his throat yet again. "No, Comrade Stalin, but those responsible for this oversight have already been . . . *reassigned*."

Anatoly followed up. "I believe that this American was sent into Brazil to find something and to stop the attack."

"Well, then obviously *he* failed, too," Stalin said, with disgust.

"Unless of course, he did *not* fail," Beria said, pausing for effect.

"Go on," Stalin said, with impatience.

"Unless the American *wanted* the attack on the Mother Country to succeed. Who can forget their General Patton, who said—"

Stalin held up a hand. "I know exactly what that presumptuous asshole said: 'After Hitler is dead, if FDR wants Moscow, I can give it to him.'"

Once again, the room went uncomfortably silent.

Stalin seemed to wave off the thought, then poured himself another glass of "water." "And we all know what happened to Patton," he muttered to himself, before turning to Anatoly. "Do you think MacCready could have been ordered to let this attack occur—maybe even to *help* it happen?"

"Difficult to tell, sir," Anatoly lied. The man was clearly trying *not* to let his response sound like a contradiction to Beria's suggestion. "According to the information we were able to gather, through Comrade Theremin's 'gift,' MacCready is, as the Americans say, a loose cannon."

"But they do find him to be a valuable asset, yes?" said Beria, before finally turning to the fourth man in the room. "So, Nikita, you were assigned to read everything this MacCready has published. Have you any predictions? What do you think is on his mind?"

An inordinate interest in horses and bats, Nikita

Khrushchev thought, and decided to keep even this observation to himself, because it was clearly far safer to play the bumbling, uncivilized half-wit only recently recovered from an extended (and nonexistent) bout of pneumonia. Khrushchev never suspected that the facade would ultimately leave him the last man standing in the Kremlin, as history hurried him along toward a game of nuclear poker with an American president. Presently, his only concern was to avoid taking his place beside those who had spoken the wrong words (or any words at all)—and who now lay buried under Beria's rose garden.

Khrushchev stammered.

"Out with it!" said Stalin.

"I . . . I don't believe I can predict anything," he said quickly. "I don't know."

Beria shook his head in an exaggerated manner. "I don't believe you know anything, either. Or that you ever will." He glanced over at young Anatoly, who laughed obediently.

Beria continued. "As *we* now know perfectly well, the Americans uncovered an ancient Roman expedition log indicating the existence of certain biological monstrosities, out there in the wild. And—"

Stalin interrupted. "And now this same Mac-Cready is on this ancient trail like a bloodhound."

"A brilliant deduction," Beria said, seemingly making a second career out of constantly redefining the word *obsequious*. "And if what we've overheard during the translation of this 'Omega Codex' is true—" He turned to Anatoly.

"I believe it is," said Anatoly.

"Then you will assemble a team immediately," Stalin decided. "Priority one—find this Mac-Cready and bring me whatever it is he is searching for. It must be important for the American military to have risked sending him in there."

"And priority two?"

Stalin smiled an undertaker's smile. "Bring me this loose cannon—or silence him for good."

What about the Chinese? Nikita Khrushchev asked himself. *What will they think of this incursion into their territory?* Of course, he left the questions unasked, though he was clearly pleased that young Anatoly had apparently arrived at the very same questions.

"I'm afraid, sir, we must risk stirring up Chiang Kai-shek's Nationalists," said Anatoly. "But I—" He looked at Beria and went silent.

"Finish your thought," Stalin commanded. "You have no enemies here."

"With pleasure," Anatoly lied, then continued: "I can explain it best by telling you what I believe this ancient Roman found, and what is going to happen in Tibet—very soon."

On the floor of Pliny's Mist Lake

AUGUST, A.D. 67

Initially, Pliny had realized with a jolt that the decision of the Cerae not to mark him with their stink doomed him to the Scythian fate.

He came to this realization during the instant in which he saw the Ceran called Teacher pouring a pot of drill-tipped worms over Severus's head, arms, and chest. Up to that very moment, he believed the creature had turned against her pet and actually thought of Severus's fate as "some justice." And yet, moved by a stubborn ember of compassion for the centurion, he turned away, bracing himself for screams that never came.

When he looked again, the worms were falling away from Severus's body. The swarm of ticks had remained near the rim of the pit for a long time, then scattered and disappeared. Proculus's moments of dread came and went in the very same way.

Finally, when Pliny's turn came, he glared at Severus. Clenching and unclenching his bound hands into fists, the naturalist watched stoically as the Ceran ladled worms from Severus's pit into Proculus's pit, and finally into his own. Pliny set his jaw—determined to accept his fate like a Roman.

But the bites for which I had braced myself were never delivered, Pliny recorded in his codex.

It seemed, to me, that no sooner had they touched, tasted, or smelled my skin, my hair, and my sweat, they were repulsed by me, and fled my body.

I understood then, beyond doubting, that we had indeed been used for a process of training the weapon. The same worms and ticks that did not attack me were collected from my pit and poured upon a Scythian captive who had been brought forth and lowered into the ground. His flesh did not repel them—could not repel them.

And it seemed to me that the unfortunate man was dead in the amount of time I would take to draw a deep breath, hold it reflectively, and exhale.

CHAPTER 17

Dilemma

*The real problem of humanity is
the following: We have Paleolithic
emotions . . . and god-like technology. And
it is terrifically dangerous, and it is now
approaching a point of crisis overall.*
— E. O. WILSON

Metropolitan Museum of Natural History
Fifth Floor

S o, do you think Pliny knew
the implications of this?" Dr.
Nora Nesbitt asked.

"Of course he knew," Patricia said, gesturing
toward the codex. "He's telling us right there the
step-by-step procedure for imprinting a biological weapon to attack an ethno-specific group."

Charles Knight held the newly assembled fragments of codex in one hand, a magnifying lens in
the other. "A race-specific weapon," he said, notic-

ing that his hands were shaking. "Two thousand years ago."

"How can this be?" Patricia asked. "It would be the biological equivalent of uranium-235."

"He must have been mad to write this down," Nesbitt said, as much to herself as the others.

"Ah, but he never *published* it," Patricia emphasized.

"Thankfully," Knight replied. He placed the codex fragment and magnifier down on a lab bench, then buried his trembling hands in his pockets—hoping to shift the conversation away from what had quickly become an uncomfortable topic.

Nesbitt, however, was not about to let the subject rest, even for a minute. "Where, exactly, did they find Pliny's book?"

"Someone concealed it under a wine cellar," Knight said, allowing a degree of impatience to creep into his voice.

"In one of Pompeii's sister cities," Patricia chipped in. "Not quite sure which one."

"And *that's* how it was preserved?"

Knight peered at Nesbitt over his glasses. "You know, I'm beginning to feel a bit like one of those contestants on *Twenty Questions*."

"Come on, Charles," Patricia said, in her best singsong voice. "You know you want to tell us."

Knight shot his friend an exasperated look, sighed, then continued. "According to Major Dropsy, the fact that the codex was sealed in an airtight, screw-top cylinder of noncorrosive metal probably had something to do with its preservation."

Patricia gave a wry smile. "See, now that wasn't so hard."

Nesbitt ignored the banter. "So Pliny's codex got buried by Mount Vesuvius, on the very same day that he died?"

"Pliny, Pompeii, and thirty thousand people," Knight said.

Nesbitt shot the artist a skeptical look. "And how come nobody recovered it until recently?"

"Well, apparently they came close," Knight replied, resigned now and back in educator mode. "Soon after the blast, Emperor Titus had begun a recovery and aid operation in the region—which included the sinking of mine shafts into sites where the wealthiest Pompeians had lived."

"Ah, the recovery of gold, you mean?"

Knight smiled. "Of course, Dr. Nesbitt. But Pliny's nephew, Pliny the Younger, was instrumental in bringing mining under the volcano to a halt."

"And why's that?" Nesbitt asked.

"Until now, historians figured it was simply a matter of too many earthquakes and too many mine collapses," said Knight. "But after reading the codex you really do have to wonder."

"Maybe Pliny the Nephew didn't want anybody poking around and finding Pliny the Uncle's little secret."

"I'd call this more of a big secret," Patricia added.

"Agreed," Knight replied. "And the only reason to hide the codex from the rest of the empire is if you know the danger is real."

"Maybe even more dangerous now," said Nesbitt. "If something like this got into the wrong hands, it could make what General Ishii Shirō and his pals did with bioweapons in Manchuria look like a church picnic."

"That's a big 'if,'" Knight replied, "but if this is true, then . . ." His voice trailed off, his mind considering thoughts that had suddenly leaped past "uncomfortable" into something darkly nightmarish.

Nesbitt carried her own thought to its next logical step. "Just imagine the Russians or the Chinese getting their hands on something like this."

Patricia shook her head. "I'm not sure I follow."

"What if they took an already fast-evolving pathogen—plague say—and then began imprinting it against Western Europeans."

"*Or* the other way around," said Patricia.

"If both sides had it, you could end up with people sending race-specific plagues back and forth against each other, until the only safe thing to be is—"

"—anything but human," said Patricia.

Nesbitt let out a long whistling sigh, and the room fell silent. "How much does your Major Hendry know about this?" she said, at last.

Once again, Knight lifted the freshly reconstructed page. "He knows quite a lot. And as a point of information, Dr. Nesbitt, he certainly isn't *my* Major Hendry."

Patricia stepped in, giving her friend a moment to cool off. "I'm sure the major's also figured there'd be more revelations, once we got going on this translation."

"Although he hasn't seen these particular fragments," Knight continued, calmer now. "Doesn't know how the pieces fit together, or the story they tell."

"But I'm sure he's got backup copies of all the fragments, right?" Nesbitt asked.

"He provided us with photos initially, so yes, it makes sense that they've got the negatives floating around somewhere."

"If only we could make them disappear," Nesbitt wondered out loud.

Patricia gave a mirthless laugh. "Good luck getting access."

"Actually," Knight said, "this *might* just work out without resorting to cloak-and-dagger foolery."

The two women turned to the artist, who continued. "What's on this page simply expands on things Pliny had written earlier in the codex. And anyone who's read this thing—even parts of it— knows that he had a tendency to repeat himself."

"That's being kind, Charles," Patricia interjected, then turned to Nesbitt. "I often get the feeling that his critics must have originated the term 'beating a dead horse.'"

The biologist nodded. "So, he rambled a lot."

"Yes," said Knight, "but as it turns out, we may

be able to use this tendency to our advantage. The point is, that saying we *think* what we found on any given page is simply more of the same—is believable. And if anyone happens to take a close look at the photos of the codex in a year or two, then we're simply eccentrically incompetent—"

"—and not traitors," Patricia said, completing Knight's thought with a dose of skepticism.

"Right," Knight said, crossing his arms. "So what do you think?"

Patricia made an unsuccessful attempt to hide her true feelings about the suggestion. "Well, I wouldn't call it ironclad, Charles, but—"

"In the meantime, maybe we can get our hands on those negatives," Nesbitt suggested. "Destroy them for good."

"You're beginning to remind me of Pliny," Knight said, looking offended that his own potential solution had been summarily dismissed.

Nesbitt, however, ignored the dig. "Let's just hope you're right about having a year or two."

"Indeed," Knight replied, latching on to the hope that they had gotten themselves unnecessarily worked up about something whose very existence was far from a given.

Nesbitt, though, wasn't quite finished. "If what Pliny describes here *is* still active, do you suppose your friend MacCready has found it?"

Patricia Wynters and Charles Knight exchanged glances, then nodded in unison.

Nesbitt pressed on. "And if he brings it back, is there anyone we can trust with it?"

This time there were synchronized head shakes. "Not exactly," Knight replied.

"Meaning, no one?"

"Exactly."

Unlike Knight and Wynters, Nesbitt did not know Mac, Yanni, and Jerry. So, it became easier for her to wish that their disappearance simply meant they were dead. She suspected that what gave Pliny's Cerae a godlike power over life was a hot-spring microbe that could, with practice, be prodded into hijacking and editing the mysterious code of life itself—essentially instantly. If the now-hidden parts of Pliny's codex weren't just a fairy tale, then there existed a lost microbe that enabled one to direct, at will, evolutionary change.

And to whom should America entrust such power?

The military?

The legislature?

The church?

None of the above?

One fact, Nesbit did know: many microbes would not find it difficult to survive whatever environmental changes nearly two thousand years had wrought, even if the valley's hot pools were now smashed and frozen.

What . . . thing might MacCready free from the ice? Nesbitt wondered. *And what will happen to the world if he brings it back?*

Perhaps, she thought, *MacCready would understand the true nature of the discovery and would refrain from bringing it back alive. But what's the likelihood of that? The man is a zoologist and finding an organism that would allow humans to conduct the symphony of life would be the find of the century.*

And so it became possible for Dr. Nora Nesbitt to wonder if there was anyone who knew a way to make sure that Captain MacCready and his friends never came back at all.

CHAPTER 18

Nursery

*The idea that science will one day be able
to read and understand DNA the way we
can now read and even rewrite music is
moonshine.*

—LUIS ALVAREZ (1982)

*One could write a history of science in reverse
by assembling the solid pronouncements on
highest authority about what could not be
done and could never happen.*

—ROBERT A. HEINLEIN

*We have become frighteningly effective at
altering nature.*

—SYLVIA EARLE

Outside the Prison Igloo
July 18, 1946

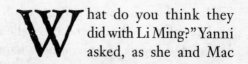

W hat do you think they
did with Li Ming?" Yanni
asked, as she and Mac

were once again marched out of their igloo prison and this time, to their relief, by Alpha and a rather unassuming duo of Morlock "dog walkers."

Mac bit down on his lower lip, then shrugged, having decided not to tell Yanni what he'd seen the day before—what he'd been forced to see.

For the moment, however, they were relieved to be out of their glorified icebox, setting off on what, except for the previous day's nightmarish detour, was now becoming more or less routine. This time, however, after trekking away from the igloo for approximately twenty minutes, they met up with a fourth creature, who seemed to have been waiting for them. There followed a brief exchange between the Morlocks, after which they moved apart, roughly delineating a small patch of ground where the humans were free to wander about.

"Is it just me, or are Alpha's friends looking even more agitated than usual?" Mac asked, wishing that his ability to decipher Morlock facial expressions were not so frustratingly small.

"You mean *nervousness?*"

"Yeah."

"Something like that," Yanni replied, squinting into the distance. Within their limited radius of view, no pallid corpse plants or plant-mimicking animals were present, and few Morlocks. "I just wish we could see more," she added, waving a hand at the ever-present mist. "I'd love to take a gander at this place without all of this."

Mac nodded, his mind shifting easily into what his late friend Bob Thorne had called "zoology mode." He began by extending a hand into the strange, snow-laden fog. Mostly, the soupy air was just a suspension of microscopic ice crystals, but like Yanni, he knew that this particular mist was home to something far more interesting than perpetually floating snow—something that was, in fact, quite unique.

As if summoned, one of the tiny snowflake mimics twirled past his face. He waited. Another appeared, then another. "Well, at least they're not avoiding me any longer," he said.

"Maybe that has something to do with not getting your face smashed down into them this time," Yanni suggested.

Even so, it was impossible to get anything like a good look at the flittering creatures. Mac gently cupped one between his hands as it flew by. He could feel a faint buzzing from within, and not wanting to injure the little whatever-it-was, he brought his hands close to his face before opening them, palms up.

There, sitting in the center of his left palm, was a new puzzle to be solved. *If only*—

He forced himself to concentrate on the creature. *The size is right*, he thought, *but it certainly isn't an insect*. Moreover, it was, to his amazement, impossible to place this particular critter into any known phylum.

Mac noted that what the ersatz snowflake *most* resembled was *a ball of dandelion fluff with something that sort of looked like a miniature bat inside*. There appeared to be jointed limbs and a distinct head region equipped with large eyes—each of which the zoologist estimated to be roughly the size of a pinhead. A magnifying glass would have answered the question of whether or not the eyes were compound—like those of an insect. Mac would have bet on the more camera-type vertebrate eye.

R. J. MacCready held his breath, not wanting to disturb the delicate enigma. After a long moment, the little animal seemed to drift off, as if being carried away by a breeze. Mac could see, though, that its departure was not wind driven at all. Instead, its flight mechanics became yet another layer of mystery involving the fauna and flora of this hidden ecosystem. As Mac watched, and all within those same few seconds, the gentle flyer darted into a Lilliputian headwind and disappeared into the snowy mist, obviously intent on rejoining its pals.

Mac turned and saw that Yanni had been watching him.

"Pretty incredible, huh?" she said, moving in to stand at his side.

"I'll say," Mac replied.

These thoughts were entirely forgotten once Alpha decided that exercise time was over, and—with the usual accompaniment of somewhat less-than-gentle prods—Mac, and to a lesser extent, Yanni, were herded back toward their prison of ice. The two prisoners gave no thought to the fact that the fourth Morlock remained behind.

Waiting until after the humans and their guards had disappeared into the mist, the lone Morlock headed off in the opposite direction, retracing his earlier steps until he came upon two figures on the ground—their outlines vague, like ancient statues smoothed by erosion.

Li Ming and his copilot had been reunited, though they were currently unaware of each other's paralyzed existence. Staked to the cold earth on their backs, their eyes stared straight ahead, at nothing.

To a friend or even a close relative, the two men might have been completely unrecognizable, covered as they were in suppurating nodules. Extremities that had been deemed unimportant by their own bodies were denied blood flow and were now blackening from oxygen starvation—the warm blood having been directed instead to the core. Had a pathologist been present, especially one with knowledge of pandemics, the doctor might have taken a special interest in the golf-ball-sized "buboes" that rose bubble-like from the necks, armpits, and groins of the staked-out men. But there were no pathologists present, at least none being of the *Homo sapiens* variety. Even so, the Morlock's eyes widened and his head tilted sideways in birdlike fascination, as a particularly large and purplish bubo continued to bud from the right side of the pilot's mouth. Straining the epidermal tissue beyond its shearing point, the balloon-like sore burst with an audible pop and a spray of red matter, laced with little white clots.

The stench of putrefaction would have been nauseating to most humans, but the Morlock expressed a typical hominid smile and reached down, projecting a finger at something emerging from the crater of flesh. Two newly born snow mimics catapulted themselves from the crater's edge and one of them came to rest briefly on a giant finger, before taking to the air. More of the tiny flyers emerged—more and more of them—rising like summoned spirits. They flitted around their giant midwife for a moment, as if celebrating their new lives. Then, in a swirl from a breeze that existed only in mechanized nonsentience, they were gone.

The caregiver took one last look down at the Chinese captives. Pale white, though still giving off faint mists of breath, these were creatures who had only recently believed themselves to be masters of the air. Now, however, they had taken on a far more important role—as the living nursery for a new arsenal of airborne weaponry.

The past seventy-two hours were a blur to Wang Tse-lin. Deprived of sleep, events tended to become mixed up in time, and only occasionally was he able to keep proper track of them.

When Captain Mung's soldiers broke camp after the first night, Wang had looked on with a combination of disgust and fascination while several men were ordered to butcher the body of the slain Yeren.

In less than an hour, two men with knives had skillfully freed large limb muscles and pectorals from their bony attachments. After some initial reluctance, Wang moved in closer and took notes, as if attending a more formal dissection of a particularly rare specimen. *Indeed I am*, he told himself, noting that "the muscles were dark red and thus obviously rich in oxygen-carrying myoglobin—a requirement for efficient movement at high altitude." Wang also observed that the lungs of the Yeren appeared to be proportionally much larger than those of a normal human and furthermore that they possessed two additional lobes ("another way to compensate for the thin air").

However, the dissection comparison broke down when a third man arrived and began salting the flesh while a fourth packed the Yeren in paper.

"The packages looked no different than what one might purchase from a local butcher," Wang eventually wrote in his field notebook.

When Captain Mung's men neared the end of their grisly tasks, the officer pointed to the considerable carnage that had accumulated. "I want no trace of this creature left on the surface. Clean your tools well and bury everything—bury it deep."

"Yes, sir," his men replied in unison.

"No blood and not a strand of hair can be left showing," he said. "Do you understand?"

The four men nodded as one.

Wang had warned his captain that burying what they left behind could not remove all of the Yeren scent from the campsite, or from anyone who had butchered or even touched the beast. It was plain to him that Captain Mung appreciated this fact. Any fool could cross points of no return without foreseeing them, and most did. The scientist understood that only one objective mattered to his captain, the same one with which he had begun—saving his family. Only an hour after leaving the camp, the captain had mapped out a new pass leading to higher ground. What seemed a very long time after that, the expedition was making progress again, and Mung moved backward along his line of men until he found Wang. Without anyone else noticing, the officer passed him one of the small, tightly wrapped packages.

"Take it," he said, "and do so without making a fuss."

Wang tucked the item into his coat.

"Though I did not think so at first," Mung said, "you appear to be a survivor type."

Before Wang could answer, the captain raised his hand in a gesture that meant a response would be neither necessary nor tolerated.

"If I am killed, I am asking you to take this package to my family. They will know what to do with it."

"Should I tell them anything else, sir?"

Captain Mung pondered the question for a moment before speaking quietly. "You're a scientist. Tell them everything—everything you have seen here."

Then, without another word, the officer turned and headed toward the front of the line. Watching Captain Mung, Wang Tse-lin wondered if it was only his imagination that the small package suddenly seemed to weigh considerably more than it had only seconds earlier. Now, beyond the prospect of having to carry dried flesh from the beings inhabiting this region, Wang had been appointed as the family historian of Captain Mung's mission. Few men besides the officer could have anticipated what had already happened—but fewer would have guessed that, while exceptional intuition defined Captain Mung, a failure of imagination could doom them all.

CHAPTER 19

Captain America

*There was a man who was interested in
the color of music—the connection between
light and music—and that was Einstein.*
—LEON THEREMIN

*The sciences throw an inexpressible grace
over our compositions, even where they are
not immediately concerned; as their effects
are discernible where we least expect to
find them.*
—PLINY THE ELDER

Metropolitan Museum of Natural History
Fifth Floor
July 18, 1946

D r. Nesbitt, the pleasure is all
mine," the smiling naval officer said, holding on to her

right hand for what she considered a beat too long. Nesbitt noted that the accent was unmistakably Bostonian, while the attitude that accompanied it spoke of something else—money.

Of course, Nora Nesbitt had recognized the famous last name. She also had to admit that "Just Call Me Jack" was as handsome as advertised. *Although on the seriously scrawny side*. But this too was to be expected. Nesbitt knew as well as anyone that when the curtain finally dropped on the Pacific Theater, thousands of Allied servicemen returned home with an array of unwelcome souvenirs that spanned many of the invertebrate groups she had come to love.

Nesbitt flashed a warm smile of her own and nodded. *Intestinal parasites*, she thought, before recalling the slight tremor in the man's hand. *Maybe even scrub typhus*.

"All right, break it up, you two," Major Patrick Hendry said, initiating a pair of scowls for completely different reasons.

The major seemed to savor the moment, before continuing. "I presume you both know why I've called this little meeting."

It was clear that they did but it was Nesbitt who responded. "Can I assume that there's nothing new on the status of Captain MacCready, Lieutenant Delarosa, and Yanni Thorne?"

"That would be a correct assumption, Dr. Nesbitt."

"But Mac being Mac, that's no real surprise, is it, sir?"

"No, it's not, Lieutenant," Hendry continued.

"You of all people should know that Mac has weathered some serious shit storms in the past."

It had quickly become clear to the invertebrate zoologist that neither the man with the Boston twang nor the redheaded major was at all convinced about MacCready's demise.

"Sir," the young officer said, "I am wondering why Dr. Nesbitt is here?"

Nesbitt decided to respond herself. "Well, Lieutenant, because of the scientific nature of this mission, it's been decided that I'm going with you to Tibet."

The young officer shot Major Hendry a piercing look, as if to see if this was all some sort of joke. But the major's expression told him it wasn't.

The lieutenant instantly changed gears, flashing another thousand-dollar smile. "Dr. Nesbitt, have you ever jumped out of a plane before?"

"No, I haven't," she replied. "Have you ever jumped out of a plane more than twenty-five thousand feet above sea level?"

"No, ma'am, can't say I have."

"Well then, I imagine it'll be a new experience for both of us," Nesbitt said, confidently. "And *please*, Lieutenant, just call me Nora."

Major Hendry cleared his throat. "I'm sorry to interrupt the fascinating banter you two are shoveling but I need you to look at these." He broke the wax seal on a large envelope and removed a pair of photographs. "A recon plane took these at thirty-six thousand feet over an especially mountainous section of southern Tibet. We think this is where Mac went in."

"What are those pairs of spokes?" Nesbitt asked.

"Helicopters," Jack replied. "Two of them, right, Major?"

"That's right. Sitting on a shelf of rock."

Jack squinted at his photo. "But those choppers don't look like ours."

Hendry smiled. "That's two for two, lieutenant. They're Russian. Although it's a safe bet they were flown in there by the Chinese army."

Nesbitt handed the photo back to the major. "So what's this mean?"

"It means that Mac and the others definitely have some company up there."

Now it was Jack who handed his photo back. "You mean in addition to the myths and old wives tales, sir?"

Nesbitt broke in. "Lieutenant, we think these creatures are *real*. And the quicker you start thinking that way, the better."

The naval officer gave a nod that was either respectful or condescending. He also apparently decided not to pursue the issue further. "But there's still no sign of Mac, Jerry, or—" He paused.

"Yanni," Hendry reminded him. "Yanni Thorne. And you're correct, there's no sign of them. No signal patterns in the snow, no broadcast attempts—just a blurry mark near these spokes that might or might not be part of *their* chopper. So this is as good a place as any to start looking."

"How many of us are you sending in?" Jack asked.

"Including you and Dr. Nesbitt, eight. Five

specialists in high-altitude combat—mostly skiers and mountain corps types."

"Who else?" Jack asked.

"Another old friend of Mac's," Hendry replied. "Seems as if you weren't the only person who got some strings pulled to get on this mission. Guy's name is Juliano—Sergeant Frank Juliano, weapons and munitions expert."

"This Captain MacCready sounds like a *very* popular fellow," Nesbitt said.

"He is!" the two officers replied simultaneously.

She offered a tight smile, hoping that she'd feel the same way when and if they finally met.

Fort Ethan Allen, Vermont
July 19, 1946

TWENTY HOURS LATER

A HALO insertion, huh? That sounds painful, sir." The comment came from a short man with a hangdog expression.

The five members of the First Special Service Force who were sitting apart from the others in the briefing room exchanged exasperated looks—several of them doing a rather poor job of stifling chuckles. To Major Patrick Hendry and a trio that included Dr. Nesbitt and the Navy officer Mac had once jokingly referred to as Lieutenant Moneybanks, these guys were an odd assemblage, looking more like north woodsmen, hunters, and lumberjacks than soldiers. The major also knew that this was primarily because that's *exactly* what they'd been before the war.

Hendry shot the members of the "Devil's Brigade" a look that immediately put an end to the little joke they were having at the expense of Mac's pal, Sergeant Juliano. The major knew the members of the elite American-Canadian commando unit had gotten their name from the German soldiers they'd terrorized, leaving behind calling cards on their bodies that read *Das dicke Ende kommt noch!* ("The worst is yet to come!").

Hendry turned toward a short, heavyset man who had an uncanny resemblance to the comedian Lou Costello. "HALO, Sergeant Juliano, that's High Altitude Low Opening."

"Gotcha sir, thanks," Juliano said, looking somewhat relieved.

Now Hendry could see it was Dr. Nesbitt and the Navy lieutenant who were exchanging bemused looks. He cleared his throat before continuing with the briefing.

"We're going with a HALO insertion because it'll give you the best chance of getting in there undetected. The problem of course is that you'll be free-falling for approximately ninety seconds and aiming for a narrow mountain pass we've identified as a safe DZ—that's the drop zone, Dr. Nesbitt."

The biologist responded with a self-conscious nod.

One of the Special Forces members raised a hand. "How are we getting in there, sir?"

Major Hendry went on. "You'll be leaving for Ireland within a week, then on to Turkey—which is where you'll board a C-47 specially equipped for the drop—respirators, special protective clothing, and the like. From Ankara you'll be heading straight to the mountains."

Hendry then turned his attention to Juliano, Nesbitt, and the lieutenant. "You three will be training with these fine men for the next few days. Eventually, you'll be jumping in tandem with a trio of them. Before that, though, you'll take a cram course to get you ready for the conditions you'll be facing *and* the jump itself. The last thing you or this mission needs is a broken leg or a snapped back."

Sergeant Juliano raised a hand, and the major nodded in his direction. Somewhat surprisingly, he stood and turned toward the surly-looking Devil's Brigaders. "Hey, you guys carry the Johnson LMG, don't you?"

Five heads rotated toward the man who appeared to stand roughly a foot shorter than any of them. "Indeed we do, Sergeant," said a thickly muscled, blond-haired man with a heavy French Canadian accent. "Are you familiar with it?"

"Familiar with it?" Juliano replied. "I'll say!" Then he gestured to the naval officer sitting next to Dr. Nesbitt. "Lieutenant, did you know the M-1941 was designed by a Boston lawyer?"

"Can't say I did, Sergeant," Jack replied. He glanced over at the Special Forces guys, a bit put out that their attention was inexplicably focused on Lou Costello's twin.

"Well, it's a beaut, Jack . . . I mean sir. Short recoil, rotating bolt, and up to nine hundred rounds per minute! It's a *real* beaut!"

"I guess we're done here," Major Hendry announced, and almost instantaneously, several of the commandos approached Sergeant Juliano, who immediately became the recipient of some serious glad-handing and backslapping.

"So, is it as awkward to carry a loaded Johnny gun as they say it is?" Juliano asked, eagerly.

One of the men pointed to a friend. "As awkward as my last date with his mom."

Major Hendry ambled over to where Nesbitt and Jack sat silently, watching the proceedings.

"It's nice to see that *someone* is fitting right in, isn't it?" Hendry said, making an effort not to smile until he had turned and walked toward the sound of raucous laughter.

AUGUST, A.D. 67

Now that the initial shock had worn off, Pliny and Proculus could fully appreciate the military significance of the very special hell they had somehow survived in the death pits.

More than three hours after the ordeal, as shadows lengthened across the gardens of the Cerae, the two Romans stood on the balcony of their prison cell. The historian was still rubbing uncomfortably at his arms. *There are no ticks*, he told himself—yet again.

"How are you holding up?" Proculus said softly.

"A little shaken."

A sudden movement drew their attention to

the adjoining balcony. Severus was pacing back and forth, and though anger and distress were clearly evident, neither man acknowledged his occasional glances in their direction.

"What do you think is bothering the traitor?" Proculus asked.

"Perhaps he hasn't forgiven his so-called Teacher for the treatment he received at the pits."

"Personally I thought he looked quite natural covered in worms," the cavalryman said, grimacing as the female Ceran made her appearance beside the centurion. Severus, though, stalked off, quickly putting as much distance between them as was possible.

"This is getting interesting," Proculus said, watching Severus begin to cross a dangerously narrow ledge that led to yet another section of the balcony.

The Ceran responded by emitting a sound Pliny never expected to hear from her kind—a strangled grunt, reminiscent of a sob. Then, with the speed of a leopard, she was behind Severus on the precarious ledge—gripping his body and contorting herself against him. There was no consideration given by either figure to the great height at which this drama was playing out. Even at a distance, the air was suddenly filled with her stink.

"Disgusting," Proculus said, turning away, though Pliny found himself unable to do so.

He gestured toward the strange pair. "You do your commander a disservice."

"How so?"

"I believe she is simply marking her possession," Pliny said sharply, watching as Severus's initial struggles quickly abated. "I have been observing him more closely since the pits. It is far more of an addiction than a romance."

"Does it matter?"

"It matters to her—which is quite certainly the only reason we are still alive."

The cavalryman shook his head in disbelief. "And all of this is somehow related to the Cerae training an army of ticks and worms *not* to attack us?"

Pliny nodded, watching as the Ceran moved into the chamber, disappearing from their view. Severus began to follow and then hesitated. He turned stiffly toward his friends, attempting, it seemed, to lock eyes with them. His face was void of all emotion but then, for an instant, there was an undeniable spark of recognition.

"Maybe not *fully* addicted," Proculus said, hopefully, raising his hand.

The moment passed.

The cavalryman's hand dropped to his side.

Pliny continued to watch as the end of this particular scene played out—feeling both fascinated and repelled by what he had seen and what he was still seeing. *Has any relationship during the entire history of the world ever begun and turned so complicated in so strange a place?*

Most frustrating for the historian was that he did not possess the proper words to describe it—

little beyond the realization that Severus was in-explicably bound to his Teacher. *To her scent*, he thought. *To something he cannot control.*

As if to prove that very point, the centurion turned from his fellow Romans and entered the chamber.

"Do not fight it, my old friend," Pliny said to himself. "To save us all, you must go back to her."

CHAPTER 20

What We Do in the Shadows

*Three things cannot be long hidden: the
sun, the moon, and the truth.*
—BUDDHA

The Prison Igloo
Seven days after the Fort Ethan Allen briefing
Two hours after the rescue team departed Ireland
July 27, 1946

M ac drummed his fingers
impatiently on the ice wall.
"Well, I guess those little
exercise runs are a thing of the past now, huh?"

"If they *were* exercise runs," Yanni replied. She
gestured to a pair of Morlocks who were headed
away from their igloo. As with similar visits over
the past few days, they had dropped off a supply
of food and water inside the doorway, without ac-

tually entering. "Something's *definitely* got them riled up."

"And no more visits to the elephant house, either."

"It's a corral," Yanni said, correcting him. "But do you see the connection?"

Mac shrugged. "Not much beyond the fact that they've got us locked down."

"We're not gettin' 'musked' anymore."

"You're right," Mac said, with a nod.

Yanni threw a thumb over her shoulder and in the direction of the grass mimics. "We're startin' to smell like humans again. And that ain't good."

"I *thought* those biters were creepin' in a bit closer."

"Yeah," Yanni followed, "too close if you ask me."

That night, Alpha arrived, but like the other recent visitors, he refrained from entering the igloo. Instead he slid open the ice door and gestured for Yanni to step outside. There were no elephants with him and although Mac attempted to follow her out, the Morlock's impossible-to-misinterpret body language quickly put an end to that venture.

Only a few steps from their prison, Alpha knelt down at a spot that had been covered by grass mimics only minutes before. As Yanni struggled to see in the difficult light, Alpha used an index finger to draw a shape in the dirt, then stepped away from her. She followed up by smoothing over his work and scratching in her own set of figures. Looking even more grim than usual, he motioned for Yanni to step away from the drawing.

"Yeah, I get it," she told him.

Alpha reciprocated by adding more figures, then erased their work. Standing, he glanced at the igloo and made something akin to a pointing gesture. Yanni took the hint.

After sealing the door behind Yanni, Alpha gave a few furtive glances before quickly receding again into the shadows.

"What was that all about?" Mac asked, noting that she appeared unusually shaken by what had just transpired.

Yanni flashed a funeral smile. "Well, the bad news is that the Morlocks seem to think we're part of a full-scale invasion."

"Kinda tough to do much invadin' when you're locked in a fucking icebox," Mac said.

Yanni held up her hand, effectively preventing Mac from entering rant mode. "Yeah, well, first, we showed up in a helicopter. Then Li-Ming. Now it appears as if there are more helicopters out there—maybe on the shelf."

"*What?*" Mac exclaimed. "Lemme guess—they're not ours."

"Nope," Yanni replied. "Evidently they belong to the Chinese."

"So we've opened up Pandora's box," Mac said, as much to himself as to Yanni.

She was unfamiliar with the term but definitely caught the drift. "If that's really bad, then yeah—I'd say our long-term prospects for survival just went from 'unknown' to 'completely down the shitter.'"

"So what's the good news?" Mac asked, hopefully.

Yanni shook her head. "You're kiddin', right?"

JULY 30, 1946

A fter they had passed three days huddling in tents and simply trying not to get blown off the side of a mountain, the weather finally cleared. Captain Mung continued to lead his men on a meandering, apparently random trek. As often as not, promising mountain passes led up to impossible, suffocating heights—essentially dead-ending and forcing them to turn back. There were no further signs of the Yeren—or of any life for that matter.

On a morning that broke clear and cloudless, Mung's party navigated around the base of another stone and ice wall—this one shaped like the prow of a mighty ship. Rounding the point, they came to a sudden halt, now able to carefully study, for the first time, what appeared to be a misty sea set against white snow. Using a pair of binoculars, Mung searched for a path ahead, finding a labyrinthine series of switchbacks that eventually disappeared into the basin of icy mist.

How much farther to the valley floor? Mung wondered as he felt someone move in beside him. It was Wang.

"The valley described by the helicopter pilot?" the zoologist asked.

"I wouldn't call what we heard a description," the officer responded. "But I believe it is where they went down."

Wang gestured toward the mist. "And you intend to lead us into that?"

"Where else would we go?"

"You gamble with our lives."

"Being born is a gamble," Mung said, turning away to address the line of men.

M ac squinted at the undulating carpet of mini-predators, now massing around the perimeter of the igloo walls. He gave a half-hearted try at some misplaced optimism. "I guess as long as we keep the door closed, we'll be okay."

"Come on, Mac," Yanni responded, with disappointment, before glancing up at the circular opening in the center of the roof. "These things *can* climb."

MacCready abandoned the ruse. "Yeah, they're startin' to already."

Yanni squatted down at the base of the ice wall. "They kinda remind me of army ants."

Mac's back stiffened at the image. Ants. Hive minds and superorganisms. *Tamara.*

Yanni continued, unaware of the memory she had evoked. "You've seen 'em, right? If they run into a chasm of some kind, or an impassable obstacle—"

"—then the action of each ant coalesces into a group unit," Mac recited, in monotone. "The group unit adapts to changes in the environment."

"Yeah, sure," Yanni said, realizing that she had struck some sort of raw nerve. "So they use their bodies to build a bridge."

Mac glanced up at the ceiling opening again. "Or in this case, a ladder straight into our execution chamber."

"Something like that," Yanni said quietly.

Captain Mung Chen and his men had followed the downward-leading switchback for several hours, invigorated that the drop in elevation had made breathing easier but growing ever more cautious as they drew nearer to the surface of the snow-laden mist. The path down presented sheer drops at regular intervals; but it ended at what looked deceptively like the gentle shore of a pearl-white sea.

The temperature has dropped, Wang thought as he donned his heavy gloves again. Glancing upward, he saw that the sky, thankfully still clear, was now bracketed on all sides by sheer walls of stone and ice. A pair of soldiers, sent to scout the trail ahead, was back. Their animated behavior, as they spoke to Captain Mung, left little doubt that they had encountered something worthy of considerable arm waving. A minute later, they saluted and returned to their fellows while Mung headed straight for Wang.

"They say there's flat ground some fifty or sixty meters below the cloud tops—a lot of it."

"The valley floor?"

"Perhaps an hour's march at best," the officer

said. "They also reported that they could make out foliage through the mist—*white* foliage."

"Interesting," Wang responded. "Any sign of the helicopter? Or the missing men?"

The officer shook his head. "No, apparently visibility is quite limited."

"So, Captain, what do you intend to do?"

Mung paused, his gaze falling on a cluster of soldiers, buzzing now (albeit quietly) at the news they'd just heard from their comrades. "Well, what I *don't* intend to do is march my men out there and run headlong into whatever attacked Po Han's crew."

"A fine idea, sir," Wang responded quickly. "And we'll be losing the sunlight in another hour anyway."

Mung pointed to a spot back up the trail. "There is a defensible piece of ground several hundred meters back. We'll camp there tonight. I'll go in with a small recon group in the morning. You will accompany us, of course."

"Of course," Wang said.

They turned whence they had come and began backtracking with slow, labored strides toward the proposed campsite. Wang Tse-lin and Captain Mung took a position at the front of the column. The scientist looked back often, drawn by the multiple enigmas of a frost-laden fog bank so flat that it gave the stubborn illusion of being a sea, and by descriptions of ghostly white plants beneath the surface. And somewhere in that white forest, he knew, angry Yeren stirred.

More than once, Wang thought he saw snowy

waves lapping against the shore and washing briefly uphill, but they were wispy and seemed to withdraw and settle quickly.

Too many worries, the scientist told himself. *Just a little snow blindness combined with a trick of the late afternoon light.* Wang was therefore able to forget about the waves until he and Captain Mung were alerted to a commotion down along the trail.

Moments later, an anxious-looking soldier arrived and gave an uneasy salute. "Sir, the back of the line seems to have run into a snow squall," he said breathlessly.

Captain Mung nodded. "I see, Corporal. And is there anything further?"

"It's . . . it's the snow, sir," the man stammered. "It doesn't really—"

Someone screamed. Almost immediately there came another cry and another—until the sounds merged into a nightmare chorus.

Captain Mung scrambled past the corporal and a pair of frightened soldiers, followed closely by Wang. Stopping for a moment, they shielded their eyes against the setting sun and were able to discern details within the commotion—just in time to witness a body falling off the side of the trail into open air. Then another, limbs flailing wildly as it bounced off a rock wall.

Wang recognized the man as one of the snipers who had brought down the Yeren. But even worse than the unreality of what he was witnessing was another thought—*These men haven't fallen and they're not being thrown. They're killing themselves.*

"What's happening?" Wang asked, but Captain

Mung could not answer. They both stood mesmerized, eyes widening at the sight of a third man tumbling off the side of the trail—a man who appeared to be tearing at his own face.

What brought Wang back to reality and the need to respond quickly was his own sympathetic nervous system. The swirling cloud of white was now moving with seemingly methodical intent. Following the rough-hewn path, the cloud advanced up the side of the overlook, engulfing more and more of Mung's increasingly frantic expeditionary force as it approached.

But now there would be no explanations, no orders given and none followed. As the officer and the scientist turned away from the madness unfolding below, there existed, for each of them, only a shared biological imperative—one that had originated and evolved over a half billion years. And so Captain Mung and Wang Tse-lin did the only thing that they *could* do—they ran for their lives.

JULY 31, 1946

Four days after Yanni informed Mac that they were being blamed for the arrival of more unwelcome visitors, the wall of grass mimics outside the igloo had risen to the level of Mac's shoulders.

The Morlocks occasionally gathered outside, seeming to watch the rising tide as humans might watch an animal in a zoo. Their captors continued to refrain from entering the prison. And yet they came and went by the dozens, in a fairly steady stream. It appeared to Yanni that they were more interested in the progress of the bladelike predators mounting the igloo walls than in the humans imprisoned within. A particularly large group of Morlocks arrived just in time to see the highest section of the living wall collapse and slide back to the ground. One of them directed a menacing grimace at the pair of humans, who were now more clearly visible through the ice. The grimace was accompanied by the surprisingly human pointing of a long index finger.

"Well, they've got gawking down cold," Yanni said.

"I feel like we're sittin' in a window at Macy's," Mac said, flashing the finger pointer one of his own digits. Then he finished dividing up what was left of their last food ration, now nearly three days old.

"Everybody loves a public execution," Yanni said, giving a brief nod to an audience that was presently departing—and looking rather disappointed. She took a water-filled earthen jug from Mac. "I wonder if this is how your Christians in the Colosseum felt, waiting for the arrival of the lions?"

"That story is bullshit," Mac replied quickly. "There's no evidence that any of the so-called *damnati* were killed that way."

Yanni threw him a skeptical look. "But people *were* torn up by wild animals—bears and tigers and shit, right?"

Mac shrugged his shoulders. "Yeah, well, that part is true."

"Just not shredded by a psychotic lawn?"

"No, I think they missed out on that one."

"Well, thanks, Mac," Yanni said, turning away from the scrabbling wall of the carnivorous grass and a new group of Morlocks who had come to watch the humans die. "I feel a lot better now."

The snow mimics on the highland trail were not cognizant of success or failure. They worried nothing about life or death or time. They were, in fact, quite incapable of worry at all. Creatures of mechanized instinct, they swarmed and subdued their prey. Hundreds of the tiny flyers had been killed—swatted and crushed by towering mountains of flesh that lumbered and bellowed and fell. Only when the prey had been immobilized—paralyzed now, and so no longer presenting any danger—did the females approach. The males, who were larger in body size and far more aggressive in their nature, were waiting for them. Equipped with a set of mantis-like raptorial legs, they had already pried open eyelids and lips, inviting the females to enter, and to feed, and to lay their eggs.

By the time the sun dipped behind mountain peaks and gales of snow mimics had retreated like a tide into the mist-shrouded valley, there were only the captain, the scientist, and a bewildered private still alive on the trail.

Far uphill of his preyed-upon crew, Captain Mung was moving forward, but he did so in silence and with a strange gait that seemed more mechanical than human. Wang feared that the officer was in deep shock. *And why not*, the scientist thought, *watching his entire force die—many seemingly driven to suicide by a living storm.*

A sudden gust gave him an involuntary start, and reflexively his head snapped back toward the sound. But the rocky trail behind them was empty now—the snow guided now by only gravity and wind. *Mindless.*

Three hours later, navigating under a faint crescent of moonlight, Wang knew that his questions about what had happened—questions that would have held at least a degree of morbid curiosity for him at any other time—currently mattered for nothing. The *real* question, the only question had become, *How can we escape this?*

"We must get back to the helicopters," Wang had informed the blank-faced Captain Mung earlier. But the officer said nothing, pausing for a moment as if deep in thought, before trudging ahead silently.

The third survivor, a thoroughly and perhaps permanently rattled private who had been listening to the one-way conversation, seemed at first only too happy to support Wang's plan. "We *must* get back to the helicopters," he repeated. But instead of offering reassurance, the phrase morphed into a mantra that the younger man mumbled incessantly under his breath.

At some point Wang took the lead, trekking even farther uphill and toward the imagined safety beyond those self-propelled swirls of white death.

As the moon passed behind a cliff and darkness overtook them, he led the others into what he hoped was a suitably deep and protective depression in among the rocks. Wang could not shake the suspicion that danger was tracking after them, so he resolved to remain alert through sunrise. By 2 A.M., exertion and thin air had done their work. His head began to slip downward and for a moment, just for a moment, he closed his eyes.

A sound jolted Wang awake. Morning twilight was strengthening toward daybreak and he immediately felt a rush of shame at his weakness. Stepping out of the crevice, the scientist began flexing his limbs, each joint resisting painfully. Captain Mung had evidently arisen earlier. Still silent, he was carefully surveying the lower section of the rugged trail they'd ascended. Wang glanced back into the crevice, then quickly up and down the trail, unable to see the private. Wang and the captain were alone.

"Where is—?" the scientist said, then hesitated, realizing that he did not know the private's name.

"He was over there," Captain Mung said, motioning toward the crevice. "He's gone now." The officer's voice was flat, and lacking emotion.

"Gone?"

"Just as I said."

Wang paused, briefly wondering why he felt no relief that the captain was speaking again.

"Do you think they . . . the Yeren . . . took him?"

The officer, whose stare remained fixed, shook his head. "If so, then why didn't they take us, too?"

"But . . . his pack is still there," Wang said, allowing his voice to trail off as alternative scenarios crept to the surface of his thoughts like dark spirits.

The captain stepped down from his rocky perch, passed Wang, and snatched up his own backpack. "We need to keep moving," Mung said, his face blank. Then, without another word, he headed off in the presumed direction of the helicopters.

Wang scrambled into the crevice, grabbed the remaining packs, and followed.

In the Igloo Prison
AUGUST 1, 1946

By nightfall, the grass mimics had climbed to within a few feet of being able to merely inchworm across the dome top, thus allowing them to drop through the circular opening in the ceiling.

Mac and Yanni had spent much of the past hour folding their coats into a makeshift manhole cover they hoped would block the entrance of grass mimics through the hole in the roof. Mac hoisted Yanni up to make the final fitting, bracing, and plugging as best she could.

"You all right up there?" Mac asked her.

"Swell," came the reply. "You know, I never noticed it before, but these things make a lot of noise."

"What kind of noise?" Mac asked, trying to hold Yanni's legs steady as she struggled to completely fill the opening.

"Kind of 'clicky,' you know, like *click click click*."

"They sound kind of crunchy from down here," Mac added.

Yanni was about to say something else when she saw, through spaces in the grass, movement outside the igloo. Someone or something was approaching the jail door.

"Get me down," she whispered.

Mac all but dropped her to the floor, then the pair made a somewhat less than effortless transition into *we-were-just-sitting-around-when-the-hole-in-the-ceiling-plugged-itself* mode.

The igloo door, which had been thoroughly coated in grass mimics a moment before, received a blast of something wet. Immediately the view through the portal of ice resolved itself. The tiny predators had been washed away and were making no effort to climb back. The source of the stream was a matching set of hoselike appendages, which were themselves attached to the stubby-tusked mammoth that Yanni had met in the corral. Accompanying the creature was Alpha, who slid the door open and ducked inside.

Without hesitating, Yanni stood and ran past her stunned friend, apparently intending to throw her arms around the giant. Alpha reacted by stepping back quickly and spreading his arms in an unmistakable threat display. His canines—bared directly at Yanni—were even more of a shock.

"Okay," she said. "I get it."

As Mac watched the strange reunion unfold, he never noticed that a double trunk had snaked in through the open door—at least, not until it sprayed the two humans with an elephant-scented shower of mucus and anyone's-guess-what-else.

MacCready shook himself off like a wet dog.

A moment later, something dropped on him from the ceiling, glancing off Mac's shoulder. He was relieved to see that it was only their coats—the desperately rigged ceiling plug had failed.

If not for that shower, we'd be dead, Mac realized. The little mammoth was suddenly at his side, using the tips of both trunks to simultaneously unfold and give their parkas a protective smearing.

Mac shook his head and turned toward Yanni, who, though apparently still perplexed at Alpha's *don't-touch-me* response, was finishing up a brief figure-drawing session with the big guy.

"Pull up your socks, Mac," Yanni announced. "Alpha says we're leaving."

As Wang Tse-lin and Captain Mung continued their trek toward the imagined safety of the helicopters, the scientist's unease about the other man soon gave way to something far more disturbing.

"Can you feel them?" the officer asked.

"Feel who, Captain?" Wang said.

"Can you feel the presence of the Yeren?"

"No," the scientist replied, trying to discern shadows in the faint glare of moonlight against fresh-fallen snow—trying to dredge up everything he knew about the symptoms of shell shock. It wasn't much. "I haven't felt any presence, sir. But I do know we're close now. Close to the helicopters. Close to leaving this place."

"The Yeren can smell us," Mung said, his voice haunted. Then he pointed to the backpack Wang was carrying. "They can smell that, too."

"I haven't seen or heard a thing, sir," Wang said, holding down his fear as a crescent moon sank behind a cliff, leaving little for him to see *except* shadows. He tried to be as quietly reassuring as possible. "Tell me about your family again. I wonder if I might meet them when we get home."

The captain shook his head. "Give me that bag," he said, quietly but firmly.

"That's all right sir, I'll carry—"

"*Give it to me now!*" Mung shouted, wide-eyed.

Wang did as he was told.

"The Yeren have been tracking this," the officer said, exchanging his own backpack for the one Wang had been carrying. "They *know* what I have done."

"Captain, if you like, we could just throw it over the side," Wang said quietly. "Then we can both go home."

"*No!*" the officer replied, clutching the backpack. "This was for my children! To cure them."

"But—"

Mung drew his sidearm, aimed it at the scientist's face, and took several steps backward. "If you try to follow, if you disobey me, you *will* die."

Wang Tse-lin stood silently and then likewise took several steps backward. Mung turned away from him and began walking downhill. "Can you feel them?" he asked again. "They can smell me."

Then, turning a corner, Captain Mung was gone.

After that, Wang lost track of the hours. Emerging onto the stony shelf on which the helicopters stood waiting, he squinted against the sunrise.

The wind was stronger here and it whipped between the two aircraft, scouring the ground and spinning up mini-tornados of snow. For a moment, Wang's mind flashed back to the swirling clouds that had engulfed the men on the lower portion of the trail. These swirls, however, did not chase him down or drive him to madness. They simply pulled apart and disappeared.

Where are the pilots? he thought.

Wang almost called out, but something stopped him. Instead he trudged a path through fresh snow directly toward the nearer of the two Russian helicopters, noting with unease that one of the engine cowlings had been removed.

Maybe the others are inside, he thought.

As the scientist approached the cargo door, he was startled at the sound of a voice. Wang felt a sudden surge of relief that the voice belonged to a human. There was no relief, however, at the realization that the human was speaking English.

"That's far enough, buddy," said the voice. But before Wang could respond, eight figures seemed to materialize before his eyes—some from behind the helicopters, others rising up from behind a low wall. All of them were wearing white camouflage uniforms and all of them were armed.

Americans, Wang thought.

One of the men approached, the revolver he carried pointing at Wang's midsection. The scientist slowly raised both of his hands, then screwed on a smile. "Chicago Cubs!" he said. "I was student at Northwestern."

"Well, that's your cross to bear," the man replied, nasally. "I'm a Haa-vid man, myself. So what team would I be rooting for?"

"Boston Red Sock!" Wang blurted out, breaking into a real smile.

Now the thin man with the pistol began to smile, too. "Well, he's okay," he announced, looking quite satisfied with himself.

The others moved in closer now, encircling Wang. He noticed that one of them was a woman, and gave them all a respectful nod. "Boston Red Sock," he continued for his captors. "They trade Babe Ruth to Yankees!"

There was a momentary pause and Wang watched with dismay as the first man's smile vanished. His colleagues, though, appeared to think it was all quite funny.

"That's right, Chicago," one of them said, patting Wang on the back. "You tell 'em."

CHAPTER 21

Night Zero

You can't say civilization [does not] advance. In every war they kill you in a new way.
—WILL ROGERS

In the Valley of the Cerae
August, A.D. 67

When Julius Caesar crossed the Rubicon, there was much about which he should have worried. He could easily have paralyzed himself with any one of those concerns, but he prevailed over them, as if they did not exist.

That was more than a hundred and fifteen years earlier, and half a world away from the realm of the Cerae. At times such as this, Pliny reminded himself how easily the temptation to obsess on any single, deadly obstacle could prevent him from doing what was necessary to survive, and succeed. Caesar's ability to cast his own psychological traps aside and to focus all of his genius on *solving* the challenges ahead, one by one, had always led him to the right decisions—until, that is, a particularly cold day in mid-March.

Pliny and Proculus stared silently across the Ceran gardens. Tonight, darkness was no longer being pushed back by phosphorescence—by living lamps that the Cerae had somehow managed to control. All the bioluminescence of the gardens, the terraces, and the pillars had been steadily dimming. The city and the entire valley, it seemed, were going black.

"They're going to war," Proculus said, looking out across the darkening terrain. "And we're about to be caught in the middle of it."

Pliny did not wish to dwell on the thought, but he knew the man was right and that any escape now (even if it was successful) would likely mean running into an invading force traveling in the opposite direction. But there was a far greater picture to be painted here and it had little to do with their escape.

"I know what you're thinking," Pliny said at last.

"Yes. But—"

"Proculus, you must abandon any thoughts of escape. To even attempt it would be to neglect a far greater duty."

"I don't understand," the cavalryman said.

"We *must* not leave Severus behind."

"And why is that, sir?"

"The Cerae cannot be given a reason *and* a means, Proculus, for aiming that weapon against

Roman blood. All other considerations are secondary. Do you understand me?"

"Yes," said Proculus quietly.

Pliny could see that, like him, the man had no difficulty picturing the Cerae killing them both long before they could ever flee the valley.

"They'll use Severus or perhaps even our own bodies to train their living weapons," Pliny said. "Then imagine this nightmare spreading along Roman roads, westward and into the heart of the empire."

The cavalryman gave a visible shudder, and after a pause, it was he who continued. "If you're right, then there is one more consideration—far greater than the rest."

"Go on."

"Not even knowledge about that kind of power can escape this valley. I mean no impertinence, but do *you* understand *me*?"

"I do," Pliny replied. "Quite clearly."

The historian waited for a response but there was only silence. "I wonder," he whispered against the night, "what this impossible valley will produce tomorrow."

The Scythian forces had spread across the mountains like a diffuse infection—their widely separated positions making a full assault by the Cerans impossible.

At one encampment, workers were slicing and packaging meat from a bull elephant and two horses—victims of the thin, cold air. The most skilled of the butchers were carefully cutting the flesh of two Ceran scouts into long strips.

Five riders soon departed on horseback to distribute the elephant and horsemeat to other encampments—but the flesh of the enemy was not part of the distribution. The power of Ceran muscle and marrow, having for generations been the substance of local mythology, was now, perhaps, proving to be more than mere myth. Whether the effects were real or imagined, the blood-bright meat of the creatures quickly restored strength and rendered the people of this individual brigade more resilient against heat-sapping winds and snow. Under such cover, the second enemy scout had crept in among them during the previous night's march. Unseen until it struck, the intruder took five arrows before it fell, and the fresh supply of meat and pelts came at the cost of six men.

Here, and at other outposts, the flesh of Ceran scouts was being secretly hoarded and consumed. Not only did it provide the Easterners with restored strength, it invigorated those who believed the stories told by elderly plains people—stories about a race of monsters whose flesh was not simply a curative but whose lair held the secrets of everlasting life.

Captive monks had confessed the existence of a lost city in which towers built from "crystalline gold" blazed under the sun—a promise whose value had become secondary, the Scythian chieftains agreed, should the magical elixirs turn out to be real.

The commander of this particular encampment could not sleep, noticing as well that the rest of the group also remained too energetic for their daytime rest period. She flexed her fingers, admiring the craftsmanship of her new gauntlet glove. Fashioned from a Ceran's forearm and hand, the fingers were still slightly too tight but she knew the leather would soften and stretch before the upcoming fight. The commander acknowledged a pair of armorers, who were even now putting the finishing touches on her new battle gear. They were stretching a Ceran pelt over the frame of a shield she herself had fashioned from its owner's rib cage.

The handiwork of the Scythians was not yet completed.

CHAPTER 22

Breaking Away

I have seen the science I worshiped and the aircraft I loved, destroying the civilization I expected them to serve.
—CHARLES LINDBERGH

The end of civilization will be that it will eventually die of civilization.
—RALPH WALDO EMERSON

There is precious little in civilization to appeal to a Yeti.
—SIR EDMUND HILLARY

The Kremlin
August 2, 1946

History had taught Nikita Khrushchev that, from the time of the Mongol invasions through Napoleon and Hitler, Russia had earned its paranoia the hard way.

To him, battles were not exciting victorious endeavors. He hated and feared war but knew that survival meant a constant state of heightened alertness.

Even in the enclosure of the Kremlin (and especially here, this night), Khrushchev understood that paranoia was often the only choice. *Be smart, but never show it,* he decided. *And maybe after Stalin, Beria, and their friends are finished killing one another—maybe, just maybe I'll still be taking in air and in my right mind.*

Unlike his associates, the fifty-two-year-old Politburo member foresaw that Mao Zedong's strategy and logistics must eventually emerge victorious in the current internal conflict with Chiang Kai-shek and the Nationalists. But Khrushchev, of course, kept this idea, like the rest of his thoughts, to himself.

After a very long night of exquisitely manufactured vodka and even richer food, Stalin finally asked, "So, tell me, Beria. Is there any news out of Tibet?"

"Hard to tell, Comrade," the man replied. "Although thanks to a new gift from Comrade Theremin to the museum, information has begun to seep out again, from New York."

"And?"

"And it seems that Anatoly did not overestimate the likelihood of some very dangerous biology."

"I see," Stalin said, "And what has happened with our MacCready problem?"

Beria allowed himself a small chuckle. "I doubt there *is* a MacCready problem anymore."

Stalin grunted approval, then accepted a slice of chocolate pecan pie from the ever-silent Khrushchev. He chewed reflectively and wondered aloud: "Now, what about the Chinese?"

"They sent in three helicopter crews," Beria said. "And are apparently set to send in more."

"Communists or Nationalists?" Stalin inquired, his mouth full.

"Does it matter?" Beria responded, taking what would have been for any man other than the marshall of the Soviet Union a risk with his own life. Even so, the man was relieved when Stalin chuckled. "Whoever they are, they cannot know what we already know about this Pliny and his codex."

"Why not?" Khrushchev asked, timidly.

"No theremin," Beria snapped at him, and after a pause, wondered aloud, "So, what *do* the Chinese know that we don't know?"

Stalin cleared his throat. "More importantly, Beria: how soon can our own team be in there?"

"Logistically, another three days."

Stalin shook his head. "Unacceptable," he said, and threw a glass, causing Khrushchev to dodge it in a comically exaggerated manner.

Stalin and Beria exchanged snide looks before continuing to do what they would do until their dying days—they ignored the man.

Beyond the Valley of the Morlocks

AUGUST 2, 1946

U nder the cover of darkness, accompanied by Alpha and one of the miniature mammoths,

316 Bill Schutt & J. R. Finch

Mac and Yanni were led away from their igloo
prison and along a rocky trail they had never seen
before. Once above the layer of mist and floating
snow, they were grateful that their path was made
visible (if only barely) by the faint glow of starlight.

Despite the danger, Mac found himself fascinated by the furry elephant—which, as the
journey progressed, had become more clearly illuminated by the rise of the crescent moon above
the knife edge of a rock formation. This was his
first opportunity to walk beside one of the creatures, and to view it up close for an extended
period. Unlike the thick, pillar-shaped limbs of
the two modern species, this one's legs were significantly thinner—*built for rapid, agile movement.*
Even more fantastical were the mammoth's feet.
Gone were the broadly flattened weight-bearing
structures that characterized all proboscideans,
past and present.

*And instead of a flat pad and some toenails, it's got
six stubby digits.*

Many hours beyond the valley—and beyond
daybreak—Alpha had scouted out ahead, while
Yanni knelt down to prepare another round of
what Jerry once referred to as "drawing stick figures in the dirt."

"You know that pandas have an extra digit,
right?" Mac whispered to his friend.

Yanni shot him an incredulous look. "Ummm . . .
that's great, Mac. But what's that got to do with the
price of tea in Cuiabá?"

"Helps 'em strip off bamboo leaves."

"Yeah, and?" she said, trying in vain to concentrate on her hieroglyphic figures.

"Well, these mammoths have six toes as well."

"Yeah, I noticed."

"I'm betting the extras are modified ankle and wrist bones—tweaked to take on a new purpose."

"Like climbing around in the rocks and stuff?"

"Right," Mac said. "Evolution doesn't invent. It tinkers with what's there already."

"That's great, Mac," Yanni said, "and speaking of evolution, I'm going to go get Alpha back here." She pointed to her handiwork. "I need to show him this."

Mac replied with a nod as she walked away. "Careful," he called after her.

Glancing down, Mac noted that her symbols had themselves evolved into something far more complex than the simple stick figures she and Alpha had begun with.

Mac caught incongruous movement out of the corner of one eye. Reflexively, he dropped and rolled to his right. A loud metallic clank accompanied by a spray of sparks exploded so near to his face that the embers actually struck him. He sprang to his feet, instantaneously assessing the threat while already leaning into his next dodge.

During an adrenalized flash of recognition, he saw everything he already suspected. It was the visage of the creature who had murdered Jerry— *back to complete his trophy case.*

In only two seconds, Mac managed three perfectly executed avoidance maneuvers, changing direction each time and increasing the distance from his attacker—but to no advantage at all. The Morlock's reflexes were quicker.

Mac glimpsed the raised pike and barely had time enough to register what was about to happen. And yet, within that same small part of a second, and in a blur of motion that Mac could not quite track, the little mammoth was suddenly between them. With its right trunk, the elephant had whipped something around the back of the giant's head, deftly caught it with its left trunk, and began to pull Scarface onto his tusks.

Mac watched the Morlock's expression change from one of snarling triumph to wide-eyed surprise as the mammoth's tusks drove through his body wall and diaphragm, expertly targeting the heart and lungs.

Scarface dropped, staring at nothing.

The mammoth, looking rather calm, given the circumstances, ignored the body and began wiping its tusks clean in the snow.

"Gotta tell ya, kid," Mac said, "just when I thought I'd seen everything . . ."

The mammoth shot him the briefest of glances before turning his attention uphill. Yanni was running down toward them, Alpha trailing behind.

Having finished cleaning itself, the little mammoth, continuing its nonchalant routine, picked up the woven cord it had used to save Mac's life. *It's the choke collar*, Mac realized.

He looked on with a combination of surprise

and awe as the creature reaffixed the restraint around its own neck.

"So *that's* why you guys wear those things."

Although Mac had been involved in the killing of a Morlock, he was relieved when Yanni informed him that Alpha regarded it as nothing more than "pest control." The short conference that followed ended with mutual nods and a bout of hieroglyph-obliterating overkill by the lead Morlock.

"Okay," Yanni announced, "we're headed back to the shelf and the Chinese helicopters. You think you can fly one of them?"

"As long as it's in one piece," Mac replied. His mind flashed back to Li Ming's colleague in the "Trophy Room." *It's a bet those Chinese pilots won't be flying us out of here*, he thought, but left unsaid.

The Navy lieutenant from Massachusetts was growing impatient with delays, brought about by the "sole survivor" from a Chinese expedition. He gestured toward the Asian zoologist. "And we're supposed to believe everything this Red shovels our way?"

In a remarkably calm voice, Wang had managed to inform the Devil's Brigade–led team as thoroughly as he could how easy it was to make wrong turns, and about some of the unique dangers they were now facing.

Of greater concern to Dr. Nora Nesbitt was the fact that, after an uneventful trek to the helicopter site, it was immediately apparent that the two Russian "bananas" would *not* be flying anywhere. Large sections of the engines had been forcibly torn out and were now missing.

"Look, our mission is to get MacCready and his two friends out of here," the lieutenant said. "As for the rest, I think this guy's whole story reeks of misinformation."

The invertebrate zoologist had already determined that, hero or not, the Bostonian was as cocky as he was enamored with the sound of his own voice.

While "Just Call Me Jack" shared his idea about a Chinese hoax conspiracy with Nesbitt, the rest of the team worked with Wang to plot a course that they hoped would lead them to Mac-Cready.

"So, Chicago," said Captain Don Pederson, a thick-necked former lumberjack, "you've seen nine-foot-tall ape-men and killer snowflakes?"

Wang nodded. "As I told you."

"And you're *not* a fisherman now, are you?" the Devil's Brigade leader asked, his men responding with an assortment of snickers and moans. The sole female member of the group looked on with a frown, while Wang looked confused.

"He means you're not prone to exaggeration," Nesbitt explained for Wang, shooting the captain a discouraging look.

"No . . . no, fisherman," Wang responded. "No exaggeration."

"I told you these creatures are real," she informed the group, allowing some annoyance to creep into her voice. "What he's telling us is simply more evidence."

"Any birds?" someone asked, and eight heads, including that of the Chinese scientist, turned to him. It was Sergeant Juliano, the incongruous-looking weapons expert and old friend of the missing Captain MacCready. Juliano scanned the quizzical faces, then shrugged. "I hate birds."

"No birds," Wang replied, as they began the trek downhill. "Birds not the problem."

L ong after moonrise on the third of August, the strangest team of travelers since *The Wizard of Oz* was on the move.

Mac, Yanni, and the other two species had neither heard nor smelled any pursuing Morlocks. Nonetheless, the pair of humans snapped into hyperalertness as Alpha, up ahead, halted suddenly.

"Morlocks?" Mac whispered.

"Don't think so," Yanni replied, scanning the shadows and stony crevices, and listening intently.

While Mac and Yanni hung back, the little mammoth moved forward, brushed past them, and stood just behind the giant. Mac watched in fascination as the odd bifurcated trunk split at its base into a pair of arm-length appendages—each with a set of fingerlike tips, and each testing the air in multiple directions.

"Something's got 'em worked up," he said quietly.

322 Bill Schutt & J. R. Finch

I f either of those things sees us, take the shot," Captain Pederson whispered to the man with the nightscope-mounted carbine. "Aim for the big guy."

As if on cue, both of the strange creatures turned their attention directly at the sniper's nest.

Pederson's eyes widened in surprise. *They can't have heard me*, he told himself. *We're a hundred yards away and downwind.*

The beasts—one of the Chinese scientist's "ape-men" and what appeared to be a miniature elephant sporting a shaggy carpet—continued to stare straight at him. *Son of a bitch!*

"Captain?" the sniper lying next to him said, under his breath.

Pederson shook his head slightly, before whispering a response. "Take the s—"

Y anni rushed forward, ahead of Alpha. Keeping one eye on the ice and bolder-strewn incline, she motioned for him to crouch down and for the little mammoth to remain still. All of their attention was focused on a rocky outcropping a hundred yards farther uphill. Then, just as Yanni was about to begin shouting, something unexpected broke the cold silence.

D on't shoot!" came a cry from behind the sniper. "*That's Yanni!*"

Captain Pederson and his sniper turned to see

the little weapons expert Juliano frantically waving his arms and running past them and into the line of fire. "What the hell is this?" the thick-necked officer muttered.

The two Devil's Brigaders exchanged exasperated looks, then the sniper turned back to reacquire his target. The giant was gone, as was a creature that reminded him of an elephant in need of a serious haircut.

"Hold your fire," Pederson said, just as Lou Costello's twin reached Yanni and at least one of the others they had been sent to rescue.

The sniper reset the safety.

T hose Ruskie helicopters are trashed," Sergeant Juliano told his friends. "Not even *you* could fly them out of here, Mac."

R. J. MacCready shot his buddy an appreciative nod.

Captain Pederson peered over the table of rock and into a thousand-foot drop. "So, you know another way down from here, Captain? Besides the quick way?"

"We don't," Mac replied, "but Yanni's friends might."

"If they aren't halfway back to that valley already," Jack chimed in. He was referring to the fact that, by the time Sergeant Juliano threw his arms around Mac and Yanni, both Alpha and the little white mammoth had vanished.

"They wouldn't do that, Jack," Mac said, shaking

his head, though his tone of voice expressed something less than one hundred percent certainty.

"They risked their lives to help us escape," Yanni added, sharply. "I doubt they even *have* a home to go back to, anymore."

"So . . . then why'd they run off?" the Devil's Brigade leader asked.

Mac watched Yanni's transition from defense to offense. "Probably because they were about to get ventilated," she said.

Mac noticed that Pederson also sensed the icy reaction and, knowing she was right, he dialed back on his tone. "Well, Mrs. Thorne, saving you two was quite admirable of your friends, but can you get them back here?"

"I don't know," Yanni replied, still on edge. "*Your* men gonna shoot 'em?"

"Captain Pederson," Mac said, "if anyone can coax them back, Yanni can."

"It's the guns, Mac," Yanni asserted. "You know how they are when it comes to guns."

Mac nodded; but he, Yanni, and everyone else present knew there was no chance that any of them would be giving up their weapons.

"Nobody's going to shoot them," Mac reassured her, while making eye contact with as many of the team as he could without being too obvious.

"It won't matter," Yanni continued. "If you're holding a weapon, you're goin' over the cliff."

"Excuse me," Pederson said, "am I missing something here? Why do we even *want* those creatures back? We've rescued two of the people we came here to rescue, right?"

There were nods all around from the Devil's Brigaders—but Mac, Yanni, and Jack exchanged looks.

"Whatever you need, I'm in," Jack told Mac and Yanni. Then, turning to Pederson, he said, "You do understand Jerry and Mac saved my ass."

"We know," Pederson replied.

Jack let out a deep breath, then continued. "So, Mac, have you learned whatever it is you were sent in to learn?"

"That and then some," MacCready replied, "as you might have noticed."

At that, Dr. Nora Nesbitt became even more "on mission" than she had at the sight of little "Dumbo," *to say nothing of a living example of Pliny's hairy bipeds.*

"Well then," Pederson said. "We're mostly mission accomplished. Let's find the quickest way out of these mountains—I'd start with downhill, no?"

Yanni gave a derisive laugh. "Look, Pally, Alpha knows the ins and outs of this region far better than we do," she asserted. "Without him, I'm certain we'll run into a slew of Morlocks."

"Morlocks?" Nesbitt asked "Is that what you're calling them?"

"Morlocks, Cerans, Yeren," Yanni addressed the group. "Whatever you wanna call 'em, they'll be happy to show you the quickest way down."

"Oh?" Juliano interjected, hopefully.

Yanni gestured toward the ledge. "Sure. Screaming your lungs out and with your rifles shoved up your asses, sideways."

"And don't forget the killing snow cloud,"

Wang added. "Only this Yeren will know how to avoid."

"That's right," Mac said. "Without Alpha, we're definitely not getting out of here alive."

"And with him?" Nesbitt asked.

"We're only *probably* not getting out of here alive."

"Well there's a convincing argument," Captain Pederson said. Then he shot Yanni a look. "But we're *not* getting rid of our guns."

"I'll see what I can do," Yanni said, throwing a dirty look at the holstered .45-caliber Colt that he was sporting. With no further comment, she headed off down the trail.

Mac's expression of deep concern turned to a mixture of pride and worry. He did not try to stop her.

"Shouldn't someone go with her?" Nesbitt asked.

"*No!*" Yanni called back without turning around.

Yanni Thorne turned the corner of a switchback and came face-to-face with the miniature mammoth. Taking her by surprise, the creature rushed forward, its bifurcated trunk resembling a pair of welcoming arms. It gathered her in against its forehead for what her late husband might have termed a "slightly less than bone crushing" hug, while simultaneously, Alpha seemed to materialize from the face of a sheer rock wall into the pre-dawn twilight.

Easy there, fella, Yanni told herself, trying to

find the breath that the little pachyderm had just squeezed out of her.

Alpha's reaction was far less friendly. By way of a greeting he drew back his considerable set of gums to reveal an even more considerable set of teeth. Then he hissed and gave a short whistling cry, which translated to, *Do not even think of coming near me*—a behavior that continued to leave Yanni perplexed.

"Yeah, nice to see you, too," she told him.

Adding to the peculiarities of the reunion, it was the mammoth and not Alpha who stepped forward to give Yanni an all-too-familiar "finger" poke. What made it even weirder was that the prod was in the wrong direction, toward the downhill portion of the rocky incline—away from Mac and the others. To emphasize the point, Alpha took a few steps, gesturing for her to follow.

"O-kay, I get ya. But I'm gonna need a little favor first," Yanni said, then pointed uphill. The response was nearly as predictable as it was negative.

Yanni decided to try another approach. Kneeling in the snow once more, she drew a series of stick figures, pointed to them, then to herself. Finishing up, she gestured that the three of them should proceed back the way they'd just come.

Alpha gave the artwork a quick glance before obliterating it with a violent swipe of his foot—the little elephant following up with a nasal-powered exclamation point.

"I knew you'd see it my way," Yanni said, then she smiled and started drawing again.

R. J. MacCready's internal alarms had started going off before Dr. Nora Nesbitt got to the question she'd apparently been waiting to ask all along.

"The only sped-up evolution I saw was probably related to the extreme isolation these species are under," Mac lied.

"You mean, like on an island?"

"Yeah, some species get smaller when there are less resources."

"Like the mammoths?"

"Exactly," Mac replied, knowing that at least *this* much was true.

"So this mist-covered valley—none of us gets to see—is really just a kind of island?"

"Right! Nothing magical going on. Just a series of small, isolated populations having no exchange of genetic material with the outside." Mac was in serious lecture mode now. "That type of isolation can produce some weird-looking shit."

"Like Morlocks and mini-mammoths with two trunks and legs adapted for climbing?"

"You got it," MacCready said, trying to be nonchalant as he gauged Nesbitt's response to what he was shoveling. And for her part, the invertebrate biologist simply nodded, appearing to take it all in.

Good, Mac thought, flashing her a smile.

"That's interesting, Dr. MacCready," Nesbitt replied, flashing her own smile. "I was just wondering—"

Her tone told Mac that the charade was over even before it actually was.

"—did you happen to run into any guinea worms that had been artificially selected to become biological weapons?"

Shit! "Guinea worms?" Mac asked, trying not to stutter.

"Yes, *Dracunculus*. Something very much resembling that very parasite was clearly depicted in the Pliny codex."

"And?"

"And it looked like ancient Morlocks had been farming them."

Jesus, Mac wondered, but said nothing. *Were the grass mimics Pliny's worms, two thousand years later?*

"I see," Nesbitt said, wearing a very different smile now, and reminding Mac a little too much of a cat who had just cornered a mouse.

There was a sudden commotion among the others and Mac took the opportunity to step away from what had turned into an uncomfortable grilling by Nesbitt. Two Devil's Brigaders stationed fifty yards down the rugged trail were frantically waving their arms, signaling something important.

An out-of-breath Sergeant Juliano was suddenly at Mac's side.

"You're gonna want to see this one, Captain," the man exclaimed, literally pulling MacCready by the jacket. And as usual, he knew that the little sergeant was right.

As they'd been ordered to do in just such an event, Mac saw that the two sentries had put down their rifles and were now stepping back against the rocky wall bordering one side of the trail. Yanni

Thorne gave them a brief nod as she passed. Mac noticed that there was little response from the shaggy-looking miniature elephant that followed her. Offering what Mac considered a slightly less than friendly response, the Morlock flashed a toothy snarl before kicking the two rifles off into space.

"Bad Morlock," Mac said to himself, then ran down to greet Yanni.

C aptain Don Pederson called a "humans only" meeting on a barren outcrop some thousand feet above their "thrown overboard" rifles. The focus of discussion was how, exactly, they might avoid dying in one of the various ways that had been recently enumerated by Mac and Yanni. On that topic, had anyone been acting as meeting secretary, he would have noted that even the Chinese biologist had gotten into the act, chipping in—repeatedly—with a rather squirm-inducing method of demise involving some rather badly behaved snow. And had the meeting secretary taken shorthand notes, the exchange between the parties would have read something like this:

"Alpha says there's only one way to get down from here without getting killed."

"And what's that?"

"He says we need to follow him."

"Where?"

"Up to a place where none of the other Morlocks will come after us."

"And where's that?"

"Ummm. . . . Alpha won't say."

"I still can't see why we don't just head down-hill. Whether your big pal there likes it or not, we're not completely defenseless."

"Just keep your sidearms hidden."

"Look, there's a valley full of Morlocks waiting for us to head in the wrong direction. And your little handguns won't matter for shit once they've pulled your balls out through your mouth."

"That sounds painful."

"But that's not going to happen, Sergeant."

"That's good, sir."

CHAPTER 23

When Three Worlds Collide

*Change is the law of life. And those who
look only to the past or present are certain
to miss the future.*
—JOHN F. KENNEDY

*I don't try to describe the future. My
business is to prevent the future.*
—RAY BRADBURY

In the Valley of the Cerae
Summer, A.D. 67

As the days passed, Pliny came
to realize that Severus was
falling even more intensely
under Teacher's control than he thought imaginable. At present, he could not determine who
the man was anymore: Severus the involuntary
traitor or Severus the Roman centurion who was

now actively assisting in preparations against the Scythian invasion.

"So you think their main force is still spread over a wide area?" Proculus asked.

"I believe so," Pliny said. "Becoming familiar with the terrain and drawing up their plans."

There was no question that the Cerae too understood what was happening—and how their every effort must be directed against this latest race of intruders. In fact, Pliny's captors were so preoccupied that it was deceptively easy to imagine that he and Proculus could simply retrace their steps to the glacial valley, past the ruins of Pandaya, and all the way to Rome without being captured—at least, not by the Cerae.

Pliny noted that on most nights, Teacher and Severus never returned to their chamber. *Doubtless making more catapults*, he concluded. *And more canisters.*

Nearly two weeks after the weapons test on the Scythians, Severus was finally allowed to speak with his two countrymen—an exchange that took place across adjoining balconies.

"Are you with us?" Severus asked. The sound of the centurion's voice surprised them at first.

"And are you helping our enemy design new weapons?" Proculus snarled. "The same enemy who butchered and desecrated your own men."

"I wasn't talking to *you*, Cavalryman," the officer replied.

Pliny suppressed a smile. *A trace of the old Severus*, he thought. "How are they treating you, my friend?" Pliny countered.

There was no response to the pleasantry, so Pliny resolved to answer the man's question. "I suppose if it is a choice between the Cerae and Scythians, we shall live longer among the Cerae."

"No doubt about who *you* will be serving," said Proculus, still agitated from the scolding. He pantomimed an obscene act.

Pliny scarcely noticed the gesture, deciding instead to offer Severus some advice. He turned his gaze outward, as if he could stare a thousand stadia through buildings and across mountain passes. "From what we know of the old Scythian predecessors, they like the dark," Pliny said. "They'll probably make their next move under the cover of a new moon and thick clouds."

Only after he finished his pronouncement did Pliny discover the centurion had gone.

When the Scythians did march against the valley, they struck during a cloudless night, with the full moon glowing balefully overhead.

It was plain that Severus had communicated to Teacher and her brethren, whether he believed it or not, that his two fellow travelers were on the side of the Cerae. On the night of the Scythian march, Pliny and Proculus had an extraordinarily clear view from the great pinnacle—which towered over the cloudy sea like a dark sentinel. The Scythian invasion force entered the valley of the Cerae from five different directions.

"Medusa's eyes!" Proculus said. "It's like watching five rivers pour in."

On opposite sides of the valley, the habitations of the Cerae were no longer in phosphorescent blackout.

A diversionary tactic or traps? Pliny wondered.

He watched Scythians approach narrow entrances into the brightly lit structures before rejecting them for what they were—decoys, choke points. In total, Pliny estimated that these tactics had delayed the Scythian advance by no more than a quarter hour.

On the ridges, elephants appeared, some of them with riders, others hauling wood-framed weapons.

"They've brought their own bolt-throwers," Pliny told Proculus.

Even as they spoke, several of the ballistae were being set in place and aimed at the very tower on which they stood.

Proculus held up one of the membranous, pomegranate-sized bags of worms that Severus and the Cerans had entrusted to them. The disgraced centurion himself had instructed that these needed only to be dropped upon the attackers, should they storm the tower.

The cavalryman gestured toward the invading force. "I'd trade all of these creepers for one of their longbows."

"Get down!" Pliny shouted. The first of the ballista-launched projectiles were already arching high over the moonlit fog.

The two men dove onto the floor of the terrace.

Two rounded stones struck above and below their position, bouncing off the ice and fiber mixture. A third shook the wall behind which Pliny

and Proculus had ducked, striking only a few arm
lengths from Pliny. The material seemed to be
holding together surprisingly well but a piece of
shrapnel had torn open one of the worm-filled
bags. Yet this too was of no consequence. De-
tecting nothing to attack, the writhing former
contents of the weapon simply moved off in every
direction, spreading like petals from a nightmare
flower.

Proculus pointed in the direction of the Scythian ballistae. "*That* way," he told the creatures.

"Let me know if they start listening to you,"
Pliny said, risking a peek across the mayhem unfolding below. "This is not going according to
plan," he declared, moments later.

Proculus managed a laugh. "For whose side?"

"Either."

The war elephants were the last to descend
with the Scythian horde. A hundred or more
of the armored giants moved toward the mist-
hidden catapults where Severus and a small team
of Cerae worked feverishly to load and fire as
many canisters as they could before being overrun. Projectiles landed in clusters along the
shore of the false sea, among the densest concen-
trations of Scythians. The riders reined in their
elephants, pausing to assess. The foot soldiers
also hesitated, and some of them were already
beginning to fall.

Simultaneously, no fewer than a thousand
Cerae boiled over the tops of the nearer ridges,

whence the Scythians had come. They charged down from the hills at a dead run, some wielding Roman swords and lances, others firing bags of Scythian-seeking death from slings. They had appeared with amazing suddenness—as if most of their army, well fed and rested, had swarmed up from beneath the mountains themselves.

The Scythians had no choice but to move deeper into the sea of fog.

On the mist-bound valley floor, the white mammoths were first to sense the approach of the new danger. They were taller at the shoulder, more muscular, and less fleet-footed than their descendants. Their fur was longer, their cranial capacity smaller, and each possessed only a single trunk. Three of them had just helped Severus and two Ceran warriors to realign a catapult, its aiming point directed by spotters above the mist. Teacher was about to give one of them an appreciative pat on its trunk when all three turned toward a sound that neither human nor Ceran could hear. Spreading their ears, the mammoths stood very still for just a moment, then ran off into the mist. All along the catapult site, the rest of the mammoths did the same.

"We don't have much time!" Severus called out. Driving home a message that his words did not quite convey, he pantomimed a rapid-fire sequence to the Cerae. At Teacher's signal, they launched what he feared would be their final volley of canisters.

With no mammoths remaining behind to help realign and reload, and realizing with Severus that they could not possibly reload before being overrun, the Cerae broke open the remaining launch canisters and spread their contents over the ground. Then they gathered hastily into the defensive *orbis* position that Severus had taught them.

The first direct encounter with the Scythian invasion force was with its foot soldiers. They stepped onto ground infested with two species of living weaponry that flowed like a liquid, up their legs and under their armor.

Severus looked on with a combination of horror and admiration as the soldiers advanced, displaying no response to pain—at least at first. More than thirty Scythians came striding out of the snow fog. Though his own sword had been returned to him, Severus found that, surprisingly, there seemed no use for it. Only three of the invaders reached the perimeter of outward-projecting Ceran lances. The last of them pushed a stubby reed between his lips and blew a high-pitched whistle before he died.

The whistle changed everything.

It summoned monsters.

Defensive formations no longer mattered.

The first of the war elephants broke through the Ceran position only moments after emerging from the mist. Clad in thick leather and metal armor, the elephant's headpiece was its most fearsome feature—*at least initially*—baring a huge, centrally located eye.

Cyclops! Severus thought, scarcely noticing its rider at all. Though part of his brain recognized that this was the work of an artisan, there was no escaping the sensation that the eye was staring directly at him and through him. For an instant the image held him spellbound, an involuntary response that had worked exactly as intended by the designers of the headpiece.

During that first instant, a Ceran warrior standing beside Severus, and similarly transfixed, was separated from his head by one of the twin blades affixed to the monster's tusks.

The Cerans who weren't crushed or slashed by the creature during those first moments of contact scattered to either side. Severus sidestepped the behemoth but was knocked to the ground by a Ceran. As the centurion glanced up, the armor-clad Scythian rider reined his war elephant into a remarkably tight turn in preparation for a second charge. One of the Cerans used his sling to launch a tick-filled projectile at the giant. Impacting solidly against a sliver of exposed flesh between thick leather plates, the spidery creatures burst forth but soon fell away ineffectively, like beads of water shaken from the back of a dog. In a moment of pandemonium, the defender had forgotten that his weapon was "trained" to follow only the scent of Scythian flesh.

"Aim for the rider!" Severus called out. Then, remembering the language barrier again, he pointed to the Scythian, who was howling and bellowing as if possessed.

Teacher released her own projectile and struck the mounted attacker square on the faceplate. Others followed her lead, but the rider's armor

covered the body so well, and was so tight fitting, that it slowed the penetration of the weapon.
During the few extra seconds required for the
ticks to find seams and eye slits, the elephant
gored a Ceran architect and two warriors with its
tusk-mounted blades. A physician was stamped
to death at Severus's side, with a warrior simultaneously tusk-flung over his head.

During the next instant Severus was airborne—
thrown out of the way by Teacher, who immediately scrabbled up the animal's flank with two
other physicians, even more quickly than Severus
had seen her kind ascend balconies and ice cliffs.

The centurion pried a lance from the hands
of a dead Ceran defender then, taking quick but
careful aim to avoid Teacher and her companions,
he hurled it at the elephant. Severus had contrived
to blind the creature in one eye or at least distract it from the trio of Cerans, but the projectile
pierced the giant's trunk instead.

Teacher and her two companions drove three
lances through the rider, flung him over the side,
and began tearing openings in the elephant's armor. Lances of Ceran steel pounded down between
its ribs and into each of its huge lungs.

At the moment the beast began to topple, it
reached behind with its wounded trunk, grabbed
one of the Cerae from its back, and pierced her all
the way through on a blade-tipped tusk. As the
dying monster fell onto its front knees, Teacher
and the other Ceran sprang from its back.

For all the death the elephant had wrought,
Severus could see that, unlike the indigenous mam-

moths with their coverings of dense fur, this relatively hairless giant had been leaking heat from the entire surface of its body. *Already dying before it ever entered the valley,* he thought.

The cries of bellowing monsters and mortally wounded Cerae could be heard from every direction, near and far. Drawn to the catapult emplacements by the sounds of battle and perhaps the scent of a sibling's blood, a second giant roared out of the mist—a bull elephant, more massive than the first. But there was something beyond its size that distinguished the new arrival. It only took Severus a beat to realize that the cyclopean eye of its headgear was completely obscured by blood and flesh. One of the brute's tusk blades had been snapped off near the base, the damage serving as a warning that this beast was even more hot-tempered than the one they had just slain.

The creature's Scythian rider was a monstrosity in her own right. She wore strange armor, more tightly fitting and oddly familiar. Apparently, the protective garments had already taken hits from tick- and worm-filled projectiles but this time the weapon was not only being slowed, it was being repelled. Now, with the rider having fully emerged out of the mist, the familiarity of the outfit became all too horribly clear.

"My gods," Severus whispered, realizing that the rider's gauntlet gloves had been sewn together from the carefully refitted hands of a Ceran. The headgear and most every other covering were also fashioned from Ceran skin. The ticks and worms that had been flung at the rider had mistaken her for one of Teacher's brethren, and now they were falling harmlessly from the armor, like dust.

With a sickening snap, Severus saw one tusk-pierced warrior flying end over end into the fog. Another Ceran stood his ground with a lance of native steel, trying to blind the rampaging beast, but he was not fast enough to escape a blow from the huge trunk. Teacher tried to save him but not even she was fast enough—suffering a slash to her thigh—the tusk blade coming perilously close to severing a femoral artery.

Severus moved in to assist, but Teacher violently flung him out of the fray, then spun back to face their attacker.

The beast charged again, the monstrous rider darting forward over its back and mounting the head as if climbing atop the prow of a ship. Her armored breastplates clothed in real Ceran breasts, the Scythian stood like a figurehead from hell.

Though Severus managed to avoid being stamped flat, a swipe from the creature's trunk cracked several of his ribs. When he looked up, Teacher was already clinging to the giant's sides, pulling away armor, slashing and stabbing.

Struggling to regain his footing and his breath, the centurion coughed blood and picked up another lance, his mind stuck on a single question: *How can I help tear a hole in this thing?*

Severus rose to his feet and staggered toward Teacher like a drunk, vowing to die for her with what little strength he had left.

By the time he stood, Teacher had climbed

atop the animal's shoulder. The enraged Scythian repeatedly struck the Ceran in the face with its shield, finally dislodging her. But as the physician fell, she reached one elongated arm behind the Scythian's shield. Locking her hand around a wrist, Teacher pulled the she-beast down with her.

Severus was almost upon them and he knew that death was surely no more than a few heartbeats away when Pliny and Proculus arrived, accompanied by half a dozen Ceran warriors with lances of their own. By the time four lances went through Teacher's torn-away segments of elephant armor and into the animal's lungs and arteries, they were down to three warriors. Within those same seconds, the Scythian's instincts alerted her to Teacher's sudden and repeated glances toward the Roman. In response, the warrior drew a blade and made a dash for Severus.

She never reached him. In a blur of blocking and swiping motions, Teacher disarmed the elephant rider. She tore away the weapon-repelling breastplate and mask of Ceran flesh, then drove the Scythian face-forward into the tick- and worm-covered ground.

Observing that the weapon was still refusing to feed, Teacher ripped away what remained of the mask, then rent the woman's face with teeth and nails—shredding skin and exposing unprotected muscle and bone.

Severus was all tunnel vision now, watching as the enemy's writhing body was driven into the weapon-infested ground.

He watched the ground feed.

Those left standing now saw that Teacher could easily have ended the Scythian's misery with a single neck twist, but the physician had something more vengeance driven in mind. And so the ticks and worms ate their fill.

At some point, Severus realized that Pliny was standing beside him. "If you survive this night," Pliny said, over the eerily human death cries of the bull elephant, "I have one piece of advice for you."

"And what's that?" the centurion replied, wearily.

"Don't *ever* get her mad at you!"

South Tibet
Beyond the Valley of the Morlocks

AUGUST 3, 1946

On a day when Mac came to believe the lost world had already produced so many extraordinary dangers that nothing could surprise him anymore, he was suitably surprised by the approach of two more Chinese helicopters.

And thus ended what should have been a brief food and rest stop, near the ledge where Mac's and, more recently, Wang's party had landed. Bristling with guns, the new arrivals zeroed in and circled one of the downed craft as if it were a wounded queen bee.

Mac had no time to appreciate that his insect metaphor was about to get stronger. In the distance, a black speck had been hovering over the

Morlock valley, but soon it too was making a bee-line for the shelf.

"What the hell?" Mac muttered, watching as a third helicopter loomed quickly into view. *And this one's different from the first two.* Instinctively, he glanced over his shoulder to make sure Yanni was okay. As expected, she and her two woolly pals were already scrambling for cover.

Jack, who had hunkered down beside him, gestured toward the third gunship. "You think somebody's crashing their party?"

"They're Russians," Mac replied. "And I definitely get the feeling they didn't come to this dance together."

"Lucky thing our rifles and Johnny guns got thrown over the side, huh?"

This time Mac said nothing, watching as his friend zigzagged away to find a more secure position. Though he had lost sight of the others, Mac did notice that Alpha was still maintaining his distance from the group. Uphill, and in open view, the Morlock simply pressed himself closer to a wall of rock and ice, quickly becoming all but impossible to see.

Mac caught a flash of movement out of the corner of an eye. Seemingly ignoring the multiple threats from above, now it was the Chinese scientist who had run up to join him. "Those first helicopters, Nationalists!" Wang shouted over the din of blades and engines.

"Yeah?" Mac replied, motioning for him to duck down. "What's the difference?"

"Third one *not* Chinese. Third one Russian."

"So?"

"Communists and Nationalists no like each other."

Before he could reply, Mac saw that, incredibly, two of the Devil's Brigaders had stepped out onto open ground.

What the hell are they doing?

Unarmed, the men waved their hands over their heads.

MacCready recognized a whole new potential for catastrophe. America's uneasy alliance with Kai-shek's Nationalists had worsened the tension between President Truman and the Kremlin. No one knew for certain the new lows to which hatred between China's Nationalists and Communists had sunk, but from the look on Wang's face, at least two sides in this curious triangle were on the verge of a new war.

With this in mind, Mac now realized that the brave men who had stepped out into the open were simply taking their best shot at deescalating the situation.

The first flare of gunfire was therefore all the more shocking because it came from one of the Chinese helicopters, from Nationalist "allies."

The two Devil's Brigaders were still holding up their hands when the back of one man's head disappeared. The other soldier moved with such swift and practiced precision that nothing worse than shards of lead-splattered rock reached him before he was safely behind a mound of boulders.

"So much for your side," Mac told Wang, wondering in the back of his mind if the Nationalists had initially come in trying to learn what had happened to the three prior helicopter crews, or if Pliny's secret codex was not quite a secret anymore. There was no time to examine the question. Mac began blazing a new trail uphill, behind the cover of limestone and ice. A quick glance told him the helicopter that had fired on the two men was now closing in on the survivor's rock shelter—clearly trying to secure an optimal angle of attack, in order to finish him off.

Next, they'll seek out the rest of us, Mac told himself. *Remove all witnesses and maybe no one will ever learn how badly you just screwed up your mission.*

Only now did Mac realize that Wang had decided to follow him.

"So what the hell are your people doing up here?" Mac snapped at the scientist.

"My captain was ordered to bring back Yeren bodies," the man replied, his voice strangely calm, given the circumstances.

Mac nodded in the direction of the choppers. "Looks like somebody changed the plan."

Indeed they had, and now, with the arrival of the Russians and the drawing of American blood, the plan continued to change—at a psychopathic rate. The Nationalist helicopter that had been pursuing the surviving Devil's Brigader found its way blocked by the Russian craft. A hyperamplified speaker system blazed to life above the man's position. In a Russian-English hybrid language that Jerry had once referred to as "Rushlish"—and even with most of the words distorted through the sweep of blades—it was easy to piece the message together. The Russians were ordering the Americans to come out and give themselves up. One word came through with particular clarity: "MacCready."

The Chinese tried to sidestep the Russian blockade, shifting to a new line of fire against the trapped Devil's Brigader. The Soviets moved again into a line-blocking position, reminding Mac of Charles Knight's sculpture of a *T. rex* and *Triceratops* squaring off for battle. The difference was that, at least for now, this standoff appeared to be all show, with little desire by either side to charge. The comparison broke down completely as the second Chinese helicopter moved steadily nearer, making it inevitable that they would soon outflank the Russian on either side.

While the aerial chess match began to take shape, Mac considered the two likely outcomes for those on the ground: *killed by the Chinese or captured by the Russians and disappearing after "Uncle Joe" tortures out all the information he wants from us.*

Mac thought again about Charles Knight's sculpture and the two ancient enemies—*neither quite willing to attack the other.*

"Maybe I can change this," he said to himself, noting that one of the Chinese helicopters was drifting into just the right geometry and was on the verge of eclipsing the Russian helicopter. Confident that the engine noise would drown out the sound of his sidearm, Mac waited for the very second the airborne geometry became perfect, then fired off three shots and quickly ducked.

Simultaneously, four puffs of smoke shot out

from behind a rock shelter on the other side of the Russian helicopter. The bullets bypassed that craft and struck the other. After a moment of confusion, Mac realized exactly what had happened—someone else recognized the same fortuitous geometry and contrived the *same* plan, at the *same* moment.

The two sides were so focused on the trapped American, and on one another, that neither saw the actual shooters. The Chinese seemed only to notice penetrating gunfire from the direction of the Russian helicopter, and vice versa.

"MacCready!" Wang cried out beside him. "Stay down!"

Mac paid him no attention and kept just low enough, peering between rocks, to prevent the now confused and distracted intruders from seeing, and guessing, what had just happened. He had hoped to trigger at least a scrimmage, but what erupted now was a runaway spasm of gunfire that increased in ferocity for the better part of a minute.

The Chinese had nothing more substantial, for protection, than a canvas-and-glue hull. And, although the Russian helicopter came equipped with several patches of armor plating, the Soviets found themselves outgunned by the Chinese.

Within that first minute, within that single sweep of a stopwatch, the crew of the nearer Chinese helicopter were dead even before it fell to the ground. The Russians gained only a brief respite—perhaps twenty seconds more of life, for both of their pilots were slumped dead in their seats from Chinese gunfire. Mac thought he could discern at least two figures struggling into the cockpit as the Russian ship rotated away from him, staggered across the sky, then dropped upon the chopper aboard which Wang had arrived. It shattered against the older machine, scattering fire and smoke and throwing the few who survived— however briefly—into a disoriented, flaming rout.

As Mac watched, the second Chinese helicopter, its engine laboring, disappeared over the sheer cliff, beyond the spot where death had by now claimed the last of the Russian crew.

Reasonably sure that there were no guns trained on them, Mac and Wang bounded down from their hiding place. They reached snow and slid to a stop.

"Stay down!" MacCready shouted, but the surviving Devil's Brigaders were already huddled around the body of their dead friend. Jack was covering them with his Colt .45 and he gave Mac a nod. Taking in the scene, Mac let out a deep breath as Yanni, unharmed, and the little mammoth came out into the open.

"Nice shooting, huh?" Jack called out. "But I'm afraid I've only got two rounds left."

"That was *you*?" Mac followed.

"Yeah," Jack replied. "What's that they say about great minds?"

But staring down at the body of the Devil's Brigader, Mac decided to say nothing.

The Bostonian, however, wasn't quite through. "So, can you tell me why the Chinese *and* the Russians are running air raids on Tibet?"

MacCready shook his head, very slowly. "That's a story for another time," he said. "If ever."

An unmistakable noise distracted them. Somewhere far below the strewn-field of wreckage, the other Chinese helicopter had survived and was—despite the rattle and shriek of an engine in distress—returning.

"Get to cover!" Mac yelled at Yanni, as the little mammoth instinctively placed its own body between hers and the onrushing sound.

Mac turned to face the roar of the approaching gunship, taking a bead on the edge of the shelf where he calculated the flying machine would emerge.

Jack followed MacCready's lead. "What the hell are these guys so hot to find?" he pressed again.

But now there was no time to stonewall or deny; there was only time to face the enemy.

God damn you, Pliny, Mac thought. *Why couldn't you have stayed in fucking Rome?*

In the Valley of the Cerae
Late Summer, A.D. 67

FIVE WEEKS AFTER THE SCYTHIAN DEFEAT

There were no celebrations among the Cerae—nothing resembling a victory party, no outward expression of triumph.

"They are not us," Pliny warned Severus. "I do not believe we can even call them people."

Within hours, after only the briefest recess for

a meal and sleep, the Cerae shifted to a widely communicated and apparently universally agreed-to plan. In response to it, they became as active as a nest of paper wasps.

The winds blew fitfully down from the hills. The mists of the Opal Sea rose and fell in waves, and in the center of the sea, the Cerae themselves were doing what Scythian ballistae had failed to do. They were bringing down the central tower.

"But why?" Proculus asked him.

"It's the most visible evidence of their existence in this valley," Pliny explained. "And a potential beacon to future invaders—a beacon they've decided to extinguish."

In only a month, the tower had been completely dismantled. Architects, warriors, and mammoths now put to the yoke hauled it away piece by piece to some hidden lair.

By Pliny's accounting, the Cerae physicians and architects had suffered something worse than a decimation—battle losses that had now led to a shortage of architecturally talented minds. As a result, Pliny and Proculus were escorted deep into a cave system where they were "invited" to assist in the drawing up of new structural designs. This surprising activity focused primarily on sketching in their own opinions on Ceran plans for underground roof supports. The system was being expanded at a furious rate, much of it branching out into and then remodeling a preexisting labyrinth of natural tunnels and caverns.

On the fortieth day after war's end, Pliny stood on the lip of the balcony he and Proculus still shared. It would be their last day here, since the building was also being systematically deconstructed. The gardens below were a hive of activity in which each of the pallid white plants was carefully uprooted for transport to a new subterranean home.

Pliny shrugged. "By the winter solstice, every trace of these buildings will be gone."

"After their encounters with the Pandayans, the Scythians, *and us*," said Proculus, "they must know that the world outside is growing larger—and closer."

"And so they've decided to hide every trace of themselves, under the fog and under the ground."

Through a space between stone arches, they watched the frozen body of the great bull elephant being carefully prepared for transport to the caves.

Pliny gestured toward the activity. "Including that monstrosity."

Proculus nodded, but said nothing.

"But what of the weapons they used to destroy the Scythians?" Pliny asked. "What if they decided to train such abominations against Rome?"

Proculus uttered a humorless laugh. "You have raised this question before."

"Yes. And on *that* day we had not yet seen the immensity of such power. I cannot bear to think of these living weapons—or something even worse—following trade routes and Roman roads into the very heart of the empire."

Next door, the balcony Severus and Teacher had shared was being carted away in pieces. Even as Pliny and Proculus watched, one of the worms, fleeing the commotion, inched toward the two of them. Then, sensing their presence, it darted away.

Pliny gestured toward the tiny creature. "The buildings are not all that's changing."

"I've noticed," Proculus replied.

Both of them were aware that physically, the worms were becoming smaller, faster, and seemingly more sleek-bodied than the ones they had seen at the death pits and during the battle.

Pliny did not understand the mechanism involved—no one would for nearly eighteen hundred years. And even then, Charles Darwin himself would neither see nor imagine evolution occurring at such a pace.

As Pliny and his friend prepared to descend from their quarters for the last time, both of them shared something remarkably close to a single thought.

No Roman, no man, can ever know that this place exists.

AUGUST 3, 1946

The helicopter was still beyond sight, below the cliff edge and rising loudly on damaged engines. The American rescuers and their rescued were hunkering down for a last stand against the Chinese—mere pistols against machine guns—when Alpha finally reappeared. From a distance, he communicated to Yanni with a series of hand signals and whistling sounds.

"What's *that* all about?" Mac called back to her, his pistol still trained on the edge of the cliff.

"Alpha wants everyone out of here," she said. "Out of here *now*!"

She was pointing uphill, unwisely, in Mac's opinion, in a direction that would make them more easily seen and fired upon.

The Devil's Brigade leader started to object, when Mac held up a hand. "Just, listen to her. Take Yanni and the others and run! Jack and I will follow as soon as we can."

The naval officer from Boston shot his friend a confused *Are you sure about this?* expression.

Yanni could see what the two men had in mind, and she rushed over to MacCready. Grabbing his arm, she began tugging. "No, Mac!" she yelled over the approaching roar. "Alpha wants us *all* out of here. Something about a storm coming."

"What?" Mac said, unsuccessfully trying to break free. "What storm?"

Yanni shook her head and tugged harder. "Not sure, Mac. You want me to stick around and figure out the particulars?"

Mac looked toward the edge of the cliff again. Twin rotors came noisily into view.

All three of them turned and ran.

The helicopter crested the cliff edge and navigated around the fringe of the Russian wreck. Coming close to a full stop, the pilot skillfully held his machine in a hover.

Mac, Yanni, and Jack picked up the pace, trying to catch up with Alpha and the mammoth, who were already far upslope of them. They caught a glimpse of Juliano and Wang, who appeared to be helping Nesbitt along. All three were reaching individual degrees of exhaustion in the mountain air.

Mac sensed sudden danger behind and his body moved instinctively—twisting to one side and knocking Yanni down in the same direction, just as a bullet burrowed through the air above their heads with the hollow sound that could only be heard (and felt) during a near miss. The crack of the gunshot came later.

Mac turned, surprised to see that the man who fired upon them was on the ground, limping. It appeared that he had jumped down more than a full story from the helicopter and decided to pursue them on foot. *Why aren't they just flying up after us and shooting?*

The man, a Chinese officer, emptied an entire clip in their direction but this time he was off target by hundreds of feet. He dropped his weapon and began swatting at himself.

Alpha's storm had arrived.

"*This* way!" Yanni said. Mac and the others obeyed without any further questions at all. Glances over his shoulder provided Mac with only bits and pieces of the picture below. Bright, sunlit streamers of snow rose vertically above the cliff face and above the enemy, as if driven by a howling wind. In another split second he saw the helicopter engulfed. During another glimpse, it was whirling away in apparent desperation—back again toward the terrain that dropped off more than a thousand feet. In the end, Mac paused and watched for nearly a full ten seconds. The Chinese on board were leaping from both sides of the machine. Mac was certain that by the time it began to drift and shudder, and fall out of view, not a soul remained aboard.

R. J. MacCready realized that the storm engulfing the Chinese was full of snow mimics. What he had no way of knowing yet was that he had just witnessed the first use of a racially tagged biological weapon in nearly two thousand years.

AUTUMN, A.D. 67

The Ceran domes and the enormous central tower were gone forever.

All of the valley's inhabitants were now involved in a strange endeavor by which an entire civilization was trying to dig a hole into the earth and pull the hole in behind itself.

As the Cerae retreated into subterranean depths, the architects and the physicians seemed to have picked up as many as two hundred words of Latin from Severus, along with the words necessary to join them together in some meaningful fashion. As for learning the Ceran language, Pliny continued to believe he might have an easier time trying to communicate with a fish or a bug.

"This much they do understand," Severus explained one day, as they surfaced into sunlight. "'Pliny,' they say. 'He can be trusted.'"

"How would they know that?"

"Whether it is true or not, they *think* it," Severus

replied. "And what if I told you that, should you or Proculus choose to leave this valley, none of the Cerae will stop you?"

"I think I would choose to stay around a while longer."

Proculus nodded. "It may be safer here."

"Nero wanted us to find the Cerae and bring one of their heads home for him," said Pliny. "Even if the ghoul is finally dead, who knows what would happen if the empire really does continue seeking the Cerae, perhaps even more vigorously? The Scythians might end up looking lucky by comparison, even if Rome somehow came out the winner."

"It's an amazement that the Cerae haven't destroyed themselves with their own discovery," Proculus added.

"And if *Rome* possessed such power?" Severus asked.

Without hesitation, Pliny replied, "I believe the empire's wings are made of wax, and always shall be. Give emperors the power to shape life itself? No. If your wings are made of wax, never fly too close to the sun."

"You, too, Proculus?" Severus asked.

"We can never tell of this place," said Proculus. "But if we leave, come with us, brother."

Severus looked down at the ground. "I cannot."

"What?" Proculus shouted. "You, a Roman, choosing these monkeys over us? Are you still a slave to the scent of your she-beast?"

Severus shook his head. "You have seen that she

is not well. For this reason, a path is being prepared for me to stay beside her."

"What is the meaning of that?"

"I do not comprehend it fully myself. It is difficult for them to explain, in our words."

What Pliny had been able to see and understand was that Teacher did not appear to be healing from her wounds with the same magical rapidity as the rest of the Cerae. Two physicians had been tending to her continually since the Scythian invasion. Such attention seemed proportional with the serious nature of her condition. There were, in fact, few in her caste left. Because her kind had taken an especially severe beating from the war elephants, Pliny wondered if their population might have been pushed to the edge of extinction.

"How bad is it?" Pliny asked. "Is Teacher dying?"

"You do not understand," the centurion replied. "Her wounds from the battle are completely healed. It's something else that saps her strength."

"What then? This strange addiction between you?"

"Cling to that if you must."

Pliny stared at Severus, then shook his head, very slowly. "Her power over you. It is not what I thought it was, is it?"

"Shall I tell you why I must stay with her, always? Shall I tell you why a path is being prepared?"

"She has softened your brain," Proculus insisted.

Severus managed a quiet laugh. "As most *Roman* women cloud men's minds, from time to time."

"Roman women?" Proculus stammered. "These Cerae are not *us*!"

"Maybe they are more like us than they appear," the centurion said, quietly.

Though the Cerae looked humanoid and at the same time quite different, Severus's suggestion could not have failed to hammer a few cracks into Pliny's presumption that they were a breed completely separate from humans.

"What exactly are you going to do?" Pliny asked.

The centurion glanced over toward the path into the earth, then back to his friend. "I must admit," he said, "I have yet to figure that out."

"Stay with her *always*?" Proculus protested. "Nothing is forever."

"Time will have its say," said the centurion. "It always does."

CHAPTER 24

The Man Who Loved Morlocks

Home is where the heart is.
—PLINY THE ELDER

*Glory ought to be the consequence, not
the motive, of our actions; and although
it happen not to attend the worthy deed,
yet it is by no means less fair for having
missed the applause it deserved.*
—PLINY THE YOUNGER

West, beyond the Valley of the Morlocks
August 4, 1946

D eath snow," Wang had called
it. And, though MacCready
had personally witnessed its
effects, he found it difficult to comprehend how
the same fluffy snow mimics that swirled so harm-

lessly around him during his entire time below the mist became the fury behind the storm that burst upon the Chinese.

He was thankful that the death snow did not follow them. It had in fact withdrawn with the last Chinese helicopter, but its arrival at the landing area communicated that the minds who had conceived a killing wind, and who commanded it, were on the move.

Past sunset and throughout the night march, Mac had not seen any other Morlocks, but from the way Alpha kept pressing the group forward it was clear that the danger was quite real, and likely gaining on them. The little mammoth, too, was looking increasingly nervous—making frequent stops to sniff the air, before heading off at an ever-more-hurried pace.

By the time the first rays of sunlight touched the ground, Alpha led them far from the cliff-side trail and into a narrow corridor through an ancient seabed of slate. Soon after, what some of the others might have perceived as claustrophobia-inducing walls gave way to an open plain. They crossed over what seemed like miles of stone flakes mixed with the shells of oysters and clams, but these mollusks had been off the menu for more than seventy million years. In silence and with great haste, they eventually followed Alpha from the flatland into a maze of mountain passes bordered on either side by vertiginous walls of rock. Here and there, the walls dripped skyscraper-sized streamers of green icicles.

No time for stopping and looking or asking ques-

tions, Mac thought, noting that other sights along the way were just as puzzling. Soaring outcrops of colorful mineral veins appeared to be studded with leafy plants, but they were really primitive lichens and mosses—ranging between blood red and purest white.

"The Hardy Boys," his botanist friend Bob Thorne had called these organisms, which had a talent for growing anywhere and under any conditions. "I've studied lichen that can grow on a dead guy's skull," Bob had informed Mac.

At this point, with the sun having passed high noon and with shadows just beginning to lengthen, R. J. MacCready was simply grateful that none of the local flora had behaved badly.

Despite the apparently desperate push for speed exhibited by the fleet-footed mammoth, Mac found time to make several more observations. He *was* disappointed that there were few if any animals among the lichen and white "moss"—though he knew this was generally the case for such environments—including the most species-diverse regions of all. He recalled the initial shock he had felt during his first trip to a rain forest, this particular one located deep within the Malaysian peninsula. As a graduate student, he'd come to study an oversize species of hairless bat by the name of *Cheiromeles*. He had been anticipating something like a Cecil B. DeMille crowd scene—this one starring monkeys, lizards, and every form of tropical wildlife he knew to inhabit the region. What he got was heat, humidity, and land leeches—hundreds of leeches. But these were not the wormlike parasites

Mac had encountered while swimming in Adirondack ponds as a child. These bloodsuckers were six-inch-long hunters, as fast as they were active. And as he soon determined firsthand, their bite made the most pain-dealing bee seem like a mosquito by comparison.

Thinking about the tiger leeches brought back far more recent and even more uncomfortable memories of inchworm grass and skin-piercing bites.

Next topic, Mac told himself

Shifting mental gears, he noticed that Sergeant Juliano was acclimating well to the harsh terrain. Mac knew that the relative lack of wildlife suited him just fine and the little guy actually looked quite content to be where he was. Even the appearance of a lone raptor, soaring overhead, went essentially unnoticed. It glided high enough on an updraft, and disappeared fast enough, that the feather-phobic sergeant never had a chance to complain about it.

Also on the plus side of the ledger was the fact that breathing was becoming easier—far easier. Mac estimated that they had descended at least a thousand feet from the zone Jerry had once called "where helicopters go to die," and now the benefits of additional atmospheric oxygen were becoming noticeable.

Another positive was the ambient temperature—which here and there seemed to have risen high enough to melt an igloo (if there'd been one present). As a result, although the tall massifs that surrounded them were topped with ice, the mountain ravines through which they passed were intermittently bare of snow.

Mac noted the change, then forgot about it until they were passing over an outwash of white earth.

Yanni had stopped abruptly and was kneeling with her hand held flat against the stark, chalky-looking dirt. She broke what had been an hours-long silence. "Mac, feel this ground."

MacCready squatted down beside her and placed his hand down next to hers.

"Jeez, this ground must be twenty degrees warmer than the air," he said.

"What is this stuff?" Yanni asked, gesturing toward the stark white soil.

"It's calcium carbonate," Mac said, noting that there were an assortment of fungal puffballs growing on it, each nearly as pale as its surroundings. And given that there were no dark-colored rocks to absorb sunlight and heat, Yanni asked the very question Mac was beginning to compose.

"So where's this heat coming from?"

"Must be from below," Mac replied. "Geothermal wet spots, maybe? I'm pretty sure carbonate needs warm water to form."

"Kind of like Yellowstone?" one of the Devil's Brigaders added.

"Yeah, kinda like that."

A pair of sharp whistling sounds and a loud grunt terminated the discussion. Mac turned and saw the same man whose question he had just answered stagger forward and drop to his knees. An eight-foot pike had torn through a point directly between his shoulder blades and now extended out through his abdomen. Surprisingly, there was no blood. The soldier's expression showed nothing like pain—only shock at the strange object that had seemingly materialized in front of him. He locked eyes with Mac, then fell forward, his body sliding toward the spear point that had just embedded itself in the white earth.

Now there was blood.

A groan caught Mac's attention and he turned toward it. Another spear had pinned Sergeant Juliano to the ground.

As near as he could tell, at least a dozen Morlocks had found them. Mac and Yanni ran straight for Juliano.

"Your two friends aren't stopping!" Captain Pederson called out, pointing toward Alpha and the little mammoth.

"And we can't, either!" Yanni shouted back, noting that neither of their guides had broken stride and, if anything, they were sprinting ahead at an even quicker pace.

Some of their pursuers were trailing along the floor of the ravine. Others were apparently making a camouflaged approach, using the surrounding cliffs as launching points for their assault. They were also exhibiting an astonishing, perhaps even desperate degree of accuracy.

Especially, Yanni thought, *since they're hurling their steel pikes from something like two hundred yards away*—a feat that would have been impossible even for the most talented warrior in her village.

As if to emphasize the point, another sharp

whistling sound provided a half-second warning, enabling Pederson to turn a kill shot from a lance into a glancing flesh wound to his shoulder.

"*Fuck this!*" he shouted as he, Mac, and Yanni bunched together in an attempt to drag the wounded Juliano out of firing range. The particular spear that had pierced the sergeant's calf was hastily removed with no time to consider the additional pain or damage they'd just inflicted and not even enough time to wrap the wound.

Seeing that Mac, Yanni, and now Captain Pederson were struggling, Jack quickly doubled back. Drawing his sidearm, he fired off several rounds into the surrounding cliffs while the leader of the Devil's Brigade took careful aim at what he determined to be the Morlock ground position. Without shifting either his aim or his gaze, he passed Jack three more bullets, announcing regrettably, "Those are the last I can spare you."

"They've tested our logistics," Jack said, making his out-of-breath pronouncement while grabbing a handful of Juliano's parka and more quickly dragging him along.

"I know it," Mac replied, still supporting Juliano between himself and Yanni. Ignoring his shoulder wound, Pederson was now bringing up the rear—ever watchful for more projectiles.

"They know that in a pinch, we'll leave our dead behind," Pederson said. "But *not* our wounded."

"Which serves *their* purpose by slowing us down," Mac added, with a grunt.

The rain of metal seemed to have paused.

"They're probably regrouping, no?" Juliano said,

exhibiting a degree of calm that belied his deteriorating condition.

"Sounds right," Pederson agreed.

Up ahead, Nora Nesbitt and the surviving Devil's Brigaders had been ordered to maintain at least eye contact with their nonhuman pacesetters, and the invertebrate biologist was now waving her arms to signal their position.

"I still can't believe you talked me into ditching those rifles," Captain Pederson told Mac, as they slowly gained ground on the rest of the team. But it was Yanni who replied.

"Listen careful-like this time," she said. "Without Alpha, we're not getting outta here. And if everybody's packin' iron, we don't have Alpha."

"So how come we got to keep our pistols?" Pederson asked, performing a rather skillful backward run, while covering their backs. It was now all so sickeningly clear that if the Morlocks maintained their distance at the two-hundred-yard limit of spear range, then the pistol, compared to the accuracy of the rifles and Johnny guns left behind, would be rendered next of kin to completely useless.

"It's called a compromise," Yanni said.

"Too bad you couldn't have negotiated rifles instead," Jack said.

Yanni ignored the remark. "What I'm wondering is why Alpha's former pals didn't just overrun us as soon as the first handgun was drawn."

"Afraid of gettin' plugged, maybe?" the Devil's Brigader replied.

"I don't think so," Yanni said. "At this distance you can't hit any of them with a pistol. There's something else goin' on—"

Their conversation in retreat was interrupted by Mac. "Incoming! Watch it!" he called, just before a metal shaft smashed down not more than two yards away, propelling a spray of gravel at them. One fragment struck Yanni in the forehead, and a moment later she casually wiped away a thin trickle of blood.

"Yanni, you okay?" Mac cried, nearly letting go of Juliano before instantly correcting himself.

"I'm fine. Just keep going, huh?"

"Their throws are gettin' less accurate," Mac observed. "Strange. I think they're falling back."

"That's good," Yanni responded, "because we need to pull up someplace soon and patch Juliano's wound." *His face is looking too pale*, she left unsaid.

"Don't worry about me," Juliano mumbled, barely coherent. "No birds, though, right?"

Jack shot Yanni a puzzled look.

"Everybody hates something," she whispered. Then she turned to Juliano. "No birds, Sergeant."

"Spear-slinging giants, we got," Mac added.

Jack realized that Mac and his Brazilian friend were trying to keep the wounded man awake and talking. "Nine-footers," he chimed in.

"Well that's good," Juliano mumbled. "I hate birds."

We know, Mac thought. *Just hang in there.* He and Yanni exchanged concerned looks and picked up their pace.

Thankfully, there were no more reports of "Incoming!" from Pederson or Mac—the last spear having fallen short by nearly twenty yards.

Up ahead, Alpha and the little mammoth had finally begun to slow the pace, but behind Mac and his friends, there appeared an unnerving sight—a line of Morlocks spread out across the floor of the ravine. The giants who had been stationed in the cliffs were presently descending to join what now resembled nothing less than a pack of alpine wolves—ready to charge.

"Jesus," Jack muttered, checking his ammo, "we're not out of the woods yet. Nowhere near it."

The Devil's Brigaders, having seen the Morlock formation themselves, moved into position for what was beginning to look like a last stand.

Captain Pederson, who was counting his cartridges, nodded toward the line of creatures. "Remember Custer?" he asked no one in particular.

"Fuhgeddaboutit," Yanni responded.

"Well, it was back in—"

"I *know* when it was," Yanni said. "But this ain't that."

"Yeah, how do you figure?" Pederson said, chambering a .45-caliber round.

"Because I don't think they're coming any closer."

The Morlock formation, which had swelled to nearly two dozen individuals, surged back and forth in the distance, strengthening the imagery of so many wolves—now held inexplicably in place. It was as if a line had been drawn upon on the ground, across which they could not advance, toward something even a Morlock warrior feared.

By the time Mac and his friends had begun closing the distance between themselves and Alpha, the Morlock and his furry little companion had come to a complete stop. Yanni approached him, and though he was still wary of any physical contact, they did undertake another bout of their strange, hieroglyphic communication—this time presided over by the mammoth and somewhat constrained by the gritty substrate they were using as a writing tablet.

As the powwow concluded, and while most of the others were keeping an eye on the distant Morlock pack, the mini-mammoth passed something to Yanni, who nodded and immediately ran back to Sergeant Juliano. Mac and Pederson had by now applied a field tourniquet just below his knee.

"Here, Juliano," she said, "you've got to eat this now, okay?"

Dr. Nora Nesbitt, who had been intrigued by Yanni's interaction with their nonhuman guides, was suddenly at Yanni's side. "What's that?" she asked, as the wounded man began to chew on what appeared to him to be a handful of leftover spaghetti.

"Just a little home remedy Dumbo picked up," Mac replied, without much thought and without looking up from checking the tourniquet.

"This stuff's okay," Juliano whispered. "Sauce sucks, though."

Nesbitt ignored the wounded man and the

chuckles his response had elicited from his friends. "What *kind* of remedy, Captain MacCready?"

Now Mac turned to face the invertebrate biologist. "Well, it's not *Dracunculus*—if that's what you were thinking."

"Who's drunk?" Juliano asked them.

"Never mind, Sergeant," Mac said. "Just eat up all your spaghetti and you'll be fine." Then he addressed Nesbitt again. "Look, if we ever get out of here, there'll be time to talk about all of this," he said. "Right now, I think we can all agree that we've gotta keep moving."

Before she could respond, he and Yanni redirected their attention to Juliano, whose breathing was already starting to come easier.

Before departing, Nesbitt also noted the improvement.

Mac double-checked that everyone else was out of earshot, then turned to Yanni. "I certainly wasn't planning on bringing out that cave pasta— or anything else for that matter. At least not until we've had time to *really* think about it."

"And time is what we *don't* have," Yanni asserted.

Mac gestured toward the sergeant. "Although your elephant pal just put a crimp on that idea, huh?" Mac said.

"Seems that way," she conceded, and making sure to keep her voice low, added, "But that might not be so bad, right? Potential cures for polio, maybe even cancer."

"Yeah," Mac shot back, "then there's Wang's

killing snow, carnivorous grass, and probably shit we haven't even seen yet—all of it sharin' that valley with Juliano's spaghetti."

Deep in thought, Yanni said nothing, so Mac continued. "Just imagine this flora and fauna being toyed with in some lab until they change it into who-fucking-knows-what?"

Yanni uttered a short laugh. "Now where have I heard something like that before?"

The answer, of course, was her late husband.

Yanni nodded toward Alpha and the mammoth. "And if anybody finds out what's really in that valley—"

"—it'll definitely spell the end of *their* world," Mac said, completing the thought.

Misenum, west of Pompeii

A.D. 79

Eleven years after Nero's death, nine years after Pliny's return to Rome

A t a quarter past eight on the morning of August 24, the first tremors rippled out from Mount Vesuvius. By noon a giant cloud covered most of the eastern sky.

A distress call was relayed to Pliny's seaside home by flag signal from Herculaneum. The city of six thousand people stood midway between Pompeii and the estate.

Proculus, Pliny thought, before instructing his

men to signal back. "We are coming to you, as swift as Mercury."

As Pliny, now an admiral, prepared to cast off, his seventeen-year-old nephew undertook an assignment that had just been given him. Its subject: what to do with the elder Pliny's original notes, the same notes from which the secret codex had been compiled. The young man implored the historian not to sail toward the very danger everyone else was fleeing. But Pliny waved him off, leaving the distraught teen with only a quote. "You may steal that one someday," the older man said, trying to make a joke of the situation. Then, in typical Pliny fashion, he repeated the phrase.

More than fifteen hours later, as the eruption reached its peak ferocity, a family friend on a mission of rescue found the boy at his uncle's work desk, surrounded by history books and apparently reading. *Is he in shock?* the older man asked himself, as all around the quaking grew worse and walls had already begun to crack and fail. The teen was *not* in shock. He had in fact spent the entire night seeking out and sorting through every scrap of paper mentioning the Cerae. He burned them all, in honor of his uncle's wish that their valley, their world, should remain lost.

When the boy, who would become known as Pliny the Younger, left the estate for the last time, he carried a single sheet of papyrus. It bore the very phrase his uncle had emphasized earlier.

It read, "Fortune favors the brave."

It was an epitaph.

West, beyond the Valley of the Morlocks

AUGUST 4, 1946

W ell, *this* certainly ain't in Pliny's codex,"
R. J. MacCready told Yanni.

"At least not in the parts we saw," said Nesbitt.

They reached the grotto an hour before sunset.

Several miles beyond their last encounter with
the Morlocks, the ravine had opened above what
appeared to be an oasis but what the "scientist
types" present immediately recognized as yet another microenvironment. Standing on the rim of
the craterlike depression, Mac was reminded of
the Roman Colosseum's arena floor and the surrounding amphitheater. *Maybe a bit steeper-walled*, he
thought, *but the dimensions are just about right*.

The grotto's most startling feature, though, was
neither its size nor its shape; it was the fact that
every surface had become covered in blood-red
overgrowth.

Alpha motioned for them to begin their descent
and they moved forward cautiously. Oddly, it was
the little mammoth who took the lead during the
climb down, while the Morlock remained atop
the rim, apparently to stand some uncharacteristic guard duty. Toward the rear of the column
were Wang and one of the Devil's Brigaders, carrying Sergeant Juliano on a makeshift stretcher.
The color had come back to his face and, despite
the size of his wound, those caring for him had

discovered that a tourniquet was no longer necessary.

Mac had to smile at Dr. Nora Nesbitt's unbridled joy at her new surroundings. The woman had immediately recognized that there were, in every direction, numerous unique life-forms to study, and in all likelihood, undiscovered invertebrates. She bounded down the rocky incline, reminding Mac of an undergraduate on a field study for the very first time.

Yanni motioned toward the other woman. "You'd better send down someone after her," she told Mac.

"Alpha wants us all down there, no?"

"Yeah, but if she breaks her ass or gets eaten by a tree, that's gonna slow us down real fine."

Mac nodded, no less anxious than Nesbitt to examine what Yanni had described as "a sort of forbidden zone for Morlocks." It was a disclosure that also helped explain why Alpha was acting so strangely. Thankfully, others were now assisting the rapidly recovering Sergeant Juliano, and so Mac was able to make his own observations.

He reached the floor of the grotto with little effort and, turning back, he noted that the Morlock was finally making the descent as well—still exhibiting what was clearly a great deal of hesitancy. The big guy's fur had also taken on something of a reddish hue, though MacCready took little notice, especially when he found himself standing in front of what looked like a cactus mimic that stood almost twice his height.

"Tons of iron-loving microbes and fungi," Nesbitt chirped, moving in to stand beside him. She gestured at the "cactus." "Oh, and mold—mostly red mold with, probably, some bacteria."

Mac took a closer look, noticing that what appeared at first glance to be tiny flower heads were actually black and red sporangia—circular structures that both produced and stored the spores, which were the equivalent of seeds.

Can't be too hard on myself for not recognizing them right away, he thought, realizing that these particular sporangia were half an inch in diameter— hundreds of times larger than anything he'd ever seen on a microscope slide.

Mac extended a finger and gently touched one of them.

Nesbitt cringed. "I wouldn't—"

The sporangium made a barely audible pop and suddenly Mac received a face full of red dust.

"*Blah!*" Mac cried, coughing and taking a step back.

"Never mind," Nesbitt said, which Mac translated as, *Stupid zoologist!*

She continued on, excitedly. "The closest thing you've seen to this was probably growing on an old piece of bread."

Just then, Yanni arrived. "Red looks good on you, Mac," she said, without smirking. "But listen, when you're done with your makeup session, Alpha pointed us to a clearing where we can camp for the night." Then she gestured for him to follow—which he did.

"There's also supposed to be a downhill path leading out of here," she said, under her breath.

"And where's that?"

"At the far side of the grotto."

"And?"

"And it'll take us out of this maze without running into any Morlocks. I don't think they'll come within miles of this place. According to Alpha, we just have to keep winding our way south and downhill. Eventually we'll run into civilization— although he didn't really call it that."

"He's turning out to be a lifesaver, that one," Mac said. "Who'd a thunk it?"

"Yeah, well, he *is* acting kinda weird though," Yanni said, unable to hide her concern. "And these red spores are getting all over his fur. You'll see what I mean."

The others were already starting to prepare for nightfall by the time Mac, Yanni, and Nesbitt rejoined them. Because they did not want to attract unwanted guests of any species, thoughts of a fire had been quickly nixed, so they simply arranged themselves in a rough circle and laid out whatever they could to act as bedding. The temperature in the grotto was nearly tropical compared to what they'd been through, and several of the Devil's Brigaders had already taken off their parkas to use as pillows or blankets.

Yanni gestured toward Alpha, who remained as far away from the humans as he could manage. The Morlock was squatting, and looking rather sphinxlike, with eyes closed. Even in the rapidly diminishing light, Mac could see that Yanni had been right—the Morlock's fur seemed to attract the red spores, in much the same way a magnet attracted iron shavings.

"What, you figured he'd be joining us for poker tonight?" Mac asked, trying to lighten the situation. "Guns, remember?"

"That ain't it, Mac," Yanni said, looking even more worried than before. "There's something wrong with him."

Though Mac silently agreed with her, his attention was soon drawn to the little mammoth, whose behavior was the exact opposite of the Alpha's. Currently, Dumbo (Mac's nickname having definitely caught on) was getting his ears stroked by Wang. An additional positive note was the fact that a rather comfortable-looking Sergeant Juliano, currently reclining against a scarlet boulder, was assisting the Chinese zoologist.

Within a few minutes, Mac too had settled in, and soon he was asleep.

The Red Grotto, Cerae/Morlock Forbidden Zone
AUGUST 5, 1946

D r. Nora Nesbitt awoke at dawn as something lightly touched her face then flitted away.

Sitting upright, she rubbed her eyes and peered around the makeshift camp. There were snores and some sleepy shuffling about, but apparently no one else was awake.

Nesbitt turned her attention to what had awakened her—what appeared to be a swirl of red dandelion seeds. These, though, were efficient fliers, moving upward and changing direction with nothing like a breeze to propel them.

Like insects, she thought, *but different.*

Rising slowly, she decided to follow them.

Jack opened his eyes and stared up at the brightening sky. He wondered how on earth he'd come to such an amazing and terrifying place.

The answer, of course, was his friend R. J. MacCready. And so despite an ever-growing, personal laundry list of ailments—ranging from what he hoped was *only* malaria, to a spine that was becoming the new definition of "completely fucked"—the naval reserve officer hadn't given even a second thought to turning down this rescue mission. Always sickly and rail thin, Jack had long ago come to believe that his time on this planet might be relatively brief. Because of this he'd resolved to live whatever time he might be granted in as full a fashion as possible—and to accomplish something important before he died.

He had no way of knowing or even suspecting that something red and foreign to modern human experience was working its way deep into his tissues, in much the same manner as the microbe with which Yanni had infected Juliano the day before. He would never have believed, on this morning, that instead of death, decades of gradual (albeit painful) healing lay before him.

Below, on the grotto floor, Nesbitt trailed the scarlet swirl—which she'd now determined to contain scores of tiny creatures. They moved like a vapor around rocks and foliage, and she followed them, making mental notes on their behavior, until at last they came to a door-sized opening in one of the sloping walls surrounding the grotto. Then, seeming to hesitate for a second or two, the living cloud dispersed, flying off in separate directions and leaving the puzzled biologist staring into the pitch-black crevice. Nesbitt moved a bit closer and squinted into the dark. She could see that the crevice was actually more like a tunnel, leading a short way into the rock wall before ending in an expanse of light perhaps twenty yards farther down.

The sensible part of Nesbitt's brain, which was usually quite considerable, told her to head back and tell the others. But there was something else, something she could not quite define, and it told her to explore the opening herself—and especially what might lay beyond it.

Before entering the miniature cave, Nesbitt grabbed the closest thing to a branch she could find. Invertebrate lover or not, she had a fear of spiders that was as strong as it was well hidden. She frowned at the flimsy-looking excuse for a stick, which would now serve to clear her way through the tunnel.

"Fuckers beware," she announced to the shadows. Then she ducked into the opening.

Jack sat up, just in time to see the furry little elephant disappearing into a thick growth of mold or fungus or whatever the hell the scientist types were calling it. To the former pampered kid from Massachusetts, who had been turned by circumstances beyond his control into a war hero, everything about this place was just plain weird. Still, he rose quietly, as something about the animal's stealthy departure compelled him to follow it into the undergrowth.

Nora Nesbitt emerged from the short and thankfully spider-free tunnel waving an ersatz twig she'd determined to be a new species of club moss. She planned to add a small piece of it to the specimens she'd already accumulated. Although the biologist hadn't told anyone yet, she intended to carry the collection out when they left the grotto. But what Nesbitt saw upon emerging into the light caused her to drop the moss sample without a thought. The little subchamber was even more thickly carpeted in red than the grotto above.

A half-dozen mold-covered, statue-like figures were arrayed across the ground of what looked like an open-ceilinged chamber. Her first thought was that they resembled the huge primates Mac-Cready and his friends had been calling Morlocks. But these individuals differed from the hulking creatures she'd already seen—*thinner and somehow more graceful*, she thought. *And exactly like the ones described in Pliny's codex.* The biologist approached the closest of the figures—which, like most of the others, seemed to be sitting on its haunches. The head was almost at the level of her chest, and its face was directed toward the tunnel from which she had just exited.

Nesbitt knelt down and brushed an index finger over what appeared to be a thin layer of red mold. She hoped to scrape away a portion of the stuff to reveal the layer beneath. But the mold, which had a fleshlike consistency, would not budge.

"It's fused to whatever's below it," she said to herself. "Shit, these things are *old*."

A rustle of what sounded like parchment from behind her caused the scientist to jump, but when she turned around there was nothing.

Nesbitt stood, took another glance at the tunnel exit, then crept deeper among the cluster of figures. She noted that four of them, like the one she had just examined, more resembled Pliny's drawings than the alpha Morlock, while the farthest arrangement—a pair of individuals—suggested something very different. Curiosity drew her closer to this particular grouping.

"This can't be!" Nesbitt said, the sound of her words amplified by the proximity of the chamber walls.

One of the figures was neither Plinean Cerae nor MacCready Morlock. The scientist moved in for an even closer look. It was clearly a Roman officer.

Nesbitt uttered a name that had not been spoken here for nearly two thousand years.

"Severus."

R. J. MacCready knew that something was very wrong the moment he noticed that Jack, Nesbitt, and the little mammoth were all missing.

He woke the others and within thirty seconds the clearing made an abrupt transition from peaceful to chaotic as sidearms were strapped on and hasty plans formulated to divvy up the search for the improbable trio.

It's definitely Severus and Teacher," Nesbitt told herself, only half-believing her own words. "And they're certainly not statues—they're mummies!"

Through the layer of red mold, it was clear that someone or something had arranged the bodies of the unlikely pair, so well documented by Pliny, into an embrace that had lasted two millennia.

Nesbitt moved in to examine the centurion's up-turned face, which held an undeniable expression of calm. Then her gaze turned toward the famous Ceran teacher, whose long, graceful arms were wrapped protectively around her pheromone-addicted captive.

"So it was true," she spoke to Teacher. "What the codex said about you was true."

Nesbitt turned back toward the face of the man Pliny had trusted, then hated, then finally come to forgive. She gave a start and took a reflexive step backward. The centurion's head seemed to have moved, ever so slightly. No, not merely *seemed* to have moved; he was definitely turning toward her in ultra-slow motion—at the rate a thin line of mercury would rise in a thermometer if she were to hold the glass bulb between two warm fingers.

"*Oh my God!*" Nesbitt cried, stepping in closer to Pliny's centurion. "*You're alive!*" Now she looked at the Ceran, lifting her head slowly toward her. "*Both of you!*"

The biologist suddenly understood more clearly than those who were pulling Hendry's strings the implications of what Pliny had found. And, since the Roman had never documented this particular phenomenon, she was the only one who knew. Nesbitt understood, better than even MacCready, what the real fuss would inevitably be, *if word of this ever gets out.*

Nesbitt looked Severus in the eyes, then reached out and touched one of Teacher's hands. It appeared to her that their cells and tissues—human and Morlock alike—had been replaced by or perhaps infused with and redesigned by the strange red mold. *The ultimate in symbiotic relationships*, she thought. *This one between* three *species.*

"You're immortal, aren't you?" Nesbitt asked the pair. Now stroking the physician's hand, she addressed the creature, whose face continued to turn, almost imperceptibly, in her direction. "And you and your kind figured this all out nearly two thousand years ago. Amazing."

Nora Nesbitt smiled and secured her grip on the Ceran's elongated index finger. Then, with some effort, she twisted it off.

Jack had watched the furry elephant with the strange legs and even stranger bifurcated trunk as it sniffed the air around a breach in the rocky wall. It did the same thing to the shadow-filled opening itself. Then, without hesitating, the little mammoth uttered an unnervingly human cry and ran into the dark.

From the other side, someone screamed. Jack ducked into the tunnel and scrambled toward the light. Emerging, he saw something wildly incongruous, the little mammoth—enraged and circling Nora, having already knocked its prey off her feet. The creature seemed ready to charge again and Nora let out another yell, whether in fear, in an effort to scare off the animal, or both, Jack could not tell. But instead of goring or trampling the scientist, it approached slowly, pausing several feet from where she had been standing, next to what looked to Jack vaguely like a statue. The animal's eyes were wide with anger and it bellowed loudly, holding out both of its trunks toward the terrified biologist.

Jack had drawn his Colt but determined that Nora was in the line of fire. Positioning himself for a safe angle, he began a careful crab walk along the red-slicked boulders, slipped, tried to regain his footing, and discovered immediately that he could not. Instead, he redirected all of his forward momentum to a shoulder slam into the pony-sized mammoth's side. The elephant emitted an audible *oofff* and, within the very same instant of that utterance, pivoted toward his attacker. Wrapping both of his trunks around Jack's abdomen, the

mini-pachyderm flung him aside with ease. Then
the mammoth turned its attention back again toward Nesbitt, who had used the momentary diver-
sion to make a dash for the tunnel. The enraged
elephant tore after her, kicking up clouds of red
mold and soil as it charged.

R. J. MacCready appeared at the tunnel opening just in time to see Dr. Nora Nesbitt fall to
the ground five feet from where he stood, the little mammoth seemingly hell-bent on trampling
her to death. Mac drew a bead on a spot to the
rear and just below the animal's front shoulder,
then fired off three shots—the roar of the Colt .45
magnified by the confined quarters.

The little elephant spun sideways and crashed
into the grotto floor headfirst, two feet from the
cowering Nesbitt. The animal's breath was a raspy
gurgle. Its legs kicked ineffectively, scraping fur-
rows in the ground, now wet from a heart-driven
pulsation of arterial blood.

On the other side of the enclosure, Jack was
struggling to stand. Observing that the Bostonian
was still in one piece, Mac knelt down beside the
traumatized biologist. He could hear Yanni's voice
now, coming down through the tunnel and calling
his name.

Nora Nesbitt glanced back at the fallen mammoth before looking into the face of her rescuer.
"Thank you, Captain," she said.

But R. J. MacCready was not in the mood for
gratitude, having just been forced to kill a sentient creature that had saved his life on multiple
occasions.

"Would you mind telling me what the fuck just happened?" he snarled.

He hasn't moved an inch, Mac," Yanni said, as they stood beside the giant Morlock they had come to call Alpha.

His pose reminded them both of what were apparently five of Alpha's ancient relatives, housed in a chamber that also held a Roman centurion.

"I don't know what got into him," a sorrowful MacCready had told Yanni earlier. "Nesbitt says she wandered in there chasing what were probably cousins of those snowflake mimics, found what she *thought* were weird statues, and got attacked."

They'd both had some time to think about what happened and now, as the others prepared to move out, Yanni's anger about the shooting of the little mammoth continued to seethe, just below the surface and barely contained. She did not know if she would ever be able to fully forgive Mac. For the moment, though, the two friends came together and stood beside Alpha.

Yanni broke the uneasy silence and spoke softly. "So, this Nesbitt, you believe her?"

"Jack pretty much backed up her whole story."

"Do you think *he* knows what's really in there? That those aren't statues?"

"No," Mac replied. "Although to tell you the truth I have no clue about what's going on with those figures. Do you?"

"Pliny's secret to life itself, I'd say."

Mac shook his head. "Hell, if it is, I say we leave this part out."

Yanni turned her attention to Alpha and nodded slowly. The Morlock had not only gone silent; its entire body was now covered in a layer of red mold that seethed and undulated, appearing (if that were possible) to take complete possession of the giant.

Mac glanced around to make sure there was nobody within earshot. "Look, Yanni, even if Alpha *could* leave—"

"—and judging by those living statues, I'd say that's a long shot."

Mac nodded. "Granted, but I don't think he would anyway. He'd never risk spreading this shit to his kind. It's why he brought us here. He knew the other Morlocks would never risk contaminating themselves."

"And it's also the reason he wouldn't touch us," Yanni added, crestfallen. "He knew we'd eventually be coming here and didn't want his scent on us—or we'd end up like him."

Captain Pederson's arrival curtailed any further conversation. "You two ready to move out?"

R. J. MacCready reached a hand out to Yanni but she looked down at his holstered sidearm and shook her head. Mac gave a last glance back toward the place where the little mammoth lay and said, "Let's get the hell out of here."

Something Wicked This Way Comes

> *There are known knowns; these are things we
> know that we know. We also know that there
> are known unknowns; that is to say, there
> are things that we know we don't know. But
> there are also unknown unknowns—the ones
> we don't know we don't know.*
>
> —DONALD RUMSFELD (PARAPHRASING THE
> 1955 "JOHARI WINDOW")

> *There's another possibility: the unknown
> knowns—which [are] the things we know,
> and then we choose not to know them or
> not let other people know we know.*
>
> —STEPHEN COLBERT (TO RUMSFELD, 2016)

> *I find the lure of the unknown irresistible.*
>
> —SYLVIA EARLE

*Metropolitan Museum of Natural History
New York
September 22, 1946*

Major Patrick Hendry entered Charles Knight's office and found it rather crowded. It was clear to him that the old artist, R. J. MacCready, Yanni, and Patricia Wynters had been deep in conversation before he walked in. The trio was admiring Knight's latest work—a portrait.

"What do you think?" Mac said, holding the painting out toward the major.

Hendry nodded at the familiar face of his friend—now deceased.

"Mac's gonna put it right next to Bob's."

"That's a great place for it, Yanni," Hendry replied. Finding himself on the verge of an uncomfortable emotion, he turned toward the artist. "You got a real future in this painting business there, Chuck," Hendry said. "If you keep working at it."

Charles Knight replied with a grunt he typically reserved for conversations with the major.

Hendry was just about to place a box down on a small empty table when a panicked look from the artist stopped him. "Don't put it there!" Knight cried.

Hendry looked down. "Hey, nice theremin," he said.

"And don't touch this one!" Knight shot back.

"Okay, okay, I gotcha," Hendry said, deciding to hold on to the box. Then he changed gears. "Well, I'm glad you're all here."

"Why's that?" Mac asked.

"First things first," the major continued. "Each of you take some of these."

Four quizzical faces stared back at him.

"They're from Jack," Hendry said, tilting the

open box toward them. "He says he wants you to spread 'em around."

"What the hell is this?" Mac replied, picking up one of the red, white, and blue bumper stickers and a matching pin.

"Your boy's running for Congress!" Hendry announced.

"Yeah, but not in this state," Yanni said, examining one of the buttons.

"How is Jack, anyway?" Mac asked.

"Thanks to your little adventure," Hendry said, "his back was completely screwed. Now, though, he says it's been gettin' a lot better."

Knight chimed in. "Yeah, I hear he's screwing three"—he glanced at Yanni and Patricia—"beautiful Tiffany lamps together."

Patricia laughed. "I've seen pictures of him with some of those lamps."

"Bad back, huh?" MacCready replied. "Anything I can do to help?"

Yanni shot him a dirty look as she attached a campaign button to her blouse.

"Guy's got an interesting future ahead of him," Hendry said, before turning to Knight and Wynters. "Okay, enough about our boy. By my calendar you guys are still on the payroll. So what else have you come up with?"

"Well," Patricia replied, "we finished with the last bits of Pliny's Omega codex."

"And by bits, she *means* bits," Knight said, pouring an envelope full of dust and fragments onto a metal specimen tray. "Most of this stuff was disintegrating before it ever got here," he lied.

Hendry continued. "I suppose all that business about how the Cerans molded life like clay got destroyed, too?"

"Funny," Patricia said, "it turned out to be the most fragile part of the codex."

Hendry gave Knight a knowing nod. "That's . . . um . . . terribly unfortunate," he said, trying his best to sound official.

Never suspecting that Hendry might really have been on their side all along, Knight and Patricia each raised an eyebrow—to Hendry's amusement.

"Did your boys from D.C. photograph those last codex sections?" Wynters asked.

"Hmmm . . . I'd have to check," Hendry replied, a response that Mac would doubtless translate into *Hendry never has to check anything. He's hidden or destroyed some of those negatives.*

The major turned to Mac and Yanni. "All right, final time I'm gonna ask this."

"Go on," came the simultaneous reply.

"Was Pliny's 'molding life' stuff still there and is there any way that it came out with any of you?"

"No, the red grotto was only death, and the stuff you're talking? It was back in that valley—if it existed at all."

"And?"

"And Yanni and I were the only ones who ever got in and out of there alive."

"So what's your assessment?"

"Never saw them doing anything like Pliny describes," said Yanni.

Clearly unable to completely trust Hendry,

Wynters said, convincingly, "We know environments in isolation often produce some strange evolutionary quirks."

Hendry shot her a skeptical look. "Like carnivorous grass, angry snowflakes, angrier Morlocks?"

"Look around this planet hard enough, Major," Knight added, "and you'll probably find even stranger examples."

Normally, Major Hendry would have challenged the pair, but he knew that this was anything but a normal conversation. It was more like a dance.

Mac nodded. "So, officially, we're assessing the key feature of Pliny's Omega codex as a naturally occurring evolutionary phenomenon, expanded into a fairy tale."

"And I'm guessin'," Yanni said, "with the Russians and Chinese suddenly having other things to worry about—"

"—like each other." Hendry completed the thought.

Mac grimaced and continued. "Because of that, I think we can keep a lid on this for a while longer."

"A couple of years if we're lucky," Yanni added. "Then somebody's gonna go back in there."

For several seconds there was silence, as they each pondered that particular problem.

"Well, at least that gives us some time to think this through," Mac said, resting Jerry's portrait on the theremin.

"Okay, now that that's settled," the major continued.

"For now," Yanni countered, stopping herself from saying anything more. She and Mac both knew—*we've stopped it for now, but this is far from over.*

"One way or another," Mac had told her earlier, "it's going to come back. Pliny's microbes—wildly adaptable and with numbers on their side."

Yanni also realized that, once again, wherever the road had divided into right decisions and wrong decisions, they had made the best available choice. Yet, once again, every path they had taken seemed, on some level, to have made matters worse.

"For now," Yanni emphasized again, with as much confidence as she could muster, "it *is* settled."

"All right, *for now,*" Hendry acquiesced. "What *else* did you figure out?"

It was Wynters who replied. "Apparently, our Roman friends stuck around in Tibet for quite a while—a couple years in fact."

"Though you'd never know it from reading Pliny's *Natural History,*" Knight added. "He covered up those missing years pretty well."

"Anything else?" Hendry asked them.

"Yeah," Knight continued. "Eventually Pliny and his Nubian friend made their way home. And we *know* what happened there."

"What about the other guy, the centurion?"

"We think Severus stayed behind," Wynters said.

Mac and Yanni exchanged brief but knowing glances, simultaneously sharing a thought. *He definitely stayed behind.*

Knight cleared his throat. "Now, Major, I've got a few questions for you."

"Go ahead," Hendry said, crossing his arms.

"So where exactly did they find this codex?"

"Herculaneum, if you want to be precise," Hendry snapped, then checked his watch. "And before you ask your last question, we found it in a cylinder made of some metal—it's probably some new alloy. God only knows why he wrote the damned thing up in the first place."

"He had to," Knight guessed aloud. "In his own way, the guy was an artist."

"Well, artist or not," Hendry said, "someone buried his codex months or maybe even years before the eruption. Buried it deep."

"And then deeper still, I imagine, *after* the eruption," Mac added.

"About sixty feet deeper than Pliny had planned," Hendry said, before turning back to Knight and Wynters. "You two finished with Twenty Questions?"

"Two questions," Knight replied, oblivious to the game show reference. "But for now . . . yeah."

Mac, however, wasn't quite done. "What happened to Tse-lin? He still in custody overseas?"

"For the moment," Hendry replied. "With all he knows, we couldn't let him go back to China now, could we?"

"Right," Mac agreed, "and then there's all that contact he had with us Americans. If he *did* go back home, he could be arrested or worse for less than that."

"Especially now," Hendry replied, "with the little war you guys almost started."

Mac shrugged.

"Yeah, yeah, I know," Hendry continued. "It's not like you sicced that Russian chopper and those two Chinese choppers on each other, right?"

R. J. MacCready summoned his best *Who me?* expression.

On the other side of the room, Yanni bit her lip, understanding that this was another of the details Mac had decided to keep from Hendry—to protect them all from an incident that was already widening the rift between China and the Soviets.

Yanni decided to change the subject. "So about Wang Tse-lin?"

Hendry held up his hand, then spoke slowly. "Everything's been arranged." The major shot a wry smile at four faces wearing the same expression of anticipation. He waited a beat, apparently to savor the moment, and then went on. "You can use a new vertebrate zoologist here, right? Especially one who's familiar with a part of Asia we might have trouble visiting ourselves?"

"Sure we can!" Yanni answered, not bothering to check with the three people who actually worked at the museum.

MacCready was momentarily relieved with the news about the Chinese scientist, but his look quickly returned to one of concern. "So, Pat, what about those Devil's Brigade guys? They saw the Morlocks, or the Yeti or whatever you want to call them. What if *they* say something?"

"I've got that covered, too, Mac," Hendry said. "Anyone who mentions your hairy pals—either species—will get the same treatment that those Night Fighter flyboys from the 415th got when they started chirping about their so-called 'fucking foo-fighters.'"

Now the nonmilitary types in the room shot the two Army guys a trio of quizzical looks.

"Unidentified flying objects they're calling 'em," Mac explained. "In this case, glowing round objects that some of our pilots have claimed to see following their planes around."

Hendry continued. "The bottom line is that everyone considers these guys to be laughingstocks now, and that's exactly what the Devil's Brigaders will face if they start flappin' their lips about fuzzy giants."

"Well, that's sort of a relief," Yanni said. "I guess."

Major Hendry, though, was clearly not finished with the topic and Yanni's halfhearted response served as a reminder. "What about our other problem?" he asked. "Your Dr. Nesbitt?"

The three museum workers exchanged uneasy looks, before Patricia Wynters spoke up, presumably because it had been *her* idea to bring the invertebrate biologist into the project.

"Ummm . . . well . . . as you know, Nora left the museum a few weeks ago," she said. "Rather abruptly."

"She get fired?" Hendry asked.

"No." Wynters hesitated. "She took another job—at a lab."

Hendry was suddenly paying a lot more attention to the conversation, and there was no way he could have missed MacCready wincing. "Where?"

Mac stepped in. "A small lab that nobody seems to know anything about."

"Something about a fruit," Knight added. "Peach Island I think it was."

"Well, that's not very reassuring," Hendry replied. "I'll see what I can do."

Mac nodded a thanks.

"One last question," Hendry said, and this one he directed at Yanni. "Your little elephants, did you get to chat them up like you did with that pair in Central Park?"

"As a matter of fact, I did," she responded. "One in particular."

"And how'd that work out?"

"Badly," she said. "But I'm not ready to talk about it yet." Yanni shot a quick glance at Mac, who was looking downcast. "But there was nothing anyone could have done," she added.

"So how smart do you really think they were?" Hendry asked.

Yanni paused for a moment. "As I've said, maybe smarter than humans," she replied, "and definitely more kind."

Hendry chuckled, then started to head for the door. "Well, personally, I'm glad I missed 'em then."

"Why's that?" Yanni asked.

"If they *are* smarter than us," Hendry said, "maybe they'll be running the show someday. And

I'd hate to wake up one morning and find humans depending on the humanity of elephants."

"Could be worse," Mac said, almost to himself.

"Could be a lot worse," Yanni said. Then she quietly took Mac's hand.

On that same afternoon, beneath the snows of Tibet, and in a way that neither the Morlocks nor the humans had ever anticipated, the little white mammoths launched a sudden revolt. It was as ruthlessly brutal as it was competent and when it was over the mammoths had displayed more human behaviors than even Yanni could have imagined.

Herculaneum Harbor
Just after midnight

AUGUST 25, A.D. 79

Finally, the architect thought, *the last of the boats have been launched.*

Pliny's Nubian friend had spent the better part of the night at the docks, comforting concerned parents and their children, and assisting them into an array of small craft he and a few friends had hauled out from beneath the stone arches of the city's marina. When the eruption began, many had refused to enter the boats. The giant mushroom cloud of black smoke was so distant that most people believed it safer to remain ashore than to set sail onto increasingly turbulent waters. Proculus ordered his artisans and slaves into the first boat—"As an example for others to follow, *and only as a precaution*," he lied. "You'll probably be home for dinner."

Many of those who had either chosen to stay behind or failed to find room in a boat were now huddled beneath the marina's arches. Each vaulted chamber was a storage room that served primarily as a drydock for an assortment of fishing boats. The arches and chamber ceilings formed the foundations of the city's waterfront buildings—a neighborhood that normally offered stunning views across the Bay of Neapolis.

Now though, the sights and sounds were of a far more frightening nature. The mountain, Vesuvio, had been rumbling for fourteen hours. And though the skies above Herculaneum were still crystal clear and full of stars, Pompeii to the east was now invisible, as were the entire eastern horizon and the stars above it. They were blotted out by an inky black cloud that had risen from the mountain—a cloud rent by forked and quivering bursts of flame, like flashes of lightning magnified a hundredfold. The constant rumbling roar was frequently joined by muffled cracking sounds, and each of these was followed by a growing chorus of moans and cries from those assembled along the shoreline or hiding below the arches.

The Roman stood on the beach in front of the marina, glancing out across the bay. His flag signals requesting more ships to aid in the evacuation had been answered almost immediately—the first from his old friend Pliny. But that had been more than thirteen hours ago and as of yet the architect had spotted no sails—*at least none headed in this direction*, he thought.

What Proculus would never know was that the admiral had set out with a small fleet many hours earlier. To their horror, the sailors found their way blocked by a massive island of floating pumice. But while others turned back or took off in new directions, Pliny continued to steer east, trying to find some way to reach his friend and evacuate anyone with him who needed rescuing. Finally, after a dense rain of walnut-sized rocks began to pelt his vessel, the heartbroken Pliny was forced to turn his ship toward the Isle of Capri.

Proculus now had one eye on the horizon and the other on two carpenters who were attempting to patch the bottom of an old wreck they'd dragged out in desperation.

He tried to stay cheerful, attempting to joke with the children of parents whose only concern seemed to be whether there would be a place for them on the small craft—if it were ever made seaworthy. Rendering everyone's task more difficult was the near-constant shifting of the ground beneath their feet.

Remarkably, those who had settled in under the stone arches, filled only hours earlier by boats, were calm now. Parents were sitting in a circle, with their children sleeping in the middle. Some of them Proculus knew; others were refugees from the direction of Pompeii, stopping here because they were exhausted, or being slowed in their progress by small children. Several women were obviously pregnant and had taken shelter here when they could walk no farther. Their footprints would still be present in the sand two thousand years later.

On the beach, a Roman soldier joined the crowd on horseback. Proculus threw the man a salute and beckoned him to come nearer. He would be a useful pair of hands for either the boat repair efforts or perhaps crowd control, once the last boat was ready to be launched.

"Give us a hand, soldier!" Proculus called to the man. "There's water for your horse and I could certainly use your assistance."

The soldier, though, did not respond. Instead he turned to look toward the volcano, then spurred his horse onward, moving with the flow of refugees.

"*Cowardly dog!*" Proculus yelled, and thought about running after the man.

But now a new sound reached him, like the crash of one mountain upon another—loud enough to hurt his ears despite being muffled and distorted by the dust cloud. Turning in the direction of the commotion, Proculus beheld a fiery red sun—wider than Vesuvio itself, shining out through the columns of black dust and falling to earth at incomparable speed.

The sight of it was absolutely horrifying, making his next thought as perplexing as it was incongruous—given the realization that whole towns beneath the new sun were dying. *Jove, forgive me. It is the most beautiful thing I have ever seen.*

The mixture of gas and lava mist burned hotter than iron emerging white from a furnace. From the moment it crashed down upon the volcano's sides, it flowed like liquid down the mountain's southern flanks and over the contours of the land—taller than any tidal wave ever recorded by history, and five times as fast. It brightened as it approached, blazing like uncountable millions of stars coming to life, and Proculus could feel their collective radiance against his face.

The disobedient soldier clearly felt it, too, and reining his horse into a tight turn he ran it at full gallop toward one of the arched shelters, giving apparently no thought at all to the people he was about to trample inside.

"*Stop, coward! Stop!*" Proculus yelled.

His command counted for nothing.

The cedar forest north of Herculaneum was being plowed up by a mighty precursor wave of compressed air, clearing a path for the fiery tidal wave. The tallest trees in the empire were snapped above the roots and flung many times their height. They turned slowly and gracefully, end over end as they flew toward the city. The radiance from the wave was so great that each cartwheeling tree was bursting into flames before it.

Proculus would never know that when death came, its touch would last no more than one two-hundredth of a second. Nor would he have cared. During the last moments of his life, he turned once more to face the sea—now illuminated out to the horizon and growing brighter.

With every instant that remained, he searched the great bay—praying *not* to see the sails of Pliny's boats approaching. His prayer answered, Proculus felt relief.

Then he disappeared into history.

Fin

Reality Check

Although the time frames in our novel shift between 1946 and the first century A.D., the tale serves as a fable for tomorrow—in particular, the danger of racially tagged biological weapons. Since 1945, the question has been whether our electronic civilization will survive its nuclear adolescence. As we learn how to read and edit the code of life itself, the genetic frontier looms ahead as another yin and yang, with great promise and great peril. As we write, curing cancer (the Black Plague of the past century) is almost within reach. Racial tagging (and even a person-specific weapon) also represents a looming reality.

What else in this tale is real, or blurs the lines between reality and fable?

To begin, some of the people:

Charles R. Knight (1874–1953) appears throughout as himself. He was arguably the greatest artist of prehistoric life who ever lived. Long before special effects mavens Willis O'Brian (*King*

Kong, Mighty Joe Young) and Ray Harryhausen (*Seventh Voyage of Sinbad, Mysterious Island*, and so on), put flesh on an array of creatures no human had ever seen, Knight was already bringing multiple lost worlds alive through his paintings. No one was more influential in stimulating the public's still-growing fascination with dinosaurs than Knight, who (as depicted in our novel) was born in Brooklyn and whose paintings and murals hang prominently in natural history museums across the country. For an amazing look at Knight's life and art, readers should turn to *The Artist Who Saw Through Time*, by Richard Milner.

Knight's granddaughter, Rhoda Knight Kalt, who makes a brief appearance while Wynters and Nesbitt are discussing guinea worms, is a real person. As a child, Rhoda frequently toured the American Museum of Natural History with her beloved grandfather, whom she called "Toppy." As an adult, no one has done more than Rhoda to perpetuate the legacy of Charles R. Knight.

Bernard Herrmann (1911–1975) was one of history's great composers. Born Max Herman in New York City, he wrote the musical scores for some of the classic films of the twentieth century, directed by the likes of Alfred Hitchcock, François Truffaut, Orson Wells, Robert Wise, and Fred Zinnemann. Herrmann, who studied at the Juilliard School of Music and New York University, began his career as a conductor. He won his only Oscar in 1941 for *The Devil and Daniel Webster*, a fact that is a little perplexing when one considers that his groundbreaking musical scores for films like *North by Northwest*, *Vertigo*, *Psycho*, and *The Day the Earth Stood Still* were never even nominated. Bernard Herrmann also worked extensively on television, where he composed some of the medium's most highly recognizable music, the themes for *The Twilight Zone* and *The Alfred Hitchcock Hour*. Herrmann died unexpectedly, not long after finishing the score for Martin Scorsese's *Taxi Driver* (for which he picked up a posthumous Oscar nomination).

Alfred Hitchcock (1899–1980) was one of the greatest movie directors of all time. As depicted in chapter 7, composer Miklós Róza used a theremin in Hitchcock's hallucinatory classic, *Spellbound* (1945). Hitchcock famously paired with composer Bernard Herrmann, whose first meeting we have fictionalized. Their collaborations produced some of their most famous works. Herrmann also wrote the scores for Hitchcock's *The Trouble with Harry* (1955), *The Man Who Knew Too Much* (1956), *The Wrong Man* (1956), and *Marnie* (1964). Hitchcock did not use a musical soundtrack for his classic *The Birds* (1963) but Bernard Herrmann acted as consultant on the creation of the electronically produced bird sounds, heard throughout the film. Their relationship came to an abrupt end during Herrmann's scoring of *Torn Curtain* (1966). Reportedly, studio producers wanted a more pop- and jazz-influenced score, which Herrmann refused to deliver. Nor would he provide a suitable title tune for Paul Newman's costar, Julie Andrews, to sing. As a result, Herrmann's score was bumped from the film and John Addison was approached to write a new one. Despite the stellar cast, *Torn Curtain* became one of Hitchcock's worst-reviewed films (reportedly Newman's Method actor style led to clashes with the director). The director and composer never spoke again. In what was perhaps an even more inexplicable snub than that inflicted upon Bernard Herrmann, Alfred Hitchcock never won the Academy Award for Best Director, although he was nominated five times.

The theremin is an early electronic musical instrument, designed about 1920 by Russian inventor Léon Theremin (born Lev Termen). Originally known as an etherophone, his device is the only musical instrument played without touching it. Its unique sound (once described as a cello lost in the fog and crying for help) results from two metal antennae attached to the wooden body of the instrument—which resembles an old radio receiver. One antenna is a straight vertical rod, usually situated on the right side (for right-handed players), and the other is a horizontal loop that extends out from the left side of the console. The antennae generate an electromagnetic field that extends about four feet around the device and the thereminist (necessitating that the instrument be separated from the rest of his orchestra). As the thereminist places his or her right hand closer to the pitch antenna, the pitch rises, while moving the left hand closer to the volume antenna causes the volume to decrease. These electrical signals, which vary as the thereminist moves his or her hands and fingers within the electric field, are amplified and sent to a loudspeaker. Generally typecast as a means to produce eerie or spooky sounds, the theremin played a major role in the soundtracks of *Spellbound*, *The Thing (From Another World)*—and Tim Burton's comedic tragedy *Ed Wood* (with Lydia Kavina as thereminist).

Léon Theremin happened to be working on a proximity detector for the Soviets when he developed the idea for electronic music. He also invented a miniature eavesdropping device for the NKVD (which preceded the KGB). One such listening device (aka "the Thing") was embedded in a carved wooden version of the Great Seal of the United States and presented to the U.S. ambassador to the Soviet Union in 1945. It hung in his Moscow residence for seven years until it was discovered by accident (an accident of the Major Hendry kind). We have taken a little creative license in putting Theremin's two most famous inventions together. Léon Theremin as master spy, however, is not fiction.

Pliny the Elder really did exist, really did travel the world as an explorer and writer, and was known for his extraordinary appetite for work. Many of his writings have survived because his nephew, Pliny the Younger, pleaded mercy for the early Christians during a time of political and social upheaval that ultimately eroded, from within, a civilization that was able to control water and steam, and was actually building multiple gearshift devices, at the time it began to fall. During the Dark Ages, Christian monks looked kindly upon the Plinys, copying and preserving many of their writings.

When depicted in fiction, Pliny the Elder has typically (and wrongly) been written as a buffoonish, decadent character. We have taken it as an honor, in this novel, to depict him in a manner more consistent with his writings, and what his nephew and others of his contemporaries wrote about him. We hope we have come closer to the real man, and how he would have reacted if thrust into the lost world of the Cerae.

From the writings that survive (notably his thirty-seven-volume *Naturalis Historia*), history has learned the legends of other lands, as told to Pliny the Elder during his travels. He was, for example, the explorer who gave the world its only detailed account of the strange celibate Essene cult, as related to him by another traveler, about the people who hid the library known as the Dead Sea Scrolls. Historians and naturalists still argue about the extraordinary animals he described from many lands—"what was merely the mythology of some distant tribe, what was real?"

Even his death was extraordinary. The last words attributed to him in this novel were actually spoken by him, as recorded by his nephew in letters to his friend Tacitus—the full content of which can be read in Haraldur Sigurdsson's excellent book about the eruption that buried Pompeii, *Melting the Earth* (Oxford University Press, 1999).

As we depicted, early during the second day of the increasingly violent eruption of Mount Vesuvius, Pliny the Younger was reportedly discovered by a friend to be behaving in a strange manner at his uncle's estate. In his letters to Tacitus, Pliny the Younger mentions that this friend found his insistence on reading history and finishing an assignment from his uncle as quite odd. He never explained this obsession with his uncle's papers, while two whole cities died within his view. In chapter 24, we provided a dramatized explanation for the famous Roman's true and inexplicable behavior.

The Roman cavalryman whose skeleton was found at the marina of Pompeii's sister city Herculaneum has, like Pliny the Elder, been maligned by modern, speculative history. Some fanciful "reconstructions" depict him as a hardened thief who at the last minute had a softer heart than indicated by his rugged features.

We have named him Proculus and, though he is the product of abstract fantasy, the skeleton of a man much like him actually was found, with the healed wounds we have described. He died under the physical conditions we have described, at the time and place we have described, with a gold inlaid silver scabbard for his sword.

In 2015, the Smithsonian Channel's *Mummies Alive* series focused on gold and silver coins in Specimen E26's side "pocket," and on his fine tools, asking, though he appeared to have died in the act of rescue, "Was he a hero or a villain?"

The "thief/villain" speculation is based on a self-perpetuating dogma that Roman soldiers were poor and unskilled and, because this man was apparently wealthy, he must therefore have been looting as the fires of Vesuvius approached. In reality, his finely crafted sword spoke of success within the ranks, and within his extramilitary career. In accordance with historical writings reaching back to the time of Emperor Augustus (including Pliny the Elder, *Naturalis Historia*, 2.93–94), there was much skill, education, and even wealth among the ranks, including Pliny the Elder himself—who, in reality as in this tale, was an admiral at the time of his death, and really did sail off toward the eruption that buried Pompeii and Herculaneum, on an ill-fated mission of rescue.

Pliny the Elder did indeed record legends about strange wildlife in lost worlds, sometimes so fantastical that they must generally be regarded as the mythology of distant lands, or misunderstood descriptions of animals (like orangutans) known to biologists today.

The civilization we have called the Cerae are a fictional people, but Pliny did record in his earlier volume, *Natural History* (chapter 24: "Taprobane"), the fragmentary legends of a people with whom we have set out to make our own cautionary mythology resonate. Sometimes called "the Seres," they were encountered during the reign of Emperor Claudius (Nero's adoptive father). There are several spellings for these strange-eyed beings (blue-eyed, it was sometimes rumored), who communicated by "an uncouth sort of noise" and had flaxen hair. The Emodian Mountains (either the Himalayas or mountains nearby) "looked toward" these legendary people, believed by an earlier Roman visitor to have no true or comprehensible language by which to communicate thoughts (and hence the communication dilemmas faced by Severus, which later prove challenging even to Yanni's exceptional skills). Their means of trade was also strange, and we have remained consistent with the ancient legend, according to which, goods were brought down from a distant spot behind the glacial barriers and left at the side of a river, to be removed by local inhabitants. They were said to be a shy and secretive people. Pliny the Elder wrote that those who went exploring ahead of him, during prior decades, were mystified by the idea that this race, with its habit of leaving valuable goods behind, might in doing so be communicating some demand—perhaps to take these goods and stay away. The drop-offs were made to the river civilizations north of Taprobane (Sri Lanka).

Fictional our Cerae are, but we have made sure to maintain a certain amount of convergence with the Greek historian Strabo, who wrote in the fifth century B.C. (in *Geographia*, book 15, chapter 1) about a race in the same region able to control nature to such extent that they converted an ancient wasteland in and around the inhospitable mountains (south Tibet) into very fertile ground, and were able to extend their lives beyond two hundred years.

Pliny also wrote (as in *Natural History* 20, "The Seres") that the race, whose homeland remained hidden, produced varieties of iron unequaled in quality. As legend told it, their forests were white with valuable fleece—which was combed from the trees and sent out to the world in secret and under cover of night. He emphasized (repeatedly) that they shunned direct trade "with the rest of mankind." They were described to him as being "of inoffensive manners," but also monstrous and capable of being provoked to great savagery.

Some ancient historians called them the Sieriz (pronounceable as "Ceres"); others named them the Sinae—later believed to be the Chinese (though there would thus have been some very misunderstood and exaggerated descriptions of the Chinese, with the white fleece combed from trees being, perhaps, a misunderstood account of silk harvested from the cocoons of tree-dwelling silkworms). For the sake of our story, Sieriz— *Ceres*—worked, in terms of describing a cold, hidden world where everything was white, yet fertile. Ceres was a Roman goddess of agriculture and fertility—formerly a Greek goddess, Demeter (a name you may recognize from an ill-fated submarine in *Hell's Gate*).

Our Prince of Pandaya, and his kingdom's mistake, is fictional. But a place much like it was recorded by ancient historians to have existed near East India. There, according to legend, a royal harbor city was lost during a great flood—approximately where we have let Pliny's expedition find it (or rather, its ruins). Pliny the Elder made mention of the capital city (which he sometimes called Korki Pattinam) while trying to compile reports about the hidden realm of the "Chera" kingdom (our Cerae). A generation earlier, Augustus Caesar received an emissary from the still-intact city in 13 B.C. The historical Pandion (Pandyan)/Tamil capital was shifted after the destruction. This surviving remnant, whose people were said to have been descendants of Hercules, moved south to the island of Sri Lanka (Taprobane) and were known much later as the "Tamil Tigers."

In the time of Emperor Augustus, the people of the doomed city were known as a source of luxuriant textiles, fleece, and spices. Pliny the Elder mentioned a wealthy "Pandu" port that belonged to the "Chera," of whom he wrote that he was unable to learn anything. (Bear in mind that a reason for multiple spellings of the same place, or people, is inevitable in texts that were bound to pick up variations when preserved mainly by recopying, mostly by hand and by monks, throughout several centuries and across different languages.) A contemporary of Pliny, Periplus, referred to an independent district of the Tamil ancestors (Pandu), which, as a civilization, fell under the mysterious "Chera/Chola/Cerothra" (whom we simply call Cerae). In A.D. 640, the Chinese explorer Yuan Chwang described this same mysterious (Chola) region, home to a once-powerful trading city wiped from the world, unpopulated except for a few lingering savages who lived a sorrowful, troglodyte existence.

There really was, in China, a belief that legendary apelike creatures in the mountains possessed flesh and bones that, if consumed, held curative powers. This, of course, became the basis for the ill-fated expedition into which our character, Wang, was drafted. Additionally, certain fossil remains from apelike denizens of the East actually have led to speculation about lost or undiscovered species as the origin of the still ongoing Yeren and Yeti "sightings." The abduction of poor Dr. Wang by something akin to a cannibal army in 1946 is thus not entirely beyond reason.

In 1935, Dutch paleontologist Gustav von Koenigswald came across a yellowish molar among the "dragon bones" for sale in a Hong Kong pharmacy. Traditional Chinese medicine had long maintained that certain fossilized remains possessed curative properties when ground into powder and ingested. Over the next several decades, researchers recovered several hundred similar teeth and even a few of the lower jawbones that held them. Eventually, and although no cranial or postcranial bones were recovered, anthropologists named the new primate *Gigantopithecus* because of its immense size. Initially thought to be a human relative, scientists determined the creature to be an ape, most closely related to modern orangutans. Certainly the most striking feature of *Gigantopithecus blacki* was its size, with males reaching perhaps ten feet in height and weighing in at nearly 1,200 pounds, actually outsizing Mac-Cready's "Morlocks." Females were significantly smaller, with a body mass that might have been half that of males—a textbook example of a phenomenon known as sexual dimorphism.

Although *Gigantopithecus* was quite possibly the largest primate that ever lived, it also exemplifies how great body size can become a detriment to a species over time. For at least a million years, as many as three species of *Gigantopithecus* lived in the forests of southern China, India, Vietnam, and Indonesia. Evidence from their teeth and jaws indicates that their diets consisted of an assortment of plants, including fruit, leaves, roots, and possibly bamboo. To support their massive bodies, *Gigantopithecus* would have needed to consume large amounts of plant matter, but when glaciers began advancing down from the north around 100,000 years ago, the tropical forests where Asia's apes thrived gradually gave way to cooler, drier savannas. It has been hypothesized that these altered environments could not provide enough food for the giant forest dwellers and they eventually died out (aided, perhaps, by *Homo erectus*, the apparent ancestors of modern humans).

Similar examples of the disadvantages resulting from large body size can be found elsewhere and throughout history. For example, in South America, changing environmental conditions around ten thousand years ago are thought to have been a contributing factor in the extinction of the giant sloth, *Megatherium*. Additionally, since they fed exclusively on blood, *Desmodus draculae*, the large vampire bat inhabiting our novel *Hell's Gate*, likely went extinct after the Pleistocene megafauna upon which they preyed (possibly including ground sloths) disappeared.

For the purpose of this story, we hypothesized what might have occurred if Tibetan branches of some unknown lineage of a once very diversified primate family tree (an ancestor or side branch of *Homo erectus* or some yet unknown group, perhaps) had come into contact with a substance that allowed them to more quickly adapt to harsh local conditions. This boost to the process of natural selection resulted in the fictional Ceran/Morlock classes (with their thick, insulating fur and masterful climbing ability) encountered by Pliny the Elder and R. J. MacCready. What our fictionalized version of the Roman historian and naturalist characterized as "the key to life itself" was also responsible for the other strange species—like predaceous "snowflakes" and lethal grass mimics.

The Yeti or abominable snowman (Pliny's Cerae or Mac's Morlock species) is a giant, apelike biped, said to inhabit the Himalayan region of Tibet, Nepal, and Bhutan. Although the scientific community considers it to be entirely a legend, the Yeti is arguably the most famous creature in all of cryptozoology. The term *abominable snowman* originated in 1921 with Calcutta newspaper reporter Hendry Newman. Evidently, Newman mistranslated a Tibetan colloquialism *metch kangmi* ("filthy snowman")—which was used to describe something rumored to have been seen during a reconnaissance mission to Mount Everest earlier that year. The resulting moniker has had universal appeal, though probably not for primatologists and other scientists attempting to determine if such creatures actually exist. Although there have been hundreds of reported Yeti sightings, photographs of strange footprints in the snow, and "physical evidence" like hair (determined to be from known species, including mountain goats) and even a famed skullcap (also a mountain goat), there is currently no tangible evidence that these creatures have any footing in reality.

The Yeren, recovered by our Dr. Wang Tse-lin, is one of the legendary "Wildman of Shennongjia," reputed to live a peaceful existence in the mountainous forests of Hubei, in eastern central China. Reportedly covered by either red or white hair, the Yeren is said to stand between six and eight feet tall. Cryptozoologists have speculated that it may be a relative of *Gigantopithecus* or a large species of ground-dwelling orangutan.

The real-life Wang Tselin, also a Chicago-schooled Chinese biologist, wrote a detailed report about an examination he claimed to have performed on a Yeren that had been shot and killed in China's Gansu region in 1940. He said the specimen was a nursing female, approximately six and a half feet tall, and covered in dense, grayish-red hair. According to the scientist, the specimen's "face was narrow with deep-set eyes" and it reminded him most of models he had seen of the famous "Peking Man" (a Chinese example of the modern human ancestor *Homo erectus*, thought to have lived between 1.9 million and 230,000 years ago [see Smithsonian Institution: http://humanorigins.si.edu/evidence/human-fossils/species/homo-erectus]). Locals reportedly told Tselin that a pair of Yeren had been observed in the area for more than a month. Unfortunately, there was no follow-up to this story (no photographs, no physical evidence), and it has been difficult to track down additional information on the scientist himself. As the Chinese civil war heated up, he seems simply to have disappeared into history (probably as a casualty). We have taken the liberty of fictionalizing Wang Tselin and his Himalayan adventure, and also given him a more hopeful future.

As with the Yeti and its North American counterpart, "Bigfoot," there is currently no physical evidence that the Yeren (as described by Wang) actually exists. Most skeptics believe that Yeren sightings are the result of misidentification. There is strong agreement among scientists from a variety of fields that any suggestion of a Yeti/Bigfoot/*Gigantopithecus* connection is untenable unless tangible, repeatable laboratory evidence becomes available—such as hair roots with distinctive DNA that does not turn out to come from goats and known species of monkeys (which, so far, has universally been the case).

Our suggestion (in the Epilogue) of a Morlock diaspora was invented to fit certain anecdotal events, actually recorded as far away as Russia. That the Kremlin would be willing (as in this novel) to send military helicopter crews out to investigate rumors of strange creatures is not far-fetched. In the May 29, 2014, issue of the *Huffington Post*, David Moye reported on a 1959 event involving the Russian military: "Mysterious Deaths of College Students Blamed on Russian Yeti." If nothing else, the article and the documentary on which Moye was reporting make for interesting reading and viewing.

While Mac and Yanni have become accidental cryptozoologists, with the exception of very large squids, cryptozoology (certainly in the case of Yeren and their kin) has the curious distinction of being the only field of exploration that has yet to prove that its subject matter actually exists.

Nonetheless, there are a wide assortment of increasingly fascinating—and surprisingly recently coexisting—side branches of our tree of human lineages to choose from as ancestors to the inhabitants of our story's mist valley. The origins of humans, Neanderthals, and other human cousins is not a single, classical poster image of descent leading from an apelike fossil called "Lucy," to something resembling "Peking Man," to Neanderthals, and finally to fully erect "Cro-Magnon Man." It makes for a visually interesting T-shirt depicting apes walking from left to right along a "ladder of evolution" to become ape-men and erect-walking humans (leading to erect-walking robots). It's a simple and tidy and popular depiction, but it is also entirely wrong.

The ascent of man is not a ladder with a few missing links inserted among the rungs. We, and the few apes that remain on the planet today, are merely the surviving branches of a once (and not very long ago) very luxuriant bush. The lost valley in the maze of the eastern Himalayas is, in this story, populated by one of those missing branches, isolated in a place where the actual process of evolutionary change could be altered.

The complexity of the human family bush is much greater, and more interesting, than previous generations have supposed. The emerging possibility of a human cousin closely related to Peking Man, surviving into recent times in the isolation of an Indonesian island, enhanced the sort of speculative journey we have taken into the isolation of a lost east Himalayan world, as isolated as any island.

In real life, as in the journey we have all just taken together, the genetic distances between our human branch and branches that used to be called "animals" or "ape-men" are being diminished and even blurred. The lessons from studies of ancient DNA indicate a surprising amount of interbreeding, for example, between Charles Knight's Neanderthal "cave men" and "archaic humans" from Africa, also between Neanderthals and a species or race traditionally graded as distinctly *non*-human (*Homo erectus*, "Peking Man").

Relevant to the relationship between Severus and a fictional race that looked so physically different as to seem nonhuman, the list of ancient hybrid events is growing: South Africa's *Homo naledi*, the "mystery human," appears to have an ancestry dating back more than two million years (close to the origin of *Homo erectus*). To judge from their fossils, they looked simultaneously very human yet carried a mixture of less human features even more ancient than *H. erectus*. Another branch—*Homo floresiensis*, popularly dubbed "the Hobbit people"—resembled a miniature and more primitive version of "Peking Man," surviving in parts of Indonesia into very recent times (probably post–Ice Age and even into our Bronze Age). Scarcely had the 2003 "Hobbit" discovery begun to be tested and resolved when yet another branch was unearthed: Denisovan Man, located primarily in Siberia. Though it is Neanderthal-like in appearance, approximately 8 percent of Denisovan DNA seems to have been derived from interbreeding with still another new (presently unidentified) human species from Asia—a branch genetically distinct from both Neanderthals and modern humans. Researchers believe that in the Middle East Neanderthal interbreeding with our modern, more thinly boned ancestors took place along the Jordan Valley.

In the November 2016 special edition of *Scientific American: The Story of Us*, Kate Wong and Michael Hammer commented at length on these truly fascinating discoveries. Wong noted that the "mystery human" of South Africa "exhibits a mishmash of traits associated with various hominin species," including some skull similarities to the more apelike *Australopithecus*, commonly known as "Lucy." And yet there is evidence of burial practices and the use of fire, possibly dating back as many as three million years, almost as far back in time as "Lucy." If so, these people could even oust australopithecines from the lineage leading to us (and, in our fiction, to the Cerae). "It may be," Wong continued, "[that] *H. naledi* originated millions of years ago and managed to persist across the ages unchanged, like a coelacanth, overlapping with other *Homo* 'species,' including *H. sapiens*. . . . Possibly, *H. naledi* interbred with our ancestors and contributed DNA to the modern gene pool, like Neanderthals and Denisovians did."

"The roots of modern humans," added Hammer, "trace back to not just a single ancestral population in Africa but to populations throughout the world. Although archaic humans have often been seen as rivals of modern humans, scientists now must seriously consider the possibility that they were the secret of *H. sapiens'* success."

And thus the picture is more complex than you might have supposed. Though it is extremely doubtful that a lost world of Yeti-like Cerae or Morlocks is living and awaiting discovery, we will not be the two people in the room who drop dead from shock if a twig on the human bush looking even stranger than Indonesia's "Hobbits" or South Africa's "Mystery Man" is found to have survived in some remote place, into the Bronze Age or even into Pliny's time.

Elephants, mammoths, and their cousins have a similarly complex ancestry, now winnowed down to only two recognized species: the Indian and African elephants.

Mutations of the kind we have described are not entirely unknown. Nearly four thousand years ago, a pygmy elephant smaller than a Shetland pony inhabited the island of Crete in the Mediterranean, contributing to the idea of the Cerae's mini-mammoths. In Alaska and along some of its offshore islands, the northwest mammoths were still alive when Egypt's pyramids were being built. Among the last of them was a "pygmy" species.

There is also real-life precedent for the "twinning" effect on mammoth appendages, in Mac's time. At the Explorers Club in New York City, visitors to the main lecture hall can examine the fully adult, fully functional-over-a-lifetime quadruple tusks of an extinct woolly mammoth (whether this was a single mutation or a previously unknown type of mammoth continues to be debated). On public display in the same city, at the Ripley's museum on Forty-Second Street, are the preserved remains of an elephant that grew to adulthood in Botswana, and lived until 2005 with a mutation that produced two fully functional trunks (both confirmed, by DNA tests, as belonging to the same individual). The mutation was clearly imperfect, and no one knows for sure whether the two-trunked elephant would have lived to adulthood if not maintained in a "preserve." In the opinion of most veterinarians, the mutation was an impediment. We have bypassed this problem in the novel by presenting as if true the mythology of fantastical Himalayan cure-alls—which, in the world of the Cerae and the Morlocks, influenced the tempo and mode of evolution, rendering imperfect mutations perfect. Thus "little Dumbo's" two trunks become the evolutionary equivalent of giving our human ancestors two hands with opposable thumbs.

As depicted in the Yanni encounters, elephants really are known to have a language at least as complex as the communications between cetaceans (whales and dolphins). Most of the communication has been recorded at low frequencies, beyond human hearing. In Africa, actual "tribal dialects" have been identified among these amazing giants. Once again, a group of animals requires us to ask new questions about the identification of intelligent species, and whether we humans really are the only potentially intelligent creatures now being evolved on this planet.

Sadly (as noted in a September 29, 2016, census summary in the British science journal *Nature*), elephant populations are being decimated. *Worse than decimated.* Between 2006 and 2015, ivory poaching alone had dropped the population of African elephants by 111,000, to only 415,000 individuals. And hence, our fitful moments of wishful thinking, on behalf of elephants: In our fable, living with a microbe that modifies life while reducing the frequent evolutionary mistakes in the raw material of natural selection (random variation), the Morlock misfortune became their failure to notice that brain growth was being enhanced for the enslaved and environmentally stressed mammoths.

When imagining the architecture of a post–Stone Age culture in the eastern Himalayas—where mountains and valleys are being pushed up by the collision of India with Asia—we had to invent architecture with earthquake resistance in mind. As with human architecture, much of the inspiration for long-lived structures comes from nature. One of the most amazing borrowed-from-nature structures on earth is Gaudí's nature- and forest-based design for the La Sagrada Familia Basílica in Barcelona. Strong by definition, Cerae and Morlock structures needed more flexibility than stone and mortar, and had to be rendered conceivable based on local building materials, including plant matter and ice.

Ice composite architecture is rooted in reality. For our own civilization, it might actually begin to play an important role in the not-too-distant future. Composites with the strength of concrete and flexibility of steel can be made from materials as simple as pulped garbage or "cotton" spun from recycled plastic.

The ice composite boats mentioned by Jerry as he examined Morlock structures really did reach the experimental stage near the end of World War II. Composite hulls and bunker walls tested well. Cotton balls in ice have proved to be a surprisingly good strengthening material, distribut-

ing the force evenly and preventing shattering of
the ice even against artillery. An ice composite
boat more than thirty feet long, after successful
testing under Churchill, was left abandoned at
war's end, on a drydock near London—where it
took almost a year to melt. (A smaller version, using old newspapers in ice, was famously tested on
the American documentary series *MythBusters*.)

The world's first, actual large-scale ice-composite
is an underground dam, built in the aftermath of
Japan's "3/11 triple disaster" (earthquake, tsunami,
nuclear meltdown). Currently one mile in cir-
cumference, the dam of ice-and-dirt prevents new
groundwater from entering the Fukushima meltdown site and carrying even more radioactive debris into the ocean. The Fukushima ice composite
dam is impermeable, non-brittle—and it can be
kept in place for centuries to come (if civilization
endures). Even in the aftermath of new earthquakes, the dam is easily repaired—in a manner
analogous to a living organism healing an injured
bone—just as we have indicated for the Cerae and
Morlock structures.

There was, in reality, a lost Roman Ninth Legion. The timing of the disappearance varies
but it is most commonly believed to have happened about A.D. 120 (and possibly as late as A.D.
160), either in Britain or after a long march east-
ward through Persia (present-day Iran). The Jordan
Valley and India are occasionally mentioned in
missing Ninth sightings. Whether they actually

wandered into some unknown slaughter, or were simply disbanded and not recorded, remains unknown. We do know, from trade goods found in the cities of Vesuvius and through DNA tracing the descent of remote Chinese villagers back to Rome, that the Romans did reach as far as China and the eastern Himalayas, in Pliny's time. (See, for example, Nick Squires on Chinese DNA, in the *Telegraph*, November 23, 2010, and National Geographic Society on the study of Chinese mummies with European features and red hair.)

A twentieth-century Chinese army like the one MacCready, Yanni, and Jerry found in "the Trophy Room" really is (like the Roman Ghost Legion) widely reported to have vanished into legend. In the realm of great mysteries, the disappearance of nearly three thousand Chinese soldiers outside of Nanking during the morning of December 10, 1939, remains unsolved. At 4 A.M., Colonel Li Fu Sein (after an inspection of men and equipment) slept for three hours in a truck and awoke to find concealed cooking fires still burning, and camouflaged artillery still loaded and aimed. With the exception of about a half-dozen men at a remote overlook, Sein's entire battalion, including its field officers, had vanished without any signs of combat. During the decades that followed, not even an impostor came forward (as in the manner of Little Bighorn "survivors") claiming to have been a survivor or deserter from China's own "missing Ninth." Farmers westward, upriver, attested that no soldiers at all, and certainly not three thousand of them, ever came through the area, as it could not have gone unnoticed during a mass desertion. To the east of their position, the Japanese never recorded a battle against Chinese defenders or (as was their tradition) the execution of men who surrendered. The most probable explanation: farmers west of the location simply kept quiet about a mass desertion upriver into the mountains, and the lookouts who remained at their post, and who never heard anything about desertion plans, were at their posts for precisely that reason.

Whatever really did happen, the Japanese occupiers of Nanking would have publicized a desertion of this magnitude for its propaganda value. They did not. They were evidently as mystified by the event as everyone else. For the sake of storytelling, we have tapped this mystery on the shoulder and blamed the Morlocks.

This was not the last mass disappearance in China. Almost exactly nine years later, on December 12, 1948, the *New York Times* reported that General Sun Yuan-lians's Fifteenth Army had vanished southwest of Suchow. While they were thought to have surrendered to the communists, or deserted, aerial reconnaissance revealed that they appeared simply to have vanished.

Only rumors survive.

O n underground realms of the Far East: Even without expansion by Morlocks and their ancestors, Asia already boasts cave systems so large that St. Patrick's Cathedral could easily be accommodated in a small corner. China's Miao cavern, which can be reached only by navigating an underground river, is the largest "supercave" currently known. It contains a stalagmite large enough to engulf the Statue of Liberty from toe to torch tip, and the main cavern is long enough to contain a jumbo jet's entire runway. In Tibet, enormous Buddhist temples have been built inside natural caverns. The cave systems of the eastern Himalayas remain mostly unexplored. The bioluminescent life in the lost world of the Cerae/Morlocks is based on organisms that actually exist—some encountered in caves, others being extrapolations of prey-and-predator relationships studied by colleagues who have visited the ocean's "deep scattering layer" of life and the hydrothermal oases still being explored at the continental spreading centers. Among the strangest observations: organisms that give off a literally blinding, bioluminescent flash to stun predators, or prey, or both.

On unknown microscopic life and strange microbial symbiotic linkages: Recent assessments using new collecting and culturing methods have revealed that 99 percent of all microbial species (not counting viruses) are yet to be discovered. A good place to begin venturing into and learning about this realm is Laura Beil's introduction to microbial "Dark Matter" in the September 7, 2016, issue of *Science News:* "Out of the Dark: Scientists Discover Bacteria that Defy Rules of Biochemistry." Beil's article is one of the clearest expositions on a field exploding with amazing new discoveries, and we cannot wait until she writes a book.

The fictional Nora Nesbitt's speculation about pheromones and microbes, and what she believed might have taken control of Severus, as reported by Pliny, is based on a strange but true microbial relationship. The cat-rat paradox occurs precisely as Nesbitt described it, in her conversation with Patricia Wynters. Kathleen McAuliffe's profile of parasitologist Jaroslav Flegr—"How Your Cat Is Making You Crazy"—in the March 2012 issue of the *Atlantic* (as well as publications by Flegr himself) would be an excellent place to begin exploring this subject.

The guinea worm parasite (minus the enhancements brought about by a microbe under control of the Cerae) follows its usual life cycle exactly as described by Nesbitt. As an example of how we do not know the measure of some national leaders until after they are out of office, former American president Jimmy Carter, along with his many truly charitable efforts, has brought the world closer than ever to eradicating the dreaded disease dracunculiasis.

The lost worlds of the Himalayas, much as we have described them, really do exist in legends older than Imperial Rome. One lost tropical valley, located east of our fictional mist valley and believed in the West to have existed in legend only, actually was discovered early in the twenty-first century.

We owe much to these long-standing oral and written traditions about mystical hidden valleys in the eastern Himalayas and Tibet, and in particular the Shambala legend. The mythical kingdom is mentioned in ancient Buddhist and Hindu texts with origins going back to at least 200 B.C. Predating Pliny's Rome, the legends spoke of magical substances and secret healing practices.

The tales first emerged into popular Western culture in the form of a novel about a man who crash-landed in an airplane, on the fringe of the hidden realm. This was Talbot Mundy's *Om: The Secret of the Ahbor Valley*, published in 1925. Eight years later, in his retread of Mundy's story (*The Lost Horizon*), James Hilton renamed the hidden world Shangri-la. This place-name never existed, until Hilton. Shambala (sometimes spelled Shambhala) is the proper name, of legend.

As further examples of how we have tried to keep our story consistent with Eastern traditions about the lost world: In China and as far north as Russia, legends actually do describe jewel-like cities hidden in the mountains—cities in which the people vary from enlightened to very warlike and even enlightened in the bodies of large monkeys. Their central hidden realm is shrouded in white mists and there are cave systems that, as tradition describes them, have spread out widely under the world. Apocalyptic prophecies are linked to the innermost realm—according to which, during a universal outburst of evil when humanity is governed by the furies of greed and war and as the leaders of all the doomed nations peer into the abyss, something spreads out of Shambala to save humanity from itself.

Shambala is the hidden realm that Westerners have been seeking since at least the time of Vatican expeditions sent during the tenth century, based on the belief that it was a surviving remnant of Eden. Evidently there were no expedition survivors. About 1534, Jesuits returned to Rome with further tales of Shambala. The Vatican library preserves hand-drawn maps of hidden worlds, encircled by mountains and strange waters, and showing encounter points with Buddhist monks, living in temples at altitudes of seventeen thousand feet. The monks had described mythical women, "extraordinarily angelic yet as wild as snow leopards," according to the twenty-first-century explorer Ian Baker.

It is Baker whose expedition discovered the strange, tropical oasis of "Pemaku," nestled deep within an east Himalayan labyrinth of valleys, with snowcapped mountains and glaciers towering overhead. Following the path of the nineteenth-century explorer John Whitehead, Baker did find a cave, river, and waterfall system consistent with one of the valleys described by Jesuits centuries earlier. The world Baker found descended below five thousand feet and was carpeted with strange, isolated plant life (members of his expedition are, at this writing, still identifying specimens with medicinal potential). More than a century earlier, his predecessor Whitehead had given up, writing that the search for the magical waters and plants of a lost Himalayan paradise "can be characterized as one of the great romances of geography and one of the most obsessive wild goose chases of modern times." Whitehead noted that not even guides could get him past the unknown (cryptic and feral) guardians: "They kill Tibetans on principle."

In 1924, the Russians sent an expedition into Tibet and the eastern Himalayas, searching for Shambala. They failed. Later, the Nazis sent expeditions (expecting to find a cave leading deep into the Earth, where dwelled the perfect, white-haired Aryan race). The German expeditions were launched in 1930, 1934, and 1938. Most of the Germans were believed to have frozen to death. (For the purposes of our fable, look in the Morlock trophy room.)

Ian Baker noted in 2016, while lecturing at the Explorers Club in Manhattan, that there are legends of other hidden realms west of his "Pemaku" site. Ancient texts speak of "the secret gate . . . The people who know the key have hidden it from outsiders and especially from the Chinese. . . . [T]he way in is guarded by a long-haired, extraordinary animal." Texts also describe tall and terraced waterfalls, and tunnels behind life-giving waters, going deep into a mountain.

According to Baker, mentions in sacred books of hidden gorges carpeted with strange plants that impart longevity and memories of past lives are part of an amazingly symbolic language—next of kin to Western civilization's oldest fables. "The big mistake is to take the texts too literally."

And thus, bold traveler, you will read bamboo

annals describing something in a remote valley "harder than a tiger, to tame. And at the heart, at the final stage of deification [and realization], the colors in the guarded place are orange and red, like a fiery tiger." *Logic and reason fail you*, the annals warn. "And an ancient figure in red fire riding with a pregnant tigress. And an image of redness beyond anything you have been ready for."

Although we have a red grotto consistent with the texts, Baker believed in, as not actually existing in physical form, a world beyond the tropical, unpopulated Himalayan oasis he discovered. "The Shambala story may even be based on *this* oasis," he said. The innermost secret realm in a more distant fog valley may, he suggested, "in the symbolic language of the region, really refer to a hidden realm that is inside of you, rather than being literally a physical place."

Paraphrasing Mircea Eliade on this subject (from *Myths, Dreams and Mysteries: The Encounter Between Contemporary Faiths and Archaic Realities*, Harper, 1975), Baker concluded, "At the commencement and at the end of the religious history of humanity, we find again the same nostalgia for Paradise. The myths by which this ideology is constituted are among the most beautiful and profound in existence. They are the myths of Paradise and the fall of immortality of primordial man . . . and the discovery of the spirit."

Or, as we have depicted it, the gates to Paradise can also swing open into Hell.

There really do exist many written warnings against seeking out and then entering the center of the most secret of the lost worlds. According to one ancient text, "Without proper vision, if unready, you bring unpredictable disaster. Disaster for all."

On racially tagged bioweapons: Fortunately, at our present point in history, the development of such weapons is restricted by the fact that viruses (the most likely tools) tend to mutate too rapidly to be practical for this kind of weaponization. However, talk of such weapons (mostly in a "defensive" context) had been in the air by the time our first novel, *Hell's Gate*, originally planned as a stand-alone cautionary tale, was purchased with a request for a sequel. Though we have described this danger in terms of a modern-day fable, as with most fables, it carries a real warning. In this case, the warning points toward a reality hiding somewhere not very far ahead, like a monster under the bridge we are approaching. If there is time enough to start thinking about what might be hiding under humanity's bridge to the genetic frontier, and to take action before we actually get close enough to be in danger, then it is logical to do so. Many aspects of our scientific fable are, in fact, science eventuality. It's time to start the conversation.

Acknowledgments

The authors would like to thank Gillian MacKenzie for continuing to be the best literary agent that anyone could ever hope for. Thanks also to Kirsten Wolff and Allison Devereux at the Gillian MacKenzie Agency for their hard work.

A very special thanks to our talented editor Lyssa Keusch and to her colleagues at William Morrow.

We are grateful to Patricia J. Wynne for the amazing figures of Tibetan wildlife that grace our novel.

Much gratitude to James Cameron and James Rollins for their support.

A special shout-out to Robert Ruotolo for generously giving his time and bringing us up to speed on all things helicopter-related. We thank our friends in the USN and USMC, and we carry with us always, alive in our memories, those who did not make it back to shore.

From Bill Schutt

I am deeply indebted to my friends and colleagues in the research community and at the American

Museum of Natural History for their advice, support, and friendship. They include Ricky Adams, Frank Bonaccorso, Catherine Doyle-Capitman, Kristi Collom, Betsy Dumont, Neil Duncan, John Hermanson, Mary Knight, Gary Kwiecinski, Ross MacPhee, Shahroukh Mistry, Scott Pedersen, Nancy Simmons (it's good to know the Queen), Ian Tattersall, Elizabeth Taylor, Rob Voss, Sean Werle, and Eileen Westwig.

A very special thanks goes out to my wonderful friend and coconspirator Leslie Nesbitt Sittlow. Leslie and my "brother" Darrin Lunde spent many hours reading through early versions of *Codex* and they were always there to provide friendship, laughs, and sound editorial advice.

At LIU Post, thanks and gratitude to Ted Brummel, Gina Famulare, Kathy Mendola, Katherine Hill-Miller, Jeff Kane, Jen Snekser, and Steve Tettlebach. Thanks also to my teaching assistants, LIU graduate students Elsie Jasmin, Chelsea Miller, and Kayla Mladinich, for making my life so much easier.

Sincere thanks goes out to Bob Adamo (RIP), Frank Bacolas, John Bodnar, Alice Cooper, Aza Derman, John Glusman, Art Goldberg, Chris Grant (Yoga Farm, Lansing), Kathy Kennedy, Lisa Kombrink, Suzanne Finnamore Luckenbach, Aja Marcato, Elaine Markson, Carrie and Dan McKenna, Maceo Mitchell, Farouk Muradali; Gerard, Oda, and Dominique Ramsawak, Jerry Ruotolo, Laura Schlecker, Edwin J. Spicka, Lynn Swisher, and Katherine Turman.

Special thanks also go out to Dorothy Wachter

and Carol Trezza—for being wonderful "second moms" to me back in the day, and for encouraging my dreams of becoming a writer.

Finally, my eternal thanks and love go out to my family for their patience, love, encouragement, and unwavering support, especially Janet Schutt, Billy Schutt, Eileen Schutt, Chuck Schutt, Bob and Dee Schutt, Rob, Shannon, and Kelly Schutt, Dawn Montalto, Donna Carpenter, Don and Sue Pedersen, Jason, Geoff, and Chris Langos, my grandparents (Angelo and Millie DiDonato), Erin Nicosia (American Cheese), and of course, my late parents, Bill and Marie Schutt.

Selected Bibliography

Baker, Ian. *The Heart of the World* (Penguin, 2006) and "The Secret River: Plants, Alchemy, and Immortality in Tibet's Hidden Land of Pe-maku," *National Geographic Adventure*, 2010. (See also, regarding Russian and Chinese legends of Shambala: http://studybuddhism. com/web/en/archives/advanced/kalachakra/ shambhala/russian_japanese_shambhala.html.)

Bisel, Sara. *Secrets of Vesuvius*. New York: Scholas-tic, 1991.

McAuliffe, Kathleen. "How Your Cat Is Making You Crazy." *Atlantic*, March 2012.

Milner, Richard. *Charles R. Knight: The Artist Who Saw Through Time*. New York: Harry Abrams, 2012.

Nielsen, R., et al. "Tracing the Peopling of the World Through Genomics," *Nature*, January 19, 2017, pp. 302–310. (NOTE: The rapidly developing discovery of unknown human-like relatives is beginning to look like only the tip of a rather large iceberg, including one species that, in a manner similar to our fictional Nesbitt specimen, is known only by a broken off finger fragment.)

Suetonius, Gaius (translated by R. Graves, M. Grant edition). Nero [in] *The Twelve Caesars*. New York: Penguin, 1979.

For a compilation of what little history survives the legend, see W. H. Schoff, "Tamil Political Divisions in the First Two Centuries AD," *Journal of the American Oriental Society* 33 (1913): 209–13, and K.A.N. Sastri, *The Pandyan Kingdom: from the Earliest Times to the Sixteenth Century* (Madras: Swathi Publications, 1972).

For an introduction to the Scythians, see Jeannine Davis-Kimball, *Warrior Women: An Archaeologist's Search for History's Lost Heroines* (New York: Warner, 2003) and A. Karasulas and A. McBride, *Mounted Archers of the Steppe 600 BC–AD 1300* (U.K.: Osprey Publishers, 2004).

On elephant vocalization, see Caitlin O'Connell, *The Elephant Secret Sense: The Hidden Life of the Secret Herds of Africa* (MA: University of Chicago Press, 2008) and Carl Safina, *Beyond Words: What Animals Think and Feel* (New York: Holt, 2015). To actually listen: http://www.cbsnews.com/news/the-secret-language-of-elephants2/ and http://news.nationalgeographic.com/animals/what-elephant-calls-mean/.

Captain R. J. MacCready returns in another thrilling adventure—this one taking him to the island of Santorini, where ancient Greek legend has come to life in the form of a super-intelligent and deadly species, and political tensions between the United States and Russia threaten to escalate into a global level conflict—in

The Darwin Strain

Read on for a sneak peek!

CHAPTER 1

Hephaestus Awakes

June 23, 1948
The Greek Isle of Santorini, Eastern Mediterranean

J acques Yves Cousteau had never been seasick in his life but something told him that this was probably what it felt like.

"*Merde alors*," he muttered, walking unsteadily away from the twin-engine light transport.

With its newly modified glazed nose, the French Air Force was grooming the ten-passenger Dassault "Flamingo" for use as a trainer and light bomber. Cousteau, a thirty-eight year-old former Naval officer, had called in a favor to be flown from Tunisia to an airstrip on the Greek island of Santorini, as quickly as possible.

Cousteau turned back to see two of the ground crew hauling his baggage out of the cargo hold.

One tall Greek was lugging an oversized canvas bag that contained his clothes and wetsuit, while the other struggled with a pair of steel air tanks.

He called a warning to the one wrestling with the cylinders. "*Monsieur, soyez prudent avec ceux.*"

The man gave him a quick disinterested wave, before muttering something to his coworker. Cousteau ignored him, turning his attention instead to the pilot, who had already climbed outside to inspect one of the plane's duel six cylinder engines.

A bit underpowered, isn't she? Cousteau thought.

Lieutenant Cousteau knew that if not for a horrific accident a decade earlier, *he* should have been the one piloting the plane, perhaps even flight-testing one of the newer models. His dreams of becoming a naval aviator had been derailed in a single moment of random chance—a car crash that broke both of his arms. Even now, Cousteau cringed at the memory, cognizant that few people knew how very close he had come to dying. The young gunnery officer had nonetheless adapted quickly, steering a new path, during the remainder of the war, toward his lifelong fascination with the sea and diving. Working with the French Resistance, he had also found time to co-develop the regulator apparatus that made Jules Verne's *Aqua-Lung* a reality.

On land, "Gravity is my enemy," he sometimes told friends. The damage to Cousteau's bones made him feel like a man at least thirty years older—*yet beneath the water, I am free, like a child.*

These days, in an alliance with the American Navy, his government was assigning him to form what someone had already christened the Underwater Studies and Research Group. Cousteau and his small team were field-testing improvements on their equipment while simultaneously exploring and mapping the remains of a Roman shipwreck—the first such scuba expedition in history. The project was not yet complete when two members of his team were instructed to fly ahead to Santorini to investigate the aftermath of seismic shifts offshore. Reportedly, the quakes were associated with "some interesting biological phenomena." Cousteau, still recovering from a serious infection he'd contracted in Tunisia, had planned to sit this one out. Now though, a message from his old friend and new business partner, Bernard, had changed the plan.

From the air, it had been easy to see that Santorini was the outer rim of a caldera nearly twelve kilometers wide, the remains of an ancient cataclysm that had literally blown a hole in the Earth. Long before the first words were written or even spoken in Greek, the northern Mediterranean filled in the wound, creating one of the planet's most picturesque lagoons. But beauty could not hide the violence or the potential for it to awaken again. During the war, British sonar had revealed cracks radiating from the crater, along the seabed—and extending out more than a hundred kilometers in every direction. As chronicled since the time of the first Greek scribes, the center of the lagoon was continually pushing up volcanic slabs and cones, with eruptions taking place every few generations. The youngest island, Nea

Kameni ("new burnt island"), had risen during the time of Napoleon. More recently there had occurred a series of small but progressively stronger quakes, and although geologists debated whether these might be ushering in a new period of island building, they all agreed on one thing—Santorini was not dead.

But volcanic islands rising do not normally attract the attention of both the French Navy and the Greek Orthodox Church, Cousteau told himself, shaking his head at the incongruity.

Twenty minutes after landing, he checked into what his driver described as "the only hotel in town." The clerk, who had a face that not only resembled tanned leather but also belonged to the identical twin of the driver, passed Cousteau a sealed envelope. The Frenchman shot him a questioning look but the man simply shrugged, feigning disinterest.

The message inside was in neat, handwritten English.

Heard you were dropping by. Have made remarkable discovery in local quarry. Your old friend MacCready should be here soon. Hope we can compare notes (and share Mac stories) tonight over a bottle of grappa. —Cordially, Wang Tse-lin

Cousteau smiled. At the bottom of the sheet, the Chinese scientist had written a phone number and the local address for a restaurant, in what was apparently another "only hotel in town."

Tse-lin was a paleo-anthropologist with a brontosaurian appetite for all things scientific—including zoology and gemology. During the war, he had lived through the darkest, most tenuous days of the Resistance against the occupation of northern China by the late Empire of Japan. Recently, he had also survived some undisclosed adventure with R. J. MacCready, apparently settling now into what the Frenchman considered to be a rather tame existence collecting fossils and gems. Evidently, the only mission Tse-lin cared about, these days, involved the peace and quiet of fossil-studded cliffs offering skyscraper-high views of the Aegean Sea.

A good plan, Cousteau told himself. *Until it wasn't.*

The Frenchman was looking forward to a meeting with the newest member of the MacCready gang—but that would have to wait. As if to drive home this particular point, he turned toward a commotion at the front door. It was Bernard, trailed by Laurent, the other professional diver. Their excitement was unmistakable, and urgent.

"Jacques, *finally!*" Bernard exclaimed, rushing in to hug him.

"Are you ready to dive?" Laurent chimed in.

Cousteau gestured to his bags and equipment, which had been deposited beside the hotel's front desk. "Yes, I am ready this very minute," Cousteau responded. "No food. No rest. Still sick. A dive sounds like great fun."

"Great!" they exclaimed in unison. Cousteau nodded, reminded that sarcasm had never been one of his talents.

The clerk had apparently moved past any concerns about the strange luggage and was now looking quite amused at what was unfolding. Shooting the man a suspicious look, the one called Bernard gestured for Cousteau to come nearer, then began whispering something in his ear. During the next minute, the newly arrived guest became even more animated than his two friends. Five minutes after that, the hotel worker was staring at Cousteau's open canvas bag—which looked as if it had just ejected a small assortment of clothing onto the floor. The strange guest and half of the even stranger tanks that had arrived with him were gone.

C*ela semble microbien*," one of the Frenchmen called out, over the protests of an aging inboard engine. His two compatriots nodded in response.

As the little fishing boat motored away from the waterfront village of Fira, its owner, Antoninus Stavracos, thought it odd that the newest member of the trio was ignoring the spectacular multicolored cliffs bordering a crater lagoon nearly eight miles wide.

"*Une espèce de Rhodophyte, peut-être?*" a second Frenchman called out. He and his friend had hired Stavracos to take them on an identical dive trip several days earlier.

"*Je ne pense pas*," the new man responded with a headshake. Though the Greek boatman could barely understand a word of French, it was clear that this one was the leader.

They're talking about the arrival of the red waters,

Stavracos thought. *His Holy Blood*. The Greek found it impossible not to fixate on the amazing events that had occurred during the three weeks since The Reddening. *The fish in the markets are larger and healthier, and those who eat them have been cured from all manner of ailments.* "A miracle," Stavracos said, beneath the sound of the motor. Then, shooting a quick glance skyward, he crossed himself.

He knew that, unlike these Frenchmen, most of his recent clientele had been locals—parents mostly, accompanied by their sick or crippled children. He'd taken them to the exact spot where His Holy Blood poured from wounds on the sea floor. Stigmata, some were calling the red plumes, though no one, save for these Frenchmen, had dared to investigate any deeper.

Nearly all of the pilgrims who hired out his boat were poor, like he was, and although he felt bad about taking advantage of their misfortune, he sometimes took a few coins or an item that had been bartered. Often though, and this was something Stavracos kept from his wife, Cara, he charged them nothing at all—the sight of mothers and fathers gently lowering their loved ones into the red water was incompatible with the collection of a fee. He shook his head, remembering how some poor souls, too weak for even a brief emersion, had been splashed with the red-tinted water.

Using the relative positions of the three islands that surrounded them, Therasia looming ahead, Nea Kameni portside, and the cliffs of Santorini far to the rear, Stavracos throttled back briefly before turning off the engine. Satisfied that he'd arrived at the desired location, he gestured toward the anchor, but none of the men took notice. They were either struggling into black rubber dive suits or adjusting the equipment and bulky air tanks that would allow them to remain submerged for nearly half an hour.

Shaking his head, Stavracos moved forward and lowered the anchor himself, feeling for and finding the bottom. He allowed himself a smile, pleased that he could now pinpoint the initial section of shallows, bordering a drop-off estimated to reach at least a third of a mile.

Several minutes later, the boat owner's concerns about the divers and their questionable motives were interrupted by a rapid series of splashes as one by one the men tumbled backward over the gunwale and disappeared.

He watched three sets of bubbles rise through the dark water. *God prevent these strangers from desecrating this site*, he thought. Then Antoninus Stavracos crossed himself yet again.

As Cousteau followed Bernard and Laurent toward a gentle slope strewn with rocks, he managed a quick review of all that he had recently learned. Three weeks earlier, there had been a small earthquake. There were no fatalities and little damage beyond some cracked masonry and smashed glassware. In the aftermath, though, the waters near the lagoon's central cluster of islands gradually began to change color, and within a day or two a sharp-eyed fisherman had determined the source—a shallow spot near the shore of Nea Kameni. Here the stained waters were indeed flowing toward the surface, warm and red—like blood. Soon after came the first claims of rejuvenation and healing, with local doctors perplexed at their apparent validity. Within a week, the Greek Orthodox Church got into the act and several senior representatives arrived from Crete to begin an investigation.

"They're calling it a Greek version of Fátima," Bernard had explained, with a shrug.

"At first we thought it was just superstitious nonsense," Laurent had added.

But the mystery only deepened after one of the town physicians discovered that the so-called "miracle" fish all contained a strange red material in their guts. It was then that Cousteau had been alerted, and by the time he arrived, his men discovered the source of the material—a series of vents on the sea floor, sixty feet below the surface.

As Cousteau equalized the pressure in his ears and descended toward a rocky incline, he could see it for himself—strange, cauliflower-like billows of red smoke escaping fissures no wider than his fist. Heard above the distant propeller whine of a fishing boat were the sounds emanating from the vents themselves—a steady rumble of water, accented by the occasional clicking and snapping of rocks trapped within.

Pulling up beside Cousteau, as they reached the bottom, Bernard pointed to a boulder several meters from the nearest vent. Like much of the surrounding hillside, it had the appearance of being covered in lush scarlet-hued velvet, and as they moved nearer, Cousteau could feel a significant rise in water temperature. Knowing that his men had taken only a tiny sample of the material on their first dive, he could also see that someone—in all likelihood a free-diver—had been there as well, apparently using a blade to scrape away sections of the red mat. Whoever did this, had exposed a series of organic strata, the outermost of which was clearly alive. The curious formation reminded Cousteau of the fossilized algal mats called stromatolites, the living varieties of which thrived in the hellish conditions of western Australia, in some of the saltiest water on the planet.

He peeled off a small piece and brought it close to his facemask. *Perhaps, this is an even more extreme life form than the stromatolites*, he thought, before turning his attention toward the near-boiling point water pouring from the vents. *Microbes from deep in the earth, thriving in the most difficult of environments.*

His thoughts were interrupted by Laurent, who swept one arm in a wide arc. Cousteau allowed his gaze to follow it. The same material covered the rocks downhill and in every other direction for as far as the eye could see.

He nodded, the message quite clear. *This has been escaping into the sea for far longer than three weeks— probably at a much-reduced rate—until the earthquake.*

Cousteau gave the thumbs-up sign, gestured for

his two friends to collect samples of the material, and then swam off a short distance to examine another formation. The Frenchman noticed more scratches on the rock surfaces, where the velvet-like material had been torn away in long strips.

Locals, searching for their miracles, he thought.

Glancing back, Cousteau could see Bernard and Laurent turning over red-tinted rocks, their wetsuit-clad bodies set against an even darker backdrop as the shallows dropped-off into deep black water.

A s spectacular as all of this might have been to his friends, Laurent was quickly growing bored.

Bringing Ancient Roman artifacts into the light for the first time in two thousand years—now that was interesting, he thought. *But a smoke-spewing exhaust pipe—not so much. And collecting more samples of algae? Merde.*

He checked his dive watch and air supply. *Great, we'll be heading up soon.*

As his hyperactive colleague Bernard continued to examine the scarlet-stained surroundings, Laurent drifted toward a relatively flattened section that fell off into a far steeper incline. He steadied himself against the current, and stared down into the abyss.

There is no red tint there, he thought, noting this with an involuntary shiver. Instead, the water was bible black and noticeably colder.

How deep is it really? Laurent wondered. *They say 400 meters but I'm betting more.*

In response to his own question, Laurent pulled loose a bowling ball-shaped stone, briefly struggled to maneuver the microbe-sheathed boulder into position, then gave a final push. Kicking gently back, he watched as it rolled down the precipitous slope, trailed by an avalanche of dust and red gravel. He followed the path of the rock until it disappeared and until the avalanche he'd created had subsided, leaving only the impenetrable darkness.

Turning, he could see that Bernard was working his way slowly uphill toward another smoke-spewing vent. The man stopped and gestured for him to follow.

Excellent suggestion, Laurent thought, before turning to take a final glance over the cliff edge.

Now though, something had changed—a section of the darkness below appeared to be shimmering—a black sheet fluttering in the breeze. *No, not black. More like a violet so deep as to only seem black. And so beautiful that no camera I know will ever capture the hue.*

Laurent spun around and began waving his arms wildly, and Bernard, obviously sensing that his friend was either excited or alarmed, swam toward him at full speed. Laurent turned back to face the disturbance from below, barely noticing Bernard's arrival. Both men stared mesmerized at the shimmering transparency, one thought from their dive training coming immediately to the forefront: *La panique et vous êtes mort!*

The shimmer ascended the slope and now seemed to hover, suspended before them like a great dark curtain.

Jacques Yves Cousteau perceived no indication of violence. It was as if his two friends were simply standing beside the drop off, in front of a gently shifting and transparent veil. He would have described the movements as graceful—right up to the moment in which Bernard and Laurent were snatched off the rim. They were not dragged downward, or dragged anywhere for that matter, as they would have if seized by a shark or another known predator. Instead they seemed to come apart—to shred before Cousteau's eyes—leaving fragments of wetsuit and flesh and a new hue of red clouding the water.

Without turning his back on the shimmering transparency—there was no one to be saved—he began backing away from the vent, moving cautiously uphill. He resisted the urge to rise too fast, a move his experience had taught him would cause a crippling or even lethal case of "the bends".

Under the direction of his sympathetic nervous system, Cousteau's body had already initiated a fight-or-flight response—the former action neurochemically circumvented by the latter. He'd decided to escape the immediate area before surfacing, but the shimmering whatever-it-was appeared to have another idea—gliding closer to Cousteau's position.

An incredibly cryptic predator, he thought, *or predators*—since he had no idea if there were more than one of them.

As if to answer this particular question, the veil seemed to split in two, each section more or less rectangular. Now they were drifting apart.

Having paused between two boulders, Cousteau was painfully aware that the breath-generated bubble trail he was producing served to advertise his position as effectively as a neon sign.

They're flanking me, he thought. *Like lions stalking their prey.*

A disturbance from above froze the shapes in place.

The boatman's seen something. And as if to affirm this realization, streaks that Cousteau immediately identified as three bullets knifed downward through the water in quick succession.

The diver's subconscious steadied him, during that critical moment, by focusing on an irrelevant oddity: *Where did the gun come from?*

The response to the gunshots was instantaneous—the sheets of distorted water streaked up toward the boat.

To his simultaneous relief and alarm, Cousteau realized that he had just been provided with a distraction. Deciding not to give away his location any more than he'd already done, he took two last deep breaths, shed his scuba tank, then his weight belt, and resumed his swim up the incline, exhaling as he advanced toward shallower water. His subconscious had already performed the vital calculations: *You can stay underwater three minutes on one lungful of air—four at the outside, if you remain calm.*

The commotion on the surface had evolved into a confusion of inexplicable movement. After initially shaking itself from side to side, the vessel was snatched downward. Through a semi-translucent blur, Cousteau could see the hull disassemble into a chaotic mélange of smashed timber, boat gear and motor parts. There was also a human body, its natural buoyancy overwhelmed by something (or several somethings) that jerked it violently.

The boatman.

The Greek was flailing and struggling some twenty feet below the surface, and in that moment Cousteau decided to swim toward him. Then, as Antoninus Stavracos reached down toward Cousteau pleadingly, his entire body was engulfed in semi-transparent sheets, now taking on the reddish-blue hues of the water's surface.

Though his lungs were beginning to ache, Cousteau had a single thought, *They camouflage themselves.* Continuing to back away from the hellscape, and uphill, he saw the roiling shape glow blindingly bright for an instant, then wink out.

Inexplicably, the man had simply disappeared— as had the sheets of distorted water.

Now the only movement came from the slipstream of the descending boat parts as they rained around the sole human survivor.

Unable to sustain a calm sufficient to provide the hoped for maximum of four minutes, Cousteau surfaced far too quickly, barely noting the painful tingling in his fingers.

He gave a loud involuntary cough, his imagination anticipating the sudden tug that would come just before his body was dragged downward. *Like Bernard. Like Laurent. Like*—

There was a loud squawking sound to his right, but a moment later he realized that it was only sea gulls. *Fighting over*—Cousteau turned away.

Now, as the Frenchman wondered what had just taken place, while simultaneously preparing himself for an array of rapid ascent symptoms that would never come, he scissor-kicked smoothly, propelling his body toward the rocky shore of Nea Kameni.

I might just survive the bends, he thought, *if I don't get eaten first.*

Jacque Yves Cousteau had already choked down several mouthfuls of water stained with the red microbes. He would swear until his dying day, that it tasted like blood.

CHAPTER 2

From the Graves of Eden

Two days later
June 25, 1948
Metropolitan Museum of Natural History, NYC

The fifth-floor office door was open, so Major Patrick Hendry decided that clearing his throat would be an effective way to announce his arrival. R. J. MacCready and two familiar "museum types" had their backs turned to him and were examining what appeared to be a pair of football-sized skulls.

As Hendry's pharyngeal house cleaning abruptly turned into a prolonged, phlegmy cough, the trio turned toward him, wearing an assortment of disgusted looks.

"I'll have some of that on a cracker," Mac said, eliciting additional groans from the pixyish woman in black sitting to his right.

"Go ahead, Mac, make fun," Hendry said, after finally catching his breath. He was carrying a shoebox-sized package and made an exaggerated showing of gently placing it down on Mac-Cready's desk.

"Well, Major, that *was* a rather unique entrance," said Patricia Wynters. She had flipped up a pair of jeweler's loupe-equipped eyeglasses and was now wearing a genuinely concerned expression. "Are you ill?"

"Sounds like he needs an oil change," grumbled a white-haired man, who quickly turned his attention back to the skulls.

"Nice to see you too, Knight," Major Hendry grumbled back.

Seventy-three-year-old Charles R. Knight was the world's foremost artist of prehistoric life. Without turning around, he granted Hendry a wave with his cigarette.

"Personally, I think *both* of you should quit smoking," Patricia said, quietly.

"Second that," Mac added, now waving his arms in a vain attempt to break up the smoke screen that Hendry and Knight were laying down.

Ignoring Patricia and Mac's comments, Hendry moved in closer to an enamel tray holding the skulls. "Prehistoric horses again, huh?"

"Yeah, and no touching," Mac added. Though the major had certainly improved over the years, Mac remained mindful of past trespasses that included the conversion of a triceratops into a *bi*-ceretops, and most infamously, tripping over and fracturing three of *T. rex's* toes. Some of Knight's colleagues believed a convergence of disease and an upheaval of the world's oceans had killed the dinosaurs. "If so," Knight had assured one of them, "It took Hendry to finish the job."

Putting down his cigar and leaning in toward the specimens, the major placed both hands behind his back—assuming the "museum looking" position Mac had demonstrated for him on too many occasions for Hendry's liking.

"*Mesohippus* and *Parahippus*, huh?" he asked.

"You got it," Mac said, with an appreciative nod.

"Show off," Knight muttered under his breath. "Ask him what species they are."

Patricia ignored her grumpy friend. "We're off to central Brazil next month, Major," she announced, excitedly. "Yanni, too."

Instead of responding, Hendry flashed her a tight-lipped smile and nodded slightly.

"What?" Mac asked quickly, his voice carrying a hint of alarm.

The major gestured toward the specimens. "Those formerly extinct horses you're looking to study have been around a long time—right, Mac?"

"About fifteen million years," MacCready replied. "And yeah, that's a lot longer than anyone believed possible."

Hendry took a deep breath then let it out slowly. "Well, then—"

"You *can't* be serious?" Mac said, interrupting what he knew was bound to be bad news.

Major Hendry said nothing.

"Come on, Pat. I mean . . . I'm on quasi-semi-active duty."

Hendry cupped a hand behind one ear. "What was that last thing?" The major turned to Knight and Wynters. "He *did* say, 'active duty'. Am I right?"

The researchers stared back at him, blankly, so the major continued. "I'm *sure* there was an 'active' in there somewhere."

"But the permits, the equipment, the . . . the—"

Hendry shook his head, still silent but wearing an expression that said, *Save it, Mac*. He turned back to the package he'd brought and opened it. "This came for you in the mail today," he said, gently removing some packing material before spreading out several items on an empty tray. "They're from Greece. Your pal Tse-lin dug 'em up."

"Wang Tse-lin? And what are *you* doing with it?"

"Let's just say, someone in your mail room gave me a call when it came in. I did them a little favor by making the delivery myself."

The three scientists moved in for a closer look. Hendry had laid out a pair of strange-looking hand-tools—obviously ancient. "They're made of volcanic glass," he said, watching as the trio reacted with something several notches below astonishment.

Knight was the first to turn away, adjusting the easel that held his latest reconstruction on canvas—a prehistoric horse species with beautiful golden eyes.

Mac picked up an obsidian blade. "Umm . . . these are nice Pat. But you can find stone tools all around the Mediterranean."

Instead of responding, Major Hendry broke

into a smile that Mac had seen only rarely—and he hated it. It said, *Gotcha!*

"What?" Mac said.

Hendry replied by lifting away another layer of cardboard and cotton packing material. Then he carefully withdrew an object and held it out to MacCready and Patricia.

"Well, here's your tool-maker, Smart Guy."

Reacting to the odd silence that followed, Charles R. Knight turned around, adjusted his glasses and stood so quickly that he knocked his easel and brushes to the floor.

"Holy shit!" he cried. "You have *got* to be kidding me."

"No kidding, Chuck," Hendry replied. Then turning to Mac, he handed him an envelope with two folded pages sticking out and jerked a thumb toward Knight. "Now before *you* get excited and start knocking stuff over, I need you to read this."

Mac read it quickly, and handed the telegram back.

"What is it?" Patricia asked, concerned.

R. J. MacCready remained silent as the Sphinx—his face giving away nothing. *Well, Pat,* he thought. *I wonder what new level of hell you're dropping me into this time.*